Indomitable

Cliff Huckleberry

PAGE PUBLISHING, INC.
New York, NY

First originally published by Page Publishing, Inc. 2018

ISBN 978-1-64298-294-7 (Paperback)
ISBN 978-1-64298-296-1 (Hardcover)
ISBN 978-1-64298-295-4 (Digital)

Printed in the United States of America

Part 1

Chapter 1

Thirty-five thousand feet up in the sky

CHRIS WOKE UP FROM a brief nap and debated whether or not he wanted to read the newspaper he brought onboard the plane. He reached up to turn on the light above his seat; a glance at the monitor showed that three hours remained until landing. The cabin area was dark. Most passengers were sleeping or watching movies. He smiled warmly as he reflected on his successful business trip. His customer was kicking off a couple of new circuit board designs that would be strategic for both parties. Another smile formed on his lips as he recalled his boss half-jokingly tell him not to return until the deal was consummated. He sighed and stretched his legs.

Chris was so grateful for his career. He appreciated how he was constantly challenged by the dynamic electronics technology, and he was also grateful that he was able to raise four children and get them through college. Well, almost. Mark still had two more years at Oklahoma University. The last couple of years, Chris would sometimes feel exhausted from the travel and the long and fast-paced hours the industry demanded. He and Carly had been talking about retirement, which would coincide with Mark's graduation and Chris's sixtieth birthday.

Chris enjoyed a fairly conservative lifestyle, so retirement at sixty years old appeared to be a viable option. He had colleagues and friends who became very sick or even died at or near retirement. They couldn't pull themselves away. Sometimes work—the lifestyle and the validation it brought—could be addictive. He always had this lingering premonition in the back of his mind warning him to not stay too long. Chris consistently exercised at the gym with weights and cycling and ate healthy to try to take care of himself.

One of Chris's colleagues made the comment in jest a couple weeks ago that this was a "young man's business," but it was the truth. Chris always said that he would rather follow "Barry Sander's route," referring to the athlete who retired in his prime at thirty-one from the NFL as a leading rusher. This was preferable; as opposed to the path of an athlete that played too long and retired as "damaged goods." So for the last few years, Chris and Carly had been modeling expenses and assets to see if they could retire comfortably. They had settled on two more years until retirement.

The next question was what to do in retirement? Carly liked the idea of staying in the same house in San Diego, working on crafts and spending time together. He had recently lobbied the idea of spending even more time together, selling everything (even the house), and placing all into investments. Possessing only their passports and roller bags, they could travel as nomads for years, then return back to San Diego and buy a smaller house closer to the beach. He thought it was romantic—the notion of going to exotic places with new adventures and traveling to various destinations. They would have the freedom to determine how long they would stay in each place while deciding on their next destination. Carly wasn't sold on his nomadic plan, but she seemed open to two trips a year, one adventuresome three-to-four-week trip and another two-week "low key" vacation. Well, Chris, thought, that was a workable plan.

Chris and Carly's big indulgence over the past ten years was travel. They had an extensive bucket list. Chris had both of them write a list of their top destinations on a page of paper, and they had worked to cross reference their lists. The process had proven very insightful on how common their interests had become. They were both interested in other cultures, history, sights, and experiences.

Their interests on the lists weren't the issue, but the size of the list was challenging. Chris had over thirty places on his bucket list.

Carly would say, "We won't be able to travel to all these destinations."

But that just made Chris more determined to do it. He figured two vacations a year times fifteen years (good health permitting) would allow them to hit their top thirty. That seemed possible to him. Chris just hoped that they could stay healthy to knock most of the destinations off their lists.

Carly had the idea that they would tackle the most strenuous destinations during the first ten years of retirement. Her logic focused on the thought that they could always join tour groups when they became older. Chris liked traveling just the two of them. The independence and freedom that came with planning your own itinerary was very appealing. Also, it required them to stretch themselves to pick up the key language phrases and customs. But Chris agreed that Carly had an excellent plan in looking at the most exotic and challenging destinations first.

In fact, all their kids were great travelers. They were interested in all the sites, culture, history and food and with these experiences, they didn't have a fear of the unknown of travel. Instead, the "children" embraced it. Their family trips were some of his fondest memories.

Chris would shop airlines for competitive flights, then he and Carly would research travel sites to determine their itinerary. Carly would book lodging with B&B's and hostels-pensions. Carly's efforts to find good accommodations at reasonable prices enabled more travel opportunities for their family and provided them with terrific family experiences.

Carly's work made vacations more economical, but it was also their preferred way to travel. They were able to get a better feel for the people in the country, the culture, and it was an opportunity to meet other travelers from around the world. The family had fond memories of meeting locals and world travelers and listening to their stories. Chris stayed at the Hyatt's and Marriott's when he traveled on business: while this was perhaps a great situation for the business traveler, it was not optimal for one seeking an adventurous vacation. Both he and Carly agreed that they didn't find this mode of travel appealing. So they researched and created their own itineraries.

As the children became adults, their work and school began to conflict with family vacations. Chris and Carly had lost one of them every couple of years to careers; now it was just Carly and Chris traveling together. The children still traveled, but with one another or with friends. Abby and Jessica had traveled together to Portugal for two weeks and had a terrific time. Ethan went to Central America with a friend and surfed while sightseeing. They were starting their careers and didn't have much vacation time, but jumped at the chance to travel when time was available.

Chris opened the newspaper—it was more of the same news on the virus. The general public was dissatisfied with the US government's handling of the outbreak. The virus from West Africa was still rampant, with another case in the United States brought over by a doctor returning to New York from Africa. The outbreak from New York claimed twenty lives, forcing the government to clamp down hard and cease entry from Africa without thorough screening.

The New York mayor and governor had to implement the quarantine and create policies to contain the virus. The White House confirmed and adopted the policies afterward and tried to take credit, claiming the policies as their own. But many felt that if it had been left to the Federal Government, the outbreak would have been substantial with many more deaths, encompassing many states.

West African countries were devastated by the virus. The first report was that the virus was a variation of Ebola, but they had not given it a name yet. Numbers tolling the dead were still increasing with many more becoming infected. West Africa had effectively been closed off from the rest of the world for a year while health officials continued to try to stop the virus. Travel was restricted within regions of Africa. Europe, North and South America and Asia had also cut many flights to and from West Africa. Furthermore, anyone traveling from Africa had to be quarantined for a minimum of twenty-one days.

An effective ten-minute test had been developed in the US, and this test had to be given and passed on the twenty-first day of exposure to enter the States. In fact, this had quickly become policy in not only most Western countries, but for most of the world. Travel changed significantly, with additional security at immigration, and the incorporation of health checks for individuals both leaving and entering countries.

Chris's trip from Europe had a mandatory health check station in Amsterdam before departure. Passports were examined closely, especially within the last month of travel to screen for visitation to Africa. Flying to Europe was becoming more difficult. Flying to China concerned him because if you had a low-grade fever, they could quarantine you for an indeterminate time at their discretion. Chris thought this was too risky. So he had pushed his annual China/Taiwan trip out two quarters, waiting to see if the virus would stay contained to West Africa and if the rest of the world would relax travel restrictions.

Chris looked down at the page, and there was more news focused on terrorism. Most of the articles referenced ISIS, but there were articles on Al-Qaeda and other Muslim terrorist groups as well. There were splinter terrorist groups all over the Middle East and Africa. Europe was experiencing protests and violence in most of their major cities with large Muslim populations. Immigration had been very liberal for the past few decades in Western Europe and Chris was hearing concerns from friends and individuals in Europe. It appeared that Western European countries were making attempts to tighten immigration policies.

In the Middle East, the Sunni Muslims and the Shiites Muslims continued their conflict that had spanned over 1,500 years. Terrorists were persecuting the Christian people in their regions and essentially were at war with everyone. Alarmingly, the terrorist groups seemed to keep growing in number and finding more recruits. There were rumors that Al-Qaeda, ISIS, and other groups might merge into one force. Chris wondered if this was more of a threat to the world than the African virus. And to top it off, there was still the sour Israel-and-Palestinian situation and the fear of Iran building nuclear weapons. The US was still trying to find a resolution to Israel-Palestinian tensions, and they were sponsoring another peace talk that week in Israel. Chris thought that a truce with Israel and Palestine wouldn't happen in his lifetime, but every year there was another attempt.

Chris and Carly traveled years ago with the family to Turkey and had a wonderful time, but the Middle East political climate had changed immensely since that trip. The majority of these regions were on the US warning list for travel. Chris and Carly hoped to travel to the Middle East in the future. Hopefully things would settle down and be more peaceful in a few years.

Chris turned a few pages and saw an editorial blasting the US government for not effectively controlling the border along Mexico. The article raised concern that terrorists could easily cross the border and reassemble to attack a military base or any strategic site. More people were concerned about controlling the border than in implementing the Immigration initiatives that were constantly debated. He felt that if the government could control and stop migration on the border, then most people would agree on a reasonable amnesty plan.

The flight attendant came by with a bottle of water. Chris politely accepted it and when the attendant passed again, he thought it was time for a bathroom break. He tried to hydrate on the flights and get up every couple of hours to go to the bathroom and let his circulation flow and give his legs a chance to stretch. One of his colleagues developed a blood clot from a long plane flight and when Chris looked on the web, he found out that it was fairly common. He had had knee surgery the past summer, so he felt he could be more at risk for getting a clot. He needed to be diligent about staying hydrated and walking the aisles.

Chris came back from the restroom and maneuvered back into his seat. He leaned over to search for his seat buckles, and his business cards flew out of his shirt pocket, scattering to the seat and the floor. He picked them up and his seatmate paused his movie to glance over.

"Sorry to disturb you," Chris said sheepishly.

"Were you at the technology show?" his seatmate asked as he picked up and studied Chris's business card.

"Yes. We finished with our meetings yesterday afternoon," Chris explained.

"How was the show for you?" his seatmate asked. "We thought the show was mediocre this year. Customers are cautious to invest; with the financial uncertainty and global issues."

"We thought it was okay, but I agree that it wasn't the best show. We have some new technology that created excitement and interest," Chris revealed.

"We're in the software business. A number of our key customers told us they'd wait a year and evaluate the economy at that time," the seatmate confessed.

"We're in semiconductors and there are some new video and wireless standards that have our industry excited," Chris explained.

"Well, we're ready to return to Southern California," the man added as he looked across the aisle to a man sleeping. "We had some customer meetings in Europe before the show and we've been away for three weeks."

They conducted more small talk, and Chris discovered the man was a nice person and knowledgeable in his industry. After more conversation the seatmate returned to his movie and Chris picked up his newspaper to continue reading.

There was an article on page six debating the status of the US economy and how the government initiatives weren't creating meaningful jobs (at least not good-paying jobs that allowed people to create a living). The article stressed that part-time jobs with ten to twenty hours per week shouldn't be calculated against the unemployment number. The paper pressed on about how current numbers were more representative of underemployment than unemployment. How could a couple, each working part-time jobs, survive? The article made sense, but politics were in play, with the current presidency and Congress determined to show a positive economy.

Chris enjoyed being exposed to different ideas. Should the US create a trade school program for teens that did not want to pursue the university path? Should everyone be working fifty hours a week before retirement? He was contemplating this thought, then smiled. *Fifty hours? What would I do with that spare time?* The final point in the article was that the unemployment and underemployment created a powder keg in the US, and was generating unrest.

Chris and Carly were more conservative on political issues: a little to the right of the middle line (if there were a midline these days). He believed in some social programs and that people needed to take their own initiative and be independent. He felt most people *wanted* to be independent. However, it seemed like the US was torn into several factions: the extreme left and extreme right were 180 degrees apart and seemed to rarely find middle ground. His concern was that moderate conservatives and moderate liberals seemed to be drifting further apart.

He shook his head and thought about his neighborhood. Everyone got along; relationships ranging from friendly to civil. Neighbors helped one another in times of need. The common denominator was that they all worked hard in their respective careers and in their home life. They respected the rights of one another.

Finally deciding that he'd had enough of the news, Chris reclined in his seat, turned off the overhead light, closed his eyes, and sought another nap.

Anyway, Chris thought, he'd be home soon, and in three weeks all the children were coming home to San Diego for Christmas holiday. Carly was so excited. She had almost all the presents purchased. Carly started Christmas lists and shopping in September, stressing herself to find the perfect gifts for each person. She pulsed each of the kids individually after Thanksgiving, asking what foods they would like to have over the Christmas vacation week to ensure that each had several of their favorites represented during the Holiday. Christmas was her favorite time of the year.

Mark would be home for four weeks during his winter school break, but Ethan and Jessica would have to go back to work after a week of vacation. They had limited vacation time with their companies. Abby taught school in a district within San Diego County and she would have two weeks of vacation for Christmas break.

He thought about his family and drifted in and out of slumber until the plane landed safely in the Los Angeles International Airport. He dreamt of coming home with Christmas music playing, Christmas goodies baking in the oven, and Carly decorating the house.

Chris was checking to make sure he had all his personal belongings in his seat area. He pulled out his wallet and brought out the ticket for the parking garage. His seatmate glanced over and saw the ticket.

"Hey, we're parked in the same garage. My colleague and I carpooled to the airport since we live ten minutes from each other. I like that garage the best, the shuttles run regularly and it has easy access to the freeway," the man shared as he pulled out a similar parking ticket.

Chris, his seatmate and the seatmate's colleague exited customs minutes apart. They chatted as they dragged their roller bags toward the exit. Chris was eager to begin his drive home to San Diego. He still had a long drive. Dang, why didn't he use the restroom on the plane before landing?

"Guys, I need to use the restroom since I have a long drive ahead of me. Why don't you, guys, go ahead, and I'll meet you at the island for the shuttle," Chris suggested.

In minutes, he was out of the restroom, pulling his roller bag to the curb. He stopped, waiting for the green light to allow him to cross to the island. He looked over and saw a group of people waiting for the shuttle and he spotted his seatmate standing at the curb.

Chris pulled out his phone to check and see how many emails and texts he'd accumulated while in-flight. The emails were loading.

Suddenly, Chris experienced a sensory overload. Instantaneously there were ear splitting noises that jerked Chris's head from his phone. As he looked back to the island, he heard screams and shouts fill the air. Chris saw smoke and debris scattered around the shuttle area. A man engulfed by the fire was running from the island down the street. No-one was left standing in the shuttle area. There were bodies strewn about.

"There was a white truck that rammed into that area!" a woman shouted, and then her voice trailed off as she was overcome with emotion.

Sirens screamed as security and police swarmed the area and tended to the injured. One security woman came over to where Chris and others were standing and directed them back inside the terminal. Chris glanced over and saw a taxi stand to the right, on the opposite side of the incident. As the others were herded back into the terminal, he briskly walked over to the taxi area. The explosion had dispersed the lines of people waiting for transportation. He walked up to a cab and climbed inside.

"Do you know where this is?" He showed his ticket with the parking garage address to the driver.

The driver nodded, and they left the airport in silence. Chris paid the driver, found his car and exited the garage. As he waited at a traffic light, he texted Carly that there was an incident at the airport but he was safe, and getting on I-405. He should be home in two hours. Chris was still rattled and wasn't ready to discuss the bus stop explosion yet. Carly would hear about the incident on the news, but at least she would understand that he was safe and out of the area.

Chris couldn't get out of his head that if he hadn't stopped to use the restroom, he would have been standing there next to his seatmate. He unknowingly dodged a bullet, and he gave thanks to God as he barreled down the freeway.

Chapter 2

Days later in San Diego

CHRIS WOKE UP, SLEEPING on his side at the edge of the bed. The clock read 5:54 a.m. Finley, their golden retriever, saw Chris move and came over to greet him. His nose was about three inches away from Chris's face, tail wagging, and eager to start the day. After all, it was Saturday morning, and Chris and Carly had the same Saturday-morning routine. Chris would get up before Carly. If Chris didn't get up quickly, then Finley would jump up on the bed (waking Carly). Carly liked sleeping until 7:00 a.m. She was finally able to sleep in most days after their youngest, Mark, went off to college. Chris quickly moved out of bed before Finley felt prompted to jump up.

As a golden retriever, Finley loved every part of the day, but especially their routines in the morning. Chris would pull on his pants and T-shirt, and his feet would find his slippers tucked by the night stand, and they would head down the stairs. Chris would open the front door, and Finley would run out to the driveway and fetch the newspaper looking around for a reason to bark. Finley would do a complete visual sweep of the street and then hurry back inside to be fed.

Once Finley's needs were addressed, Chris would grind his Costa Rica beans and start his morning pot of coffee. When he turned around from the kitchen counter, Finley would be watching him. A lime-green tennis ball in his mouth, Finley would look at Chris with his tail wagging. With a cup of coffee and the Sports section they would go outside to the backyard. Situated in a wicker chair, Chris would throw the ball for Finley. This was Finley's favorite time of the day, and the truth was, it was the same for Chris. It was quiet, birds were chirping. It was just delightful.

After a bit, they would go upstairs to the bedroom and Finley would get up on the bed and lick and wake up Carly while Chris got ready for the gym. For twenty-five years now, he and Jim would exercise together every Saturday morning unless one of them was injured, sick, or away on travel. Meanwhile Carly would go for a six-mile run with her good friend Diana and with Abby their oldest daughter.

Chris and Jim used to run on Saturday mornings. However, as the years went by, the miles took their toll. Now their routine was to lift some weights and then cycle. Their preference was to cycle on their own versus the spinning classes because they could talk and catch up on the week. They had tried a few months of spin, but part of their exercise routine was social.

The two were very good friends, yet they were so very different. Chris was more outspoken, fiery, and conservative. Jim internalized things that bothered him. He lived conservatively but voted liberally and was empathetic toward the plights of others. They were perfect for each other. Over the years, Jim softened some of Chris's political and world views and Jim became more fiscally conservative. Jim and his wife Joan were extremely nice; Chris was sometimes concerned they were too nice and could be taken advantage of by others. They were terrific friends.

Jim had retired two years ago from his job as an accounting manager. After a brief spell of inactivity, Jim took some counseling courses at a local college, and then started a second career working for a nonprofit. He really liked it there and had the chance to counsel many people. One of his former clients, Mike, was a vet from Iraq suffering from PTSD. Mike was a good guy who joined Chris and Jim at the gym to work out. Chris grew to like Mike but, in some ways, felt that he didn't know Mike very well.

Mike was originally from Iowa, but when he joined the marines, he was stationed at Camp Pendleton. Now that he was out of the service, he considered San Diego his home. Mike had a job, but he was still struggling to fit into civilian life. Mike couldn't pinpoint exactly what the issue was, but talking about his experiences with Jim and Chris seemed to help. It was more like he just didn't feel he fit into society after returning from his tour. Chris and Jim would encourage Mike and were always rooting for him. Mike was strong and liked to max out on weights while Chris and Jim cycled.

Chris climbed in the car and found a parking space in the side lot by the gym. He checked in at the front desk, entered his code, and found a stationary bicycle that had an empty bicycle on either side. He arrived before Jim and adjusted the bike seat height and climbed atop. Jim would come to the gym with his wife, Joan. She would go through her exercises elsewhere in the gym and they would go through their own routine, catching up on the week and discussing current events, mutual friends and work up a good sweat.

Chris started pushing the pedals, adjusting the machine to his desired strength level while watching the TV screens overhead. There was a sports station and a news station displayed overhead on the two TV's. If he positioned himself in a good spot, Chris could see both easily. The sports channel was focused on today's Bowl game and the sportscasters offered their predictions of the outcome.

Five minutes later Jim arrived, climbing up on the bike to his left without a word. Then discussion revolved around a checklist status of their families. Chris had four children and he felt guilty that he took most of the air time. Jim and Joan had only one son, Clark. Clark had had a couple of challenging years trying to get settled into a good routine and discover what he wanted to study. He had recently been hired at a local store for part-time work, this seemed to be a positive boost in his life. The job gave Clark confidence and he seemed to be progressing well in school.

Jim had been in the service for four years before he started college. He had a soft spot for military veterans and San Diego was a promilitary town. Chris's father and father-in-law served in the navy and army, and Chris's uncles also served in the navy. Chris had appreciation for the armed services and felt compassion for Mike's postwar struggles.

Chris and Jim were both concerned about some of the prolonged wars involving the US in the Middle East. Jim felt good about trying to help combat veterans assimilate into civilian life and Chris had admiration for Jim's work and dedication.

Chris had something bothering him. He waited until they were near the end of their cycling.

"Jim, did you hear about the terrorist van at LAX?" Chris asked.

"Yes, it killed and injured a lot of people who were waiting for shuttles. Airport security has now extended checkpoints outside the airport," Jim shared.

"Yes. I missed that explosion because I needed to use the restroom. The passenger that I sat next to and his colleague were there, and they died. I was traveling with them, and in a minute or two, I would have caught up to them and would have been standing there. I can't shake the irony, and I don't feel comfortable talking to Carly about this in detail," Chris confessed.

Jim was quiet, and they cycled for another minute. Chris looked over at Jim.

"Why was I spared from the explosion? I wonder if there is a reason why I am alive," Chris shared what was truly bothering him.

"Your time hasn't come," Jim surmised.

There wasn't more to say, and they were quiet as they finished their last few minutes on the stationary bicycles.

Finished with cycling, Jim and Chris walked over toward the part of the gym with the weights. Jim was a little over six feet one inch with long legs and a runner's build. Today he was wearing a gold sweatshirt, blue shorts, and new sport shoes that were so clean they looked like they came right out of the shoe box. Chris was wearing Mark's old high school basketball shorts with a generic blue work-out shirt.

Mike was easy to spot in his gray T-shirt and black shorts. Positioned at the bench press pumping a quick set, the thirty-two-year-old single man stood out as very buff. Mike was a hair under six feet and a little over two hundred pounds. He had just finished benching a set; sweat dripped from his face and arms. They spent a few minutes chatting as they set up the tricep machine. Chris and Jim worked lighter weights and more reps than the younger guys, but they could lift a respectable weight. Alongside Mike, they would adjust up/down depending on whose turn it was. There were times when Chris wished he were twenty-five years old again for thirty minutes so he could crush a power circuit in the gym, but then he realized how lucky he was to be able to handle the simpler workout ahead of him. There were others in their fifties that he worked with that had a lot of health issues and couldn't do what he was about to do.

Mike reminded them that next Saturday they'd skip the gym to go shooting instead. Mike had quite a collection of guns that he was willing to share. They would all pitch in for the cost of ammunition, and Chris would bring some hot coffee in a thermos for the three of them. They had done this a couple of times in the past. Carly was not happy when Chris went shooting, but it was a good bonding experience that also allowed them to be outside. The best part was that this environment put Mike at ease, back in his comfort zone.

They spent another thirty minutes in the weight room and finished the last set. With the cardio and weight workout complete, it was a good start for the weekend.

Chris said goodbye to Mike who stayed behind to warm down and stretch. Chris said goodbye to Jim and Joan outside the gym; Joan asked Chris to say hi to Carly. They waved and headed toward their respective cars.

Joan had a smile every day, and Chris had known both of them for almost thirty years. They used to be neighbors who lived across the street from each other. That was Chris and Carly's previous house and where all four of their children had been born. Thirty years ago they were all young with limited funds, bonds had been forged as they worked together to build fences, decks and walls, and as they watched each other's children in times of need.

It was a great house and neighborhood—all the immediate neighbors helped each other and became fast friends. Although some had moved away, they were still in touch. They saw each other less frequently but were friends for life.

Chris drove the back roads home, pulled into the garage, and walked into the kitchen. He grabbed a cereal bowl, spoon, milk from the fridge, and a box of cereal from the pantry. As he started to eat breakfast, he looked at the weekend's chore list. Mow the lawn, trim the trees in the front yard, take out some trash, and then check in with Carly. Carly was refinishing the cabinets in the downstairs bathroom, which would consume at least half of her day. Carly loved a good home improvement challenge. She and Chris typically had a list of things to accomplish each Saturday for the house. She had refinished cabinets before and they turned out looking terrific. Her work was excellent and in many cases better quality than the contracted work; not to mention it saved them money since they only had to pay for the supplies. They were regulars at the local Home Depot store.

Chris finished eating and changed from his workout clothes to his yard clothes. Pushing the lawn mower out of the garage, Chris paused, to appreciate the birds singing and the sun shining. He was thankful for this life he built.

Chapter 3

Coffee shop near the tech center in San Diego

CHRIS SET HIS COFFEE down on the patio table outside the coffee shop. Pulling out a chair to sit down, he thoughtfully considered his colleagues. He had known Will for fourteen years as the manager of the application engineers. Typically steady, Will had been unsettled this past year. Will struggled to decide if he should relocate back to North Carolina to be near his elderly parents and within close proximity to his sister and brother-in-law. To do this, he would need to sell his house in San Diego and move his two dogs across the country. The biggest thing holding Will back was his great job in the Southwest.

Will was about six feet and slim, with dark, short hair and wire-rimmed glasses. He graduated from the Midwest and was a great engineer. Chris had the utmost respect and confidence in Will's technical capability. He could drill down on a problem and resolve it every time. Will had technical expertise in customer support but also managed the other application engineers, Dan and Jack.

Sitting next to Will was Dan, the wireless application engineer. He came from a large family, with brothers and sisters all throughout southern California. Dan loved the water, boats, fishing, and water sports.

Dan had a forty-plus-foot boat back at his house in Florida. Dan had two homes: he had rented an apartment in downtown San Diego, and he owned a house in Florida. It was the perfect situation for Dan: he could head back to Florida once every couple of months to sail away for the weekend. His backyard included a dock on a canal where he housed the boat. While Dan's current work required him to be based in San Diego, his long-term goal was to eventually retire in Florida and go out on the boat several times a week to fish. He felt uninhibited and free on the water.

Dan had been with the company for over ten years now. He was about five feet eight inches and slender, with a contagious smile and a great attitude. There were many guys that listened intently to Dan's retirement plan and envied him. Dan had never married, but he had a girlfriend in Spain. They had met two years ago, and Dan seemed very interested in her, even naming his boat Maria in her honor.

Dan had met Maria in Barcelona a couple of years ago while visiting a friend. She was an architect and looked pretty in the photographs. She had a big white smile and long dark hair. She seemed to be a good match for Dan because she was active. She was also family oriented; Chris thought that Dan's long term Florida plan could turn into a European plan in the future if things became more serious between the two of them. Over the holidays, Dan and Maria would take turns flying to see each other. A couple of times they met in the Caribbean for a short vacation.

Chris, Will and Jack didn't pry, but Dan's next step was to ask Maria's parents for permission to marry her. It sounded like he was getting ready for this step. Everyone was waiting for him to announce a trip to Spain.

Jack filled the fourth seat at the table. He was the video expert and had been with the company for seven years. Jack exercised often and was quite involved with the latest workout fads. He was very dedicated to the workouts and typically sported an injury or two. Lately he had a bad right elbow and didn't know if it was tendonitis or something more serious.

Chris could relate to Jack. Years ago when he'd attempted Krav Maga with his sons, Chris was always nursing one or two injuries. Jack seemed happy with his life and was an avid football fan. Chris enjoyed talking a few minutes of football with Jack and trying to problem solve on how to get their team to the playoffs.

The foursome spent a little time talking about current events and conversing about what was happening in the technology industry, but a couple of times a month, they would grab a coffee or sandwich and share notes and go through action items or future meetings with their key customers. Their largest customer had design centers throughout the world, and while there were other people completing the world wide team, these guys worked closely together at the San Diego facility to support customer sites outside San Diego, including Europe. Chris also worked with the China and Taiwan locations with their respective Sales and FAE teams.

Will spoke now about someone in their company becoming a roadblock from sharing critical information with their customer: information that was critical to get the customer's final product to production. Despite the frustrating circumstance, Chris thought, I'm in San Diego, the sun is shining and I'm having a cup of coffee with some guys that I really enjoy—life is wonderful.

Chris had worked with engineers for over thirty years and in that time he surmised that engineers tended to be a fairly conservative group. Chris reflected that this had probably influenced his life greatly since he felt so comfortable surrounded by his engineering colleagues and customers. Chris tuned back to Will's conversation and noticed Will was getting fired up. Chris took the action item to make a call later in the day to try to get the document in question released.

At the end of their meeting, Dan confirmed with Chris and Jack that they would take three of their key customers out on a fishing day trip in two days. Will didn't like fish (or the idea of fishing), so he opted out of this event. Chris thought that he should stop and get some Dramamine patches on the way home in case of rough weather. He wanted to avoid being seasick at all costs!

Chapter 4

San Diego coast two days later

It was still dark in the early morning; the customer wanted to head out early. It had been reported that the yellowtail were biting, so expectations were high. Chris looked for a parking space and found one across the street at the far end of the parking area. He pulled in and parked, taking a last swig from his coffee mug before getting out. He had on a shirt, sweater, and a jacket so that he could layer up and down depending on the weather. According to the forecast, it was going to be a beautiful day.

Chris's task was to bring food (which translated to mostly unhealthy snacks). He had the cooler packed with their food including beef jerky, bags of potato chips and pretzels. Jack was in charge of the drinks and Dan had arranged all the fishing equipment along with the chartered boat. The scenario had been preapproved by Chris's boss, Dale, so the excursion would be expensed.

Chris walked down the pier with the cooler on his right shoulder looking for Dan and the boat. He had never seen this particular boat before but he had a good description. He finally spotted Dan and he walked over to the boat. It appeared that Chris had arrived before Jack and the three customers. He looked up at Dan while boarding and saw another person that he assumed was the captain.

With a playful smile, Chris announced, "Good morning. Permission to come aboard?"

Dan looked down and smiled as the captain replied, "Permission granted." One more curt nod, and Chris brought the cooler aboard.

Chris wasn't too knowledgeable about boats, but Dan often spoke about his forty-foot boat. Dan went back to Florida every few months to check on his house and boat. His Floridian boat was built in 1998: a Pacific Seacraft 40 Voyager. That didn't mean anything to Chris, but Dan told him that it was large enough to really sail anywhere around the world.

Dan had been working on the boat the past couple of years to get it in shape for a long journey. To date he would only take it out for two days at a time. He told Chris that the bottom was newly painted and that he had recently rebuilt the engine and replaced some of the rigging. Dan explained that he had a Spectra 380C 12 VDC water maker on his boat. While no specific trip had been planned, Dan was thinking of an extended trip through the Caribbean.

Jack and the customers arrived fifteen minutes later. Everyone came onboard and once they were all settled, Dan asked, "Is everyone ready?" He received some sleepy grunts, hand waves, and a thumbs-up, all signaling they were ready to go. Dan signaled to the captain, and they were on their way!

As the boat headed toward open water, Jack pulled out the coffee, instantly becoming the most popular guy on the boat. Jack allowed the group to grab a cup while the captain navigated their watercraft out of the harbor.

It was relaxing, the men drank their coffee, listening to the hum of the engine as the cool wind brushed their faces. Everything was quiet and still as they left the harbor. The boats left behind began to look like toy boats as they left the harbor toward the ocean. Off to the east, they could see the sun trying to peak over the mountain as they headed out further to sea.

* * * * *

It was a successful outing, and Dan and Chris assisted the captain with last chores before leaving the boat Meanwhile, Jack and the customers cleaned the fish. Their total catch amounted to fourteen fish, but a few fish were oversize, weighing in at twenty-five pounds or more. The terrific part was that each of the customers had caught a twenty-plus pounder that they were excited to bring home to their family. Even more terrific, Jack volunteered to clean Chris's fish and to take them home to his own freezer. Carly was a vegetarian and wouldn't want the fish stored in their freezer. Chris would eat fish and poultry outside their home.

Chris reached into the front pocket of his Levis and found the cash he had set aside. Walking over, he slipped a tip to the captain, who had him sign an invoice with the company credit card. The business transaction complete, Chris carried the now empty cooler and approached the others.

"Have you ever thought of buying a boat?" Dan asked him out of the blue.

Chris looked at him and paused. "Thirty years ago I thought about retiring some day and sailing for a couple of years around the world. Then I got married and learned that Carly gets really seasick—on our honeymoon we went out on a Hawaiian excursion and she became ill quickly. It's not something that she can get used to; she had an ear operation when she was a young girl, and her equilibrium also prevents her from scuba diving. It seems to bother her most swaying in the water."

Chris asked if Dan was thinking about sailing away someday. He just smiled and his mind seemed to drift.

After a couple of minutes, Dan responded, "You know Chris, I do think about it and I think I'm going to test myself by taking a two week trip to the Caribbean. I'm talking to Maria about coming over for a nice vacation with her brother and sister-in-law. If that's successful, I may try crossing the Atlantic." Chris smiled and nodded.

Their conversation halted as they reached Jack and the customers at the end of the pier. Everyone looked tired but pleased that they were returning home with fish. They said their goodbyes, declared the day a huge success, and walked to their vehicles. Chris remembered that he was parked in a lot across the main street.

He paused at the curb, looked both ways and started to take a step. *What was that ahead?* He saw a swerving car coming toward him, straddling both lanes.

Chris focused on the car, a white sedan. The driver was a young man. As the car got closer, the driver looked petrified and the person riding in the passenger seat was animated and pointing straight ahead.

Were they pointing at him? Chris was about to run back to the dock when he saw that the car was now steady in one lane. As the car passed, he saw the name of a driving school on the side of the door. Chris shook his head and felt foolish. *This is one incident I will keep to myself.*

Chris started the drive home by tuning the radio to a local sports-talk station. The local college football team was fighting for the league title, and it was all football talk with people calling in and giving their opinion of whether they would win their last game. Chris listened in and out of the talk show; cycling through the back of his mind was the conversation with Dan. What an adventure it would be to sail away in the Caribbean!

Chapter 5

Christmas Day

CHRIS ASKED ETHAN TO uncork the two wine bottles on the counter and let them breathe. Ethan was becoming a wine connoisseur, knowledgeable in the treatment of cabernets and merlots. Most of the family liked a good red wine, but Carly and her father, Pa K, preferred white wine, so Chris made sure he had a nice bottle of chardonnay ready for them.

As Ethan uncorked the Cabernet, Chris was struck by how grown up his oldest son was. Ethan had graduated two and half years ago from Baylor with a finance degree and had been working as an analyst in Dallas for the past two years with a hedge fund. He loved the job but worked long and hard hours. Ethan still looked strong, a result of early workouts at the gym before starting his grueling thirteen- to fourteen-hour work day. As a freshman at Baylor, Ethan had found some "workout" buddies; he'd quickly gained thirty-five pounds of muscle in two years—a lot for his six-foot-two-inch frame. He had blond hair, blue eyes, and 210 lbs of muscle—he was strong and could move quickly.

With a smile, Chris recalled seeing Ethan that Thanksgiving of his freshman year. He and Carly pulled up to the curb of the airport, trying unsuccessfully to spot Ethan while he was standing only twenty yards away. They didn't recognize him because he was twenty pounds heavier, decked out in a cowboy hat and cowboy boots. Chris chuckled. When they had dropped him off months before in August, Ethan was wearing a T-shirt, shorts, and flip-flops. Three months later, he looked so different in his western garb.

Standing next to Ethan was his younger brother, Mark, who would turn twenty in March. He was an inch or two taller than Ethan, but fifteen pounds lighter. Mark worked out intensely each day in an attempt to catch his brother in bulk and strength. There was no doubt that he would surpass Ethan by the time he graduated from OU. Mark was a basketball player in high school, and while he played, he was slim from all the running on the court. He had blond hair and blue eyes, a prominent chin, and a splattering of freckles. Chris thought that he could probably increase to 220 lbs and still look slim; he just had that type of frame.

Chris looked at his two sons with pride, wondering where the time had gone. Mark grabbed two beers from the fridge for the grandfathers who were talking in the family room. Chris liked IPA's and had stashed a number of them in the refrigerator earlier that morning. Mark popped the tops off both and carried them into the other room.

Mark had started as an accounting major but had recently decided to switch to finance. Ethan and his sister Jessica both had finance degrees, and Mark had been asking them a lot of questions about their work. Jessica was in corporate finance, but she was looking into investment banking and had made a couple of contacts through Chris's brother Jeff in San Francisco. Mark planned to take a couple of upper-division finance classes in the spring semester; if he liked them, he'd officially switch his major to finance. One thing Chris made a mental note to discuss with Mark later was the idea of majoring in one field and minoring in the other.

Mark followed the path of his siblings and took advantage of the high school AP and college courses offered. He started at OU with a semester under his belt, allowing him the option to graduate in three and a half years or entertain a major/minor combination in four years. Mark attended Oklahoma University which was in Norman, Oklahoma. He loved the school almost as much as Ethan had loved Baylor. And of course, they were Big 12 conference rivals. Ethan had driven up to Norman in November when Mark had secured two tickets for them to attend the OU vs. Baylor game. Talking smack the whole time, but all in fun. Chris loved hearing the banter back and forth between the two of them.

Carly's mother, Ma K, went to Kansas University, so the three of them would talk about sports throughout the day. Ma K focused on basketball because of KU's success, but that didn't stop her from talking about their respective football game vs. KU. She would give them a "Rock Chalk, Jayhawk," and they would respond with a "Sic'em Bears," or a "Boomer Sooner." After all these years, Chris still didn't know what "Rock Chalk" meant, but his mother-in-law shouted it with authority.

Suddenly there was laughter in the family room. Chris finished setting up the wine glasses on the table and continued into the family room. Carly's parents (Pa K and Ma K) were laughing with Abby. Abby, their oldest daughter, was a schoolteacher and always had fun stories to share. Abby was very creative: Chris and Carly were amazed at all the creative lesson plans she taught to her students. She was five feet nine inches and had long blond hair. As a girl, she had had a lot of freckles—now she had just a few. In school she had always been strong in math, writing, and public speaking. They hadn't known what area she would focus on in college. She chose a finance major at Cal Poly and did extremely well. But after a year she decided that she didn't want to work in business finance and she went back for her teaching credential at night. Abby was in her fourth year of teaching and she loved it. She was a very strong teacher in the best school district in San Diego County. She was a beautiful, confident, and successful woman.

Carly's parents had been teachers themselves. Even Carly had taught a couple years as an elementary school teacher, so they could relate to the stories. In addition, Chris's father, Grandpa H, was a school administrator. There would be a lot of teacher stories today.

Ryan, Abby's fiancé, was nearby tossing the ball to Finley. Ryan and Abby had been dating for two years and were to be married next summer. Ryan was an electrical engineer at a local technology company in Sorrento Valley. Ryan was a low-key guy and a good balance for the outgoing Abby. He liked sports, worked out, and he got along great with the family. He had a mother and sister on the east coast, but no one had heard too much about either of them. Chris felt that Ryan was his third son and he knew that Carly felt the same. Ryan was six feet three inches with more of a slim build. He had short brown hair and a crooked smile. Abby was animated as she told her story, and Chris felt so happy that she had found teaching because it was evident that she loved it.

Chris and Ryan had a natural bond because they both worked in the technology industry. Ryan could bring up a topic for conversation and Chris could follow and add to the discussion.

Carly had been a kindergarten teacher many years ago before they had built their family. She loved it so much that Chris recalled constantly reminding her to bring home the monthly paycheck in her school mailbox. There were times where she would forget to bring it home for two weeks. When they were first married they didn't have much money, so they needed that paycheck! One year after they were married, they bought their first house and spent two years' worth of weekends working on the house.

They were either decorating the inside of the house or landscaping the outside. Chris learned to build retaining walls, to install sprinkler systems, to build patio covers and fences, and he even became experienced with laying bricks. They quickly became valued customers of Home Depot. When they grew to be a family of six plus a big dog, space grew tight. Carly told him one day while cooking dinner in the kitchen that they needed a bigger house, and that was that.

Not long after, they moved to their current house. The move was only five miles, into the next community of Poway, to a more spacious home. He and Carly really liked the area north of San Diego; they wanted to keep their family in the general area. It was a good family community with a lot of activities for the children. Both of their houses had decent sized backyards where the kids could play safely in the backyard. That had always been a hard requirement; to have plenty of outside space. This was as important as Carly's inside house requirements.

Through the years, Carly always had books available for the children, so entertainment largely consisted of reading or playing outside. There was also a swing set, a large trampoline, a basketball court, and a large grass area for playing soccer. Carly limited TV and computer games, and Chris was so thankful that they stayed firm on this point. Carly deserved the credit for holding the line when their young kids asked for more TV and computer time. Carly had a technology limit per week for each child, and she did not compromise. The result was that all four were good readers: Abby and Jessica preferred fiction, Ethan liked nonfiction, and Mark read a little of everything. Mark's favorite was learning all his trivia from the "Bathroom Reader." Chris chuckled to himself remembering that Mark used the "Bathroom Reader" as a reference on one of his high school term papers. At first Chris thought he was a joking, but then Mark showed him the paper, proud that he had earned an A. So it became a running joke when Mark or anyone would have a piece of random trivia that the source was the "Bathroom Reader."

Years ago, Carly kept the children supplied with reading material but even now she often made trips to the library. Chris thought the interest in reading probably started with the grandparents, who always had reading material on hand. Within the family, they often kept magazines floating and books rotating from home to home. There was always an abundance of material available to read.

Chris looked out on the patio and watched his parents, Grandpa H and Grandma H, talking to Jessica. Jessica had graduated a year early from

Cal Poly San Luis Obispo and was in a program with her company where they moved her each year to a new division for a total of three years. The plan was for her and the others in the program to learn more about the company's business at each location, which operated as a separate entity. Her first assignment was in Seattle and she didn't care for the weather. Growing up in southern California, it was difficult to lose the sun for nine months out of the year. Last summer she had transferred to northern California—now she enjoyed the weather change and fit in better with the people.

Jessica was two inches shorter than Abby at five feet seven inches and also had blond hair and freckles. She seemed quiet and shy, but that was misleading. Jessica was a very fiery and competitive person. She did well at Cal Poly and had also majored in finance. In fact, the dean had expressed disappointment that Chris and Carly didn't have more of their children through Cal Poly's program. Both girls had attended Cal Poly, and both boys had chosen central US for their college studies. Jessica was another beautiful and confident woman who was finding success in the corporate world.

As part of corporate training, Jessica traveled every four months. She loved this aspect of her job and was excited that her company had acquired another small company in Italy for their European market. The next training would be in Rome. Carly had expressed her concern with the situation in light of recent air travel restrictions, the Middle East conflict, and with Rome in close proximity to North Africa. Jessica countered by pointing out that she would be traveling with a group of twenty colleagues. Chris had just returned from Europe and thought it should be safe. Besides, she was an adult working in the corporate world. He could only advise her to be careful in public places and to move quickly through the piazza's, avoiding crowds and tourist areas as much as possible.

The African virus was another issue to consider. However, with all flights cancelled between Africa and Europe, the risk that it could spread to Europe was minimal. Jessica told them that she was considering tacking on one to two weeks of vacation at the end of her training to see some sights in northern Italy, Slovenia, and Croatia with a couple of colleagues. This sounded like fun. Carly and Chris had taken Jessica and Mark to Italy a few years ago, but they had not seen northern Italy. Carly and Chris had recently visited Slovenia and Croatia, and they had really enjoyed it. As a result, they shared their travel books and stories (probably more than Jessica wanted to hear).

Chris walked over and asked if Grandma H and Jessica wanted a glass of hot cider. They both agreed that it sounded good. Chris went over to the crockpot that Carly had set up early in the morning with the cider and all sort of spices mixed. Grabbing two mugs from the cabinet, Chris poured two cups. Carly looked over with one finger in the air and Chris poured a third and handed it to her.

Walking back in the room, Chris handed the drinks to the ladies. His father, Grandpa H, pulled him aside to give an update on their property, in Brownfield Texas, which was a little south of Lubbock. Chris's father inherited a little over one thousand acres—1,200 acres to be exact. They had a couple of wells and two farmhouses, one older house and the other one somewhat newer.

Grandpa H had inherited the farm, which had been in the family for a couple of generations. The farm was passed by Chris's grandmother, who split it between her three boys. Grandpa H was her youngest son. One of Chris's uncles did not have children, so Grandpa H inherited that parcel when he passed away. His other uncle's kids hadn't wanted their share of the property. They lived on the east coast, and Grandpa H bought that remaining parcel from them. Chris recalled as a young boy visiting the property, but it was a vague memory.

Grandpa H leased the farmland to a local farmer who had determined to grow maize the past couple of years. The area had been dry farmed for over ninety years. Grandpa H informed Chris that the farmer had a good spring and summer crop the past year. The lease had been written so that Grandpa H would get a percentage of the profit, so a good year for the farmer was a good year for Chris's parents.

Ten minutes later, Carly came over and told Chris it was time to cut the turkey. Carly was still very attractive to Chris. Carly's auburn hair had a trace of red, and her blue eyes sparkled and set off her many freckles. At five feet four inches, she was by far the shortest in their immediate family with the exception of "Rock Chalk" Ma K who might hit five feet on her tippy toes. Carly was still very slim from running several times a week. The children had all inherited Carly's freckles.

Chris loved Carly as much as when they had first married. Sometimes he thought he loved her a lot more. There was so much history after thirty years of raising four children: shouldn't the love grow stronger?

Carly was concerned about Chris continuing to push hard on the job and had asked him to back off to ease into retirement. He couldn't communicate easily to Carly why it wasn't an easy job, and with his personality, he couldn't ease up. It was an "all or nothing" situation in his mind. Carly's response was, "Let's get you retired!" Hence the plan to line up retirement with Mark's graduation.

Over the past couple of years, Chris had relinquished the cutting of the turkey to Ethan. Chris glanced across the kitchen toward Mark and asked Ethan if Mark should try cutting the turkey for Christmas dinner. Ethan agreed, so Chris walked over and asked Mark to assist, pulling an apron out from the drawer and setting up the electric carving knife.

Chris grabbed an IPA out of the fridge, opened it, and told Mark exactly how to carve the turkey. Ethan also grabbed a beer and started talking about a local hedge fund acquiring water rights to expand the port-folio. Chris often joked with his colleague Will that he often felt relieved if he were the "dumbest guy" sitting in the room for some of the technical meetings. Chris's joy was that he was surrounded by such smart and capable people. Ethan was talking, and Chris was thinking, "I may be the dumbest guy in my family," listening to the hedge-fund details by Ethan and corporate finance jargon by Jessica. Mark was learning and participating in the conversation, and Abby was talking about writing composition. The tactics seemed to exceed what Chris had learned in college over thirty years ago. He took a drink and thought that he got through school in the nick of time!

After Mark finished carving the turkey, the platter was full, signaling everyone to gather around the kitchen island to say grace. The family circled the kitchen island and held hands, according to holiday tradition. Chris gave thanks for all their health and for all that they had been given.

Then they started a line with their plates in hand: women first, moving counterclockwise around the island, loading their plates with the delicious food that everyone contributed for the Christmas feast. Chris stood back to go last, listening to the continuous chatter as the family move around the kitchen island and back to their place at the table. Carly was seated close to the island, ready to refill any platter or bowl that became half full. Carly and Chris always went last in the line. They had done this for years, and it worked perfectly. They refilled bowls and platters so people could go back for "seconds" at their leisure. Then they filled their plates and joined the others.

As people sat, Chris sauntered over with the wine that Ethan un-corked and asked red or white before pouring a glass.

Carly had acquired the "big farm" kitchen table years ago. With strong legs and a rustic appearance, it was perfect for holidays and special family occasions where they could add a couple of leaves to really lengthen the table. When fully expanded, it spilled over from the eating area into some of the kitchen, but it was a comfortable set-up.

Mark had helped Chris add two leaves to the table earlier in the morning. As Chris sat back in his chair, he paused after a bite and listened, watching all the conversation and laughter. Years ago, they often had their four children plus their grandparents over for each family function, enjoying dinner on this table. Now it was a rare experience to have everyone together, and it was good to see the table full again. It made Chris feel good.

The grandparents were all doing well. Chris's dad, or Grandpa H, had been diagnosed with a type of leukemia: chronic lymphocytic (when the body's white blood cells attack and destroy the red blood cells). Chris recalled how at one of Mark's Christmas basketball tournaments (when they hadn't seen Chris's dad for a couple of weeks). It was disturbing how yellow his skin looked. At the family's urging, Grandpa H had gone to the hospital, where he required a blood transfusion and weeks of chemotherapy sessions. Grandpa was in maintenance mode now and had to go in every six months for a week of chemo. He had always been an active individual, so it was a major victory that he could now enjoy some of his past activities and go on local hikes in the San Diego area. You wouldn't know by looking at him that he struggled to keep the CLL in check. Grandpa H loved outdoor activities and a large variety of sports.

Chris's mother Grandma H was also doing fine. She had had an issue recently in one eye with Glaucoma and had undergone an operation to relieve the pressure. The operation had been successful: she was doing well, and the improved vision gave her more confidence. She joined Grandpa H for some hikes, but her preference was to read a good book.

Carly's parents were both doing well. Pa K had had a hip replacement two years ago, but was moving around well (much better than prior to the operation). This was critical because Pa K was not one to stay still. He loved to putz around the yard and to shop in the local malls. He was happy if he was in motion. Chris noticed that Carly had inherited a little of this from her father.

Ma K had brought some concern with her heart six months ago, but that had turned out to be okay after a series of tests. She did have to take some meds for a thyroid condition. Ma K kept her mind sharp by participating in multiple bridge clubs and by watching the city council meetings on TV.

Carly and Chris often reflected how fortunate they had been with their parents' health and the fact that their own children were able to grow up with the grandparents nearby, to share in big moments. After talking to their friends, they knew this to be a unique situation.

Chris flashed back on his own path: he had gone to Community College and then to San Diego State, probably the least expensive path to a degree. His parents were able to pay for his education and Chris didn't have any debt when he graduated. Carly had taken similar path through school. Chris had met Carly when he was a young man, he flashed back for a moment to when he and Carly first met and started dating—to their marriage and the purchase of their first house.

In two minutes, Chris flashed back thirty-five years, to the life in front of him. Abby's birth had been a major moment, bringing further purpose to his life that had been reconfirmed with each child's birth. The miracle of birth, along with the responsibility and purpose, caused him to work with Carly to ensure that they raised good and independent children who'd blossomed to become responsible adults. The best decisions in Chris's life had been to marry Carly and to start a family. All four children were adults with different personalities; all of them had a plan for their lives and no fear to face their life adventures. Life was not perfect for any of them, but they were fortunate.

Chris snapped back and noticed how alive and animated the grandparents were with the children. The display of youth made life exciting again for the grandparents, who couldn't get enough of the stories and future plans of their grandchildren. "Let's face it," Chris thought, "Carly and I aren't that exciting at this time in our lives. I have work and business trips, Carly exercises and keeps the house and kids together, and works on her projects."

With retirement on the horizon, Carly had been tackling rooms in the house that needed remodeling. It had been time consuming. She'd started when Mark left for college; now they were halfway through. But Carly and Chris planned for the next chapter of their life to have less drama (although this did mean it might be more boring). Chris was contemplating some hobbies and had developed a list of potential diversions. Carly enjoyed crafts and repurposing. They envisioned the retirement life: a couple of trips a year coupled with time with the kids and grandkids.

With Abby two miles away and Ryan in an apartment five miles away, both were very close to Chris and Carly. They talked about getting a place in the general area when they married. Chris and Carly would have to see where the others ended up to see if they would need to travel a few times a year to see them. However, Jessica had stated that she wanted to come back to San Diego, and Ethan had his surfboards stored in the garage. Carly thought he could end up on the west coast again one day. Mark was still in college; they would need to see where his first job took him.

Ethan had had a serious girlfriend but had broken up with her just two months ago. Ethan had made the decision that they were too different in their lifestyles: Ethan loved the outdoors, but she did not. He was a camping type of person and she was more of a "Hilton" person. Apparently that was just one example. He cared for her, this had been a painful decision. It was a topic that they would avoid this holiday unless he brought it up. Ethan worked long hours each week in the office. When not working, he wanted to be outside as much as possible: hiking and surfing with his old high school friends in San Diego were some of his favorite pastimes. Chris and Carly loved the outdoors and could understand why Ethan felt that way.

Jessica didn't have a boyfriend at the time, but was currently living in the Bay Area. She had had a boyfriend at her first assignment in Seattle, but they had broken up before she was transferred down to the Bay Area. Jessica was talking to investment banks in San Diego and San Francisco trying to decide if she should make the switch. Recently she had really started to like her work. Jessica missed home and San Diego because she also loved the outdoors and adventure, but at least northern California was more conducive to her lifestyle than Seattle.

Chris and Carly stored two of Ethan's surfboards in the garage, a longboard and a shortboard. He and his best friend from second grade would surf when Ethan was in town. His friend worked locally as a civil engineer; while they were two very different people they shared a love for catching waves in Del Mar and had remained good friends. Ethan voiced his long term goal of buying a place near the beach (perhaps Solana Beach or Encinitas) to start his own hedge fund and surf on the weekend.

Chris felt something graze his pant leg while he was sitting at the table. It was Finley who had placed his head on Chris's lap expectantly. Chris looked to make sure that Carly wasn't looking, then gave Finley a piece of turkey. Chris spoiled Finley; he couldn't help it. Chris had been against getting Finley five years ago, when their other golden retriever Cody had passed away. He hadn't felt ready to get another dog. However, soon after bringing the puppy, Finley, home, they started to become buddies. Finley loved tennis balls and in the garage they had many cans of tennis balls ready for use. A visitor would think they were avid tennis players, but these were all for Finley!

Every morning, Chris fed Finley his scoop and took him out into the backyard to do his business. Finley was relentless, Chris estimated that he threw the ball sixty or more times per morning—enough to feel the ache in his shoulder. The ball bounced through the wrought-iron fence occasionally, an event that made Finley distraught. Finley would have Chris follow him to the edge of the fence, where they could both see the ball twenty feet below on the slope. In these moments, Chris went into the garage and brought Finley a new ball. Instantly, life was good again.

Chris and Finley would sometimes repeat this routine at dusk, substituting the coffee for a glass of wine or beer. It was a good way to relax after a long day; Chris would sit outside and rifle through the remaining emails on his phone. Finley and Chris loved their routine together.

Chris never thought of himself as finicky or an elitist, but ever since they had taken a family trip to Costa Rica years ago, Costa Rican coffee was instantly Chris's favorite. He would search for and buy these beans, grind a little at a time, and make a fresh pot each day. The dark, bold taste was unforgettable—he felt it was by far the best coffee. Friends would have him try their Kona or French Roast, or Ethiopian or Columbian brew but he was hooked on Costa Rican coffee. Chris got up and went over to the coffee maker and started a pot—it would be ready for dessert time.

In addition to its excellent coffee, Costa Rica was remembered as one of the families' favorite trips. With white water rafting, horseback riding, and a zip line through the forest at Lake Arenal, it had been a great adventure for an active family. The food was probably the weakest part of the trip: rice and beans were served every meal whether it was for breakfast, lunch, or dinner. However, the exciting adventure more than made up for the poor food.

Chris often thought of the Costa Rican trip while drinking his morning coffee.

Chris looking over at Carly, Chris felt thoughtful that through thirty-plus years of challenges, she had always been supportive and by his side. He had tried his best to reciprocate, but felt that she was his better half. Because of Carly and the family, he had stayed focused on his career and family. He loved them all so much and he thanked God for what he had been given. He silently thanked God, paused, took a bite of turkey and cranberries, and tuned back into the conversations.

Chapter 6

Three days after Christmas

ETHAN AND MARK HAD just returned from visiting Chris's parents, and Ethan was ecstatic. Grandpa H had given Ethan the Winchester Model 1886, a rare rifle that was over one hundred years old. Chris recalled seeing this hung on the wall at his grandfather's house as a boy. It was a beast of a rifle and Ethan wanted to hang it up in his apartment back in Dallas. Before he left, he said that he would pay the cost of packing and shipping the rifle to his apartment. Carly was not too excited about this, but Ethan and Mark were beside themselves in excitement. Chris heard Ethan tell Mark that they would take it out shooting when Mark visited Ethan in Dallas during his next break.

Later that evening, the six of them sat around the fire pit out in the backyard. Ryan was meeting with one of his friends, so it was Chris, Carly, Abby, Ethan, Jessica and Mark sitting around the fire. Jessica was talking about her upcoming trip to Italy. Jessica confirmed that she would have one week of training in Rome before a vacation that would include two of her Californian colleagues. They would spend two weeks visiting Northern Italy, Slovenia, and Croatia.

Jessica shared information on their planned travel destinations: one of her colleagues in the Rome division was from Slovenia and he was considering joining them in Ljubljana, Slovenia, to show them some of the attractions in Slovenia and Croatia. Jessica was clearly very excited about the trip.

Carly and Chris had spent some time in Slovenia and Croatia and they loved all of it. Slovenia had the mountainous terrain bordering Austria and Italy, and the clear lakes of Lake Bled and Lake Bohinj, along with the eerie aquamarine clear water in Vintgar Gorge. Croatia was incredible; the Plitvice Lakes had the same clear aquamarine water with numerous waterfalls and pools, and of course the Adriatic coast.

Jessica shared that because of time constraints, they would only go down to Plitvice Lakes in Croatia, but they would spend a number of days in Slovenia. They would take a train to Venice, spend a day there, spend a day or two in the Italian Alps, and then they would travel to Ljubljana. Drago, her Slovenian colleague, would join them on this last excursion and drive them to the Plitvice, Croatia destination and then introduce them to the sights in Slovenia.

Chris thought of how much he liked having the family together, they only had two more days before Ethan and Jessica had to fly back to Texas and northern California. Carly had received a phone call from her father Pa K earlier in the day, confirming that her parents would be flying back to Wisconsin in March for a two-week trip to visit family.

Pa K's sister and husband lived up in Door County, Wisconsin, in a small town called Fish Creek. It was a northern finger of Wisconsin with only Lake Michigan separating it from Canada. The grandparents were getting older and recognized that time together was getting short. Opportunities to see loved ones were not to be missed. Carly's folks also planned to visit other nephews and nieces who lived from Racine, Wisconsin, all the way up to Fish Creek. Carly wrote their flight information on her master calendar and told them she'd shuttle them to the airport and pick them up at the end of their trip.

Carly reminded Chris that it had been a long time since they had last visited Wisconsin. Chris reminisced that their last visit had been in early October when Abby and Ethan were very small. The leaves on the trees had turned to vibrant reds and yellows that floated effortlessly to the forest floor. They had rented bikes with carriers attached to the backs of the bikes. The carriers were little seats on wheels with a covered canopy to shield Abby and Ethan from the pounding rain and wind. Carly and Chris leisurely cycled their family through the park on the Lake Michigan shore. It was a special moment. They stopped and let the children stretch their legs, and they both ran through the forest trying to catch the falling leaves as they danced to the ground. Chris and Carly knew how special these moments were—the simple things were often the best things in life. Fortunately Chris and Carly had a collection of these wonderful but simple moments.

He tuned into the current conversation regarding the supply and demand of coffee and cocoa. Chris listened, enjoying the glass of cabernet that his children had brought out for him. He wondered if that would be a good retirement plan: buy land in Panama or Costa Rica, and plant a coffee or cocoa plantation? He envisioned himself in a safari hat with khakis in an open-air jeep, with Finley riding shotgun as they traveled through their plantation. He could picture this.

Chapter 7

Two days later

CHRIS PULLED THE CAR up to the terminal departure area of the San Diego airport. Ethan and Jessica had flights in the next two hours to their respective homes, he drove them together to the airport.

Ethan would fly to DFW and then drive to his apartment in downtown Dallas, and Jessica would fly to the Oakland airport and then take a short drive to her apartment in Pleasanton. Ethan had the first flight so they dropped him off at the curb before grabbing a refreshment with Jessica—and then dropped her off at her terminal. Having them all home for a week was fantastic—it would be next Christmas holiday before they would have the entire family back together.

In a couple of days, Chris and Carly would take Mark back to San Diego Lindbergh field for his flight to Norman, Oklahoma, to begin his spring school semester at OU. Abby's fifth grade class would start back in a few days, so she was working in the classroom that weekend preparing for the first couple of weeks of January. This was hard for both Chris and Carly. They easily got depressed when they dwelt on the end of the Christmas Holiday: the aftermath after everyone left. The bright side was that they had a busy January ahead of them. Chris had the Consumer Electronics Show in Las Vegas after the New Year, and Carly planned to start researching for the remodel of their kitchen.

Their kitchen appliances and counter tops and back splash would all be replaced. The cabinets were in decent shape, so they would have them painted with new hardware. The entire process would take a few months, the goal was to be done by the end of Mark's spring semester in May.

Both Ethan and Mark loved Texas and Oklahoma, respectively. They loved their schools and the friends they had made. Carly and Chris had to admit that the people in Texas and Oklahoma were very nice and down-to-earth. Chris's uncles had lived in Texas along with many of his other relatives. As a boy, he visited Texas a few times with his parents. His sons had never visited Texas or Oklahoma until high school when they took university tours with Carly.

It was uncanny how the boys felt at home in Texas and Oklahoma. They loved the people, lifting weights, attending football games, camping with friends, and shooting guns with friends on the weekends.

Carly did not like guns which probably coincided with living in California her whole life. Chris would comment every once in a while about the laws in California being too soft on the criminals, he thought that someday he would need to get a gun for their safety. Carly was adamant that they would never have a gun in the house. When the kids were young, he conceded to her argument—there was danger in having guns around children. Now she admitted she was just fearful of guns. Chris often took his customers shooting at the CES show; he wasn't antigun, and he felt that they may need one in the future for protection.

Chris thought of his grandfather's guns. His father had inherited them all and had just kept the Colt .44 and Winchester. He sold the others when Chris's grandfather passed away. The Winchester could take down a bear or buffalo; he wondered what Ethan planned to do with that gun. It was an impressive rifle, and he recalled just staring at the gun that hung on the family room wall at his grandparent's house for five to ten minutes at a time as a boy. It was definitely reminiscent of the old Wild West. Ethan had arranged to ship the rifle back; it was already en route to his apartment in Texas.

Ethan had an appreciation for the classics. He had recently bought an old 1972 Land Rover as his weekend vehicle. He acknowledged that it wasn't the most practical of vehicles, but he loved that Rover. His ex-girlfriend wasn't too fond of it, and Chris and Carly wondered if that could have been a contributing factor to the breakup. Ethan didn't have too much time available during the week, but he enjoyed spending hours each weekend working on the Rover. He was saving up for the snorkel to allow him to drive through small rivers. Chris thought the rifle belonged in the same category: it was over one hundred years old and could be considered a classic.

Chris had always enjoyed the Dirty Harry series with Clint Eastwood; he contemplated asking for the Colt .44 down the road. However, knowing that Carly would be 100 percent against keeping it in their home, he thought perhaps Mark might inherit it from his Grandpa H.

Jessica had her training in Rome coming up in mid-March. She told Chris and Carly that her friends had confirmed their trip after the training, they had all requested and received approval for the additional two weeks of vacation. She had purchased a travel book on Northern Italy and asked Carly to borrow the Slovenia/Croatia travel book. The colleague from Slovenia, Drago, was reviewing and tweaking the proposed itinerary for them.

Carly bit her tongue. Nervous about terrorists in the Middle East and the virus in Africa, she listed out all her concerns to Chris but did not tell Jessica. Italy was close to Africa. Carly followed the news that large European cities had had sporadic terrorist activities and demonstrations. London and Paris were taking the lead in cracking down on any behavior that could lead to violence. Russia had invaded Ukraine and seized Crimea a year ago, and now there were more rebel activities in eastern Ukraine. Ukraine claimed that Russian Special Forces were working with the rebels, and the fear was that the ex-KGB leader of Russia would try to recreate the old USSR. Chris listened and tried to calm her, but he knew that there was some risk and her concerns were valid. However, there was risk at home as well.

* * * * *

Chris returned home from an afternoon work meeting and changed from his work clothes to his gym attire. Carly was convinced that he needed to lose twenty pounds by the time he retired. This was his New Years' resolution, although he thought ten to fifteen was more realistic. She monitored what he ate at home and she was correct that he needed to drop a few, so Chris went along with the plan and followed her proposed regimen.

Carly even solicited the children to push on Chris. Jessica especially was a fitness fanatic, and she really rode Chris to take the challenge to lose weight. Mark's graduation and Chris's sixtieth birthday were perfectly aligned, so Chris had a two-year plan to shed the weight. Chris had had knee surgery recently for a torn meniscus and to take care of some other "cleanup," as the surgeon called it. The doctor explained in detail (and sold Carly) how losing the additional weight would help Chris's knees in the future. It was all logical and good, and Chris needed to do it. As he changed into his gym shirt, he hoped that he could lose the weight in the waist and butt and go down a pant size. Yes, he would accept Jessica's challenge. He thought he may do a little more cardio and more reps with lighter weights this next year to help slim down.

Chris worked hard at the gym, drove home, and ten minutes later was still sweaty as he walked in from the garage into the kitchen and family room. He switched on the news briefly to get an update on the epidemic virus, to hear more on ISIS and other terrorist activities, and to review polls showing public anger in the US with regards to politicians and especially the White House. The final clip honed in on the concern over Russia's intentions with Ukraine.

Chris turned off the TV and headed upstairs to shower, hoping that the next election campaign would offer a conservative Democrat candidate and a moderate Republican candidate. He wanted to have two good choices to choose from. In the past couple of presidential elections, he hadn't been too excited with either of the choices.

After his shower, Chris came down to the family room and turned on the football game. He lost himself in the game relishing in the chance to rest up before the next week at CES in Las Vegas. The CES show was too big. It was almost impossible to meet someone if you weren't located in close proximity. Taxi lines could be two hours long if you were in a tough location. However, it was a "must show" for key players in the tech industry. Chris was definitely not a fan of Las Vegas, and he hoped that his Vegas trips were numbered.

Chapter 8

At home in San Diego, many weeks later

CARLY WAS TALKING TO Jessica on the phone, and she motioned to Chris, who walked over. Carly announced to Jessica that Chris had walked in as she switched to speakerphone. By the strained look on Carly's face, Chris assumed he was walking into a stressful discussion. It must have been an impromptu call, or they would have scheduled a "face time."

Chris discovered that Carly had expressed her concern about the Italy trip. The ISIS, Al-Qaeda, and other terrorist activities had accelerated in Europe, and in the Middle East and Asia there seemed to be a pattern where these groups merged into one group effort with ISIS. There had been several incidents all throughout Europe with terrorist activities. England, Germany, France, and Spain appeared to have the most activity, with terrorist bombings and incidents where innocent people had been attacked in a market, plaza, or office building.

While the terrorist activity was accelerating, there were antiterrorist groups forming in Europe. It had first started in Scandinavia two months ago when a group announced a plan similar to the eleventh-century crusades. A group of bikers planned to go to Syria to assist the Kurds in fighting ISIS. The concept of a crusading army made the Western European governments uneasy. To date, the key European countries (along with the US) had supplied the Kurds and the Iraqi army with some weapons and had sent some special forces to train and aide their forces. The reports all came back negative. The US was not making progress.

Chris thought that the general public had given up on the US government's ability to make effective choices with regards to international situations. In Europe, many of the countries had not recovered from the economic crisis adding to the lingering stress on many of the countries.

It was hard to understand if the news accurately represented the situation in Europe. Russia occupied Crimea by force, and it was proven that they had been sending special ops into eastern Ukraine to support terrorists. Some reports predicted Russia would invade other countries that comprised the old USSR. It seemed as though another Cold War could be on the horizon. Russia, supplied a lot of the oil and natural gas to many of the countries in Europe, and that created an economic dilemma. If Europe pushed back on Russia, they ran the risk of losing gas and oil.

Would the European Union, NATO, and the United States express their displeasure and let it go from there? Or would they implement economic sanctions on Russia and possibly assemble forces on the border to support the Ukraine and Baltic countries? All were good questions posed by both TV and newspaper editorials.

Carly wanted Chris to join the conversation so he could give his "father speech" and ask Jessica to promise that she would be cautious during her trip. Chris asked Jessica for her detailed itinerary and requested she check in periodically via text message to confirm that she was fine. Jessica endured Chris's quick speech and agreed to keep them informed.

The conversation ended on a high note. Chris and Carly discussed that Jessica was an adult; there were different boundaries now. Chris also pointed out that Jessica was working for a Fortune 500 firm: her company should have a good pulse on the safety for Rome and Europe since they had a division there.

Chris had an easier time connecting with Jessica on "touchy subjects." Carly was the mom and so focused on all the possible negative outcomes. Chris mused that there must have been a "Mom class" where all moms learned to uncover all potential dangers to warn their children of.

Jessica was a risk taker like Ethan; they mostly saw the challenge and excitement of opportunities. For example, a year ago when Jessica had gone skydiving, only telling Carly and Chris about her adventure after the jump (instead of letting them know beforehand). Certainly Chris was not a skydiving candidate, but he generally saw more opportunity than danger.

Abby was a little more like Carly, a bit more cautious. Mark seemed in between, but he was still developing. Chris had the feeling that he would end up a little toward Jessica and Ethan. While Chris said this to Carly, he contemplated whether or not to try to convince Carly (or himself) that Jessica would be safe.

After the call ended, Chris climbed upstairs to change and to put on his jeans to get more comfortable. Finley was there in the doorway, the tennis ball in his mouth and his tail wagging profusely. His body language strongly suggested that they both needed time outside. Chris took his phone and poured a glass of wine; then the two of them went outside to the back of the yard. Chris threw the ball and cleaned out his open emails to ensure a fresh start the next day. Carly walked out fifteen minutes later to sit with Chris and Finley under the giant tree.

When they had moved into the house almost twenty years ago, there had only been dirt for both the front and back yard. The tree in their far backyard was only six feet tall when they had planted it—now it was about fifty feet tall and forty feet wide, with a beautiful and shady canopy. They had placed a couple of Adirondack chairs under the tree on the lawn facing the house about one hundred feet away. This was Chris and Finley's early evening spot. Finley knew that this was the evening spot and the patio by the house was their early morning spot. Chris thought again that Finley might be smarter than a lot of people in the world.

Chris looked up and glanced around the yard, taking in a full panoramic view. When they had first moved in, they had designed the backyard for the kids: a big lawn, a large swing set and fort that his father-in-law and Chris built, a tetherball in the far back corner, and a large trampoline in the other corner with a mini basketball court near the side of the yard. Now only the basketball court was left, and the grass area was a little smaller where Chris had reduced its boundaries a couple of years ago. The trees and vegetation had grown the past seventeen years, so they had shade and privacy from their neighbors.

Not that many years ago, Chris and Carly had had children running around with balls scattered throughout the yard. Chris had enjoyed coaching children's youth teams in soccer and basketball, and he was looking forward to watching his grandchildren play a sport one day. Maybe he would help coach his daughter's or son's youth team. Abby had mentioned in the past that Chris would need to develop some hobbies. If Chris retired and they had grandchildren someday, he agreed that could be a fun thing to add to his hobby list. But what other hobbies could be interesting?

Chapter 9

Mid-March

CHRIS AND CARLY WERE on the phone with Jessica, who was over-the-top excited. The first two days of training had gone well. While it was 8:00 a.m. in San Diego, Jessica had just finished her day in Rome and had a team dinner in one hour. She was in her hotel room and had ten minutes to chat before she needed to get ready for her dinner event. Chris and Carly decided just to listen to her report and not ask questions. She said that the weather was cool but pleasant, and that her new colleagues from Italy were interesting and competent. Her travel colleague Drago from Slovenia was about her age. Jessica guessed he was in his midtwenties, and noted that he enjoyed the outdoors. Drago was from a small town outside Lake Bled in the Lake Bohinj area. Carly and Chris looked at each other—they had been there and had enjoyed that area of Slovenia. Drago planned to join Jessica and her friends at the Slovenia capital of Ljubljana.

After the meeting, Jessica and two friends would take a train to Venice and spend a day visiting and exploring the city. Chris had a flashback of eating gelato and walking the small walkways with Carly over the quaint bridges crossing the Venetian canals, before taking a gondola ride and eating dinner in a restaurant right off St. Mark's square while listening to the musicians. He recalled the gypsies wandering around the square, they had had to keep an eye on their backpacks.

Chris quickly turned back to the conversation in time to hear Jessica advise that after Venice, one of her California colleagues would rent a car. They would spend two days up in the Italian Alps before driving over to Slovenia to drop off the car in Ljubljana and meet Drago. Drago had planned an itinerary for them which consisted of spending a day or two around Lake Bled and then heading to Croatia and visiting Plitvice Lakes.

Chris recalled that the pristine water allowed for visibility to a depth of twenty feet or more. The fish below looked close; it gave the illusion that you could just reach down and grab them. Jessica advised that after Plitvice, their group would head up to northern Slovenia right on the border of Austria and Italy, before dropping down into northern Italy. Drago planned to bring them back to Ljubljana where his three US colleagues would continue by train to Rome.

The other two colleagues from California, Sam and Nancy, were both in their mid to late twenties. The young man and woman were in the same program as Jessica. Each year for three years, they rotated to a new division and learned about the operations and idiosyncrasies of each. They were both working in other Northern California offices. Jessica thought that Nancy was originally from the Los Angeles area and Sam was a local from San Jose. Chris and Carly were excited for Jessica, but they couldn't help but remind her to avoid standing around in public places and to be aware and cautious.

Chris didn't know when the switch turned from being carefree to a concerned adult: perhaps it was after he'd had his first child. Chris tried to imagine how he and Carly would have responded to all that advice at Jessica's age. Chris had a feeling he wouldn't have taken it as well.

Jessica needed to get ready for her dinner event in Rome so the conversation ended abruptly.

Her excitement had transferred to them, and Chris said to Carly, "We should discuss locations for our next vacation in the fall."

Carly informed Chris after the call with Jessica that Mark had decided to stay at OU for the spring break. Mark planned to spend the week with his friend Ray on his parents' ranch. They intended to help Ray's dad repair the horse corral and complete a few other odd jobs at Ray's family ranch located forty-five minutes northwest of Oklahoma City. Chris concluded that the free time would include shooting rifles and handguns on the ranch. This meant they wouldn't see Mark until the second week of May, when his semester ended. Chris was bummed, but he understood that Mark had choices to make.

Chapter 10

A week later, 8:00 a.m.

CHRIS WAS WORKING IN his home office, trying to catch up on email before his weekly conference call. Finley was lying on the tile floor beside him. Carly was downstairs working on a project and Chris could hear the faint sound of music in the background. The music helped Carly to relax and concentrate on her projects. Chris received a text from his colleague and friend, Will, instructing him to check the news. Walking over to the TV in the bedroom, Chris clicked it on and tuned to a local news station.

At first Chris couldn't figure out what was going on. There was camera footage of the White House, and a news reporter gesturing animatedly. But then the footage reverted back to a studio and another reporter came on. A terrorist attack. Chris walked out of the bedroom to the top of the stairs and shouted down to Carly that there had been some sort of terrorist attack near the White House and that she should turn on the TV to watch in the family room.

There had been multiple episodes this past year during which individuals attempted to scale the fence and break into the Capitol, but all the attempts had foiled. The would-be offenders were either delusional or without a real plan or purpose. This was different: the reporters at both the local news station and the reporters on-site in DC appeared to be frantic.

Chris could hear static noise as he saw smoke in the background. Switching to a live report, Chris learned that there had been a large scale terrorist attack on the White House. Reporters were still gathering information, but they had a witness on TV saying he had seen terrorists wearing black clothing similar to the Islamic State, or ISIS, and they had been carrying a similar flag.

Chris headed downstairs to watch the news with Carly. The local news moved back to the reporter at the capitol, who informed viewers that it had been a large scale attack: thirty to forty terrorists, all dressed in black, had entered the White House. The terrorists had used a truck to break through the fence surrounding the White House and then stormed the grounds. The terrorists were well armed, their arsenal included rocket-propelled grenade launchers.

The news program switched back to a local San Diego newscaster who stated that there were now multiple incidents being reported throughout the United States. While Chris and Carly watched the monstrosity unfold, Chris texted their children to update them on the white house event and to follow the news.

The news moved to another reporter in Washington, DC, who verified that the president and his Cabinet were in a meeting at the time of attack. There was no confirmation that everyone was okay: the fighting lasted over thirty minutes, and many people were feared dead.

A break back to the local news revealed a map of the US marked with the locations of terrorist attacks. There were confirmed attacks on many state and local government buildings, assaults on military bases, and many random acts of aggression throughout the US. Every major city was lit up on the map.

Chris switched to another news channel and learned that two commercial airplanes had gone down. One from Atlanta Hartsfield-Jackson International airport had been en route to Europe when it exploded and was lost in the Atlantic Ocean; another plane from SFO went down in the Pacific en route to Beijing. It was reported that three other airplane hijack attempts were thwarted. One attempt from Chicago's O'Hare airport and one each from JFK and Dulles were unsuccessful.

There had been a similar situation as in 9-11, when two terrorists were part of the flight crew. Another incident involved two terrorists attempting to board a plane with a concealed bomb in a small stroller. There had been a terrorist bombing at LAX; fifty to one hundred people were dead at the International terminal ticket counter area. Two terrorist bombers hit Detroit, and it was reported that another one hundred or more were dead. The news stories continued, reporting of terrorist attacks at bus stations and train stations, of train tracks blown up. It became difficult to comprehend all the carnage.

An hour later, they received an update on the White House. The president, vice president, and many cabinet members were dead—along with eleven secret service men and fourteen other administrative personnel whose names were withheld. There were thirty-two terrorists in the attack: twenty-nine were dead, and the three wounded were currently in custody. It was confirmed that the terrorists had had missiles and grenades, all were heavily armed with bombs strapped to their chests.

A news center reported that the state capitol in Sacramento had been attacked. They were in the process of gathering information regarding how many people had died. Another break in the news reported that in Albany, New York, there had been a plane crash into the capitol. There were two suicide bombings in Detroit malls. A video clip showed a small terrorist group in New York City attacking civilians randomly with knives. Bodies sprawled out on the street in Times Square, and similar news filtered in from Los Angeles, Chicago, and other major cities.

The reporter explained that military bases and government buildings appeared to have been prime targets. They had a growing list of attacks. Some were unsuccessful. It was obvious that this had been a coordinated attack on the US. A reporter asked an official how the terrorists were able to travel into the US, and how they were able to acquire heavy weapons in the US, and organize the attack. Information had been gathered that some of the terrorist activity had been from US citizens. Two newscasters had been asked how this could happen with the CIA, FBI, Homeland Security, and other organizations monitoring terrorist activity—wouldn't they have uncovered the plot?

Carly and Chris sat glued to the sofa in the family room, stunned. How could this have happened on US soil? It was confirmed again that the president, vice president, speaker of the house, and president of the Senate had all been killed by the attack on the Capitol. The secretary of state was the next in line for succession. He had been on a Middle East tour in Israel for an attempt to make progress on the Israeli-Palestinian issues, but was on a flight back to Washington. All military personnel were on high alert on military bases; all reserves and off-duty personnel had been summoned and dispatched to all government buildings. There was a standing warning that any individual who approached a government facility without authorization would be fired upon.

Local and state updates confirmed that the city, county and state police had been assigned to all city and state government buildings, including schools and utilities. Everyone in the private sector was instructed to go home and to wait for further instructions.

It was reported that there was a message from Washington, DC, to each state governor. Each governor was told that they were to take complete control of the safety of their state. In California, all police and sheriff departments were on high alert, ordered to protect any state and city buildings. Police were sent to all utilities to ensure that water and gas /electric facilities were safe. All airports and public transportation (including trains and buses) were evacuated with police or military personnel on-site. All transportation routes were cancelled; the public was notified not to enter the facilities until further notice.

Chris turned to Carly, they needed to contact family immediately to tell them to go to a safe haven. Carly sent a text message to Mark and told him to stay safe in his apartment located one and half miles from the OU campus, and Chris texted Ethan at work and asked him to leave soon and drive to his apartment in downtown Dallas. Chris encouraged him to be careful. Carly sent a text to Abby checking in—she assumed school would be in lock down mode.

Abby responded immediately: schools were in lock down, and all parents had been contacted to come immediately to take their children. After her last child was picked up, Abby intended to drive home. Chris tried to text Jessica in Europe, searching for any news of events in Italy, Slovenia, or Croatia. He couldn't find anything online. Jessica did not respond. Meanwhile, they received confirmation from Mark and Ethan that Mark was safe and Ethan was caught in gridlock traffic on his way back to his apartment.

After further digging, Chris found on the internet that there had been some attacks in Europe (but not of the magnitude of the US attacks). Chris and Carly called their parents and confirmed that they were safe at home and glued to their TV news stations. Chris's parents were at their home in Rancho Bernardo and Carly's parents were up in Wisconsin with family.

Carly received a text from Ryan: he was leaving his office and would go directly to Abby's apartment to wait for her. Chris and Carly spent the next few hours listening to the news and continuing to text family and friends. A few texts and calls seemed to have trouble going through, but they did ultimately make it through. Chris assumed that communication might be problematic for a few days.

Turning to local news, a reporter shared that there had been two terrorist attempts at military bases in San Diego that day. They were unsuccessful at both Camp Pendleton and the Miramar Air Base. In both cases, a small group of armed terrorists tried to enter the grounds. At Miramar, the terrorists made their attempt at the entrance off Miramar road. One marine was shot and injured and was in critical condition. The base was on high alert but confirmed they had killed the four terrorists. They showed a picture of a bullet-ridden black SUV. At Camp Pendleton, eleven terrorists tried to hike in from the I-5 freeway but were quickly spotted. Five were killed and six captured with no marine casualties. There was hope that the prisoners could reveal more about who was the mastermind behind these attacks.

Shocking footage interrupted this report to show a terrorist group in Detroit storming a local TV station and beheading two newscasters while on air. The executioners were all dressed in black. The video footage and pictures were now on the internet and all news stations. All local police called for reinforcements in every city. All businesses were warned to keep their facilities locked and were encouraged to leave private security guards on-site. Individuals were instructed to travel only when necessary. A list was posted of the type of essential facilities that would remain open with a reduced staff.

A late breaking news report interrupted the newscast. Terrorists had seized the San Onofre Nuclear power station on the Pacific coast near San

Clemente, California. Local police were positioned outside the facility and would soon be joined by special armed forces.

The news switched to a reporter interviewing a professor at a nearby university. The professor shared his opinion that in the event the nuclear reactors were blown up, the radiation would affect people and animals within a fifty-mile radius. The wind was currently blowing from the coast toward inland, so the expert explained that evacuation distance should be increased in that direction another fifteen to twenty miles. This region encompassed all of the Riverside and San Bernardino counties. There were over ten million people that lived in this radius. Chris pulled out his smartphone and looked at the map. His family was in danger.

A channel change brought an update on San Onofre: it was believed that the terrorists had plant workers held hostage.

The San Onofre Nuclear plant had been no stranger to the press the last few years. The utility company had scheduled it's dismantling because of safety concerns. Chris thought that this potential danger may have been overlooked for a possible terrorist attack.

Chris telephoned his brother Scott on his cell phone and assumed he was still at work. Scott answered on the third ring.

"Chris?"

"Scott, have you heard about San Onofre? Terrorists have captured the power plant, and they have hostages. We are both inside the radius for contamination. It's at least a minimum of a fifty-mile radius in the Irvine area. You are well within the radius."

Scott was quiet for a couple seconds. "Chris, thanks for the call. I need to call Stefanie."

Chris heard the click and turned to Carly. He didn't have anything to say. Chris called his brother Jeff in San Francisco. He was following what was happening in Sacramento: there had been some isolated attacks in San Francisco. He and his wife Helen were at their home with their two sons watching TV and reading the news online. Jeff felt that they were safe at that time and they were locked down until things changed.

Chris's phone vibrated; it was a text from work advising all employees to seek safety. Chris and Carly stayed glued to the TV station and their phones for the rest of the morning.

Chapter 11

Noon

THERE WERE TOO MANY stories in the news now. Coverage was focused on the United States. The secretary of state had landed in Washington, DC, and armed forces were on high alert and dispatched to the nation's capital. Federal, state, and local authorities had been dispatched and were on alert at every federal, state and local city facility. News outlets recommended once more that people stay home. Every ten minutes, a reminder played, "Do not drive to work. Do not go to school. Do not leave the house unless there is an emergency." Banks, grocery stores, and a limited number of gas stations would remain open with a skeleton crew and armed guards on-site.

There were reports of more terrorist activities in the United States, unfortunate reports of locals deciding to join in terrorist activities. What was disconcerting was that neighborhood criminals were taking advantage of the chaos by looting stores, attempting robberies, assaulting innocents, carjacking vehicles and carrying out other conceivable crimes. Gangs were taking over neighborhoods; news stations were attacked, and random attacks were carried out in shopping malls and typically safe neighborhoods. The news report in San Diego had the police chief asking people to stay calm and to remain locked inside their homes. Vigilante groups began to form in response to the mayhem with armed neighborhood-watch programs.

Chris and Carly still hadn't heard from Jessica. Carly looked at the itinerary: Jessica was supposedly at Plitvice, Croatia or possibly in the Slovenian mountains (or perhaps somewhere in between these two locations). Carly searched but she didn't have contact information to try to reach Jessica's fellow travelers. Chris and Carly did have a list of the places Jessica had planned to stay. Carly decided to email the Plitvice and Slovenian locations to inquire if Jessica had checked in. Chris told Carly that at this moment, the countryside in Europe looked a whole lot safer than the United States. The odds were that Jessica and her friends were fine.

Carly looked at Chris. "I think we should take money out of the bank if it's open. If it's not, we should use the ATM to pull out cash. And we should stock up on food."

Chris agreed to venture out to obtain the essentials. Meanwhile, Carly texted family members and made the same suggestions.

"If it's too dangerous, tell them not to go out." Chris added. "But if they can make it to a bank or ATM safely, they should withdraw cash."

Carly wrote Chris a grocery list, and Chris went to their travel drawer and retrieved a money belt and put it on underneath his pants. He would try to pull as much cash as possible from the ATM.

Locking the house, Chris went into the garage and took off in his somewhat-new BMW and headed straight to their bank. The BMW was a gift Carly and Chris gave each other, a statement that they were almost done with college tuitions. He had sold some of his last stock options three months ago and the proceeds were currently sitting in their money market account. He had been waiting to invest the dollars, but now that plan seemed irrelevant. It was most important to have the money in cash.

The streets were empty. At each red light, Chris looked around, ready to run through the traffic light if anything looked menacing. Turning into a shopping center, he was struck by how eerie and deserted the theatre, restaurants, and mom and pop stores were. Up ahead, he saw cars parked in front of the bank. Chris walked purposefully to the bank noticing that the typical solitary security guard had now grown to two guards; they were armed, hands positioned on their guns.

A small line of about six deep had formed outside the bank. Before permission to enter, each person was frisked. Only two individuals were allowed inside the bank at a time. Fifteen minutes later, Chris was frisked and allowed to enter. He went inside only to pass another armed guard before encountering one of two working tellers.

A young girl about twenty-two with dyed red hair, heavy eye shadow and pink lipstick greeted Chris. "Can I help you?' She asked in a practiced voice.

Chris gave her his account information, and she asked Chris what he wanted to do. "How much cash can I pull out of my account today? I want to pull the maximum from both our checking account and our money market."

Without explanation, the teller called over the manager, who explained to Chris that the daily limit was $10,000. Without arguing, Chris pulled $10,000 out of their accounts.

Crisp bills in hand, Chris walked over to some well-loved lounge chairs, sat down and divided the money into four stacks of hundred-dollar bills. One stack went in his wallet in the front pant pocket of his Levi's, another wad went in the other front pocket, and the final two piles were buried in the money belt hidden beneath his pants. Without another word, Chris walked out, got in his car and drove to the grocery store.

The grocery store was busier than the bank. Two guards were stationed at the only entrance and exit. Chris pulled out a shopping cart and quickly worked on Carly's list. There were a few other purposeful shoppers, but Chris was struck by the fact that some were shopping as though it was a regular weekday as they strolled the aisles. Chris loaded the cart, purchased the items (with his credit card to preserve the cash) and went out into the parking lot. Opening the trunk, he packed the items in tight; he had to also use the back seat to pack the groceries.

Although Chris had been away for less than two hours, there was now a roadblock a mile from his home, manned by Poway Sheriff's. There were two cars and four armed law enforcement officials with one lane open for traffic in either direction. One deputy was stationed to ask questions, another was armed with a shotgun positioned some twenty feet back. Chris was behind a green truck and silver corolla. When Chris finally pulled up to the deputy, he showed him his driver's license and explained that he lived up the hill and was returning from getting supplies.

Chris was motioned through, and he headed straight home and drove into the garage. He unloaded the food, then gave Carly three of the money stacks. She would keep one in her purse, and found discreet places to store the other two cash reserves.

Chris took inventory of a few knives that he had accumulated over the years. They were mostly collector items—they wouldn't be of much use, considering what other weapons he might access. His thoughts traveled to an old baseball bat stored in the garage. He brought it out to the living room area.

They had a very open house with a lot of windows to let in the sunshine; this was always a delightful feature of the home. For the first time in seventeen years, Chris wished that they could have all the windows boarded up. He had no idea of what to expect in the next couple of days, and that made him nervous.

Together with Carly, Chris turned on the news to see an update on the same situation. The military and police had been distributed amongst the public facilities and utilities to ensure that the public water was safe and that gas and electric working. Each community was responsible for establishing a roadblock at key points to monitor people coming and going. The lower economic areas were predictably bedlam and communities were having difficulty establishing entry and exit points. The troubled areas were highlighted in red on the map, people were told not to travel in these areas.

Chris and Carly kept the news on in the background as they organized within the house. The Texas governor had authorized town sheriffs to deputize a number of people in their respective communities to help keep order. There was a rumor that Oklahoma would join with Texas to create a larger safe zone. Kansas, Nebraska, New Mexico, and Arizona were also discussing joining Texas. The Texas governor was known as a powerhouse. He asked the sheriff and police chiefs to deputize a large force at their discretion: they were bringing back the Texas rangers in force. All media outlets distributed the warning to all in the territory that the rangers were authorized to shoot on sight. Texas and Oklahoma temporarily considered themselves a sovereign entity.

There were parts of large cities that were considered unmanageable. Large areas of Los Angeles were considered war zones. Local San Diego news showed red highlighted areas on a map to indicate places to avoid. Yellow areas were regions of concern that could easily transition to red. Authorities advised civilians to avoid yellow regions if at all possible. Meanwhile gangs built checkpoints on major roads in their neighborhoods to collect money and episodes of drive-by shootings were reported on freeways. As each hour passed, the nation plummeted into deeper chaos.

Chris looked at Carly. "We need to have a gun," he announced matter-of-factly.

She started to protest, but he gave her a look. Carly's nod of resignation was all it took: Chris got in the car and headed to the local Walmart, where he recalled seeing guns displayed in the sporting goods department. The last time he had been in that department was when he had bought a protective cup for Krav Maga classes.

Krav Maga, an Israeli martial arts program, was an art that Chris's boys loved instantly. They talked about it constantly, then invited Chris to join class with them. They assured him that he wouldn't be the oldest student, and they had been correct; he was the second oldest. He had to admit that a year in that Krav class was very worthwhile. He had learned a lot and it was great exercise, but his body was often punished.

Chris walked up to the Walmart counter where guns were displayed. The man working in the department was about fifty and balding, a little heavy set, clad in jeans, outdoor shoes, and the Walmart vest. He explained to Chris that current firearm law required a background check that could take in normal times up to two weeks, but with the current state of things, he was unsure if that was a valid benchmark. He understood Chris's pressing need for a gun, but there was nothing he could do.

Chris walked out to the parking lot and called his friend Jim. The phone rang four times and then Joan answered. "Joan, is Jim available?" Chris asked.

Chris waited about thirty seconds before Jim came on line.

Chris cut to the chase. "Jim, do you have Mike's phone number?"

Jim said, "Yes," and to give him a minute to retrieve it. He came back and read Chris the digits for Mike's cell phone.

"What's up?" Jim asked curiously before they disconnected.

Chris told him that he felt that he needed a gun, and wanted to see if Mike would sell him one. Chris shared his failed attempt at the store. Jim felt it was a good idea, and he was also concerned.

Chris telephoned Mike on his cell. Mike answered within two rings. "Mike, this is Chris."

"How are you doing?" Mike asked.

"We are okay for now. However, I am concerned about how safe it is out there." He paused before adding, "I would like to buy or borrow a gun."

Chris explained that he wanted to find a gun for both Ryan and Abby and then for Carly and himself. When he left the house, he wanted Carly to have something to protect herself with. Mike said that he had several guns and that Chris should come over. Chris planted the idea that Jim and Joan might also need a gun, and if it was fine with them, then he would swing by to pick Jim up before heading over. Mike agreed, and it was. Chris drove home. He took one wad of money, told Carly where he was going, and then called Jim to let him know that he was swinging by his house to pick him up.

Chris pulled up into Jim's driveway and walked up. Jim answered the door, Joan next to him looking worried. Chris warned Joan that things might get worse in the next few days, and he thought everyone needed protection until things were restored. Jim came out the entry to the doorstep and told Joan to lock all the doors after he left.

Streets were still deserted as they drove to Mike's place. He lived in a gated community within Carmel Mountain Ranch in a complex with nice attached homes and amenities like a community pool, gym, playground, and park. Jim and Chris drove up to the gate and punched in the code that Mike had given earlier. Driving up to his place, they parked in front of his yard. Mike had a small yard with plants and a sidewalk leading to the front door. All the homes in the complex had a similar front yard design, some with just plants and some with a small plot of lawn.

Chris got out of the car; they walked to the door and rang the doorbell. Mike answered, walked out, and looked around with a quick 180-degree scan before telling them to come in. He walked from the living room to his back bedroom, Chris and Jim following closely behind as he went in his closet. Mike explained that he had his weapons all locked up and in special containers. Mike asked what they had in mind for protection, and Chris answered that ideally he wanted a couple of handguns and a shotgun. Jim confirmed that a handgun was also good for him.

Mike came out with a twelve-gauge shotgun and handed it to Chris. He also brought out three boxes of ammunition and put them on the bed. He had a Ruger P89, a Berretta, and a Glock. Chris looked at Jim, and they both shrugged. Mike handed Chris the Ruger and Berretta and Jim the Glock. He went back in and brought out more ammunition—enough rounds to keep them armed.

Chris asked Mike how much he wanted for the guns, but Mike waved him off, pointing out that they could return them later, when things had settled down. He joked that with his military background he was always semi-ready for the Apocalypse. Chris and Jim thanked Mike profusely. Before they left, Mike asked them how comfortable they were with the guns. Chris explained that he had gone shooting a few times in Las Vegas at CES and his experience shooting with the three of them. He thought Abby and Ryan had minimal experience at best and Carly had none. Jim mentioned that his major experience was thirty years ago when he was in the military.

Mike suggested that they hold a quick shooting lesson on how to hold and treat the guns. Everyone agreed, the plan was to meet at Chris's house at 8:00 a.m. the next day, then find a place in the country to shoot. They said their goodbyes, and Chris dropped Jim off at his house, and then he continued on home.

Chris brought the guns into the family room and called Abby to tell her about the guns he had borrowed from Mike. He asked if she and Ryan could come to their house the next morning at 8:00 a.m. for shooting practice. Abby had been shooting a couple of times with Jessica at the shooting range, and she said that Ryan had a little experience.

Chris called Ethan and then he called Mark. Chris recommended that they research their respective state gun laws and consider purchasing a handgun at the local store. Ethan had the Winchester rifle, and Chris suggested that he buy several rounds of ammunition while he shopped for a handgun. Chris informed him that he had borrowed some guns from Mike and explained their plans to go shooting. Chris determined to bring Carly along to learn to shoot despite her protests.

By the evening, Carly and Chris had checked in with Abby, Ethan, Mark, and the grandparents. Still no response from Jessica. Carly had reached her parents in Wisconsin—they were safe with relatives up in Fish Creek. Chris told Carly that in some ways it was good that they were on vacation and in a desolate area. Carly's cousin was a retired detective, and he was with them in Fish Creek at the reunion. Chris knew that he'd be a cautious, tough guy, not to mention armed. He believed they were in good hands.

Chris left the cell phone by his bed stand, hoping that Jessica would contact them in the night. They had a restless sleep, each of them waking up every hour or two to check to make sure they hadn't accidently slept through a phone call or text message. However, as of 3:30 a.m., there was still nothing from Jessica.

Chapter 12

Next morning, 7:50 a.m.

ABBY, RYAN, CARLY, AND Chris were all in the family room. Chris placed the two handguns and a shotgun on the table. He told the others why he had suggested they participate with Mike for practice shooting.

"Mike is an expert with armed weapons, and we want to ensure that each of us feel comfortable shooting. Ryan, since you have some experience, please assist Abby. I'll work with Carly."

Carly gave Chris a look, but before she could say something, Chris blurted, "Look, hopefully we won't have to use these, but the violence has been escalating by the hour. It's better to borrow the guns and not have to use them. But we must be able to defend ourselves."

Chris received nods of approval. There was a knock on the front door and when Chris answered it, Jim and Mike were standing on the front step. Chris invited them in and noticed right away that it was only the two of them.

"Are Joan and Clark joining us?" Chris asked.

"They don't think that guns will be necessary, so they told me to go ahead without them," Jim replied with a shrug. "And Joan is taking her mother to her doctor's appointment." Jim added.

Chris knew that Joan's parents had a few medical issues and that Joan was the dutiful daughter that took them to their appointments.

Chris waved them inside and they joined Carly, Abby, and Ryan in the kitchen. After a few greetings and some small talk, Chris led the group through the kitchen and laundry room and out into the garage. Pushing the button to open the garage door, Chris pulled out some water bottles and passed them around. Mike and Jim excused themselves and went back to their vehicle and came back with a black container. Chris pulled out their eight-year-old Toyota minivan and opened the back hatch for Mike to load the container with additional guns and ammunition. It was the third minivan that Chris and Carly had owned, and this Toyota was the best of the three. They didn't use it as often now, except for big shopping sprees and for home improvement supplies. It wasn't always necessary, but it came in handy at times like this.

Chris drove until he was stopped at the Poway Sheriff's roadblock; he showed his ID and shared where they were going, and the group made it through. Continuing on to the east part of Poway on Scripps Poway Parkway, they took a side road off I-67 and found a desolate area.

Mike had brought a bag of empty soda cans for targets, and Jim and Chris set them up on rocks while Mike opened his container and took out the weapons for target practice.

Mike was very patient. Chris wouldn't say they walked away as experts, but Chris made sure that he, Abby, Ryan, and Carly had ample experience with both of the handguns and the shotgun before they returned back home.

They thanked Mike many times throughout the shooting session. Mike was a tough guy with a soft heart. Chris didn't know if shooting practice was therapeutic for Mike, but he seemed pleased that he'd taught them all how to protect themselves.

When Mike and Jim left the house to head home, Chris suggested that he and Ryan go to Walmart to buy ammunition for the guns. Carly told Chris not to buy too much, but he wanted to err on the side of caution and have more than they needed to sustain them for a long period of time if needed. Chris felt that it could be months before normalcy returned to their lives.

Before Chris took off, Carly turned the news back on. Chris went numb. Too many episodes; too many attacks and killings. They heard a news update on the San Onofre reactor: four security guards had been killed during the skirmish with the terrorists. The terrorists had confirmed that they had twelve workers hostage; they were demanding $2B dollars and a plane with a flight crew at an airport within twenty-four hours. If their demands were not met in time, they announced that they would start killing hostages. They had further warned that they had explosives placed all throughout the nuclear plant, including inside the two nuclear reactors. If any attempt was made to rescue the hostages, they threatened to detonate the reactors. Chris made a mental note of the time the demand was made. Twenty-four hours was not a lot of time.

Ryan and Chris drove back to the Super Walmart and purchased many rounds for both the Ruger and Berretta, along with several boxes of shells for the shotgun. The streets were still empty, and so far, the Poway sheriffs appeared to have the area in control. Chris was thankful for Poway, the country vibe, and the separation from most of the other communities that were experiencing mayhem.

When they returned home, Chris suggested to Ryan that since they had four empty bedrooms, that both he and Abby move in immediately. Chris pointed out that it would be temporary, but he thought it would be safer to be together. Abby lived a couple of miles away in Sabre Springs; Ryan was a bit further northwest in 4S Ranch in an apartment complex; neither lived very far away.

The TV called to them once more, this time with another news update reporting chaos in Los Angeles. It was also reported that San Diego had some Mexican gangs that had traveled over the border into Chula Vista. So far it looked like Southern California was one of the worst regions in the West.

Chris, concerned, called his parents. His father answered on the first ring and Chris asserted, "Dad, Ryan is gathering his things and moving in with us until things settle down. I will be going with Abby in a few minutes to get her valuables so she can stay with us." Chris's mom joined in on the other telephone, and Chris continued, "I would like you to come and stay with us for a while. We have the empty bedrooms, and I think it will be safer for all of us to be in one location. We can discuss contingency plans when you get here."

There was silence on the line. "Well, maybe that is a good idea," Chris's mom replied hesitantly.

Chris was afraid that his dad could kill the momentum, so he interjected, "We have a lot of room and if things settle down, you can move back, but it will help us some with you here."

Chris's dad spoke up, "Well, I guess we could come over for a few days."

"Great," Chris was quick to reply. "Why don't I move Abby from her apartment, and then I'll come by and meet you at your house? If you can pack now, that will save us some time. We'll bring your computer and important financial and health documents along with some clothes and other valuables. Dad, do you have the .44 pistol that was Grandpa's?'"

"Yes, I have it loaded and ready," Chris's father answered.

"Great, please bring it, along with your ammunition," Chris commented.

Chris informed his parents that he'd borrowed some guns from Mike and that they'd gone shooting that morning with Carly, Abby, and Ryan. It was agreed that Chris would come over when he was done moving Abby in approximately two hours. Chris's mom asked if he had been following the terrorists' activity at San Onofre. Chris responded that he had been following the news and that they needed to talk about the fifty-mile safety radius when they were all gathered together later that day. Recognizing the urgency of the situation, Chris's parents ended the call to start packing.

Chris asked Carly if she and Finley would be okay alone. Before he left, he would make the rounds to ensure everything was locked up. Carly thought she would be fine, Chris loaded the shotgun and discussed with her how to use it. If a stranger tried to enter the house, she promised him that she would shoot. Chris left the Ruger with her on the kitchen island.

Beretta in hand, Chris slipped into a shoulder holster that Mike had loaned to him. Chris grabbed an OU jacket that Mark gave him last Christmas and put it on concealing the holster.

Finley knew the climate had shifted; he was agitated. Chris went over and gave him a few pats and then went to the freezer to give him his favorite treat: pumpkin ice cubes.

Carly bought pumpkin (without sugar) and put them in ice cube trays as a treat and Finley would instantaneously drop anything for a pumpkin cube. Chris thought that Finley's great hearing capability would be an asset for them down the road; they just needed to watch him to make sure that he didn't get hurt.

Chapter 13

Fifteen minutes later

ABBY AND CHRIS DROVE down to her apartment in the family van. Chris acknowledged that they'd been using the van a lot more lately. It now had one hundred thousand miles on it; most of those miles had been logged when he and Carly had shuttled their children around to their activities. However, they had kept it well maintained and it had recently been serviced with new brakes and tires.

Abby's apartment complex (and the parking lot) was half empty. Chris pulled into a space that was closest to her apartment, and Abby and Chris walked toward her complex. The winding sidewalk had grass and trees on either side, creating a little park area. Chris recalled seeing parents with young children there in the past. Now, it was eerily quiet. Abby went to the front porch and used her key to open the door. Her apartment was on the first floor, across from the swimming pool and exercise area. As a father, the ground floor was one of Chris's safety concerns, although Abby insisted that the location was great. The complex was nice, and it was located in a good area of town.

When you walked in the front door, there was a little dining area to the left and beyond the dining area was the kitchen. If you walked straight eight steps, you were in the living room. To the left of the living room and behind the kitchen was a patio with a sliding glass door. The small patio was enclosed by a six-foot wall housing the washing machine and dryer. To the right of the living room was a short hallway. Abby's bedroom was straight back and to the left and Nicki, her roommate, was a turn to the right.

Abby's roommate was in the hallway between her bedroom and the kitchen; it appeared that she was packing her roller bag. They said their hellos; Chris liked Nicki. Abby asked Nicki if she was going to her parent's house, and Nicki confirmed that she was heading to their home.

Chris suggested to Abby that they pack her electronics and financial records along with some clothes and toiletries; she started packing right away. Abby pointed Chris to the laptop and shared that the laptop carrying case was behind the stand. Chris went over and put it in, stuffing in the power cord.

Their progress was interrupted by a heavy knock on the door. Chris and Abby walked quietly to the hallway, where Nicki was walking toward the door. She was two steps away from opening it when Chris whispered "Wait!" Nicki turned around and Chris held out his hand with the palm extended to emphasize the wait.

Chris walked over and peeked through the peep hole but didn't see anything. Walking over to the kitchen window that was about ten feet away, he saw two rough-looking characters pressed up against either side of the door to avoid being discovered by the peephole. Chris put a finger to his lips and then raised two fingers, and pointed to the door. Chris knew he didn't want to answer the door, but he was trying to decide if he should say anything.

There was suddenly a small noise. Abby looked from her spot in the living room in the direction of the patio and pointed toward it. Chris nodded and took the Beretta out of the holster and went over to the sliding glass door. From the side of the door, he stole a quick peek. He saw an arm and leg catapulting over the top of the wall.

All Chris could see was a tattooed arm, leg, and the top sliver of a head. He needed to time this correctly. Quietly lifting the lock latch on the sliding glass door, Chris opened it an inch to make sure it wasn't stuck. There was a screen door, but luckily, it was half open, so he could get out without touching it or making noise.

When the body was hoisted half way down over the wall, Chris opened the door and abruptly stepped out, gun leveled at the man's chest as he landed on his feet.

Chris was only three feet away from the intruder. He whispered with authority, "Freeze!" which was the only thing he could think to say. The guy saw the gun and froze, putting his hands up. He was African American with cornrows and he was wearing a baggy gray sweatshirt with the sleeves rolled up and baggy jeans with white tennis shoes and studded earrings in each ear. Chris told him to lay on the ground face first with hands behind his back. The man complied and laid down on the cement patio floor while Chris kept the gun trained on him. Chris patted his back and then patted his front—discovering a handgun. Standing up, Chris motioned for Abby to come over.

"Abby, tell Nicki to find some rope or wire, and to come back right away." Abby left for 15 seconds, then returned.

Chris gave her the other gun, "You remember how to shoot?"

"Yes, Dad." Abby answered.

Chris kept his focus on the intruder as he said, "keep the gun pointed right here." Chris had the gun directed on the intruder's back.

Chris continued," I'm going to empty his pockets, pat him down and take off his shoes. If he moves one inch you shoot three times, got it?"

She nodded and Chris bent over and told the man, "Listen carefully. You need to stay perfectly still. We will shoot—if you move. Understand?"

The intruder sneered, "If you think—" he began

But Chris silenced him, "Listen, I'm not playing around."

Chris emptied his pockets and found car keys, some cash in a money clip, a pocket knife, and a couple of joints. Chris left his pockets hanging inside-out and then took off the guy's shoes. He didn't find anything on his legs or shoes, so Chris figured the burglar was now clean.

Nicki walked outside with rope. Chris told the man to keep his hands behind his back, then motioned Nicki to come over. "Have you ever fired a gun?" he asked her.

Nicki nodded, and Chris told Abby to hand her the gun. "Nicki, be quiet, stand in the living room, and point the gun at the door. Don't go outside, but if you hear a noise like they are trying to force their way in through the door, then shoot through the door. That will give us time to come in the living room," Chris told her.

Nicki left the patio.

Chris reminded Abby, "Same thing with the gun focused on his back. Shoot him multiple times if he moves."

Chris took the rope that Nicki gave him and started wrapping it around the robber's wrists. This wouldn't last long, but it wouldn't allow him to easily move his arms or mobilize. Chris wrapped the rope tight, the guy grunted each time he pulled on it. Chris finally tied a knot.

"I'm going to help you stand up. No sudden movements!" Chris threatened.

Chris pulled him up onto his knees and then further up to his feet. Grabbing one shoulder, Chris brought him in from the patio to the living room. He told him to stay still as Chris approached the intruder's chest and lifted his baggy sweatshirt up and over his head. Chris could easily see the tattoos that decorated his chest and arms: the guy had a lot of ink. Chris asked Abby to close and lock the sliding glass doors.

"Will you move two steps toward the hallway with your gun still pointed in the direction of the front door?" Chris directed Nicki.

"Hand me the gun, and move behind Nicki," Chris added, signaling Abby.

Chris took the Beretta and pushed the guy toward the door. "When I tell you to, yell to your buddies and tell them you're opening the door and coming out. Anything else and I'll shoot you. Nod if you understand!"

The tattooed burglar nodded.

Chris pushed him up to the side of the front door about two feet away and stood beside him. Chris was in position with his gun and pointed at the man, who prepared to open the door.

Chris whispered to him, "Tell them that you're opening the door and coming out?"

"I'm opening the door and coming out," the man shouted.

Chris opened the door with the gun pointed at the man and slid over behind him, he watched as the friends had moved to the front of the door. They had a shocked look on their faces. Chris pushed Mr. Cornrows toward the door and stood in place waving his gun at the three intruders.

Chris directed, "Put your hands up real slow." The two friends put their hands up, and Chris told them to take slow steps back off the front porch as Chris pushed the patio robber to the porch and front step. Now all three of them were eight feet away from the front door.

"Put your hands slowly behind your neck and then get on your knees. Remember to keep it slow."

One of the intruders was about five feet six inches with similar baggy pants, and a white T-shirt on that resembled a wifebeater tank. The man had unruly dreadlocks.

"Man we don't want trouble, we're just coming to the door to ask—" the man began.

Chris cut him off. "Save it! Everyone will be okay if you do what I say. I need to warn you that if I get nervous, I plan to shoot first and then ask second. Do you understand?"

Dreadlocks was thinking of saying something and thought better of it. He looked at the other guy who was taller, about six feet one inch and thin, with a shorter afro. There was something Chris couldn't make out etched on the side of his head.

The two men followed Chris's instructions and put their hands behind their neck. Slowly, they dropped to their knees.

Chris yelled for Abby and Nicki to come outside onto the front porch to join him. Chris pushed the patio guy with the sweatshirt over his head down to his knees. The girls came out and Chris asked Nicki to point the gun on the patio guy. Chris looked at the other two men.

Chris asked Abby to come over; then told the short guy and taller guy on their knees to lay down face first. Chris handed his gun to Abby and brought her closer to them.

Chris told both girls, "Shoot if they move. Understand?" He spoke loudly, ensuring that the intruders heard the directive.

"Yes!" they responded in unison.

Chris explained to "Dreadlocks" and "Afro" that he was going to check their pockets and pat them down, and that if they moved they would be shot, so it was critical for them to stay very still.

Chris checked on "Dreadlocks" first. Chris thought that he might be the leader of the three. The man had a revolver tucked in the back of his pants, a switchblade knife in a front pocket, and a wallet with a lot of hundred-dollar bills, and some miscellaneous coins. Chris patted down the pant legs but didn't find any additional weapons. Chris took off his shoes, they were empty.

Chris moved to the taller one and found he also had a gun tucked in his pants with just a pocket knife in a front pocket and a money clip with some dollars. Chris left his pockets inside-out like the others. Stuffing the two knives in his own front pocket, Chris had a gun in each hand. Chris tucked one gun in the back of his pants, then grabbed the patio guy and brought him right next to his pals. Chris pulled the sweatshirt over "Afro's" head and asked the girls if they had an old sweatshirt or beanie. Chris also asked Nicki if she had more rope and if not, if she had extension cords.

Nicki went inside and brought out two extension cords and a blue beanie hat with a tassel on top. Chris tied "Dreadlocks'" hands behind his back and then "Afro's" hands behind his back. Once face down, Chris went over to the short leader and pulled the beanie down over his head and tight over his eyes and face. Chris asked Abby for the Berretta; he knew it was fully loaded and in good working order. Mike was meticulous on keeping his guns clean and oiled.

Chris told Nicki and Abby to be thorough and quick as they finished their packing. The girls quickly went back inside the apartment and got to work.

Fifteen minutes later, they had their roller bags, computer equipment, and a few boxes packed and ready to go. Chris asked Nicki if she was going straight to her parents and she confirmed that she was. Chris suggested that he watch the three robbers while they helped each other pack their cars. Chris gave Abby the Beretta and suggested that one stand guard while the other loaded the bags in the car.

They loaded Nicki's SUV and returned. Chris gave Abby the keys to his van and they next loaded Abby's things in the van before returning.

Chris asked Nicki if she would go back inside to call the police and tell them that there were three people trying to break into their apartment. Nicki came back out five minutes later, stating that the response time could be a couple of hours. The police were stretched thin. Chris had anticipated this response. Chris instructed Nicki to keep the gun and to get in her car and not stop until she reached her parents' house. She hesitated, searching for words to say. She ended up smiling and waving to Abby as she walked toward her car.

Chris then told Abby to lock the apartment, get in the van, put the key in the ignition, and prepare to drive.

Chris had multiple thoughts of what to do here. In one scenario, he thought about shooting and wounding the three criminals. He was certain that they would run away the moment he turned the corner and that they would continue looting. *Should* he shoot them?

In the end, Chris decided to pull their baggy pants down and off their legs. He soon had a pile of three pairs of pants and three pairs of shoes.

"I have decided that we're going to wait for the police, so stay still," Chris informed them.

Quietly, Chris picked up the money clips, the shoes and pants, and headed toward the van. Chris waited until Abby opened the door then put down his load and got in. Abby immediately started driving home.

About a mile down the road, Chris spotted a trash can and asked Abby to pull over so he could throw the robbers items in the trash. He knew the guys would escape, but hoped his tactic would delay them.

When they got home and opened the garage door, Chris helped Abby bring in her things. Carly was relieved; she had expected them back sooner. Ryan was there in the family room with Finley. Chris told Abby to keep the revolver, it was now hers. He put the other gun down on the table and told Carly that it was now hers to keep. Chris asked Ryan to remind him to take Abby shooting in the next couple of days to test the two new guns.

Pulling out his cell phone, Chris called his parents. "I'm on the way," he let them know.

Chris walked out to the garage and pulled out the car, driving over to his parents' house in Rancho Bernardo. It was twenty minutes away, but he didn't have to drive on the freeway. Chris drove to the north end of Poway, then continued driving down Pomerado road. He pulled up to his parents' house and backed in the driveway.

Chris looked around and didn't see anyone, so he walked up and knocked on the door. It took about a minute before the door opened. His parents had been very busy and were loading up their own van with some of their belongings. They had bought their van years ago with the idea that they would take it on road trips, the reality was that they didn't use it much, and now they were less interested in driving. However, it was like new and Chris's dad kept it well serviced. They typically drove their sedan around town.

Chris ensured that they locked the front door, then checked to make sure they had their computer, financial documents, prescriptions, and other key items. They had their roller bags packed and also some scrapbooks with pictures. They rechecked that all the doors were locked before Chris suggested that they follow him back to his house.

The streets were quiet, and they made it back to Poway and past the roadblock. Chris showed his driver's license to the sheriff so that they could verify his address; he explained to them that he was bringing his parents to stay with him. They arrived at his home and Ryan came out to help them unpack.

Carly arranged Chris's parents in Ethan's old bedroom; Abby was in her old room, and Ryan was in Mark's room. One empty bedroom was left: Jessica's, and it was decided to keep everyone's additional packed items in this room. It was close to the top of the stairs, so it was convenient.

After unloading everything, Chris and his dad locked the van in the driveway and Chris went over and sat down, smiled and said "all right." Ryan went over to the refrigerator and grabbed three beers, flipping off the tops as he handed one bottle to Chris and one to Grandpa H.

"What a day," Chris thought. Little did he know that this was just the beginning of an adventure that would change their lives forever.

Chapter 14

Later in the afternoon

CHRIS ANSWERED HIS CELL phone. It was his brother Scott. "Chris?"

"Yes. Scott?" Chris replied getting straight to it.

"Los Angeles has been labeled a war zone right now with no control in sight. Interstate 5 North and Highway 101 are sealed off. Interstate I-5 South is closed because of the San Onofre terrorist activity." Scott paused. "Our neighbors are leaving and heading east."

"I've been looking at the radius." Chris responded. "I wonder if we should also think about leaving. Even if they give the terrorists the 2 billion dollars and an escape route to freedom, I'm worried that they still might detonate the bombs around the reactors,"

Scott agreed. "We need to leave. We're heading to Stefanie's uncle's place outside Carson City, Nevada. We're taking Stefanie's mom. Her sister and brother-in-law will be following with their children. Her uncle reports that things are calm in Carson City."

"When are you leaving?" Chris inquired.

"In less than an hour. We're packing the SUV now with our essentials, then we're heading out. We'll stop and pick up my mother-in-law in Palm Springs on the way. Are Mom and Dad with you?"

"Yes, they are. We also have Abby and Ryan here. We'll all sit down soon and decide if we should move outside the radius surrounding the San Onofre Nuclear plant. Take care of yourselves. Do you have a gun?"

"No, we don't but there is a caravan of neighbors heading out to Palm Springs so we think it will be safe. Stefanie's uncle has a couple of guns, and so do his immediate neighbors. They live ten minutes outside of Carson City and it's very quiet." Chris wished him well and then hung up.

Carly listened in on the tail end of the conversation. Chris turned to her. "Scott and Stefanie are heading to her uncle's place in the Reno area. Scott substantiated that Los Angeles is a mess and that all the northern highways are closed. Also, as we expected, the I-5 South is closed because of San Onofre—it will be closed on the north side as well. They'll travel east, pick up Scott's mother-in-law, and head toward Stefanie's uncle in Carson City, Nevada. They're concerned about the terrorists, gangs, and looters in Los Angeles that are pouring into Orange County, and also about the situation with the terrorists at San Onofre."

Chris paused and looked at Carly. "Can we get everyone at the kitchen table to strategize our next steps?"

Before Carly has a chance to respond, the doorbell rang. Walking over to the front door, Chris looked through the peep hole. It was their next door neighbors, the Callahans. They had children the same ages as Abby and Ethan, and Chris and Carly had lived next to them for many years.

Chris opened the door. "Hi. Is everything okay?"

Mrs. Callahan responded, "Yes, the neighbors are gathering in the cul-de-sac across the street to discuss the recent developments and to share information."

Carly was standing behind Chris. "When is it?"

Both of the Callahans answered in unison. "Right now. We've heard that the marines are evacuating Camp Pendleton."

Chris responded, "We'll be out in five minutes."

Mr. Callahan nodded. "Good, we'll see you in a couple of minutes." They turned and briskly walked away.

Chris closed and locked the door and shouted out at the base of the stairs. "Mom, Dad, Ryan, and Abby, can you come down right now?"

They had been unpacking upstairs; Chris heard footsteps pad down the stairs in response to his request.

"Scott called. They are packing and leaving Orange County shortly. They'll pick up Stefanie's mother in Palm Springs and then head to Carson City to stay with Stefanie's uncle. Scott says that they can only travel east out of Los Angeles and Orange County, and that all their neighbors are leaving."

Chris continued, "The Callahans just stopped by. All our neighbors are gathering in the cul-de-sac across the street to share the current news. I think we should all join to listen and share what we have heard, then we should come back and strategize." Chris didn't get a response but received several nods.

Grabbing his OU jacket, Chris put it over his gun/holster and waited for the others to exit and then locked the door and walked across the street. There were almost fifty people gathered, filling the cul-de-sac. The people had broken into smaller groups and as Chris and family walked over, he could tell that the discussion was animated. Chris paused and looked at his neighbors. Unfortunately, he hadn't spoken with some of them for a while. Their neighborhood was a true melting pot: Indian, Jewish, Egyptian, Chinese, Japanese, Latino, black; it was a potpourri of neighbors and friends that had lived together for over fifteen years.

On his IPhone Chris received an email announcement from his company's HR department. Their corporate headquarters was based in Orange County and they had offices around the world.

The email put forth a strong recommendation for all employees in Southern California to evacuate their families and head east toward Arizona. The email confirmed that all northern freeways were closed, and that Los Angeles was regarded as unsafe. Finally, they advised that there would be follow up emails in a week with further instructions, but the corporate team would temporarily move to San Jose.

One of the neighbors climbed three steps up onto his stepstool and started shouting over the commotion. "Neighbors, please gather around. I would like to suggest that we share information of what we have heard so each family can make informed decisions on whether to leave or stay here in the neighborhood. Perhaps we can all take a turn and share key information?"

They all took turns sharing information. One neighbor confirmed the information that the marines were moving off the Camp Pendleton base. There were reports of marine vehicles caravanning from the base across Highway 78 down I-15 south and moving east' on I-8 toward Arizona. Another neighbor shared that Miramar base personnel were also moving. He had heard the planes take off earlier today from his house. He assumed they were flying to another base. Another neighbor confirmed this news: he found a vantage point near the freeway and had seen the vehicles leaving the base. The consensus among all gathered was that this was a significant warning sign.

Chris relayed his brother's information along with his corporate email: that people in Irvine and most of Orange County were leaving, and Los Angeles was a war zone. All northbound freeways were closed as well as I-5 because of the San Onofre terrorist situation. One neighbor asked about the radius of contamination if the nuclear reactors were destroyed; Chris had the information on his iPhone and showed them the fifty-mile radius. He shared that it could travel farther, depending on the wind. Almost everyone in the cul-de-sac knew of the terrorist demands and the time limit threat to kill hostages. Then, for a few minutes, people shared what was happening in the rest of the US.

One of the neighbors shouted out what most were probably considering. "I think we need to leave soon, at least temporarily, until the hostage situation at San Onofre is resolved."

People nodded.

Another neighbor interjected. "We should leave San Diego quickly. We don't know if the terrorists will blow up the reactors on a whim or if our armed forces plan to attempt a rescue." People generally agreed, and the meeting was over as they quickly headed back to their homes.

Walking back to their house, the Callahans asked Chris where they planned to go. Chris commented that they would have a family meeting right away for discussion. Mrs. Callahan shared they were considering

Colorado so they could stay with their relatives. Chris promised that they would be in touch after their family meeting.

The family walked in and sat around the big country kitchen table. Ryan, Abby, the grandparents, and Carly sat down first. Chris started a pot of his Costa Rican coffee, knowing that his dad and Abby and Ryan would join him with a cup. Finley was in the kitchen and lying down below a chair.

Chris walked over and suggested that they go around the kitchen table and brainstorm all possibilities. Chris shared that he would go last. Carly suggested heading to Portland where her brother lived. Abby threw out the idea of San Francisco where Chris's brother Jeff lives. Chris commented that all northbound freeways were closed, and that they would probably need to head east toward Reno/Carson City (similar to Scott's family) and then attempt to cut over to San Francisco or head further north to Idaho and then cut over to Portland. Chris cautioned that most cities seemed to be dealing with terrorist issues; not just Los Angeles. Chicago, New York, Philadelphia, and Atlanta were other cities with major trouble and described in the media as war zones.

Wisconsin was voiced as an option since Chris's in-laws were staying there with relatives. It was a long trek, but a feasible option if they had room for them.

Grandpa H shared, "On our farm property in Brownfield, we have two houses that are vacant. One is older and would need repair, but the other should be habitable from the start. That could be an option."

Chris glanced over at Carly and responded, "Okay, one positive is that there would be space for us, and Texas is one of the few states that seems to be safe right now."

Chris added that he had heard of some unrest in Dallas and Houston and also El Paso, with some crime coming over from Mexico. However, with the increased enrollment of Texas rangers, the area seemed to be contained. Carly commented that it was closer to Ethan and Mark. One negative about west Texas was that it was 1,200 miles away, and they would need two full days of driving without delays. Maybe three full days, depending on any obstacles. Ryan added that the Callahans were heading to Colorado and perhaps they could caravan for half of the way.

Carly suggested that a vote be taken to decide. "Does everyone agree that we should leave the radiation radius area?" she queried.

They all agreed.

"So what are the valid alternatives?" Chris asked. "Texas? Reno? Portland? Fish Creek, Wisconsin? Perhaps we can pass out pens and paper and we each write down our preference? Or do we all verbally agree that one is better than another?"

Chris added, "It doesn't mean that we have to stay there forever, but we do need a destination outside of Southern California."

Chris looked at Ryan, Abby, Carly, and then his parents. "We just need to go somewhere safe temporarily."

"Texas." Carly shared her choice. Abby and Ryan agreed, and so did the grandparents.

"I think we need to pack tonight and leave first thing in the morning." Chris suggested. "The twenty-four-hour San Onofre terrorist time limit is 11:00 a.m. tomorrow." They all agreed on an early-morning start.

Chris asked Carly if she would call the Callahans to share what time they were leaving.

"They are heading for Colorado; they may want to drive with us for a day or two and then head north." Carly reported back.

Chris needed to call his boss and some colleagues and friends. He suggested that the others make any necessary calls and suggested that his dad and Ryan to take the lead on logistics.

"Try to determine the best route, avoiding all big cities and any areas that could be problematic." Chris suggested. "Right now, we're hearing reports of problems from white supremists and motorcycle gangs, ethnic gangs, and Muslim terrorists."

Ryan pulled out his phone for information and Grandpa H went into the den and pulled out a World Atlas. The two of them gathered at the end of the kitchen table to devise a plan.

Chris proposed that they call Ethan and Mark to see if they could meet them in Brownfield.

Chris dialed Ethan first. "Hi, Dad," Ethan answered on the second ring.

"Ethan, is everything okay?"

Ethan provided a status on Dallas: there were skirmishes in downtown Dallas, but from what he had heard and read on the news, it seemed like it was not as bad as other major cities. He said that they had shut down work for at least a week.

Chris told Ethan that they were leaving and heading to Brownfield and that they planned to stay at Grandpa's farm. He added that they were heading out early in the morning and they planned to stay in the houses on the property until things calmed down. Chris recommended that he and Mark join them. Ethan thought about the offer and said that he would consider it.

"Have you heard from Mark?" Chris asked.

"I've been texting with him back and forth. He seems to be okay. OU and all colleges and universities have suspended classes until further notice," Ethan replied.

Chris shared with Ethan that he'd call Mark next. Ethan proposed that he drive from Dallas to Norman to pick up Mark and then head over to the farm in Brownfield. Chris thanked him for the offer since Mark didn't have a car at OU. He lived about one and a half miles from campus and walked or took the shuttle to classes.

Chris dialed Mark next, and Mark answered on the fifth ring. "Mark, this is Dad. We're leaving early tomorrow morning from San Diego to go to Grandpa's farm in Brownfield."

Chris informed Mark that they had a family caravan of vehicles, possibly more if neighbors joined. Chris shared that Ethan had offered to pick him up and meet everyone at the farm. Chris then asked Mark if he would be able to buy or obtain a gun. He replied that he'd borrowed one from a friend. Chris recommended Mark pack his roller bag with necessary clothing along with his valuables, laptop, and handgun. Chris asked him to work on logistics with Ethan and to be extremely cautious.

Chris called Ethan back, "Ethan, I spoke with Mark. He has a gun and he's packing his roller bag and valuables. Will you work out logistics with him?"

Ethan had been to Mark's apartment. They had both attended the OU-Baylor football game last fall in Norman. Chris asked when he thought he would leave, and Ethan said that he'd leave Dallas the next day. They'd spend the night at Mark's apartment the first night, then head over to the farm the next day. Chris told him that they'd arrive before the caravan; he'd text both of them directions to the ranch. Chris made a mental note to get this information from his dad, Grandpa H.

Chris had a sudden thought. "Ethan, do you have the Winchester that your grandfather gave you?" Ethan replied that he was going to bring it along with the handgun he'd been able to purchase.

Chris reminded Ethan to use his Krav Maga training. "Keep your eyes open, and don't trust any person or situation," Chris advised. He also told them to stay armed and to carry all valuables en route.

It might not materialize into a long stay, but Chris suggested they pack as though they'd be gone for a couple of weeks. "Ethan, hopefully, it'll only be a week or so, but I don't think anyone really knows what will transpire.

Before Chris made his next call, he mentioned to the others something he had been contemplating. "It is not practical for all of us to take our cars," he ventured.

Ryan had a truck. Chris and Carly owned a van, and Chris's parents had a van. They could transport more of their belongings in these vehicles. Chris proposed that Abby park her Mustang in the garage by the BMW. Chris received minimal responses from the others: more nods and what sounded like "yeses" and "okays." Everyone was preoccupied with their own tasks. Chris's father and Ryan went back to the map, and Abby, Carly, and Grandma H went back to making their phone calls to relatives and friends.

Chris's next call was to his friend Jim to tell him of their plans to leave at 7:00 a.m. for Texas. Chris invited them to travel along. Jim was appreciative of the offer: he said that he would discuss it with Joan and his son Clark. Jim shared that Joan was concerned about leaving her parents and their doctors. Chris mentioned that Lubbock wasn't too far away from the farm; they would have access to all the type of medical facilities that they currently had access to in San Diego. Jim said that he would call back later to let him know.

Chris dialed Mike on his cell phone and laid out the evacuation plan once more with an invitation to join. Mike didn't hesitate. "I'm in, and I'll be at your house at 6:30 a.m."

Mike had a truck and stated that he would start packing his things right away. His last comment was that he would bring his whole arsenal of weaponry with him.

Working his way down the list, Chris called Will next. Will had read the company email about the evacuation and commented that he should travel all the way to North Carolina where his parents, sister and brother-in-law lived. Chris suggested that Will travel with them to Texas, then rest a few days and continue on to Asheville. Will had a Toyota 4 Runner. His two dogs were loyal companions that would make the journey with him. Will paused, then said, "Why not?" He announced that he'd start packing and be at the house at 6:30 a.m.

Next, Chris spoke with Jack. Jack had read the company email and said that they had decided to head toward Reno, then make their way up to Idaho. His older son and wife were up in Boise, so they would stay with them until things settled down. He'd take his other son and girlfriend with him. Chris wished him luck and both parties agreed that they'd stay in touch.

Chris had barely ended the call with Jack when his phone lit up with Dan's name displayed. Chris answered, and Dan got straight to it. He said he had read the company emails; and he planned to travel to his home and boat in Florida. Chris explained his plan of going to Texas and invited Dan to travel with them to Texas; from there he could head to Florida. Dan agreed, and Chris provided his address.

On a roll, Chris figured he had one more call to make. He punched in the familiar number of his boss, Dale, in New Jersey. Dale lived in a small town in Southern Jersey, near one of their main customer divisions. He understood the Southern California situation and the evacuation recommendations. Chris explained that Dan and Will were joining him on the trek to Texas and then continue to their eastern destinations; and that they were leaving in the early morning. Chris further shared that Jack was heading to Reno and then on to Boise. Dave offered his approval of the plans; it was his belief it'd be a minimum of two weeks before work could resume.

Chris set his cell phone on the table and Carly looked at him intentionally. "The Callahans will be traveling with us tomorrow. I told them to spread the news to others who might want to join our caravan."

Chris acknowledged Carly, then provided an update on Dan, Mike, and Will traveling with them—and hopefully, Jim and his family. Overwhelmed, Carly put herself in motion; she turned and gathered Finley's leash, toys, food, and water dish along with his big bag of dog food. Chris mentioned that they'd need to bring all the bottled water from the garage, then headed to the garage to begin loading.

Abby and Grandma H had started a pile of things by the front door. They had everyone's roller bag (except Carly's and Chris's), and they were packing food items Carly had listed for them to assemble.

Walking over to the kitchen table, Chris watched Ryan and Dad H with the Atlas. They were looking over the maps and considering potential routes.

"Can you take a break and write down how to get to the farm in Brownfield?" Chris asked his dad. "Ethan and Mark will join us there, and I need to text the directions. Who should they see to get a key to the farmhouses since they'll arrive a day or two ahead of us?"

Grandpa H began to copy directions onto a clean piece of paper Chris provided. Chris continued by requesting that his father call the farmer that sub-leased the farmland to let him know that Ethan and Mark would be coming to stay on the property in a couple days, and that the family planned to arrive a day or two afterward. Chris also asked his father to ask the farmer to inform other neighbors of their arrival. Chris knew that this wouldn't affect the farming, but with all the craziness, he wanted to make sure that they didn't surprise the good people in that community.

While his father made the courtesy calls, Chris reviewed what Ryan and Grandpa H had planned as their route. They would leave Poway to I-67, then take that north through Ramona to the historic gold town of Julian in the mountains. From there they would drop down to Borrego and the desert, then turn northeast to take the I-40 through Arizona and New Mexico. They'd take I-40 all the way to Amarillo, Texas and I-27 south to Lubbock, then on to Brownfield.

The planned route allowed them to bypass Phoenix and other major cities (including El Paso) where they knew there were problems. Chris went up the stairs to his bedroom to pack alongside Carly. They had to pack light; it would be a challenge to discern necessities from luxuries.

While Grandpa H talked on the phone, Ryan and Chris took a break from studying the map to start packing all the vehicles with the roller bags, food, and other supplies. When they finished, Chris's mother and Abby checked and verified that they had all the valuables ready and waiting in the living room. They'd move these to the vans and truck in the morning. Ryan and Chris finished loading the other items, then pulled a tarp over the bed of Ryan's truck.

Chris moved Abby's Mustang into the garage next to the BMW. Chris thought for a brief second that he should take his newer car, but then reasonableness set in. A BMW wouldn't be of use to them on the journey they had planned.

Six p.m. crept up, and the group started thinking about dinner. Chris suggested that after dinner they rotate; taking two to three hour shifts watching the packed vehicles in the driveway. The news had emphasized looting taking place throughout San Diego.

The bonus room above the garage had two French doors leading to a balcony overlooking the driveway and street. Chris suggested that they use this area for their sentry. Two large trees outlined the front yard. On either side of the three-car garage, the trees had grown quite tall over the years. It was easy to see below from up above on the balcony; but, from the sidewalk it was difficult to determine there was a balcony.

A plan was created: Carly and Abby would take two hour shifts, Ryan and Chris committed to three hour shifts. The intent was to let the grandparents get a good night's rest before the trek. Grandpa H pushed for a shift and Chris relented—modifying the schedule so Ryan and Chris took shorter shifts.

The order for the sentry began with Carly and then progressed to Abby, Ryan, Chris, and then Grandpa H with the final shift from 4:00 a.m. to 6:00 a.m. Chris figured if they had trouble, it would be in the middle of the night. Chris walked outside into the front yard and noticed that there were a lot of garage doors open at 6:30 p.m. Neighbors were busily packing their vehicles; Chris could only imagine how the block would look tomorrow evening once so many of them had moved out.

Walking back into the house, Chris confirmed with the others that they had their guns, understood their shift windows and knew how to use their weapons. If they saw suspicious activity, they were instructed to wake the others and to not confront anyone alone. They dined on a hodgepodge dinner, eliminating all perishables from the refrigerator. Soon after, Carly was up on the balcony for the first watch at 7:00 p.m.

Chris sat at the table with Ryan, Grandpa H, Grandma H, and Abby. They were marking their route using the Atlas and had a yellow marker, highlighting the Atlas pages. They planned to use Chris's copier on the Western US page showing the route from San Diego and through California, Arizona, New Mexico—all the way until their destination in Texas. Many copies would be made, one for each car in the caravan plus extra copies to be packed in Ryan's vehicle. The intention was to preserve their cell phone battery life; and not all cars had Navigation systems. Ryan had made the point earlier that a phone map application drained the battery quickly, so it was better to go low-tech unless they had an emergency.

At 9:00 p.m., Abby took the shift for Carly, and Chris's mom and dad headed for bed. Ryan ascended the stairs to take a nap before his 11:00 p.m. shift; Chris and Carly had a similar idea when Chris's cell phone rang. Chris looked at the display and saw that it was Jessica. Without hesitation Chris answered and pushed the button for speakerphone.

"Jessica! Is everything okay? We have been worried!" Carly blurted anxiously.

"Yes, we're safe, but there's been a complication," Jessica replied. "Nancy, Sam, Drago and I were at Plitvice Lakes when the terrorists attacked in Europe. Similar to the US, there were incidents in all the major Europe cities at government buildings, airports, train stations, and bus stations. Countries like Bosnia with a heavier Muslim population had even more trouble."

Jessica paused to let this information sink in. "The four of us are still together. Drago, our friend from Slovenia, and Nancy and Sam from Northern California are with me. For the past two days Drago has guided us on back roads. We made it across the border to Slovenia, we're currently in his hometown in a house in Lake Bohinj."

Jessica continued that public transportation was down in Europe, and that heading to Rome or any major city didn't seem like a viable option at the time. Then Jessica gave them a real shocker, "there are reports of Russian troops sighted in various locations inside the old Soviet Union. We haven't run across any Russians on our way back to Slovenia, but we heard the rumors often enough that we believe them. This is why Drago was cautious and intent on getting us to Lake Bohinj. The rumor was that many paratroopers had dropped along the borders of the old Soviet Union and that the Russian army had crossed over and occupied most of Ukraine."

Chris glanced over at Carly. He didn't know what to say. Chris explained to Jessica the current status of the United States. He then explained the specific situation in Southern California, and San Onofre and filled her in on how they were scheduled to leave the next morning for the grandparents' farm in Brownfield, Texas. They chatted for another ten minutes, and Chris asked Jessica to keep them informed of her status in Bohinj, a text or quick call would suffice. Anything to keep them apprised of what was happening! Jessica asked for the same courtesy as they traveled, and Chris and Carly both agreed.

Chris ended the phone call. He and Carly were relieved that at least Jessica was safe. Chris and Carly both agreed that Lake Bohinj appeared to be a good place for Jessica to lay low.

At 9:45 p.m., Chris suggested they go to bed. Chris first went upstairs and headed through the bonus room to the balcony to check on Abby. She was sitting up in the wicker chair, scanning out into the darkness. He asked if she needed anything, but she had her hot tea and was doing fine. Chris reminded her to wake Ryan at 11:00 p.m.

Walking from the balcony, Chris quietly made his way down the hallway to his bedroom. He picked up the clock and set the alarm for a 1:25 a.m. wake-up.

Carly was already ready for bed; she walked out of the bathroom and headed to her side of the bed. Chris stripped down to his boxer shorts and climbed in bed, rolled over to her. She snuggled in. Finley lay content in his doggy bed underneath the window. He lifted his head once to check on Chris, and then dropped it back down to sleep.

Chapter 15

Middle of the night

THE ALARM WENT OFF, and Chris hit the Off button. Carly groaned and pulled the covers close around her, Chris quickly dressed, pulled on his light jacket, slipped the holster on, and grabbed the shotgun in the corner, walking quietly out of the bedroom. Anxious not to miss out on the fun, Finley jumped up and followed him out. Gently closing the bedroom door, Chris and Finley walked silently down the hallway to the balcony.

All the others were asleep. Chris walked silently into the bonus room and stuck his head out onto the balcony, tapping the door in a little knock. He didn't want to startle Ryan, nor make a lot of noise. He whispered, "Ryan?" and then looked around the door.

"Chris, come on out," Ryan responded. Finley found a place in the corner of the balcony with his nose in between the vertical wrought-iron bars. His head was pointed out toward the street. Chris sat down next to Ryan, put down his shotgun, and asked "Everything quiet?"

Ryan answered in a hush. "All except for an old pickup truck that's been driving up and down the street a couple of times in the past thirty minutes. It doesn't appear to be a car from our immediate neighborhood, and it's not a sheriff's car or a military vehicle. Perhaps it's someone who lives a couple of blocks away. But 1:00 a.m. is an odd time to be driving." Chris nodded.

"What type of truck?" he queried.

"An older truck—it looked like an old rusty American-made truck, but I can't tell if it's a Ford, Dodge, or Chevy," Ryan described.

"Okay, good observation," Chris responded. "Why don't you get some sleep? We'll need you fresh for tomorrow when we work our way out of California into Arizona."

Twenty minutes went by. Chris was walking through the next day's route in his head to keep awake. An old truck drove by slowly at about five to ten miles an hour. The truck passed Chris and then pulled over two houses ahead and parked. There was complete silence, but Finley's ears were up and he stared right at the black shape of the truck.

Chris tried to listen carefully. His eyes had now adjusted to the dark. He heard what he thought were two doors opening and closing. It was very quiet, but the old truck doors betrayed the riders with squeaks. Then, nothing. Finley continued to stare at the edge of their property that bordered with the Callahans; a low growl from deep within his chest hinted at a bark to come. Chris reached down to touch Finley in a signal—to stay quiet, knowing that their location would be compromised. Reaching for the shotgun, Chris quietly laid down near Finley. Chris figured that he needed to minimize his body as a target, so he laid on his stomach with his legs and feet splayed out at forty-five-degree angles under the wicker sofa.

Finley's eyes focused on the pickup, Chris assumed that whoever was at the edge of the property had now moved back toward their truck. He supposed that Finley's growl may have altered their plans. One of Chris's concerns had been the presence of the two vans and Ryan's truck with the tarp parked in the driveway. From his perspective, it made them targets for vandals or burglars.

Chris and Finley were perfectly quiet for the next fifteen minutes. Then, from a distance, maybe three or four houses away, Chris heard broken glass, some shouts, then a shot. Jumping up off the balcony floor, he and Finley ran out of the bonus room. Chris knocked on bedroom doors as he ran by, and stopped when he reached his bedroom to see Carly. She was groggy; her head was up, but she stayed put in bed. Ryan was first out into the hallway, and Chris turned to him. "Ryan, that truck came by and parked up the street two houses. I heard glass break and a couple of shouts followed by a gunshot."

As he spoke, four more shots crackled, making the hairs on the back of Chris's neck stand on end.

"Ryan, I'm going out front to look. Lock the door after me, and keep Finley in. Please have everyone stay inside—you go out on the balcony. I'll shout up to you if I can determine anything."

Carly was now coming out of the bedroom, but Ryan and Chris were already down the stairway. Chris instructed her to stay put and Ryan would fill her in. Giving Finley the command to stay (he was poised to run out the front door with him), Chris squeezed out and reminded Ryan to lock up behind him.

Chris was out in the courtyard; he paused to let his eyes adjust again to the darkness. Walking over to their chest-high wrought-iron front gate (the entry/exit to their front courtyard). Chris didn't see anything out front save for the minivans and truck, which blocked most of his view. He did notice a lot of house lights were now on across the street in the cul-de-sac. The neighbors had obviously heard the noise but were electing to stay inside.

Chris moved slowly down the length of the van to look around. He still didn't see anything. Another shot rang out, again from up the street—it sounded like it could be the Jennings' or the Al-Jeeris' home. The shotgun aimed in front of him, Chris moved briskly up the sidewalk. He approached the old truck and saw that it was empty. All the houses now had lights on, and Chris was concerned that he was now visible. Continuing up the street, he heard another two shots; now he could definitely discern that they were coming from the Al-Jeeris' house.

Chris peered up the walkway through the Al-Jeeris' courtyard and saw that the front door was closed. He crept up the steps and tried the door handle but found it locked. Moving out of the courtyard, Chris hugged the garage and traveled to the other side of the house. He stuck his head out from behind the garage toward the side gate and saw that it was ajar. Walking through the gate and down the side of the house, he stopped at the kitchen window and peered inside. A shadow! Ducking down quickly below the window, Chris assumed a low crouch and headed to the back kitchen door. He could strategize well—the floor plan model was identical to Chris and Carly's.

Chris saw that the glass on the patio French door had been broken and that the door was now half open. He quietly opened it a little wider as Chris took two steps in, then stopped and pressed his back to the wall. From here he could see the kitchen, the laundry room further ahead and the family room to the left. Chris knew the layout of the home, he focused his efforts on studying the placement of the furniture.

Chris could see what looked like a body on the floor. It was dark, and he could only see silhouettes; but he didn't see anything suspicious in the kitchen or laundry room. Entering the family room, Chris approached the body on the floor. It was a man dressed in a sweatshirt, jeans and boots. He had dirty, long, scraggily hair, and some facial hair. The man appeared to be dead. Chris took a couple of steps to look around the corner toward the living room and stairway, where he could see two more bodies. Crouched low, Chris moved along the closet wall in the direction of the stairwell. He leaned down to examine the bodies and identified them as his neighbors. The husband and wife were dead, and there was a gun lying next to the husband. Chris was trying to make sense of it. He assumed that the husband had shot and killed one of the intruders before he and his wife were killed themselves.

Chris was unsure how many intruders were left in the house. The truck had still been parked out front when he had walked up, so there were most likely more vandals still in the home.

Chris thought about his neighbor's two sons. Ali went to a local university in San Diego, and Chris wondered if he was home. The other son was married and living somewhere in the Northwest. Chris thought there may have been two armed vandals, and he worried that Ali might still be in the home.

Looking around the stairwell, Chris saw that the dining room was empty. The dining room wrapped back around to the laundry room and kitchen, so he backtracked and headed into the den and downstairs bathroom by the den. Once had he confirmed that nobody was in either room and the downstairs was empty, Chris glanced upstairs. The stairway curved and there was a wall separating it from the hallway, which split into two directions. One hallway led to the master bedroom; around the corner, a longer hallway led to the other bedrooms, bathrooms and the bonus room. This was similar to their floor plan.

Chris knew that he'd be exposed on the stairway, so he decided to take the stairs low and quiet. He'd only made it up two steps when he'd heard footsteps up above. Stopping in his track, Chris heard some rummaging coming from the master bedroom. Chris continued quietly, pausing at the top stair.

A light was on in the master bedroom, but Chris didn't see anyone. He advanced to the bedroom, leaning against the wall by the double doors to the master bedroom. He heard drawers open and close and froze in place. Chris cautiously moved to the side of the doorway, shotgun poised and ready to shoot. Scanning to the left, he saw a man with his back to him. He had long hair tied back with a bandana, boots, Levi's, and a flannel shirt. Chris noticed a tattoo running around the back of the man's neck. The intruder was rummaging through a drawer and held a necklace in his right hand and a handgun in his left.

Chris took two quiet steps from the doorway to the left wall to disappear from sight. He was still concerned there could be another robber in the house. He didn't see or hear anything else. Chris was tense and poised, he quietly took two steps into the master bedroom and said "freeze." The long-haired man turned his head toward Chris and then whipped around quickly with the gun, ready to shoot. Without hesitating, Chris aimed and fired his shotgun at the man's chest. The man's body sprang back several feet before landing flat on his back. It took only seconds for the body to become very still.

Chris walked over quickly and nudged the man, swiveling his head to make sure there wasn't a third robber in the house. When he could not find a pulse, Chris confirmed that the robber was dead and reached over to grab the robber's gun and tucked it in at his waist. Walking quickly back to the door, he pulled out his Beretta with his right hand—carrying the empty shotgun with his left. Nobody was in the hallway. He walked carefully up the two steps to the bathroom and closets. Peeking into the walk-in closet, Chris checked the toilet and shower area of the master to make sure there wasn't anybody hiding in there.

Satisfied that it was clear, Chris came back to the master double doors and went over to the next bedroom. The door was open, so he looked inside and saw that it was clear. He went down the hallway, checking each bedroom along the way.

In fact, everything looked clear; the only room left was the last bedroom with the door closed. Chris decided to take a chance. Hovering in the hallway about four feet down, gun pointed at the bedroom door, he yelled. "Ali, this is your neighbor Chris. If you are here, please come out." He thought Ali could be inside, a third robber might be inside, or the house could be empty.

Chris waited and the door opened. Ali stuck his head out. Chris lowered the gun and asked if he was alone. Ali nodded.

Chris walked over briskly and pulled Ali in for a quick hug. Pulling back, he looked at him. Physically, he looked fine. Chris told him that there appeared to have been two robbers and that they were now both dead. Laying the shotgun down on the carpet, he sat on the edge of the bed, close to Ali. Ali's eyes were locked with Chris's, waiting for him to tell him more. Chris tried to find something to say, but all he could say was, "I'm sorry." Tears formed in Ali's eyes, and Chris's eyes were misty. Ali was crestfallen. At a loss for what to do, Chris leaned forward and hugged Ali. They stayed in this position, and not a word was spoken. Ali knew. Finally, they both stood up, and Ali ran out the door and downstairs to his parents' bodies. Chris followed him and watched as Ali knelt down to the tiled floor, hugging his parents and crying.

Chris felt queasy and sat down on a stair and rifled his hands through his hair. *What happened?* Chris knew he shot the intruder in self-defense, and the man had killed Ali's parents—but still Chris had killed a man, and it bothered him. He knew he had to be strong and keep moving. This was something he would just have to live with and deal with over time.

After ten minutes, Chris went over to Ali and touched his shoulder. Whispering gently, Chris told Ali that when he was ready, Chris wanted to know what had happened.

Wiping tears from his eyes, Ali said that they had all been asleep and were awakened by glass breaking at the back of the house. His dad had a gun and told Ali and his mom to stay upstairs, but his mom followed his dad. Ali said that he had heard a gunshot, then it was quiet, then he heard four shots and then the final two minutes later. Afterward, he heard noises upstairs, and was concerned because his parents would have told him as soon as it was okay. He'd been sitting in his room trying to decide if he should confront the killers.

Ali's family had already packed and had planned to leave in the morning, but they had been unsure where to go. They'd thought of traveling to Las Vegas and then up north to Seattle, where Ali's brother lived with his wife. Looking at Ali purposefully, Chris told him that he could come with them the next morning. He explained that they were heading to Texas where his dad had a farm. Chris handed Ali his father's gun but Chris kept the two guns from the robbers. He thought that he might need them in the future.

Before Ali had a chance to turn down the invitation, Chris suggested to Ali that they take his valuables and clothes over to Chris's house. Chris helped Ali to gather his things that were already packed in the family car. Without much deliberation, Ali agreed, and walked over to Chris's house.

They slowly walked up the driveway, yelling up to Ryan (who was standing on the balcony with Finley). "Will you open the front door?" Chris asked.

Carly, Abby, Grandma and Grandpa H, and Ryan looked expectantly at Chris and Ali as they walked through the open door. Chris told Ali to set his things down, then he asked everyone to gather in the living room.

Chapter 16

Early morning

At 3:00 a.m., Carly, Abby, and Chris's mom and dad traveled back upstairs to return to sleep. Ryan thought of going back to sleep; he and Ali were up on the balcony with Chris while he finished his watch. Ali had understandably been very quiet. He looked over at Chris, his eyes moist.

"I can't leave my parents lying on the floor in the house. I have to bury them."

It was quiet for ten seconds. Chris tried to understand what Ali was saying.

"Ali, what if we could bury them in your backyard?" Ryan suggested.

Ali looked away and stared at the side of the house. "Yes, that would be fine. My mom had a garden in the backyard that she enjoyed."

Chris thought about the good rain they had a week ago—hopefully, the soil would be soft. He silently worked to figure out how long it would take them to dig the graves. They had only a few hours before they had planned to leave.

"At 4:00 a.m., I'll wake up my father for his shift. We can go back over to your house and bury your parents. We have to be back here at 6:00 a.m. Hopefully, the soil is still loose from our last rain," Chris spoke up.

Ryan looked over. "I'm going back down to the family room to nap until 4:00 a.m. Wake me up and I'll help you," he said with a yawn.

Chris nodded and suggested that Ali try to take a nap for an hour as well. "We have a sofa in the family room with a lot of space … and you should get some sleep," Chris pointed out.

* * * * *

An hour passed, and Chris gently woke his dad up while trying not to disturb his mom. Chris's father, Grandpa H, stirred and then sat up to put on his shoes.

Chris left the bedroom to wait outside, and his dad joined him in the hallway a minute later. Chris asked if he was alert enough to take the watch, and he said he was fine. Chris asked him to come downstairs to grab a coffee so he could explain the agreement he had with Ali.

Chris explained while pouring the cup of coffee. "Ali, Ryan, and I are walking up the hill to Ali's house to bury his parents. This is important to Ali. While we're there, we'll try to dispose of the looter's bodies as well."

Chris asked his father if he wanted the shotgun. His father shook his head. "No, I think I'm fine with the .44."

Grandpa H headed up to the balcony for his watch. Ryan, Ali, and Chris walked through the laundry room into the garage. Opening the garage door, Chris made sure they were still armed as they carried two shovels and a pick axe. Chris took the garage remote-control off their lawn mower and closed the garage door after they exited into the driveway. With a quiet wave to Grandpa H that they were off, the three of them walked up the hill.

Chris noticed that most of the houses still had their lights on. He guessed that the gunfire was the culprit and that his neighbors were having trouble falling back asleep. They felt safer with the light.

Walking through Ali's gate, Ali reached through the sliding glass door and turned on the back porch light. He walked over to his mother's garden. Chris suggested that one person begin digging the hole while the other two brought the bodies out. Without further prompting, Ryan grabbed a shovel and started digging.

Entering the house with Ali, Chris watched as he approached his mother, who was lying on the family-room floor. Chris heard a sob escape from Ali as they worked to straighten her out on her back. Gently they carried her out to the patio to lay her near where Ryan was digging. They put her down carefully, then headed back into the house to retrieve his father.

Chris suggested to Ali that they take the two looter's bodies outside to the patio. They walked upstairs to the dead looter in the master bedroom. Dragging him downstairs, they carried him to the other side of the patio and dropped him down. Chris felt it was disrespectful to lay him in proximity of Ali's parents. Chris had shot the man with the shotgun, and his remains were a bloody mess. Then, they dragged the last looter out of the house.

Chris was not certain what had happened: he had heard Ali's account, and now he had been running scenarios through his mind of how the last stand had gone down. His best guess was that Ali's dad had shot and killed the looter downstairs, and a gun fight with the other looter had come next. Somehow, the robber had managed to shoot and kill Ali's mom and dad.

Ali walked over to Ryan, grabbed the second shovel, and asked if he needed a break. Ryan had made good progress outlining a hole about six feet by four feet. With a nod, Ryan climbed out of the hole and set down his shovel; Ali promptly jumped in and continued to dig the hole deeper.

Chris suggested that Ryan look in the laundry room for a liquid cleaner, a mop, and some rags to clean up the blood in the house. Ryan nodded and walked inside. Grabbing Ryan's shovel, Chris glanced over to the other side of the yard. He picked up the pickaxe in his other hand and walked over to the opposite side of the yard.

"Ali, are you okay if I start digging a hole over here to bury the looters? I think we should leave this house like it was abandoned. We don't want to have the police try to solve this possible crime."

Ali nodded but kept at work.

Twenty minutes later, Ali shared, "I think the hole is good."

Chris dropped his shovel and walked over toward Ali, peering down into the hole that was now about four feet deep. Chris nodded to Ali and helped him delicately place his parents inside the hole, side by side.

After they were placed, Chris walked over to the door by the kitchen and called to Ryan to come outside. Ryan was out within ten seconds. "Ali, do you want to say anything? Or would you prefer I say something?" Chris asked kindly.

Ali asked Chris to say a few words; he didn't trust himself to keep it together. Chris found that this was difficult. They had been neighbors for seven years (Carly and Ali's mom had been friends; Ali's dad frequently traveled for work and Chris would see him periodically and wave). Chris reflected that it was unfortunate that he had never been able to really get to know either of them.

Ali and Chris buried Ali's parents while Ryan left to finish the cleaning inside. When they had finished shoveling the last of the dirt, Chris suggested to Ali that he find something personal from his mother and father to take with him.

Ali agreed, and Chris walked over to the other side of the patio, hopping into the hole to finish the grave for the looters.

Five minutes later Ryan came out and said things looked clean—the master bedroom had been the worst. Chris advised that the hole was large enough, and he asked Ryan to help him bury the looters. As they worked to lift the looters into the hole, Chris thought about the truck.

"Ryan, help me find the truck keys."

A quick search of the looters, and Chris found the keys in the right front pocket of the looter they had found downstairs. Chris tossed the keys onto the patio, and they finished burying the men.

Ali walked out of the house just as they finished. He showed them what he had decided to bring with him: a necklace of his mom's that had been passed down a few generations, a small photo album, and his dad's briefcase. These things all held a personal connection for Ali. He told a quick story about each item—Chris hoped that with time this would help Ali move forward.

Placing the album and the necklace in the briefcase, Ali grabbed a shovel. Ryan bent down and took the second shovel, and Chris took the pickaxe and bent down for the truck keys. They walked out of the backyard and back down the sidewalk to Chris's house.

As they passed the looter's old truck, Chris mentioned to Ryan, "We should move the truck down a couple of blocks after we drop the tools off in the garage."

When they made it to Chris's driveway, he spoke just loudly enough for his dad to hear. "Dad, we're back. Ryan, Ali and I are heading up to the garage."

Chris saw his dad's silhouette up on the balcony. "How did it go?"

"We were able to accomplish what we set out to do," Chris responded.

Chris looked at Ali and told him to put the briefcase by his roller bag near the front door. Looking into Ali's eyes, he suggested that he go inside and rest—if at all possible, to take a nap.

Chris shut the garage door behind them as they walked in the direction of the truck. He needed to move the truck far enough away so that police would not link the truck and the looters to their street. The truck doors were unlocked, so Chris and Ryan climbed in. Starting the engine, Chris drove the truck down the hill three blocks closer to the busier intersection. Once parked, they climbed out—Chris left the car keys in the ignition.

Walking back up the hill to the house, Chris noticed that the evening was quiet and spectral. The houses lit up the blackness of the night like fireflies in a black lagoon. As they approached the house, Chris acknowledged his father and reopened the garage door and went back into the house.

Ali was spread out on the sofa; Chris glanced at the clock in the family room and noticed that they had worked quickly at Ali's house. It was only 5:10 a.m.

Chris grabbed a sofa pillow and sprawled down on the carpet. Settling in quickly, he thought, "Just ten minutes of sleep." In a matter of seconds, he was sound asleep.

Chapter 17

Morning in San Diego

A KNOCK ON THE front door set Finley barking. Chris tried to wake up and come back to the world. His body ached and protested as he looked at the grandmother clock, 6:05 a.m. Chris stood up groggily and saw his dad coming down the stairs.

"It's Jim!" exclaimed his father, peering through the peephole of the front door. Chris walked to the door and looked through the peephole to be sure. The last two days had made him extremely cautious.

Chris opened the door and saw Jim and Clark standing on the porch. He welcomed them inside to the living room. Chris surveyed the courtyard before closing the front door. Chris looked back to Jim.

"Is Joan waiting outside?" Chris asked.

"No," Jim responded simply.

They walked further into the house; Jim asked Chris if he could talk to him privately. Chris suggested the den and motioned for Clark to sit down in the family room. Chris turned to his dad before going in the den.

"Dad, will you ensure that everyone is up and ready by 6:30 a.m.?"

His father gave him a curt nod, and then Jim and Chris walked into the den. Chris closed the door and studied Jim's face: he was clearly in angst. Jim was quiet for an awkward amount of time; he did not make eye contact with Chris.

"I need a favor from you, Chris. Joan will not leave without her parents—and her parents will not leave San Diego. We talked about this all through the night. I am asking you to take Clark with you to Texas. If things settle down here in the future, we will see you again. If they don't, we would like him to start a new life with you." Jim's eyes were moist, and he struggled to vocalize those final words.

"Jim, should I drive over and talk to Joan!" Chris asked anxiously. He couldn't bear the thought of leaving Jim and Joan behind.

Jim shook his head. "It's no use; she will not change her mind. She will not leave her parents. I need you to take Clark, keep an eye on him, and help him get a new start."

Tears formed in Chris's eyes, and he hugged him. "Jim, yes, of course."

Jim pulled away while offering his thanks. Chris opened the door, and Jim walked out of the den and headed over to Clark. Jim hugged Clark and said something to him privately. In seconds he turned and walked toward the front door. This event had clearly taken everything out of him—now that his business was finished, he wanted to leave. Opening the door, Jim stepped outside. He never looked back.

There was one roller bag and a backpack on the porch. Chris brought them inside the door. Chris's heart felt heavy—he had a feeling that this could be the last time he would see his friend Jim. Stepping over to Clark, Chris informed him that people would be gathering at 6:30 a.m., which left him only fifteen minutes before departure. Chris suggested that Clark help himself to coffee or anything he could find in the refrigerator or cupboards for a quick breakfast.

Taking a step away, Chris had a thought and walked back over to Clark. He asked Clark to ride with his parents and help with the driving and suggested they split it fifty percent. Clark nodded and headed to the kitchen in search of coffee.

Chris moved quickly upstairs to check on Carly and his parents. Reconvening with his parents, Chris explained that Clark was now coming with them and shared his idea of the driving trade-off. Chris suggested to his dad that Clark could drive half of the time to spell him and let him rest, explaining that everyone needed to be fresh. There could even be a scenario where it would be best for his dad to be armed and riding shotgun while Clark drove. Chris added that Clark had a roller bag and backpack and asked if they could find room for it.

Everyone was preoccupied, with the final packing of the vehicles. Mike drove up the street in his truck and pulled up in front of Chris's house. Jumping out of his vehicle, he walked over and said hello.

Chris gave him a high-level update about what had happened last night with Ali. Chris asked Mike if he thought it might be good for Ali to travel with him on the drive. Mike had seen a lot in Iraq, and Chris wondered if that could be a good fit for both of them. Mike smiled and nodded, so Chris motioned where Ali was standing, without further prompting, Mike walked over to introduce himself.

Will pulled up next in his 4 Runner, he parked on the other side of Chris's driveway near the Callahans'. As he got out, his two dogs came bounding up through the garage. He had one lab/retriever mix and one that looked like a husky with something else mixed in. Introductions were made and Finley wasted no time and greeted the other two dogs.

Dan was last to arrive in his Mercedes. He parked behind Mike's truck and got out. Chris smiled when he saw that he looked dressed for a beach party in shorts, a T-shirt, and flip-flops. Dan went straight toward the group that was gathered at the back of Ryan's truck. Ryan's lift gate door was down and formed a table for the maps spread out before them. Chris put his hand up to silence the group and took a moment to introduce the members of the caravan.

After the introductions, Ryan shared the day's route and the goal to reach Flagstaff, Arizona, or beyond by the end of the day. Chris suggested that each car have someone armed, and that they travel as a caravan.

Ali shifted uncomfortably but waited for a pause before approaching Chris. "I need to check on something at the house," Ali blurted out.

Chris nodded dismissively. "If the lead car pulls over, then everyone pulls over. Does everyone have a full or at least three-fourths tank of gas?"

Everyone nodded. Chris confirmed the travel groups. When the logistics were through, Chris looked up—Ali was out of sight. "I need to tell you all something. Two looters entered Ali's house last night. There was a shootout and they killed his parents. Obviously Ali is upset; I am not sure when he'll be ready to talk about it. I just wanted to be sure that everyone knew—it's probably best not to bring up his parents for a couple of days."

Chris confirmed that Mike and Ali would drive in Mike's truck, Ryan and Abby would ride in Ryan's truck. They would be the lead vehicles in the caravan.

Clark would travel with Chris's parents in their van. Carly and Chris would be last in line, driving in their van.

The Callahans had their SUV packed and ready to go in their driveway. Chris walked over and asked them if their children would mind splitting up with Will and Dan to help them drive. They agreed.

Most of the group had gone inside for a last-minute bathroom break. Ali had returned from his house and stood by Mike's truck. Chris pulled Mike, Ali, Ryan, and Abby over and suggested that they alternate on taking the lead position. Chris shared that the lead vehicle must be fresh and observant, and asked if there were any questions or concerns about the caravan they needed to discuss before they take off.

Mike reiterated that they needed to expect the unexpected on the road with possible terrorists, gangs, etc., or the condition of the road. Carly noticed the time and instructed people in the caravan to head to their vehicles. Abby spoke with each vehicle to confirm their order in the caravan.

The neighbors poured out into the cul-de-sac and walked across the street to the caravan. After a few conversations, it appeared that many of them would take I-8 toward El Cajon to Yuma, Arizona. From Yuma, many were looking to continue to Phoenix or Tucson. Chris had Ryan share their route—anyone who wanted to caravan with them was welcome to do so.

Two families that had a final destination in Utah walked over; when they heard details about the route they decided to join Chris and the team for part of the journey.

Chapter 18

Leaving San Diego

THE CARS WERE LINED up and ready to go. Every car was equipped with a copied page of the route and an armed passenger. There were at least two people per vehicle.

At 7:56 a.m., Chris stressed that they needed to get moving. They needed to make it to at least Julian by the terrorist's deadline to get beyond the fifty-mile distance that was considered the danger zone. Chris had shared with his family earlier that morning his desire to get down to the desert for the extra buffer. There was minimal wind, but what if the experts on radiation had their calculations off a little? Some critics said that it was an overreaction for residents to leave their homes and that people would just need to return. But it was something that Chris and the caravan felt was worth the effort. Yes, there was a good chance that they would return once the terrorist situation had cleared. Each person hoped that this would be the conclusion!

The group agreed to stop briefly in Julian. They would check to make sure the vehicles were okay and take a bathroom break only if necessary. They would only make time for a fuel stop if required, then move quickly down to the Anza Borrego desert where they would be able to take a longer break.

At 7:58 a.m., they moved out, with Mike and Ali in the lead vehicle followed by Abby and Ryan. Chris and Carly waited for all the cars in their caravan to move down the road, and then they took the rear. Chris wanted to ensure that they didn't lose anyone on the trip. At a minimum, he wanted everyone to reach Borrego.

There was some traffic, but they moved along on I-67 and left Ramona. By 9:00 a.m., they had reached Santa Isabella and passed the iconic Dudley's bakery. At 9:30 a.m., they were in Julian.

Carly received a text from Ethan that he would be in Norman, Oklahoma, in another hour. They were two hours ahead at Central time zone, so that would be around 12:30 p.m. Central time when he arrived.

A few people needed a bathroom break, so the group decided to also fuel up during this break. It didn't take long as they used two fueling stations a block apart. After fueling up, they fell in line behind Mike on the side of the road. By 9:50 a.m., they were on the move again on their way to the desert.

The next leg was only thirty-one miles, but it took forty-five minutes to drive from Julian down the mountain to Borrego Springs. There was significant traffic including trucks and large vehicles that slowed them down. They reached Borrego just inside an hour. As 11:00 a.m. approached, they took another break. Their progress was significant, and Chris felt relieved. Whether San Onofre was safe or not, they were now out of immediate danger. His mind lingered on Jim and Joan—he shook the thought from his head and focused on the immediate tasks at hand.

There had not been any vehicle maintenance issues, so things were going well. Mike had highlighted vehicle problems as one of his concerns, they'd need to be prepared to abandon a vehicle in a moment's notice on the road if necessary.

Mike pulled over near the store and the caravan followed and parked. A number of people took off to buy grocery items. As they shopped, the remainder of the caravan rested or checked their phones for current news reports. Some small groups were clustered for conversation. Chris suggested that they use the restroom again.

At 11:30 a.m., they prepared to leave Borrego Springs. Ryan had the group gather to confirm the next stretch. One of the Callahan girls had some news on her phone regarding the San Onofre situation: the terrorists had killed a hostage at eleven that morning. He was a male, middle-aged worker. A picture of him standing with some coworkers gleamed dully on her phone. He appeared to be a little under six feet, with short hair. He could have been any number of neighbors or colleagues that Chris associated with on a daily basis.

A video was released by the terrorists showing the beheading; it ended with a threat that they'd kill another hostage in six hours. Watching this barbaric act on home soil created additional emotion. The entire group was speechless; not a word was uttered. It was a somber reminder of the reality they now faced. Quietly, the group dispersed and continued on the trek.

It was about 220 miles to I-40 when Chris broke the silence. "It's important to share all the news on California, but also we must keep moving forward. Please keep an ear out for information for where we are heading, especially traffic information. Let's see if we can reach I-40 in three and a half hours, at around 2:30 p.m. Hopefully, we won't hit much traffic."

The next stretch was light on scenery and uneventful. They moved quickly through the desert, traveling on the I-10 to Blythe and then up north to Needles. There they merged on I-40 and crossed the border into Arizona. In March the desert weather was nice, they were comfortable traveling along without air conditioning. After a couple of hours, the lead vehicle pulled over at a rest area to provide the opportunity to stretch legs and use the restroom facilities.

At 2:45 p.m., Chris and the others were standing at a picnic table stretching their legs and discussing the next stretch of road. A loud scream immediately captured their attention. Chris followed the wail to Clark, who was about ten feet from the restroom, down on his knees.

Chris and the others rushed over to Clark, who appeared to be fine physically but who was crying uncontrollably. His phone was lying a couple feet away from him, face up, in the grass. Ali picked up Clark's phone and his face turned white. Mike took the phone from Ali and stared at the display. It was a report sent out from a news station in Northern California: the terrorists had detonated the San Onofre reactors.

Mike relayed the news to the group and many scrambled for their phones. Ali took a step toward Clark and gave him a long hug, but nothing could stop Clark's grieving. Chris instantly realized with a sinking in his chest that he had lost his best friend. They all had lost many friends.

Everyone within the fifty mile radius of San Onofre had died, or would soon.

Chris looked over at Carly, who stared at him.

"We can never go back to our home."

There was pain in Carly's eyes, but she didn't' say a word. Carly had been born and raised in San Diego, and now she would never return. Ethan would never surf in Del Mar. They would not grow old in that town. Jessica could not move back to San Diego. It was devastating news—although they had known it was a possibility, they found themselves in shock.

With assistance from Mike, Ali lifted Clark off of the ground and sat him down at the picnic table. Chris glanced around: all the others had a lost look in their eyes. He could tell they all felt similar emotions: their home was gone forever.

In the next thirty minutes, more information on what had happened at San Onofre trickled out. After the hostage execution at 11:00 a.m., the state government had made the decision to attempt a raid and kill the terrorists. The governor had approached the navy commander in San Diego to select a SEAL team from Coronado to stage a rescue attempt.

Apparently, there had been a debate on whether to wait for nightfall. It was determined that waiting for nightfall would mean another hostage beheading, so the decision was made to attempt the raid in the afternoon.

All the terrorists had been killed in the raid, but the terrorists had managed to detonate the explosives before death. All living things within the radius were now dead or exposed to lethal levels of radiation.

Northern California had officially sealed off all travel into or out of Southern California at Ventura on Highway 101 and also at Cajon pass on I-5. Each location had armed troops along with a barricade. One report suggested that Arizona would barricade on I-8 around Yuma and I-40 and I-15 would have barricades in the near future. Most of Southern California would become a wasteland for many years to come.

Now 3:30 p.m., they had about 190 miles to travel before they reached Flagstaff. Ryan estimated they had another three and a half hours of driving. Chris didn't know what to say, but he felt they needed to keep moving forward. He suggested that everyone gather around for a prayer for all the friends and family exposed to the radiation.

"We're alive, and we need to keep focused on what is ahead of us," Chris shared.

"I'm very sad and I don't want to be disrespectful but I believe we need to keep moving forward. But let's decide as a group: we can make camp here or we can go closer to Flagstaff," he offered.

Everyone agreed, mumbling that it would be best to keep going. They felt vulnerable, and moving seemed safer than staying at a rest area in the middle of nowhere.

"Is everyone okay to drive?" Chris asked. The last thing they needed now was an accident.

More heads nodded, and people slowly started walking to their vehicles. Mike was a big help, he went from one group to the next making small talk with each group.

Chris walked over to his van and reached through the window to pet Finley. This was calming for him. While petting Finley he spoke privately with Carly about temporarily trading places with Clark so she could rotate driving with Grandpa H. Chris was fine driving the final stretch for the day.

Carly was fine with the plan; they walked up to Clark to suggest that he switch vehicles for the rest of the day. But Clark spoke up that he was okay and that he wanted to stay in the same vehicle. Chris looked him in the eye, evaluating if he was okay, Chris nodded and turned with Carly to go back to the van.

Carly suggested on the walk back to the van that they stop the caravan before dark and not drive more than two or three hours at most. "We are emotionally drained. Don't push them too hard," she said wisely.

Chris listened. "Yes, I agree. However, we need to make sure we stop somewhere safe."

Chris requested that Mike, Ryan and Grandpa H come by Ryan's vehicle for a quick meeting. They studied the map and the decision was made to head to Seligman, Arizona and then evaluate how they were doing. This stretch was only a little over one hundred miles.

They moved out with their vehicles in single file. The sun was starting to move down the horizon in the west. Looking behind them, unique colors were visible in the sky as they left Southern California further behind, forever.

Chapter 19

Arizona

THEY MADE GREAT TIME, arriving in Seligman, Arizona, in a little over one and a half hours. Seligman was a very small town; after a brief meeting, the group decided to move ahead to Williams. Williams had less than three thousand people, but it was only about thirty miles from Flagstaff. Williams was known as the most common route to the Grand Canyon.

They arrived in Williams, Arizona, with still a little daylight left. Some yellow and slight tangerine orange and purple skies splashed beautifully against the western landscape. As they traveled through town, Chris noticed that each motel had No Vacancy listed in front of their offices.

The lead vehicle pulled into a gas station that was also a mini-mart. Two vehicles pulled forward to pump gas, and the others queued in line. Those not driving popped out of the vehicles to use the bathroom, purchase snacks, or stretch their legs.

They called a meeting to determine where they would spend the night. Very few of the group had sleeping bags or tents, so most of them would be sleeping in their cars. Williams was at a higher elevation, and it looked like it would be a cool March evening.

Chris asked Carly if she could fill the van with gas so that he could walk up ahead. Mike and Ryan had filled their tanks and pulled their vehicles off to the side and parked while the others behind them filled up. Abby and Ali stood to the side, stretching their legs and talking.

Chris motioned to Ryan and Mike, and the trio walked over to the van of Chris's parents. Mike and Ryan held back ten feet from the van as Chris approached. Clark was driving and Chris confirmed with him and Chris's mom that they could pull up and fill the tank.

"Do you want to stretch your legs?" Chris asked his father.

Grandpa H opened the passenger door and stepped out. Chris knew his dad had driven this route a number of times, and he thought he might contribute in choosing a location for the night. As they approached Ryan and Mike, Mike spoke. "Looks like all the motels are full of other travelers leaving California."

"Let's go inside and see if there is a park or a place they recommend for the night," Chris suggested. "Many of us didn't sleep much last night, and I slept very little on the drive today other than a quick five-to-ten-minute nap. We need a safe and quiet place."

The others nodded and the group walked over to the mini-mart. The building looked like it had been built in the 1940s—the building was clearly old and coated with thick layers of paint.

Entering through the door, Chris heard Johnny Cash's "Walk the Line" belted out over the speakers. Behind the counter were two women; at the register was an American Indian girl who looked in her early twenties. There were a number of Indian reservations in the area, so their presence made sense. Standing next to the girl, about four feet away, was a grizzled-looking woman that looked to be about eighty years old, but who was probably in her sixties. She had a cigarette hanging from the right corner of her mouth and she was hunched over the counter, looking at an inventory report.

The young girl looked at the group and nodded in a way that asked what she could do for them. Chris noticed that she wore a name tag with the name Rosa.

Chris tried his best to be charming. "Ladies, while we fill our gas tanks, we'd like your advice on a couple of matters."

The older woman didn't look up from her inventory report, so Chris continued, "We are continuing on I-40 eastbound through Arizona. Have you heard of any problems or issues that we might encounter?"

The older woman reached for her cigarette, flicked it in the ash tray, and then peered up at them. She tried to size them up as it was obvious they were visitors. "What kind of trouble?"

"We had to quickly leave everything behind in Southern California. Before we left we experienced terrorist attacks, gang warfare, looting, and general lawlessness. We would appreciate any information on potential problem areas. All we're trying to do is to travel to a safe destination," Chris explained.

Taking a long drag from her cigarette, the woman exhaled smoke as if she were contemplating each and every word. Chris hoped her response wouldn't be in smoke signals.

"I'm sorry to hear about your home. Things have been very quiet around here. There have been some rumors of Latino gangs coming up from the South and roaming around and looting, but folks around here are armed. We think the gangs were probably just looking for easy targets." She paused for a few seconds but continued. "There aren't any motel rooms open for the night—too many others passing through from California."

Now that Chris had her in a chatty mood, he pressed on. "We've had a long day. Is there a park or somewhere quiet and protected for us to rest for the night?"

The older woman confirmed that there was a county park outside the town, and she volunteered Rosa to point out its location on a local county map. Without another word, she turned back to her important inventory sheets.

Rosa pulled out a laminated piece of paper that proved to be the map of the county. Chris stepped back a bit to allow Ryan and Mike to discuss directions in detail with her.

Chris patted his dad on the shoulder to get his attention. The two turned and walked out the glass doors and stepped outside.

Grandpa H smirked. "Well, I could hardly process all that information."

Chris smiled and chuckled. A couple of minutes later, Ryan and Mike stepped out and stated that they knew where the park was located. The name was Cataract Lake County Park. Mike suggested that they head over immediately before it got completely dark so they could survey the park and then decide on a location and set up. Based on the information from the older woman about possible gang activity, Mike suggested that they consider a defensive position.

Carly finished pumping gas, and all the other cars were now fueled. Chris walked over to the van and screwed on the gas cap while Carly put away the nozzle. Carly climbed into the driver's seat and pulled up behind the rest of the group.

Mike and Ali took the lead and drove the caravan out a few miles to the park. The entrance fee was fifteen dollars for overnight camping, but the ranger kiosk was deserted. As they drove a loop, there was no ranger in sight and the park appeared to be deserted other than a single family tent on one side of the campground about one hundred yards away. The park had a few trees and a river that fed into a nice lake.

Mike and Ali pulled their truck over and got out, walking toward the caravan. Chris climbed out of the passenger side of the van and walked over to Mike. Mike mentioned that he would like to walk around before recommending a spot to camp. Chris asked Mike if he would like help: Mike selected Ali and Ryan, then walked down the caravan and drafted Dan and Will to also join.

Chris appreciated Mike's thought process. It made sense that they lean heavy on engineering for camp set up. Chris walked back along the line of vehicles and stopped to chat for a couple of minutes with each car to share information from the mini-mart woman and to let everyone know that Mike was scouting the best location for the night.

Twenty minutes later, Mike and his team were back to report. They gathered around a picnic bench as Mike summarized the team's advice.

"There is a stretch of camping spots along the river leading to the lake. The recommendation is for us to take a number of the contiguous spaces with vehicles parked closely in a line. We will have the river and lake behind us to lessen the chance that someone can sneak up behind us. The place we chose has bathrooms across the small road adjacent to where we plan to stay."

The group agreed with Mike's recommendation, and they headed back to their vehicles. Mike wasted no time driving to the chosen location.

Parking his truck, Mike popped out and directed the rest of the group one by one, building the formation he had in mind. When he had finished, there was a line of vehicles with one vehicle on each end going perpendicular so they were protected by the vehicles with their backs to the river and lake. The area was not large; it covered three picnic tables, and Chris guessed that it was about 120 feet long.

The sun was setting and they were minutes away from complete darkness. Mike suggested that everyone get settled quickly and decide if they were sleeping in their cars or outside. Then they fixed something to eat, used the bathrooms, and filled up their water containers. He recommended car windows to be powered up with all doors locked.

Mike created a sentry plan for the adults. Every adult was armed, and going to the bathroom needed to be done in pairs with someone on guard at all times. Mike suggested to Ryan that they introduce themselves to the other family in the park and warn them about the banditos traveling in the area. Ryan grabbed Clark and they headed over.

The tent group turned out to be a family of four with two children aged eight and twelve, a boy and a girl. They were from the Temecula area and were moving toward Santa Fe, New Mexico, where the mother's parents retired a few years ago. They appreciated the update from Ryan and immediately decided to move their camp over to the caravan for the night.

The San Diego caravan welcomed the family warmly; each group came up and introduced themselves. Clark helped them move their camp over and assisted in rebuilding the tent in the middle of the compound. Mike had the father move his vehicle over to extend the fortress. The Temecula father had one gun, so Mike added the father to one of the sentry slots before everyone disbanded for the evening.

A number of people had the foresight to bring flashlights and camping lanterns that ran on propane. As the sun traveled down fast, it soon became pitch-black. The lanterns were positioned on the picnic tables for light, and the flashlights were saved for sentries and bathroom visits.

Mike had the detail scheduled with two sentries in the middle of the fortress: one on each end of the fortress, and one sentry that patrolled the water behind them. Five people were on guard at all times; this was broken down into two hour shifts. People were exhausted—this allowed everyone to get at least eight or nine hours of sleep. Everyone sixteen years and older had a shift. A number of the individuals started sleeping at 7:00 p.m., the beginning of the first shift.

Chris and Carly elected to sleep outside underneath blankets and with Finley. At 9:43 p.m., Chris was in a deep sleep. He awoke instantly to the faint roar of car engines and Finley's low growl.

Chris felt someone shake his shoulder and realized it was Mike looking down on him. Chris immediately became alert.

Mike whispered, "We may have trouble. I think the banditos just entered the park."

Chris stood up, strapped on his holster, and grabbed the shotgun. Carly was up now, and Mike suggested that she fasten the leash on Finley. She went quietly to wake each family and tell them to arm themselves and to get in position.

Ryan and Grandpa H were sitting at the center picnic table. Dan, Will, and Callahan came over and in seconds were standing, waiting for orders.

Mike went through his suggestion of placement. "Dan, you take Ali and two others and take the right edge of our fortress. Will, you take Clark and two others and manage the left edge. Callahan, you and your family patrol the water edge: two on the lake and two on the river. Ryan, you and Abby, Chris, and Carly, and the grandparents take the center. We'll fill the two Utah families between the edges and center. Have the Temecula mom take the children in back of us twenty yards, behind the trees and picnic table. We'll have the Temecula father positioned with one of the Utah families."

This one-minute instruction from Mike was all they had time for. The car engine roars grew louder, and everyone moved to their positions. Mike acted as the floater, walking the perimeter of his defense.

Mike ensured that each edge position had at least one rifle. He gave Ryan a rifle for the center position, and Chris saw that Mike had two shotguns in addition to the shotgun Chris was carrying. Mike handed one shotgun to Grandpa H, then took off as he continued to walk the perimeter. Mike checked to make sure everyone was in place and that all lanterns and flashlights were out. Ryan and Abby were on the left center, Grandpa H and Grandma H were on the right of center; Chris and Carly looked straight ahead.

Finally, the noisy cars made their way along the loop, coming down the stretch of the road that housed the caravan. Noticing the vehicles lined up in a defensive position, they stopped their cars at the left edge of the camp. They left their bright lights shining on the fortress. Chris counted four cars. After a minute, the car doors opened and Chris saw the silhouettes of bodies. He couldn't get an exact count, but thought there might be twelve of them.

The silence suddenly broke. A voice called out with a Latino accent.

"Hello, my friends, my name is Guillermo, and I welcome you to my park."

The announcement was met with silence from the caravan. Chris whispered to Carly that he would join Mike at the left edge. Grandpa H wanted to travel with Chris, but Chris explained, "Dad we need armed people in the center. We have to be alert for a surprise attack. We don't know if this is a diversion—if they have others in position to attack our center or right edge, you have the shotgun and we need your firepower in the center."

Chris's father agreed with this logic and Chris quickly moved to his left. Clark was over on the left with Will. For a brief instant, Chris recalled Jim's wish for him to keep an eye out for Clark. All this ran through his head as he approached the left edge.

Chris whispered to his colleagues, "It's Chris," as he approached.

Will was frozen; he had his rifle aimed at one of the silhouettes. Chris could see Clark nearby, his gun aimed in the same direction. Then Chris saw Mike.

Guillermo was getting agitated from the lack of response. "You are trespassing in my park."

Mike shouted out, "Guillermo, this is a county park."

Guillermo responded, "Perhaps we should talk."

"Do we know how many there are?" Chris asked no one in particular.

"I counted about twelve," Will answered.

"Do you think they have more bandits in the park?" Chris asked Mike.

Mike said he didn't know, but he thought this might be the aforementioned group that had been cruising the territory. There was little doubt that they were opportunists.

"What do you want to talk about?" Mike shouted back to Guillermo.

"Amigo, I want it face-to-face," Guillermo retorted.

Chris looked at Mike and Will. "Let's consider our options. Can we get them to leave? We have our laptops, phones, guns, and cars—we can't give them any of these things. A firefight would lose people on both sides.

Is it possible to talk them into leaving us alone? I don't like the sound of a confrontation—too dangerous."

"I don't think we should send more than one or two people to negotiate. I probably should be one of them," Mike reasoned.

Will quipped, "This group of banditos will most likely want to avoid a big fight. It's probably an attempt for an easy score. Perhaps we should show strength and then they might back down?"

"What if Mike and I go out with our shotguns?" Chris thought out loud. "If anything goes wrong, we'll empty both barrels. Mike, you can take one side, and I'll take the other. Perhaps we can have Will lock in on their leader with his rifle?"

Will shrugged like it was a mediocre plan, but he didn't have a better alternative. Mike looked at Chris and advised, "If I smell trouble, I plan to shoot both barrels and then drop to the ground with my handgun. I suggest you do the same and follow my lead. Will and Clark, if we drop, you start firing. Will, after you shoot the leader, you go left to center. Clark, you go right to center."

"Guillermo, two of us are coming out. We need your group out in front of your cars. If you don't come out, we won't come out," Chris called out.

Guillermo said something in Spanish, and some of the guys came out and fanned out to either side of him. Chris quickly counted ten in their group, none had a shotgun, but they all seemed to have revolvers. Chris looked at Mike, who nodded.

"Please have the other two come forward!" Chris shouted to Guillermo.

Guillermo smiled and said something in Spanish. Two more armed banditos walked out to the front of the cars.

"Guillermo, we are coming out," Chris announced.

Mike and Chris walked about four feet apart, their shotguns pointed to the ground. Guillermo was about one hundred feet away from the fortress. They went about sixty feet toward him then stopped forty feet away. Guillermo was leaned up against an old green Dodge Dart. Before they had walked out, Mike had confirmed that Will would fire at the leader first, then start shooting from the left. Mike would have left center, and Chris would have right center with their shotguns. Clark had the right side all to himself.

Guillermo was five feet six inches, about 165 lbs, and looked like he'd never been within a mile of a gym. He smiled at Chris and Mike.

"I think we can create an arrangement here. This is our park now, and for two thousand dollars, we will allow you to rent a spot for the night."

A big smile appeared at the end of his proposal, but when Guillermo noticed the red dot on his chest, his smile vanished.

"Guillermo, we know this is a county-owned park. There is a slight problem: we only have basic supplies and weapons. We don't have $2,000 to spare for your rent. We are tired and cranky, but I think I have a good offer for you," Chris replied. He paused to let this sink in.

"What is your counter offer?" Guillermo had to ask.

Chris smiled. "We are all armed and have nothing to fight for but our lives. We'll let you leave the park now if you promise not to return until midmorning. We'll be gone early tomorrow, and then you can have your park back. If this is not acceptable, consider that we have a rifle pointed at you and guns pointed at the others. You can see we're carrying double barrels. You may kill us, but we'll die killing all or most of you. It's your choice, but our offer is to let you live."

Guillermo sneered, and Mike and Chris raised their shotguns. They had each shotgun pointed on a group on either side of Guillermo. Anyone could see by the looks on their faces that this hadn't gone as they'd intended. Chris could also tell that they weren't ready to die for a few cars and guns. Will had been correct that they were looking for an easy score. Guillermo said something in Spanish, and his men started to retreat to their cars. Will had his rifle trained on Guillermo; the red dot visible on the front windshield as he climbed in the passenger seat of a car. Chris and Mike kept their shotguns up while the banditos put their cars in reverse and left the same way they had entered.

Chris and Mike stayed frozen for two minutes as the cacophony of the car engines became faint. Chris released a big sigh, and Mike looked over and smiled.

"We called it right."

They lowered their shotguns, turned, and walked back to the camp. There was no celebration in camp, but general relief.

Mike continued on with the sentry detail as planned. Chris walked over to his family.

Carly gave him a hug, and he smiled. "We just have to make it to Brownfield," he commented.

Carly shared that she had received a text from both Ethan and Mark. They were leaving early the next day from Norman to travel to Brownfield.

Minutes later, Chris had Carly on one side of the blankets and Finley on the other. Chris was exhausted, but he couldn't sleep. He was thinking. What had happened to their lives? They had had everything planned for the future: plans for a relaxing and fun retirement. But everything had changed and now they had no home. Their only goal now was to just try to survive. They'd survived one day, but what would they face tomorrow?

Chapter 20

Norman, Oklahoma

ETHAN WOKE UP AT 6:00 a.m., temporarily confused about where he was. He quickly recalled that he was on the sofa in Mark's apartment in Norman. He'd arrived in Norman yesterday evening at 5:00 p.m; he'd brought his possessions into Mark's apartment and then they promptly walked north of campus to eat at one of the many restaurants.

The drive on I-35 from Dallas to Norman had been uneventful other than the typical traffic. The only change had been a new checkpoint on the Texas and Oklahoma border manned by the Texas rangers. However, since Texas and Oklahoma were in alliance for this critical moment in the US, it was not a problem and it didn't waste much time. Ethan wondered if the checkpoint would disappear in a week or two.

Two of Mark's roommates had left days ago to return to their parents' homes in Oklahoma. Both were short trips, with one at forty-five minutes and the other at one a half hours. The fourth roommate from Ohio was still at the apartment. He was packing and planned to drive home that day. Ethan had met the Ohio roommate last night after they'd eaten dinner. Last night the OU campus had been unusually quiet; Ethan guessed that 75 percent or more of the students had left for home. The restaurant had only a few patrons in what Mark said was typically a very crowded establishment.

Ethan cycled through some work items along with the day's trip in his head as he lay on the sofa. Twenty minutes later, Mark appeared from his bedroom hallway. Mark grumbled a "good morning" as he walked into the living room and then sat in the chair opposite Ethan.

Ethan and Mark had gone through the travel route last night. It was fairly easy: they would take I-40 West and reach Amarillo, Texas for 250 miles, then they would head south on Highway 27 to Lubbock for one hundred miles, then down to Brownfield. Ethan had driven the old Land Rover, which traveled about fifty to fifty-five miles an hour, he calculated about eight hours' worth of driving for the day.

Mark started a pot of coffee and together they pulled out all of Mark's food that was perishable and placed it on the counter island. They created an odd breakfast as they cooked a veggie Omelette using eggs and vegetables with a couple of turkey slices chopped up and put into the pan. They decided to pack and take the fruit with them for the journey. Mark also used up his bread and made peanut butter and jelly sandwiches for their lunch. These were hungry young men—both knew their trek would go sour fast if they didn't have enough food!

Mark had packed late last night; now he placed his travel bags in the living room near Ethan's bags. He had a roller bag of clothes and two backpacks with some school materials and laptop.

When they had finished eating breakfast, both got dressed and then washed and dried the dishes and put them away. They then loaded the Land Rover with the roller bags and backpacks. Ethan kept the Winchester rifle positioned in the back seat; they would keep their handguns and lunch with them in the front of the Rover.

The Land Rover wouldn't move fast on the freeway, but it would be able to go over any terrain. This was the tradeoff that Ethan had made when choosing which car to take on the trip. If there were roadblocks or traffic jams, they would be able to travel off the road.

Once packed, Mark went back to the apartment to say good luck to his last remaining roommate. They left the apartment complex at 7:05 a.m. Ethan drove along with his Baylor cap and sunglasses; Mark with his OU cap and crimson shirt riding shotgun. It was a nice spring day for a ride. They left Norman, Oklahoma, behind them, thinking that they would return to school or work within two weeks. Both assumed their lives would go back to normal. How bad could things get?

Chapter 21

Brownfield, Texas

ETHAN AND MARK SAT in the Land Rover that was parked off to the side of a gas station. Ethan had filled the gas tank while Mark called the phone number that their father had relayed from Grandpa H. Mr. Wilson was the lawyer that Grandpa H had used for his lease and other legal matters. He supposedly had an office in town.

Mr. Wilson told Mark that he had received a call from Grandpa H and that he'd expected to hear from them. It was four fifteen in the afternoon, Mr. Wilson encouraged them to drive over to his office right away so he could provide them with directions to the farm and the keys to the houses. Mark had given Mr. Wilson the name of their gas station, and he'd pointed out that they're only three blocks away. Mark gave Ethan the directions and address—without hesitation, they headed over and parked in front of the building.

Ethan and Mark walked into the small lobby. The front desk was unmanned and Ethan guessed the receptionist had left for the day. The door had a bell that rang when opened or closed, this announced their entry.

Within thirty seconds Mr. Wilson walked out of his office. He was six feet two inches and about 260 lbs, with a long-sleeved shirt, bolo tie, slacks, and boots. He looked to have been in his midfifties with gray-and-black hair. He was clean-shaven and sported a big grin. Walking over briskly, he pumped both Ethan's and Mark's hands with a hearty handshake, then beckoned them back into his office. Pointing at two empty chairs, he walked around and sat behind his desk. An older map of the state of Texas was framed on the wall, along with several pictures of Mr. Wilson over the last few decades posed with several different people. Ethan thought that they must be significant people, the photographs were hung in prominent areas of the wall.

Mr. Wilson reached across the desk and handed Mark two sets of keys. He explained that one house on the property was newer and although it hadn't been recently used, he thought they would find it in relatively good shape. The second, older house would require some work. Mr. Wilson recommended that the brothers check the houses thoroughly before their family arrived.

Mr. Wilson further explained that the farm land was leased to Mr. McGregor on an annual contract. He provided them McGregor's phone number and encouraged them to call to let him know that they planned to stay at the houses and that more family members were arriving in the next two days. Mr. Wilson had left McGregor a voicemail message on his cell phone, but he had not spoken with him. He went on to say that this lack of response was typical, McGregor was no stranger to working long days.

Wilson advised that they had a well on the property for water, and the house had a propane tank and electricity for cooking and lighting. He had arranged to have the propane tank checked and filled earlier in the week after the phone call from their grandpa. Wilson took a blank sheet of paper and drew a crude map with the road names and markers to find the driveway off the road. He told them to call if they needed anything as he scribbled his cell phone on the map. This was the signal that the meeting was over. Ethan and Mark stood up, gave their thanks, shook hands and then headed out of the office. As they stood on the porch, they paused and noticed that the sun had started to set in the West.

Ethan and Mark drove out of town and headed southwest. Mark had the map in his hand, looking diligently for each landmark. Through a series of rights and lefts on county roads, they eventually found themselves driving down a long straight dirt road. A half mile down the road, they could see trees, houses, and buildings looming. At the end of the road, they saw a larger house on the left. It had a wide, wraparound wooden porch; its charm surpassed that of the house on the right, which was older and smaller with a smaller front porch.

Ethan drove the Land Rover up to the larger house and parked it. This was the house that Wilson had described as the main house. Ethan and Mark climbed out of the Rover, walked up the steps to the porch, and exchanged a quick look. Since Mark had the keys, he opened the front door.

Grandpa H had had a cleaning service come in periodically to do some of the basic cleaning and maintenance. Ethan and Mark walked into the living room or family room and they saw that some of the furniture had been covered in sheets. The window coverings were closed, and the house was dark.

They continued to walk through the house. Off the living room, there was a hallway with four bedrooms and two bathrooms. In the other direction from the living room, there was a huge country kitchen with an oversize distressed farm table. It was essentially a huge kitchen and eating room combined into one large open area.

Directly off the kitchen was a mud room to put dirty shoes and hang jackets. The mudroom continued out to the back of the house, where there was a path to the barn.

Ethan and Mark opened the window coverings, then walked back outside. They moved their bags and personal possessions into two of the bedrooms. Next, Mark took the covers off the furniture while Ethan checked the plumbing and power for both the lighting and the stove. As a nice touch, Mark swept the front porch.

They knew they had arrived early, their first chore was to get the main house ready, to check the surrounding area, and then check the older home. Ethan and Mark planned to check the older home the next day. There was little sunlight left in the day. They had been very productive that early evening in uncovering the furniture, sweeping, dusting, and checking the lighting and plumbing of the main house.

Minutes later, they sat eating dinner on the front porch. Dinner was a continuation of lunch; both gobbled down the sandwiches Mark had made along with the leftover fruit. They were both exhausted, from a full day of travel and went to bed early, knowing they had a full day ahead of them the next day.

Chapter 22

Plitvice, Croatia, a couple of days earlier

JESSICA AND HER COLLEAGUES had just finished hiking the lakes, returning late afternoon to their bed and breakfast location just outside the park. Drago pulled the car into a spot outside the home, where they saw the proprietor in the front yard sweeping his porch. He had a strained look on his face.

"Is everything okay?" Jessica asked as they got out of the car.

The older man looked at them each individually, then motioned for them to come and sit down at the picnic table under the tree. Twenty feet from the tree was a creek that fed into a river that traveled through Plitvice

Park. His house was in an idyllic park setting: the big tree, sound of the babbling creek, and the spectacular mountain backdrop made quite the scene.

Once they had sat down, the proprietor sat down next to them and announced, "We have big trouble. Russians are coming—and with them, maybe another war."

Drago, Jessica, Sam, and Nancy had many questions, but out of respect, they elected to just sit and listen to the man. They learned that the Russians had invaded Ukraine; Russian paratroopers had dropped along borders in key government locations. Russia had announced that past USSR boundaries would go into effect immediately; any opposition would be considered an enemy to Russia. Russia demanded military, police, and government officials to comply and there was a rumor floating that they had offered Serbia and Montenegro a key role in the new USSR if they assisted with the management of Croatia and others who might reject Russia's attempt for a united Eastern Europe.

He went on to explain how his grandfather had built his house over a hundred years ago—in WWI it had burned to the ground, but the proprietor explained that his grandfather rebuilt it again. His father had to rebuild the house again when it was destroyed in WWII. The current house had been—resurrected after he had been forced by a Bosnian to burn his own house down during the Bosnian war. He proceeded to tell the story of how he had hidden his wife and children in a drain pipe to get them out of the area and to Slovenia, and then on to friends in Italy. Meanwhile, he'd been tortured in a prison camp during the conflict.

The proprietor appeared to have aged since breakfast that morning. Jessica thought it must be memories, and the anticipation of what might be on the horizon. He suggested that they leave early the next morning and head back to Slovenia. He went on to say that he would cook them dinner tonight: since it might not be safe to go into town. He confirmed with Drago to take only back roads back to Slovenia en route to his hometown in Lake Bohinj.

Sam and Drago went up to their room to pack while Jessica and Nancy walked over to the stream, allowing them to revel in its beauty for a couple minutes. Nancy looked at Jessica thoughtfully. "What are you thinking?" she asked.

Jessica turned and smiled. "This might become more of an adventurous vacation. Let's go pack and get ready for dinner."

It was quiet at dinner. The proprietor and his wife were pleasant but clearly distracted and deep in thought. Jessica noticed that an old rifle and a handgun were now positioned by the front door. She wondered if the man had decided to make this his last stand.

Chapter 23

Croatia to Lake Bohinj

A KNOCK ON THE door at 5:30 a.m. woke Jessica from a deep sleep and a terrific dream. Jessica had been walking the Del Mar beach on a summer's day with the family, including Finley. She had been throwing Finley's tennis ball and laughing as he chased it in the water.

Groggily, she turned on the light by the bed and had to reset herself. She was in Plitvice, Croatia—not on the Del Mar beach. Nancy groaned something unintelligible and Jessica acknowledged the knocking with a "Come in."

The bedroom door opened; Drago peeked through the opening. "You need to get dressed, packed, and then bring down the bags."

They had discussed last night that they would need an early start. The plan was to have a quick breakfast and take off on the road before sunrise.

The girls came down the stairs to the kitchen for breakfast. They placed their roller bags and backpacks by the front door, then walked through the doorway into the kitchen to find Sam and Drago at the kitchen table with the proprietor. He had a map spread out on the table, his finger on the map as he traced a route for Drago.

Jessica noted that Drago seemed comfortable taking charge. He was an interesting guy; at the work conference, he had been so easygoing, but now he seemed confident and decisive. He had brown hair and blue eyes, and she guessed he was around six feet two inches in height. He had a slim but powerful build. As though realizing Jessica's thoughts were on him, he looked up and smiled at the girls in acknowledgement, then dropped his head back to what the proprietor was showing him.

A moment later, they had finished with the map. The proprietor got up from the table and poured them coffee and juice before walking over to the stove for eggs.

Drago took a drink of orange juice, set down the glass, and looked at the girls.

"We'll have one more passenger for part of our trip."

The proprietor came over to their table and put down two plates of eggs, toast, and sausage. He left to grab the other two plates and Drago continued.

"He asked if we would take his wife to Trieste, located on the Adriatic Coast. He has a contact there who can slip her on a boat to Italy so she can be with her sister and family. I said yes, so it will be tight in the back seat for the first part of our trip."

Jessica nodded. "Of course. Will he be okay here, alone by himself?"

Drago smiled and continued. "Apparently, there was an emergency meeting in the hamlet last night. These men know these mountains and lakes well—they've been hiking them from a young age. They voted last night to fight when the Russians and Serbs arrive. Many are finding ways to send their wives and children to a safe place."

The group was quiet as they ate their breakfast. A couple of minutes later, they could hear the wife come down the stairs. She entered the doorway to the kitchen sporting a suitcase, a bag, and moist eyes.

Drago pushed up from the table and looked over at Sam.

"Let's pack up the car, Sam." As Sam stood up, Drago looked over at the girls. "We'll be ready in less than five minutes."

The men walked out of the kitchen. Through the doorway Jessica could see them grab two roller bags as they walked out the front door.

The wife of the proprietor walked over and poured herself a cup of coffee. She ate quietly, staring into her plate in a way that discouraged conversation. Feeling uncomfortable, Jessica and Nancy finished the last bites of breakfast and took their plates and left them by the sink.

Sensing that the proprietor and his wife needed some time alone together, the two of them walked out of the kitchen. By the front door they grabbed backpacks and the wife's suitcase, then opened the front door. Sam reentered the house to grab the suitcase from Jessica and carried it back to the car. As Jessica and Nancy approached the car, they saw that Drago and Sam had left a spot in the trunk for the last suitcase. They spent some time arranging the backpacks and finally determined that a number of them would need to be stashed inside the car.

The proprietor and his wife walked out the front door a few minutes later. They couldn't understand the words, but they knew what was being said. The wife was talking, the proprietor hugged her as she was still talking, tears streaming down her face. He said a few words in response and walked her over to the car.

Jessica and Nancy climbed into the back seat. Jessica was the smallest, so she volunteered for the middle seat. Sam rode shotgun with the map on his lap. Drago started the engine, signaling for them to buckle up. Drago backed out of the parking space, and they were off. Jessica glanced once at the proprietor: he was still standing in his same spot, staring after them, offering a slight wave. Jessica hoped that he and his neighbors would survive in the beautiful park.

The drive led them through the country; they passed many villages and hamlets. The proprietor's mapped route avoided cities and large towns, and crossing the border into Slovenia proved to be easy. The proprietor had packed sandwiches for them, so they ate lunch as they drove to save time. Eventually they came to the outskirts of Trieste.

Drago pulled the car over at an overlook with a panoramic view of the Adriatic. He handed his cell phone to the proprietor's wife, who pulled a piece of paper out from her pocket and punched in the number that was written on a scrap piece of paper. She was on the phone for a few minutes. The others piled out of the car, using the opportunity to stretch their legs and enjoy the view of the sea. It was a deep blue with the sun shining and reflecting off of it.

The wife climbed out of the car, instructing them to stay where they were on the overlook. Her husband's friend would drive over to get her. In ten minutes, a car pulled up. An older man with gray hair, average height, and some girth that had been established over the years struggled out of the driver's seat. He spoke to all of them in broken English, then walked over and shook the wife's hand with both of his hands clasped around hers. They seemed to know each other.

"When do I travel to Italy?" she asked her friend.

The man shook his head. "I don't know. Serbian and Russian troops have shut down the harbor, and there are Russian boats out along the coast. I told your husband that we couldn't take you to Italy, at least right now. We will have to wait for an opportunity."

The wife looked at him in disbelief. This was information that her husband hadn't shared. Drago opened the trunk, pulling out her suitcase, Sam offered up her other bag.

The friend continued, "I told him that you are welcome to stay with us here. He felt it wouldn't be safe in Plitvice. Things in Trieste will be quiet, like in the past. I promised your husband that we would look after you, and I promise you that as soon as we can safely get you to Italy, we will."

Drago initiated the goodbyes and the others joined in, then jumped back into the car. They left the two at the overlook; the friend had taken the suitcase and bag and placed them in the trunk of his car. The wife was still quizzing him about when they might be able to leave for Italy.

Jessica felt sorry for the wife, but understood they needed to keep moving. Drago told Sam that he didn't need a map for the next portion of the trip; he would navigate all the roads and avoid Ljubljana, heading to Lake Bohinj instead. He was in his country, his home, and this was all familiar to him now.

The drive was scenic, and Jessica lost count of all the small villages that they drove through. Finally, they arrived in Lake Bohinj. Drago took some lefts and rights until he drove straight into the driveway of his family home. A woman came out of the house to the front step as Drago pulled up. She walked down the steps and headed toward the car, hugging Drago and welcoming each of the others warmly. She had Drago's piercing blue eyes, blonde hair with some streaks of gray, and a stout frame with a smile worn ear to ear.

The house was on a slope with a view of the lake. It was a two-story structure with flower boxes outside all the lake-facing windows. It was still a little early in the season, but there were a few flowers blooming. Behind, on the side of the house, was an outline of trees which helped the home blend into the country. Drago's mother quickly got them settled. She showed them to their rooms providing each of them with fresh linens and towels. She then left them to freshen up while she worked to prepare dinner.

Drago's father came home from work after dark. Their merry group all sat around the wooden dinner table before dinner until the father excused himself. In less than five minutes, he returned with a couple of bottles of wine. He uncorked them both, offering everyone a glass as he took a glass to his wife who was working less than ten feet away in the kitchen. Finally, he poured himself a glass and sat down, eager to hear about their day.

When they had finished with the day's events, Drago refilled the wine glasses. At this point, Drago's father shared all the information that he had gathered throughout his day.

Since Drago's father owned and operated one of the ferry lines that traveled across Lake Bohinj, many people opted to hike from one end of the lake to the other end, then take the ferry back. On one side was a small village; on the other side, a campground with a few lodges and B&B's. Both the hike and ferry ride were scenic. The best part of the lake for hiking was opposite the main road, where the trail hugged the lake, tracing the numerous inlets. It was a shady trail that offered great views of the lake and the mountain range.

Drago's father had carried several passengers on each trip as he traveled from one end of the lake to the other continuously throughout the day. The quantity of passengers increased significantly in the summer, but in the spring time, the crowds were a little lighter, allowing for more conversation with the passengers. This provided him with all the latest news in Slovenia and Europe.

Drago's father confirmed that there was immediate concern regarding the Russians. It appeared that the Russian army had dropped paratroopers along multiple borders, including the Slovenian border between Italy and Austria. All major roads had checkpoints now, with Russian soldiers halting traffic in and out of Slovenia. They had heard that this was also occurring in Croatia, Hungary, the Czech Republic, and Poland. Essentially all countries along the old USSR border and Western Europe had Russian troops.

He had also heard that the Russians were moving in large forces to secure Ukraine. It was assumed that the plan was to continue west until the Russians had claimed all the original Soviet Union. Serbia, who had strong ties with Russia, had announced their allegiance to the new Soviet Union that day; this brought immediate tension to Croatia and Bosnia, who still had fresh memories of the past Bosnian war. The rumor was that Serbian troops planned to march into Bosnia and Croatia any day now. Jessica looked at Drago, Sam, and Nancy; they were all thinking of their proprietor in Plitvice.

Drago's father stressed the point that the Slovenians did not want to be under Russian rule again. He said that there had been discussion in town that day among many of the locals. He took a deep sip from his wine glass before he spoke.

"Slovenia is a small country, and we are a small population. Still, we will not conform again to Russia."

He went on to say that many people had talked about forming militias to initiate underground fighting. They planned to establish bases at higher elevations in the Julian Alps.

Drago offered his thoughts: he planned to take Jessica, Sam, and Nancy to Lake Bohinj to walk around the lake the next day. Drago's father agreed that this was a good idea. He encouraged them to observe what develops in Slovenia the next few days, but he thought that Bohinj would be a secondary target for Russia.

His father looked over and held eye contact with Jessica and Nancy and Sam for a moment. Jessica found it hard to look away his piercing blue eyes.

"I think you should buy some clothes in town tomorrow. You need to blend in, look more Slovenian."

Jessica, Nancy, and Sam looked at one another and noticed that they were indeed dressed differently from the people they had seen during the drive that day. They nodded.

After dinner, Jessica, Nancy, Sam, and Drago helped clear the table and offered to clean the dishes. Carrying the dirty dishes into the kitchen, Sam washed, Jessica and Nancy dried, them, and Drago put them away.

Once everything had been cleaned, they put away the dishtowels and walked into the living room. The mother and father had on a local Slovenian TV show. Drago motioned with his head to Jessica, Sam, and Nancy and they walked out onto the front porch.

Jessica looked at Drago. "Is there a way for us to cross the mountains into Austria or Italy?"

Drago waited a couple seconds, then turned to her. "Yes, there are trails, but we may need another couple of weeks or months for the snow to melt so the path is passable. We may need a couple of days to determine where the Russians are, and what their next move may be. Tomorrow I plan to show you Lake Bohinj—you each need to buy hiking boots, warm jackets, and Slovenian pants and tops. The next day we can take the tram to the mountain lodge to break in your boots. I can talk to friends there and ask about the condition of the mountain trails. We had a lot of snow this winter."

It was quiet; they all looked up and gazed at the stars in the sky. They were in a valley nestled by the mountains, with very few houses and lights in sight, so the night was pitch-black. The stars and moon were out in full brilliance. After gazing at the stars for five minutes, Sam said he was tired and Nancy agreed with him. They both gave "good nights" and left to prepare for bed.

A minute after they left, Jessica commented on the quiet and beautiful view of the valley. Drago didn't respond but nodded and stared out into space.

Finally, he commented. "My family has lived here for many generations. This is a wonderful place to grow up as a child. During the seasons

I could hike, ski, row, skate, and sail. However, at this stage of my life, I would like to see more of the world."

Jessica looked at him. "It appears there will be many changes in store for all of us in the next few months."

Drago looked at her. "Don't be worried. I will get you out of Slovenia so you can return to your family in the US."

Jessica looked up into his eyes and nodded. "Thank you. Yes, I believe that you will."

She said good night and went through the front door and up the stairs to the bedroom. As she went up the stairs, she thought there might be something special about Drago.

Nancy turned to Jessica once she was back in the room. Nancy got straight to the point pulling her back to reality. "Jessica, are you worried?"

Jessica thought for a moment before responding. She looked over at Nancy, who was propped up on one elbow, looking at her intently.

"Well, from information I received talking to my parents, the US is a mess right now. We seem to be in a good spot, considering the terrorist problems. This is Drago's home, and the Slovenians know the mountain range. I'm sure they have many trails that the Russians don't know about. I think we take it one day at a time. But we do need to buy good mountain gear tomorrow. Right now I don't think I'm worried."

Satisfied, Nancy turned off the light by her bed and laid her head down to sleep. Jessica wondered where her parents were, and if they were having problems getting to Texas. Somewhere in that thought, she started to drift to sleep.

Chapter 24

Lake Bohinj

THE SOUND OF BIRDS singing outside the bedroom window woke Jessica up. She still felt sleepy and it took her a few minutes to wake up. Staring at the thick wooden beams above her on the ceiling, she wondered how old the house was. Looking over, she saw that Nancy was still asleep in her bed across the bedroom. Jessica recalled the previous day's journey traveling to

Bohinj and the plan to explore Lake Bohinj that day. She got dressed quietly and navigated down the stairs.

Drago's father had eaten his breakfast, the only evidence of his meal the dishes sitting on the table. When Jessica entered, she saw him talking to Drago, who sat at the table directly across from his father. They both looked up and said "Good morning" in unison. Walking over, Jessica pulled out an empty chair and settled in. Drago's mother, who had heard the hellos came in to greet Jessica with a beaming smile and a cup of coffee.

"What would you like for breakfast?" Drago's mother asked.

Jessica noticed she had a fruit basket and a plate of pastries ready on the table. Near the fruit was a pitcher of freshly squeezed juice.

"The fruit, pastries, and juice look delicious," Jessica said appreciatively, her stomach rumbling in anticipation.

Drago's mother smiled and nodded, then went back over to the kitchen counter. Drago's father finished the last of his coffee, set his mug down, and stood up.

"I need to get down to the dock." Nodding to Jessica, he added, "Enjoy your day at Lake Bohinj. The weather should be pleasant today."

Walking to the front door, he paused at the coat rack, pulled his jacket on, placed his woolen hat on his head, then walked out the front door.

Drago explained that his father had told him to be careful in the village. In years past, there had been spies or people who were willing to become spies. Information that there were American tourists in the Bohinj area would eventually be relayed to the Russians.

Within fifteen minutes, both Sam and Nancy were down in the kitchen eating breakfast. They ate quickly while Drago and Jessica sat and chatted. When they had finished eating, they cleaned up and made plans to leave within ten minutes for town. Drago drove them to town but purposely parked on the outskirts, close to the lake.

Drago pointed toward a trail, and the others followed him without protest. They started the hike around the lake, which was opposite of the main road. Passing a large grass area that could be used for picnics or play, they continued on as the trail became narrower. Soon, they were shielded by trees; invisible from across the lake as they traveled the trail along the shoreline.

Jessica really enjoyed the hike. Drago stopped frequently so they could enjoy the view and try to spot fish. The sky was partly cloudy with a little sun peeking through. They didn't come across too many other hikers on that weekday morning. As they took their time, Drago would point and comment on the mountain peaks surrounding the valley. They took their time walking along the lake.

Approaching the other end of the lake, they walked adjacent to a closed campground. As they walked along, Jessica noted some lodges and beach areas. Drago followed her line of sight and commented that in the summer, the places would open with snack bars and shops that offered rental canoes and boats.

Drago led them to a dock farther down where they could enjoy the view of the lake from a different vantage point. Pointing to a boat halfway across the lake, Drago cleared his throat.

"That is my father and his ferry. We will take his ferry back to the village."

In fifteen minutes, the ferry docked and unloaded a few passengers. Drago, Sam, Nancy, and Jessica then climbed up the ramp to board. Apparently, one of the perks of traveling with Drago was a free ferry ride. Climbing onboard, they gave a good greeting to Drago's father and followed Drago to the very back of the boat to the last center row. From there they could see both sides of the lake along with the mountain range. Drago pointed out the tram leading up the mountain, explaining that they would take the tram the next day. From the lake, the tram looked like an ant crawling up the side of the mountain.

The group disembarked at the village, and Drago brought them to a café. As they sat down at a table outside, a server who knew Drago walked over to give him a big hug, followed by two minutes of conversation in Slovenian that appeared to be just catching up. Drago introduced everyone, explaining that the owner was his mother's cousin. He shared that he didn't get much time off for Christmas, so he hadn't seen that friend since last summer.

They had an early lunch; Jessica was able to people watch to try to determine what was different with her appearance versus the Slovenians. With a few tweaks to her wardrobe, she thought she would be able to fit in.

After lunch, Drago led them down a couple of blocks to a sporting goods store that his best friend's parents owned. A woman at the counter came around, shouting at the sight of Drago, then enveloping him in a giant hug. There was a rapid Slovenian exchange, after which Drago pointed to his three friends and spoke a few sentences. The owner nodded, motioning for them to follow. Once seated, she encouraged them to take off a shoe. Soon, they were outfitted with new hiking boots. Next, the owner took them to a corner of the shop and had them try on some coats. These appeared to be heavy-duty; Drago assured them that they would need these types of coats on the mountain.

Outfitted with new boots and coats, they paid with their credit cards. The transaction complete, Drago took them to another store in search of tops and pants. Another friend with another greeting, and quickly they had jeans and other pants and tops that would repel water.

Looking at Sam and Jessica, Nancy proclaimed, "Now we are starting to look European."

They had purchased two pairs of pants and four tops each. Each chose to wear a new outfit with the boots as they wandered the town to see if they could fit in with the locals.

When they arrived at Drago's home, Drago's mother was excited. Looking them up and down, she offered her approval as she announced "Slovenian." Jessica knew this was a compliment, and they all took it that way. Later in the evening they enjoyed another great home-cooked meal with equally pleasant conversation.

After dinner, they retired to the family room and sat around and chatted. Drago's father brought out a Slovenian brandy which they all sipped, hypnotized by the dance of the fire in the fireplace as they listened to Drago's mother and father tell stories.

Although the evening was lovely, Jessica was anxious for the next day; to see some of the mountain range, and to determine if they could devise a plan for how to leave Slovenia. She thanked Drago's parents for a lovely evening and excused herself for bed.

Nancy followed her upstairs to the bedroom; there was some small talk as they undressed and brushed their teeth. Jessica could tell that Nancy was nervous—when they got in bed, Jessica looked over at her.

"Nancy, tomorrow's going to be a good day to test our boots and clothes, to prepare for our way back home."

Nancy nodded but looked unconvinced. Jessica wanted to relieve her concern.

"Nancy, Drago won't push us too far tomorrow. We'll get a chance to see the scenery and try to break in our boots, that's all. You'll do fine."

Nancy smiled weakly. There was nothing more that could be said. Jessica smiled back and flipped the lights off. She wanted to be well rested for the next day's adventure.

Chapter 25

Farmhouse; Brownfield, Texas

THE SUNLIGHT WOKE ETHAN. Opening his eyes, he collected his thoughts, got out of bed, and pulled his Levi's on. When he had his socks and boots on, he walked out to the front porch where Mark sat looking out at the farm.

"Good morning, Ethan."

"Good morning," Ethan replied, plopping down next to Mark.

"Do we have any food left?" Ethan asked, getting straight to the point.

Mark informed him that they had some fruit and a couple of bagels. Ethan left for the kitchen, then brought out the bagels, two bananas, and two apples. After a bite of banana, Ethan paused.

"After we eat, we should walk through the house, plus the old house, the barn and the surrounding area to see what needs fixing and inventory of what materials we may already have at the farm. Then we can go into town and get supplies and groceries."

"I already walked the barn. There are a lot of tools and a workshop in the corner of the barn," Mark shared.

After breakfast, they started exploring. The new house had working toilets, a shower, and a tub. The kitchen had water but the faucet had a small leak below the sink. The furniture looked okay, and the heater was working. The refrigerator was old, but they plugged it in and found out it still got cold.

The old farmhouse needed more work. The front porch had sections with rotted planks that needed replacing. The kitchen sink and faucet worked but needed major scrubbing and cleaning. The bathroom toilet was okay, but it had trouble flushing so they would need a kit to replace the inside of the tank. The house was dusty, and while they both figured they would probably discover more items to be repaired, right then they were focused on getting it habitable for their family and friends.

Venturing to the barn, they found the shelves of wood in good condition. They decided to use the planks to replace some of the porch on the old house. They also found nails, a few different types of saws, and four hammers. There were other tools like wrenches, pliers, and screwdrivers.

The workshop had all the tools available to maintain a farm, barn, and house.

Behind the barn, Mark could see that a couple of stalls and pens required repair. The grounds around the house and barn would need to be cleared of weeds, and there were a couple of fruit trees on the side of the house that were overgrown. They were alive, but in need of some pruning.

Things were in better condition than they had thought at first glance. Quickly they prioritized a list of repairs. Cleaning, fixing the bathrooms and kitchens, and fixing the front porch on the old house surfaced as the top items. The others items could wait until the group arrived.

Ethan and Mark grabbed their hats and wallets, then headed for the Land Rover. In less than fifteen minutes, they drove into town and stopped at the local hardware store. With the assistance of one of the employees, they found all the plumbing supplies they needed, grabbing two new pairs of gloves just in case.

When they came to the checkout stand, there was a distinguished man at the counter. Mark thought he was the owner of the store: he was in his fifties and wore a flannel shirt, Wrangler jeans, boots and a cap that showed salt and pepper hair sprouting out on the sides. The man looked them over and asked if they were new to the area. Ethan told him that they had just arrived at their grandfather's farm and that family and friends were en route from California; he and Mark were trying to get some things repaired before their arrival. The man touched his Jim Deere cap and pushed it further back on his head. He asked where the farm was, and Mark provided him the location. The man nodded and acknowledged that he knew the farm. He seemed friendlier as they checked out and paid their bill. As they left the counter, he even wished them luck.

After loading the supplies in the Rover, they drove two blocks to the grocery store. In twenty minutes, they had a full cart of food. Mark worried that they would need even more food for when their family and friends arrived.

At the checkout counter a pretty girl around twenty with long blondish-brown hair. She was a petite five feet five inches and wore a badge that said her name was Lindsey. Looking at the guys and all the food, she asked if they were having a party. They told her their story and the girl asked if they were going to stay in Brownfield.

Ethan smiled. "I live and work in Dallas, and Mark goes to school at OU. We don't know how long we'll be here, but more family are heading our way. We're guessing we'll be here a week or two."

The exchange complete, the brothers drove back to the farm with their supplies. They unloaded the groceries in the kitchen; Ethan was please to find that the refrigerator and freezer were ice cold.

Ethan offered to work on the kitchen faucet first. He found some plumbing wrenches in the barn, scrounged for some rags in the laundry room, and set to work.

Mark volunteered to pull up the rotted wood on the old farm porch. Pulling on his new gloves, Mark went into the barn and came out with a crowbar and hammer. From left to right he worked to yank out the rotted planks. When he finished, he had torn up about half of the porch. Mark took the old rotted wood and placed it out in an open area away from the house. He didn't know if they would take the refuse to a dump or if they would burn it. He hadn't seen evidence of termites; it looked to be just old wood.

Mark was bringing the good wood out from the barn to the porch when he saw a trail of dust in the distance. A truck was heading up the long drive from the main road.

"Ethan, we have a visitor!" Mark called out.

Ethan came out a minute later and stood on the porch. The Winchester was cradled in his arms and across his chest. Mark had his handgun nearby and strapped his holster on. It was understood that they would be extra cautious. The truck grew closer, finally pulling up in front of the newer house. A big man about six feet four inches and 250 lbs climbed out. He wore a long-sleeve flannel shirt, overalls, and working boots. He had a wide brimmed hat partially covering a face with a ruddy complexion.

"Hello, my name is McGregor. I farm this land. I lease it from your grandfather."

Ethan and Mark moved toward McGregor, lowering their weapons. They shook hands and shared their names.

"Fixing the porch on the old house?" McGregor asked.

"Yes, we're trying to fix it up before our family arrives," Mark replied.

McGregor nodded, took his hat off, and tapped it against the side of his leg.

"Do you, guys, need anything?" he asked.

"I think we have everything we need. We went into town this morn-ing to get a few supplies. Thank you for the offer," Ethan replied.

McGregor nodded again, then stuck his hat back on his head. "I live about two miles from here."

He went into the truck and pulled out a piece of paper and pen. "You have my phone number, but let me draw you up a map on how to get to my house. Stop by if you need anything, but I would like to invite you over for dinner tonight. You boys will work up a good appetite, and my wife is a good cook. She cooks big portions for our large family."

Ethan and Mark looked at each other, and Ethan responded, "That's a very nice offer. We would like that."

McGregor nodded again and suggested, "Six thirty?"

Mark replied, "Great," and with that McGregor climbed back in his truck. He took off with one hand waving, the other on the steering wheel, and a dust trail followed him out to the main road. The boys smiled at each other and then turned back to their work.

Ethan finished both the kitchen and bathroom repairs, then joined Mark who was out in the barn cutting new planks. He had a few boards that would fit "as is," but about one third of the repairs needed to be cut to size. They agreed to take turns sawing while the other nailed the planks into place.

They finished the porch at about 5:30 p.m. and put all the tools in the barn. Walking into the kitchen, they grabbed a couple of drinks and sat on the porch.

"Hungry?" Ethan asked Mark.

Mark looked over with a frown that suggested that Ethan's question was the dumbest remark of the day. Mark was *always* hungry.

Ethan followed up, "Well, we have thirty minutes to shower, get dressed, and get over to McGregor's."

Jumping up, they went to take showers in the new farmhouse. They shaved before they left; they looked clean and crisp for Mr. and Mrs. McGregor.

Ethan drove his Land Rover down the paved country road as Mark held McGregor's map in his hand and gave Ethan directions.

"It should be the next driveway on the left."

Ethan took the left turn and they drove half of a mile down a dirt road until they came to a white painted farmhouse with gray trim. The home was surrounded by trees; a red barn was located about one hundred yards south of the house.

Ethan pulled up and parked next to McGregor's truck. Two dogs that looked like mutts promptly rambled over to greet them. The brothers got out of the Rover and walked up the porch, the dogs escorting them to the house. McGregor opened the front door and shook each of their hands vigorously. He had changed into a short-sleeve cotton shirt, Levi's, and brown slippers. He welcomed them into his home and they walked into the living room.

McGregor's wife came in. She was in her forties and pretty with blondish hair. She wore a scarlet-and-black apron that said Texas Tech across the front. Ethan and Mark made a mental note that they weren't in OU or Baylor Country. She was very nice as she offered them a beer and had them sit down on the sofa in the living room insisting that they "make themselves comfortable." She informed them that dinner would be ready in twenty minutes, in the meantime they could meet the rest of the family.

Within a minute, Ethan and Mark heard voices and feet coming down stairs. They noticed that Lindsey from the grocery store checkout counter came around the corner. She had been pretty in the store, but now she looked stunning in a simple dress, sandals, and her long blond hair loose. Close behind her were three more girls. Mark thought they appeared to be around twenty-two, twenty, eighteen, and sixteen years old, and they definitely favored Mrs. McGregor. They were all blond, beautiful girls. Ethan wondered if the dinner was southern hospitality, or an attempt to matchmake for Mark and himself. Ethan and Mark looked at each other. There were worse things in life than having dinner with several pretty women.

The evening was delightful. McGregor had as many stories than either of their grandpas. The girls and Mrs. McGregor were pleasant to talk with, and there was never an awkward moment at the table. Ethan sat between Lindsey and Cali; Mark sat between Megan and Allie. They found out that the two older girls, Lindsey and Megan, went to Tech. The third, Allie, was just finishing high school and was considering Tech, and the youngest, Cali, had two more years in high school. Even Mrs. McGregor was an alum of Texas Tech!

After dinner, they returned to the living room where they had pecan pie for dessert. The McGregors were interested in Ethan and Mark: the next hour was spent questioning the boys about their family. Soon Ethan felt tired, and Mark looked exhausted. He hated to break up the evening, but they had another full day ahead of them.

Ethan stood up and nodded at Mark. Mark understood the gesture and pushed up from the sofa.

"We really appreciate the delicious dinner and the wonderful company. We have a full day ahead of us tomorrow to make sure we are ready for our family," Ethan thanked them.

Mark added, "It would be great to have you meet our family when they arrive."

Mr. and Mrs. McGregor agreed that they would like to meet the others. Ethan and Mark shook hands with each McGregor as they were escorted to the front door. It was a quick drive back to the house; once there, sleep came quickly to both Mark and Ethan.

Chapter 26

Arizona

CHRIS COULD FEEL FINLEY stir. Quietly he got up and moved away with Finley, careful not to wake Carly. By the fire ring he made out the profile of the Temecula man along with Mike—they both had a cup of coffee in hand. Chris walked over and their new Temecula friend offered him a cup, thanking Chris again for letting them stay with the caravan. He mentioned how it would had been trouble for his family to have been caught by Guillermo and his band. Chris and Mike agreed that at the moment, it was better to travel in numbers. They suggested that he continue to travel with them that day.

"I appreciate the offer—we would like to travel with you until you reach Albuquerque," the Temecula man shared.

Mike set down his cup and looked at Chris. "Before we leave this morning, I'd like to take a small group to scout the grounds to make sure Guillermo didn't leave any of his men behind in the park."

Chris nodded. "That's a good idea. Any concern of an ambush after we leave the park?"

Mike thought for a moment, "I think once we reach the freeway, we'll be okay. The park itself has a lot of places to hide, and maybe a few places along the park road exit until we reach the main road."

Chris added, "I'd also like to go over the map with you and Ryan this morning. I think our two Utah families will head north when we reach Flagstaff. Then at Albuquerque, our Temecula friends will head to Santa Fe and the Callahans will head north."

They sat in silence for a couple of minutes enjoying the warmth of the coffee and thinking about the day's route. Five minutes later, Chris saw

Ryan, Abby and his parents up and about. Chris excused himself, walked over and grabbed Ryan and his dad, bringing them back to the picnic table.

Chris wanted to walk through the logistics. The goal was to make it to the Texas border by nightfall. They finished discussing the route, and Mike and Ryan made tentative plans on where they would switch off as the lead car. Mike saw Dan and Ali eating breakfast and immediately recruited them for his morning patrol. He brought them together and discussed how he wanted to scout the park. Chris noticed that Ali and Mike already seemed to be forming a tight bond.

Mike, Dan, and Ali were armed and walked out together to patrol the park to the exit. Mike had them in a triangle formation with himself as the point. Meanwhile Ryan, Chris, and Grandpa H encouraged people to get up, use the bathroom, eat, and get packed up. Everyone needed an early start so that they could cover a lot of distance.

Forty minutes later, Mike, Dan, and Ali reported back that the park was empty. They finished packing; ten minutes later the cars were lined up in formation. The Temecula family found a spot before Carly and Chris near the rear of the caravan.

Mike walked over to Ryan and asked him to follow. Together they walked the caravan line down toward the last car and Chris. Chris got out and walked to them and met them by the Callahans' SUV.

"When we get to the edge of the park, we have two miles before we reach the freeway. Ryan, when we get to the edge of the park, I want you to hold the line of cars back. Ali and I will go up ahead to make sure things are clear to the freeway. We'll come back in view and flash our headlights if it's clear for you to proceed," said Mike.

With that they took off with Mike driving and Ali riding shotgun. At the edge of the park, Ryan stopped, and the rest of the Caravan paused with him. Five minutes later, Mike and Ali returned, flashing their bright lights and turning the truck around. Ryan started his truck, and the others followed until they caught up with Mike, who led them to the freeway entrance to Flagstaff.

Chris looked over and smiled at Carly. Their adrenaline was flowing, and they were on the move. With any luck, they would reach Texas by nightfall.

Mike stopped at a rest area before they reached Flagstaff. The two Utah neighbors would head north at Flagstaff, and this was an opportunity to say their goodbyes. Ryan and Abby swapped with Mike and Ali as the lead car, forging the way to Albuquerque.

As planned, Ryan stopped at Winslow for gas and to allow the group to stretch their legs. After Ryan finished at the pump he pulled up ahead, parked and waited for the others. A sheriff's car pulled over and two men climbed out of the car, ambling over to Ryan's truck. Mike was at an adjacent pump, Chris was waiting in the queue at the end of the caravan. They saw the two men from the sheriff's car head over and walked themselves over to join Ryan and Abby in case of trouble. The sheriff and deputy greeted them as they approached.

"Where are you coming from, and where are you headed?" the older sheriff asked.

They told the story of how they left San Diego and mentioned that they were headed for Texas; others in the caravan were traveling to New Mexico and Colorado. Mike mentioned that they had stayed in a park on the other side of Flagstaff.

"There was a crime spree last night by a bunch of banditos west of Flagstaff. There's a high alert through the state of Arizona," the sheriff reported.

Ryan explained their encounter with Guillermo from the night before, and the sheriff listened intently. He spent ten minutes asking for descriptions of the cars, the number of men, and any physical characteristics they could recall. Apparently most of the complaints had been about robberies and attempted robberies, but there had also been an incident of rape.

Chris looked back and saw that the cars were fueled up. Carly drove the van away from the fuel pump and parked on the side of the road with the others. They said their goodbyes to the sheriff and followed Ryan's vehicle toward Albuquerque.

Chris and Carly noticed when they passed by the turn-off for the Petrified Forest National Park, they enjoyed the scenery. Before they knew it, they were leaving Arizona and entering into New Mexico.

Ryan had them turn off to refuel and take a bathroom break in the city of Gallup. Ryan found a gas station with multiple pumps and they moved forward in a line to fill their tanks and use the restrooms. While Chris was queued in line, Mike walked down to Chris's car and pointed out to a bar across the street.

"Does that look familiar?" he asked.

Chris looked over, trying to decipher what Mike was talking about. Then he spotted an old green Dodge Dart parked along the street.

While everyone finished with the fuel pump, Mike and Chris walked inside the gas station. There was a middle-aged woman at the register counter.

"Will you call the local sheriff? We think we spotted a wanted criminal's vehicle," Mike asked.

The woman grabbed the phone and started to key in the numbers. Mike had a change of mind, and he put his hand up abruptly.

"Will you tell him to meet us a block down the road?"

While they waited for the sheriff, Mike and Chris walked up to Ryan and filled him in quickly, asking him to lead the caravan a half mile up the road to a safer place. Mike suggested that he arm everyone and keep them on high alert. Mike instructed Ali to drive and follow Ryan in the truck. Chris approached Carly and shared the plan, promising that he would be careful and allow the sheriff to handle Guillermo and his band.

Mike and Chris were armed. Walking back a block from Guillermo's car, they stood by a tree and waited for the sheriff.

A sheriff car pulled up and stopped. The driver stepped out of his vehicle, revealing a very unimpressive officer. He was young (thirty at most) and weighed about 140 lbs with five feet nine inches of height. Chris glanced over at Mike and caught himself before he said anything. Mike briefed the sheriff about their last night and shared the conversation with the sheriff in Winslow, Arizona.

The sheriff excused himself and made a call for two deputies. Chris explained that there could be up to twelve banditos in the establishment. The sheriff asked for descriptions, and they offered a thorough description of Guillermo. They could recall a few banditos that had been standing close to Guillermo at the park, but the others had been silhouettes in the shadows. The sheriff asked if they had others in their caravan, and if he could deputize the two of them.

Mike and Chris looked at each other, contemplating how involved they wanted to become. Chris thought about Guillermo and his band terrorizing other people.

"Yes, you can deputize me," Chris answered.

Mike nodded. "We can probably get a couple more."

Mike and Chris walked the half mile to the caravan and shared the sheriff's request. Will, Dan, and Ryan agreed to come along to back up the sheriff. Chris grabbed the shotgun in the van, and Mike found his shotgun and two additional handguns. Chris asked Abby to drive Ryan's truck and lead the caravan at least a mile off of the main road until they called for them. Ryan and Mike went through the map with Abby and Ali and Grandpa H.

"If you don't hear from us within an hour, you must proceed to Texas," Chris explained. Carly interjected that they should all just continue and let the sheriff deal with Guillermo.

Chris shared what they had heard in Winslow. "A woman was raped last night and there were robberies. We need to help them stop Guillermo. There aren't a lot of sheriffs and deputies out here. We'll be careful."

The five of them walked back toward the bar with resolve. Chris reminded them to be decisive but careful.

Mike followed up with additional advice. "Shoot steady and accurate. Not wild." He paused for five seconds. "Find a good place for cover so that nobody gets hurt or killed!" He further demanded.

Two deputies arrived minutes after they reached the sheriff. The sheriff revealed his plan: one of the deputies would walk into the establishment with the sheriff while the other deputy covered the back door. The sheriff wanted two of the group to travel behind the establishment with the deputy. Will and Dan agreed to help the deputy and left immediately to find cover behind the bar.

The sheriff suggested that Mike, Ryan and Chris position themselves to cover the front door. Mike suggested that he position himself behind the few trees to the right side of the parking lot, and that Ryan and Chris go to the left side behind the retaining wall. He reminded them not to be stationed at or near the gas station. The sheriff had arranged with the manager to close the station for a long lunch.

They were set in position at their designated spots. The sheriff and his deputy were positioned at the front of the tavern, and they entered through the front door. The deputy had his shotgun ready as he entered through the door behind the sheriff. All was quiet for a minute. The silence was so long that Chris thought that it must have been a false alarm with the old green Dodge Dart. There must have been another car just like it.

The silence was suddenly broken by gunfire.

A series of rounds abruptly stopped, followed by silence. They heard gunfire at the back of the tavern followed by another ten seconds of silence. Then they saw banditos spill out through the front door toward the parking lot. Two banditos ran for the trees, and Mike shouted for them to stop and put down their guns. They paused just long enough to bring their guns up to shoot. Mike hit the first bandito, then the second.

The next three banditos out the front door saw their two comrades down and made a move in a different direction, toward Chris and Ryan.

"Put your guns down!" Chris shouted a warning.

The men stopped to trace the location of Chris's voice, pointing their guns at Chris. Ryan and Chris both shot, and one bandito fell down. Chris and Mike kept shooting, and a second bandito went down. The third bandito immediately dropped his gun, hands held high over his head.

Mike moved quickly; he was behind the bandito in seconds. Pushing the bandito's face to the ground, legs spread and hands behind his head, Mike patted him down. Mike requested that Ryan focus on the front door to ensure other banditos didn't attempt to exit out the door. He suggested that Chris circle to the back of the building to check on the others.

Chris cautiously walked around the outside of the bar to the rear of the building, peeking around the corner. He could see three banditos lying on the ground, but he didn't see his colleagues. "Will? Dan?" he called out.

In seconds they responded to let Chris know they were fine. They cautiously walked out from behind their trees, guns pointed at the exit. The deputy walked over to the bodies and checked each bandito to see if any were alive. Within a minute, he confirmed that they were all dead. Chris explained that Mike had one captive in the front.

The deputy requested that Will and Dan remain positioned and cover the rear of the building while he walked with Chris around to the front. When they reached the front of the building, the deputy didn't break his stride as he approached the bandito lying on the ground. He bent his knees, dropping down close to the bandito and placed cuffs on his wrists. Mike confirmed that he had patted the bandito down and he was clean. Turning to Ryan, the deputy asked him to escort the bandito into the back seat of his car. He tossed his car keys to Ryan and ordered Ryan to stay with the car and watch him. Ryan left with the bandito in front of him. The deputy then asked Mike and Chris to take cover again and keep watch on the front of the tavern.

"It's been too quiet. I'm going to look inside. Your friends are watching the back; you watch the front of the building. If you hear shots and I don't come out, call our local office and ask that they dispatch the sheriff from the next county here immediately."

He gave a fake smile. "There's only three of us in the county: a sheriff and two deputies. I need to see who is alive inside."

He walked cautiously to the door, paused for ten seconds, then gathered enough courage and disappeared inside. In three minutes he was back outside the door. He waved Mike and Chris to walk toward him and motioned them inside as he reentered the bar.

It took Chris almost a minute to let his eyes adjust to the dark bar. He and Mike scanned the bar from where they stood. There appeared to be six dead banditos inside the bar: one of them near the restroom exit, four around a table in the back corner, and one lay near the long wooden bar. The dead sheriff was five feet from where Chris stood, a middle-aged wait-ress with jet black hair lay in the middle of the bar, and the second deputy was about three feet from the wooden bar. The bartender had been shot in the shoulder but appeared to be alive, propped up on the floor in a corner behind the bar.

The deputy called for an ambulance and applied pressure on the bartender's wound with a white towel that quickly turned crimson. Mike checked on each of the others on the floor, looking for a pulse. The deputy asked the bartender to tell him what had happened.

Chris decided to check each bathroom and the back storage room. The storage room and the men's room were empty. Walking in the women's restroom, he saw the washroom area was empty and got down on his knees with his head low, but he didn't see any feet under the stall. He continued through the cursory check to make sure the bathroom was empty. As he opened the second stall he received a jolt. Raising his gun in a quick reflex, he stopped himself before he shot. Standing on the toilet with her knees bent was a waitress in her midtwenties with brown hair tied back in a red bow. She wore a green top with a long red skirt, and she had tears rolling down her cheeks. It took Chris a few seconds to regain his composure, then he was able to lower his gun.

"It's over. The deputy is in the bar speaking with the bartender. Let's walk out of here so you can talk with him."

Chris and the young waitress walked out of the women's bathroom over to the sheriff behind the wooden bar. Mike gave them a second look as he checked the dead waitress for a pulse. The young waitress saw the dead older waitress on the ground and whimpered as they navigated around the bodies on the floor toward the deputy. Chris walked over, stopping near the deputy and bartender in the corner.

The deputy glanced up in question. "I found her hiding in one of the stalls in the restroom," Chris offered.

The deputy nodded as he applied more pressure on the bartender's wound.

"Will you take her to a table and have her sit down? I'll want to talk with her. Then please come back here and help me with the bartender."

Chris returned, found some clean towels, and applied considerable force on the bartender's wound. The bartender whispered the story to the deputy, who pulled his book and pencil out of his pocket and took notes.

"The banditos walked in an hour ago. They selected the tables in the back corner and they were drinking whiskey and tequila. I had a couple of regulars at the bar when the banditos walked in, but the regulars quietly finished their drinks and left within minutes. It was just the twelve banditos at the back tables drinking. When the sheriff and deputy came inside, I could tell there would be trouble because I knew the guys were armed. I made sure I had my gun ready behind the bar, and I motioned to Denise to head back to the bathrooms. Our other waitress, Rosarita, was at the table serving another bottle of tequila. She couldn't make it back to the bar before the shooting."

The bartender winced and paused for a few seconds. The deputy glanced over to Chris, who was still applying pressure on the wound. The clean towels were becoming crimson.

"The sheriff asked for IDs, and the small guy shot him. The deputy emptied both barrels of the shotgun and took four of them out in the corner. Then he ran to the bar for cover. They shot the deputy before he could reach the bar, and that's when Rosarita was also hit. A number of them ran out the back door. We heard some gunfire and only two banditos returned back inside the bar. They joined the others, then headed for the front door. One stopped and turned toward me, so I shot him, and there was an exchange of crossfire. The last three banditos made it out the front door."

Sirens blasted and lights flashed as the ambulance sped to the front door. A young female and male paramedic jumped out with the stretcher and Mike positioned himself at the front door, waving them over to the bartender. Chris stepped away as they approached and placed the bartender on the stretcher while the woman paramedic applied pressure to the wound. Mike assisted them with the stretcher and he walked out the door with the medics.

The deputy was now the acting sheriff in their small town. He walked over to the table where Denise, the young waitress, sat in a chair. Dropping down in the chair across from her, the deputy looked at her and waited to hear her story of what had happened.

Before she started, Chris walked over to the deputy, stopping four feet away.

"Sorry to interrupt, but we have to leave soon. Some of us have a long trek to make before nightfall."

The deputy asked if they could provide testimony of the last hour. He would wait for the investigators to lock down the crime scene, then he would take the prisoner to jail. He asked if Chris could gather the others to meet at his car. He would head out there in five to ten minutes, but first needed to take Denise's testimony and let her leave.

Chris walked out the front door as the ambulance left. Mike and Chris proceeded to the rear of the building and motioned for Dan and Will to come out and join them.

Will had an inquisitive look on his face. "What happened?"

Mike motioned and started walking toward Ryan, who was standing outside the deputy car. Within seconds, they were standing alongside Ryan by the car. Mike and Chris explained what they had seen in the tavern and Chris continued with the bartender's story. Will in turn provided details on the action at the rear of the building.

A few minutes later, the deputy and the waitress walked out the front door and down the sidewalk. The deputy escorted the young woman to her car parked under a large tree in the parking lot. As she drove away, he turned and walked to his vehicle. Ryan reached out and returned the car keys to the deputy. The deputy peered in his car, confirming his captive was still sitting in the back seat.

The deputy required a short deposition from each of them; they told their stories of what had happened, then gave their cell phone numbers in case there were further questions. The deputy was positioned with Dan and Will at the rear of the building, so their story was the same as what he had witnessed himself. Chris and Mike and Ryan explained what had happened at the front of the establishment and the deputy interrupted a few times with questions.

Chris became agitated with the amount of time the deputy had taken. He knew that they were losing considerable travel time. Finally, they were finished. The deputy waited for the crime scene unit to arrive, he shook their hands, and the five men left.

Ryan called Abby to let her know that they were fine and the area was clear. He asked her to drive down and pick them up at the gas station. In five minutes, Abby and Ali arrived in both Ryan's vehicle and Mike's vehicle. Climbing in the trucks, they rode back to join the caravan.

Gathering everyone, they agreed to provide a quick synopsis of what had happened and then continue their journey. Chris condensed the story to five minutes with Mike, Ryan, Will and Dan standing by his side. There were a few questions, and they helped with the responses.

Chris noticed that Mike had brought a bottle of whiskey from the bed of his truck. As they answered the questions, Mike opened the bottle, took a swig, and passed it to Will. Will took a shot and glanced at the others who shook him off.

Chris sat in the passenger seat in the van as Carly drove. He was relaxed in the passenger seat and offered her more details of the shootout. Chris looked at her for minutes as she cruised down the interstate.

"Carly, I've always liked action movies. You often ask me if I could ever get enough. I think in the past couple of days, I've had too much action. I may have to pause on the action movies for a while and watch those romantic comedies that you enjoy so much."

Carly smiled and drove them east toward Texas. Chris was suddenly tired; he stopped resisting and finally succumbed to a short but deep sleep.

Chapter 27

New Mexico, en route to Texas

CARLY CALLED CHRIS'S NAME loud, suggesting to Chris that she'd called his name more than once. Opening his eyes, Chris sat up, straightened in his seat, and took a minute to orient himself. They were closing in on Albuquerque, that much he could tell right away. Chris pulled out his phone to check the time and noted with surprise that he had slept for a couple of hours.

Fifteen minutes later, Ryan, the lead vehicle, pulled over at a rest stop. The caravan followed and parked their vehicles. Jumping out of the cars, they stretched their legs, visited the restrooms, and said some goodbyes.

The Temecula family was heading north to Santa Fe, New Mexico to stay with relatives. The caravan wished them the best. Even though they had only met them two days prior, they were a nice family and Chris really wished them well.

The Callahans would caravan with them to Santa Fe, then spend the night before heading to their final destination in Colorado the next day.

Chris and Carly had lived next door to the Callahans for over seventeen years. They had each other's cell phone numbers listed in their contact folder. But neither of the families knew their future—or final destination. The only thing certain was that they couldn't go back to the past and their home in San Diego. Hugging at a picnic table in front of their vehicles, they wished each other the best of luck and offered to host each other when they once again became settled.

As the Callahans climbed in their SUV, Chris looked over at Carly. "I hope they make it to Colorado."

The rest of the caravan assembled in their cars and trucks, then continued on their journey. Mike was now in the lead as they passed through Santa Rosa and then through the town of Tucumcari. The sun was setting behind them, but they were determined to make it to the Texas border.

The sun disappeared and they drove on in the dark. Chris noticed that the caravan ahead of them slowed down and pulled over to the side of the road. There was enough space on the shoulder to pull 90 percent off the road, so Chris pulled his van behind the car ahead. He left the keys with Carly and suggested she move over into the driver's seat. Opening the door, Chris walked to the front of the caravan. Ryan, Mike, Abby, and Ali were up ahead talking amongst themselves.

Chris's father had rolled down his window.

"Do you have any idea what's going on?"

"Dad, why don't you come with me. I'm trying to find out."

They walked forward to join the others. Mike's car was stopped at a roadblock. Lanes in all directions were closed, except for one lane. There were four officers, and no other traffic in either direction.

As they approached Mike's truck, he walked over to meet them. He quickly debriefed the group.

"They're concerned about the size of our caravan. They're peppering us with questions about where we're headed, who we are, and why we want to enter Texas."

Chris asked who was in charge, and Mike pointed to the man wearing the biggest hat. He was standing behind two deputies positioned at the barricade.

Chris asked his father and Abby to join them as they turned and walked toward the barricade. Chris walked up to one of the deputies.

"May we speak with the person in charge?"

One of the deputies nodded and left the barricade to speak with the man with the big hat. After a minute of conversation between the deputy and the sheriff, they both walked over. Chris greeted him.

"Good evening, Sheriff."

"Actually, we're Texas rangers. I'm a captain of the rangers."

Chris introduced his father, daughter, and Mike. He explained to the captain that the caravan was from San Diego. The Texas ranger was listening so Chris expanded his story and provided a five-minute synopsis of their trip. Chris paused, and the ranger took the opportunity to speak.

"It's tragic about San Diego, Southern California, and the nuclear reactor at San Onofre," he agreed.

"My father has a farm in Brownfield, Texas, and we are en route there to join our sons. They have traveled from Dallas and Norman, Oklahoma, and have already arrived at my father's farm. We're trying to meet up with them," Chris explained.

This seemed to carry some weight. Chris continued, "Some of the friends in the caravan plan to rest with us in Brownfield for a few days, then continue on to their own families in North Carolina and Florida."

Chris paused and waited for clarification questions from the ranger. Grandpa H added to the conversation and provided a detailed description of the farm, explaining how it had been handed down through a few generations.

The ranger had heard enough. He motioned for the second deputy to walk over. The captain had made a decision. "I will need to check everyone's ID!"

Chris responded, "Of course. We all have California drivers' licenses. Would you like everyone up here or would you like a deputy checking ID's at each vehicle?"

The ranger was quiet for a couple of seconds, then responded.

"We would like to check ID's at each vehicle and then search each vehicle."

"Okay, we'll head back to our vehicles and get our ID's ready. I want to inform you that we are armed, but your deputies can search each vehicle."

Chris glanced at the others as they walked back to their vehicles. They explained to the others what was about to take place, instructing them to have their IDs ready, and to let the rangers inspect their cars.

The process took about thirty minutes. One of the deputies had a clipboard with a document where he recorded driver's license numbers, cell phone numbers, and the address of the Brownfield destination.

Once they had that information, one of the deputies motioned for Mike to lead the caravan through the roadblock. The caravan slowly made it through, with Chris and Carly heading up the rear. The captain tipped his cap in farewell, and Carly and Chris responded with a wave.

A sign said that they were close to the exit for Amarillo. Mike chose an exit and turned off the road and stopped at a gas station. They fueled up and decided to buy food at the market for dinner. Ryan and Mike confirmed that they would head south from Amarillo toward Lubbock, then continue on to Brownfield.

The group looked exhausted from their long day. After reviewing the map, Ryan estimated an arrival time of 10:00 p.m. They took a quick vote whether to continue or call it a day; the majority voted to continue even if it meant reaching the farm early the next morning.

Carly telephoned Ethan at 7:00 p.m. He was with Mark at dinner with the McGregor's. She gave him advance notice that the caravan planned to arrive at the farm around 10:00 to 10:30 p.m., assuming that they didn't' run into any issues.

Chris asked Grandpa H if he could navigate them to the farm once they arrived in Brownfield. Grandpa confirmed that he knew the way, and Chris shared with Mike and Ryan that when they reached Brownfield city limits, they should all pull over to let Grandpa H lead. Everyone was quiet. They bought their groceries and elected to eat as they drove. Chris understood that fatigue was setting in. The caravan continued south through Lubbock and then reached the final stretch to Brownfield.

Clark was driving with Grandpa H providing directions. They left Brownfield and moved down some deserted two lane roads. Farmland surrounded them with an occasional house and barn in the distance outlined by a light. Grandpa H suggested to Clark to slow down. Ahead they could see a dirt road, which Grandpa H guided Clark down. Clark turned on his directional, signaling for the rest of the caravan to follow. He turned down the road, going only ten miles per hour.

The caravan kicked up dust as the road led toward the trees and farmhouses up ahead. In a minute, they were at the front of the house, and Chris and Carly could see Ethan's Rover as they parked. Abby honked the horn in Ryan's truck as a greeting. Mark was out the door first and Ethan joined him on the porch seconds later. There were family hugs and handshakes with friends. Finley gave Mark and Ethan a terrific greeting.

Mark and Ethan suggested that everyone enter the farmhouse. They provided a quick tour of the living room, kitchen, and bathrooms. Some individuals needed immediate access to the restroom and a small line formed.

Ethan and Mark brought in their grandparents' luggage and placed it in the master bedroom. Afterward they showed Carly and Chris a bedroom, Abby a bedroom, and Ryan a bedroom. They informed the group that they would sleep on the sofas in the Family room. Chris and Ryan left to bring in the luggage, and Finley lingered outside with Chris, taking in all the new smells. Will had his dogs outside and they were marking every post on-site.

Mark took Mike, Dan, Ali, Will, and Clark to the older farmhouse. They walked out to the parked vehicles and removed their luggage. From there, it was a short walk to the old farmhouse.

Mark showed the newly rebuilt porch with pride, opening the door and turning on some lights in the living room. He succinctly explained the layout. Mike, Will, and Dan decided quickly they would each get a bedroom, and Clark and Ali agreed that they would flip a coin for the last bedroom. The loser would sleep on the sofa. Mark gave them a good night and closed the door, walking back over to the main house.

Clark won the toss and took the last bedroom. Shortly after, he felt bad and offered it to Ali. Ali shook his head.

"No, you won the flip, I'm fine with the sofa. I'm so tired, I think I could sleep almost anywhere tonight."

Everyone was exhausted. Will brought his dogs in; they would stay in the bedroom with him. They took turns with the bathroom and cleaned up in record time. Within fifteen minutes, every man and dog in the old farmhouse was asleep.

When Mark returned to the main house, he and Ethan shared with Carly and Chris that they had food for breakfast but they'd have to grocery shop the next morning to buy provisions for the next couple of days. They outlined all that they had accomplished in just that day. Chris and Carly were appreciative and thanked them several times for arriving early and for their considerable effort.

They agreed that they would serve pancakes, sausages, and coffee in the morning. At breakfast they would gather input to develop a working chore list for the next couple of days.

Mark yawned and Chris thought that even with the nap in the car earlier, he was tired. They said their good nights, and Chris and Carly entered their bedroom with Finley. Chris unbuckled his gun and started to undress, so Carly beat him to bed. Finley found Chris's jacket on the floor to use as a bed, snuggling in quickly. Turning off the light, in one minute Chris had joined Carly and Finley in a sound sleep.

Chapter 28

Brownfield, Texas

EVERYONE GATHERED IN THE large country kitchen of the newer farmhouse. Fortunately, Ethan and Mark had bought coffee along with the eggs, sausage, and pancake mix for breakfast. Carly was cooking pancakes, and Abby was serving them. Grandma H was actively pouring refills of coffee. The young men at the table were working on their second stack of pancakes as Grandpa H drank his second cup of coffee.

Ryan and Dan pushed away from the table, relieving Carly and Abby from the pancake duty. Will offered to take over the coffee duty so the ladies could sit down.

Chris had a comprehensive list of chores that he was reviewing. Ethan and Mark provided items that they had noted for repair.

Chris and Grandpa H had woken up early, and walked the property line before breakfast. Chris verbally shared his list, making additions and modifications as needed. He was now in the house going through the list, jotting suggested names next to each chore.

Clark and Grandpa H would drive the two vans to the market with Carly and Grandma H. There was an extensive grocery list of provisions that should last them the week. While the ladies were grocery shopping, Clark and Grandpa H would visit the lawyer Mr. Wilson. After checking in with Mr. Wilson, Grandpa H would stop by and check in with the sheriff and let him know the group were in town and living at the farm. After these two visits, Grandpa H and Clark would return to the market and meet the women, load up the groceries, and drive back to the farm.

Abby, Ryan, Dan, and Will volunteered to work on a garden. They would create a list of vegetable seeds to purchase along with fruit trees to plant. Ryan and Dan would begin at morning by turning over the soil in the garden area on the side of the house. Meanwhile, Abby and Will would head into town and purchase the seeds, fertilizer, top soil, and soaker hose, along with chicken feed and a few fruit trees. They would take Ryan's truck into town. When they returned, Will would work on the irrigation system for the trees and garden. It appeared that there were a couple of mature apple trees that had been neglected over the years; these would require pruning, but they were expected to produce with a little care.

Ali offered to clear the area around the farmhouse and barn. He would trim shrubs, whack weeds, and add the debris to the pile of rotted wood that Mark had already stacked. When Clark returned from the market, he would prune the apple trees in the afternoon.

Ethan and Mark planned to repair the hen house, then repair the barn stalls. They had plenty of wood and all the tools and supplies available in the barn.

Mike and Chris would attempt to buy chickens and two milking cows. They planned to take Mike's truck, and their goal was to bring the chickens back with them. Ethan and Mark thought that they would be finished with the hen house by midday; if Chris and Mike found milking cows that day, they would need to arrange for a delivery.

This was the agreed-upon plan. Chris thanked everyone in advance for their participation. The ladies finished breakfast and the men cleaned up; within ten minutes people were off running their errands.

Everyone worked hard through the day. Carly and Abby brought back bags full of fruit from the grocery store, placing two large bowls of fruit on the front porch. This was an easy snack that allowed people to take breaks on their own throughout the day.

Carly found an old bell on the front porch, and at 6:00 p.m., she clanged the bell. Within five minutes, she had everyone gathered around the front porch. Carly informed the team that she and Grandma H had done a lot of the preparation for dinner and that they would be eating in thirty minutes. She asked for everyone to finish what they were doing, to clean up, and then assist them on last-minute details. Dinner was grilled chicken, potato salad, green salad, BBQ beans, and a choice of either lemonade or the beer that was chilling in the old farmhouse refrigerator. Everyone scattered immediately but returned back to the kitchen within the thirty allotted minutes.

Chris suggested that the ladies sit at the table for dinner with Grandpa H, Mike, Dan, Will, Ali and Clark. There were nine chairs around the table. Chris asked Ethan and Mark if they would help him serve; as they did so, Chris asked if everyone would report individually on what they had accomplished and what still needed to be done the next day.

Ethan and Mark were the first to report: They had finished the chicken coop, and the chickens were now in the coop. They had also finished repairing the stalls in the barn, including the outside corral for the cows.

Mike announced that they had two milking cows scheduled for delivery the next morning along with some bales of hay. He shared that the delivery window was between eight and nine the next morning.

Abby, Ryan, Will, and Dan reported that a vegetable garden had been planted along with four fruit trees; and irrigation was in place. Clark announced that he had trimmed the two apple trees, and Ali had weed-whacked and trimmed around the farmhouses and barn, clearing all trash. He had combined his refuse with the rotted wood from the porch.

Abby and Carly shared that they had stocked the food for the week, and Grandpa H shared his conversation with the sheriff: No concerns to report.

They went through more detail, but it had been very productive day for everyone. Chris, Ethan, and Mark brought three chairs in from the living room and sat down, eating dinner with the others.

Chris inventoried a list of tasks for the next day. Mike and Ali would inspect the roofs for leaks and repairs. Mark shared that he had spotted some shingles in the barn, but he had not been able to examine their condition. Mike and Ali would look at them after dinner to determine if they could be used. Mike would also receive the cows in the morning.

There was some miscellaneous plumbing and repair work in the house that Dan and Will volunteered to work on. As engineers, Chris knew these men to be perfectionists; they would inspect the inside plumbing of the homes in detail.

Grandpa H would drive with Grandma H to town to buy linens and towels and toiletries. They had a consolidated list that Carly added to: some other household items that had been missed earlier in the day.

Chris planned to travel with Abby and Ryan to town to buy paint and paint supplies for the houses and barn. Carly and Grandma H chose the color white for the outside of the houses with gray trim to complement the main color. They selected a light beige for the inside walls and traditional red for the barn.

Clark, Ethan, and Mark planned to go through the outside of the homes to inspect and make sure all the wood was in solid shape, and to replace anything suspect. When they had finished with the outside, they would move to the inside of the houses to look for anything that required patching. Chris made a note on the list that he would need caulking for around the windows and to also purchase wood putty and drywall patch.

Grandma H brought over a large, heaping plate of chocolate chip cookies that had been baked in the afternoon. Abby brought over two gallons of milk and everyone cheered.

Chris rose from his chair and walked over to Will and Dan. He asked them if they were okay hanging around for a few more days. They agreed and shared that they were enjoying themselves. They understood that they had a long trip ahead of them, so they were happy to stay for a few more days of farm life.

Chris had been watching Ali and Clark the past few days. He knew they were hurting; he felt that they must be processing some strong feelings. They had been working hard and had been getting along well with the others. Chris thought there had been so many changes in a short period of time that they hadn't had a chance to properly mourn.

Carly spoke with Ma K and Pa K later that evening. It was late and many had already left for bed. Carly sat in a chair on the porch and Chris had a cup of coffee in hand as he sat in a chair adjacent to her with Finley lying below him. He half-listened to Carly's end of the conversation, gazing into the darkness.

After the call, Carly shared that her parents had confirmed that when it was possible, they would like to come to the farm in Texas. They felt that would be an easier adjustment than moving to Portland and living in Oregon near Carly's brother. However, they were unsure of how they would get down to Texas from northern Wisconsin.

"What are your thoughts?" Carly asked when she had finished sharing her information.

"I think we first need to get settled here at the farm. We're getting a lot accomplished with the extra hands. In a couple of days, we can discuss how to get your parents here. We'll need to check on whether it's safe to drive up to Wisconsin."

Something piqued Finley's interest, and he lifted his head up, ears perked. Chris tried to see into the darkness, but after a minute, Finley laid his head down to rest. Chris had another thought.

"Carly, it would be great if we could find out how to get Jessica back to the United States. If we could get Jessica home and your parents here to the farm, then we could truly begin to start over."

Carly thought in silence for a couple minutes. She looked over at Chris and Finley, who were both about to fall asleep.

"Let's go to bed. We have a full day again tomorrow."

Chapter 29

Julian Alps

Jessica, Drago, Nancy, and Sam took the tram up the mountain. Once they made it to the top, they exited the tram, and Drago took them to an overlook. From the overlook, Drago pointed out to Jessica, Nancy, and Sam the view of Mount Vogel and then the view below the lake. The Julian Mountains were on one side; down below they could see Lake Bohinj and the village Stara Fuzina.

Jessica wore her new boots and warm coat and Nancy and Sam were also wearing their new clothes. Drago had recommended the olive green and brown jackets rather than the brighter colors. Jessica knew that Drago was working to have them blend into the landscape.

Drago knew the young man at the snack bar. Excusing himself, he walked over to chat for five minutes. Jessica, Nancy, and Sam remained at the overlook, admiring the view.

Drago walked back to them and inquired, "Are we ready to go?"

"Did you get any information from your friend on the mountain conditions?" Sam asked Drago.

"It appears that we may need a couple weeks before the trails are clear. He's unsure about the higher altitudes. Let's take a hike to give you a chance to break in your boots."

And with that, they were off following Drago. About fifty meters down from the lift, there were two signs posted with trails headed in different directions. Drago paused, then took the trail toward the "cheese house." The other trail led to the ski lift and they could identify some skiers sloming down the slopes.

They hiked up and down trails that were steep. It was beautiful with the trees surrounding them. After an hour of hiking, they walked around a bend and spotted two wooden buildings. Drago called out a greeting in Slovenian as they approached the structure. In a minute, Jessica saw an older woman and man walk out the door. There were more excited exclamations between Drago and this older couple along with hugs and handshakes. Drago pointed at Jessica, Nancy, and Sam while he was communicating and on queue they nodded to the couple and returned their focus on Drago.

There were picnic tables available outside the house, and the couple motioned for them to sit down. The woman went back in for a couple of minutes, returning with a pan of apple strudel. The man walked into an adjoining building and returned with a flask and six glasses. He poured each glass from the flask and gave a toast that Jessica didn't understand. Jessica could feel the liquor warm her as it traveled down her throat into her tummy. She guessed it was a Slovenian whisky. The couple were smiling and happy. Drago continued talking to them—a few times he pointed up toward the mountains.

After the delicious strudel, the couple took them inside the adjacent building and showed the guests how they made the cheese. After a brief cheese tour, they brought them to the main building. The main building had bunks for people to spend the night after they cross-country skied or hiked for the summer. The terrain was free of snow in the immediate vicinity, but Jessica could see the mountains above blanketed in white.

Walking back out to the picnic tables, Drago told them that they should take an hour to relax. Sam took a nap, Drago went inside for more conversation with the couple and Jessica and Nancy discussed the strudel and their favorite desserts of all-time.

After an hour, Drago walked out of the main cabin. "Are you, guys, ready to continue?"

Sam opened his eyes, and Jessica and Nancy rose up from the table. It was time to say goodbye and continue the hike. Drago led up the trail and they followed him in a single-file formation.

Drago shared that they were continuing with a loop that would end back at the tram. They hiked for another one and a half hours at a brisk pace—it was a good workout. When they reached the tram, Sam suggested that they rest, have a drink, and enjoy the view. He bought four hot chocolates and they sat at a private table off to the side and away from the group of skiers.

After Sam handed the hot drinks to his friends, he asked, "Drago, were you able to gather any information at the cheese house?"

Drago inhaled deeply and exhaled slowly. He took a drink of hot chocolate before setting it down and looking at the others. Jessica, Nancy, and Sam stared at Drago.

"They had a group stay a week ago—they went on a hike for a couple of days. They had poles, crampons, and were outfitted for the weather. They came back after two days and said that they would try the hike again in a few weeks. The mountain passes are closed right now."

It wasn't excellent news, but Jessica and the others knew that there was more information. They didn't say anything but waited patiently for Drago to continue.

"The patriots, my friends and neighbors, will start conducting some training exercises on the weekends. There are other huts and houses scattered in the mountains to allow soldiers to hide from the Russians."

Jessica knew that this was not good news either. It appeared that the Slovenians were preparing to fight the Russians.

They finished their hot chocolates and rode the tram down the mountain. Drago led them to his car and drove them back to his parents' house. They took showers and rested in their bedrooms for the rest of the afternoon.

In the evening, the news from Drago's father was concerning. There were reports that the Russians had seized all government buildings in the Slovenian capital of Ljubljana, and that some Russian soldiers had been spotted in nearby Lake Bled.

Drago's father looked at them with seriousness in his eyes and voice.

"From this day on, be careful in town. Avoid people when you can."

That night, Jessica went outside after dinner while the others were still in the living room. Calling her parents, Carly put Jessica on speakerphone and found Chris who was outside painting the barn. Jessica provided them with an update.

"We're staying at Drago's family house in Lake Bohinj. We are all fine. We hiked in the mountains today, and Drago's friends reported that there was too much snow on the trail to Austria to make it through."

"Is it safe?" Carly asked. "Do you have an update on the Russians in Slovenia?"

Jessica paused. "Well, Drago's father heard that the Russians seized all government buildings in Ljubljana. There are also rumors that the Russians appeared at Lake Bled today. Drago's father warned us to keep a low profile, and Drago took us into town the other day to buy boots, a warm coat, and a couple of Slovenian outfits to blend in with the locals. We wore them today on a hike in the mountains and it went well."

Carly and Chris knew how close Bled was to Bohinj and their eyes locked. Jessica turned the conversation back to Texas and asked for a status on how they were doing. After five minutes, she was ready to get off the phone. Jessica assured them that she would try to update them each evening.

Jessica pressed End on her phone and looked out at the stars for several minutes. She heard the front door open and Drago walked outside and leaned against the railing, gazing at the stars over the lake.

Jessica looked at him. "What is our plan if Russians come into Bohinj?" she asked.

Drago continued looking straight ahead. "We will pack up and go up into the mountains. We have an invitation to stay at the cheese house for as long as we want."

Jessica now understood that there had been more to the trip that day—there had been more discussion and development than they had known about. Drago had made contingency plans.

"The bonus is that we can eat all the apple strudel and cheese in the house," he added.

Jessica chuckled. She was concerned, but somehow Drago understood already what the stakes were; he was always a step or two ahead. She found it comforting—he was different than many of the young men in California; he seemed more mature and grown up. Jessica found that an attractive quality—Drago was becoming more interesting the more time she spent with him.

Chapter 30

Lake Bohinj

THE GROUP SAT AT the breakfast table; Sam wasted no time in asking Drago what the plan for the day was. Drago responded that they would make another trip into town.

"We need more supplies, including additional clothing and two backpacks."

Drago explained that he had a backpack, and Sam could use Drago's father's pack. However, they needed to purchase two packs, one for Jessica and one for Nancy. They finished breakfast, cleared the table, and cleaned the dishes before they went upstairs to brush their teeth. In minutes they met downstairs, ready to go into town.

Drago parked the car a couple of blocks from the main street and they walked to the store. Drago had written a list on a crumpled piece of paper.

As they entered the store, they bought backpacks for Nancy and Jessica and found canteens for Sam, Nancy and Jessica. Drago took them down a block and they bought a few pairs of wool socks and a couple of sweaters.

Next on the list was to buy food. Drago acquired nonperishable items that could last a while; the group followed, walking up and down the aisles as he loaded the cart. Drago often stopped and asked his friends for their food preferences. They carried their bags back to the car and placed the packs, clothes, and food in the trunk. Returning to the main street, they noted that it was 1:00 p.m.—they were hungry for lunch!

The weather was crisp but pleasant. They had their coats on, so they were comfortable with the weather outside. They elected to sit outside at a table on the corner of the street. Drago positioned himself so he had excellent visibility up and down the main street.

They were halfway through their meal, enjoying their salads and sandwiches, when Sam asked a question about the valley. He stopped mid-sentence as he noticed Drago stop chewing and freeze.

Drago put down his sandwich. Speaking quietly but firmly, he said. "We have to leave now."

"We haven't finished eating," Nancy pointed out, flustered.

"Don't panic, and don't look right now, but a military vehicle with Russian soldiers parked one block down from us. It appears that the soldiers are getting out of the vehicle and waiting for orders. When I give the word, rise up slowly from the table and follow me."

Drago reached to the back of his pants and grabbed his wallet, opened it and threw some euros on the table. He spoke as he put his wallet back in his pants pocket.

"Get up casually and walk behind me. We'll then turn at the corner. Do not look back as we walk away."

It was the opposite direction of where their car was parked, but nobody argued. Drago rose from the table and the others got up and followed him.

They walked down the block, turning the corner off of the main street where Drago picked up the pace. Walking another block, Drago turned left again and started heading back down a parallel street. Finally, they reached the car and climbed in. Drago drove quickly out of town and when they were safely out of town, he pulled over to the side of the road.

Sam had been quiet until now.

"How many soldiers were there?"

Drago looked at Sam. "I counted four."

"How could you tell they were Russian?" Jessica asked.

"They're easy to spot. I am certain they were Russians. We'll go to my parents' house and then we'll pack and prepare to leave," Drago responded.

They drove quietly back to Drago's home, and nobody spoke. They had many thoughts swirling in their heads, all revolving around a single question.

What am I doing here? I should be home. Jessica thought. *What's the next adventure ahead of them?*

Jessica was now hiding from Russians, putting her complete trust in a young Slovenian man she had met only a few weeks ago. Riding shotgun in the front seat she looked over at Drago. He returned her look and smiled, showing no sign of nerves at all.

Chapter 31

Brownfield, Texas

It was late afternoon. Chris stood in front of the new farmhouse and took in the sweeping view. It had been a couple of days since they first began their work, and they were running out of things to do. The place was looking good.

Grandpa H had visited all his relatives in the area the other day. He had been able to share and receive family news and updates. Chris also had some uncles and aunts and a lot of second and third cousins in the area. He knew that Carly and his mother were not convinced that this would be their final destination, but both farmhouses were clean, updated, and painted. They also appeared to be safe at the farm: they now had chickens producing eggs and two milking cows.

Chris knew that Will and Dan would continue on to North Carolina and Florida, respectively, in a couple of days. Chris and Carly spoke with Clark about registering at Texas Tech for the next fall semester to try to finish his education. Ryan planned to check on possible engineering jobs in Austin, Dallas, and Houston. Abby was trying to figure out if she should apply for a teaching position locally or wait to see if Ryan could find a good job in Austin, Dallas, or another city in Texas.

Ethan still had a reprieve from work, and OU had notified Mark that they would resume classes in another two weeks and add two weeks to the May academic calendar. Mark would take finals late in May and finish the semester a bit later than usual.

The two that seemed restless the past couple of days were Mike and Ali. They both had been told individually by Chris and Carly that they could stay permanently at the farm. Chris had spoken to Ali about enrolling at Tech with Clark, but he was undecided about what to do and didn't seem interested in enrolling for the fall. They had all agreed to have a discussion that night after dinner about the future.

Last night, Carly had spoken with her parents. She'd been told that there was gang activity up in northern Wisconsin that concerned locals; her parents were not sure if the gangs were from Chicago or Milwaukee. Carly's cousin, a retired detective, thought about heading back home with his wife to Racine in southern Wisconsin. Carly felt that her parents weren't too comfortable staying up in Fish Creek for much longer.

Chris and the others had gathered news over the past day. There was disarray in most of the United States: Oklahoma had officially joined Texas, and the rumor was that Kansas and Nebraska had made a decision to join Texas too. Arizona, Utah, and New Mexico were also discussing whether or not to join the Texas Union.

As a number of their group sat down to share news, the consensus was that Illinois, Wisconsin, and Ohio were unsafe. There were advisory warnings not to travel to or through these states. Chris wondered how to get Carly's parents to Brownfield.

The report on the south was inconsistent: Will and Dan would travel through the south once they left Texas—there were a number of safe counties, but there were an equal number of unsafe areas. They would have to be cautious and choose their route carefully until they reached North Carolina.

Carly walked out onto the front porch and continued down the steps to where Chris sat. She had a troubled look on her face.

"Chris, we need to talk."

Chris smiled and asked "Now?" He pulled himself off the steps and followed her into the living room where they were alone. When they stopped, he looked up at her expectantly.

"Ryan has an ex-colleague in Austin who was able to get Ryan in touch with the VP of engineering. The bottom line is that Ryan has a good job offer in Austin, and they want him to start in a week."

Chris thought that sounded like great news. Ryan had a promising job offer. But Carly's tone told Chris that there was more to this.

Carly continued, "Ryan suggested to Abby that they marry now so that she can go to Austin with him. Once they move, she could search for a teaching job."

She stopped and studied Chris as he processed the information. Chris was stuck on the marriage part.

Chris nodded. "When are they thinking of getting married? After he moves to Austin and she finds a job?" he asked slowly.

Carly blurted out, "They're thinking about marrying in the next couple of days, before everyone leaves. Mark and Ethan leave soon, but my parents aren't here and Jessica isn't here. I understand their situation, and I want them to start fresh—but it's not what she and I had planned."

Chris knew it wasn't time to talk yet. He looked at Carly and held his tongue.

"What do you think?" she asked.

"I agree with all your points. Losing our home and lives in San Diego has been hard on everyone. Our children, along with Ali and Clark, all have a chance to start a fresh life. You and I will start over, but it'll take more effort. It's hard to say this, but I think it's best for them to start fresh as soon as they are able to do so."

There was no response from Carly. Chris paused and then continued, "Well, we have a crowd here now. I have a lot of cousins in the area. What if we had a quick wedding here with a BBQ reception at the farm? We can schedule another family reception later, to celebrate with your parents and Jessica when they return."

Carly looked at Chris and thought this through. The issue was not this particular surprise, but all the changes that had taken place over the past few days.

Nodding, she agreed. "That may work. Let me go talk to Abby. If she and Ryan like the idea, we can discuss it in more detail tonight."

Chris added, "Ryan's sister and mother are in the Northeast—perhaps they could come down for a delayed family reception. Maybe transportation will be back to normal in a few months, and it will be safer to travel."

* * * * *

That evening they ate another hearty dinner. It was pleasant weather that allowed for them to sit on the front porch. Some of them had a beer, a few had a postdinner coffee, and others had hot chocolate drinks.

They shared their thoughts. Will confirmed that he and Dan would be ready to leave in a couple of days, they would caravan to Asheville, where Dan would stay a day or so and then continue to his place in Florida.

Dan then added some news. "I will first ensure my boat is in good condition, but I'm thinking of crossing the Atlantic to Barcelona to ask Maria's parents for their blessing to marry Maria. If so, we'll get married and I'll bring her back to Florida."

Everyone was quiet as they processed Dan's plan. After a minute Chris popped up and walked over and shook Dan's hand.

"Congratulations, Dan! Do you feel you can cross safely back and forth? Especially bringing your bride back to the US?"

Dan stood up and replied optimistically while scanning and connecting with everyone on the porch.

"Yes! I've been getting the boat ready for a long journey. I was preparing to take a couple of Caribbean Island voyages as test runs followed by a trip to South America. But the boat is in good shape and I can sail it across the Atlantic. I'll just need a couple of people for a crew. I'll ask some friends in Florida if they want an adventure. I think I can make it to Portugal in two weeks."

Abby and Ryan couldn't hold their news. Ryan blurted out, "I've asked Abby to marry me. Now—I mean sooner than planned."

Heads turned, and Abby added, "We'll have the wedding at the farm here in two days. We would like all of you to be here to participate."

Carly shared the rest of the wedding plan. "We'll have another family reception when Jessica and my parents arrive. Hopefully, Ryan's mother and sister can safely travel to Texas in a few months."

Abby had more to share, "Ryan has accepted a good engineering position in Austin. We'll move there right after the wedding and I'll look for a teaching job in Austin."

Chris left the porch area by Dan and walked over to Abby. He first hugged and kissed his daughter, then stepped over and shook Ryan's hand. In seconds, everyone was standing and congratulating Abby and Ryan and Dan. Some came over to Carly and Chris to share hugs and to offer their congratulations.

"So should we target the wedding for two days? How about an afternoon BBQ? We can all help to prepare tomorrow?" Chris asked.

"A BBQ?" Abby laughed as she glanced over at Carly. Chris knew there could be some resistance from the women.

"We will have to discuss the menu, but we'll be ready for a wedding in two days," confirmed Carly.

They weren't able to finish the discussion as many other related topics and conversations cropped up.

Chris noticed that ever since Dan had stated that he would need a crew member for his Atlantic voyage, Mike had looked deep in thought. He sat on the edge of the porch with a smile that Chris had seen before.

Ten minutes later, Carly and Chris retreated to the kitchen with Abby and Ryan. Carly started writing a list of what needed to be done with action items and assignments. It would be their responsibility to draft others if assistance was required.

Fifteen minutes later, Chris and Carly were walking down the hall to the bedroom. Carly had a spring in her step as they walked in, and Chris closed the door as they prepared for bed.

"Carly, this is a great surprise. We need a nice event—I think it will be good for everyone to have fun and to focus on something positive."

Chris received no response from Carly—she was deep in thought about the wedding plans. As usual, she was five to ten moves ahead of Chris on the planning.

Chapter 32

Brownfield, two days later

THERE WERE AROUND ONE hundred people at the farm. Chris and Carly had rented tables and chairs that were now positioned under the shade of two large trees near the front side of the house. Relatives arrived with a multitude of side dishes and neighbors brought gifts for Abby and Ryan. Drinks were available on the couple of tables set up on the porch. Clark and Ali were in charge of serving beverages.

One neighbor had prepared and transported the barbeque. Mike sampled it and spread the word that it was the best barbecue he'd ever tasted. Carly prepared a vegetarian option with grilled vegetables and veggie burgers for herself and Abby. The weather was beautiful with only a few clouds in the blue sky. It would be an informal and intimate reception.

Carly and Abby found a wedding cake and a wedding dress on short notice. Abby looked beautiful, and Chris marveled at what a captivating young woman his firstborn had become. If things weren't happening so fast, Chris might have been more melancholy that his daughter was getting married and moving away.

Ryan was handsome, dressed in his charcoal-gray suit. Chris was thankful to inherit him as a son. Chris looked around and saw the McGregors, numerous cousins, and neighbors enjoying the festivities. A number of folks were individuals he and Carly had met in the past couple of days.

McGregor had two daughters who gravitated to Ethan and Mark for most of the wedding. The local sheriff and his family talked to Chris's parents, and up on the porch Chris saw the deputy and his family talking to Will and Dan. Everyone appeared to be having a grand time, Chris tried to recall if he had ever been around so many nice and genuine people.

A local pastor conducted the ceremony. The ceremony was conducted on the new porch that Ethan and Mark had built at the old farmhouse. With the houses freshly painted and the yards cleared, it was a nice setting: The two old trees at the front offered a lot of shade on that spring day.

Just prior to the wedding ceremony, Carly called her parents and put them on speakerphone. She placed the phone on the porch so they could hear the ceremony, then focused on Abby and the wedding. Mark tried to reach Jessica but was unsuccessful.

Now it was approaching sunset. Ryan and Abby left the wedding in Ryan's truck to spend the night in town at a boutique hotel. It was an older hotel, but it had a lavish honeymoon suite. Carly and Chris had arranged this for three days and nights. Ryan could only spare a few days before leaving for work, and Carly and Chris agreed that the newlyweds shouldn't have to share two farmhouses with eleven people. Ryan had assured Abby that they would have a better honeymoon in the future, when it became safe again to travel.

Soon after Abby and Ryan left for town, guests started to leave. They echoed the good wishes and insisted that Chris and Carly contact them if they needed help. In twenty minutes, the party went from one hundred people on the farm to eleven.

It was anticlimactic, now that the wedding was over, and everyone was quiet as they changed their clothes and began to clean up. With so many people assisting in the cleanup, it didn't take long to finish.

Leftovers were stashed in both refrigerators, and enough food was stored that it would last a while, even considering the appetites of the young men. Some people snacked, some enjoyed a postwedding drink on the front porch.

Will and Dan were on the porch with a beer, when Will turned to make an announcement.

"We regret being forced to leave our lives in San Diego. However, we really appreciate all the support and friendship you've shown us this past week. Tomorrow Dan, my dogs and I will head to North Carolina. From there Dan will continue on to his home in Florida."

Chris knew that they had waited until after the wedding to make this announcement, and he appreciated the gesture. He nodded and Mike spoke up.

"I've been talking to Dan the past two days. I am going to join Will and Dan tomorrow morning—I plan to assist Dan on his voyage to Europe, and then I'll return back to Florida with him. I can't let this type of adventure pass me by."

Mike looked at Chris and then Carly. The porch was quiet, waiting for more news.

"Chris and Carly, I would like to leave my truck here in the barn. If that is okay?" Mike added. "I'd like to return back to the farm once we get Dan and Maria situated safely in Florida. Then I can decide where I'll settle down."

Ali spoke up, "I would like to go along with Dan and Mike to Europe."

Chris could tell that Carly was about to say no and he touched her arm to stop her.

"Have you been able to discuss with Dan and Mike the work involved? And what to expect during the journey?" Chris asked him.

Ali looked at Chris, then over at Mike and Dan.

"Yes, I have. I need some time to process all that happened in San Diego, and I need time to reflect and determine what I want to do. Perhaps after this trip, I may be ready to go back and finish college."

Chris looked at Carly and nodded.

"I think he has to do this," he whispered to her.

"What do you need to pack for the trip?" Carly asked Ali.

And so it was established that the four of them would leave the next day after breakfast, as soon as Ryan and Abby returned from Brownfield. There was not much else to say, so they quietly finished their drinks. Will, Dan, Mike and Ali left to pack and discuss their route to Asheville.

Five minutes later, Ethan walked out onto the porch, talking to Carly's parents. Pa K and Ma K had called and he walked over to Chris and Carly, placing the call on speakerphone. Pa K was talking.

"Some gangs have taken over Sturgeon Bay in Wisconsin. Local people are worried that some gang activity will make its way up to Fish Creek."

Carly looked at Chris with a frown. Minutes later, Ethan and Chris offered their goodbyes to Pa K and Ma K and left the porch, walking into the house. Carly continued the conversation with her parents, describing Abby's wedding.

Chris and Ethan sat down in the living room, where Ethan shared his thoughts.

"Dad, Mark and I have some time left before we need to report back to work and school. Maybe Mark and I should go and bring Pa K and Ma K back to Texas."

Chris immediately thought of all the reasons why it was a bad plan. Ethan could see the concerns rifling through Chris's head, and so he quickly continued.

"Dad, we can plan out a safe route. We'll be back in days."

"Ethan, we don't know how safe some of the routes are. We know that Chicago and some of the big cities are labeled as war zones," Chris countered.

Ethan walked over to the coffee table where maps were stacked in a corner. He found the one he was looking for and unfolded it. Chris moved over toward Ethan to look at the old central US as he pulled up a website on his cell phone that offered the latest information of the trouble spots in the United States. Red was to be avoided at all cost," yellow was "high warning"—they needed a green path. Using a yellow highlighter, they started highlighting a path through small towns north in the direction of Fish Creek, Wisconsin.

Carly walked back through the front door and asked what they were doing. Chris explained that Ethan wanted to take Mark and drive up to Fish Creek to bring her parents back to the ranch. Carly suggested that she be the one to travel to Fish Creek, but Chris explained that it seemed better to have Mark and Ethan go so she could stay and run the ranch with his parents. He reminded her that he would have to confirm with his company if he had a similar job in Texas.

Carly walked over closer to Chris and Ethan to see the route they had created. Chris told her that he thought they could do this without any problems.

Chris looked over at Ethan. "It may be better to ask Mike to borrow his truck for the trip. It has four-wheel drive, and you may need to accelerate and drive faster than is possible with the Land Rover."

Ethan left to talk to Mike about borrowing his truck, then ventured to find Mark to let him know that the trip was a go.

Chapter 33

Brownfield

AT 1:45 A.M., CHRIS's phone rang. He grabbed his cell phone on the night stand and answered the phone groggily. "Hello?"

"Dad, I can't talk long right now. A Russian patrol moved over into Bohinj, and we're concerned that they know we're in town. Drago is taking us up the tram and we're heading into the mountains. Drago has some spots identified where we can stay until we can attempt to cross into Austria or Italy. We have all the necessary supplies and Drago is armed. I may not be able to call again for a while. I love you, guys," Jessica blurted.

Chris tried to filter through all this information. He was silent, and Jessica could sense his bewilderment.

"Dad, I'm okay."

Chris found his voice. "Jessica, are you sure you have enough supplies?"

"Yes, Drago anticipated that we might need to move quickly. He knows the area well and he has friends in the mountains since this is his home. I think we'll be fine."

Carly started to stir, and Chris asked Jessica to hold on for a minute while he relayed the update to Carly. Carly took the phone from Chris.

"Jessica, be safe!"

Chris overheard Jessica assure Carly that she would be fine. Chris asked Carly to return the phone and almost had to pry it from Carly's fingers.

"Jessica, take care of your feet, and make sure you change your socks often. Be very aware of where you are and respect the mountains. Learn as much from Drago as you can."

"Dad, yes, I have to go, love you!"

"I love you, Jessica," both Chris and Carly called in unison as the phone clicked off.

Carly looked at Chris, tears in her eyes. Chris hugged her and they sat in bed quietly for a couple of minutes.

Chris pulled back a little to look at her. Their eyes locked and Chris's mind raced. It gnawed at Chris that he needed to do something. Suddenly, it became clear.

"I need to go get her. I need to travel with Dan, Mike and Ali and go to Europe and bring her back."

Carly didn't say anything, but pulled away, climbed out of bed, and stood on the floor with her back to Chris. After a minute, Chris left the bed and walked over to her. She could feel his presence as he approached and turned around.

"We need to get our family home. Go get her and bring her back. Ethan and Mark need to bring my parents back."

They went back to bed but couldn't sleep. Chris was thinking about what to pack and what to do once he arrived in Spain. Finally, at 3:00 a.m., they decided that sleep was futile and they gave up.

Chris packed a travel bag while Carly went to the kitchen to start a pot of coffee. Chris brought his bag, backpack, jacket, gun, and ammunition and sat it down at the side of the door between the kitchen and living room as he walked over for a cup of coffee. Carly decided to cook breakfast and began working on pancake batter.

Walking to the pantry, Chris brought syrup to the table. He pulled out a stack of plates and silverware and brought them to the table.

"After you bring Jessica back, and the boys bring my parents back, no travel is allowed unless I give the okay!" Carly exclaimed.

Chris turned and was going to make a wisecrack, but he saw the look on her face and understood that this was a serious statement. Perhaps more of a mandate than statement. It was the way it was going to be. He nodded.

"Yes, let's just get everyone home, honey," he said as he lowered his face and kissed her.

Chapter 34

Brownfield

AT 6:00 A.M., FOLKS began to filter into the kitchen for coffee, bacon, and pancakes. At 6:30 a.m., they had the full crowd eating breakfast. Chris shared about their call from Jessica last night, and Chris turned to Dan.

"Can I join you on your trek to Europe?"

Dan answered quickly. "Yes, four of us on the boat will be ideal."

Chris explained that he was packed: he had a bag, backpack, ammo, and his gun was freshly cleaned.

Walking into the living room, Chris followed Ethan and Mark. They were packed, bags against the wall, and going over the map one more time. Chris's dad joined them as the four studied the route to Wisconsin.

Chris looked up at Ethan and Mark.

"Sons, this is very important—I need you to listen. You need to be aware of your surroundings for the whole trip up and back. This is not a fun trip. There are parts of the US in chaos, and if you have any doubt, then do what you have to do. Trust your instincts. You are armed for a purpose. Bring your grandparents and yourselves back safely and remember all the Krav Maga training. Avoid trouble if possible, but if you have to engage, make it count."

Ethan and Mark looked at Chris, and he knew what they were thinking.

"Yes, and I have to do the same," he acknowledged.

Grandpa H cleared his throat and the three of them looked up at him. He was older, but Chris could still see his strength.

"Boys, you do what you have to, to survive. Do you hear me? You survive!"

Chris nodded and left the others and headed to the bedroom to see Carly. She walked over to Chris, misty-eyed, and grabbed his shoulders.

"Come home! Find Jessica, and come home. Do whatever you have to do, but bring both of you home."

It was 7:30 a.m., and the sun was shining in west Texas. Ethan and Mark stood by Mike's truck with their bags packed in the back. They were both armed with handguns; Mark had a shotgun that he laid down in the back seat alongside Ethan's rifle. Mike's cab had a back bench seat for three people and they planned to clear the back seat on the return trip for the grandparents. Their route should be safe through Texas and Oklahoma— from that point, they would need to be on high alert. The reports they had gathered confirmed that they should avoid the cities. However, some towns could prove to be dangerous as well.

Carly, the grandparents and Chris hugged and shook hands with the others gathered around the truck. They took time for Chris to lead them in a prayer for a safe journey.

Five minutes later, Ethan and Mark climbed into the truck and with a wave, they took off. Chris stood frozen as he watched the truck take off— he followed the dust trail as Ethan and Mark approached the main road. Finally, the dust trail disappeared, and they were gone.

Turning around, Chris saw Dan, Mike, and Ali packing Dan's car. Mike placed Chris's bag in Will's trunk—they would still travel to North Carolina first, then leave Will and drive south to Florida.

It was time for goodbyes. Chris walked over to Clark and shook his hand.

"Clark, you'll need to help run things here until I return. I know you're up to the task and will do well."

Chris hugged his mom, who had some tears, but who did her best to remain composed. Chris tried to give her a reassuring smile, then he hugged his dad, who returned the embrace. His dad had only one word to share.

"Survive!"

Chris walked over for a long embrace with Carly. He thought how much he loved this woman—he was sorry that he had to leave her.

The embrace was long, but not long enough. Carly didn't say anything until they broke the embrace.

"Come back with Jessica!"

Chris looked deep into her eyes, gently kissed her, then dropped down to his knees and gave Finley a hug. Finley was perceptive: he knew something big was happening. Chris received a doggy kiss for good luck and he turned away to place his backpack in the back seat of Will's car. Waving, Chris climbed in the passenger's seat. Carly, his parents, and Clark stood there, looking like a small, forlorn group. Chris was quiet for a couple of seconds, then looked over at Will.

"Will, what in the hell happened to our lives this past week?"

Part 2

Chapter 35

Texarkana

CHRIS, WILL, MIKE, DAN, and Ali gathered around a table at a local coffee shop in Texarkana drinking hot beverages. They had driven across the entire state of Texas that day, switching drivers every two to three hours to keep themselves fresh. They were mentally exhausted and were hoping the caffeine drinks would erase some of the fatigue.

Mike teased Ali that he appeared to have more whipped cream than drink in his cup. Chris, Will, and Dan knew their coffee drinks of choice from working together over the years! It was always black and bold, and the bolder the better.

The coffee shop was virtually empty that early evening: two girls conversed at a table across the room and one older gent read a newspaper, enjoying his brew as he sat by the large window at the front of the store.

Mike had the map spread out on a table in a back corner of the establishment. An hour earlier they had crossed the Texas border. The helpful Texas ranger at the border had asked them about their intended route, then shared the latest regional reports on areas to avoid and which areas appeared to be safe for travel. They listened carefully and were now trying to use the ranger's useful information to construct a safe route.

The original plan included a route to Atlanta consisting of driving through Shreveport in Northern Louisiana, on toward Jackson, Mississippi, and then through Birmingham, Alabama, arriving in Atlanta. One option was to split with Will in Atlanta—he would travel northeast to Asheville, North Carolina, the others would head south to Dan's home in Florida. This appeared to be the quickest route to Florida, and Dan was anxious to reach his home and embark on his journey to Spain. The ranger advised that this was a dangerous path covering a lot of areas of lawlessness and unrest. Now, at the coffee shop, they redrew their route, heeding the ranger's advice as they created a northern route through Arkansas and Tennessee.

In fifteen minutes, they had a new plan. They'd bypass Little Rock and Memphis by taking surface roads to Nashville. The report on Nashville was favorable—it was considered safe and stable. From Nashville, they would head to Knoxville, and then to Asheville. They would spend a night in Asheville before they left Will and drove down the coast to Florida.

They broke their drive to Asheville into two segments, making the decision to continue driving until they reached Nashville, then they would look for a place to sleep. They would reach Asheville the following day.

Everyone agreed with the new plan, and Mike folded the map up. Ali made some sounds with his straw sucking down the last of his whip cream signifying the end of their meeting.

Before Chris, Ali, and Mike walked over to a deli to buy sandwiches, chips and bottled water for their late evening travel, they wrote down Will and Dan's preferences for sandwiches. Will mentioned three times "no green peppers and avocado," and it was written and clearly marked on their napkin. Meanwhile, Will and Dan would drive the cars down the street to fuel up.

The five guys were getting along tremendously. They were all pleasant and respectful to each other and in a typical situation, each had a good sense of humor. The jokes and lightheartedness had stopped the moment they left Brownfield: now they were focused and serious about making it safely across the country.

Will thought about reaching his relatives in North Carolina, Dan thought about reaching his fiancée in Spain, and Chris thought about getting Jessica back home. Meanwhile, Chris hoped that Carly, his parents, and Clark would be fine in Texas, and that Ethan and Mark would bring Carly's parents' safely home.

Mike and Ali were also serious, but for different reasons. Mike was on high alert as a result of his prior military training, and he felt Chris's concern to bring Jessica home. Chris could tell that Mike was deep in thought.

Ali needed a distraction to allow his bottled "hurt" to dissipate: he seemed to be a little better each day, his steps a little lighter. Chris felt that they would need Ali on this adventure—somehow Ali understood that he wasn't just tagging along.

Mike highlighted the detour areas around Little Rock and Memphis on the Arkansas state map and kept it visible in his hand. He rode shotgun in the lead car; Ali would assist Dan with the driving since Mike was the navigator for that portion of the trip. Will and Chris planned to switch off and follow in the second car.

After an hour on the road, they saw lightning strike in the mountain range ahead. Dark clouds were heading into their path. Chris looked at Will and they nodded to each other in acknowledgement. They would head into the storm. In only fifteen minutes, a downpour began. They drove through, keeping an eye on Dan's taillights.

The driving was very slow since visibility was poor. Mike had to pull over several times as they reached forks in the road to ensure that they were making the correct turn. The lightning never approached too close for the travelers, but the rain pounded. The heavy rain, black night, and unfamiliar small roads made the travel tense.

As they bypassed Memphis on a smaller road north of the city, they were blocked by a tree that fell across the road. Mike jumped out of the car first, followed by Ali and then Dan. Each was armed and ready. Mike did a peripheral scan around the road to make sure it was not an ambush, and Will pulled up, stopped his car, and then joined the others with guns drawn. In a few minutes, Mike had walked the area and confirmed that all looked clear.

Mike asked Dan (the smallest of the group of five) to stand guard. The other four grabbed the top side of the tree and dragged it over until it was parallel to the road. Then they positioned themselves on one side of the tree and pushed it to the side of the road. This was their exercise for the day: it felt good to stretch their legs and work their upper bodies.

The mission complete, they quickly assembled back in the cars where it was warm and dry. Chris brought his backpack to the front of the car and rummaged around for a sweatshirt. Chris and Will used the sweatshirt to dry their face and hair as Will turned up the defrost and heat to high. Slowly they followed Dan's car past the fallen tree.

They continued their route bypassing Memphis and then heading on toward Nashville. Dan and Ali did a great job driving; if they moved left or right to avoid something, Will was easily able to follow.

They only saw four other cars on the bypass route the entire night. It was a good night to be safe and warm in your home—not to be out on the road. A person would only go out in this weather for an emergency or an important mission. And they had a mission.

Chapter 36

Nashville to Florida

THEY APPROACHED THE CITY of Nashville in the early morning. The previous night's trek had been uneventful: the only adventure had been moving the fallen tree and driving in torrential rain. Having said that, they were extremely tired. Chris had switched driving with Will about three hours ago, and he felt exhausted.

A mile before entering Nashville city limits, Dan's car pulled into a driveway and stopped at a motel. It was an old motel, built maybe seventy years ago, but you could tell the owners had pride of ownership and had worked hard to maintain it. Lights provided some visibility of the grounds and the motel. The yard was manicured and the motel had been recently painted. Ali drove and, per Mike's suggestion, had pulled in. It was still raining hard and the rain echoed off the rooftop. One quarter of the parking lot was a small lake but there were still many parking spaces available.

They rented two rooms side by side, situated between the pool area and the office. The motel had a four-foot overhang and a sidewalk connecting the rooms to the office. Mike suggested that four of them sleep with one individual awake to keep guard of the vehicles. They could leave their belongings in the vehicles, but take the guns into the motel rooms. Dan did a quick calculation in his head and decided that they would switch watch every one and a half hours. They needed the sleep and were willing to sacrifice a later start the next morning if it meant they could be well rested.

Walking over to the pool area, Will opened the gate and took a lawn chair and brought it under the overhang. He placed the chair between the two rooms, and Ali promptly took first watch. He was armed and promised he could stay awake. Ali quickly created a schedule for guard duty, assigning each man to a time slot. Once they received their assignment, each left quickly to make the most of every minute of sleep.

Chris was exhausted, he hadn't slept the prior night. Trudging inside the motel door to their room, Chris dropped his backpack to the floor, set his guns on the chair, and stripped his damp clothes down to his boxer shorts. Pulling back the covers of the twin bed, and climbing in, he was soon fast asleep.

Chris dreamt that he was in an earthquake. It was unsettling and he tried to register his location. He soon realized that he was being gently shaken. Opening his eyes, he saw Dan shaking him gently by the shoulder.

"Chris, it's time for your watch."

In a few seconds Chris got up, looked in his bag, and pulled on a dry pair of pants and a shirt. He attached his holster and gun, grabbed his jacket, and walked out. Walking outside the motel door holding his shoes and socks and jacket, Chris turned around and noticed Dan was already half-asleep on the bed. Chris wondered how four and a half hours of sleep had seemed like a minute. But he felt mildly refreshed and was thankful he'd had some chance to rest.

The rain had turned to drizzle and Chris carefully surveyed the area. Their two vehicles were side by side, and the chair was now located ten feet closer to the office. If someone had approached their vehicles, they would have a clear view. Chris assumed that Will had moved the chair during his second shift.

It was 5:30 a.m., and the fourth watch. The rooms formed an L with the adjoining office, and extended away from the main road. Chris looked toward the main road about fifty feet from the office and noticed that mature hardwood tree's surrounded the parking lot. By looking at the cars in the parking lot, Chris guessed the motel looked to be only a quarter full. Walking the perimeter of the parking lot just to get a clear picture of the place, Chris noted that the drizzle was light, but the darkness was becoming lighter. He checked both vehicles to make sure they were secure, then came back to the chair outside their rooms and sat down.

At 5:45 a.m. he saw someone move in the office. Chris walked down five doors to the office and peeked in the window. A hotel clerk was busy putting out a fresh pot of coffee.

Glancing at the empty parking lot, Chris didn't see any movement, so he decided to step into the office. The clerk had his back to Chris as he pulled out Styrofoam cups from the cabinet below, placing them up on the counter. Chris cleared his throat, startling the clerk, who jumped a few inches.

Chris nodded with a greeting. The clerk paused a few seconds, gained his composure, and returned the salutation.

"Good morning."

"Do you mind if I try the coffee?" Chris asked.

The clerk waved him over, placing the cups on the counter before he walked over to the register counter, and regained his composure.

"Please help yourself. We'll have muffins and bagels by 6:30 a.m."

The clerk then disappeared behind the door into an adjoining room. He reappeared moments later with a stack of newspapers that he placed on another table to the side of the counter.

Chris poured a cup of coffee and walked over to the windows and looked out at the parking lot. It was a great vantage point: he could see a lot better looking out than others could see peering in. He recalled that when he had first seen the clerk, all he had seen was a dark shadow. For ten minutes, Chris stared outside and saw no movement.

Finishing his drink, Chris walked back over to the coffee table and poured himself a refill. He took a sip and walked over and grabbed a newspaper, scouring the headlines. Tucking the paper under his armpit, he walked back over to his vantage point at the window.

Wait, movement! There was some activity as a young man brought out his suitcase from a motel room and placed it in his car trunk. Instead of heading back to the room, he walked over to Dan's car. He stopped and looked around to see if anyone was watching, then moved close to the back car window and peeked into the car.

Chris dropped the paper and moved swiftly to the door, exiting the office. He took another sip of coffee with his left hand as he pulled out his handgun from the shoulder holster with his right hand, holding it close behind his back as he walked casually toward Dan's car about sixty feet away.

After a few steps, a second guy came out of the motel room and put his suitcase in the same car trunk. Gently closing the trunk to his car, he had a quick exchange with the first guy looking inside Dan's car. Then the second man walked over to Dan's car.

Chris kept the car between them as he approached the two men. In seconds, he dropped his Styrofoam coffee cup on the ground.

"Can I help you?"

They were startled; that much was obvious. The first guy spoke.

"We were just admiring the car. Looks like you're all packed up. Where are you headed?"

The man wore a beanie hat and a light blue windbreaker with light blue faded Levi's. Chris saw that his hands were exposed. The second guy was hatless, his brown hair badly needed a haircut. He wore a heavier coat; one hand rummaged around in his coat, making Chris nervous.

Chris smiled and responded crisply.

"Just passing through."

The first one asked again.

"Where to?"

At the same time, the second guy pulled his hand from inside his jacket. Chris quickly pulled the gun from behind his back and pointed it at his chest.

"Slow."

They looked at Chris, puzzled. The first guy froze, and the second guy pulled out his beanie very slowly.

"We don't want any trouble, mister."

Chris slowly shook his head and smiled. He dropped his arm with the gun to his side.

"I apologize, gentlemen. It's been a tough week."

They both turned and quickly got into their car. The first guy drove; he started the engine and they closed their doors quickly. Staring at Chris, they peeled out of the parking lot.

Chris thought that he would never have suspected those guys (nor would he have pointed a gun at them) two weeks ago. But that was then and this was now. It was time to survive.

* * * * *

At 6:30 a.m., Chris woke Mike up. Mike dressed quickly, and Chris wondered how he could be dressed and ready to go in five seconds.

Chris couldn't go back to sleep for an hour and half. His adrenaline was still running from the episode in the parking lot, so he decided to stay up with Mike. Chris directed Mike to the coffee pot in the lobby and was delighted to see muffins and bagels had been put out.

Mike and Chris came out of the office with cups in one hand and pastries in the other. Walking over to the pool area at the end of the complex, they stood alongside the wrought iron fence while they drank their coffee. Mike looked at Chris.

"Chris, have you thought about what you will do when you reach Europe?"

"I'm not sure, Mike. I thought I would get across the border to Slovenia and then move toward Lake Bohinj. Jessica told me that Drago's father runs a ferry boat on the lake."

Chris paused to see what ideas Mike might offer. Mike listened and was quiet for a minute before speaking up.

"Getting into Slovenia will probably be easier than getting out. We should get a small reference book with words and phrases dictating Slovenian to English and learn some phrases."

Chris almost choked on his coffee as he looked over at Mike, a surprised look on his face.

"Mike, I can't ask you to risk your life by coming with me to Slovenia. I'm thankful you will help us cross the ocean. I can't ask you to join me past that."

Mike looked intensely at Chris for a few seconds. His eyes were piercing, almost as if he could see through Chris. He grinned, his smile extending from ear to ear.

"Hell! Someone has to make sure you come back alive."

Chris nodded and sighed. His odds for survival had just increased substantially. Mike was an experienced soldier and would be a valuable asset in Slovenia. Chris was just a "tech sales guy" trying to get his family back together. That was a lot of motivation, but he would need to take lessons from Mike on how to survive.

An hour later, they woke everyone up. Within thirty minutes they were on the road with coffee and muffins, en route to Asheville. The report from Nashville to Asheville was clear, and they cruised along the highway without any trouble. They stopped and bought some sandwiches and drinks along the way, fueled up, and that was all they stopped for until they reached Asheville.

Dan pulled over, and Will took the lead now navigating safely to his sister's house. She welcomed them warmly and graciously invited them into her lovely home. Will's sister and husband suggested that the four of them spend the night, and take hot showers after their long day. After the shower, shave, and a fresh set of clothes, they looked more presentable.

Thankful for this gesture, Chris pulled Will to the side and asked if they could take Will's sister and brother-in-law out to dinner. Will mentioned that they had a favorite restaurant, a family Italian restaurant nearby. After the final shower, they piled into the two cars and made their way to the neighborhood establishment.

After a hearty dinner with a couple of bottles of wine, when they could not fathom one more bite of food, they quickly called it a night. Chris asked for the check and they drove back to Will's sister's house for the night.

Will's sister had two spare bedrooms, a sofa, and two sleeping bags. Will took a bed, and the rest of the group flipped a coin for the other bedroom. Ali was lucky and won the other bed. Chris and Mike grabbed the two sleeping bags and gave Dan the sofa.

They fell fast asleep. Chris awoke to the smell of coffee and pancakes. Will's sister was cooking breakfast and soon Will, Mike, Dan, and Chris were in the kitchen.

Mike and Dan were studying the map. Chris walked over and they shared the intended route to Florida. The first destination was Columbia, South Carolina and from Columbia they would drive down the coast until they reached Dan's place outside West Palm Beach.

When Dan was done with the map, Chris and Will suggested that they call their boss, Dale, with an update. Chris dialed Dale's cell.

"Hi, Dale, this is Will and Dan and Chris."

"Hey, guys, what's happening? Still in Texas?"

"No, that's why we called. We're now in Asheville."

Will jumped in, "I'm here for good and should be settled within a week."

Chris continued, "We're heading to Dan's house in Florida this morning with two other friends."

"Chris, why are *you* going to Florida?" Dale asked.

"A change in plans. My daughter Jessica is in Slovenia: the border is closed and she cannot leave. I am traveling with Dan on his boat to Spain. He plans to propose to Maria and bring her back to Florida. Mike and I are going to find Jessica and bring her home."

"I've been preparing my boat for this type of voyage. With the four of us, we should be in good shape to make it," Dan added.

Dale wished them luck and asked them to check in periodically if they could. He said it was too soon to discuss logistics and details with their company, but he would make his best effort to get Will a spot in Asheville, Dan in Florida and Chris in Texas. These were Dale's last words: "Be safe and do what you have to do. Let me do the work on my end; hopefully I'll have good news for you when you check back in."

They hung up and Chris looked at Dan and Will.

"We're so fortunate to have such a terrific boss."

Dan and Will nodded: fifteen years of history working together as a team, a team considered to be one of the top in the company.

After breakfast, they helped clear the dishes, then packed all their bags in Dan's trunk. It was now just the four of them: Dan, Mike, Ali, and Chris.

They thanked Will's sister and husband for the hospitality and Chris shook Will's hand and gave him a hug. They had worked together closely for 15 years. Chris didn't know what the future would hold, but he hoped that they would see each other again someday.

Will wished them the best of luck as they jumped in Dan's car with Mike as navigator. As they pulled away from the house, Chris saw Will wave slowly, his whole arm stiff and extended. It was odd how the small details were often those that were stored in your memory.

Dan drove them out of Asheville, Mike rode shotgun with the map on his lap. Chris looked forward to relaxing in the back seat for a couple of hours. Ali sat directly behind Dan and Chris noticed that he looked like he was preparing for a nap.

They stopped every three hours to stretch and switch drivers or to buy a coffee or sandwich. They encountered no problems: it was clear sailing down the freeway and they made great time.

It was evening when they closed in on their destination. Dan suggested that he drive the last stretch since they were now in his neighborhood. Chris tried to follow the turns and landmarks so he would know the route, but he didn't feel confident. It was too dark to find landmarks, and Dan made too many left and right turns.

Soon they approached a gated community. Dan lowered the car window to punch in a numerical code and the gate opened. He drove a couple blocks inside the development, then pulled his car into a driveway.

"We are here!" he exclaimed.

They brought their luggage out of the car trunk and set it on the driveway while Dan pulled his car into the garage. Once he parked, they walked into the kitchen from the garage and dropped their luggage in the living room.

Dan's home had three bedrooms and two baths, and it was in very nice condition. The front yard was small with low-maintenance landscaping. His backyard had a large patio and some lawn that the gardener mowed every two weeks. The highlight was his private dock on the canal. Along the dock was his pride and joy, the boat that would hopefully transport them safely across the Atlantic Ocean to Europe.

After they unpacked and showered, they drove out of the community one to two miles to Dan's favorite pizza shop where they enjoyed beers and pizza (except Ali who drank a root beer). Dan told them that if they worked quickly and didn't encounter any unforeseen problems, they should only need two full days of prep before departure. On a napkin, Dan scribbled down everything they would need to do.

They agreed to divide the tasks: Ali and Chris would shop for supplies the next day while Mike helped Dan with the boat. Dan wrote a detailed list of what he needed and where to shop. He told Chris and Ali that they might need to make several trips.

Chris called Carly that evening when they returned from the pizza restaurant to tell her that they had arrived safely in Florida and planned to leave in a couple of days. Carly replied that she had made an appointment for his dad to see an oncologist in Lubbock.

"He was looking a little yellow, but other than that, we're all fine. I haven't heard anything from the boys on their Wisconsin trip," she offered before they wished each other a good night and hung up.

Chapter 37

Wichita to St. Paul

ETHAN AND MARK HAD the map unfolded on the surface of a table at a sandwich shop. Mark found the table in the corner of the establishment, his Krav Maga training leading him to select a spot off the main thoroughfare with high visibility and his back to the wall. He always identified all exits before settling down.

Their water bottles held the edges of the map down, the condensation forming a wet ring on the crinkled paper.

They had traveled from Brownfield and had left the state of Texas, continuing through Oklahoma until they had reached Kansas. Each border stop from Texas to Oklahoma to Kansas had had minimum border security. All three states were a part of the new Texas Federation.

The ranger at the last border crossing between Oklahoma and Kansas had advised them not to travel through northern Illinois or southern Wisconsin. The issued travel warning was to avoid the two states entirely. Gangs from Chicago had spread through northern Illinois and southern Wisconsin; gangs from Racine and Milwaukee were in the south and central parts of Wisconsin.

Ethan and Mark explained that they would need to bring their grandparents back to Texas from Fish Creek, Wisconsin. The last ranger at the Kansas checkpoint suggested they continue northeast; he thought that they should travel through Kansas and Iowa until they reached Minneapolis/St. Paul, then assess their route once again in St. Paul.

The travel had been easy so far. Mike's truck was easy to drive and was a comfortable ride. Ethan and Mark had switched off driving every few hours, so they were becoming comfortable driving the large truck. They had driven through some refreshing rain: light and steady, the air was now clear and fresh.

They spent the night in Topeka, Kansas at a motel off the highway. The only thing to be seen in Kansas was miles and miles of fields. With a fresh night of sleep logged, they headed out to Minneapolis/St. Paul and were soon at the Iowa border. Iowa was part of the Texas Federation and they stopped at the next small town. Switching drivers, they grabbed coffee and sandwiches, then filled the gas tank.

Ethan and Mark reached Minneapolis in the evening. Driving through Minneapolis and St. Paul, they found a motel and pulled into the parking lot. They checked in at the office, rented a room with two twin beds, and brought their roller bags, shotgun and rifle into the room. Stashing the guns under the bed, they exited the room and walked back into the motel office, asking the clerk for directions to the nearest police station.

Ethan pulled the truck up to the police station, where there were a few open parking places. Stepping out of the truck, they walked through the glass door entrance into the station lobby. There was one policeman at the four-foot-high front counter. Ethan and Mark surveyed the room: off to the side of the room, a policeman and policewoman sat with their heads down, sitting at their respective desks filling out some paperwork.

The policeman at the counter looked to be forty, with dark hair and some graying at the temple. He was about six feet tall and about two hundred pounds. He looked fit. At their entrance, he glanced up with inquisitive eyes.

"My brother and I are heading to Green Bay—we'll continue on to Fish Creek tomorrow to get our grandparents." Ethan started. "We've traveled from Texas and have received warnings by rangers at certain checkpoints along the way that part of Wisconsin isn't recommended for travel. We'd like your recommendation on the best route and areas we should avoid," Ethan explained.

Mark had a map of Wisconsin ready; he unfolded it and spread it out on the counter. The whole state of Wisconsin was exposed to the officer.

The policeman and policewoman compiling reports suddenly stopped writing. Their heads jerked up and they looked at Ethan and Mark, sizing them up.

The policewoman rose and walked over to the desk. So did the other policeman. They were younger, in their thirties. The policewoman had short red hair, was about five feet eight inches and was big-boned but not fat. The policeman was six feet two inches and about 220 lbs, and had a buzz haircut. He was comparable in size to Ethan and Mark.

The policewoman reached the counter before her colleague. The man at the counter let her take the lead as she spoke first, pointing to the map.

"All of Southern Wisconsin up to Green Bay should be avoided. There are gangs roaming in Green Bay, and there's conflict between the gangs, police, and local militia in that whole region."

The younger policeman was now at the counter and he leaned over the map.

"The route from St. Paul to Duluth is what I would recommend. Travel east along Lake Superior to Lake Michigan to Escanaba," the policeman added.

He pointed at the map with his finger, tracing the route that he suggested. As his finger reached Escanaba, he looked up.

"At Escanaba you should stop and get an update from Sheriff Krieger on the Green Bay situation. He's my Uncle and knows that area well."

Ethan and Mark thanked them graciously for their advice. Mark folded the map up and they walked outside. Some partial clouds blocked most of the stars in the sky; streetlights highlighted the mature trees that outlined the street. Ethan noted how quiet and peaceful it was. He had heard good things about the Minneapolis area that were now confirmed. Hopping in the truck, Ethan drove them back toward the motel. The next objective was to find a place for dinner.

Mark spotted a little family restaurant along the way. They stopped, walked in and found the place only half full. They were shown a booth with laminated menus, confirming that the menu did not change weekly. They were hungry and ordered a substantial dinner. As soon as the waitress left, Ethan looked at Mark and shared what was on his mind.

"The past couple of travel days have been very easy. I think the next couple of days may be difficult. We need to be aware of our surroundings and the situation at all times."

Mark agreed. "When we go back to the motel, we should clean our guns, then go to bed to get a good night's sleep."

Dinner was good—when they were full, they left the restaurant. Ethan drove them back, and in ten minutes, they were at their motel room. As they cleaned the rifle and shotgun, they listened to the news on television.

Before they went to sleep, they called their mom to let her know that they were fine and had made great travel time. There was not much to report other than that they were getting closer to Fish Creek. Promising to call back in a couple of days, they hung up the cell phone. Turning off the lamp, they settled in for a good night's sleep.

Chapter 38

Escanaba, Wisconsin

MARK PULLED THE TRUCK into the sheriff's station. There was one vehicle marked Sheriff in the parking lot. They had an enjoyable drive from St. Paul: there were some clouds, but the sun peeked through. The air temperature was crisp and cool, but pleasant.

They walked into the lobby and paused, they didn't see anyone. Ethan looked for a bell on the counter but didn't see one. They decided to wait. Mark spotted a framed photo on the wall: Sheriff Krieger and Mayor Linscomb were featured at a city celebration. After a minute, they heard a flush and a door opened around the corner of the room. In seconds, they saw a man in his early sixties emerge. He had white hair, stood a little less than six feet tall, and had a small pot belly.

He saw them at the counter and walked over to them. Offering a big smile and a hello, it was obvious to Mark and Ethan that this was Sheriff Krieger at the counter.

Ethan provided the sheriff with their story, explaining that they were on a mission to retrieve their grandparents. Sheriff Krieger pulled out a detailed map of his region of Wisconsin, unfolding it for Ethan and Mark. Every dirt road was detailed on this map. He explained that there were gangs from Milwaukee and motorcycle gangs from Sturgeon Bay down to Illinois. They were fighting each other and also terrorizing private citizens. Residents were forming a militia to fight these gangs along with the local police in Green Bay in an attempt to drive them from their towns and cities.

Sheriff Krieger felt it was dangerous to drive through Green Bay and Sturgeon Bay to Fish Creek. There were many roads closed with check points. Some checkpoints were manned by the gangs and some were managed by the militia and police. His recommendation was to wait for a week or two to see if things settled down.

Ethan and Mark left the sheriff's office dejected. They needed to get their grandparents and head back home.

Ethan spoke first. "We can't sit here for a couple of weeks."

"And it could be worse in two weeks," Mark added.

They got in the truck and pulled out of the parking area. Mark drove them over to the harbor where they found a place to park. They got out and walked along the shore, Ethan rifling through the pros and cons with Mark as they tried to brainstorm how to break through the roadblocks to Fish Creek. The biggest con was that if they were fortunate enough to arrive at Fish Creek, they weren't sure if they would get lucky the second time as they departed. It sounded like a long shot.

Mark selected a rock on the beach, threw it, and was rewarded with three skips on top of the water. He spotted a boat returning to the harbor and heading toward the dock.

A thought burst through. "Ethan, what if we travel by boat across the bay to Fish Creek? On the sheriff's map, it didn't look like we were too far away by water. What if we left the truck here, arranged for passage on a boat to get Pa K and Ma K, and then traveled back here? Then we could retrace our trip and drive back the way we came to Brownfield."

Ethan looked at Mark, then back to the boat that was now arriving at the dock. "Mark, that's a great idea. Let's go down and talk to the guy that's pulling into the dock."

Ethan and Mark walked down to the dock. The boat owner and his wife were tying down their boat. They were a middle-aged couple in their midfifties. Dressed in shorts and long-sleeved shirts. He had a Packer's hat on, and she had on a pink hat with a wide three-inch brim on all sides.

To ensure that they didn't startle them, Ethan gave them a hello at the beginning of the dock. This allowed a few minutes before Ethan and Mark reached the boat.

Mark and Ethan stopped at the edge of the boat and waited a few seconds. Finally, the guy looked up at them.

"Have you ever taken this boat across the bay to Fish Creek?" Ethan asked.

The man adjusted his Packer's hat with his right hand and looked at his wife before answering. "Sure, many times. It's just across the bay."

There was quiet for ten seconds that seemed like five minutes. Ethan and Mark were deep in thought, and the man and his wife anticipated a follow-up question. Finally, the man asked, "Why?"

Ethan and Mark told the story of why they were looking for passage to the town of Fish Creek. They shared the sheriff's warning not to drive.

"I'll take you across to Fish Creek for $300, but only for a day trip. I'll drop you off, take off and fish, then come back to the pier to pick you back up."

"When?" Ethan asked.

"I can do eight tomorrow morning," the boat owner responded. He looked at his wife first, she nodded.

Mark and Ethan nodded, then stepped over and shook his hand and made formal introductions. They found out the man's name was Mac Wilson. Mac, the Packer football fan. They planned to meet him the next morning at eight with $300. After exchanging goodbyes, they walked back to the truck.

On the drive back, Ethan spotted a bank and an ATM and asked Mark to pull over. They both withdrew cash, then drove back to the motel.

Mark and Ethan returned to their hotel room, took a shower, and then walked across the street to eat dinner at another local mom and pop restaurant. It was nice to see more family-owned establishments and less chain restaurants. On the walk back to their motel room, they stopped and chatted with the motel clerk. He confirmed that they had room availability and that Ethan and Mark could stay for a couple more nights. Ethan pulled out some cash and paid the clerk in advance.

They now had a plan to arrive at Fish Creek the next day. They called their grandparents on Ethan's cell phone and shared the plan. Pa K and Ma K were at first confused about the plan with the boat, but they knew that the roads were dangerous in Wisconsin. Ethan and Mark explained it again, slower, and with more details, and then they understood. Ethan instructed them to be packed and ready late the next morning. Pa K and Ma K were both excited to see their grandsons, and to finally leave Fish Creek. They told Ethan and Mark that they were getting really concerned: there was a rumor that a motorcycle gang could head up to Fish Creek any day now.

Pa K told them to hold for a minute; he came back on the phone with his brother-in-law standing by. Handing his brother-in-law the telephone, he gave Ethan and Mark directions to their home from the pier. As Mark wrote the directions down, they heard more voices in the background. When the directions were fully relayed, Pa K took the phone again He confirmed that their nephew who recently retired and built a house on a lot adjacent to his parents; was over now, and visiting with them.

"We'll be packed and anxious to see you tomorrow," Pa K said before the boys ended the call.

Ethan and Mark went through the directions over and over. They had them written down and would take the paper, but they both wanted to memorize the directions in order to move quickly.

Chapter 39

Julian Alps, Slovenia

JESSICA DRANK A CUP of coffee by herself and took time to reflect. She had ten more minutes before their hike. Ever since they had left Lake Bohinj and relocated up into the mountains, things had been quiet. The four of them had been hiking a couple of hours every day; each day led to the discovery of a new trail.

Drago brought two rifles: his own personal rifle, and another rifle he had borrowed from a friend. He set aside time each day for Sam, Nancy, and Jessica to practice shooting in the afternoon. He told them that it would hopefully not be necessary, but that their lives could depend on knowing how to shoot accurately.

They quickly fell into a daily routine: after breakfast, they went on a hike and were back by lunch. They would eat and rest; in midafternoon they had thirty minutes of shooting practice. Drago spent time after the shooting exercises talking about how to load and care for the rifles and handguns. Then, before dinner, Drago would go to the top of the nearby mountain and scan down below them. He did this every morning and each evening, and sometimes Jessica elected to travel with him. They hardly spoke on top of the mountain, but she knew what he was looking for.

On their morning hikes they sometimes ran across smaller groups of Slovenian men. Drago explained that these men were fighters who called themselves "Patriots." Their mission was to drive the Russians out from Slovenia. These teams operated as Commando teams; often there were five to six men in each group. Dressed as mountaineers, they carried themselves as mountaineers: all the Patriots were armed with handguns, knives and rifles. They trained on the mountain in preparation for future attacks on the Russians.

Jessica found that her shooting had improved immensely over the past days; she was also getting comfortable hiking up and down the mountains. She was a runner, but the elevation was a lot higher than what she was accustomed to and so the past couple of days had allowed for her body to adjust. She thought she was getting acclimated. At first the daypacks felt heavy, but now she could easily carry one for a few hours. Drago had them carry a heavier load each day, and she guessed that they were now up to twenty-five to thirty pounds.

Every time they crossed a Slovenian Patriot group, Drago took a break for a couple of minutes to speak Slovenian with his countrymen. There were animated discussions between Drago and the other men as they shared information about the Russians, trails, and mountain passes.

* * * * *

The next morning, Jessica glanced up at the mountain as she drank her cup of coffee. She wondered when Drago would attempt a full day hike to the adjacent peak. She had seen Drago look at it many times—during his discussions with the Patriots, he often pointed at the peak.

Drago walked out of the house that instant. Jessica turned to him and pointed at the peak.

"Drago, are we going to attempt that peak some day? Can we do it in a full day?"

"It's too soon, Jessica. When we come across the Patriots and I share information, I ask them each time about the passage out of Slovenia and the conditions at the higher elevation. The Russians seem to be preoccupied with Ljubljana and their new borders. There isn't any activity in Bohinj other than a little outpost that now has six soldiers. We're fortunate that we can wait for the weather to change and the snow to melt. In the meantime, we're getting fit for our trek."

Nancy walked out of the house five minutes later and asked if they had eaten breakfast. They hadn't, and followed her back inside to a breakfast of a little cheese, along with bread and prepared meats. Nancy and Sam were already eating so Jessica and Drago grabbed a plate and joined them.

Jessica longed for a giant green salad with fresh spinach, lettuce, tomatoes and cucumbers, but she would just have to wait. She thought how wonderful it would be to be there under different circumstances. The mountains were so beautiful and majestic with their snow-covered peaks. This would be a beautiful place to vacation.

Chapter 40

Cheese house, Slovenia

THEY HAD JUST FINISHED eating dinner and were sitting outside enjoying the last half hour of light. Drago spotted a Patriot squad in the distance: they stared as the group walked single-file toward them. Watching the five men as they approached the house, they were one hundred feet away before Drago asked Sam for assistance. Quickly they went inside, and Drago brought out a bottle and Sam carried several shot glasses. As the Patriots approached, Drago greeted them and motioned for them to come over and sit at the picnic benches. There were smiles and handshakes, Drago then took the cork off of the bottle and poured some drinks. A quick toast was given by Drago in Slovenian, then all of them raised their glasses and took a shot.

Jessica took a sip and felt it burn down her throat. Deciding quickly that she only wanted that partial shot, she asked Sam and Nancy if they wanted to take a short walk up the knoll. They agreed, went inside and grabbed their flashlights, then climbed the knoll. They left Drago and the Patriots to have a few more shots of whiskey along with discussion.

Sam was first up the hill. From the knoll you could see several peaks through the filtered light. The drawback was that if you stood up you could be noticed from miles away. There was a clearing on the knoll and they sat down and admired the peaks and valleys before them. The air was cool, but with their jackets on, they were warm enough. Besides, they were adjusting to the cooler temperature.

As they stared ahead, they talked about their families back home. Nancy worried about her mom and dad and little sister, who was still in high school. She wondered how they were doing. Sam had just his mother back home—he worried about her being all alone. He explained that his father had died when he was a young boy, and that it had been just he and his mother since the age of four. Jessica shared about her family: it would be different never going back to San Diego, but if she were with her family, it would be home no matter where they were.

After an hour they walked back down to the hut using flashlights to guide the way. The Patriots had already left, and Drago sat at the table, looking deep in thought. When they walked up, he motioned for them to sit down at the table.

"The Patriots shared that the Russians now have fifteen soldiers in Bohinj." He waited for a moment. "Also, the Russians were questioning people about the tram up to the mountain."

After a minute Drago continued. "The Patriots have heard that the Russians will soon send a patrol up here to check the surroundings. They think it'll happen in the next day or two. They recommend that we move, at least temporarily, up to a different cabin at a little higher altitude."

They all sat in silence. "I think we need to pack tonight. Tomorrow morning we should clean all footprints and any trace that we've been staying here, then leave for a few days. The Patriots suggested a hut that is about a six-hour hike from here. We've been training each day, so we'll all make it easily," Drago added.

Sam and Nancy excused themselves to pack and get ready for bed, knowing it would be all-uphill hike the next day. They wanted to have a good night's sleep. A nonstrenuous hike for Drago would be plenty strenuous for them.

Jessica stood up and looked up at the stars, wondering if any of her family members were looking at these same stars thousands of miles away. Drago got up and walked over, sharing her view of the sky.

"More Russians in Bohinj is not good news for us, is it? Russian patrols in these mountains are not good either," Jessica shared her thoughts aloud.

"I'm not sure if they are looking for us. They've heard of the Patriots preparing and training. I think they may be looking to see if they can see any evidence of the Patriots."

It was quiet for a minute. Drago turned his head and looked at Jessica. They were about a foot away from each other. Jessica could feel his arm as it rested next to hers.

"Don't worry, I will protect you."

They continued to look at each other, and then Drago bent down and gave Jessica a kiss. It was soft: not long, but full of meaning. Jessica felt stunned—she looked up into Drago's eyes and nodded, before she turned and went inside to pack.

What a strange place and circumstance to have romantic feelings for this young Slovenian man. Why were these feelings growing between the two of them at this time? Would the feelings still be there once they left Slovenia? Thoughts bounced around Jessica's head as she packed, brushed her teeth, and went to bed. She dreamt of her family in the backyard for a holiday BBQ, Finley parading around with his tennis ball.

Chapter 41

Julian Alps, Slovenia

DRAGO'S VOICE SHOOK JESSICA from her dream. "It's time to move."

Jessica's eyes opened, and she saw Nancy stir on the other side of the bedroom. They were in wooden bunks with a number of blankets piled on top of them to keep them warm at night. It felt good in bed, and Jessica had to force herself to get out from under the warm blankets and quickly get dressed. They had packed the evening before, so they just had to eat and clean the area before taking off.

Jessica came down the stairs to discover that Drago had made coffee for them. There was some bread and cheese and sausages on a plate for breakfast. Sam was already seated and eating. Jessica put her pack against a post and walked over, pouring a cup of coffee. She didn't need too much to eat in the morning, but she would have some bread. One thing she had discovered about Europe was that the bread tasted so much better than in the United States. Her mom thought this was because the European bread didn't have preservatives. Whatever it was, the bread was delicious. A minute later, Nancy came down the stairs with her pack, which she set next to Jessica's. She started for the coffee first, poured herself a cup, and then sat down with the others.

As they ate, Drago took the opportunity to go through his list of the morning's tasks. "Sam and Nancy, I'd like you to take a branch and remove any footprints within fifty yards of the house. Double check to make sure we didn't leave anything behind outside. Jessica, go through and make sure we didn't leave anything behind inside the house. Take a wet rag and wipe off any smudges, and get rid of crumbs," the owner will return in a couple weeks. "Clean anything that shows we stayed here. I'll climb up the hill here and get one more view before we head up the mountain. Be ready to travel in thirty minutes."

Everyone nodded. After they finished eating, they washed and dried their cups and dishes, putting them away in the cupboard. Drago wrapped up the uneaten breakfast food and put it in his pack: this would be part of their lunch. They had more food to take along and Drago distributed it evenly among the four of them, who each packed their portion in their backpacks.

In less than a half hour, they were all in front of the house. Sam kept a branch and held it in his hand. He was instructed to erase their footsteps for the next hundred yards as they left the cheese house for the peak.

Drago led them. They followed in single-file formation: Nancy first, then Jessica, and then Sam. While Sam erased their footprints, Jessica carried the second rifle. They walked slowly while Sam worked behind them. When they came to the fork, Sam chucked the branch about thirty feet into a thicket. Jessica gave him the rifle, and they took off for an adventure.

They started up the right fork and immediately the trail climbed. About ½ mile up, they heard a screeching. Drago stopped and they watched as an eagle soared above them, disappearing among the tree tops.

Drago looked back at them. "It's a golden eagle. As we climb in altitude, we'll see more wildlife."

They continued the climb. Drago let them stop every mile for a quick drink, then it was back to hiking the trail. Some of the trail was slow—the loose shale made it tough to get a foothold. They covered three miles in the first two hours and they finally approached an overlook with a good view. Drago gave them a longer rest and the chance to snack while he pulled out a pair of binoculars and scanned below.

After their snack, they continued hiking at the same steady pace so they could handle the increased altitude. They reached the peak around noon and celebrated with some water. Drago kept their rest brief, suggesting they eat lunch in the valley. Ten minutes later, they continued on the trail. It dropped down into a small valley, patches of snow clung to the side of the mountain. Jessica saw larger snowcapped peaks looming behind the valley.

Drago led them through the small valley. There was a fast-moving stream running through, and they caught a glimpse of a rustic cabin at the end of the valley, off the trail fifty meters. The cabin was on a knoll twenty feet above the valley floor.

Hiking over toward the cabin, Jessica's first impression was that this new place looked more rustic than their previous cabin. Drago walked over and opened the front door. They walked in and saw that there were eight wooden bunks and a primitive stone fire place. The fireplace was a necessity that would allow for warmth and the ability to cook food. There were two windows with wooden shutters that opened up. Sam discovered that the toilet was an outhouse one hundred feet away.

Drago noted the running water from the stream was their water source: they would need to boil the water before drinking it. This would be a daily chore.

Drago suggested that they unpack, have lunch and rest a little. They brought their packs into the cabin and unpacked a portion of it using their bunk beds, there were four on each side: Nancy and Jessica picked one side, and the guys chose the other.

As they walked out onto the small porch and sat down, they brought their canteens. Drago pulled out that morning's breakfast and added more bread and cheese. It was quiet: they were tired, and it was nice to sit down and look out over the valley. A couple of squirrels moved up a tree ten meters away.

"After we rest, we should explore the valley together," Drago stated, breaking the silence.

"What preparation do we need to do before nightfall?" Jessica asked.

Drago thought for a moment. "We'll need to start a fire and boil drinking water. I'd like to hike up above us for a mile or two and explore. Someone should hike up to the peak we just climbed and check down below us. In fact, we need to do this a couple of times a day."

"Is it possible to take a bath?" Nancy chimed in.

"When we walk around the valley, let's see if there's a good place to take a bath—preferably downstream from where we gather our drinking water," Drago agreed.

They rested an hour, then packed away the remaining food. Closing the cabin door, they walked to the stream where it rushed down the mountain. There were some small waterfalls that cascaded until they dropped into a pool. From the pool, the water continued as a stream through the valley floor.

They decided to walk along the stream. They left their packs, but still carried the two rifles.

"Are there fish in the stream?" Sam asked Drago.

Drago shook his head. "I'm not sure if there are fish, but we can try. I don't know if they stock fish this high in the mountain range."

They continued along the river and found a small pool further down the valley that was sheltered and secluded. It looked good for bathing or swimming. They all agreed that it would feel good to take a bath later in the day.

Following the stream to the end of the valley, they decided to walk the perimeter of the valley. It wasn't large, and they walked back toward their cabin and crossed the trail that led through the valley. Drago crossed the stream, hopping on a few rocks at the narrow part of the water and beckoning the others to follow. Drago discovered a small cave and suggested that they come back to explore the cave with a flashlight later, perhaps the next day. They continued the perimeter, then hiked back to their cabin.

"I'd like to take a bath. Jessica, do you want to join me?" Nancy asked.

"I think that's a good idea," Drago agreed. "I'll hike a mile or two above us on the trail. Sam, will you take the rifle and binoculars and go back to the peak to see if you see anything below us? We can all meet back in an hour," Drago instructed.

Jessica and Nancy brought a towel and a bar of soap as they walked to the pool they had spotted earlier. Sam took the rifle and binoculars from Drago and went back on the trail through the valley toward the peak. Drago walked over to the trail and ventured in the opposite direction, upward in the direction of the next peak.

In an hour they met up again, the girls were clean and proclaimed that the water was cold but refreshing. Sam confirmed that he hadn't seen anything below them, and Drago agreed that he hadn't seen any fresh footprints on the trail. He had run into snow about a mile up: It was still walkable, but he felt that farther up on the peak they *would* need crampons or snow shoes.

They gathered firewood and placed it to the side of the cabin. Drago started a fire in the fireplace and Nancy was to maintain the fire. Sam and Drago discovered a bucket and a pot in the cabin and they traveled to the stream, making two trips to fill the pot. Nancy and Jessica planned to boil the water so they could fill the canteens later that evening.

Drago and Sam announced that they were going to take their baths. They quickly headed down to the stream with the damp towel and a bar of soap. In thirty minutes, the guys returned clean and refreshed. They discovered that Nancy and Jessica already had the water boiling, so the four of them now had time to relax and enjoy a leisurely dinner.

The evening sky was clear and the stars were out in abundance, shining brilliantly against the black sky. When they had finished eating dinner, they just relaxed under the stars, sitting on some tree stumps in front of the cabin. They could hear some of the nighttime noises common to the wilderness; Jessica thought nature's music offered comforting sounds.

Drago suggested that they take turns the next day watching for potential activity from the peak. They could each take four small shifts: early morning, midmorning, midafternoon, and later afternoon.

Drago also suggested that they make a fishing pole with a stick. He had a hook in his pack along with some twine for a line. Sam seemed to be the one interested in trying his hand at fishing.

"Drago, if you can create a fishing pole, I'll volunteer to fish. I can look for worms, crickets, or something for bait."

Drago explained that he would set a trap for rabbits using some of the same twine. He had had some success in catching rabbits while camping with his father. All this talk made Sam excited.

"I'd like something different to eat besides bread, cheese, and sausage tomorrow. Having a fish or rabbit would be delicious," Sam added.

* * * * *

Nancy was tired and turned her head to the side, in an attempt to cover her mouth with her hand. The big yawn did not escape her friend's notice, and soon the others yawned themselves. They were all getting tired.

Jessica went into the cabin, found a ladle, and brought it outside. Nancy, Sam, and Drago brought their canteens and she poured the boiled water into their canteens. They had some additional water available and poured some into a cup to use later to brush their teeth. Covering the pot, they saved the rest of the water for the next day.

After brushing their teeth, they took turns visiting the outhouse with the flashlight. Safely back in their bunks, Drago was the last person in their shelter. Approaching his bunk, he turned out the flashlight.

"Good night, everyone."

Chapter 42

Texas

CARLY PULLED THE VAN to a stop in front of the farmhouse. Opening her door to get out, her in-laws followed her lead as they opened and closed the doors. Clark, up on the second story of the barn with a pitchfork, waved to them. There were bales of hay stacked in the barn on one side; on the other side there were openings to the pens for the milking cows and horses. Clark had opened a couple of bales and was pitching some hay into each pen. A neighbor had gifted them a horse the other day, so Grandpa H had discovered a couple of saddles and riding equipment in the barn. Carly had taken the horse for a ride and found out that she enjoyed riding. She planned to take a ride once a day around the perimeter of the property. Their quaint farm was coming along: they now had a horse with their two milking cows and chickens.

Finley was lying on the porch and came down to greet them, his wagging tail and body contorted in the way that golden retrievers do when they meet friends. Finley ran to each person, acknowledging their return. They had just returned from the oncologist in Lubbock. Some bloodwork was performed on Grandpa H and his red blood count was low. The hospital had scheduled him for chemo the next week: he had been on a maintenance plan in San Diego for his CLL, a type of leukemia. He had missed a treatment, and now he was a little low. Unfortunately the hospital in San Diego was no longer in existence, and the new doctor didn't have the medical records. The oncologist in Lubbock wanted to do a full exam and blood work. Grandpa H was exhausted from the treatment, and they were watching him and testing him each day. The doctor recommended that he stay close to the hospital for the week.

After the doctor visit, they found a hotel less than a mile away where the grandparents could stay for the week. The hotel would give them a free shuttle ride back and forth to the hospital and there were two restaurants nearby: one family restaurant next door and a steak house across the street. The doctor scheduled the chemo treatments for Monday, Tuesday, Thursday, and Friday. Their plan was for Carly to take them early Monday, to try to visit on Wednesday, and then pick them up on Friday late afternoon. The distance to Lubbock was a significant commute, and she needed to watch and maintain the farm with Clark.

Clark was becoming a big help. He took responsibility for feeding all the farm animals and for cleaning the coop, stalls, and pen. He picked the apples off of the existing fruit trees and Grandma H had rewarded Clark's apple picking with a couple of apple pies that past weekend. Clark milked the cows with Grandpa H in the morning, where Grandpa H told stories from when he had been a young boy on the Texas farm. Carly collected the eggs each morning.

Carly had more eggs and milk than they could consume. An immediate neighbor to the east came by twice a week and exchanged fruit and vegetables for milk. Their neighbors had a milk container that held up to four gallons of milk: they came by the farm on Monday and Thursday. They had a family of four small children and they had more fruit and vegetables than they could eat from their garden, so it was a good exchange for both families.

Carly had discovered there was a farmer's market in Brownfield each Saturday morning—she took the excess eggs and sold them there. Clark would load up the van with a folding table and chair, and she would take the van into town with her in-laws. The eggs were packaged in cartons of twelve and stacked on the table. Grandpa H sold the eggs and talked to the other locals as Grandma H and Carly walked the farmer's market and bought different fruits and vegetables. Later in the morning, they would stop at the grocery store and buy bread, meat, and other food supplies for the week. It was a pleasant way to spend Saturday morning, and it also let them meet more of the folks in town.

Abby had called on Friday night to announce that she and Ryan had moved into their apartment in Austin. Ryan was ready to start his job, and Abby had two interviews for elementary school teaching positions. Abby sounded excited over the phone. Carly placed her on speakerphone so the grandparents could listen in and join the conversation. Abby's enthusiasm was contagious; she and Ryan represented hope for the future.

Grandpa H took Clark out to the back of the barn a couple of times a week and taught him to shoot. He told Clark that he hoped he would never have to use the gun, but he needed to learn how just in case. Clark was reluctant at first, but he now looked forward to these sessions. He had improved since the initial lesson and now felt more comfortable holding and shooting the gun.

Clark missed his parents and San Diego. He hid it well, but sometimes, it was a little overwhelming. Having chores on the farm gave him time to think, mourn, and recover. This new life on the farm was very different from his previous life, but he was adjusting, and he liked the responsibility that he had been given. His life was changing, he now felt that his life had a purpose. Clark knew that he was depended on here at the farm. He was excited to start school at Tech in the fall and had recently found out that there were a few other Tech students in the community.

Chapter 43

Florida

IT WAS THEIR THIRD day in Florida, and they planned for an early departure the next morning. Dan's buddy was a mechanic: even though Dan felt the boat was in good condition, he had his friend check it thoroughly. Dan had everything inspected: the Avon six man raft and the desalination machine were both given the thumbs-up yesterday. They were taking a long voyage; it was important that everything was in working order.

Chris and Ali loaded food and supplies onto the boat and Dan directed where things should be stowed. It was midafternoon, and it looked like they were going to get a downpour any minute. Dan directed Ali to where the canned food should be stashed. Chris was directed to the storage area for all bottled drinks along with pharmaceuticals: he had bought all the basics at the pharmacy to fight headaches, the flu, the common cold, and had added some miscellaneous first aid items.

Mike was in the house cleaning all the weapons. He had bought more ammunition today at the store and was in charge of making sure they were sufficiently armed. The hope was that they wouldn't run across pirates or trouble on the voyage. Mike wasn't too sure what they might encounter once they reached Europe: they would have to navigate between Portugal, Spain, Morocco, and Algeria to safely reach Barcelona.

Chris had also purchased fishing gear. Dan had two fishing poles on the boat—the goal was to catch fish on the voyage for lunch and dinner. They bought a lot of fresh fruit and vegetables and planned to restock once they reached port in Puerto Rico.

The four had poured over the map in detail the past night. The plan was to leave West Palm Beach early the next morning and head toward the Bahamas, then continue to Puerto Rico. If they had any unforeseen trouble with the boat, Puerto Rico was their last chance for repair. This would be their test drive. They would restock food, especially fruits and vegetables in Puerto Rico—then head across the Atlantic to the Madeira islands off the coast of Portugal. Other than some rain along the way, the weather report at this time looked good. Dan cautioned them that the extended weather report should be taken with a grain of salt: in his experience, the weather could be unpredictable.

Dan's friend finished checking the engine, smiling and nodding in approval. Dan shook his hand, and gave him a brief hug. Minutes later, his friend walked away. Dan came over and helped direct Chris and Ali to the next section of supplies. They continued working for another hour; when they finished packing, it was time to double-check Dan's list.

Dan had a checklist that he brought out: he would shout an item out loud and wait for Ali and Chris to confirm where it was packed. Dan made a notation, then moved to the next item. Everything was accounted for and in the correct place. The three went inside the house to check on Mike.

Mike saw them enter and looked at Dan. "Are we ready to go, boss?"

"Yes. We're checked and rechecked." Dan smiled.

Mike handed each of them their guns. He had two shotguns and rifles lying on the dining room table.

After handing them their handguns he remarked, "These are now your new best friends. Take care of them and they will take care of you." They responded with smiles.

Two defrosted chickens from Dan's freezer sat in the sink. Dan walked over and peeked at them.

"Guys, are we ready to cook dinner?"

They quickly went to work. The goal was to finish off anything from inside the refrigerator. Ali made a fresh salad with the lettuce, tomatoes and any fresh vegetable remaining in the refrigerator and Dan turned on the oven as he told them about his secret chicken spice that he conjured up and mixed into the bowl. Chris and Mike found some potatoes that they baked in the oven. On the stove top, they cooked a frozen veggie medley package that Mike found in the freezer.

Dan finished his secret sauce and applied it liberally to the chicken before setting it to cook in the oven. He walked into the other room and came back with a bottle of wine, uncorked it, and found four wine glasses. Leaving the bottle on the table to breathe, he walked over and found some salad dressing in the pantry. They waited for the chicken and potatoes and veggies to cook; Dan walked over and poured glasses of wine. He took his time and handed everyone a glass with the exception of Ali who had grape juice.

Dan held up his wine glass and searched for something to say. He struggled, so Mike raised his glass and said, "Salute."

They all answered in unison with "salute," then took a drink and looked at each other and smiled. Sitting down at the table, they ate their salad and engaged in some small talk. Most of the conversation focused on their route as they confirmed timelines and places they would visit. They didn't want to mention what they were all thinking: that this might be their last meal at a dining room table.

Chris had faith that Ethan and Mark would bring their grandparents back to Texas. He had faith that Carly would ensure that his father continued to receive the chemo treatment to get his red blood cell count up to a safe level. He had faith that Ryan and Abby would be safe and successful in Austin as they started their new lives. He had faith that Jessica and her colleagues could evade the Russians for a while in the Julian Alps. Now, as he looked around the table, his group had to successfully cross the ocean. He needed faith that they could make it across successfully. He had to find Jessica and bring her home safely to Texas.

They finished eating and cleaned up—when they finished it was still early in the evening. Walking into the family room, Dan turned on the news to receive an update on the situation in the United States. The Texas Federation was growing: Arizona and New Mexico had joined from the west, and North and South Dakota had joined along with Nebraska. Idaho and Colorado were considering joining and would make a decision in a couple of weeks. California, or what was left of it, had held a major vote inside the state government. They had declared themselves as an independent country. Oregon and Washington were in a quandary: The Texas Federation was a conservative country while they were traditionally more liberal. Would they fit in with the Texas Federation, or would they join California? Or would they create their own country?

In the South, Florida, South Carolina, and North Carolina were forming an independent country. They only needed to agree on the name. Georgia wanted to join, but they needed to stabilize the Atlanta area before they would seriously be considered. This was a common theme: state entry required that you not only agree with the new countries' policies but that you also enter as a stable state. The consensus was that if Georgia joined, Alabama and Mississippi would follow. Louisiana was leaning toward joining the Texas Federation, but they were trying to contain New Orleans. Arkansas could go to either country, but they needed to contain Little Rock before either federation would look at inviting them in.

The Northeast was a mess. New York City, Camden, New Jersey, Philadelphia, and all the way down to Baltimore; Washington, DC; and Richmond was a war zone with little chance of stabilization. Maine, Vermont, New Hampshire, Connecticut, and Massachusetts were looking to form their own Federation. Pennsylvania wanted to join, but they would have to clean up Philadelphia or redraw lines to cut Philadelphia off of the new Pennsylvania.

In the Midwest, the news targeted central and southern Wisconsin, Illinois, and Ohio as dangerous areas. Chris thought about where Ethan and Mark were at this time and wondered if they would need to modify their original route. Some previous states, like Indiana and West Virginia, and Delaware and Rhode Island were islands among the chaos, waiting to see if they could join a stable group.

After forty-five minutes of news, they'd heard enough, knowing they faced a long day, the four of them turned in early for bed. Dan announced that he would set his alarm for four the next morning. Chris must have fallen into a deep sleep, because the next thing he heard was Dan's voice beckoning him to wake up. It was time to head out.

Groggily they moved about and got dressed. They brought their packs onboard the boat with their guns. Everything else was packed and ready to go on the boat.

Dan locked his home and set his alarm. His neighbor had promised to keep an eye on his home while he was away.

At 4:15 a.m. they slowly pulled away from the dock to head down the canal that led them to the Ocean. Chris looked around: everyone had their game face on as they passed the dark homes of Dan's neighbors. Other than a neighbor's dog barking, everything was still and quiet as they made their way out. Chris thought he saw some eyes from the bank of the shore and pointed them out to Dan.

"Gators" was the only response he got from Dan. The boat's motor hummed as Dan navigated them along.

Dan had them out in the ocean by 4:30 a.m. The course was quickly set for the Bahamas. Dan had the wheel, and Chris suggested that he make them a pot of coffee. Ali gave him a hand and they made a big pot. Chris put in a couple more scoops for extra strength. Within twenty minutes, they walked out of the cabin holding two cups each: Chris handed one to Dan and Ali handed one to Mike.

Chris took a few steps toward the stern, took a sip, and looked up into the dark sky. There were still stars blinking brightly and he could see the crescent moon. The warm breeze tickled his face and felt refreshing.

Mike motioned for them to gather around.

"Until we leave Puerto Rico, we can't have the boat on autopilot. There are many reefs that we need to avoid but just as important, there are reports of many pirates through the Bahamas and Puerto Rico," Dan spoke up.

"Dan and I were thinking that we should implement two man shifts. We need one person at the helm and another armed and on look-out at all times. Dan and I were thinking of six hour shifts—the navigator and guard could switch off after three hours each," Mike suggested.

Ali and Chris nodded. "Are there ideas of the pairings?" Chris asked.

Dan answered, "I know this boat well. I thought that Chris and Mike could be one pair, and Ali and myself as the other."

He glanced ahead. "I'd like to train each of you during the day today on how to handle the boat and what dangers to keep an eye out for. After dinner we can start with the six hour shifts. If we do 8:00 p.m. to 2:00 a.m. and 2:00 a.m. to 8:00 a.m., then we'll each hopefully get sufficient sleep with the option to take a nap during the day."

"Anything to bring up before Dan begins his training?" Mike asked.

Chris gazed out in the direction that Dan had set course. "I've never been to the Bahamas."

They looked at him and laughed.

Chapter 44

Bahamas

THEY WERE MAKING GREAT travel time. So far, Dan was pleased; there had been no issues with the boat. Moving south along the Florida coast, Dan steered them east toward the Miami shore, then guided the boat between the Grand Bahama and Nassau islands. Dan was very patient and had already taught the crew a lot about sailing.

Dan and Mike also described some worst-case scenarios as discussion points for possible solutions. They would hold a group discussion on each case, talking over options until they could agree on the best approach. Dan focused on the boat emergency situations while Mike focused on potential confrontations with other boats or bandits.

When he was off his shift or sleeping, Dan tried his luck fishing. Ali joined him at every opportunity. Chris wasn't sure if it was due to Dan's instruction or to beginner's luck, but Ali had so far caught ten fish to Dan's three, including some large ones. So far, they had caught enough fish for both lunch and dinner, leading Chris to wonder if they might be able to keep their canned food on the shelf.

One item that Chris, Mike and Ali didn't possess were sun hats and long-sleeved T-shirts to sufficiently protect them from the sun. They lathered on the sunscreen several times a day, but they needed more protection against the sun. The three agreed that they would stop at the island of Great Inagua before leaving the Bahamas to purchase a few of these supplies. With big hats, long-sleeved shirts, and sunglasses, they would have proper protection for the journey across the Atlantic Ocean.

Later in the afternoon, Dan had the boat approach the harbor of Matthew town on the island of Great Inagua. Pulling a yellow flag out from the storage compartment, Dan had Ali help him raise the flag. Dan explained that it was a yellow quarantine flag that you were expected to fly as you entered the port. Dan brought them into the harbor and had them docked within thirty minutes; as soon as they had the boat tied down, they had a visit from Customs. Grabbing his passport, Dan was about to leave the boat, but turned around and told his fellow sailors to stay put and to keep all guns onboard.

Twenty minutes later, Dan came back with two Customs representatives. Both representatives appeared to be in their thirties, a man and woman. They smiled beautiful smiles that revealed very white teeth. Dan explained that each of them must show their passport to the agents; they would also have to show the guns onboard and have them registered (but they could not take them off of the boat). Chris, Mike, and Ali retrieved their passports from the cabin below and brought out the rifles and shotguns, displaying their handguns for the custom representatives. The agents worked quickly, writing down serial numbers along with the gun descriptions. Within fifteen minutes the Customs agents were finished and departed with a Welcome to Inagua.

Dan suggested that Chris, Mike, and Ali leave the boat first to shop for shirts, hats, and sunglasses while he remained behind to keep an eye on the boat. There was a guard stationed on the dock, but Dan felt more comfortable having one of them on guard at all times.

As they left the marina, Mike asked a local food vendor for the best place to buy long-sleeved shirts and hats. The vendor gave them directions to a shop two blocks away. Mike followed the directions and took them down a block, cut right at the intersection, went down a block, and then stumbled upon the store on a corner. Walking inside, they found a girl behind the counter who approached them.

"Can I help you?"

"Where are your long-sleeve tees?" Mike asked.

"Are you looking for a specific color or design?" the girl asked helpfully.

"Where are the least expensive shirts?" Chris asked, identifying their objective in a single question.

The girl took them to a rack in the back with a "Sale" sign attached. It appeared to be a wild selection of shirts—the odds and ends of past shipments. Ali walked over and started browsing the "medium" section for himself and Dan, Chris and Mike headed over to look at the XLs.

"How many do you think we should get?" Ali asked.

"Three or four is what I'm looking for. I'd recommend getting the camouflage green, brown or black so we don't stand out." Mike offered.

Chris looked at the signage for pricing. It was inexpensive: advertising four for $25.

"We should get four," he suggested, gesturing to the sign.

They found four shirts each and laid them on the counter. Chris asked about hats and the sales girl showed them a big collection on the other side of the counter. Chris asked for a hat with a wide brim and she pulled out some hats that were very nondescript.

Chris put on a khaki hat and looked in the mirror. "Well, it looks nerdy, but it should be functional."

Ali and Mike chose their hats within five minutes. Chris and Mike already had sun glasses, but Ali needed a pair. The sales girl showed him the display case and Ali tried on a few before he found a very dark wraparound pair that he liked. They paid for the hats, shirts, and sunglasses and thanked the sales girl for her assistance.

Walking out of the store with bags in hand, they followed Mike as he walked back to the main street. They decided to walk up and down the main road to get a feel of the place before heading back. They didn't see anything unusual or interesting, so they walked back to the boat and showed Dan their purchases. Chris went down below deck and packed three of his new shirts, he wore the fourth long-sleeved T-shirt with his new hat. Climbing the stairs to the deck, he walked into an ongoing discussion between Dan and Mike on what to do next.

Dan was talking to Mike. "I had to pay for one night. It may make sense to stay the night and get a good night's sleep. We can grab dinner tonight on shore?"

"Who will stay behind and guard the boat?" Ali asked.

"Three of us can go and order dinner—after one of us eats quickly, he can switch places with the one left behind on the boat, who can then come and eat dinner while the other two finish. Does that seem workable?" Mike asked.

"I'll be the guy waiting and coming in later," Chris volunteered.

"I'll be the guy that comes back early," Mike replied.

The port had a shower, so they took turns showering and shaving. With their new T-shirts on, they looked presentable. Chris waved goodbye and sat on top of the deck—he was looking forward to some alone time. He decided that a beer sounded good, so he went down to the icebox and pulled out a beer, popped the top, and went back up to the deck. He called to check in with Carly for five minutes. Carly was in the middle of something and they promised to talk later in more detail.

After ten minutes, a family returned from town and walked past security toward the boat adjacent to Chris. There was a father, mother, a girl that looked eighteen, and a boy that looked around fourteen. They carried bags of supplies and as they passed, Chris gave them a slight wave and said, "Hello." They hadn't seen Chris and were startled. After a few seconds, the man spotted Chris and replied with a "Hello." They were an attractive family, dark haired with olive complexions, and the women had very thick and beautiful hair. They proceeded to go aboard their pristine white boat named *Layla*.

As soon as he said *Layla* in his mind, Chris thought it was a tribute to the Kinks. In actuality, he guessed it was the man's wife's name. A couple of minutes later, the father came out on top of his deck with his son. Leaving their boat, they walked over to Chris.

"We stored our food supplies and now the ladies are trying on some of the clothes they bought."

Chris looked at them and smiled. "Can I get you a beer and soda?"

The man said, "Yes," then looked at his son, who nodded. He added, "My name is Gillespie."

Chris went down the hatch and came back with a beer and cola. Hopping off the boat, he landed on the dock and handed the beverages to them. The man took a drink from his beer. "Thank you very much, very nice of you. Where are you headed?"

Chris told him that he was with a few other guys and they were headed for Europe. He gave them some background on how they had traveled from San Diego. The man knew all the news of San Diego, San Onofre, and the terrorists. He listened intently and then proceeded to tell his story.

"We are from the Norfolk area. After a week of turmoil, I decided that we had to leave for the safety of my family. We always had a boat because I come from a long line of sailors. We packed up, boarded our house, and headed down to the Bahamas. We're headed over to the Turk and Caicos Islands and will leave as soon as the ladies finish below and we have some dinner."

They chatted a while longer. Chris found out the son was fifteen and would be starting high school next year. The daughter was a senior in high school and had been accepted to the University of Virginia. But things had changed and they were going to stay on the boat for at least a couple of months to see if their home area could stabilize or if they should relocate.

Chris, Gillespie, and the son chatted for forty-five minutes before the daughter called out from the deck that dinner was ready. They said good-byes, and Chris wished them both the best of luck.

Fifteen minutes later, Chris saw Mike's profile as he stepped down the dock. Chris reported about the family near them and told Mike that everything else had been quiet. Mike gave Chris the name and location of the restaurant where Dan and Ali were sitting, and Chris was off.

Chris found the restaurant easily and walked over to their table. Dan and Ali had finished dinner and Dan was nursing a beer as Ali drank a soda. They made some small talk and Chris told them about the boat docked nearby. Chris ordered a chicken sandwich special that was advertised to have the best spices in the Bahamas.

When he had finished eating his sandwich, the three of them headed back to the dock. Chris noticed that *Layla* had left. He hoped that the man would end up finding a good destination for his family. Chris thought about how some of the new federations were being formed and that in a few months, things would hopefully be more settled. Perhaps the old United States would become three to five different, independent countries.

Chapter 45

Turks and Caicos

THEY DEPARTED FROM INAGUA at six thirty in the morning, well rested and prepared for a full day on the water. The plan was to go across the Turks islands to try to create a safe distance from Haiti and the Dominican Republic. The Bahamas agents told Dan that there could be trouble in those waters. The sun was out and shining, creating a glare from the water. Chris was at the helm, Mike was on watch, and Ali and Dan tried their luck with fishing. Ali had already caught two and Dan seemed to be less amused that Ali consistently caught more fish than him.

As they moved through some uninhabited islands, Chris reflected on Brownfield, Texas. He wondered if Carly would be happy living there long term or if they'd need to move in the near future.

Chris saw Mike point to his immediate left as a flare went up. It came from the opposite side of the small island they were passing, the other side was not visible. Dan and Ali immediately reeled in their lines, and Dan took the helm from Chris. Mike was armed with his rifle and Chris went below deck and came out with the shotgun. Ali had the other rifle. Dan guided the boat past the island, providing himself a lot of clearance to avoid the reef.

As soon as Dan came about with the sailboat, he brought them to the other side of the island. Mike quickly spotted two boats in close proximity to each other. They heard a series of gunshots, and Mike had the binoculars out within seconds, as he tried to gauge what was happening.

"It may be pirates attacking another boat," Chris suggested.

Mike looked at Dan. "Dan, I would go as fast as you safely can."

Dan nodded and started the engine as they dropped the main sail. Once they had the sail down, Mike motioned for Ali and Chris to come over to him. Mike laid down on the bow and Chris and Ali mimicked him. Mike confirmed that the green boat on the right appeared to be attacking the white boat on the left.

As they approached, Mike handed Chris the binoculars.

"Be ready with the shotgun as we get closer, okay!" Mike told Ali to follow him and to keep the green boat in his sights.

As they approached, Mike pointed his rifle to the sky and shot a round as a warning. In response, he received a couple of shots fired back at them from the green boat. This was confirmation to Mike that the green boat was attacking the white vessel.

"Find someone on the green boat and shoot," Mike told Ali.

Mike found someone in his sights and fired. Chris saw a man on the bow of the green boat tumble down and fall into the ocean with a splash. As they got closer, Ali and Mike shot at random and they received some return fire. Dan hunched down as he brought them alongside the white boat. Chris noticed some bodies lying on the deck.

Chris saw a man from the green boat hide behind a box. The return fire from the green boat ceased. Chris wondered if they were waiting for them.

Twenty yards away, they approached the two boats. Mike eliminated another bandit who peeked out from behind the box on the green boat.

Chris looked now at the white boat again. It was *Layla*. As they came close, two men that weren't in the Gillespie family came out from below the deck. Chris popped up from his knee and fired the shotgun. The two pirates went down instantly. Chris set the shotgun down on the deck and reached for his handgun as Mike jumped onto the white boat. Chris followed him. Mike shouted back for Ali to stay put and to focus on the green boat. Chris noticed that Dan had cut the engine, quickly dropped anchor, and had his handgun out and ready to assist Ali.

Chris looked on deck and saw bodies that he assumed were dead. Gillespie lay across the bow, his son lay by the hatch, and his wife was propped up at the stern. Chris couldn't tell if she was still alive.

They heard a girl scream below, and Mike eased down the hatch with gun raised—Chris followed right behind him. Inside was a man with dreadlocks and a scruffy beard, no shirt, and ragged shorts, holding a knife at the daughter's throat. She was partially undressed and it was obvious that he was trying to rape her. Her shorts were torn off and she was wearing panties and a torn T-shirt showing most of her bra. The man looked back at Mike and Chris and smiled, blinding them with his gold front top tooth surrounded by white front teeth. The gold-toothed pirate motioned the knife toward the girl's throat, communicating that he would kill her if Mike came closer. Mike had his handgun out and steadily pointed it at the man. It seemed like an hour but it must have been only ten seconds. This was a standoff between Mike and the pirate. Unexpectedly, Mike fired and shot the man in the middle of his forehead. The girl screamed as blood splattered her from the pirate. She continued screaming as Mike walked over and hugged her, giving her reassurance. Chris turned and climbed back up the steps to the deck.

Confident that the girl was safe, Chris raced up to the deck to check on Mrs. Gillespie. She had been shot in the chest and having difficulty breathing. Chris took off his beige T-shirt and pressed it on her chest wound. In seconds, the T-shirt was crimson red. Chris pressed hard, but he couldn't stop the bleeding. Seconds later, Chris yelled for Ali to bring the first aid kit. Ali reached Chris in less than a minute. Ali shared that Dan was watching for pirates on the green boat, but they'd not seen anyone else move on the boat.

"Check each person on deck to see if anyone is alive. Be careful with the pirates and make sure they're dead. They could be playing possum," Chris instructed Ali.

Chris pressed down on Mrs. Gillespie's wound with his left palm as he opened the kit with his right hand. Looking for something to clean the wound, Chris found a towel and tore her blouse a little more so he could expose the wound. He applied disinfectant liberally as he searched for a bandage.

Mike and the daughter were now on deck. The daughter sobbed as she ran over to her mother. Leaning down, the daughter took her mother's head and began to stroke her hair. Chris applied pressure with the towel but it was red now just like his beige T-shirt. The mother was trying to talk. In a feint, raspy voice she told her daughter that she loved her.

She then focused her eyes on Chris. "Please promise me that you will take my daughter to safety?"

Chris nodded. "Yes, I promise."

The mother stared into her daughter's eyes as she struggled to breathe. No words were spoken, but the love between mother and daughter was obvious. A minute later, Mrs. Gillespie closed her eyes and died. Chris hadn't been able to help her. He hadn't been able to stop the bleeding, and he hadn't been able to stop her from dying. He kept applying the pressure with the towel, hoping for a miracle. Chris marveled that less than twelve hours earlier, she had been trying on new outfits with her daughter, and then the family had eaten dinner together. Chris had a reality check in this moment, thinking of his own family.

Five minutes passed. Chris stood and looked at Ali, who had returned from inspecting the pirate bodies. Ali nodded to signal that he had checked all the people on deck. He also confirmed that Gillespie and his son were dead. Chris looked over at Mike, who was still trying to comfort the daughter.

"Ali confirmed the *Layla* deck is clear. I'm going over to the green boat to make sure it's clear below deck," Chris told Mike.

Mike motioned for Ali to come over and comfort the girl while Mike pried himself away. Chris reloaded the shotgun; Mike had his Glock out and they climbed aboard the green boat. They only found three dead pirates on deck—the cabin was clear. The boat was older and worn and was in worse condition than *Layla*. Chris concluded that the pirates wanted the boat and cargo, but not the people. They were either taking the boat for themselves or selling it for the money.

Fifteen minutes later, they transferred the girl over to Dan's boat. Ali discovered that her name was Lisa. They introduced themselves to Lisa, but she needed more time. They would ask her questions later. Mike asked Ali to stay with Lisa while he, Dan, and Chris went over to *Layla* to search it thoroughly.

They found nothing but basic supplies. When they came back onboard Dan's boat, Lisa was quiet, but responding with a few words to Ali.

Dan, Mike, and Chris sat down next to them. Lisa said that she recalled seeing Chris at the last port speaking with her father and brother. Chris told Lisa that they needed a plan, and proposed that they gather her family and bury them on the island. They'd try to give their graves a proper marking.

There was some discussion on what to do with the pirate bodies. Dan was inclined to dump them overboard, but Mike was concerned that this would attract sharks. Chris thought they would have to report the pirate attack to island authorities, and it would be better to be able to show the pirate bodies if required. The final consensus was to bury them in one common grave away from Lisa's family. Lisa didn't say anything but she provided a small nod of approval with tears.

Lisa climbed back over to *Layla*, and she would stay with Dan. Mike was concerned that there could be more pirates in the area, so Dan's job was to watch Lisa and watch out for pirates.

Mike, Ali, and Chris would take the bodies ashore and dig the graves. Once ready, they'd come back and bring Lisa ashore for the burial. Chris found a blanket to lay the bodies on—to avoid smearing blood on Dan's raft. They boarded Dan's raft with Lisa's family members and rowed to shore.

They landed and dragged the raft ashore. Ali found a nice knoll ten feet above sea level and back one hundred feet from the shore. It looked protected and secluded. Mike thought that this would be a protected area from the storms. They didn't have shovels, but Ali found some palm fronds, using the wide part of the palm to dig. Mike and Ali said they would start digging three graves for Lisa's family. Chris would return and shuttle the six pirates to the island. Grabbing the blanket and heading over to the raft, Chris pushed it into the water and started rowing toward the boats.

Chris made two trips back and forth with three pirates per trip. After he had all six pirates on shore, he walked over to where Mike and Ali were digging. They had almost two graves outlined— they just needed to make them a little deeper. Looking for a burial place far from the Gillespie graves, Chris walked one hundred feet down from Mike and Ali and found an area inland that looked suitable. The area was not as nice as the graves on the knoll, but it had soft dirt and sand.

Chris dragged the bodies to the location one by one. By the time he had brought over the sixth pirate, Mike and Ali had finished the two graves. They put Mr. and Mrs. Gillespie in the first two holes, and Mike suggested that Ali work on the third grave for the boy. Mike helped Chris with the mass pirate's grave.

Mike and Chris started digging. Ali finished his third grave before they finished, so he came over and assisted them. They finally had a big hole that was deep enough for six bodies. Dragging the pirates into the hole, they lined them up side by side, then quickly covered them with dirt and sand. They decided they wouldn't leave a marker here. Perhaps nobody would ever find them.

Walking back to the other three graves, they found that Ali had already put the son in the last grave. All three bodies were placed on their backs with faces pointed up to the sky. They covered them up and then got in the raft and headed over to Dan and Lisa. Lisa was now staring into space, and Chris told Dan that they needed something for markers.

Searching the pirate boat, Mike found a crate that was almost empty. He found a hammer and started taking the wood apart from the crate. While Mike dismantled the crate, Ali and Chris found a small can of white paint along with a brush. They found a couple of nails and Ali nailed three crosses. After Ali finished each cross, Chris wrote the name on top with the paintbrush. Chris confirmed with Lisa their first names: Jim, Layla, and Lyle.

They had the crosses up and were all ashore by dusk to witness the unbelievable sunset of orange and red hues on the horizon. Since Chris had spoken with Jim Gillespie at the port and knew some of their history, he gave the eulogy. His heart felt heavy doing this: this was a good family, one that shouldn't have been destroyed. Lisa stared at the graves but it didn't look like she was really seeing anything. They finished and waited a couple of minutes for reflection. Ali touched Lisa's shoulder and she looked at him. He hugged her and then turned her toward the raft.

Back on deck, Dan, Chris, and Mike fixed dinner even though no one was hungry. Layla and Ali went to sleep right after dinner, but Mike, Dan, and Chris cleaned up, grabbed a beer, and went above deck to talk.

"What should we do with the Gillespie and pirate boats?" Dan thought out loud.

Chris had already thought about it. "It's too bad we can't sell *Layla* and give the money to Lisa."

Mike thought for a few seconds. "Why couldn't we do this? Maybe the pirate boat will provide us some money that we could split evenly, too."

"Perhaps we could take them to a harbor and sell them, then put the money into an account for her." Dan chimed in.

Dan pulled out a map of the area. "We can stay somewhat on course and take the boats to Puerto Plata in the Dominican. You, guys, have become decent navigators. You could each take one of the boats and follow me into the harbor, where we could attempt to sell the two boats and continue on our course. We should be able to find a safe place for Lisa in Puerto Rico before we head across the Atlantic."

The plan was the best they could come up with considering the circumstances, so they all agreed. They would get a good night's sleep and then start out at first light, each would take a two-hour guard shift. There were other pirates looming in these waters. Mike, Dan and Chris, determined to search the pirate boat one last time before retiring to sleep.

Chris took the first watch. He was very tired, but he knew he wouldn't be able to easily sleep, at least not right away. An hour later, Chris was in deep thought, scanning the ocean by moonlight. At times he was certain that he had spotted pirates approaching them, but before he woke anyone he found out it was his imagination playing tricks. Around this island, they were the only people alive.

Chapter 46

Bahamas to Puerto Plata in Dominican Republic

THEY LEFT THE ISLAND at the crack of dawn. Lisa agreed with the plan to sell the boats but insisted that she receive only the proceeds from her parent's boat and not from the pirate boat. She wanted to travel on *Layla* en route to Puerto Plata.

The pirate boat was the smaller of the crafts at thirty-three feet, and Dan could handle it solo. He decided to lead the fleet with the pirate boat, Mike and Ali would follow with his boat, and Chris would bring up the rear, navigating *Layla* with Lisa.

The previous evening they had searched the pirate boat. Dan, Mike, and Chris searched it thoroughly for an hour looking for illegal contraband before taking it to port. They found ten thousand dollars in US cash, some miscellaneous drugs that they threw overboard, and a cache of weapons. They decided to keep the weapons and divided the cash amongst themselves, about $2000 each.

Lisa was a great help with the sails, but she was quiet the whole day. Chris understood—he appreciated a day of quiet while he reflected on the next couple weeks. It was a beautiful day: the sun was out, there were some wispy white clouds high in the sky and a nice breeze that assisted in their sailing toward the Dominican Republic. Everyone was armed except for Lisa who refused a gun. They kept their heads swiveling left to right, concerned that they could run across more pirates.

Finally, they saw the harbor ahead of them. Chris guessed that it was a mile away. Dan pulled down his sail and waved to Mike and Ali. Ali waved back to Chris, and Lisa brought down their sails. For the rest of the way into the harbor they'd use the engine. They maintained their spacing as Dan brought the pirate boat to port first. A dock worker gave him a hand, grabbing the rope and cinching the boat down. After Dan's boat was secure, Mike and Ali approached the dock, and Dan helped them to secure his boat. Lisa and Chris came in last while the others waited on deck. Once they arrived, they helped Chris and Lisa secure the boat.

Dan recommended that they wait by the boats—he walked ahead to the customs office. He returned fifteen minutes later with a customs agent who initiated the process with Dan's boat. The agent was black, about six feet tall, thin, and with gray hair, a weathered face, and a goatee. A cigarette hung from the left corner of his mouth. Dan introduced them to Pedro. Chris guessed he was in his sixties. Dan showed the agent his boat's registration and paperwork. While the agent reviewed it and checked it off, Dan told them that they'd called the police at the customs office.

Pedro finished up with Dan's boat, and Dan asked Lisa to come over closer. Dan explained to Pedro what had happened with *Layla*, and Lisa showed them where her parents had kept their paperwork. The customs agent listened to the story and made notations on his paperwork.

When Pedro completed the *Layla* paperwork, he smiled. "Okay, we are finished."

Dan pulled Pedro to the side of the dock, out of earshot of the others. As they talked, Mike and Chris had a sense that Dan had reached an understanding with Pedro. Chris motioned for Ali and Lisa to join them.

"We should let Dan take the lead with the police questioning," Chris suggested, nodding in Dan's direction.

Ten minutes later, two members of the policia arrived, strolling toward them. These two men were the same height but a little thicker than Pedro: one was thirtyish and one was in his midforties. Pedro took the lead with Dan standing next to him; they spoke Spanish for five minutes. Some of the conversation was animated, with Pedro pointing to *Layla* twice during the conversation.

The policia came over to where the others were standing and asked Lisa where her family had been attacked. Dan had the map laid out and he showed them the area in the Turks and Caicos region.

There was another ten minutes of conversation. The police asked what happened to the bodies of Lisa's family and what had happened to the pirates. Dan told them about burying the bodies on the island. Pedro would translate or add more information in Spanish. They nodded and then the older one suggested that they take a trip out there in a few days. Chris looked at Dan and Mike, and Mike explained that they were in a hurry to travel across the Atlantic to Europe. Pedro translated in English and the officers slowly nodded. Chris quickly explained about retrieving his daughter. Finally, the policia said they would be in touch and left.

Pedro told them that he had suggested to the police that one of them travel with the policia tomorrow to the location and wrap up the inquiry. The police would consider this and confirm their decision that afternoon. Pedro took his clipboard and walked back to his office.

Dan told Chris and Mike that he would meet Pedro after his shift. He confirmed that they would meet in one hour across the street from his office and down a block at a local bar. He'd provided Dan with directions to the bar. A group had docked their boat down at the end and were now walking by. Dan didn't want to continue the conversation, so he motioned the others over toward his boat.

They climbed aboard and Dan smiled and looked at them. "Pedro will provide names of three potential buyers that he feels will give us the best price for *Layla*. I'll meet him at the bar at 6:00 p.m. to confirm. He will try to arrange meetings tomorrow with all three to come by and inspect the boat. We'll sell to the highest bidder."

Dan looked at Lisa. "You'll receive the money, and you can either take it with us to Puerto Rico or we can try to find a bank here in town. The banks here make me a little uncomfortable, but Pedro gave me the two he liked the best. What do you think?"

"My first thought is to take it to Puerto Rico, but I'd like to sleep on it," Lisa responded carefully.

"You'll be here with me when we meet the potential buyers in the late morning." Dan advised. "We'll visit two of the banks in the afternoon. We're supposed to get the offers by 4:00 p.m. tomorrow and all the money will be in cash. You should move your possessions tonight from *Layla* to my boat—everything you want to bring with you to Puerto Rico. Everything else we can try to sell here in one day, or we'll say it's sold with the boat. Lisa, you'll have to make that determination. If you need assistance, please ask any of us to help."

Lisa nodded and Dan looked at Mike, Ali, and Chris. "The pirate's boat is a little different. Pedro will help us to sell the boat. As you know, neither Pedro nor the policia recognized the boat. Pedro will help us sell the boat, and he will get 25 percent, the two policia will get 25 percent, and we will all split the balance five ways."

Lisa shook her head about splitting the pirate boat funds five ways. Chris knew that she didn't want anything associated with the pirates.

"He's arranging for buyers to see the pirate boat tomorrow as well," Dan continued. "They'll negotiate with Pedro and me. Pedro thinks we'll fetch about $80K, so that would be $8K for each of us. Lisa, I've chatted with Mike and Chris and we insist that we split our half of the money five ways."

Dan wasn't finished. "I also explained to Pedro that we'd like to sell some items. What's left on the pirate boat, and whatever Lisa doesn't want to take to Puerto Rico. Tomorrow is Saturday, and there's a market in town in the early morning. I propose that Mike, Ali, and Lisa take everything we want to sell to the market early tomorrow. Lisa can keep the cash from her family's items and we can split the money from the pirates' merchandise."

"Chris, I volunteered you to go with the policia tomorrow." Dan added. "They have to make the trip and have someone join them. We pushed for tomorrow, and they weren't too happy. This means they miss time with their family on a weekend day. I figured that tomorrow we sell the boats, the merchandise, and you wrap up the police report. Then we can leave the day after."

Mike looked over at Lisa. "Do you have relatives in the US? Someone that we can contact to let them know you are okay? When we reach Puerto Rico, we need to figure out how to get you safely back to the US."

"Maybe you can use the Custom agent's telephone in his office tomorrow and contact them?" Chris chimed in.

"I have elderly grandparents staying in an assisted-living home in Raleigh. I have an uncle, aunt, and nephews in Minneapolis, and I have an uncle in Montana and another aunt in San Francisco," Lisa told them.

Chris shot a look at Dan and Mike—they were all thinking the same thing. This wouldn't be as easy as sending her on a boat to Florida. They knew the situation on the old continental US and that there were pockets of turmoil. Also, per the news they'd heard in Florida, the old United States might soon be a few different countries.

Mike and Ali left the dock to find a restaurant and bring back dinner. They left Lisa to have some time on *Layla* to go through things and to figure out what items she would keep. Dan reminded her that they had limited space and to take only what she needed or what had sentimental value.

Dan took off to meet Pedro at the bar, promising to be back as soon as possible. Chris went aboard the pirate's boat and pulled everything from the cabin out onto the deck to see what they had to sell. When Mike, Ali, and Dan returned, they would eat dinner and gather the merchandise for sale at tomorrow's market.

An hour later, they ate dinner aboard *Layla*. Dan confirmed that the buyer's viewing times would be staggered, starting at 10:00 a.m. the next day. Pedro confirmed that the policia would take Chris to the island early the next morning. He told Dan that the market opened at 7:00 a.m. and to get there early for the best location.

They finished eating and diligently began the process of consolidating the merchandise on the pirate's boat along with Lisa's items from *Layla*. They had a full night and a full day ahead of them.

Chapter 47

Puerto Plato

THEY WERE SITTING AT a table on the main street across from the harbor. It was early evening and they were sharing their stories of the day. Mike paid five dollars to a twelve-year-old boy to stand in front of Dan's boat with instructions to run immediately to them if anyone even looked at the boat. Mike offered twenty dollars in additional money if the boy performed his guard duty well. In this area, twenty-five dollars was a lot of money for a couple of hours watching the boat, and the boy looked motivated. He was small for his age, thin in stature with a smile that reached ear-to-ear. He didn't wear shoes and wore baggy tan shorts and a red tank top. Chris initially thought he was ten years old but the boy said he was twelve.

Chris went first with the recap of his day because it wasn't too exciting. He had left in the early morning with the policia on a boat—they'd traveled back to the island where they had encountered the pirates. Chris had showed them the marked graves for Lisa's family and then the large grave with the pirates. He had done his best to recreate the scene. They wrote his testimony in Spanish and had him sign the document. After that, they were finished and headed back to port. On the trek back to the harbor, the policia pulled beers from the cooler—drinking several on the return.

Mike, Lisa, and Ali had found a shopping cart that morning to move the heavy merchandise. They'd used bed sheets to carry the lighter merchandise. The market was held in a park a few blocks away from the main intersection. They explained that they were able to spread out a sheet, distribute some merchandise in the middle of the sheet, and then grab all four corners and carry it over their backs to the market. They had arrived early enough to secure a good spot.

Mike and Lisa had spent time spreading out their inventory from *Layla* and the pirate boat. Meanwhile, Ali took the shopping cart and made a few trips back and forth until he was able to bring everything. Lisa had stayed at the market until it was time for her to join Dan and the potential boat buyers. They had Lisa's merchandise on one side, and the pirate's items on the other side. Mike kept the *Layla* cash, and Ali held the pirate's cash, keeping the funds separate.

They priced the merchandise aggressively to sell; soon had a crowd of people making them offers—they even had buyers making counter offers. It became a mini auction with active bidding.

By midafternoon, they'd sold almost everything. At that point, Ali made a deal with the vendor right next to them, who bought their remaining items at a significant discount. By 3:30 p.m., Mike and Ali had a wad of cash in each of their pockets as they headed back to the harbor.

Dan had had a very busy day. He'd met with Pedro early to confirm the meetings to show the boat at 10:00 a.m., 11:00 a.m., noon, and 1:00 p.m. Pedro had found four potential buyers, with one more confirmed late the past night. Pedro told Dan that they were serious buyers.

Pedro had made calls on the phone to find prospective buyers for the pirate vessel: he'd found five interested parties and he made arrangements for them to all meet at the harbor at 2:30 p.m., when they were finished with the *Layla* appointments.

One requirement for the pirate boat was that they had to bring cash for the purchase. The price and the transaction would take place immediately. They understood that there was limited paperwork on the vessel— this reduced the asking price, but it was the best way to proceed.

The noon appointment didn't show, but the other three buyers arrived as scheduled. Lisa and Dan and Pedro showed each buyer *Layla*. They received three good offers by 4:00 p.m. They took the highest bid and were given the cash transfer at the bank. Lisa signed over the title before 6:00 p.m., then hid the cash in her backpack. Mike advised her to keep it with her at all times until they reached Puerto Rico, where they would search for a bank to deposit the cash.

Dan shared that all five of the prospects for the pirate bid showed up at 2:30 p.m. It had become a bidding war: Pedro started at what he considered the low end of the price range and two of the men bidding were really interested. The resulting final price was in the upper range of what Pedro had been expecting. The cash was received immediately. Dan received 50 percent of the cash and the two policia were there to collect their portion. Dan gave Mike the cash and he merged it with the sale of the pirate merchandise. He would divide the cash amongst the others when he had the opportunity.

Chris, Dan, and Mike had a cold beer in hand and toasted themselves (along with Lisa and Ali, who had cold sodas in hand). It had been a very productive day. Dan shared privately with Chris that Lisa had melancholy moments during the day but that she and Ali had really seemed to bond. Dan thought it was perhaps because of their similar ages—Ali was only a year older. It might also have been that they'd both undergone the traumatic experience of losing their family.

Although Ali was forming a tight bond with Lisa, he still had his bond with Mike, a different bond than with Lisa. Mike and Ali both felt each other's pain and they soothed each other in some way. Chris wasn't a psychologist, but he accepted that they somehow helped each other.

After eating dinner and conversing about Puerto Rico (their last stop before venturing across the Atlantic), Dan suggested they head back to the boat. Walking back across the street, they found their little guard on high alert. Mike walked over and thanked him, handing him a $20. The boy's smile was ear-to-ear, displaying the whitest teeth known to man. He asked Mike if he might be needed the next night. Mike said that he doubted it, temporarily dampening the boy's spirits. The young boy shook each of their hands and walked away with a spring in his step.

After climbing aboard, Mike decided that they should split their dollars from the pirate boat and belongings right then and there. The cash was a nice boost to their funds—Chris knew he might need it for his trip to Slovenia. Lisa consolidated her dollars and found a place in the hatch to place her backpack.

Dan had advised the harbor police, Pedro, and the customs agents that they planned to leave early in the morning. He had also told them that they had decided to return to Florida to send Lisa to her relatives. Dan, Mike, and Chris went up on deck to chat. It was 8:30 p.m., and they were concerned that there were too many people that knew they had a lot of cash on them. They were aware that they were staying in a very poor country.

"Why don't we just take off now?" Mike suggested.

Dan nodded. "We would be obvious right now. Maybe we should wait a couple of hours?"

They made the decision to pull out at 11:00 p.m. They were afraid that they might otherwise have unwelcome visitors in the middle of the night. Their concern included the Policia—in this territory, there was a fine line between the pirates, the bandits, and the police—so fine was the differentiation that they were not able to understand at times where the line was drawn.

Quietly they prepared the boat and made sure they were all set to depart from the harbor. At 10:45 p.m., Ali walked up to the harbor building to check if things were very quiet. He motioned back with a thumbs-up. Across the street, the parties were just starting for Saturday night.

Mike believed this noise would help them to escape. Dan started the engine. They were fortunate because the clouds were coming in for a potential evening rain—the moon was covered, and the sky was dark. Mike went over to the closest light on the dock and cut the electrical cord, so their boat was in the dark. Mike had them armed with handguns and rifles ready. The shotguns were nearby if needed. Ali watched Dan and Mike closely, and after five minutes, Dan gave Ali a wave with the flashlight in his hand. Ali had them untethered and was back swiftly, climbing back onboard.

Dan guided them out of the harbor, and nobody seemed to notice. They were now out to sea, where there was a nice breeze. They put up the sails and set their course for San Juan, Puerto Rico. If they were fortunate, the Dominican agents or police wouldn't check on them until the early morning. Assuming there was a sinister plot in play, then they would have had a several hour head start en route to their next destination.

Chapter 48

Lake Michigan

MARK SPOTTED A STARBUCKS on the way to the harbor, and Ethan pulled the truck in. They bought a few muffins and scones in addition to coffees for breakfast. Ethan suggested that they take it with them and arrive early at the bay.

Ethan and Mark were at the harbor at 7:30 a.m. sharp. They had $300 in cash and they discussed between themselves that they would pay $150 each way. They wanted an incentive for Mac Wilson to return for them later in the day. Taking their coffee and muffins, they ate at a picnic table that overlooked the bay. They then took a walk around the pier, scouting it out. There wasn't much happening that weekday morning.

They both had small backpacks that contained some snacks, an extra pair of socks, and a spare shirt. Inside their light jacket, they had handguns hidden from public view. They also wore their running shoes, and Mark had suggested they double knot their shoe laces. They were ready to begin the day.

They had left the rifle and shotgun under the bed in their hotel room and Mark placed the Do Not Disturb sign on the outside of the door. Ethan had made a phone call to the front desk telling them that they didn't want the maid service that day.

Mark spotted Mac walking down and whistling out loud as he made his way from the parking area to the dock. He saw them and waved hello. He had on a green and gold Packer windbreaker, the same hat from the day before, khaki shorts, and deck shoes.

Following him to his boat, Mac commented, "It's a nice day to be out on the lake."

Mac stepped onboard his boat and looked over at them. "Please come aboard." Mark and Ethan hopped aboard and shook hands. Ethan suggested they pay half up front and half on the way back, and Mac was fine with the plan. Ethan pulled $150 in cash from his jean pocket, and Mac took the handoff from Ethan, slipping the cash down the front pocket of his shorts.

They asked Mac if they could give him a hand. He responded that he needed only ten minutes to get ready and he would welcome their assistance. Quickly he involved Mark and Ethan with his checklist; in fifteen minutes, they were out in the bay. Ethan and Mark quickly found out that he was engaging. Once he was out on the water, Mac told them that he was a retired professor from Madison, Wisconsin, the University of Wisconsin "fighting badgers." Mac and his wife had always enjoyed activities at the lake—they'd purchased their boat and a summer home for weekend getaways and holidays. When he'd retired, they'd sold their house in Madison and remodeled their cabin into their dream home with a modern kitchen and bathrooms.

After a condensed version of his life story, Mac commented, "I've never been happier in my life. My wife and I go out three to four times a week on the lake if the weather is nice. She reads and I fish, or we stop at a harbor and grab lunch. We just love it. We visit our children and grand-children a few times a year, but I'll stay here until I die."

Mac asked questions about Ethan and Mark. He'd taught economics at the University of Wisconsin, and since Ethan worked at a hedge fund in Dallas and Mark was enrolled in finance at OU, he was extremely inter-ested in them. He asked Ethan about his work, then asked Mark if he knew a specific finance professor at OU. They discussed the current situation in the world and the financial impact, finally Mac broke the discussion off and advised that they would reach their destination in ten minutes.

Ethan and Mark watched the land as Mac steered the boat closer. They noticed that the little harbor was very quiet. They could make out from a distance only a few "ants" moving about that minutes later became visible as people getting ready to take a trip out onto the lake. Ethan looked over at Mark and they both nodded. It looked clear.

As they approached the harbor, Mac asked Mark if he could jump out onto the dock when they were within a few feet. He instructed Ethan to throw Mark the line. Mac maneuvered the boat within a couple of feet and Mark jumped and landed on the wooden dock, turned around, and received the line from Ethan seconds later. Within minutes, he had the boat cinched. The plan had started out perfectly—Ethan and Mark were both quickly on the dock and ready to transition to the next phase of the plan.

Mac joined them on the dock. He looked at his watch and they synced up to make sure they had the same time. Mac confirmed that he'd sail out in the lake to fish and be back in exactly four hours. Mac told them that he'd stay for ten minutes, clean his fish, use the restroom, and then he'd be off.

The boys waved to Mac and moved off the dock. They'd been told by their grandparents that their great uncle and aunt's house was approx-imately four miles away. They had directions to find their home from the town. Ethan and Mark walked out of the parking lot toward the main road and noticed a red SUV pulling out. Ethan waved to the SUV and the young man driving pulled up next to them, pushed a button, and brought down the passenger window.

"Are you heading to town?" Ethan asked.

"We just landed here on the dock and we could use a ride into town."

The guy was in his early thirties, and he motioned for them to get in his vehicle. Ethan took shotgun and Mark opened the side door to the second row of seats. They climbed in the SUV with their backpacks sitting on their laps. The driver told them that he wasn't going into town.

"The latest news as of last night, is that the town is now under control by a motorcycle gang. It's considered unsafe to enter the town. Most people have left town and are staying with neighbors outside the city limits."

He paused and then continued. "Do you really need to go into town? If so, I can drop you off within a mile of Fish Creek. If you want to be dropped off somewhere else, I can take you there if it's close by and doesn't involve driving through town."

Ethan reached into his pocket and pulled out the paper with his uncle and aunt's house address written down and shared it with the driver. The driver recognized the address and volunteered to take them there.

"It'll be about ten minutes. It's a little longer because I need to skirt around the town of Fish Creek."

Ethan and Mark thanked him profusely for the ride. He was a genuine and amiable guy. "No problem," he insisted as he took off.

On the ride to their great aunt's house, the SUV driver explained in more detail about the changes in town. He shared that many residents were leaving Fish Creek and staying in the country with friends. However, there were many gangs between Fish Creek and Green Bay, and people were trapped and unable to leave the peninsula. He'd heard speculation that the gangs had made an agreement amongst themselves to divide up towns and territory. The driver shared that he had some friends from town staying with his family right now.

"I'm trying to figure out how to get my wife and child out of here. That's why I was driving to the dock—I wanted to see if I could hire a boat off the peninsula. Many folks with boats have already packed up and left. That's why the dock is scarce of boats."

He approached the house and stopped his vehicle. They wished him luck and thanked him again as they got out of his SUV.

Ethan and Mark marched up the gravel rock walkway to the single-story home in the woods. They rang the doorbell, and in ten seconds, the large wooden door opened and they saw their grandparents, uncle, and aunt. Ethan and Mark hugged each one and were then ushered into the house. They were motioned to enter through the hallway and to take a seat in the family room. As they sat down, Ethan advised them that they could visit for a while, but their boat to take them back across the bay would be leaving in less than four hours.

Pa K told them that they were packed and ready—they didn't need time to prepare. He thought they had time to visit for a while. Greg, the uncle and aunt's son who lived in a house a half of a mile away, was coming over soon to meet Ethan and Mark. Aunt Helga asked if they were hungry: she'd already prepared lunch for them.

They all sat down and Aunt Helga told them that she'd cooked a roast and potatoes, vegetables, and a special dessert for afterward. They'd eat as soon as Greg arrived. Mark and Ethan asked each one how they were doing.

After each person had a chance to speak, Mark mentioned the ride they'd received from the young man in the SUV and the news about the gang that had rolled into town. This was all new information for them: they only went to town on Sundays, and they hadn't met with anyone from town the past two days. Sunday consisted of church in the morning, lunch with friends afterward, and then grocery shopping and any other shopping in the afternoon before they returned home. It was midweek, so their news was stale.

In twenty minutes, Greg came into the family room. He was tall, about six feet two inches and trim at about 190 lbs—in great shape for someone in his mid to late sixties. Ethan and Mark had never met him before, so there were formal introductions, then they sat down again. Ma K brought up the gang in town, and Greg mentioned that he'd received a call from a friend thirty minutes ago, with the same news.

"My friend advised that the gang was already harassing retailers and private citizens. Our sheriff left town, fearing for his safety, and many citizens have already left or are leaving now with only their most important possessions. The concern is that you may be safe in the countryside, but eventually you'll need food or something in town. This gang appears to be here for the long run."

Mark and Ethan shared what they had heard from law enforcement on their way to Fish Creek. Originally, they had planned to drive to Fish Creek.

"The news from the sheriff made us change our plan—so we took the boat across the bay instead of driving into town. We were warned that there were gang roadblocks on the road," Ethan explained.

Ethan told them about meeting Mac at the harbor. Mark looked at his cell phone and noticed they only had three hours and fifteen minutes left before Mac returned.

"We have to be back in a little over three hours," Mark shared.

Pa K looked over at his sister and brother-in-law and nephew.

"Based on the news we heard, perhaps you should leave with us across the bay." He looked at Ethan and Mark. "Do you think there is room for three more?"

"Yes, and it's a short trip across the bay," Mark responded.

A fifteen minute, heated discussion followed. The key concern for the uncle and aunt was that they didn't want to leave their home. How long would they need to leave? Nobody knew if it were a week, a month, a year, maybe longer.

Finally, Greg suggested, "Why don't we pack a suitcase or two to take with us. We can bring key financial documents with us. We can cross the bay and find a place to stay in Minnesota until it's safe to return. We'll turn off all water to our home and lock it down."

This seemed acceptable with the uncle and aunt. Lunch was soon forgotten.

Greg left to walk back to his house, pack, lock up, and drive over. He would then drive them all to the dock in his SUV that seated seven.

Ethan and Mark asked if Greg needed help and he took them up on the offer. Ethan elected to go with Greg to help him secure his home; they would be back right away. Meanwhile, Ma K and Pa K helped the uncle and aunt pack some clothes and documents. The uncle told Mark what to do to secure his home.

Two hours, later Ethan and Greg arrived driving a large beige SUV into the driveway. Opening the back trunk, they put in the suitcases and backpacks from Ma K and Pa K and the uncle and aunt. It was loaded up to the brim—the backpacks would need to fit in the passenger area on their laps. Ethan and Greg went over to help Mark, who was busy locking down the guest cottage and turning off appliances.

Finally finished, they had forty-five minutes left before Mac returned. Before they got in the SUV, Ethan asked Mark to come over to the side.

Ethan looked at Mark, "Instead of four of us including our grandparents in their eighties, there are now seven of us with two more in their nineties, and one in his mid to late sixties. We won't be able to do any quick getaways."

Climbing into the SUV, Mark sat in the front passenger seat and reminded Greg to avoid the town. He took the same route as the young man earlier in the day, and in ten minutes, they approached the harbor. Greg was about to turn off the exit into the parking lot when Mark noticed a couple of motorcycles and a few people on the dock. He immediately told Greg to stop, to put the car in reverse, and to go backward to the main road. Greg shifted the car in reverse and backed up toward the main road. As he approached an area where the road was wider, he stopped and performed a U-turn and started driving away from the dock. Mark suggested that he stop at a pull out situated off the main road about a mile down the road and under a grove of trees.

Greg found the pull out and parked. Ethan and Mark got out of the SUV and told Greg, their grandparents, and uncle and aunt that they were going to take a look and that they should all stay in the car. Ethan told Greg that if anything looked troublesome or if more gang members arrived, they should leave immediately and would plan to meet at the uncle and aunts' house.

Mark chose a dirt trail that headed to the lake. When they reached the lake, they walked along the lake for half of a mile. The trail split in two: one along the lake toward the dock and another that went away from the lake. They took the trail that moved them back closer to the road. They could still see the dock. They stopped and stood alongside some trees that had a good view. They couldn't make out the conversation, but it appeared that the two gang members were hassling and stopping a family from disembarking on their boat. The gang members were big, had long hair, tattoos on their arms, and wore vests with jeans and boots. One of them had a gun out and was threatening the family.

During this argument, Ethan saw Mac's boat on the horizon. He was coming in toward the harbor. Ethan nudged Mark and pointed at Mac. Mark nodded and they returned their gaze to the confrontation between the gang and family.

The family was getting off the boat and the father had the suitcases on the dock and they were prepared to return to the parking lot. There was more debate and finally the man handed over the boat keys to one of the gang members. At that time, Mac, was about to lower his sails, but he was watching the exchange and saw the man hand the keys to the gang member and grab his suitcases and head with his family for their car. Mac suddenly had a change of heart, he "came about" and headed back out into the bay.

Ethan and Mark looked at each other. "We just lost our transportation off this peninsula," Mark said.

They continued watching the man, his wife and family as they loaded their luggage in the back of their van and took off. The two gang members were laughing at the incident as they pulled up chairs to sit down. Ethan looked at Mark. "It appears they are planning to stay here for a while."

They walked back along the trail toward Greg and their relatives. The man and family who had left their boat with the gang members had pulled his van alongside Greg's SUV and was talking with Greg and the others. They were telling them the story as Ethan and Mark walked up.

"We saw what happened," remarked Ethan.

"We were trying to leave and now I'm not sure what we will do," the man responded.

Ethan noticed that his wife looked distraught—they had three kids in the van ranging from six to eleven years old. His question was pointed to both Greg and the man in the van. "Do you both live near each other?"

"Yes, they live about a mile further down the road from my parents," Greg responded.

"Do you have a second pair of keys for the boat?" Ethan questioned.

The man leaned out of the van. "Yes, at home in my desk drawer."

Ethan had one more thought. "If Mark and I come up with a plan to seize control of your boat and get us all onboard, are you capable of sailing us across the bay to Escanaba?"

The man nodded to Ethan. "If you can help me get my family off this peninsula, I'll take you anywhere."

Ethan looked at Mark. "Mark, I think we should stay for a while."

Ethan looked at Greg and the man. "I suggest you, guys, drive over to my aunt's house. Don't unpack the vehicles. Go inside and eat and rest. Greg, will you come and pick us up at this exact spot at 7:00 p.m? Mark and I will stay here and watch the bikers from the woods."

Ethan added, "Let's see if we can form a plan so we can leave tonight."

He looked at the man in the van. "I assume you can navigate us out of the harbor in the middle of the night?"

The man nodded, yes. Mark and Ethan stepped back from the vehicles and gave them a wave. The man and family took off, and Greg followed him in his SUV. Mark and Ethan turned and headed back on the trail toward the harbor.

As they walked, Ethan thought out loud to Mark. "We need to watch these guys at the pier and observe their behavior to find patterns, like how often they go to the bathroom, when and where they eat, and then come up with a plan on how to take the boat back and temporarily control the harbor. With children and older people, we'll have to take care of these guys before we can take off."

They walked along and stopped at the same spot in the trees where they had watched the gang members before. Instead of standing they sat down to observe both of the men. Ethan and Mark didn't say a word; they were so intent and focused.

Chapter 49

Lake Michigan

At around 6:00 p.m., they heard a loud noise that sounded like motorcycles: soon there were two bikes pulling into the empty parking lot at the harbor. The two arriving gang members looked like the other two, with beards, long hair, tattoos, denim vests, pants, and boots. They walked over to the two members sitting in chairs by the dock entrance. The four chatted for five minutes before the two that had been at the harbor walked over to their motorcycles, started them up, and took off.

Mark leaned over to Ethan, "Looks like a new shift. Someone's determined that this harbor has importance. It looks like they're using shifts."

Ethan nodded. They'd watched the first group for a couple of hours—they would get up periodically to go into the restroom located about two hundred feet off the beginning of the dock up on a little knoll. Other than that, they would sometimes get up and walk the length of the dock. They constantly smoked and had a cooler stocked with a seemingly endless supply of beers (which they drank continuously). The trash bag hanging by the office was bursting with beer cans.

Both Ethan and Mark had observed the first gang member's behavior and now they were gone. They had another hour before Greg picked them up off the side of the road. They would observe these two new gang members to see if they had the same routine. They had about thirty minutes before it got dark.

At 7:00 p.m. they quietly walked the path using their cell phone as a flashlight. They saw Greg pull his vehicle off the road. He reported that they'd eaten dinner and that Aunt Helga had dinner waiting for Ethan and Mark. Some of them had tried to take naps unsuccessfully, everyone was on edge. Mark shared that the two gang members were relieved at 6:00 p.m.

by another shift and he felt that these men would guard the dock through the night. Ethan looked over at Mark.

"Should we go eat dinner, compare notes, and create a plan? Greg, we'd like to do this in private, but perhaps you can join in, as our sounding board," Ethan suggested.

Greg drove them back to the house. As expected, everyone had questions. Ethan and Mark shared that the two gang members left at 6:00 p.m., another two had replaced them. They kept guard of the dock and never left their station other than to visit the restroom. Ethan asked if they could have dinner privately so that he and Mark could compare notes and ideas. The uncle, aunt, Pa K, and Ma K got up from their seats. They were reluctant but agreed. Aunt Helga went into the kitchen with Ethan and Mark to show them their plates that were kept warm on the stove. Before they left the family room, Ethan looked at Greg. "Greg, maybe you can join us for a few minutes? In case we have some questions of the area," he explained.

As they sat down at their plates, there was a knock on the door. The uncle and Greg went to look out the peep hole of the front door and sighed in relief. It was the man from the van. He walked through the opened front door.

"Is there is a plan?" he asked.

"Mark and I are sitting down now to eat and discuss a plan," Ethan responded.

"Can I listen?" the man asked. "I promise I'll be quiet. I have my wife and three children that I'm thinking of. I'd like to understand the plan." Ethan and Mark looked at each other, and then nodded. Ethan looked at Mark and asked his grandparents, uncle, and aunt if they wanted to join. It didn't seem to matter anymore.

Ethan and Mark were so hungry that they didn't speak for the first two minutes as they tackled the food. They had six people sitting around and staring at them intently as they ate, waiting for them to begin the discussion. Finally, the brothers started sharing their thoughts—Mark went first. "They stay at the dock and only leave for the restroom. The door to the men's room faces the road and isn't visible from the dock. So when one of them goes to the restroom, he's out of sight of the other."

Ethan added, "They smoke a lot. There's a light at the office about twenty yards from the entrance to the dock: they have two chairs there and they sit there while they smoke and drink beer. If they walk down to the dock to stretch their legs, you can only follow them by their cigarette light. They have a large cooler of beer they were drinking from. I counted at least two beers per hour, and I'm thinking that they won't be at the top of their game later tonight."

Mark added while looking at the van man, "After your family left, there weren't any other people approaching the harbor. We see only three boats left in the harbor, including yours. I think they could be caught off guard in the right situation. The dock is calm, without traffic or people, and the bikers are drinking a lot of beer and getting bored."

"It would be best to isolate them one at a time," Ethan shared. "That would be the least dangerous. I'm wondering about the bathroom as an ambush spot for one."

"Perhaps one of us could be in the restroom and attack him at that time," Mark chimed in. "There's a small motion light at the entrance of the bathroom. Greg, have you been in the bathroom before?"

It was the boys' uncle who answered. "I've been there many times: it's a small bathroom with two urinals, a sink, and a stall with a toilet."

Mark digested this information. "Thank you. Ethan, maybe one of us could be in the bathroom in advance to take out the light in the front, then eliminate or lessen the lighting inside the bathroom. One of us can hide in the stall and attack at the urinal."

"Do you have a baseball bat?" Ethan asked.

"I have one in my house," Greg answered.

"Both Ethan and I are armed, but firing a shot will warn the other gang member," Mark added. "Knocking him out with the bat would be best because then we'd have only one left, and he wouldn't be forewarned of danger."

They finally came up with a plan that everyone thought was viable. A number of them thought there was danger and risk involved, but no one had a better option.

At 11:00 p.m., they drove up in the two vehicles and stopped a mile away at the same turn off so the headlights wouldn't show. The van man stayed with his family in his vehicle, Pa K was situated in the driver's seat of Greg's SUV. If anything went wrong, he'd drive back to his sister's house. Greg would assist Mark and Ethan with their plan.

Greg and Mark planned to walk alongside the road in the dark past the turn off road to the dock and then they would approach the restroom. Greg had his baseball bat, and Mark carried rope that his uncle had found in the basement along with a flashlight and rags from his garage. Mark stopped periodically to listen; he kept checking to make sure the gang members were down at the dock.

The gang members were still drinking beer, smoking, and talking in their chairs by the small building twenty feet down the dock. Greg and Mark stood at the side of the bathroom, where Mark looked at the motion light. It wasn't up high, just to the side and above the door. He'd be able to reach it easily. He went to the corner, which was only three feet to the light, but as soon as he moved, it would go on. This was one of the first risk areas of the plan. Mark put down the rope and other items he was carrying. Greg watched the dock to make sure none of the gang members had an immediate nature call. Mark flashed his cell phone light and saw the switch on the light. Cell light in his left hand, he sprang out quickly and reached with his right hand, turning the switch. There was at most a few seconds of light. Mark breathed deeply and looked at Greg. Greg gave him a nod: neither of the guys on the dock had seen the light go on for those seconds.

Walking into the bathroom, Greg and Mark went inside and turned on the flashlight, keeping a rag over it to keep the light filtered. The light over the sink had two bulbs: Mark unscrewed one bulb and left one in place. Greg noticed that there was a bulb over the stall; he climbed on the toilet seat while Mark pointed the flashlight onto the ground with the rag still over it to give him deflected light as he removed that bulb. Now there was just one bulb over the sink that would give minimal light.

They both went into the stall and closed the door, but didn't lock it. Their plan was for Greg to knock the biker in the head with the bat while at the urinal. The backup plan was that Mark would use the gun in an emergency and shoot the gang member. Now, they just had to wait.

Ethan crept along the lakeshore in the dark by himself, quietly crawling underneath the dock on the land side. The dock started about ten feet on the land and extended over the water. He moved along quietly in the dark until he reached the dock. There was about a three or four-foot clearance under the dock, and he swung his body underneath the wood. He was now only about twenty feet from the motorcycle gang.

They bikers were in their chairs talking smack about how boring it was up in this part of Wisconsin and how they would rather head back south. Finally, after fifteen minutes, one said, "I have to go piss." Ethan heard someone get up from the chair and then heard footsteps walking down the dock. The biker walked over to where Ethan sat underneath the pier. The biker paused and lit a smoke, and then continued to the bathroom. Ethan waited anxiously for the right moment. He saw the remaining gang member stand up, light a cigarette, and walk down twenty feet toward the water and look out over the lake.

Mark and Greg heard the gang member walk in the direction of the bathroom. There was crunching and crackling on the crushed stone as he made his way on the path. They were in the stall, waiting for the man. Mark climbed on top of the toilet seat so his feet wouldn't show. He crouched a little, gun out. Greg was over to the side of the stall so his feet wouldn't be seen easily under the stall. He had one hand on the bat and one on the door. He'd be ready to open the door, take two steps, and swing.

They heard the restroom door open and some muttering about the light or lack of light. The man paused and farted—they stood frozen, waiting for a sound confirming the gang member was peeing at the urinal. All of a sudden, the stall door opened. The guy had to do more than pee—and the gang member and Greg both stared at each other. This wasn't the plan. They'd assumed (because of the beer consumption) the man would need the urinal. Now face to face, Greg froze. The gang member yelped, punching Greg. Greg went flying into the corner, losing control of the bat. The gang member kicked Greg in the ribs and pulled out a knife. At that point, Mark jumped down from the toilet, grabbed the gang member's beard with his left hand, and jerked his head down, hitting him in the back of the head with the Glock. The gang member fell to his knees but was not done. Mark was in "Krav mode" and kneed the man up to his chin. The gang member went backward through the stall door, landing on his back. The knife scattered to the ground by the stall door, and Mark scooped it up and then pulled Greg up.

"Bring me the rope and rags," Mark called out to Greg.

Greg brought them over, and Mark took the rag and put it in the dazed motorcycle member's mouth. Flipping the body over, Greg reached back to tie his hands. Mark patted the man down and found a handgun, which he gave to Greg, instructing him to tie the guy's feet and then watch him. Mark was concerned that the other gang member might have heard the noise and could arrive soon. He had his gun ready as he walked out of the bathroom door, peeking around the corner.

The gang member on the dock had heard the yelp and immediately threw his cigarette into the bay. Pulling out his gun, he waited to hear if there was any more noise. His colleague could have fallen down or hit his head, or was there something wrong? He decided to move toward the bathroom. He passed the chairs and moved toward the end of the dock.

Ethan was down below the dock waiting, knowing that he'd have to improvise. As soon as the man was ten feet off the dock, Ethan popped up so that the upper half of his body was above the dock. Pointing the gun at the member, he said, "Freeze and put down the gun."

The gang member turned around quickly, drawing the gun toward Ethan. He was drunk, slow, and unsteady. Ethan fired. He aimed for the heart and missed a little to the left side. The gang member was winged, but he had the gun in his right hand and tried to aim. Ethan fired again, and this one was centered. He fired a third round and the man dropped to his knees and then onto his face.

Ethan walked slowly to the man. He wasn't moving, but Ethan didn't want to take a chance. He was ready to shoot again, and his adrenaline raged.

As soon as the gang member on the dock turned toward Ethan, Mark tried to decide if he should shoot. He was farther away: if he missed the gang member, he could hit Ethan. He positioned himself on the other side of the bathroom and cautiously trotted down to the shore so he wouldn't be in the path of Ethan's gunfire. Mark saw Ethan shoot the man and watched the man fall to the dock. He approached the dock and jumped up, joining Ethan as he approached the gang member. Mark picked up the gun and Ethan kicked the guy in the side to see if there was movement. It looked like he was dead. He knelt and felt for a pulse on the neck but couldn't find one.

Greg walked the path toward them, bat and gun in hand. He moved gingerly from the kick in the ribs and Mark wondered if some were broken. At a minimum, they were bruised. Ethan looked at Mark and without verbalizing his question, Mark told Ethan that they'd tied him up with rope in the bathroom. Mark told Greg to watch the guy by the dock. They left the dock and walked briskly to the bathroom.

Ethan and Mark dragged the gang member from the bathroom. He wasn't moving. They tried to check for a pulse: Ethan thought he found a faint one, but he was not sure. They brought him all the way to the dock and laid him down near the man that Ethan shot.

As soon as they dropped him down, Mark suggested, "I'll run down the road to help Pa K drive the SUV back to the parking lot."

About ten minutes later, Ethan and Greg saw two vehicles drive into the parking lot. The man with the van unloaded his family and suitcases and brought them on the boat. Pa K and Ma K and the uncle and aunt headed over, and Ethan told them to climb aboard the boat and to get settled. Greg, Mark, and Ethan worked to clear the luggage out of the SUV and to carry them to the boat.

The rest of the plan went into action: Greg lowered the back seat of the SUV, and Mark and Ethan spread out a blanket and carried the two gang members one at a time, laying them out on the blanket. Mark went through the guy's pockets and retrieved their motorcycle keys. Ethan and Mark guessed that two colleagues would relieve them in the morning. They thought it was best if these two men were just missing, with no trace of their motorcycles.

The van friend and his family focused on the boat, prepping it to sail across the bay. Greg climbed in his SUV, Mark had the keys for the van, and Ethan drove one of the motorcycles. They had a few stops according to the plan: the first stop was at a dumpster that Greg had identified two miles up the road. Reaching the dumpster, Mark and Ethan dragged the gang members out and threw their bodies in, closing the lid. Perhaps one would live, but they wouldn't hang around to find out. Mark pulled the van into the garage, exited, and locked the garage door. He then climbed onto the back of the motorcycle and Ethan drove him back to the boat in the harbor.

Meanwhile, Greg drove his SUV to his house, parked in his garage, and locked up. Once Ethan dropped Mark off at the dock, he headed for Greg's house. Ethan swung on the motorcycle and picked Greg up and brought them back to the parking lot. Greg hopped off and boarded the boat. Mark waited for Ethan.

Mark started the second motorcycle: they drove slowly on the trail by the shore. After a mile, they turned off the engines and walked the bikes off the trail and up a small incline away from the lake and into the forest. Mark stopped and turned around to speak with Ethan.

"There's some brush up ahead that may be a good place to leave the motorcycles."

They brought the motorcycles by the brush, pushed the kickstands down and left the keys in the ignition.

"I hope some hikers find these and take them for a joy ride," Ethan commented.

"If the motorcycles are found by the gang, they'll have to find the bodies in the dumpster and then try to piece the story together," Mark responded.

"With the cars parked safely in the garages, the parking lot is empty. And there will only be two boats remaining in the harbor," Ethan agreed.

Ethan and Mark walked briskly back to the trail, using the flashlight to guide them as they jogged back. They could see the others waiting for them on the boat. When they arrived, and climbed onboard, they discovered that the boat was ready to leave. The engine took the boat one hundred yards out into Lake Michigan and then Ethan, Mark, and Greg helped with the sails. Soon they were sailing away from the harbor and away from the peninsula.

Ethan and Mark walked down the stairs into the cabin. Pa K and Ma K were anxious to hear everything that had happened however, Ethan and Mark were exhausted. They answered a few questions but soon leaned back in their seats. Minutes later, they had their heads on their arm, and within ten minutes, they had fallen asleep. It was the first opportunity they'd had to rest all day.

The Grandparents nodded to each other without exchanging words. They'd hear the rest of the story later—the way things were happening lately, their grandsons would need their rest for the next day.

Chapter 50

Texas

CARLY WAS DRIVING BACK from the hospital toward Brownfield. She'd dropped Grandpa and Grandma H off at the hospital for Grandpa H's chemo treatment, and she'd come back later in the week to bring them home. They'd done a blood test on Grandpa to check his hemoglobin levels and he'd gone down further. The medical plan had been modified to have chemo each day. Carly planned to return on Friday afternoon and bring them back home to the ranch for the weekend. Before entering the hospital, she'd checked them into the hotel down the street and dropped off their luggage. It was too early to get a clean room, but the concierge held their suitcases for them in a backroom off of the lobby. The concierge agreed to take them to their room later that day after the room was available. The hotel was very close; Grandpa would welcome the opportunity to walk the two blocks to maintain his strength.

Carly had music playing but soon drove out of range of the Lubbock radio station. She'd been switching channels, trying to find a clear station. She turned to a channel with a news alert: eight prisoners had escaped from the correction center in northern Louisiana and they had information confirming that all eight had crossed into Texas. The Texas rangers had caught three outside the city of Fort Worth, who were now in custody. The rangers had shot and killed one escapee in Plano, and were now searching for the other four escapees. They asked the public to call with any leads.

The Texas rangers' current theory was that the escapees had split up. They didn't know if some were traveling in pairs or if they were going solo.

While Carly drove, she listened to the news report. She was thankful that she'd had her gun stashed in the glove compartment. Before he left, Chris had stressed the importance of keeping it with her all the time. Texas was probably one of the safest places in North America now, but there would still be danger for a while. Meanwhile, a good portion of the US was still in turmoil.

Carly drove along the empty road, thinking about her conversation with Ethan, Mark, and her parents last night. She was relieved that they were out of Wisconsin. She didn't get the whole story, and Ethan told her they would give her all the details later, but she could sense that they'd had complications.

Abby and Ryan were doing well in Austin. They'd rented a place downtown and both had found employment. Abby found an elementary school teaching position for a teacher that was out on leave, and she was enjoying it. Carly felt comforted that they appeared to be in a safe bubble within Austin, newly married, and ready to start a new life.

She hadn't heard from Jessica for some time. In their last conversation, Jessica had reported that Drago was taking them higher up into the mountains for safety.

Carly hadn't heard from Chris since he and the other men had left Florida on Dan's boat. He'd given her his route through the Caribbean, explaining that Dan marked it as a test run before crossing the Atlantic. She prayed each day for the safety of Chris, Jessica, Ethan, and Mark—she hoped they would come home soon.

Carly stopped at the market in Brownfield to pick up some groceries and run some other errands while in town. At the checkout counter was the cute McGregor girl that was also their neighbor. Carly couldn't recall her name, she wasn't wearing a name tag, but the girl knew who she was and asked about the boys. Carly explained that they were bringing their grandparents back from Wisconsin to the farm. She gave the girl a warm goodbye and pushed the cart out of the store to the parking lot, found her vehicle, and loaded the groceries into the back of the van.

Carly looked at her to-do list. She had to walk across the street and over a block to the hardware store to pick up miscellaneous items that Clark had requested.

As she crossed the street, she thought about Clark. Clark was really a big help—if you had seen him a month ago, you wouldn't have noticed he was the same young man. He now had short hair, was clean shaven, and had slimmed down. Clark's upper body was getting strong from the chores on the farm.

Since living on the farm, each day they recognized additional things that needed repair. Every day, Clark and Carly would tackle a couple of small repairs along with the rest of their daily chores. Grandpa H tried to help Clark, but he was weak from the past couple of weeks.

Carly thought about how Clark had adjusted to his new setting. He'd gone to his first dance in town on Saturday night and had come back excited that he'd made new friends. He was learning to two-step, and with his Levi's, boots, and clean-cut but rugged appearance, he was starting to look more like a local.

Carly finished her errands and drove down the dirt road to their house. Pulling up, she saw that the barn door was open. Finley had spotted her from a mile away and he was waiting by the porch to greet her. She'd trained him to stay on the porch until the engine stopped. The porch was his lookout post, and she had a gigantic water bowl and a dog bed for him in the shade of the porch.

While she was getting out of the vehicle, Carly saw Clark walk out the barn door, and take off his gloves.

"Hey, Mrs. H., do you have anything to unload?"

"Yes, Clark, groceries and a box from the hardware store."

Clark came around and found the box of hardware and picked it up, heading for the barn to put it on the workbench. Dropping it off, he then came back to help Carly with the groceries. It was now midafternoon. "What are you working on?" Carly asked.

"I was repairing the workbench and replacing some wooden rungs on the ladder to the loft."

Carly nodded, then went into the kitchen and put food away in the refrigerator and freezer. Clark knew which food items went in the pantry and he helped put things away on the shelves. As soon as Carly had finished, she brought out two cold bottles of lemonade and opened them, handing one to Clark when he walked out of the pantry. He leaned back on the counter and took a long drink.

"Do you need any help out there?" Carly asked.

"No, I'm wrapping up the work and then I'll clean up and feed the cows. I'll be done in forty-five minutes."

Carly nodded. "Okay, I'll start dinner in about thirty minutes."

Clark paused. "Grandparents checked in okay at the hospital?"

"Yes, they have a room at the nearby hotel. Grandpa went in for the first chemo treatment this morning."

Clark went back outside to finish up, and Carly grabbed the book that she'd been reading and went over to sit down at the sofa to read a chapter. She noted that they now ate dinner earlier than in San Diego. Dinner was now typically served at 6:00 p.m., whereas back home it had been between 7:00 p.m. and 8:00 p.m. Life was not easy here in Texas, but it was a simpler life.

Chapter 51

San Juan, Puerto Rico

THE GROUP APPROACHED THE harbor in San Juan. Sail's down, Dan had the engine running as he guided them in. As they approached the dock, they were within three feet when Ali jumped out of the boat and landed effortlessly on the dock. Chris threw the rope and Ali caught it, cinching down the line. Chris walked quickly toward the aft and repeated the same sequence with Ali. They arrived safely in San Juan without any problems. Dan took the most direct route in hopes of trying to make up some lost time in the Dominican and Turk islands.

The crew now knew the drill: Dan gave them some chores and then disembarked, walking to the customs office. Within ten minutes, he had an agent who came aboard and looked at everyone's passport, guns, and boat documents. The custom agent was quickly off the boat, so they gathered on deck to review their chore list. Lisa had a lot of cash on her, and a visit to the bank was a priority. They didn't want to walk around nor spend the night holding a significant amount of money.

They would go ashore in two groups: Dan, Lisa, and Ali would be the first to go into town, and Mike and Chris would go afterward. Since Lisa and Ali were almost inseparable, this appeared to be a natural grouping.

They would leave immediately and open bank accounts in order to place most of the dollars in the account, then swing by a market and shop quickly for staple items and fresh fruit and vegetables. They'd return back to the boat so that Chris and Mike could visit the bank before it closed. The two of them had a shopping list for any remaining items.

Dan had asked the agent about banks in close proximity and was pleased to learn that they had the same banks that they were accustomed to in the US. They decided on Bank of America, which had their corporate office based in Charlotte, North Carolina. They felt it was less risk than some financial institutions based in New York. They'd heard days prior, that New York was still unstable and they were unsure of the status of the general northeast.

They had to leave their guns on the boat per local law, so Dan, Lisa, and Ali moved quickly, unarmed, down the four blocks to the bank. Once inside, Dan noticed the bank had only two customers for business. He asked for a manager who came out from his office promptly. The manager was the only one wearing a suit in the facility: he wore his beige suit with a white shirt and dark brown tie with a design Dan couldn't decipher. Pulling the manager to the side, Dan explained that they wanted to open three accounts and they wanted to ensure that they could withdraw funds whether in Europe, the Caribbean, or the US. The manager assured them that they could withdraw their funds from anywhere in the world. He called a clerk over and they ushered them to a desk where they opened up the bank accounts.

The process only took about thirty minutes. Before they departed the manager came by to thank them. Dan told him that they had two friends that would stop by in an hour to open up similar accounts. He asked the manager how a person could safely make passage back to the US from Puerto Rico. The manager wrote down a name and number on a Post-it and handed it to Dan.

"My cousin Rafael is aware of all boats heading to the States—he can arrange a safe passage. Of course, there is a fee, typically $500 per person, and it will take a week or two, depending on the stops along the way."

Dan looked at Lisa, put the Post-it in his pocket, thanked the manager, and the clerk that helped them, shook hands, and walked out the door. They were all relieved to have the majority of their cash in the bank. They noticed a market on the way back to the harbor, walking inside, their first objective was to buy fresh fruits and vegetables. They'd need two weeks' supply at a minimum. Ali and Lisa found a shopping cart and walked down the aisles, loading up the cart. Meanwhile, Dan took another cart and bought some beer and soda along with large sacks of beans and rice. Dan hoped that they could continue to catch fish along the way for dinner and prepare the rice and beans with the fish along with the vegetables.

In ten minutes, Dan had two cases of beer and soda and two bags of rice and beans. He checked on Ali and Lisa, who had two bags of potatoes and a lot of other vegetables and fruits. Ali and Lisa had some fruit that Dan couldn't recognize but he was game for eating something new. As they checked out at the counter, Dan noticed that they were not busy. He asked the guy at the checkout if they could get some assistance carrying their purchases. Dan pulled out a couple of bills and soon they had two young men assisting them. The five of them carried the bags of food toward the harbor. They made it to the dock and set the groceries down by the boat. Dan, Ali, and Lisa thanked the young men and Chris and Mike helped them bring the groceries onboard.

Dan handed Mike and Chris directions to the bank and market. Dan looked at the food and suggested that if they find another market to purchase more fruit and vegetables. He thought they might also need bakery items, canned meats, tuna, peanut butter, and jelly.

Mike and Chris left for the bank while Dan, Ali, and Lisa packed the groceries in the cabin. After they packed, they planned to relax and wait for their comrades.

Mike and Chris walked into the bank. The manager and clerk were aware of their arrival and ushered them over to the desk, where they both unloaded the cash from their backpacks and opened new bank accounts. Before they left the bank, Chris asked for directions to the best bakery and inquired where they could buy the best produce and meat. The manager wrote down a bakery name and gave detailed directions by going out the front door and pointing to the left twice.

The fruit stand was a right turn out the front door and then four blocks down. The locations were in opposite direction. There was also a butcher a block from the fruit stand.

Chris and Mike decided to split up and meet back at the bank in thirty minutes. Chris went to the bakery, and Mike went for the fruit and veggies and butcher shop. He planned to buy a few items, but were planning on eating fish for most of the voyage.

Chris took two lefts and immediately found himself off the main thoroughfare. Continuing on, he saw a few guys lingering on the corner. As he approached, he was on high alert but they nodded and smiled at him. He took this as an opportunity to ask them about the bakery and they pointed up ahead and to the left. He gave them a "gracias" and walked down the residential street. There was a small bakery there. As he walked inside, he saw bread and pastries on shelves and racks. There were five people in front of him, four women and one man stopping on the way home from work to buy bread for the family dinner.

In the ten minutes standing in line, Chris decided what to buy. When his turn came, he pointed and said, "Dos" or "Tres" or "Quatro," and soon, he walked out of the bakery with his hands full. He had about ten loaves of bread and a dozen pastries. In four bags: two in each arm along with his backpack, pastries safely tucked inside. He made it back to the bank and found that he was the first to arrive, so he dropped his bags of bread against the bank wall and sat down on the bank porch with his back to the wall.

Ten minutes later, a man approached carrying two boxes stacked on top of each other. On the top box, he had a large bunch of plantains. His head was hidden by the boxes, but Chris could tell by his walk that it was Mike. Chris picked up his bags of bread and joined him in stride as they continued the four blocks back to the boat. Dan was up on deck and spotted them from a distance—he yelled down for Ali and Lisa to help Chris and Mike bring aboard the bread and fruit.

After they stored the food in the galley, they all went on deck. Dan brought up three beers and Ali brought a soda for himself and for Lisa. They sat down and Dan said they still needed some canned meats, peanut butter and other miscellaneous nonperishable foods. They agreed that first thing the next day, two of them would revisit the markets to gather these items. Meanwhile, Dan would check the engine and fill up the gas tank with the objective to depart the next afternoon for Europe.

At this point, Dan pulled out the paper with Rafael's name, the cousin of the bank manager. Dan looked over at Lisa.

"Shall I call him and arrange passage to Florida?"

Lisa looked each of the men straight in the eyes and said, "I'm not going back to the States."

They were stunned. She continued, "I'm going with you to Europe."

Dan spoke first. "Lisa, this may be a difficult trip across the Atlantic— and there are major problem areas in parts of Europe and certainly in the Middle-East and Africa."

"We are expecting this to be a dangerous trip," Mike added.

"I don't have anything left for me in the States. I've given this a lot of thought: I need to restart my life again. I could use the time on the voyage to think things through and decide what I want to do going forward," Lisa responded.

"I'm going to get my fiancée in Spain and spend a couple of weeks with her family and then I'll bring her back to Florida. Chris and Mike are going to try to locate Chris's daughter in Slovenia, which is now Russian territory, and bring her back to Florida and then to Texas. We have serious objectives here," Dan advised.

Ali looked at Chris and Mike. "I thought I would go with you to Slovenia."

Chris shook his head. "Ali, we can't take you with us to Slovenia. We have to travel in small numbers—we can't attract any attention and more importantly, I can't have you risk your life. This may be a very dangerous situation. It would be best for you to stay with Dan when we reach Barcelona. Dan has agreed to wait a few weeks for us to find Jessica and her friends and bring them back across the border."

Ali looked at Mike. "Mike?"

Mike looked uncomfortable. "Ali, I agree with Chris. We spoke about it back in the States—we want you as part of our team beyond this mission, but it's best for just the two of us to take this risk to find Jessica and the others. We may have more dangerous situations just trying to reach Barcelona, so we'll need you on this trip."

Lisa wanted to close her situation. "So you'll take me with you?"

Dan and Mike and Chris looked at each other and Dan spoke. "Yes, I'm okay with that as long as the others are."

Mike and Chris nodded, and Lisa had the first big smile that they had seen from her. They sat up on the deck and finished their drinks. Mike informed them that he saw a jerk chicken stand a block from the harbor.

"Does jerk chicken sound good for dinner?" Mike was closing the deal.

Everyone agreed, and Mike, Ali, and Lisa left to buy dinner and bring it back to the boat. Dan and Chris would use some of the fresh produce to make a salad and have it ready by the time they returned.

Dan waited until they left the dock. "Chris, do you have a plan after we arrive in Barcelona?"

"I've discussed possibilities with Mike. The current plan is that we'll head into Italy. Once we arrive, we'll buy clothes and equipment and gather fresh information on the best way to get inside Slovenia. Once inside Slovenia, we'll have to make our way to Bohinj. Bohinj is where we'll find

Jessica's trail. Of course this all must be done without being discovered by the Russians," Chris answered.

There was silence for thirty seconds and Chris added, "Of all the big obstacles I have overcome during my life, this appears to be the biggest. I feel guilty that Mike is joining me, but in all honesty, my odds would be terrible without him. He's a true friend to volunteer and insist that he travel with me. I can't have Ali risk his life. Ali and Lisa have both recently lived through tragic situations. They're young and I hope they can start new and productive lives."

It was quiet for a minute as they watched another boat enter the harbor. Dan broke the silence. "I originally thought I would go to Barcelona, make sure my relationship with Maria was still terrific, then take her back to Florida where we could be together for a year or two and then marry. However, with all the events happening, I've realized that life is short. I've decided that I'll meet her family and spend a few weeks with her—if it feels right, I'm going to marry her in Spain and then take my bride back to Florida."

Chris looked at Dan and smiled. "If you have the right woman, then don't let her get away. I have no regrets," he agreed.

A few minutes later, Mike, Ali, and Lisa came back with chicken and rice and beans. Chris went below and pulled out some more beers and sodas. Dan brought up the salad and they ate on deck, enjoying the nice weather.

The conversation for dinner was light and cheerful. Ali talked with Dan and Chris about the BBQ stand. The guy at the food kiosk had barbecue grills behind him with a stove to the side of the grills with rice and beans. He had a cooler with drinks on the other side. It was a two-man show with just the cook and his wife, but he had a decent line of customers buying dinner. Ali was laughing that the proprietor had a crazy hat with a propeller that spun with the breeze. Lisa teased Ali that they should open an outdoor barbecue similar to the guy back in the States. Ali laughed and thought that was funny. Chris found it interesting that Lisa was thinking about a future with Ali after the voyage.

They sat on deck, and the stars began to multiply, the moon in the distance half full. The night was hypnotic with a nice, warm, breeze. Chris thought that this would have been ideal if he had his whole family here with him. He'd had all these dreams that had been shattered, and now he, like everyone on this boat, had to start a new life. Would this new life be in Texas, or somewhere else?

Mike broke the silence and suggested that they create two-and-a-half-hour guard shifts starting at 10:00 p.m. Lisa would be exempt but that would give them all seven and a half hours to sleep until 8:00 a.m. He found a pen and paper and wrote down time slots and put them in the empty salad bowl. Chris lucked out and pulled out the 10:00 p.m.–12:30 a.m. shift.

To prepare for his shift, Chris put a pot of coffee on for everyone to share throughout the course of the night. At 10:00 p.m. the others went to bed and he was out on the deck by himself. He had his shotgun nearby, but the dock was quiet. No activity at all.

At 12:30 a.m., Dan had a cup of coffee followed by a series of three yawns. He had some serious bedhead going. He said he was awake and Chris went down and jumped into an empty bunk. Soon Chris was sound asleep. He dreamt of his home in San Diego, and then about the farm in Texas. Some nightmares woke him up at 3:00 a.m., but he was finally able to fall back asleep before he woke up for good at around 7:30 a.m.

By 8:00 a.m., everyone was awake. Breakfast was fruit and coffee and some of the pastries from the bakery. Dan would do some maintenance on the boat that day as planned. Mike and Chris asked if he needed assistance.

"No, I'm good at this time. I may need some help mid to late morning."

Ali and Lisa left after breakfast to buy the canned goods. The group decided that they could use more pastries, so Chris took off to the bakery. Mike said he had an errand to run and would be gone for at least two hours.

By 10:30 a.m., everyone was back. Chris had a couple more loaves of bread along with more pastries. He tried to find creative places to store these bakery items. This was especially difficult since they already had fruit and veggies tucked in every nook and cranny throughout the cabin.

Ali and Lisa had more canned food to be stored and they hid it anywhere they could, hoping they would remember where they'd stashed it. Their next task was to fill all the water containers.

Chris checked with Dan and confirmed that the boat looked good: all that was needed was fuel on the way out. Chris turned and asked Mike, "Were you successful finding your item?"

Mike motioned for them to come over near him. On the stern of the boat he had a blanket and something wrapped inside. Pulling the blanket back, he revealed a weapon and a carrying case.

"What is it?" Chris asked.

"It's a M72 Law," he answered.

Chris gave Mike a confused look. Mike raised his hands up, trying to find the right words.

"It's an antitank rocket launcher," he said.

He had two ammo shells. "We'll be out to sea. After we reach Portugal, we'll have to sail between Europe and North Africa. This is our equalizer. We may need something more powerful than our Glock's, Shotgun's and rifles," he added.

Chris looked at Dan as he raised his eyebrows.

"Mike, thank you for the preparation. And I mean it sincerely," Chris spoke up. Mike smiled and wrapped the rocket launcher back up in the blanket.

"I need to store it somewhere in the cabin," Mike added. Chris wondered if someone would have to sleep with it in a bunk.

Ali and Lisa confirmed that the fresh water containers were full. Chris looked at his phone and it was 11:30 a.m. Ali untethered the lines and pushed the boat out and jumped aboard. Dan guided them to the gas pump to fuel up the tank. Mike jumped off the boat and assisted him. After they were fueled, Dan took them out about two hundred yards in the ocean where they put up the sails. Dan looked at his navigation equipment to make sure they were on course.

"Where are we heading next?" Ali spoke up.

"Madeira," Mike responded.

Ali and Lisa looked puzzled.

"It's a Portuguese island on the Atlantic in the direct path to the Strait of Gibraltar, the narrow strait between Spain and Morocco," Mike added.

Dan laughed. "If I miss to the north, we'll hit the Azores, and if I miss to the south we'll hit the Canary Islands," he said.

Ali and Lisa were enthralled with the Azores, Canary Islands, and Madeira and launched many questions. Chris hoped that Dan had the course correct. Chris kept feeling that he had a time clock that he was racing against to find Jessica; the ball game was advancing to the second quarter. They couldn't waste time by steering off course. Hopefully Dan had his calculations correct.

After a couple of hours, Ali took out a fishing rod to see if he could catch some dinner. Chris was rooting for Ali—in a week's time they would finish most of the produce and bread they'd acquired in San Juan. It would be tough living on just rice and beans.

Chris recalled a joke he'd heard in Costa Rica. "We have options." Chris had responded, "How so?"

"Today we have rice and beans, and tomorrow we have … beans and rice!" The guy had thought it was more humorous than Chris and his family, who had grown tired of rice and beans at every meal for a week. But now the memory gave Chris a chuckle.

Chapter 52

Escanaba, Wisconsin

THEY WERE DROPPED OFF at the harbor late at night. The family continued along the lake toward another destination farther away from Fish Creek. Ethan and Mark retrieved their truck in the harbor parking lot; since they didn't have enough room for all the passengers, Ethan drove Pa K, Ma K and the uncle and aunt to the same motel that he and Mark had stayed in before. They were very tired—Ethan was amazed at how well they had handled the past twenty-four hours.

After the grandparents, uncle, and aunt were checked in, Ethan drove back to the harbor to pick up Mark and Greg. He was tired enough that he decided to power down the windows to feel the cool breeze. It was early morning and Ethan decided that they would sleep until noon the next day, then gather in the lobby for lunch. He would share this update with Mark and Greg, then leave a message at the counter for the others.

The drive from the motel was a short distance back to the harbor. Ethan approached Mark and Greg standing on the sidewalk. They wasted no time jumping into the truck. As they drove to the motel, Greg asked about their plans.

"We plan to take Pa K and Ma K back with us to Texas. Unless there are new problem areas that have developed, we'll drive back the way that we came," Mark told him.

They could tell Greg was contemplating his next move. Ethan added, "I'm sure you can travel with us to Texas and stay with us. We have two farmhouses—if you're interested, I can call my mom to let her know."

"I need to talk this over with my parents," Greg responded. "I think my father will be reluctant to travel too far from their home—they've lived there since he retired."

As they pulled into the motel parking lot, Greg went inside the lobby to check in. Before he left, Ethan shared the plan that they would all sleep until noon and then gather to eat lunch.

Ethan and Mark walked up to their motel door, pulled out the key, entered the room, and dropped their backpacks. Ethan requested a wake-up call for 11:50 a.m., and Mark jumped in the shower.

In two minutes, Mark was out and Ethan went in for his shower. The hot water felt refreshing, but he was exhausted, so the shower was brief. He walked out of the bathroom minutes later to find Mark already fast asleep.

Walking over to his bed, Ethan pulled back the covers and stretched out, feet and legs extended to each far corner of the bed. He suddenly remembered the rifles that they'd stored in the room: jumping up, he looked under the bed and confirmed that they were still there. Within a couple minutes, he was sound asleep. He was dead to the world until he heard the alarm.

Mark punched the alarm so it would stop. He was groggy, but quickly put on a new shirt and jeans and stood up, looking at Ethan. Ethan required a couple more minutes to wake up, but five minutes later they left their room and walked across the parking lot to the lobby.

Everyone was gathered in the lobby. Pa K had asked the clerk at the desk for directions to the closest sandwich shop, which happened to be just down the street. They were soon walking two blocks down to the delicatessen. It was busy inside the deli, but they discovered an empty outside table and brought over a few additional chairs so they could seat seven people.

They soon had their sandwiches, chips, and drinks—and the food was delicious. They were very hungry—for five minutes no words were spoken as they tackled their food.

Ethan broke the silence. "Our plan is to rest for a day or so then take Pa K and Ma K back to Texas with us. Aunt and Uncle, I'm sure you can join us there at the farm, and we would love to have you."

"Well, that is a nice offer," their aunt replied.

"I think we should stay in this area and wait until we can return to our home," their uncle spoke up quickly.

"What if it's not safe for a long time?" Ma K asked.

"There are a lot of cities and major towns that are warzones in the old United States. If police and armed forces are available, they'll focus first on the worst areas," Mark added.

Their aunt was nodding. Greg listened, and Mark and Ethan could tell he was really thinking this through. "I'll need to get a car. I'm not sure if I can rent one or if I need to buy one. However, I'll need a car for any option we choose. The offer is very nice—I need to discuss this privately with my parents. Perhaps we can discuss it this afternoon and evening and then meet you for breakfast in the morning. We can have dinner separately so you can make your preparations for your return to Texas."

Everyone agreed. They walked the two blocks back to the motel and Mark suggested to his grandparents they try a pizza place for dinner. According to the guy at the counter, it was supposedly only a half of a mile away. They went back to their rooms and Ethan called his mom.

Carly answered in just a few rings. "Is everyone okay?"

Ethan put the cell phone on speaker and told her that Mark was also there.

"Yes. We had some complications, but we brought Ma K and Pa K out of Fish Creek and off the peninsula. We had to take a boat across the harbor. We have your uncle and aunt and cousin Greg with us—your uncle would like to stay here in this town on the bay and wait for the sheriff to clear out the gangs, but I'm not sure that will happen for a while."

"Bring them back with you to Brownfield! We have a lot of room here, and things seem fairly safe," Carly jumped in.

"We suggested that scenario—they're thinking about it and will let us know tomorrow morning. Regardless of what they decide, we'll probably head back in a couple of days," Mark responded.

Ethan and Mark asked about the farm and how everyone was doing. Carly filled them in and shared how helpful Clark has been. She told them how Abby and Ryan had settled in Austin and how they both now had jobs and a place to live. She also told them about their Grandpa H requiring chemo, and ended by telling them that she hadn't heard from Jessica.

"What about Dad?" Mark asked.

Carly paused. "Well, he called a few days ago. They left Puerto Rico and are traveling across the Atlantic toward Portugal. I'm worried about Jessica and your dad. I'm worried about you two also, but I'm glad that you are now in a safe place. Please come home safely."

They finished talking on the phone and Mark and Ethan decided to take a nap before meeting their grandparents at 5:30 p.m. in the lobby. Ethan thought that they would need a day or two to catch up on sleep before driving back to Texas.

They were more refreshed after their nap. Ethan drove them to the pizza place. The hostess guided them to an empty booth in the corner of the dining room. The room was decorated with wood paneling on the walls and had old wooden tables covered in white and red checkered table-cloths. Old photos from Italy hung on the paneled walls—it appeared to be the proprietor's extended family through several generations, their history displayed and shared with their patrons. Mark looked for a painting of a Roman Centurion, but the oldest display seemed to be photographs from the early 1900s. A few photographs showcased the family with a volcano in the background—Mark wondered if they were from Sicily.

They ordered soft drinks and agreed on the toppings for a large pizza. Midway through dinner, they talked about traveling back to Texas. Pa K shared his thoughts first.

"I would like my sister, brother-in-law, and nephew to travel back with us to Texas. But I know that is their decision to make."

The others agreed that would be best. Ma K added, "Well, at least this is a safe area if they decide to stay."

"We can only wait a day or two at maximum before heading back. I'll have to return to work and Mark has to finish his semester at school," Ethan confirmed.

It was a relaxing evening as they finished dinner, when they finished, they drove directly back to the motel. Ethan and Mark decided to go to bed early—they were still tired, even with their naps earlier in the day. Their bodies were trying to regain strength.

* * * * *

The next morning, they all gathered for breakfast at the same family diner two blocks away. The place was nondescript and looked as though it had last been remodeled in the '60s. They had two pots of coffee sitting on the Formica table with stacks of empty dishes and remnants of toast, eggs and pancakes cluttered on the middle of the table.

Greg shared their decision: they would stay and see what developed in Fish Creek.

They hoped that law and order would prevail in the near future. Pa K looked disappointed, but he knew this was likely going to be their decision. Pa K and Ma K would be happy themselves when they could return to their home.

Greg asked Ethan and Mark if they would be willing to drive him around for a few stops. He had researched purchasing a car and he wanted to evaluate buying versus renting a car. He had called yesterday and had received weekly rates from three agencies. He thought buying a car would be the best option—he could drive it back to Fish Creek when it was safe. Greg advised that he'd like to check a couple of dealerships, private parties, and then the bank. Finding transportation was his first priority.

He'd also looked at renting a small house. If he couldn't find a car today, he would need a ride to a few vacant rentals. He had made some appointments for later in the day.

After breakfast Ethan and Mark drove Greg around to look at cars. It took the entire morning, but by midafternoon, Greg had his car. Greg finally settled on a four-year-old Camry from a private party. They headed back to the motel where Greg picked his parents up. He called the property manager to confirm the appointments and they drove off to meet her and see a few houses available for rent.

Ethan and Mark relaxed for a few hours, then took their grandparents to another diner. They were all rested now and ready for the trek south. They wanted to confirm that Greg, the uncle and aunt had found a place. Pa K expressed that he would feel better leaving if he knew they had a permanent place to stay.

After dinner, Ethan drove them back to the motel. Greg and his parents were waiting for them in the lobby. Greg asked if they could sit for a while with a smile on his face. Ethan and Mark's aunt shared that they had found a three-bedroom house about two miles outside of town. The property included a couple of acres, and they'd signed a six-month lease. After six months, it would convert to month to month. The exciting news was that it was vacant—they could move into the house the next day. They had left everything behind in Fish Creek except what they'd managed to pack in the suitcases. They would shop the next day for cooking utensils, bathroom supplies, food, and clothes. The house was furnished so they wouldn't have to shop for furniture.

The uncle asked the clerk at the desk if it would be a problem to make a pot of coffee. The clerk's response was a big smile and she started brewing a full pot. The family sat in the lobby and talked. Pa K and Ma K asked questions about the house and reveled in all the details. After an hour, they said their goodbyes with hugs, kisses, handshakes, and best wishes. Ethan and Mark explained that they would leave early the next morning for Texas.

Ethan, Mark, Ma K and Pa K agreed to check out at 6:30 a.m. Breakfast would be the motel's cup of coffee—they would stop and find something to eat along the way. They were anxious to start their journey to Brownfield.

Chapter 53

Julian Alps

AFTER A FEW DAYS in the valley, Jessica was ready for a change. Each morning Drago would take a hike further up the mountain to check on the trail conditions—he would take a companion with him on each trip. He alternated between the three of them to keep everyone's mind fresh.

The report from Drago on the condition of the trail to the other two was always, "Not yet, but it's getting better."

They had explored every foot of the little valley and it was beautiful. Each day they would watch from their lookout, but they never saw anyone.

One day Drago decided to hike down to the cheese house. It was Jessica's turn to travel with him. They would cautiously venture down—hoping they could come in contact with nationals with a status on the Russians.

The cheese house was in a good location for a couple of reasons. It was easier to get supplies, and there were more routes across the Alps that originated from this area. They had limited routes from their current location in the valley, hidden and out of the way—but they only had one route down and two options for climbing to a higher elevation.

Drago and Jessica departed right after breakfast. They passed Sam who had already positioned himself as the lookout. Drago explained to Jessica that they shouldn't talk on the hike down the trail, as their voices could carry. As they moved down the trail, Drago stopped periodically and pulled out his binoculars, scanning below them.

Drago and Jessica were halfway down the mountain and making great time. They were approaching a fast running stream below that they could hear from a distance. Drago froze about one hundred yards away from the stream, motioning with his arm for Jessica to squat down. He pulled out his binoculars and they were frozen for five minutes as he scanned below. Finally, he turned his head toward her and whispered, "Stay here, and be very quiet!" Moving cautiously, he walked down the mountain, his rifle ready.

After two minutes, Jessica heard some loud greetings and then some laughter. In about five minutes, Drago hiked up the one hundred yards to where Jessica had remained hidden, crouched down behind some trees.

Motioning for Jessica to come join him, she walked down the trail and near the stream. Jessica saw four people that she thought were nationalists scattered around the stream, and sitting on rocks and eating lunch. Drago pointed up the hill and she saw a fifth person that was on lookout.

Jessica waved to each nationalist and said hello. She was surprised that one of the nationalists was a young woman in her midtwenties. She was dressed in her mountaineering gear, her pistol holstered to her waist and her rifle leaning against a tree. The only difference between the girl and the other four was that she wore her hair in a long ponytail. The leader of the group had a small beard and was about six feet three inches and over two hundred pounds. He had blond hair and reminded Jessica of her two brothers. He was probably in his early thirties. The other two also had beards, but their hair was brown and they were in their late twenties or early thirties. Drago pulled out some of his food for a midmorning snack and motioned for Jessica to do the same. Sitting down, he started talking to them.

All through lunch there was conversation. A couple of times Drago said something and they would stop and look at Jessica. Jessica didn't have much of a reaction: by now she used to it. Finally, the leader waved to the guy on top of the hill and he came down. Jessica noted that he looked like he was about eighteen years old. He had no beard, but he did have a few scraggily hairs on his chin. He had short sandy hair and was outfitted like all the others. They had special pants, shirts and jackets made from a light material that Jessica thought was water repellant.

The leader spoke to his team. The nationalists carefully packed away the leftover food in their packs, then slung them over their backs and grabbed their rifles. The leader said something to Drago and they waved and headed off down the trail. They were out of sight within a minute's time.

After the nationalists' departure, Drago told Jessica that there had been a Russian patrol in the mountains two days ago. The Russians had covered the lower trails, spent one night in the mountains, and then headed back down into Ribcev Laz in the Bohinj area. The nationalists watched the Russians but did not engage in contact. The nationalists had then moved to higher ground like Drago and Jessica had earlier. However, since the Russians had left the mountain, the lower trails were now considered safe. The nationalists were all moving back down the mountain.

A few minutes later, Drago told Jessica that the nationalists had mentioned that they were gaining in numbers and they were training hard, getting organized for early summer. As soon as the mountain passes were open, they would have many routes through the Alps. When this happened, they planned to engage in combat and fight the Russians.

They were hiking for only an hour when they reached the cheese house. When they arrived, they saw a few other nationalists at the picnic table eating. Drago sat down and engaged in some discussion with them. The nationalists offered them a shot of something in a flask: Drago accepted and Jessica thanked them but said no and drank from her canteen. They rested and conversed for twenty minutes and then Drago motioned that they were done. They said their goodbyes and headed up the trail back toward Sam and Nancy in the upper valley.

By late afternoon they reached the lookout area. This time it was Nancy who was watching down below. She had been tracking them for more than a mile. As they approached, Nancy stared at them, waiting for a report.

Drago told her to come down, and they soon found Sam fishing in the stream. Drago called out to Sam—the four of them situated themselves by their cabin, sitting down on a few big rocks below the mountain. Drago went through what he had shared with Jessica, providing the reports from the two nationalist patrols. He then confirmed that they would head down to the cheese house the next morning. If they were lucky, they would be able to stay there for a couple of weeks—then, with good fortune, the passes should open up.

Sam successfully caught two trout. They cooked the fish on the open fire with some of the other food. Jessica was happy that they would move down to the lower trails tomorrow: she felt less confined in that area. From the cheese house, there were many trails—they could hike in any direction to Italy or Austria. She could sense that all of them were getting a little anxious, they were ready to begin their journey out of Slovenia.

Jessica wondered if Drago would be happy long-term living in another country. He was adventurous and she had noticed how he was really at home in these mountains. You could tell that he had spent a lot of time up in the Julian Alps as a child and young adult.

They cleaned up after dinner but they returned to warm themselves by the fire. They each shared some of the things that they missed from home, then played games where one of them would bring up a topic and they all had to answer a question. It could be a favorite dessert, car, television show, least favorite vegetable, or class from school. They shared their best vacations and some of their most sincere dreams. Without TV, work, and other distractions, they were becoming close, they were starting to know each other at a deeper level. After a few hours, Sam yawned, signaling that it was time for bed. They said their good nights and went to bed, dreaming about climbing the mountain.

Chapter 54

Ribcev Laz

JESSICA WOKE AND WENT quietly down the wooden ladder from the loft. She smelled that someone had made coffee, and she knew it wasn't Nancy, because she was still sleeping in the loft. She poured a cup and walked outside, glancing from left to right before she hiked to the knoll overlook. She saw a figure up ahead and even halfway up the path she recognized the shape and how he stood. There was something unusual about the way he looked over the landscape. She had seen it often by now. He heard her coming up and turned around, giving a short one-motion wave with a smile before turning back around and bringing his binoculars up to his eyes for a more detailed review of the landscape. Jessica thought that Drago always looked around: he was always aware of his surroundings.

When she was within a few feet of him, Drago turned around.

"Good morning."

Jessica took a quick sip of her coffee. "Good morning to you. Thanks for starting the coffee."

He nodded. They had been sharing the cheese house the past two days with another group of nationalists, a very easy and very friendly group. There were two lofts: one for the guys and one for the ladies. Each loft had ten bunks that were fully booked during a normal winter for cross country skiing. The nationalists sharing the house with them were six men, so Nancy and Jessica had the women's loft to themselves.

Drago had spoken to many people on the trail, and he'd been watching. He explained to Jessica, Sam, and Nancy that they needed to restock their supplies. He estimated that they needed to stock for four weeks with at least two more weeks at the cheese house and for up to two weeks leaving Slovenia over the mountain trails. They would need to shop for groceries in town. He had heard that the Russians now had fourteen soldiers stationed in Ribcev Laz—they were using a small hotel as their station and headquarters. Drago was uneasy about preparing to go into town one last time.

Drago looked at Jessica. "Today, we'll go into town. Go wake up Nancy and dress only in Slovenian clothes. Empty your backpacks of everything but your handguns and some money. We should leave in thirty minutes."

They walked back down the hill to the house together. Jessica climbed up the stairs to the loft to change her clothes and to wake up Nancy. Drago went upstairs to the men's loft to wake up Sam. Nancy was in a deep sleep, but Jessica was able to get her up in a couple of minutes. Jessica surveyed what she was wearing in the mirror and decided that she only needed to change her shirt.

Within fifteen minutes, they were out by the picnic tables. Drago instructed them that it would be crucial to be aware of everything around them. He had heard that there was a meeting in Bled today and the Russian Lieutenant of the Bohinj outpost was traveling to Bled with an escort of some of his soldiers. Therefore, he anticipated minimum security around Ribcev Laz.

Drago had their attention and he provided the plan for the day. They would go down the tram and borrow a car from a friend who managed the restaurant at the top of lift. Sam would be the driver—he would drop them off at the grocery store. Nancy, Jessica, and Drago would shop, and Sam would come back at a prearranged location and time. They would divide up in the store to buy groceries. Drago said the girls would be less suspicious than Sam in town—Drago himself, knew a little Russian to get by if confronted by a soldier.

They hiked over to the tram. Drago told them to wait as he walked to the back of the restaurant and through a door that said Employees Only. Emerging back through the door two minutes later with car keys, he also had some paper and a pencil. Gathering the others at a picnic bench, they created grocery lists.

They developed three lists. Once inside the grocery store they would be quick: each would shop for only the items on their list. One person had fresh produce and bread, another had dairy and meat, and the last list was for canned goods. Drago would cross the street and buy them more socks before he started working on his grocery list.

Sam had rehearsed that he would come back exactly thirty minutes after the drop off. If there were Russians on the street, Sam would abort and come back in thirty minutes. He would always operate within thirty minute intervals. Drago had created a crude map on one of the blank pieces of paper and had given it to Sam. It showed the tram parking lot, the road to town, and details in the town on the drop off and pick up.

They rode down the tram, the others following behind Drago as he looked for his friend's car. Once they reached the car, he flipped the keys to Sam and jumped in the front passenger seat. The girls climbed in the back seat.

Sam drove into town. Everyone was quiet and watched carefully out their windows. They were getting close to the drop off when they spotted two Russian soldiers walking down the street. Sam kept his cool and drove the speed limit and they looked away from the soldiers as they passed. Two blocks past the Russian soldiers, Sam stopped the car in front of the grocery store and the other three moved quickly out of the car. Sam left them instantly and turned left at the next corner, quickly out of sight.

Drago immediately walked across the street, leaving passersby with the assumption that the two groups didn't know each other. Nancy and Jessica walked into the store and started on their grocery lists; Drago was in the store in five minutes with a small package of socks. He started shopping for items on his list without speaking nor acknowledging the girls.

Meanwhile, after dropping off his friends, Sam drove to a pull-out area adjacent to the lake. He could relax now, but had to be aware of the time. A Russian patrol might decide to stroll around the lake—he needed to keep an eye out.

Jessica and Nancy had been successful in gathering the produce and canned goods and were ready to check out. Drago had some meat on the counter and carried a big bag each of rice and beans. They had cheese at the cheese house, so they didn't need too much dairy.

They checked out together at the register. Drago did the talking and paid the woman at the register. They packed what they could in their backpacks, and Nancy and Jessica had a heavy bag each of canned goods. Drago carried a bag of beans in one arm and a bag of rice in the other. They kept an eye on the clock above the register—they had ten minutes before Sam would drive by for pick up.

Drago looked out the window before taking a step out of the store. Turning around quickly, he spoke to the owner in Slovenian. Drago unzipped his pack and handed Jessica his handgun. The owner moved from behind the counter right away and motioned for the girls to follow. They followed her quickly to the back-stock room, and there was a closet. She had them go inside. She put a finger to her lips communicating the universal sign to be quiet, then closed the door. Jessica and Nancy heard her footsteps walking away. Jessica turned on the overhead light for five seconds to pull out her gun, pointing it toward the door. Once in place, she turned off the light.

Ten seconds later, they heard the bells on the front door ring followed by some voices. Jessica strained to hear. She heard Drago's voice briefly and then the shop owner's voice, along with two different men's voices that she had not heard before. After two minutes of conversation (which they couldn't understand), there were another two minutes of silence followed by a minute more of conversation and then they heard the bells on the door again. Jessica wondered if someone had left, or if more people had entered the store. After five minutes of quiet, they heard footsteps approach the back room and toward their door.

Jessica had her pistol pointed at the door. As the doorknob turned, she heard a voice.

"Girls, the Russians are gone," Drago announced as he opened the door.

He saw the Glock pointed at him. "I'm glad I said something before opening the door."

Jessica lowered the gun and stepped out with Nancy. She put the gun in her backpack and they followed Drago out to the store. The shopkeeper was there at the counter, smiling. Drago walked over to edge of the window and looked across the street to the far side.

"They walked in the store and asked many questions of our friend here about her customers," Drago told them. "I passed myself off as a customer buying groceries. They asked me where I worked, what I was doing. I told them I lived in Bled and was on holiday staying by the lake. If they follow up on my information, they'll know that I'm lying. The good news is that they walked up and down the aisles, then left the store. The bad news is that they walked across the street and down two shops to the café, where it appears they are having a coffee and pastry while sitting out on the sidewalk. We can't go out the front door and meet Sam on the street."

A minute later, and thirty minutes after they had been dropped off, they saw Sam cruise slowly down the street. Sam didn't see them on the street but he moved slowly, giving his friends the benefit of the doubt to make it out to the curb. Sam suddenly looked over to the other side of the street and saw the two Russians at their street side table looking at him. Picking up some speed, he looked straight ahead and drove out of sight.

Drago spoke to the store owner in Slovenian and they had a series of exchanges, in which the store owner pointed to the back of her store. She moved from behind the counter and waved for them to follow.

Drago looked at Nancy and Jessica. "The store owner has a back door that is used for her suppliers to deliver food. The Russians know that I'm in the store. I'll need to leave the store soon from the front door. We also can't have Sam cruise by again slowly in thirty minutes with the chance that they are still at the table. They'll be suspicious the second time he comes around."

"So what should we do?" Nancy asked.

"I assume that Drago leaves through the front door and we'll go out the back door and we meet at an agreed-upon spot." Jessica jumped in.

Drago nodded. "You will go out the back and turn left and walk down three blocks until you come to a house on the corner with a giant tree. Wait for me there. I'll walk out and go to the right and then turn the corner and meet you. We'll need to intersect Sam before he heads down this street again in twenty-five minutes."

Drago said something to the shopkeeper, then took the bag of beans and the bag of rice and walked out the front door. He did not look at the Russians but was aware that they watched him carefully. The grocer walked to the back of the store, motioning for the girls to follow. Jessica and Nancy had their backpacks on and were carrying a bag each as they followed past the stock room. The owner stopped at a wide metal door, pulling out keys for two locks. The door opened up, and the girls walked out the door.

"Thank you," they said in unison as they turned left, following Drago's instructions. The shopkeeper smiled and gave them a small wave.

It only took five minutes to reach the tree—Drago was there waiting for them. He had his two bags leaning against the tree trunk. Drago explained that he wanted to walk back to the main street to see if he could find a safe place to wait for Sam. He came back in ten minutes and shared that there weren't any good locations to hide: there were mostly cafes or restaurants in the area. He thought it might be best for them to stay put and wait. He could go back to the street to try to flag Sam down. Together they could drive over to pick up the girls and supplies.

There were only ten minutes left until Sam would come by again, so the girls agreed to wait for Drago. He left the sacks of beans and rice leaning against the trunk of the tree, then moved down the street with just his backpack.

The instructions from Drago were for them to wait unless something seemed dangerous. If they ran into danger, they were to walk in the direction of the tram to Mt Vogel and leave the supplies behind. Drago was now out of Jessica's eyesight as he approached the main street.

Drago walked slowly, hoping to kill some time. He wanted to come upon the street with only two minutes before Sam arrived. When he reached the street, he decided to walk back a block toward the grocer, then cross the street and come back up the street, so he was on the same side of the street as Sam. He wanted to be able to jump in the passenger seat quickly. He also knew that Sam would not be looking for him in that spot, so he might have to walk out in the street to flag Sam down.

Drago walked down a block; then, while crossing the street, he saw the two Russian soldiers walking back in his direction. They must have finished their drinks and were now a block away and approaching him. Reaching the corner, he started walking away from them and toward where Sam might approach with the car. He made it one block and looked at his phone. It was time for Sam to come by. Drago paused—out of the corner of his eye, he could see the Russians approaching, and now they were only two thirds of a block away. They were focused on him.

Drago continued walking, maintaining a good pace to ensure the Russians kept the same distance away. He walked one more block, then saw Sam's car up ahead turning onto the street and approaching him. He kept his stride steady, hoping Sam would see him. He needed to keep his distance from the Russian soldiers, and he was going to have to flag Sam down at the last minute. Anything too early would have the Russians running after him.

Sam was now thirty meters from him, and he didn't show any recognition of spotting him. Drago immediately jogged out onto the street several steps toward the car. He had his backpack in his left hand as he waved with his right hand. Sam had to slam on the brakes before he instantly noticed Drago. Drago was carrying his pack now. The car door was unlocked, and Drago opened the passenger car door and jumped in, his backpack on his lap.

"Quick, turn left at the next block," he blurted.

Sam sat still, stunned.

"Now," Drago shouted.

Sam continued the half block and made a sharp left. Drago saw that the Russians were trotting after them. They had just turned the same corner, and they shouted something that Drago couldn't understand, but he knew they weren't asking for directions to Lake Bohinj. The Russians continued trotting down the street after them. Two blocks later, Drago told Sam to hang a right turn and then one block further, he had Sam stop near the tree.

Drago told Sam to open the trunk of the car as he jumped out. Running to the bags, Drago grabbed one of them and yelled for the girls to get in the car quickly. Jessica and Nancy ran with their backpacks and bags of canned goods, put them in the trunk, and quickly got in the back seat. Sam was back in the driver's seat. Drago had one bag in the trunk and was going for the second. Jessica looked back and saw two Russian soldiers running at them about one and a half blocks away. They were shouting something that she couldn't understand. Drago dumped the last bag in the back, slammed the trunk closed, and threw himself in the passenger seat.

"Go!" he shouted.

Sam stepped on the gas. Looking back, Jessica saw one Russian drop down and point his rifle at their car.

Jessica shouted, "Heads down!" and placed her arm around Nancy, pulling her head down with hers as a shot rang out. The car was not hit, but it was a close call. Sam made another quick right turn, and then slowed down to the speed limit a few blocks later. He had memorized the map that Drago had drawn for him and he drove straight toward the tram parking lot.

Parking the car in the same place where they had found it that morning, Sam gave Drago the car keys and grabbed the sack of rice and the sack of beans. Drago took the two bags of cans along with his backpack and Jessica took the bag of socks and her backpack. Quickly, they made their way to the tram area. They would have to wait ten minutes to take the next tram up the mountain.

It seemed like forever, but finally after fifteen minutes, they were moving up the mountain. Drago and Nancy and Jessica emptied some of the cans from the bags into Sam's backpack. Drago and Sam would carry a sack each of rice or beans to the cheese house. Jessica had the bag of socks and Nancy had a small bag of cans that hadn't been able to fit in Sam's backpack.

At the top of the tram, Drago gave the keys back to his friend. He explained the close call and the possibility that the Russians may have identified their car. Drago gave his friend some money and a quick hug. As they left, Drago added, "He'll need to garage his car for a while and use other transportation for the next two weeks."

It was an hour hike to the cheese house. As soon as they arrived, they emptied their packs and put away their supplies. Drago explained that they would eat a lot of the rice and beans now and wait to eat anything canned so they could save it for their final trip over the mountain pass. They were tired, so Sam decided to grill some of the meat from the market with their rice and beans. Drago cooked the rice and beans and Nancy set the table. Jessica made a green salad with the fresh produce. They ate dinner outside at the picnic table with some of the nationalists.

As they shared their story with the Slovenians, the nationalists reported that the Russian meeting in Bled was to discuss more Russian patrols in the mountains as they approached summer.

After dinner, the nationalists poured each of them a drink. They held up the glasses and one of the nationalists said something in Slovenian. Others gave credence with words of affirmation, then they all clicked the glasses and tossed the shot. Jessica, Sam, and Nancy didn't need to know what was said: it didn't matter. They were all toasting themselves for living, for hating the Russians, and for a good day to follow. Perhaps, Jessica thought, that is the meaning of it all. Perhaps what everyone should toast for each night was life itself.

Chapter 55

Atlantic Ocean

CHRIS HAD WORKED WITH Dan long enough to know when he was nervous. He wasn't sure if the others had caught on. The past week had been terrific as they had covered a lot of distance. Ali was becoming a good fisherman! He caught fish each day to supplement their daily rice and beans.

However, yesterday Dan had watched the radar intently, frequently listening to the weather report. Chris was aware that a big storm was heading their way from West Africa. Dan had changed their course last night to a little more north than northeast to try to avoid the brunt of it, and he was now following the storm every hour.

Dan had inspected the boat again the past couple of hours to make sure that everything was buttoned down and properly stowed. He had them switch the sails to the storm sails, and he instructed Ali and Lisa to confirm that the cabin was clear and secure.

It was now 2:00 p.m. and getting darker by the minute. The waves were strong, but they were still able to keep their course. Dan shouted for his colleagues to come toward him.

"We weren't able to outrun the storm, but hopefully we'll catch just the edge of it."

"We will try to sail through. If it gets really bad, we'll need to take the sails down and use the engine to ride into the wind and waves. I'll have the wheel." He continued.

He gave Mike and Chris their tasks during the storm: at his command, they would quickly take down the sails. He gave instructions of how to safely secure the sails: Mike should assist in starting the engine. Chris's stomach quickly became uneasy from the bouncing in the water. Ali was getting sick and had vomited once already. Looking at Ali made Chris feel worse—he felt fortunate that he hadn't eaten all day and had only consumed coffee earlier in the morning. It was an excellent moment for an empty stomach.

The group was concerned that they might lose Ali overboard, so Dan instructed Lisa to take him down below to find Ali a bucket. He asked both of them to remain in the cabin.

The waves were now ten feet high, and the wind was picking up. Dan was at the wheel in his dark-gray raincoat, hood on. Chris couldn't see his face, but he could hear Dan shout encouragement that they were doing fine. Chris and Mike had their jackets with hoods on, and they wore the orange life vests fastened over their coats. Chris knew that falling overboard would be problematic, even with the life vests.

Chris had the jib, and Mike had the mainsail. Dan shouted instructions as he turned the boat east into the storm. The storm had caught them and they were no longer trying to run from it. Their mission now was to survive it.

Dan frantically shouted something to them, but by now the wind was so loud they had trouble hearing him. Mike looked back to try to make out some words; Chris looked ahead and saw a monstrous wave approaching. A sudden gust of wind suddenly changed direction, and Chris held firm and ducked down as Mike was hit. He got a sweeping boom on the side of his head and was instantly knocked down. Mike lost balance, but held the line firmly as he slid six feet along the deck. The boat was now coming down from the wave, and Mike slid back several feet the other direction toward Chris. Chris looked and could tell he was hurt badly. A streak of crimson dripped down the side of Mike's forehead. Chris freed one hand and grabbed Mike's right leg, which was the closest limb to him. Chris held on to Mike tightly while also holding onto the rail with his other arm. He tried to pull Mike over to him until they were side by side. Mike looked up at Chris—he seemed to be trying to shake off the confusion. Mercifully, the boat began to climb up another wave. Another steep drop, and the wind shifted again. The boom was traveling back over Mike's head.

"Take down the sails!" Dan shouted.

Chris gave Dan a thumbs up, and even though Mike's head was only five feet away, Chris shouted to him, "Mike, are you okay? Can you hold on?"

Mike nodded. He hung on tightly to the halyard, but Chris could tell he was in pain. While Mike was holding on to the main sail, Chris took down the jib. Chris had to time his actions in between the sets of waves; he secured the sail and was quickly back on the mainsail with Mike. Chris told him that they'd pull it down just as Dan had instructed them earlier, and Mike nodded again. They were slow and steady in their work, but finally they brought it down. Chris told him to hang on as he timed the waves. Somehow, he tied and secured the mainsail. Mike tried hard to keep focus as Chris tied it.

They slid a few feet each time the boat dropped with the wave. Chris asked Mike to continue to hold on tight as he made his way over to Dan. Dan asked Chris to hold the wheel and to keep it on the same course. Coming behind Dan, Chris put his arms over him and placed each hand next to his. Once Chris had full command, Dan ducked under Chris and went over to start the engine. It took a couple of minutes for him to get it up and running. Chris's only focus was to keep the boat headed straight into the waves. Chris thought randomly of whether someone could simulate this exercise at the gym: it'd be a good arm and core workout. He felt fatigue within just a few minutes.

Once Dan started the engine, he came back and took the wheel. He nodded to Chris to take care of Mike and shouted, "I'm good for right now."

Chris left the wheel with Dan and slid over to Mike, who was barely conscious: he was on his knees, holding onto a railing with both hands. Chris shouted to him that they were going to take him down below to the cabin. Chris asked if he thought he could walk and he received a weak confirmation. As soon as the boat climbed the next wave, Chris grabbed Mike and together they staggered in the direction of the hatch. Chris realized that they weren't going to make it down below by the time the boat dropped, so he stopped short, holding on tight as the boat dropped down once more. On the next wave, Chris was able to get Mike to the hatch and down into the cabin.

Chris shouted to Lisa, who joined them in seconds at the stairs. She helped Chris get Mike down. Mike was a mess. The whole side of his head was covered in blood, and Chris asked Lisa to bring the medical kit and a clean towel as he brought Mike to the bunk to lie down.

Chris asked Ali, who was sitting down and holding a bucket, to help watch Mike and make sure he didn't fall out of the bunk. Ali braced himself against the bunk, and set the bucket down. One hand holding on and one hand on Mike, Ali watched as Lisa came back with the towel. Gingerly, she dried Mike's head, wiping the blood and water from his head. Soon, they could see a gash about three inches long on the side of his head. It receded one inch into the hair line and two inches up the forehead. Chris looked at Lisa.

"We need to sew him up. Lisa, keep his wound clean. Ali, please put some disinfectant on the wound but don't let it get into his eyes," Chris instructed.

Fortunately, Mike kept his hair very short—so the wound was easily exposed. Chris didn't have clippers or a razor to shave the wound area, so he would just have to stitch it the best he could.

Chris found the bottle of whiskey that Mike had brought for a special occasion. This appeared to be the special occasion. Chris opened the bottle and brought it to Mike, who raised his head.

"Take a couple of swigs," Chris encouraged. Mike took the bottle and took several gulps.

Needle and thread in his hand, Chris recalled how Carly had instructed him when they were first married how to mend his socks. In spite of all the boats movement, Chris patiently threaded the needle. When he was ready, Chris started slowly on one side of the wound and worked his way across to the other side. He stopped periodically so Lisa could dab the blood away. Chris could time the movement and get one stitch when the boat was up. Fifteen minutes later, Mike had twelve stitches.

"Lisa, will you put a bandage over my sutures? I'm confident that Mike has a severe concussion. You can let him have another drink or two of whiskey, but then put the bottle away. Mike can't sleep right now—talk to him and keep him awake. This is very important. I need to help Dan on deck."

Chris moved up through the hatch and almost stumbled out as the boat crashed at the bottom of the wave. Stumbling two feet to the right, Chris held on. He staggered over to Dan, who was still holding strong. Chris offered to give Dan a break, and Dan agreed that a ten-minute break would be terrific. They switched and Dan watched Chris for two minutes to make sure he was steady before disappearing below in the cabin.

Chris felt very small out there at the wheel in the violent ocean. He could finally relate to the ancient stories of Greek mariners in the seas and then later other European explorers crossing vast bodies of water, at the mercy of the oceans and seas. Dan had a good-sized boat, yet the ocean tossed them around like a toy boat.

Somehow Chris experienced peace as he firmly held the wheel. He talked to himself out loud, but nobody could hear save for the ocean and the wind. "We can't die out here today; I can't die. I have to find Jessica."

Chris became quickly in tune with the waves and the storm. Chris was small, the boat was small, but they were all a part of the ocean.

Dan climbed out of the cabin. A few minutes later, he was standing by Chris and had regained control of the wheel.

They traded off a few times as they battled the storm. After an hour, Chris could tell that the storm was subsiding. The wind didn't appear as strong, and the waves were still substantial but a little smaller. In another hour, they saw more improvement. Three hours later, the ocean waves and wind were almost back to normal. The skies, however, were still dark since it was now evening.

Chris went down in the cabin and found Ali talking with Mike. Mike wanted desperately to take a nap and was getting cranky with Ali.

"Mike, are you hungry?" Chris interrupted.

"I can eat something," Mike grumbled.

Chris asked Lisa if she would mind fixing Mike something to eat. They could tell that they were not being tossed around the cabin anymore, and Chris confirmed that it was likely they had ridden out the storm.

Chris told Mike that he was certain he had a concussion and that they wanted to keep him awake a little longer. Ali was feeling better and he assisted keeping Mike alert. Mike grumbled that he still had a headache, and Ali interjected that he had given him four aspirin an hour ago.

"Ali, perhaps get him a couple more?" Chris suggested.

Chris went back up to the deck and Dan asked him to take the wheel again so he could check on the status of the storm. He wanted to make sure they were clear and then he would rechart their course. Dan had changed their course to North and then East during the worst part of the storm. Their destination was Madeira, and he wanted to make sure that was where they were still headed.

Dan paused. "I think we are fine, but I will also need to inspect the boat."

Thirty minutes later, Dan had some bread and cheese on a plate in one hand and a beer in the other as he walked over to Chris. He offered Chris the food and Chris shook his head no.

"No, thanks. I think I'll skip food today and then restart with breakfast tomorrow," Chris explained.

Chris hadn't been sick that day, and he didn't want to take any chances. Having an empty stomach had to have helped. But he wasn't a sailor like Dan and he needed some time to become a veteran of the sea.

They finally let Mike go to sleep at midnight, only because he was so tired that it seemed inhumane to keep him up further. He had been awake for ten hours.

Dan and Chris took turns at the wheel throughout the night. Ali had recovered and he graciously made a pot of coffee. Chris was slowly coming off his adrenaline rush. At 1:00 a.m. Dan and Chris were both on deck while Mike, Ali, and Lisa were asleep below. Dan was at the wheel and Chris sat about four feet away.

Dan looked over. "Chris, I'm nervous about arriving in Barcelona. I'm so anxious to see Maria, but we haven't seen each other in a while. What if she doesn't love me anymore? What if things have changed?"

Chris took a sip of coffee and looked at him. "Dan, I wouldn't worry about it. You two have known each other for two years. You've told me that you've discussed all the main topics: you are willing to become a Catholic, which is big for her and her family. She is willing to come with you back to Florida to start a new life. You both agree you want to start a family. Your life goals seem aligned—it appears to me that you've discussed the priority items."

"But I think you're right that you should take some time to get reacquainted," Chris added. "You know that Mike and I will have to leave soon after we reach Barcelona?"

Dan was quiet and nodded. "Chris, how long do you think you'll need to find Jessica and return to Barcelona?"

"I don't know, Dan. I've discussed this a little with Mike—we think it could be two to three weeks. However, the Russians are re-creating their old Soviet empire; with the border checks and Russians occupying Slovenia, I'm not sure how difficult it'll be to get in, move around the country, and then escape."

"But I'll tell you something, Dan. With Mike joining me, I think my chances for success may be good. He's not as comfortable with sailing, but I have a feeling once we land in Barcelona that he'll be in his element," Chris continued.

Dan looked over at Chris and smiled. "Chris, why don't you go down and try to sleep for a few hours and then come back up and trade off? We dodged a bullet today, and we need to be strong for tomorrow."

Chris took his last sip of coffee. "Good night, Dan. You were outstanding today. Thank you."

Chapter 56

Texas

CARLY HAD DROPPED HER in-laws off at the medical center in Lubbock Monday morning. The report so far showed that Grandpa H's red blood cell count was increasing. The oncologist said that after that week of chemo, they'd hold off further treatments for two weeks. Carly had stayed for the doctor visit, then left around noon as they prepared her father-in-law for his treatment. She would be back on Friday to bring them home.

Carly planned to stop by Brownfield on the way home to get some groceries and a few supplies. It was early afternoon, and the radio was on. A news bulletin declared that local law enforcement had caught two more prisoners from the Louisiana prison breakout.

They'd recovered the convicts in Amarillo, Texas. There was a shootout at a motel with one prisoner shot and hospitalized in critical condition. The other was in custody. The news story reported that the other two prisoners had split from these two about a day ago; they had no idea which direction they had gone. The news reporter shared that the last two escaped prisoners could have traveled south and deeper into Texas, or they could have headed west into New Mexico or north into Oklahoma, Kansas, or Colorado. However, the authorities surmised that they were heading northwest and that they were probably in Colorado by now.

Switching the news channel to an interview of a local Texas ranger, Carly listened as he reported that he thought there was a strong chance that the escapees would try to continue southwest into Mexico.

Carly pulled into the parking lot at the grocery store. Approaching the store, she grabbed a cart and pushed it with grocery list in hand. Carly moved her cart up and down the aisles: she didn't need a lot of things, so she was able to go quickly. She stopped at the produce area for fresh veggies and fruits to compliment the items from the farmer's market.

The Texas Federation had resumed trade with Central and South America, and some of the produce was starting to come in via rail from Mexico or on boat from the Gulf. She checked each week: the selection of fruits and vegetables was improving. At the checkout counter, she saw that line two was open and pushed her cart forward. The checkout girl was very cute, she recognized her from before; her name tag said Lindsey.

When she was ready to pay, Lindsey saw Carly's last name on her credit card and introduced herself.

"Hi, I'm Lindsey McGregor. My father leases your farmland."

Carly recalled hearing about McGregor and his four daughters.

"Hello, nice to meet you, Lindsey."

"How are Ethan and Mark?" Lindsey inquired.

"I just heard from them," Carly replied. "They are up in the Midwest, bringing my parents back. I'm hoping they'll be back here in a few days."

Lindsey seemed very interested in this information, "Will Ethan return back to Dallas to work?" Lindsey paused. "And will Mark return to college at OU?"

Carly was honest. "I think Ethan will return back to work soon, but I'm not sure if Mark will return until the fall semester. He is waiting to hear how he can finish spring semester. There's some discussion about starting midsummer in July, finishing the spring, and then rolling into the fall. We'll know more when they return."

Carly asked Lindsey how her family was doing and got a quick report that each family member was doing well. By now all the groceries were bagged and ready to go. Carly got the sense that Lindsey would have liked to talk more and find out more about her sons, but there were now two more people in line. They said their goodbyes and Carly pushed her cart out to the parking lot.

As she was putting in the last bag, an older man and woman pulled up near her vehicle. They nodded and said "hello." Carly responded, "Hello" and the woman blurted out. "Have you heard the two convicts at large could be in our area if they decide to head south to Mexico?"

Before Carly could think of a reply, the old farmer added, "Make sure you are armed—these last two escapees are very dangerous."

"Both of them have killed people," his wife went on. "One appears to be a rapist who killed his victims, and the other has killed during robberies."

Carly thanked them for their advice. She was shaken for a minute but calmed herself down while driving back to the farm. She had one pistol in the glove compartment and one inside the house, and she carried the rifle with her around the farm. Besides, their farm was outside of town.

She pulled up to the farm and saw Clark repairing the chicken coop. It looked like a coyote or dog had tried unsuccessfully to get in the coop—some of the wood holding up the mesh was damaged. This was on Clark's to-do list for the day, and it appeared that he was finishing up. He waved and walked over to her as Finley ran out from the porch.

"I'll help you bring in the groceries, then I'm almost finished with this coop. I'll put away the tools and clean up. Remember that I'm going to the dance in town tonight."

"Thank you, Clark. I'll put away the groceries and then start dinner soon. We will eat around six, so you can head out after. Does that work?"

Clark nodded. "Yes. I'll feed the cows before dinner."

Since it was just the two of them, Carly didn't want to cook too much. They ate burgers, veggies, and baked beans for dinner. Clark came into the house after finishing his chores and Carly told him he had ten minutes to shower. Finley was nervous because it was getting close to his dinner so Carly decided to feed him ten minutes early. Finley attacked the food in his dish like he was going for an Olympic medal; in less than a minute, he was done, burped, and came over to thank Carly for feeding him. He could now relax and lay down near the side of the table waiting for Clark and Carly to eat with hope that he might get a few morsels after dinner. Carly thought that if Chris were there, Finley would enjoy secret bites under the table. She was a stickler: she would only feed Finley after dinner, with the leftovers placed in his bowl.

They had a quiet dinner. Carly asked Clark who he was meeting at the dance. Clark didn't like to share much, but she knew he had been quickly welcomed by the locals and that he had made both guy and gal friends. The Monday night dance had drinks half off and it consistently drew a big crowd for a weeknight. Monday night was a hit, especially with the under twenty-five crowd that needed to stretch their dollars. Carly knew that Clark would limit himself to one or two sodas. His parents didn't like alcohol, and he was determined not to break his vow to his mother.

Clark went to the bathroom to brush his teeth, then he left the farm for the dance. Carly checked the front and back of the house and made sure the doors were locked. Walking into the living room, she sat in a chair and picked up the book that she was reading. She found a bookcase at the farmhouse that had some old classics. Abby was an avid reader and had taken a few books with her to Austin; she'd vowed that she would bring them back and exchange them for a few more. Carly found the classic *Tale of Two Cities* by Dickens and was about one hundred pages into the book. She thought she could make a big dent in it tonight. Finley decided to nap in front of the fireplace where it was cool.

Two hours later, she was starting to nod off when she saw Finley raise his head. Ears cocked, he stared outside and a low growl escaped from his chest. Carly walked over to the front window and looked out. She had the porch light on for Clark, but no other lights were on. From what she could see, there wasn't anyone on the porch—she didn't see anything strange in front of the house.

Her mind raced, trying to figure out what Finley could be upset about. *Were there coyotes? It wasn't the rabbits. Finley was now used to smelling and seeing rabbits daily. Could it possibly be the escaped convicts? But why would they be out here?*

After two minutes, Carly heard a noise in the barn that sounded like the gate. She thought that Clark had fed their two cows before dinner— could the gate be open?

Finley was still frozen and focused in the direction of the barn. He had not stopped growling. Carly tried to remember all the times that he had acted this way and recalled that it typically involved another animal. She wanted to stay in the house, but she thought, *What if the cows are loose? Or what if the cows are in danger?*

Carly walked over to the corner of the living room and grabbed the rifle and flashlight. She decided to leave Finley inside in case there were coyotes outside. He was a wonderful dog, but he would be mismatched against a pack of coyotes. She wouldn't be able to shoot the rifle in fear of hitting him.

Carly opened the door, stepped out, closed it, and walked out on the porch. She held the flashlight out with her left hand, her right hand perched on the trigger of the rifle.

She waited on the porch for a minute to let her eyes adjust. She heard the knocking sound again and was able to identify that it came from inside the barn. Stepping off the porch, she started walking toward the barn slowly. The front of the house was cleared of brush when they arrived, so visibility was great. She did not see a person or animal, so she walked across the gravel driveway slow and steady. Carly eased up as she approached the barn entrance.

She paused for ten seconds—which seemed like two minutes—and then she walked in the barn door and stopped. From there she panned her flashlight to see if she could spot the source of the noise. She flashed the beam toward the gate for the cows. The gate was open and one cow was half in and half out. Clark was in such a hurry for his dance that he wasn't paying attention when he fed the cows, she thought. He forgot to close their pen. Carly walked over to the pen and started talking to her cow Daisy who was half in her pen. Hopefully Daisy could easily be talked into getting back in.

"Daisy, what are you doing? You need to be safe in your pen with Roxi. Why did you open the gate? What were you looking for, more food?"

The hay was kept in the second story, and Clark would pitch it down, so the cows wouldn't have access to more hay if they escaped their pen.

Carly set her rifle down and patted Daisy on the side to get her to turn and move in. She got her turned and into the pen, then pulled the gate closed and dropped the rope loop over the post.

As she turned away, Carly felt a hand on her shoulder. She dropped the flashlight and jumped. It was a man's hand, and it was rough. The flashlight was still on, but it was lying on the barn floor and everything she could see was through filtered light. Visibility was poor.

"Look what we have here, Leroy."

Leroy was quick to respond. "TJ, let's keep our focus on what we have planned. Let's get the keys to her vehicle and keep moving."

TJ had other ideas. "First I want to have a little fun with the missus."

Carly's mind raced. *These are the convicts. TJ is the killer rapist—he will rape and then kill me.* More thoughts rushed in her head. *Leroy is between me and the rifle. Visibility is poor and I know the barn. I have to try something. I need to stay alive for my family.* More random thoughts. *I have to get my in-laws in four days. They are going to find Finley and kill him.*

TJ had her by both shoulders. "If you cooperate, then you will be okay," he told Carly.

Carly knew this wouldn't be the case. He kept his left hand on her shoulder while his right hand went down to her pants' zipper. Carly knew she needed to act quickly and she couldn't go for the rifle. However, opposite of the rifle and Leroy, on the other dark side of the barn, was the ladder to the loft on the second story. She kicked swiftly, her right foot launching upward to TJ's groin. She kicked as hard as she could, knowing that her life depended on it. As soon as she made contact, he howled and let go of her instantly as he crouched over in pain.

Carly immediately took two steps, swooped up the flashlight, and ran for the other side of the barn. She turned the flashlight off leaving the barn in darkness. Running to the ladder, she put her hands out after ten steps and felt for the ladder. In a few seconds, she found it and scurried up the ladder as fast as she could. While she was running, she heard Leroy come over to TJ to check if he was going to be okay.

TJ was in pain, but he was rallying around, cursing, and shouting, "Missy, you're going to pay for this!"

"She ran over to the other side, and it sounded like she went up the ladder. I think she is in the loft," Leroy told TJ.

"Well, then she's trapped," TJ said.

Carly's first thought was that she was safe. But now she realized that she had to protect herself or climb out of the second story to the outside. There was a window with a pulley: perhaps she could cinch and climb outside. But then she thought, "*They have my rifle, and they can wait for me.*"

Leroy and TJ found the ladder in little time. "I'm going up to get her. When I'm done, you can have a turn before I finish her," TJ told Leroy.

Leroy made another attempt to change TJ's mind. "TJ, let's just get her car and leave."

Carly didn't want to turn on the flashlight. Her eyes had adjusted to the dark, and she saw the pitchfork that Clark had used earlier in the day embedded in a bale of hay. She walked over and struggled, but on the third attempt she pulled it out. Clark was becoming stronger each day at the farm and had pushed the pitch fork deep in the bale.

She heard TJ climbing up the ladder—it sounded like he was halfway up to the loft. Carly held the pitchfork out in front of her and slowly but surely walked toward the ladder until she was positioned three feet away.

She heard TJ cackling like this was the most fun he had in a while; it was an eerie cackle that sent shivers up her spine. The man was crazy. In two seconds, she saw the top of his head, then his whole upper body was exposed.

He paused as he looked at her. "Now we are going to have some good fun." Starting to come off the ladder and up into the loft.

Carly was frozen for two seconds. Her mind argued with itself. *"I can't! But you must!"* Her inner voice went back and forth ten times. Finally, she knew she had no choice if she wanted to see her family again. Carly would have to do some things she didn't think she could do. Gritting her teeth, she took two steps forward and with all her strength, thrust the pitchfork in TJ's chest. His verbal threats were replaced with gurgles. Carly took two steps back and pulled the pitchfork out from his chest. It came out of TJ, and he fell and dropped to the ground with a thud.

She stopped and waited for Elroy to climb the ladder. Seconds after TJ fell to the floor in a thud, she heard Elroy ask, "TJ?"

Then, "You crazy bitch!"

Carly waited with the pitchfork. Her adrenaline was pumping and she was ready for Elroy. She could hear every noise in the barn, from the cows to the crickets. Her body and senses were on high alert. She didn't hear him coming up the steps, but she could hear footsteps. Then she heard the sound of running footfalls outside the barn door.

She walked over to the barn window and tried to cautiously peer out to the side of the window. Carly saw a shadow of a figure running toward the main road. The front porchlight was the only light source and Elroy soon disappeared from sight. Carly turned the flashlight on and shined it on everything in the barn below and then again out the window into the farmyard. It looked clear. She went back to the ladder and climbed down quickly. The rifle was gone. Elroy had taken it.

Carly ran across the yard, opened the front door, and went inside the house and locked it. Finley was prepared to give her a big greeting but she couldn't stop and enjoy it. She found her pistol in the bedroom and opened up the closet and got out the shotgun. Once she had her weapons loaded, she grabbed her cell phone.

Carly called the sheriff's office and told them what had happened, then called Clark to let him know. Clark didn't pick up, and she guessed he couldn't hear his phone ring over the music. The dispatcher was going to call the sheriff and send someone over. Carly now sat down with her pistol on the end table and shotgun lying on the floor. She hugged Finley and cried, crying out of relief that she was alive and crying because she was forced to take a life.

Chapter 57

Brownfield Texas

Fifteen minutes later Finley heard a sound in the distance. He trotted over to the front door with his ears up and tail wagging. Thirty seconds later, Carly heard cars approaching the house. She went to the window: with the porch lights on, she was able to identify two sheriff's cars. She kept Finley inside the house and had her shotgun positioned over her left arm as she walked out onto the porch. There were two deputies: one that she recognized who was about six feet four inches and slim with sandy colored, close cropped hair, clean shaven and young. Carly thought that he looked twenty-five, but he must have been thirty. The other deputy was about six feet, with dark hair and an average build. He looked even younger. He must have been in his early twenties.

The tall deputy got out of his car and walked halfway from his car to the front porch where Carly was standing. He was cognizant that she had the shotgun draped across her arm, but Carly didn't care. She wasn't in a mood to trust people she didn't know.

The tall deputy stopped ten feet from the porch. He looked up at Carly. "Ma'am, did you call 911 fifteen minutes ago?"

Carly nodded. The other deputy remained standing by his car. The tall deputy decided to risk coming another ten feet to the edge of the porch. He looked at her expectantly, waiting for her to speak.

Carly told a quick version of the story: Finley hearing the noise, Carly walking to the barn, the open pen door, getting the cow in, being attacked, getting away, and killing one of the convicts while the other got away. She was talking fast—in two minutes, the deputy's mind was swimming with questions.

When she was finished talking, he waited five seconds to make sure that was all she had to report. "Which way did the other guy run?"

Carly pointed down the road. "He was running down the road and I eventually lost sight of him."

The tall deputy told the younger one, "Why don't you take the flashlight and walk along the road and see if you find any tracks?" The deputy opened the car door and found his flashlight. With gun in hand, he followed the road, looking at tracks and stopping periodically to look around the area.

The tall deputy turned to Carly. "The sheriff will be here in about ten minutes. Why don't you take me into the barn and show me step by step what happened." Carly led him to the barn and on the way her phone rang.

"Clark."

"Are you okay?" asked Clark.

"Yes, Clark. The deputies are here now—be careful when you come back."

"I'm leaving now," said Clark.

Carly continued into the barn and brought the deputy to the body of the dead convict. She showed him the pen and how she had found the gate open with Daisy. She showed him the spot where TJ had accosted her, and then went through her escape to the loft. As the deputy came down the loft, she heard another car pull up in the driveway. She followed the deputy out the barn door. The sheriff had arrived. He stepped out of his car, surveyed the area, then looked at both Carly and his deputy as they approached him. The tall deputy told Carly that she could wait on the porch while he filled in the sheriff.

Carly walked to the porch and opened the door for Finley. He came outside to check the visiting cars and to visit the two law officers, who both pat him on the head to satisfy him. They continued into the barn and Finley came back and settled down near Carly as she sat down on a porch chair.

In minutes Carly saw three cars come up the drive. One vehicle was Clark and there were some other young men and women in the other two vehicles. Clark pulled up, climbed out of his vehicle, and came over and gave Carly a hug. Finley acted like he hadn't seen Clark for days—he had to get recognition from Clark before he settled down. This evening held more excitement than Finley was used to.

The sheriff and deputy came back out and saw that they now had eight more people gathered. Clark looked at his friends and told the sheriff, "We would all like to help find this guy."

The sheriff looked at them. "I will need to talk to Carly alone right now to clear a few questions. I may need your help if you can wait ten minutes."

Clark and his friends went up and sat on the end of the porch. The sheriff took Carly off to the side and had her repeat her story. He wanted to see if there was anything new from what she had told the deputy. He told

Carly that they'd have a medical examiner out to check the crime scene, so it was important not to disturb the barn. As they wrapped things up, the dark-haired deputy returned from down the road. Walking quickly with his flashlight, he motioned for the sheriff and tall deputy to come over, and they had a two-minute discussion.

Finally, the sheriff came over to Carly and motioned for Clark and his friends to gather around him. He pointed to the younger, smaller deputy who spoke. "I found a car broken down about a mile down the road. We'll need to examine it thoroughly, but it appears they were driving down the road and had car trouble. They left the car and hiked back to your turn off with the intent to steal a vehicle and continue. It would seem that one of them got sidetracked and focused on you."

The sheriff looked at Clark and his friends and then back at his two deputies. "The three of us are all that is available tonight in the county. We have one deputy out on personal time off, and another ill at the hospital. I could use some help. I need armed people that I can deputize. We need to find this convict. These convicts have been a high priority for law enforcement in Texas. I have someone contacting the prison for photographs. I could use twenty people right away. If you could call neighbors or friends that could come here right away, that would be appreciated. I'll deputize all of you at once, and we'll split up routes to search for the convict."

Clark and his friends got on their phones. One car left with the three girls and the two guys took off in the other car and advised that they were grabbing their rifles and would return. Clark looked at Carly. "I'm going to join them."

"Clark, I would like you to stay here," Carly responded.

Clark had his jaw set. "No, this needs to be done. We are in Texas now. Our lives have changed and now I'm here. This is something I want to do and *must* do to make sure he doesn't hurt anyone else."

The two deputies left the farm to look at the convict's broken down car for clues. The convict was traveling on foot, but they hoped they might find something helpful for the search. Carly looked at the sheriff and suggested that she make some coffee. Clark, the sheriff, Carly, and Finley went inside to the kitchen. Carly had the sheriff sit down in a chair by the kitchen table as she started a fresh pot of coffee and gave Finley one of his favorite dog biscuits.

Within thirty minutes they had about twenty-five people out in front of the ranch house. It looked like a parking lot with about fifteen cars parked outside. She saw neighbors, including McGregor, and others she recognized from the town. There were a number of Clark's friends (all in their early twenties) and behind McGregor was a man that looked to be seventy-five years old. He stood perfectly straight and tall, his Stetson perched upon his head.

The deputies drove back down the road to the farm and found a place to park their car. They took the sheriff into Carly's living room, where he listened to their verbal report before he walked outside to the porch.

"Gentlemen, my deputies didn't find much in the car. It was stolen, and there was a map of Texas. It appears they were en route to El Paso and then across the border to Juarez."

All of a sudden, the sheriff was interrupted by his phone. He received a text message to call the dispatcher immediately. Walking to his car, the sheriff asked everyone to give him a minute.

He called in and had a brief conversation. When it ended, he quickly got out of his car and addressed the crowd assembled in front of the farmhouse.

"A truck was just carjacked four miles down the road by a guy with a rifle. It was Jensen who was hijacked—as he was shutting the gate to his farm. Sounds like it could be our convict. He shot Jensen and then took off south in the direction of Wellman. Jenson is in critical condition: they don't know if he'll make it but he was coherent and talking when they found him. He said he got one shot off but doesn't think he hit the convict."

"Jenson drives a white F150," the old man offered.

The sheriff had all the men raise their hands and he deputized them on the spot. He had a few rules: that they travel in twos or threes, that they drove safely and didn't do anything reckless that could hurt the citizens in Brownfield's county, that they make sure not to get killed and that each group had to call in every thirty minutes.

The sheriff planned to stay at Carly's farm and use it as a command center for the night. His young dark-haired deputy would take one of the sworn deputies with him to the entrance of Jenson's farm to get more information on Jenson's truck and what had happened. They left immediately.

The tall deputy took two sworn deputies and traveled toward Wellman.

There were multiple dirt roads and directions leading to Wellman. The sheriff took the sworn deputies and gave each a route. Each pairing was given a team number with their names and a central cell phone number for them to call and check in every thirty minutes. Each group wrote down their personal phone numbers on the sheriff's notebook.

In five minutes, the dark-haired deputy called the sheriff. He had the description of Jenson's stolen truck confirmed as the white F150, but he also had the license plate number.

The sheriff had a detailed map of his county and had them follow what he thought was the main route. Now that they knew the convict was in a vehicle, he would put out an alert to all towns within a fifty-mile radius to look for Jenson's truck and plate number.

It was now just the sheriff and Carly—she was busy making another pot of coffee for the sheriff. The medical examiner would arrive in thirty minutes. Carly thought that it was getting late and the ME might also want coffee. She brought the sheriff another fresh cup outside to his car and noticed he looked animated. As she came closer to the sheriff, she heard the excitement in his voice as he called several of his deputies on the phone. He finally paused and told Carly, "The truck was spotted going through Wellman—he's headed for Seminole. From there he will most likely go south to Odessa or east to Hobbs, New Mexico."

He called the sheriff's at both locations and shared this information. He asked them to set up a roadblock outside their towns and emphasized that the man was armed and dangerous.

The sheriff called all the deputies, who were abandoning their previous routes and moving toward the latest sighting. The deputy teams would be divided: half en route to Odessa, and the other half to Hobbs. The sheriff had a hunch and asked his tall deputy to head toward Hobbs.

The ME arrived and was shown to the barn by the sheriff. After a couple of minutes, the sheriff left the medical examiner to do his work and returned to his car and radio.

Clark was riding with one of his buddies in a truck. The tall deputy gave them instructions to continue to Hobbs. They were following behind the deputy and had four other cars following behind them. As they rode along, they looked for a white Ford F150 truck. Clark looked for any road or sign of a truck pulling off. They were driving along and suddenly the deputy in front of them was heavy on his brakes as he slowed down. They could see another car ahead of the deputy blocking the road. There was a man standing alongside the road, waving for the deputy.

They saw a nearby dirt road and assumed the man was a deputy from Hobbs. Their tall deputy pulled his car over, parked and peered down the road as all the cars behind him pulled off the road and waited for instructions. The deputy waved for all the men to come toward him.

After they were gathered, the deputy informed them, "Our convict saw the roadblock before entering the town of Hobbs, so he stopped and turned the truck around. A deputy followed and saw him turn down this road. This road goes down a mile to a farm. I think from here we need to go on foot. The Hobbs deputy heard some shots, but it's been quiet since."

The Hobbs deputy and two sworn deputies remained at the road entrance. The Hobbs deputy parked his car to create a roadblock on the dirt road to the farm so that the convict could not drive out. The tall Brownfield deputy had eleven deputies in his posse, and the Hobbs deputy advised that there were some trees around the farmhouse. There was also a barn and a few sheds. If they continued down the road, they would approach the front of the house.

The deputy planned to take four men with him and travel up the road. He had one group of three men to the left of the road one hundred yards, where they would watch the left side of the house and also keep an eye out for a backdoor exit. The remaining five would walk carefully one hundred yards to the right. Off on the right were the barn and sheds, which they would have to examine thoroughly. Clark and his buddies were in the group of five: they walked one hundred yards to the right of the road and fanned out ten yards apart from each other as they started moving toward the farm.

They walked slow and steady through the fields. The plan was to give them twenty minutes to clear the barn and sheds before they would text confirmation to the tall deputy. The tall deputy would be waiting in position fifty yards outside the house. Clark and his two buddies planned to first clear the barn; when they were done, the other two friends would clear the two sheds. If both the barn and sheds were clear, the five of them would move into position at the right and rear of the house.

Clark and his friends also had a plan. The three of them would step inside the barn, one on the right and two on the left. The other two would be on guard outside the barn. They'd need to move fast. They had their flashlights ready as they went in and searched the ground floor of the barn. Clark was on guard to the left as he and his friend searched through the pens and farm equipment. When he was finished, Clark motioned that he would climb up to the loft. He went slowly up each rung on the ladder, his eyes just above the loft floor. He scanned his flashlight left to right, and it looked clear. He pulled himself up all the way and searched more carefully. The loft stored just a few bales of hay, so Clark quickly gave a wave which signaled "all clear." The two men outside the barn searched the two sheds. Within five minutes they signaled that the sheds were clear.

Clark texted the tall deputy that the barn and sheds were clear. He received a quick response: he and his friends were instructed to get into position. Three of them continued and positioned themselves behind the house. Clark and one of his friends took the side of the house: Clark got on one knee by the barn door, his rifle focused on the front door. His friend focused on the side window.

The tall deputy hid behind bushes forty meters in front of the house. He called out, "You are surrounded! Come out with your hands up."

Within seconds the tall deputy received gunfire as a response, with a bullet striking his leg and causing him to fall down in the dirt. Another sworn deputy standing nearby also dropped down to his knees—shot in the arm.

At this point, all the deputies began firing toward the source of the gunfire which came from a front window. After thirty seconds, they paused. The tall deputy sent a text message communicating their next move: they should hold their position, wait, and then shoot again in two minutes. This message brought relief to the others that the tall deputy was okay.

Suddenly, in the silence of the night, they heard the convict's voice from inside the farmhouse. "I placed my gun down and I'm walking out."

"Keep your hands up high and where we can see them," the wounded deputy advised.

In ten seconds the convict walked out the front door, his hands empty and up in the air. Clark and the others kept him in their sights. Two of the sworn deputies in front of the house walked over to the convict and had him lay on the ground spread eagle. After searching him, they had him put his hands around his back and handcuffed his hands. Clark and the others surrounding the house came in as the deputy shouted for Clark and his buddies to go check inside the house.

Clark walked onto the porch. Glass scattered everywhere from the front window—in fact, there wasn't *any* glass remaining in the window, only shards sticking out from the window edges. As Clark and his team left the porch through the front door, they saw more glass on the living room floor. They went from room to room, saving the kitchen for last. There they found an older farmer and his wife. The farmer sat in a kitchen chair slumped over on the table with his head in a pool of blood, his wife dead on the kitchen floor under the sink. It looked like they had been surprised by the convict, who had shown no mercy but immediately shot and killed them both. Later it would be confirmed that the convict had left his car a half mile off the side of the road and surprised this couple in the kitchen. The couple had farmed and lived on the land their whole life.

Clark started to feel sick. He walked quickly out of the house to get some air, where he was followed by his two friends. The others gathered around the convict who was lying still on the ground.

Clark shook his head and one of the sworn deputies by the prisoner asked, "What did you find?"

"The husband and wife were shot and killed in the kitchen."

The group looked to the deputy hobbling on one leg. The other sworn deputy had a cloth tied around his wounded arm, which he said was just a flesh wound.

"What do we do now?" Someone asked.

"We'll take him back to Brownfield," the tall deputy answered matter-of-factly.

"Look, he killed two innocent and unarmed senior citizens tonight," one person commented. "That could grow to three people, if Jenson dies. He and his partner almost raped and killed a fourth person, and he also shot two of us."

"I say let's take care of this here and now," someone else suggested.

Clark looked around—he heard affirmation and saw others nodding in agreement.

"How should we do it?" One of the younger men asked.

An older, stocky farmer said, "Let us take him to the barn." He nodded at his friend who pulled the convict up to his feet and escorted him to the barn. As they held him in the barn, another sworn deputy found a rope, and then the older farmer took the rope and in minutes, created a noose.

Now everyone was in the barn, and Clark was speechless. They put the noose around the convict's head. The deputy had stopped protesting knowing that one of their farmers could still die along with the couple murdered in the farmhouse. He was guilty, and the punishment would be swift. The rope was thrown over a beam and then placed over the convict's neck and tightened. Six of the big farm boys grabbed the rope and hoisted the convict off the ground and then tied the rope to a post.

Clark watched for some time as the man choked and struggled—then he no longer moved. The mood wasn't celebratory in the barn: another life had been taken, but it had to be done. A few left to take the deputy and the other man to the hospital. After an hour, Clark and the rest of the sworn deputies left and walked up the road. They got into their vehicles and started back to Brownfield.

The sheriff knocked on the door. Carly answered and came out onto the porch. He looked at her and said abruptly, "Well, they caught him."

Carly waited for more information but realized that this was all he was going to say. "Are they bringing him back? Were others hurt?" She asked.

"No," he said. "They aren't bringing him back. He shot Jensen for the truck, and he killed a farming couple near Hobbs. He shot them dead in their kitchen."

Carly tried to digest the information. "So they shot and killed him."

He waited a few seconds. "No, they hung him."

Carly looked at him perplexed, hoping he would divulge more information.

"Ma'am, my preference was to bring him back to our jail and face a judge, but this is how things had been handled in Texas years ago. The last few decades we housed a lot of criminals in prison. But the world has changed, and we may be embracing some old traditions that were effective for many years. And one thing is for sure, we don't believe in repeat offenders in the Lone Star state, perhaps it's best to just take care of things."

With that, he turned and walked to his car. He slid into the driver seat, turned on the ignition, and left in a hurry down the dirt road. Carly stood at the door and watched his taillights until they were no longer visible. The ME had left earlier so now she and Finley would wait for Clark to return home.

Chapter 58

South Dakota

ETHAN DROVE ALONG THE Interstate. After they left their relatives in Northern Wisconsin, they traveled across the northern part of the state into Minnesota and down the eastern side of North and South Dakota. Ethan and Mark received the latest news report from the sheriff of Escanaba: he thought it would take a little longer, but suggested they avoid Minneapolis,

Des Moines and Kansas City to be safer. So they traveled further west for the return trip to Texas.

They were having a good time traveling with their grandparents: there was a lot of time to update them on the farm in Brownfield, and about Abby and Ryan and what they knew about the situation with Jessica and her friends. They also shared what they knew about their father trying to cross the Atlantic to find Jessica.

Mark and Ethan went through all the details of the farm as they described downtown Brownfield and the people they had met. Their grandparents seemed excited to try a new adventure. Carly had warned Ethan and Mark before they had left that it could be difficult for the grandparents—losing their home and all the memorabilia would be difficult for them. Instead, they found the opposite reaction: perhaps it was all a good show, but Pa K and Ma K appeared to be excited to go see their daughter and the farm in Texas.

Once they reached Omaha, they stopped for lunch and to fuel up. As they waited for their sandwiches at the deli, Mark studied the map with Ethan. They would take smaller farm roads from Omaha to Wichita to avoid Kansas City. There was a concerted effort to clean up Kansas City, but the current guidance was that it was best to avoid it.

They finished eating their sandwiches and drinks and were back in the vehicle to continue their journey. The sun was peeking out through the clouds. Grandma had lived in Kansas as a girl—she warned the boys that it would be flat and mostly miles and miles of farmland.

Two hours later, as they neared the border of Nebraska and Kansas, steam started to come up from the hood of the vehicle. The two-lane road was deserted as Ethan pulled over to the shoulder of the road. Grabbing an extra T-shirt from his backpack, he and Mark jumped out of the car to raise the hood. Pa K also came out and looked over their shoulders. Ethan told them to stand back as he raised the hood and jumped back two steps as hot steam escaped. Pa K suggested to look at the upper or lower radiator hose.

Grandma came out of the car, and they chose to sit down off the road for a few minutes to let the car cool off. It was an opportunity for her to tell them about where she had lived in Kansas and share some of her adventures as a girl.

After the truck had a chance to cool and the steam was gone, Ethan, Mark and Pa K walked over to look under the hood. They found the upper radiator hose had a crack and the truck had lost most of its coolant. They didn't have a spare hose, so they were temporarily stranded. Mark noticed that he didn't have cell coverage: he mentioned it to Ethan, who confirmed that he didn't have coverage either. They were trying to find a cool place to sit but there weren't any trees, and Ma K looked uncomfortable. Mark looked inside the truck and pulled out some bottled waters that they kept for an emergency and handed one to each of his grandparents.

After about thirty minutes a truck approached from the opposite direction. They waved their arms and the truck stopped on the road. A man that appeared to be in his midforties powered down his window. A Deere baseball cap covered his brown hair and he wore a brown and green flannel shirt with the sleeves rolled up.

"Having trouble with your vehicle?"

"Yes, sir, our upper radiator hose needs to be replaced," Ethan responded.

The farmer pulled over to his side of the road, got out, and walked over. Ethan showed him the hose and where it split.

"The closest town, if you can call it that, is about ten miles away. You go about four miles, and it's six miles off this road. I'm headed in that direction. I can drop one or two of you off at the garage and hopefully they can tow you in. It's midafternoon—I would suggest getting over there before they close up," the farmer suggested.

"Why don't you go with Ma K, and I'll wait with Pa K," Mark suggested.

Ethan nodded and asked Ma K what she wanted to bring. Ethan grabbed his backpack with handgun and walked over to Mark for a few words.

"Mark, be careful and stay armed. I'll be back as soon as I can. I'll try to get us towed to the garage. If not, I'll borrow or rent a car."

Ethan helped his grandmother climb into the middle of the truck and then hoisted himself into the passenger seat, backpack on his lap. The farmer took off toward the town. He made small talk and asked where they were from and then proceeded to say he was a fourth-generation farmer. Ma K shared with him where she had lived in Lawrence, Kansas as they exchanged stories.

Before long they came across a little town that had two motels, a grocery store, a sit-down restaurant, a fast food place, and two gas stations. One of the gas stations had a garage in the back. The farmer drove into this gas station. He got out and walked to the back of the garage while Ethan and Ma K climbed out of the truck. They followed the farmer about ten steps into the garage when Ethan saw that he was already returning with an older man in coveralls.

The coveralls may have been blue at one time. Ethan thought he saw a glimpse of blue on the shoulder straps, but the coveralls were all gray with grease and oil. The little old bald man must have been in his seventies. He wasn't completely bald—he had little white tufts of hair springing out on the edges of his head. The farmer made the introductions and then pre-pared to leave them. Ethan thanked him for the ride and shook his hand.

Ethan turned to the mechanic who had the name Earl fixed on his coveralls. The name of the gas station and garage was also Earl's, so Ethan surmised he was the owner. Ethan told him the story of what had happened and what he had observed with the hose, explaining that his grandfather and brother were stranded on the side of the road with the vehicle.

Earl listened, excused himself, and went back into the shop. He came out with a guy about 40 with dingy coveralls that also said "Earl." The older Earl pointed at the man. "This is my son, Earl Jr., and he will use our tow truck to pull you to the garage. What kind of truck are you driving? I'll most likely have to order the hose, but I can look through my inventory while you are gone.

Earl pointed at a small lobby. "Perhaps your grandmother would like to wait in there for you while you bring your brother and grandfather back? It's air conditioned and we have cold water."

Ethan looked at Grandma—she looked uncomfortable. He thought it was a good idea, so he took her over to the office. He got her a cold glass of water and found some magazines that were old but looked interesting enough to read. As he went back outside, the middle-aged Earl pulled up in the tow truck. Ethan walked over and opened the passenger door and climbed in.

Thirty minutes after Ethan and Grandma left, another truck came by with three young guys traveling at high speed. They stopped off the road and shouted out to Mark and Pa K, "You, guys, picnicking?"

Then to his friends, "We've got some folks from out of state here." The driver chuckled and got out of his vehicle with his two buddies. They walked toward Mark and Pa K.

Mark sized them up—he thought they were somewhere around his age. He could tell by their smirks that they were looking for trouble. Mark had his backpack near as he and Pa K sat under the cornstalks trying to escape some of the heat.

Mark realized the situation: he couldn't leave the truck with their rifle and shotgun. They couldn't outrun the guys and they were outnumbered as well. He had one advantage that they might not anticipate: his handgun.

He and Pa K rose from the ground. Their truck formed a barrier between them and the locals. Mark quickly took out his gun behind the truck and placed it behind his back. He whispered, "Pa K, don't get between them and me."

The guys approached the front of the truck. "So what's the problem?"

"A problem with a radiator hose. We have help on the way," Mark answered.

The young guy was about six feet one inch and 190 lbs. He acted like he was the hotshot in this part of the country. To make it worse, he thought he was a comedian as well. "We can check out the truck for you. It looks to me that you may be carrying too much stuff."

The hotshot looked at his friends. One was about five feet eight inches and weighted 150 lbs at most, while the other was about six feet two inches and 250 lbs. They didn't say anything, just smiled, chuckled, and nodded.

Hotshot started walking toward the truck door and the other two headed to the back of the truck to look at the luggage. Mark took a series of quick steps to the front of the truck so he would be on the same side as their visitors. As he did this, the ringleader stopped from opening the door.

"Guys, we don't need any help here. We just want to be left alone. Our preference is not to have any trouble," Mark said.

The ringleader spoke. "Well, you're refusing our hospitality. I feel insulted."

They were now about six feet away and the ringleader took a step forward. Mark slowly reached his right hand to his back and gripped the gun handle, ready to pull it out.

With perfect timing, they heard the tow truck approaching. They froze in place as Earl and Ethan drove up. Earl Jr. popped out and asked, "Is everything okay here?"

"We just stopped to offer our help." The ringleader answered.

"Thank you, I have it now." Earl Jr. responded.

The ringleader and his guys turned slowly and headed back to their truck. In a minute, they were gone. Earl Jr. looked at Mark and Grandpa. "Those guys are trouble. One of these days that boy is going to hurt some-one or get himself really hurt. He's the sheriff's son and he feels like he owns the county. My advice is, if you are able to, stay clear of him."

Before long they were headed back to the shop with Earl Jr. pulling their truck. Pa K and Mark rode with Earl Jr. in the tow truck and Ethan rode in their truck as it was pulled along to the garage. Once they arrived, the old Earl came out of the garage and if it were possible, it looked to Ethan like he had gotten more grease on him in the hour they'd been gone. Ma K saw them approach and walked out of the small lobby, grabbing Pa K's hand as she brought him into the air-conditioned lobby.

Mark and Ethan stood by and were quiet as the Earls opened the hood of the truck and looked around inside. After five minutes the old Earl said, "Looks like you, guys, are correct that you need an upper radiator hose. The lower also looks worn, and I would recommend changing both out at the same time."

He waited a few seconds. "Now the bad news. I don't have the parts and will have to have them shipped over from Omaha. I may need two days to get them here; then I'll need two hours to change them, fill your radiator with coolant, and run your engine for a ten-minute test."

Mark and Ethan looked at each other. They'd hoped to be home in two days—not stuck in this nameless farm town. They were tired and ready to end this trip.

Earl could see the disappointment in their faces. "There are two hotels, but I would choose the one on the north side of the town. It's very clean and not too expensive. Tell them that Earl is working on your truck and sent you over. My cousin owns it and she'll give you a good rate—they have a breakfast buffet, too. The burger place in town is good for lunch, and you can head to the diner in the evening for dinner. The proprietors own both the bar and the diner. On Friday and Saturday night the bar is hopping and the food is good. I'll try to rush the shipment of the hoses."

They thanked Earl and started to take their roller bags and suitcases from the truck. Then Ethan pulled out his Winchester, and Mark pulled out his shotgun. Earl raised his eyebrows.

Ethan needed to say something. "Earl, we've had quite the adventure the past two weeks. We're on a trip to bring our grandparents back with us to Texas, and we've had to travel to unsafe places."

Earl nodded. "I wouldn't walk around with those while in town the next couple days. Sheriff may get nervous with people in town walking around armed."

They thanked him again and Mark went into the air-conditioned lobby to get the grandparents. They had each grandparent pull their own roller bag and Ethan and Mark took two suitcases each along with their rifle, shotgun, and backpack. The town was small and nobody was on the street at that time of day.

In two blocks, they walked up to the motel. It was a single-story complex painted green and yellow, about seventy-five years old but well maintained. They left Mark with the rifle, shotgun, and bags while Ethan and the grandparents walked inside to the counter. There was an older woman filing some paperwork in a brown metal file cabinet, her back to the counter. When they opened the door, the chimes rang to alert her. She slowly turned around with a big smile and took the few steps to the counter.

Ethan greeted her with a "hello" and then added, "We are here for two or three nights while Earl orders some parts for our truck. He told us to come here and that you would take care of us."

She had a big smile that matched her twinkling eyes. She had long white hair that was thick and pretty. "Of course, I always take care of my cousin's customers. I'll give you a special rate. Would you like one room or two rooms?" She responded.

"Two rooms, please. One with double beds and one with a king or queen bed. My brother is waiting outside with our bags."

Within five minutes they had their keys to the rooms and were carrying their luggage through the doors. They were given adjacent rooms. It was now late afternoon, so they agreed that they would shower and change to fresh clothes. At 6:30 p.m. they would meet in the lobby and walk to the diner for dinner.

At 6:30 p.m. they met outside the doors and walked two blocks to reach Earl's. They walked one block further and found themselves at the diner. The parking lot was full and many of the tables were occupied. However, they were able to locate a booth and they piled in.

The table countertops were Formica and the seat cushions in the booth required reupholstering, but it was clean. The menu had comfort foods like pot roast, meatloaf, fried chicken, and pork chops. Mark looked at the menu and remarked, "Good thing Mom, Abby and Jessica aren't eating here."

They all laughed because it was definitely not a vegetarian friendly menu. They ate a hearty meal and the weather was nice walking back to the motel. They would have to kill time in town tomorrow and then hopefully the day after next the hoses would arrive so they could continue their journey.

In the motel room Ethan and Mark called their mom to give her the latest update. She was disappointed that they'd been delayed but relieved that they were fine. She was anxious for them to be home. They told her they too were ready to be back in Texas.

After the phone call ended, Ethan looked at Mark. "What was happening back at the truck when we pulled up?"

"Those guys were looking for trouble, and I was about two seconds from pulling my gun when you drove up," Mark responded. "Earl Jr. is right: they are trouble. We need to avoid them until we can get out of here."

They watched some old uninteresting TV reruns to unwind. Ethan and Mark were asleep within an hour.

Chapter 59

Farm town in Nebraska

THE NEXT DAY WAS boring. The group ate breakfast, and then read magazines in the motel lobby. Midmorning, they went to the grocery store and bought some picnic items, then walked to the city park. The park had some large trees with a couple of picnic tables where they sat around and relaxed. Pa K took a nap in the shade of the tree and afterward they had lunch and relaxed further until about 3:00 p.m. Then they packed the rest of their food in the backpacks and walked back to the motel. On the way back, they stopped by Earl's and he told them the parts had shipped from Omaha and were scheduled to arrive at ten the next morning. With any luck, they'd be on the road between noon and 1:00 p.m.

After showering and watching the television in their rooms for a couple of hours, they left for the diner. It was Friday night and the parking lot was packed with patrons for both the diner and the bar. All the tables were full, so they put their names down at the register. After a thirty-minute wait, they were seated at a booth.

The menu was the same, so they chose their second choice from the menu. The food was delicious but heavy. It was definitely not low calorie, so they were secretly happy that this would be their last meal there.

When they were only halfway through their meal, there was some commotion in the parking lot. Ethan, Mark, and the grandparents had a booth by the window and could see a bouncer from the bar ushering three young guys out to the parking lot. There were words exchanged that they couldn't understand.

Mark quickly recognized them and told the others, "Those are the guys that stopped by the truck and were trying to cause trouble."

The young guys stood in the parking lot for a couple of minutes contemplating if they should challenge the bouncer or go somewhere else. One of them spoke and they turned and started walking toward the door of the diner. Ethan and Mark watched them closely as they walked up to the counter and ordered coffees. A waitress at the register left them temporarily to pour coffees to go. The ringleader leaned against the counter and surveyed the dining room. Ethan and Pa K had their back to them and Mark tried not to look at the guy who was forty feet away. But he could tell that the guy's eyes were locked on him.

The ringleader said something to the others and pointed over at the corner booth. The guys continued with the comments and then the three walked over.

Mark looked at Ethan and said, "They're coming over. All three of them, and they look drunk." Ethan and Mark were sitting at the ends of the booth: they stood up and Ethan turned around.

"Don't get up and don't say anything. But when you have a clear path, quickly exit the restaurant and walk the block toward Earl's. We'll follow," Ethan told the grandparents.

The ringleader was in front, his two sidekicks at his hip. Ethan and Mark gave themselves some room with their hands loose and in front of their bodies as the guys approached their table. Ethan and Mark had left their guns in their rooms, so their first choice now was to avoid any confrontation.

The ringleader came within five feet. "Guys, look who is still here in our town. More trouble with your truck?"

"It's getting fixed and we'll be leaving town soon," Mark responded.

It was obvious that these guys were looking for trouble. "So you don't like our town, and you can't get out fast enough. Are you trying to insult us again?"

"No insult intended," Ethan chimed in. "We are on a journey and so we'd like to continue as soon as we're able. We've enjoyed our stay here and soon we'll move on."

Ethan and Mark moved their hands up to their chest high with the palms facing out. Nobody noticed but they slowly positioned their feet in a good balanced stance. They were both cycling through possible options if they couldn't diffuse the situation. Independently, they noticed the fire extinguisher five steps to the left. There were two exits. The front door and counter were blocked by the three troublemakers. With the grandparents in tow, they knew they couldn't make a quick escape.

They weren't going to go away easily. "Where are you headed to?" The short sidekick asked.

"Look, we don't want any trouble. We just want to finish our meal and move on. Perhaps we can buy you a cup of coffee?" Ethan offered.

The manager of the diner came over. She was about thirty-ish and small, but she had some spunk as she spoke loudly to the three punks. "Your coffees are ready over at the counter."

The ringleader didn't take her bait—he couldn't let it go. "These guys have insulted us too many times now."

The ringleader took a swing at Mark. Mark was waiting—he reacted quickly and pushed the guy's right wrist away with his left hand so that it missed his face. Simultaneously Mark hit him in the nose with his right open palm. After successful contact, Mark hit the face again with his right fist and used his left fist for a solid blow to the man's ribs, followed by a right forearm to the ringleader's Adams' apple. In seconds the ringleader was down on all fours, gasping, blood pouring from his nose.

At the same time, the big friend came at Ethan. Ethan kicked him in the groin as he approached and the big guy dropped to his knees. Ethan used his knee to come up to his chin and heard some crunching. In a second the guy was out and lying on the floor. Ethan moved a couple of steps to his left and in seconds pulled the fire extinguisher off the wall to use as a weapon.

After the ringleader went down, the small guy took a step toward them, then thought twice, as he took two steps back and looked at his friends on the floor. He looked at Mark, who was in a ready fighting stance, and then at Ethan with the fire extinguisher. He did a quick calculation and then put up his hands and said, "We are done," before exiting the diner.

Mark helped his grandparents climb out of the booth and escorted them out the door. Ethan followed with the fire extinguisher and walked to the front door. He asked the manager who was now standing behind the counter, "How much do we owe for dinner?"

"It's on the house and I'm so sorry." Then she added, "Here, take the coffees." Ethan set down the fire extinguisher, took the tray with the three coffees and walked out the door.

Neither of the grandparents wanted a coffee, so Ethan threw one in the trash. He gave Mark one and kept one for himself as they quickly walked back to the motel.

At the end of the parking lot, Ma K stopped. "Where in the heck did you learn those moves?"

"It was over in seconds. It happened so quick, it was like a blur," she added.

"Was that the martial arts class that you, guys, took? And that you invited your Dad to join your training?" Pa K interjected.

Ethan nodded as they continued walking out of the parking lot and down the main street toward the motel.

Once inside the motel lobby, they went to the counter and hit the bell. The owner came out smiling. Ethan quickly told her the story and she agreed that she wouldn't confirm to anyone whether on the phone or in person that they were staying at her motel. She knew the sheriff's son and his friends and called them hoodlums. She went into her register and erased their names and reentered different names.

Ethan and Mark told Pa K and Ma K not to open the door for anyone and that they would see them in the morning. Mark and Ethan went back into their room and checked their handguns and rifle and shotgun. They were ready for more trouble tonight if it came, but they really just wanted to get out of town and on the road to Texas.

As they were preparing for bed, Mark looked over to Ethan. "I never knew whether we'd ever use it, but our Krav Maga training has paid off. All those hours of training and the bloody mouths that we regularly gave each other in the classes equipped us."

There was a pause as each recalled the hard work they had put in with two hours of training three times a week. The repetition had made the reaction natural.

Ethan nodded and added, "I hope Dad recalls the Krav training in case he needs it in Slovenia."

Mark nodded. "I think he will. Remember that special weekend where they had one of the top Krav trainers from Israel? He was having us go hard at Dad while Dad was defending. He was shouting at us, "Go harder! You may be saving your Dad's life! Go harder!"

Ethan smiled and got into bed and turned off the light at the end table. "Hopefully, we helped him."

* * * * *

The next morning, they ate breakfast in the lobby and then returned to their rooms. Ethan had called Earl's at 10:30 a.m. to make sure the parts had arrived and confirmed when they would be ready to leave. They checked out of the motel at noon and walked with their luggage to Earl's.

Earl pulled his head out from under the hood when Mark greeted him.

"I'm almost done. I've replaced the hoses and I just filled the radiator with coolant. I'd like to run the engine and if there aren't any leaks, I'll recheck that you have enough coolant in your radiator. Then you can be on your way."

Earl added, "By the way, the sheriff came by asking about you, guys, early this morning. I told a white lie that you wouldn't get your truck until midafternoon. I heard his son and friend went to the county hospital last night. The sheriff is angry, despite everyone in the diner telling him that his son picked the fight, and you guys attempted to stop it. Anyways, my advice for you is to get in the car and to drive hard and get out of our county and over into Kansas."

In fifteen minutes, they had packed their bags in the truck. Earl gave them a "thumbs up" and Ethan paid him and shook his hand. Both Ethan and Mark were armed and ready and the grandparents were tucked in the back seat.

Ethan pulled out of Earl's and headed down the main street maintaining the speed limit and then once outside the city, he increased speed and moved the truck along at a good clip. They were not stopping in this county for the sheriff or anyone else. He finally relaxed when he saw the sign that they were entering Kansas.

Ma K now popped up and leaned forward from the back of her seat. She would be the tour guide through the state of Kansas.

Mark looked over at Ethan and said, "I'll be glad when we are in Oklahoma and then, Texas."

Chapter 60

Madeira Island, Portugal

THERE WAS EXCITEMENT TODAY from everyone. Dan had shared yesterday evening that he thought they would reach Madeira the next day. They had been out to sea for a while, so this news brought a little spring in everybody's step. Lisa and Ali had spotted seagulls midmorning, and Dan told them to keep an eye out for the Island. Lisa and Ali had been looking for two hours now and Ali shouted that he saw some land: an island in the distance.

Other than a couple of days with the storm, they had been able to catch fish to supplement their food. They had eaten well. Chris couldn't wait for fresh fruits and vegetables as it had been five days since they had eaten their last produce. Lisa created a few different lists for them once they reached port. She had food lists and a supplies list to make sure nothing was forgotten. Dan had placed her in charge of this and when the guys thought of something they needed, they went to Lisa during the voyage to make sure it was on the list.

Mike and Chris were on deck and stood next to Dan who guided them toward the island. Chris brewed a fresh pot of coffee and they enjoyed a cup in the sun as they closed in on the south side of the Island. Dan told them that they would dock at Funchal, the capital of Madeira Island.

Funchal Harbor was considered one of the two most spectacular harbors in the world: considered on par with Rio de Janeiro. The harbor and port had been popular with guests since the fifteenth century and early explorers. Funchal's population was a little over 100,000, so it was not a small town. Before the terrorist attacks, it had been a frequent stop for cruise lines.

"I can't wait until I can walk on land!" Lisa exclaimed.

"I can't wait to eat an apple or orange," Mike added.

The harbor was soon in focus and the mountains were a spectacular backdrop. They froze and watched as Dan brought them close to the harbor. When they were close enough, they dropped the sails, and Dan started the motor, bringing them into the harbor and dock. Mike had the passports and boat documents ready for the officials.

Within thirty minutes of landing, they had the port official on the boat: he checked their papers and welcomed them to Funchal. Dan asked who could give them a safety report regarding travel to Barcelona and the official recommended that they visit the port office midafternoon for the latest update.

It was decided that Mike, Ali, and Lisa would head out first to eat lunch and to shop for groceries. Mike would use his ATM to get some euros for shopping and they would reimburse him later.

Chris would help Dan on some of the boat maintenance, then they would wash off and dry the sails. Dan was a stickler for boat maintenance. After experiencing the storm at sea and how they were at nature's mercy, Chris was supportive of Dan in making sure the boat was in tiptop condition.

In three hours Mike, Ali, and Lisa were back from their errands and had many bags of groceries in their full backpacks. They brought them aboard, and Dan suggested that Ali and Lisa put away the groceries while he, Chris, and Mike visited the port office.

Walking down the pier, they found the office. Mike opened the door and the three of them funneled on through. There was a woman at the counter, and the officer that had been on their boat three hours earlier was on the phone at a back desk. Another officer was positioned at a front desk where he was focused and swearing at a computer screen.

Dan, Mike, and Chris walked up to the counter. The woman glanced up.

"Olà," Chris offered.

Chris figured hello would be his only recognizable word in Portuguese and so he asked, "Do you speak English?"

"Yes, I speak English," she responded. "My name is Matilde." She was about thirty with dark, thick black hair. She was five feet maximum and had big brown eyes, a medium build, and a great smile.

Dan took the lead. "We just traveled from across the Atlantic. We plan to stay here two days, but then we must move through the Strait of Gibralter to Barcelona. We'd like to know if there are any concerns for us, and we'd welcome any safety or traveling advice."

The man at the front desk had stopped looking at his computer screen and now looked at them and stood up: he was about six inches taller than the woman at the counter, had short dark hair, an olive complexion, and a short goatee. He walked over to them and said something to the woman in Portuguese.

When he finished talking, she translated for the three of them. "Rodrigo understands English but is more comfortable speaking in Portuguese. He gathers all the reports for the Strait and the Mediterranean Sea."

She reached under the counter and pulled out a map, spreading it out on the counter in front of Dan, Mike and Chris. Rodrigo walked over to the counter and took his right index finger and pointed to where they stood in the city of Funchal. Tracing his finger toward the Strait, he said something to Matilde as he continued his finger along the coast of Spain until he came to Barcelona. After about two minutes of conversation, he was quiet.

Matilde shared, "The path to the Strait should be easy. However, once you're near the Strait, you must be careful. First, you must pay attention to the traffic as you travel through the Strait. Second, be careful for other boats that may try to board you. The boats could hold pirates, but there are also a lot of refugees trying to escape Africa. They will be on rafts and small boats looking for safe passage to Spain or Portugal. It may break your heart, but you should not stop and let them board. This could be very dangerous."

Dan, Mike, and Chris looked at each other. Matilde added, "Not only could they be armed, but they could carry the virus that is not contained yet in West Africa."

At that point, Rodrigo lost interest and went back to his computer screen. Matilde looked at them, waiting to see if she had answered everything or if they would have more questions.

Chris took the opportunity. "How safe is it in Europe?"

Matilde thought for several seconds and Chris thought perhaps she wouldn't answer. "Portugal is safe. Spain is dangerous in Madrid and Barcelona. Most large cities are still having issues with terrorists. Airlines are still grounded, but most trains are running. The trains are heavily guarded and if you buy a ticket, they can search you at their discretion. The coast is dangerous because of refugees trying to escape Africa. And you probably know that Russia is trying to create the old Soviet Union. They've claimed all their old borders and we hear that some countries have resistance fighters in rural areas."

She added, "Of course, do not think of traveling to those areas."

Chris thought that she had provided a lot of terrific information to them, and he felt by the expression on her face that she wanted to know more about them. "Why brave the trip over the Atlantic at this time?" She couldn't help to ask.

"I have my fiancée in Barcelona and I came to get her. My friends came to help," Dan responded.

"Mike and I have business meetings in Europe, so it worked out well for everyone," Chris added.

Matilde looked at Mike and Chris. They hadn't shaved in a while and Chris was certain they smelled bad from being out in the ocean for a couple of weeks. Chris could see her mind working as she tried to figure out what kind of business they were in and why conducting business at this time was so important. However, she let it go.

Mike wrapped up the conversation. "Thank you, Matilde." He looked over at Rodrigo and waved and said, "Thank you."

They received a half wave from Rodrigo, whose eyes were glued to his screen. Matilde was frozen at the counter watching them leave as they walked out and closed the door.

Chris looked over at Dan and Mike. "She seems suspicious of us. We haven't done anything illegal, but she makes me nervous. Let's make sure we keep alert—be ready for an impromptu search."

"We need to make sure our money is hidden." Mike added. "Lisa deposited most of hers, but the rest of us are all still carrying a significant amount. Should we put some more of our money in the bank?"

Chris and Dan nodded.

Dan responded, "Yes, we should use the bank as long as they have branches in southern Europe."

Chris thought about this. "I need to keep enough cash because we may not be able to use the banks in Slovenia."

They walked back to the boat where Lisa and Ali were sitting on a bench next to Dan's boat, talking. Mike asked, "What is next on the list for today?"

Dan had no question about the top three items on his list. "Laundry, showers, and dinner."

They quickly agreed with a plan. First, they had to take showers. Then they would visit the bank, and afterward run their specific errands before dinner on shore that night.

They grabbed soap, shampoo, and towels and headed to the shower area. The men shaved and showered and in twenty minutes they felt refreshed, even if their clothes were still musty. Meanwhile, Lisa took a full fifteen minutes in the shower.

Dan had a couple of items that he wanted to buy at the supply shop for the boat. Since the boat was the top priority for their transportation and safety it was on the must-do list.

Ali and Lisa had laundry duty. They would be responsible for everyone's laundry, to wash and dry the clothes and then return to the boat. They wasted no time procuring directions to the laundromat.

Mike used the water hose at the pier and started washing the top deck of the boat. He had the bucket and brush to assist on any sticky or difficult spots for cleaning. He planned to stay behind for the first watch as the others left the boat.

Ali and Lisa had three pillow cases of laundry for themselves and Mike. Dan and Chris each carried their laundry bag along with their backpacks and money. They stopped at the bank first, where Dan, Ali, and Chris deposited money and took out some euros for spending. Chris took out 1,500 euros because he thought he might need the money in an emergency. The process took only thirty minutes because the bank wasn't crowded.

Two blocks away they came to the laundry area: they left Ali and Lisa with the five pillow cases of laundry and some euros for the wash. Dan headed to the boat supply store on his own and said he would meet everyone back at the boat. Chris planned to head back to the boat to relieve Mike and let him go to the bank before it closed.

Matilde unsettled Chris a little and he didn't know exactly why. Perhaps he was now always alert and on edge.

Mike was finishing his work on the deck as Chris arrived. Chris took over for Mike and gave him directions to the bank. Mike would also shop and buy breakfast items.

After he finished cleaning the deck, Chris brought up his gun and thoroughly cleaned it as he waited for Dan and Mike. If the boat was the top priority, then the guns were a close second. Chris assumed that Lisa and Ali would be with the laundry for a while.

Thirty minutes later, Dan showed up. He stored away his supplies and fifteen minutes later, Mike returned from the bank and grocery store.

Dan and Chris left Mike with the boat and headed back to town. Dan said he had been dreaming of a steak for the past week, so they walked along until he found a place that met his approval. They grabbed a table and ordered beers and salads. Dan had a steak and Chris had half of a roasted chicken. They needed a break from fish for a day. They had a nice table on the porch overlooking the street where they could people watch. Sitting at a side table, however, everyone noticed them. Many glanced over—even people walking down the street spotted them as they passed by.

Chris tried to understand why. "What do you think it is? Is it the clothes?" He asked Dan.

"I think it's the clothes." Dan agreed. "We need to buy some new clothes tomorrow."

After their dinner, they stopped by the laundry area. Ali and Lisa had three bags of laundry done. Lisa's, Chris's, and Ali's were ready. Lisa shared that they were almost finished with Dan's and Mike's.

Dan and Chris took the three finished bags back to the boat, where Mike was enjoying the fresh air and cleaning his guns. Dan put Lisa's bag on her bunk and went up to the deck; Chris heaved Ali's laundry onto his bunk and then Chris took the time to put away his fresh clothes.

When Chris had finished packing his laundry, he climbed the wooden steps up to the deck and sat down next to Mike and Dan. Dan was talking to Mike about the next day.

"Tomorrow, I'd like to buy some paint and have you guys paint the boat where it needs touch up. I have a couple of things to fix and I think we should all buy some new clothes. Yes, we may need more underwear and socks, but we also need some European shirts, pants, and shoes."

Ten minutes later they saw two silhouettes carrying a bag each. It was Lisa and Ali with the rest of the laundry. Chris stayed up on deck while the other four put away their clothes.

Ali, Mike, and Lisa left for dinner. Chris and Dan had enjoyed their meal so much that they gave directions and the name of the establishment.

After they left, Dan went down and grabbed two beers. They sat up on the deck and enjoyed the trade winds, talking about their work back in the States, about their company and if they would change work, or even if work would be available since their territory in San Diego was now gone.

After some thought, Dan spoke. "I'm ready for a change. If Maria is willing, we'll stay in Florida and start a family. I don't want to travel for work. I'd like to stay in tech, but will look for something closer to home."

"I thought I was near retirement," Chris volunteered. "When I get back, I'll have to discuss with Carly and understand what opportunities are available. There are too many loose ends right now. My only goal for now is to get Jessica back to Texas and hopefully have the whole family safe in the US,"

As he concluded his thought, Chris saw two figures approach them. He checked to make sure that he had his gun and felt relieved when he felt it. The two figures were walking toward them and Chris didn't know why, but he knew they were heading specifically for them and not for another boat on the dock. Dan noticed that Chris was fixated on something and turned his head to follow his gaze.

As the two people came closer, Chris could see that it was Matilde and Rodrigo. They were both armed and walking toward them. Dan and Chris stared at them and when they stopped at the dock ten feet from them Chris said hello.

"Is everything okay?" Matilde asked.

"Yes, we had dinner and now the rest of our crew is eating while we relax. We like Funchal," Dan replied.

Chris held up his right arm to expose his beverage and asked, "Do you want a beer?"

Rodrigo obviously knew the word "beer" because he smiled and said "Sim," as he climbed aboard.

Matilde had no choice and followed him aboard. Chris set his beer down and went below into the cabin where he grabbed two cold ones, popped off the bottle caps with the opener and came up and handed the beers over. Rodrigo took a big gulp and smiled, raising his hand for a salute before draining the rest of the beer. He looked at Chris like he was ready for another.

Chris thought they might have to go buy more beer if Rodrigo planned on staying awhile. Chris went down below for another—as he reached for the beer in the fridge he noticed Matilde coming down.

Chris grabbed the opener and popped the cap off. "Is there something on your mind? Something troubling you?" he asked.

She looked at Chris and took a swig to give herself more time to think of a response. "Yes, I don't think you are telling me the truth. Madeira has always been a popular place, but in the last few months, nobody travels the ocean, nobody is going on vacation, and business is at a standstill. You are traveling for Dan's fiancé and you and the other gentleman are on business? Meanwhile, you have two young people traveling with you. Why are you really here in Madeira?"

Chris smiled and explained. "Dan does have a fiancée in Barcelona, and I do have some very important business that I have to take care of—it can't wait three months or six months or whenever the airlines open again. Ali is a friend and neighbor, and Lisa is his good friend. We don't want any trouble and we have nothing to hide."

Matilde took another drink. "I don't believe you. I will keep an eye on you."

She turned and went up to the deck, Chris following as he handed Rodrigo his beer. Rodrigo smiled back and Chris wondered, *Is this a good cop and bad cop routine? Or will Rodrigo become friends with anyone with a good supply of beer?*

Matilda was asking Dan where in Barcelona he was traveling to—Dan gave her the location of where Maria lived, hoping to satisfy Matilde for the moment. Chris wondered if she really knew Barcelona or if she would go back and double check the address.

Rodrigo took five minutes to finish his second beer. As soon as he was done, Matilde said something in Portuguese and he stood up. She said, "Thank you for the beer. It was refreshing after a long day. Have a good night," and then she looked pointedly at Chris. "Please keep in mind what we talked about."

They left and Dan looked at Chris. "She doesn't believe our story and she thinks that we're up to something." Chris explained. "She told me that this place is typically hopping, but nobody is traveling here with the current situation in Europe with terrorists, the virus in Africa, and Russia reestablishing the Soviet Union. Matilde said she'll be keeping an eye on us."

An hour later Mike, Ali, and Lisa were back at the boat. They looked happy, relaxed, and well fed. Dan shared the chore list for the next day and suggested they shop for European-styled clothing. Mike scheduled guard duty between the four guys into two-hour increments. Chris received the midnight to 2:00 a.m. shift, so he went to sleep right away. Dan got the first shift from ten to midnight, so he made a pot of coffee. He was also exercising on deck to stay alert for his shift; mixing in some lunges, jumping jacks and squats.

It felt good to Chris to not rock; he fell asleep dreaming of a family BBQ in their San Diego backyard. Suddenly he awoke: Dan was shaking him. Chris thought he must have been in a deep sleep as he tried to recall the dream. When Chris realized that the dream was now impossible and they couldn't ever return to their home in San Diego, it put him in a sour mood.

He went up on the deck in a dangerous frame of mind. Why was Matilde giving him a hard time? Did she think they were running drugs or guns? They weren't doing anything illegal and he was tired of being hassled. It was a good thing that Matilde and Rodrigo did not show up in the early morning, he wasn't sure how he would respond. Chris was in a foul mood and he missed Carly. This was by far the longest that they had been apart.

After thirty minutes, he looked up in the stars and thought about whether he would get the family together. Maybe they would enjoy a BBQ somewhere else? He reflected on this topic until it was 2:00 a.m., and then he went down and woke Ali for his shift.

Chris laid down in his bunk and told himself to gear up for the next phase of the journey. They were now in Europe and they would have to finish their voyage to Barcelona. Then he and Mike would have to find a way into Slovenia. He fell asleep deep in thought.

Chris awoke to the smell of coffee and bacon. It was 6:00 a.m.: Mike had started a fresh pot of coffee and was cooking some fresh eggs with bacon that they had bought yesterday at the market. Soon they were all up and eating heartily as they went through what they would accomplish that day.

Dan and Chris visited the paint store and gathered some paint and brushes. Then Dan, Ali, and Lisa went shopping for clothes while Mike and Chris started painting. Dan had given them his priority areas on the boat for painting. It was a warm and sunny day and the paint dried quickly.

Around one thirty, Dan, Ali, and Lisa returned. They bought some more fresh produce and meat along with a couple of bags of clothes. They purchased a pair of shoes each for Dan and Ali and then two pairs of shoes for Lisa. She told them that there was one pair that was too cute to pass up. They had purchased a few outfits that would make them look native to Portugal or Spain. They'd also stopped for a quick lunch on the way back to the boat.

Mike and Chris showed Dan where they had painted. They looked at what was left on his list: Lisa would store the food and then join Dan and Ali to finish painting. They thought it would be an hour or two at most to complete the paint project.

Mike and Chris took the names and directions for the best clothing retailers. When they left, they all agreed that they might leave Madeira this late afternoon. Chris felt with Matilde scrutinizing each move that it would be best to move on. Besides, he was anxious to get to Slovenia. It also helped that Dan wanted to arrive in Barcelona as soon as possible.

Chris and Mike walked along the street. They saw a bar serving food and noticed that many locals were eating there. They walked up to a small but high table and a waitress came up within a minute.

"Do you speak English?" Mike asked.

She nodded and held up her thumb and index finger showing ½ inch of space, which told them she spoke a little. Encouraged, they pulled out the menu. "Any recommendations?" Mike asked.

She pointed at "Bolo do caco" under the starters menu and then at "Espada com banana frita," they nodded and asked for two beers.

She came back with two Coral lagers. The bolo was wheat flour bread with garlic bread and parsley: the food was amazing. They scarfed down the beer and bread in minutes.

Minutes later their waitress returned with two more lagers and the main course: black fish with fried banana. They had fish almost every day on their voyage across the Atlantic, but this was served and cooked in a different way. They finished their meal and asked for the bill, and were surprised by how cheap it was. After leaving some euros on the table, they left for the clothing stores.

Chris and Mike stopped first in the store that Dan, Ali, and Lisa had recommended. Mike surveyed the store and Chris noticed that there were a couple of employees by the counter: one was a blond haired, blue eyed girl. The two others had dark hair. The one girl stood out not only because she was blond, but also because she was tall, about five feet eight inches, and was slim with long legs. The other two girls were five feet and had dark complexions as well as hair and eyes.

Chris walked over. "Do you speak English?" he asked. He hoped the blond girl was from Western or Central Europe.

She smiled. "Yes, of course."

"Excuse me for asking, but you don't look Portuguese. Where are you from?" Chris asked.

"I'm from Austria," she responded. "I came here three months ago between my studies to live in a warm climate and to work part-time for a pseudo holiday. I was originally returning to school next fall, but I've decided to stay here for a while longer. It's safe here on Madeira with healthy living. It's a good place to be while many cities in Europe try to recover from the terrorist attacks."

She looked at Chris as Mike walked over to join them. "And what brings you two Americans over to Madeira? And how did you get here?"

Chris asked her to follow him and they walked toward Mike and met him halfway. Chris introduced Mike now that they were outside earshot of all others in the store.

"We came over with some friends on a boat. I have some relatives over in Europe and some business that we need to attend to. I would appreciate a big favor. We'd like your help in finding some outfits and shoes that will help us look less American and more European. But not just in Portugal or Spain. We will also be heading to Northern Italy, Switzerland, and Austria. We want to fit in and look local in those regions as well."

She looked at the two and gave them a good once over. "No problem."

"We need clothes for hiking as well." Chris added. "If the clothes could have us blend in for both cities and towns and function for long hikes in the mountains, that would be perfect."

She spent an hour with them. Chris and Mike left with two pairs of shorts and pants and several long-sleeved and short-sleeved shirts. They also purchased hiking shoes that looked casual, and a rain jacket. They paid at the register and had two bags each. They decided to wear an outfit outside the shop. As they walked away from the register area, Chris looked at the girl who was the age of Jessica, and gave her a fifty-euro bill for her assistance.

"Thank you for spending so much time with us and for helping us find the proper clothes. I wish you well on your extended stay here on Funchal and I hope you get the chance to continue your studies in the near future."

She pushed the euro bill back to Chris. "No, it's my job and pleasure. Good luck on your business trip."

She looked Chris in the eyes and held it for seconds that seemed like minutes. "My town is outside Graz, which is near the border of Slovenia. I get reports from my family often and the Russians have secured the border. Be careful, I understand that this must be very important for you to travel such a long and difficult distance. If Russians find Americans in their new territory, they'll be shot on-site."

Chris felt that she had read his mind. How did this young girl know? All he could do was nod.

She added, "Viel Gluck!"

Chris turned around with his bags and walked out of the store with Mike. After a block, Mike asked, "What did she say?"

Chris didn't turn to look at him—he was just focused on getting back to the boat and off this island. She said, "Good luck."

"She guessed where we were going. Now that we are dressed European, hopefully, we'll blend in better. I have this strange feeling that we'll have to work hard to blend in," he added.

In fifteen minutes, they were on the boat. The others had finished painting and had cleaned up. Dan was checking a couple more things on the boat and then they would be ready to leave. Mike and Chris packed their clothes away and slipped into their old sailing clothes. Chris and Mike discussed that they would keep their purchased clothes nice for when they landed in Barcelona.

Dan went to the office and reported that they were leaving the port. Matilde was watching them as Dan guided the boat out. They were ready to reach Barcelona. The sky was beautiful, and Chris turned back to admire the cliffs overlooking the harbor. Perhaps, Chris thought, he could bring Carly back there someday.

Hoisting the sails, Dan turned off the engine and they sailed toward the Strait. Mike reminded everyone what they had been told in Funchal. "Keep an eye out for pirates and immigrants for the rest of the voyage."

Chapter 61

Strait of Gibralter

THEY WERE APPROACHING THE Strait. Since leaving Madeira they had spotted more boats in the ocean. They debated among themselves why the flurry of activity; their conclusion was that the lack of air travel required boats to transfer more goods.

Mike ensured that they had all guns in working order and cleaned on a consistent basis. It was midafternoon—they would make it through the Strait by the end of the day. The distance between Spain and Morocco was 7.7 nautical miles at the narrowest point, which was only around nine miles. Chris had never known that the Strait was so narrow between Europe and Africa.

As they approached, the number of large boats on the waterway increased. Dan kept them on course as they moved through the Strait; Ali and Lisa had fun identifying the flags of passing boats.

Dan hadn't said a word for an hour—he was focused on getting the boat safely through the Strait. Mike and Chris were positioned as lookouts: Mike watching the port side and Chris watching starboard. Chris wondered if they'd been psyched out by the warnings in Madeira: they were focused to make sure they didn't run into any trouble.

Dan guided them through the Strait and into the Mediterranean Sea. He set course to head for Majorca Island: they wouldn't stop in Majorca, but this would place them en route to Barcelona. They remained on high alert but agreed to switch teams for the rest of the day. Two people would be on break with the other three on deck: one navigating and one each watching port and starboard. After leaving the Strait, they saw fewer boats.

The sun started to go down over the Strait as they sailed away. Dan recommended they have two man teams for the rest of the voyage: one navigating and one armed and on lookout. Chris, Mike, Ali and Lisa agreed with Dan's plan. Lisa offered to cook and clean up after meals if she could skip the night watch and the guys agreed it was a fair trade. Dan and Chris would be one crew and Mike and Ali would be the other. They would work six hour shifts from 8:00 p.m. to 8:00 a.m., and within their team, they would trade off three hours navigating and three on watch in an attempt to keep the mind and body fresh.

Dan and Chris went to sleep from 8:00 p.m. to 2:00 a.m. while Mike and Ali kept them on course. They had been on high alert the whole day through the Strait and into the Mediterranean; Chris was more tired than he'd thought and he was soon fast asleep.

Voices. Chris heard some voices and a shout. He started to wake up and immediately knew it wasn't a dream. He sat up in his bunk and looked over at Dan, who was trying to wake up. Chris stood up, pulled on his pants and shoes, and walked over to Dan and shook him.

"Dan! Something is happening—we need to get up to the top." Chris was armed with his handgun and he also grabbed the shotgun as he climbed up on deck. Dan followed behind him and they left Lisa behind in the cabin trying to wake up.

Chris identified Ali at the wheel, Mike was positioned on the starboard side, armed and with his rifle raised. He was warning someone. "Back off! I will shoot you if I have to."

Chris and Dan scurried over to Mike. Through the darkness, they could make out the outline of a boat. It was hard to see in the dark, but Chris thought he saw smaller shapes that must be bodies. Dan had a flashlight out and turned it on and pointed it at the boat. They were stunned to see so many people crammed into the boat. There were children, women, and men. Chris and Dan now saw the problem: the boat had men with oars who were trying to broadside and board Dan's boat. Mike kept his rifle tracking them alongside the boat.

Mike spoke to Dan and Chris without turning his head toward them. "The wind died down about an hour ago. Maybe we can start the engine and move farther from them. Recall the advice we were given in Madeira: these people could be carrying the virus. We can't take them onboard."

Lisa was now up with them on deck, and she saw all the bodies in the boat.

"Look at some of the children, they look sick. We have to do something."

Dan was quick to respond. "We can't take them onboard. But we can give them water and some food. That's the best we can do."

Lisa jumped on this. "Okay, let's do that."

"Dan, while you and Mike stay on guard, I'll help Lisa. They can't cook on their boat so we'll unload our bread and fruits with some water and anything else that they can eat on the boat." Chris suggested.

Chris went down to the cabin and brought up two containers of water and then returned to bring bread and crackers. Lisa brought up two bags of apples and bananas that they had bought in Funchal. Mike handed the water containers to two of the men in the boat as Chris handed over a bag with bread. He assisted Lisa by merging the fruit into one large bag and then handed it over to an oarsman.

As soon as the bags were transferred, the boat became chaotic with people clamoring and fighting over the food. Dan went over to Ali and started the engine as he took Ali's spot at the wheel. Ali came over to stand with the others. The food kept the migrants preoccupied—at first, they didn't notice that Dan was pulling the boat away from them and toward the Spanish coast.

As they started pulling away, two of the men on the boat panicked and jumped into the water and started swimming for the boat, but the boat was moving quickly in the opposite direction. Dan had the boat turning away from them. One of the migrants was an older man, at least he looked old. He had gray hair and was thin and must have been weak because he stopped swimming and started shouting. He was soon ten yards from both the boat and his boat and he started to sink. He went below the surface and then he would pop up gasping for breath. He bobbed up and down a half dozen times and then finally went down for good.

By now Dan had them forty yards from the boat and was leaving it farther behind. The other migrant was younger and stronger and he was tracking them. He was close to reaching their boat. Mike had his rifle on him shouting "Stay back." The young man didn't stop and he was soon reaching and grabbing for the side of the boat. Mike warned him with the barrel down at his head. The migrant said something they couldn't understand and then tried to boost himself up onto the boat. Mike put the sole of his shoe on the migrant's head and pushed down hard while the migrant was trying to lift himself up and over. The migrant lost his balance and barely held on with one hand. Mike pushed down again with the butt of the rifle and the migrant lost his last grip and fell back. They saw him drop in the water and then he bobbed up a few seconds later but now he was ten yards away. He bobbed again and in five seconds reappeared—now they were even further away.

They stopped shining the light on the migrant. Lisa shouted in desperation, "What if he also drowns?"

Chris looked at Lisa. "We can't take him onboard. We did everything we could. He made a choice and now he will have to swim back to his boat!"

Lisa had tears in her eyes and Chris hoped that the migrant boat would land somewhere safe. He knew there was a lot of political controversy and these people were desperate. People couldn't fault the migrants for trying to escape economic as well as political strife along with the virus. However, people also understood that bringing the migrants would spread disease and issues to their homelands.

Chris commented out loud, probably to make himself feel better, "Hopefully, with the water and food, they can stay alive and make it to land."

Those were the last words that anyone spoke for the next hour. No one wanted to sleep. Dan was stoic at the helm; Mike and Chris watched and periodically shone lights out to the sides of the boat, imagining more migrant boats trying to board. Ali hugged Lisa, where they sat on the deck looking out into space. After an hour, Lisa and Ali went down and came back up with cups of coffee for Dan, Mike, and Chris.

Chris took the cup and then gave Lisa a hug. It was dark, and neither one of them knew that the other had tears in their eyes. It was another little scar that would remain in their lives.

Chapter 62

Barcelona

THEY ARRIVED IN BARCELONA. It took about one and a half hours to get checked in with the authorities because of all the activity. It was in the afternoon, and Dan couldn't contain his excitement. He had given Maria's parents address to the officials when he checked in, they told him the house was only a few miles away and they allowed him to use their phone. Dan was able to reach Maria's mother and minutes later he was on the phone with Maria. Dan explained that the entire family was coming down to the harbor to see them. Maria's mother felt it would be too difficult for Dan to find the house on his first visit.

Dan decided to hang back at the boat in case the family arrived early. The rest of the team had a mission to replenish their produce. They would only buy enough for snacks and to buy some water containers to replace the drinking water they had given the immigrants. Mike and Chris planned to get the water containers and fill them with clean water. They'd heard from the port officials that there was a maritime store just blocks away. They found the store and purchased some containers, then walked to a public fountain and filled them up before returning to the boat.

Ali and Lisa planned to explore Las Ramblas and find an outdoor market in order to bring back fresh fruit. The port officers had told them that most of Barcelona was safe now, but to be aware and to avoid any large gatherings. Dan told Ali and Lisa not to dawdle in the open market and to shop and move out of the area. Terrorists liked crowded areas like the markets.

Ali and Lisa brought back some exciting fruit and also some delicious bakery items that they decided to eat immediately. As the rest were unpacking below, Chris kept watch above. Minutes later, Chris saw a big group of people approach the boat. He called down for the others to come up on deck. The group included both women and men and they weren't port officials; Chris could see some children. There were about twenty people approaching them.

Dan stared at the group of people for a minute, then got a big smile and moved off the boat and onto the deck. He trotted toward the group and a woman broke out and ran to him in her heels. They met and embraced in a big kiss. By then, the rest of the group had moved in closer: Chris could make out what looked like the mother and father, uncles and aunts, brothers and sisters, and nephews and nieces. He counted twenty-three people, including Maria.

Dan motioned for them to come off of the boat and Chris, Mike, Ali, and Lisa were introduced to all the relatives. Chris didn't understand any of the words spoken, but the hugs were the best greetings that they had received since leaving Brownfield.

Dan and Maria were talking—in between pauses, her mother and father conversed in Spanish. In five minutes, the father left and went to the port office. In a few minutes, he came out with an officer who walked with him toward Dan and Maria. There was more conversation.

Finally, Dan came over and said, "They have a small private harbor down the coast, and we'll pay more to stay there, but the boat will be well guarded. The port worker called and they have a space for us. We will go over to the other pier. It's only about one and a half miles from here. We are all invited to stay with Maria's family."

Chris looked at Mike and then Dan. Dan replied, "It's not really a request but more of a mandate. They want to get to know my friends."

Maria came onboard the boat and said she would travel to the small port with them and lead them to her parents' house. They all waved goodbye and the family left to go prepare for their arrival.

Dan started the engine and Maria stood by him as they navigated in the direction of the small pier. Chris looked over at Maria: she was tiny and pretty with thick black hair, a pretty smile, and large brown eyes. She was about five feet two inches and Chris thought she wasn't much more than one hundred pounds.

They made it to the small pier and were welcomed by a guard who'd been expecting them. They were settled in thirty minutes. Dan and Maria walked up to the office where the pier was gated with someone at the office twenty-four hours a day. In addition to the office, they had a guard walking the small pier.

Dan paid a week of rent. Mike was nervous leaving the guns behind, so he hid the shotgun, rifle, and heavy artillery by splitting it up within the cabin. They agreed that they'd carry their handguns with them. They just couldn't be caught with them so they wore jackets despite the warm weather. Dan locked the cabin and performed another quick walk through on the deck to make sure everything was in place.

Even though Dan had paid for a week, Chris went over to the guard and gave him a twenty-euro note and pointed at the boat and made a motion with his index and middle finger to his right eye indicating for the guard to keep an eye on the boat. The guard smiled and seemed pleased. He nodded and responded, "Si."

As they were walking away from their boat, Dan explained that this smaller pier was closer to Maria's parents and they only had to walk a little over a mile to reach her home. They were wearing their Euro clothes that they had bought on Madeira Island and they hoped that they were blending in.

In twenty minutes, they reached a street. Maria explained and pointed out where her relatives lived on the block. Chris figured out that all the people that they'd met at the dock earlier that day lived on this street—it was intentional to have family in close proximity.

They followed Maria as she walked into a house and they were greeted again by Maria's mother and father. Another round of greetings and hugs followed. Maria and her father brought them behind the house to a nice patio with a couple of large trees and tables. Maria explained that this area stayed very cool—it was where they spent a lot of their time. They were all encouraged to find a seat and sit down.

Maria's father said something in Spanish. Maria translated, "My father is asking if we would like some red wine. He has some Rioja wine, a famous wine made in Spain. The first wines from here dated back to the eleventh century BC by the Phoenicians. Many vineyards were planted by the Romans. When my father heard that Dan and his friends were coming over to visit, he bought some cases for a celebration."

With that intro, it was hard for Chris to decline. Ali abstained and they gave him a glass of sparkling water. Lisa wanted a small taste of the wine and then she asked for a glass of sparkling water as well. Chris and Dan and Mike had to try this wine—it was as good as advertised.

Maria's father wanted to know about the trip. They let Dan be the story teller while Chris and Mike poured their second glass of wine. Maria assisted Dan by translating back and forth. Dan was a good story teller. He purposely left out the part about the pirates and immigrants, and he modified Lisa's story that she was a friend of Ali's and the two of them joined the journey for an adventure. They wanted to know more about Chris and Mike. Chris had prepared a white lie that he and Mike had family business in Milan. Chris had to concoct a location somewhere en route to Slovenia: Milan was a financial and business center, so it was a good location. Chris made up a story that they had some key business venture and they needed to come over and meet with their partners. Chris had told his companions that he would use this story and that he'd say that Mike and Chris couldn't go into any details and hope that this would be a sufficient explanation and not draw many questions.

Maria's father seemed to accept this explanation. He focused his conversation with more questions on Dan: he wanted to know more about his future son-in-law. Maria excused herself and said that she would help her mother prepare the meal.

Chris and Mike asked Maria if they could help with the preparations. When they insisted that they wanted to help, Maria had Mike and Chris follow her to the kitchen where Maria's mother and sister were working quickly and efficiently. Lisa and Ali followed them to the kitchen. Maria showed Ali and Lisa the glasses, plates, and silverware and they were given the responsibility of setting the tables on the patio.

Maria's mother had Chris positioned at a cutting board with eggplant, peppers, tomatoes, onions and a sharp knife. She had Chris chop up the veggies and place them in the big pan on the stove. She turned the burner on low and added vinegar and salt and olive oil as Chris filled the pan with the chopped vegetables. Chris was instructed to keep chopping and adding the veggies to the pan then to pause and stir the vegetables every two minutes. She gave him all instructions in Spanish, but the pointing gestures and what sounded like threats got his attention and Chris felt he understood.

Mike was helping the sister with the Paella: he was chopping up garlic, onion, and chicken with tomatoes. She was concentrating on Mike as well as the oil and garlic sauce. She was a carbon copy of Maria: maybe an inch or two taller, but with the same beautiful thick black hair, long eyelashes, and smile. She knew some English so Chris could hear the two of them talking on the other side of the kitchen.

Maria's mother was cooking a dessert that looked like a Spanish version of crème brûlée that Maria's mother called Crema Catalana. Every five minutes she would come over and check Chris to make sure he wasn't making an error, and then he would get a pat on the back or a pinched cheek. Chris was wondering what he would get if he messed up. The pinched cheek would probably be replaced by a kick in the butt. Chris stayed on task, stopping occasionally for a sip of wine. The last thing he wanted was to cause a big incident by ruining the vegetables. It was pleasant working in the kitchen with the others and Chris thought that they were preparing a lot of food.

Maria's brother and sister-in-law and two young children came over for dinner. It would be a subset of their family and just the immediate family for dinner. For the seating, Maria and Dan were seated together with her parents sitting at the center. There were three tables that formed a big U. Mike was seated with Maria's sister Carmen at one end. Those two were connecting and oblivious to all others. Seated with them were Lisa and Ali, who were happy it was just the two of them at that end of the table. At the other side of the table sat Maria's brother and family. Chris was seated between Maria's brother and Maria's mother and across from Maria's father and sister-in-law.

The dinner was exceptional; all the flavors enhanced by cooking with oil, garlic and spices. After a couple glasses of wine and the finale with the Crema Catalona, Chris felt stuffed. He had smiled often to Maria's parents and every once in a while, Maria's mom would pat his shoulder and say something. Chris talked to Maria's brother and sister-in-law. Maria's brother would travel some on business and often to Milan. He was helpful and advised that a train was reliable from Barcelona to Milan, traveling through the south of France. Chris gathered as many tidbits as he could on Italy without drawing suspicion.

After dessert, the brother's young boy and girl were tired, so the brother, wife, and children said their goodbyes and left. Five minutes later, Maria rose from the table and announced that she was going to show Dan some of Barcelona on a walk. They asked if anyone wanted to join but everyone was quick to say "No." Carmen spoke with Mike and then also announced that she and Mike were walking down to the water and asked if anyone wanted to join. Lisa and Ali looked at each other and volunteered.

Chris thought, a walk sounded nice. Maria and Dan were gone and they were obviously trying to reconnect after many months. He noticed Carmen and Mike as a couple and Ali and Lisa had been evolving into a couple. He could only rain on everyone's parade, so he said, "No, thanks," and remained seated. Everyone left and Chris got up with Maria's mom and father and started clearing dishes. Maria's mom had hot sudsy water in the sink and Chris brought the dishes and silverware in and dropped them in the sink. Maria's mother washed and the father dried. The system worked well.

After all the dishes were brought in, Chris volunteered to take the mother's task and wash. Maria's mom gave him another pinch on the cheek and then she started putting the dishes away. Twenty minutes later they were finished and back out on the patio. Maria's father had poured them another glass of wine and they sat out there in the beautiful evening. Nobody spoke, which was just as well since they couldn't understand each other.

Chris was feeling melancholy. He missed Carly, he missed his family, and he missed throwing the ball for Finley. He gave himself a few minutes to feel sorry for himself, then he remembered that Jessica was somewhere in the Julian Alps. He flashed through the last comments from Carly to find Jessica and come back alive and he recalled his father telling him to "survive."

He didn't know it but he said out loud, "I'm trying."

Maria's parents looked at him, puzzled, and wondered if he was trying to share something. Chris looked at them and smiled, lifted his wine glass and reached over and clicked it with theirs and shared one of his few Spanish words: "Gracias."

Chapter 63

Barcelona

CHRIS WOKE UP DISORIENTED but recalled that he was at the house of Maria's parents. He got up, shaved, dressed, and walked downstairs and out to the courtyard patio. Maria's mother had coffee and a continental breakfast prepared. Maria, Dan, and Mike were sitting around. Apparently, Chris had slept in. The many glasses of wine must have knocked him out. Carmen and Maria's father had left for work, and Lisa and Ali had left to explore. They had with them a map drawn by Maria and were going to reexplore more of Las Ramblas.

Maria was taking the next couple of days off from work and she had a day planned with Dan. Apparently, there was still a strong connection and they didn't want to share their list of errands. Chris asked Maria where he could get a map: he wanted to visit a bookstore and the train station where he and Mike would depart for their travel to Milan.

Maria walked into the house and came out a minute later with some paper and a pen and drew a crude map of where they were and some main streets. She made a great map for Chris and then she and Dan left. Chris finished his coffee and had a roll before he was ready to go. Mike had eaten earlier and was ready and waiting. Chris offered to help Maria's mother clean but she motioned for him to leave.

As they walked out the front door, Chris told Mike that he wanted to go to a bookstore to get some detailed maps of Slovenia, Italy, and Austria and how he wanted to see if they had a "translation" dictionary for English to Italian, German, and Slovenian. Then Chris wanted to look at train schedules from Barcelona to Milan—how frequent were the trains and how many stops were along the way?

Maria had written down the names of three bookstores and Chris saw that they could hit two on the way to the train station. They took off on their adventure dressed like Europeans. It was warm out but still there were some men with jackets. Chris and Mike were armed and required their jackets but they still tried to blend in. They were clean shaven, but Chris noticed that he could use a haircut.

"Mike, how about we hit a barber on the way?"

Mike agreed and they found one that was not crowded—they were able to get in and out quickly. Now, they were clean cut.

They approached the first book store: Chris was disappointed that he couldn't find any good maps. The storeowner showed them on Maria's map that there was a cartographer on the way to the train station. They did find a small translation book for English and Spanish, Italian, German and French. Chris asked about Slovenia and the shopkeeper looked at him like he was strange. Chris didn't know if it was an oddball request or if the shopkeeper was wondering why anyone would go to Slovenia.

When they walked out, Mike suggested to Chris, "We may need to find some words and phrases on the internet and then print them using Maria's computer."

Chris thought it was a great idea—they would ask Maria if they could access her computer that night. They took off for the cartographer and they found a Slovenian map along with Italian and Austrian maps. They bought all three and continued to the train station.

Stopping for a quick lunch of tapas, they arrived at the train station early in the afternoon. They went in and made their way to a short line. When Chris reached the window, he asked if the man spoke English. The middle-aged man shook his head and pointed to a window two away to the right. Chris and Mike got in that line and noticed the ticket-master was a young man in his midtwenties.

When it was their turn they walked up and asked if he spoke English. Chris then asked, "What is the best way to Trieste, Italy?" Chris and Mike had pulled out the map while eating lunch and determined that this Italian city near Slovenia would be their best starting point.

The young man looked at his computer. "This is the best route," he offered.

He gave Chris and Mike the prices for the different classes. Chris looked at Mike, "Second class?"

Mike nodded. "Is this available tomorrow?" he asked.

"Yes, it is available, it will leave at 9:30 a.m. With many stops you will arrive later in the evening." The young man responded.

Mike nodded and Chris said that they would like two tickets all the way to Trieste. The young man spent the next ten minutes booking them on a few different train segments and then went over the itinerary completely with Mike and Chris. They paid the man in euros, took the tickets, and returned to Maria's parents. They knew that they had to be back by 7:30 p.m. There was another family get together that night.

Chris and Mike found another tapas bar about half a mile from Maria's parents where they ordered a beer and a couple of tapas at a table. They mostly wanted a table not at Maria's parents' house where they could open their maps. They sat in the far back corner. The place was empty because it was later afternoon; in Spain, they typically ate late in the evening. After they received their beers and tapas, they spread out the maps of Slovenia and eastern Italy and marked Ljubljana, the capital in Slovenia, and Lake Bled and Lake Bohinj.

They would need to pack that night and leave the shotgun and rifle behind. They would dress European from now on and leave everything else on the boat. The issue was that they would have to wing it on how to get across the border. Mike commented that the Russians may be more focused on stopping people from leaving rather than coming *into* the countries at this point. Chris thought about it and felt that Mike may have a good point.

They finished their research and paid their bill and walked a short distance to Maria's parents' house. They walked in and Maria's mother was excited and brought them out to the patio where Dan and Maria were sitting. Chris and Mike didn't know what was happening but knew it must be good because Maria was beaming and Maria's mother was smiling and crying at the same time.

Dan had to help them. "I asked Maria to marry me—I'll ask her father for his blessing tonight before the relatives come over. All her family will be over tonight at 9:00 p.m. If her father gives his blessing, then we'll announce our marriage tonight. Today we looked for reception locations and we are thinking a midweek wedding in three weeks. Their church in this neighborhood is open and we found a hall where we could have a reception."

Mike and Chris jumped up and shook his hand and gave Dan their sincere congratulations, then walked over and hugged Maria. Chris was so happy for Dan. He was marrying late, but he wanted to find the right girl and start a family and now he was on his way. The mother excused herself to attend to something and Maria left with her.

Chris looked at Dan. "Dan, we're leaving tomorrow morning. We need to get on the boat tonight and pack. We'll leave the rifle and shotgun, our sailing clothes, and any American-looking clothes. We bought our tickets for the morning train and tomorrow night we'll be on the Italy and Slovenian border. You can't tell anyone where we are, just that we will be in Milan."

Mike looked at his watch. "Should we go to the boat now?"

Dan said he was available until 7:30 p.m. He had an hour before his future father-in-law would be home. He left them to find Maria to let her know he would return in time.

Dan was back in five minutes. "Let's go."

They were at the boat in twenty minutes and Dan checked in at the office. The guard who Chris slipped the twenty-euro note the other day to keep an eye on Dan's boat saw them and Chris gave him a thumbs-up, and they climbed onboard. Everything looked in order and Dan unlocked the cabin. Chris had all his money with him but he packed his Euro clothes and all his ammo. Chris looked over and Mike was packing similar to him. They each had one backpack.

Mike went through where the rifle and shotgun were stashed away. Dan locked up and they left the pier and headed back up toward Maria's parents' house.

They walked in the house and it was a little before 7:30 p.m. Mike and Chris went to their bedrooms. Maria intercepted Dan and told him her father was home, he was changing his clothes, and would be on the patio in five minutes. She whisked him away.

As they climbed the stairs, Chris shared with Mike, "In some ways, the timing is great. With all the excitement, they won't notice our departure. See you downstairs in fifteen minutes?"

Chris sent a text message to Carly. "We arrived in Barcelona. Mike and I will leave tomorrow. All is good. Dan proposed to Maria. Love, Chris."

Chris went down to the patio and to witness more excitement. Chris guessed that Papa had given his consent. Carmen, Ali, and Lisa were all there celebrating, and Mike was standing near Carmen. Maria's father had more of his excellent wine flowing and Chris thought that it needed to be a lighter drinking night. He would have one now and one later. He had to be very alert each day now.

Happiness was flowing and so was the wine. When relatives started arriving, there was more shouting and hugs and Mike and Chris chose this time to pull Ali and Lisa over to the side to talk.

Mike started. "Ali and Lisa, Chris and I are leaving tomorrow morning. You two should stay here and enjoy Barcelona. Perhaps Dan and Maria could use some help in planning the wedding? You can't say anything about where we are going other than to Milan for business. If everything goes well we will back for the wedding."

Chris could tell Ali was conflicted. He had a strong bond with Mike and he originally wanted to come with them, but he and Lisa were now inseparable and he knew that two weeks with her in Barcelona would be fun.

"You, guys, need to be very careful," Ali spoke.

"Of course," Chris answered. "We want to be back here for the celebration."

The night was a big party. Chris estimated that fifty people were over and he met each and every one. He made his rounds and shook hands and hugged many. He was now by himself; he noticed that Ali and Lisa were holding hands and then he saw that Carmen was introducing Mike to all her relatives. Romance was definitely in the air.

At midnight, relatives started leaving and Chris started taking dishes to the kitchen. He had some stacked in the sink and some on the counter. He ran some water and found the dishwashing liquid and started washing dishes and putting them in the strainer. A little later, Dan's future father-in-law came over and started drying the dishes. Mike came in and told Chris that he and Carmen were taking a walk, and so were Ali and Lisa. Chris thanked him for letting him know and to have a good evening. Chris confirmed that he would see Mike at 7:00 a.m. the next day.

Five minutes later, Maria's mother came in. She was excited. Chris had both his hands in the soap water so he couldn't defend himself as she came over and pinched his right cheek. It was the only one for the day so Chris thought he could tough it out. She started putting away the dishes and spoke to her husband a million words a minute. The Spanish language sounded very pretty, like an instrument. They were so happy.

Chris finished washing the dishes and Maria's parents finished drying and putting them away. Dan sat under the tree and Maria sat on his lap. They just sat there. Chris didn't have much of an opportunity to see Maria during the party because it seemed like a relative was telling her a long story each time he tried to approach. Now, Chris walked over.

"I'm really happy for the both of you. I would like to give you my congratulations and best wishes for your marriage."

Maria and Dan thanked Chris.

"Dan knows this, but Mike and I have to leave tomorrow to take the train to Italy. We bought our tickets today. We have urgent business. We will make our best effort to be back for the wedding."

Maria nodded and Chris smiled and added, "Good night!"

Chris walked up the stairs and took a hot shower and put his clothes out on a chair for the next morning; then he repacked. It would be a long day and all they had to do was look inconspicuous and get to Trieste. Chris feel asleep in ten minutes.

Chris woke early, and by 6:00 a.m., he was ready to go. He made his bed and quietly went downstairs and approached the courtyard. Mike must have not slept or slept well because he was already there.

"Mike, my gosh, you got up earlier than me," Chris said.

"Chris, I never slept. Carmen and I didn't get back until 5:00 a.m., and I just took a shower, shaved, and came back down."

Chris smiled. "You are a better man then me."

Chris found a piece of paper and wrote a note to Maria and her parents thanking them for their hospitality and explaining that they were sorry to leave on short notice but they had to travel to Italy that day on urgent business. He did add that they were planning to be back for Maria's and Dan's wedding.

"Should we wait until seven to see if Dan says goodbye?" Mike asked.

Chris thought for a few seconds. "No, let's go. They have a lot to do and we'll be back in a couple weeks."

Mike and Chris looked at each other, both were thinking the same thing. They didn't know if they would be back. However, Chris felt they had said their goodbyes earlier to Dan.

They grabbed their backpacks and quietly headed out the door. They saw Maria at an inside doorway; she was in her bathrobe and slippers as she walked over to them.

"I don't know what urgent business you have but please be careful. Dan thinks the world of you two and I would really like you both at the wedding."

There was nothing to say. Both Mike and Chris walked over and gave her a good hug and then didn't look back as they continued out the front door.

They walked to a bus stop and found a coffee place that was open. They bought a coffee for takeaway and then caught the bus to the train station. They had some time to spare and they found another coffee and pastry at a kiosk. Mike looked tired in spite of the caffeine, and they finally were able to board the train. On the platform, they saw a big variance from the business people on travel to the locals going on a trip or holiday.

In second class it was first come, first serve and they luckily found two seats by each other. They had their guns in their backpacks and decided to keep their backpacks on their lap. Mike took the window seat and he was asleep even before the train pulled away.

* * * * *

They were past the first leg. Chris stayed awake for thirty minutes into the second leg, then slowly lowered his head on his backpack and used it as a pillow. He thought he should rest while he could—he would need it."

Chapter 64

Trieste

IT WAS LATE IN the evening when Chris and Mike arrived at the train station. They had a few layovers and train connections, but finally they arrived in Trieste very tired. They pulled on their backpacks and went to the taxi line and grabbed a cab to the port. Chris paid the taxi driver and they took a couple of minutes to survey the landscape. They chose to stay at a higher-end chain hotel.

Chris and Mike had discussed on the train that business travelers would most likely pick a nice chain hotel since it could be written off as a business expense. They spotted one with name recognition and headed over. They wanted to leave the impression that they were on business, however, not having a roller bag could be considered suspicious.

They walked into the hotel lobby and stood in line behind another couple checking in. The exchange at the counter sounded Italian so Chris determined the guests were native. After two minutes the couple received their room key and Chris motioned Mike to come to the counter with him.

"Do you speak English?" Chris asked.

The woman at the counter responded. "Yes, of course. How can I help you?" She was about five feet five inches with long brown hair, big brown eyes. She was very trim and wore the hotel uniform which consisted of a long-sleeved shirt and skirt.

"Do you have two rooms?" Chris asked. "We don't have a reservation. My partner and I were in Milan when we had this last-minute business meeting come up for tomorrow. We will stay two nights. We left our luggage at our other hotel and only packed for one meeting and two nights."

Chris tried to explain the lack of luggage and hoped that he wasn't overplaying it. The young woman busily looked for rooms—after three minutes she handed each of them a little packet with the key inside.

Chris took his packet with the hotel key. "I know it's late, but we haven't eaten much all day. Is there a place where locals go for dinner that you would recommend? A local tavern would be fine too, if they served good food."

The woman thought and then pulled out a map of the immediate area. She highlighted a couple of places on the map and used the pen to write down the names.

Mike and Chris walked to the elevator. "Down in the lobby in ten minutes?" Mike asked.

Chris took a quick shower, changed his clothes, and was in the lobby ten minutes later. He saw Mike standing outside and Chris walked out with the map in hand. They looked at the two places on the map and they chose the one closest to the port. Mike knew the intent was more about information gathering than eating. They had spent some time in a few harbors during their voyage and they listened to the locals in that area. Tonight they would listen for news about Slovenia, and how Russia was impacting travel and trade by sea. They had heard on the train that day that all roads and trains into Slovenia were very tight with Russian security.

They walked a couple of blocks and found themselves in front of a tavern. They walked in the doorway where there was a long wooden bar that was fairly crowded. As they had thought, most of the patrons appeared to be dock workers gathered around the bar. Most of the tables were empty with the exception of two couples enjoying a bottle of wine. It was getting late for dinner.

A man in an apron came over and welcomed them. There were some menus on a little stand at the front of the establishment and Chris took one of them and motioned to it. The man nodded and asked with his waving hands where they wanted to sit. Mike and Chris picked a table very close to the bar. The man brought another menu for Mike, and they sat down. He asked in broken English if they wanted something to drink.

Chris asked, "Birra?" and the host pointed to the counter, and he saw there were eight beers on tap.

Mike asked, "Local?" and the man gave them a name, and both of them nodded acceptance. In two minutes, they had two beers on tap by their jovial bartender. He asked if they wanted to order, and Chris pointed at something that said pollo, and Mike pointed at something else on the menu. The bartender went off happily to deliver the order to the kitchen.

They were both tired but they tried to keep conversation going. Chris and Mike often looked at the bar and if they made eye contact with someone they smiled. It finally worked. One guy saw Mike smile and held up his beer and walked over to their table.

He asked, "Dutch?" and you could see all the people at the bar turning to watch as he asked where the two men were from.

"No, American." Chris pointed to one of the empty chairs, inviting their new friend to sit down and join them.

The man looked at them and raised both hands, including the right one with his beer. He pulled out a chair from under the table and two of his buds grabbed their beers and came over from the bar counter. One took the other free chair and the third man found a chair at the nearby table and pulled it over. The table was becoming a party.

It was evident by looking into his eyes that he wanted more info. "We are originally from California but now we are from Texas." Chris started. That generated some ahs.

"We are here for business and we just arrived. We were told this was a good place to eat." Mike added. The bartender liked that comment and he gave a bigger smile from his perch on the counter where he was watching and listening.

Chris and Mike conducted small talk with their new friends. When they finished dinner, they moved to the bar. After a couple of rounds, they discovered that many of these men supported the port with either supplies or services. They confirmed that Trieste was one of the leading coffee ports that supplied a lot of Italy's coffee. It was also a major route to Istanbul and other areas of the Mediterranean. A major portion of the trade between Turkey and Europe took place through Trieste.

They also confirmed Russia's invasion to the old USSR. The borders on land were heavily regulated now by the Russians. Truck and train transportation of goods was heavily scrutinized and civilian travel was very difficult. Visas were now required and issued from Moscow. However, the boat trade along the Adriatic coast had not been as heavily impacted. They felt that more restrictions would be coming in the future for the larger boats. At this time, the smaller fishing boats and smaller boats were not impacted.

Mike found out through a side conversation that there was another bar where fishermen and small traders frequented. After they finished their second round at the bar Mike gave Chris a tap on the shoulder. They said their goodbyes and pulled out.

Once out of the establishment, Mike looked at Chris. "I got the name of a bar near the port where the fisherman and small operators hang out. I think we should get some sleep, pretend we are leaving for our meeting tomorrow, and then head to the port and find the location of the bar."

Chris nodded. "This confirms what we thought—the best entry into Slovenia is probably by sea."

They walked the old streets and found their hotel. The lobby was empty except for one person at the check-in counter. They waved to the person at the counter and walked to the elevator, then headed to their rooms and prepared for sleep.

Chris lay in bed, tired, but with anticipation building within him. He had felt this before in business, but this was for higher stakes. The type of anticipation or excitement where you knew something big was going to happen and it required you to be at the top of your game. You didn't know exactly what would happen, other than you would have to perform well. Chris knew Mike was feeling the same; he was definitely ramping up. Chris could see Mike listening and watching intently that night.

On the walk back, Mike gave Chris specific details on each of the patrons at the bar. Chris thought he had performed well, but he would have to work harder to keep up with Mike.

Chris fell asleep dreaming of Jessica hiking in the Julian Alps.

Chapter 65

Brownfield, Texas

ETHAN AND MARK TURNED onto the dirt driveway off the main road to the house. In a couple of minutes, they pulled up in front of the farmhouse. Finley barked on the porch announcing their arrival. Ethan put the vehicle in park and saw their mom come out of the house with a shotgun. Clark walked out of the barn with a pitchfork. As soon as Carly and Clark saw who arrived, the gun and pitchfork went down.

Ethan and Mark climbed out of the truck and opened the doors for their grandparents. Finley was on Mark in seconds as he jumped up, wagging his tail before running around the vehicle to greet Ethan. Carly ran down the porch to hug her parents and then gave long hugs to her sons. Soon Clark was there with a handshake and greeting along with Grandpa and Grandma H.

Carly took her parents into the house while Ethan, Mark, and Clark followed them with the luggage. After they brought in the last of the luggage, the three of them went into the kitchen and sat down at the table with Carly; and the four grandparents. Carly started a pot of tea and Finley had his tennis ball and was hopeful he could entice someone into a game of throwing the ball. After a couple of minutes, he gave up and decided to lie down on the cool tile as he squeezed the ball gently in his mouth.

They sat for two hours trading stories. When the tea pot and the stories were finished, Carly got up and showed her parents their bedroom. Ethan and Mark asked Clark what chores were on the list for the day and the three of them left for the barn.

After a couple hours, the chores were finished and the boys came back to the house. Carly was still in the kitchen with her parents. When they lingered at the doorway, Carly advised that dinner was in thirty minutes, enough time to take a shower and get cleaned up.

"Are you going to the dance tonight? Carly asked Clark.

"I was thinking about it." Clark answered.

He turned to Ethan and Mark. "Do you, guys, want to join me?"

Ethan and Mark looked at each other and then at Carly and their grandparents.

"I think it's a good idea. You, guys, could use a fun night." Carly spoke up.

Mark nodded.

"Yes, sounds fun," Ethan replied.

They left to take their showers. "Tomorrow I can show you the property and we can head into town. The neighbors are very nice and good people. I've started to appreciate this place. We don't have the beach and weather of San Diego, but I could see Texas as home now," Carly told her parents.

At dinner Ethan broke the silence. "I'll need to head back to Dallas for work in a couple of days. I spoke with my manager yesterday and things are up and running."

Mark spoke next. "I checked in at OU and they'll continue the semester starting next week. I plan on riding with Ethan and he'll drop me off in Norman. The summer will be shorter because of the extension of the spring semester. I may look into an internship but with a short summer I'm not sure what will be available. If not, I'll be back here for a brief summer."

Clark shared that he had enrolled at Tech for the fall semester. The conversation went toward the status of the old US. Carly provided them an update.

Washington, Oregon and Northern California were thinking of forming a Pacific Union with Hawaii. Maine, Vermont, New Hampshire, and Massachusetts were thinking of forming their own country. New York State minus New York City was thinking of joining the New England states.

The South was in discussion with Texas about joining the Texas Union. Alaska was in discussion with Texas and the Pacific Union. Indiana was sandwiched between Ohio and Illinois but were in discussion with the South. A number of states were now vying to be part of Texas. If the South were to join Texas, it would be a large and powerful country—places like Chicago; Detroit; Philadelphia; New York City; Camden; Washington, DC/Baltimore, were all troubled areas.

It was interesting to Ethan and Mark to hear the latest in politics. The Texas Union was a conservative new country with a simple doctrine. The tax code and government all started with a clean slate and a focus on human rights and fiscal responsibility.

After dinner, Ethan, Mark, and Clark took off for the dance. Grandpa H and Grandma H decided to watch a TV program. Carly and her parents went out on the porch with Finley and sat down to enjoy the cooler evening. Finley's ears perked up every once in a while, as he spotted a bunny hopping.

Pa K spoke. "We are glad to be here. I hope that my family can return to Fish Creek soon."

"Is your brother okay in Portland?" Ma K asked Carly.

"Yes, you can call him tomorrow. The northwest is stable and he's back at work," Carly replied.

* * * * *

Ethan pulled up in the parking lot, and they got out of the vehicle. He noticed that Clark's wardrobe had changed a lot since they had seen him last. Clark now wore boots, jeans, and a western shirt. Ethan and Mark had their boots and jeans but they had few clean shirts. Mark had a crimson OU golf shirt and Ethan had a blue button down work shirt with the sleeves rolled up.

They walked up to the structure that appeared to be a converted barn. There was a table stationed at the entrance manned by a couple. The guys paid the entrance fee and walked in. Clark stepped in and looked around and spotted his friends. He brought Mark and Ethan over for introductions.

Within a couple of minutes Clark was out dancing with his group of guys and gals. Ethan motioned for Mark to follow and they went over to the refreshment area to get a couple drinks. They took their drinks and walked over to a less crowded area and were watching Clark two-step.

Then they heard a female voice. "Hi, I'm Lindsey, you had dinner at our house two weeks ago." She gestured to the girl standing next to her. "You remember my sister Allie?"

She continued, "Our sister Megan is out there dancing with her friends."

Mark noticed that the "friends" they had referenced included Clark. Mark got a smile seeing Clark two-stepping—how he had transformed. He was leaner and more outgoing.

Ethan and Mark looked back at the young girls. They saw two beautiful blondes dressed in cowgirl outfits. Ethan thought that Lindsey was stunning. He had seen her in her store outfit and at their home and each time she looked great. He nodded and shook hands and told each of them how glad he was to meet them again.

Mark went through the same thing with both girls and offered to get them something to drink. He came back with three lemonades and handed one to each girl and set the last one for Megan at a nearby table. They turned to look at the others dancing and Lindsey asked, "How was your trip to get your grandparents?"

"Good, they're home now with our mom." Ethan replied.

Lindsey asked further, "No problems?"

The music had stopped. Some of the crowd stayed on the floor while a few others came off.

Ethan looked at Mark. "Yes, we had some issues, but we got back safely."

The music was about to start again, and Allie put her drink on the table, grabbed Mark's hand, and said, "Let's dance," and they headed for the floor.

Lindsey looked at Ethan. "That sounds fun." Ethan took her drink and put it on the table and took her hand and led her to the floor. He saw Mark and Allie dancing and then focused on Lindsey.

After five straight sets of dances, Ethan asked Lindsey to sit one out. They walked over and got two fresh lemonades and watched as Mark and Allie dance another set. Megan walked over with a couple of her friends and said "Hello" to Ethan.

The current dance stopped and Mark and Allie walked over toward Ethan and Lindsey. Mark spotted Megan and said hi as Megan and her friends went back out to the floor.

Mark offered Allie a fresh drink. They rejoined Ethan and Lindsey and Mark thought all three girls looked similar with their cowboy boots, jeans, and hats. The cowgirl hats and tops in different colors was how he could easily tell them apart. Lindsey dressed in blue, Allie in pink, and Megan in purple helped him immensely. But now that he had spent time with Allie, he found her voice distinctive, and that she was two inches taller with green eyes. Lindsey had blue eyes.

Allie told him that her parents wanted her to go to Tech like her sisters, but she had applied to other schools and she asked Mark questions about OU and Norman, Oklahoma.

Two guys in their early twenties sauntered over and looked at Mark. The largest was about six feet four inches and 240 lbs. His eyes rested on Mark's shirt. "Are you an Okie?"

Mark laughed. "Yes, I go to OU."

The other one was about six feet tall and 180 lbs. "We think all OU guys are assholes."

Mark didn't say anything and turned his attention to Allie. Ethan was watching nearby and he and Lindsey stopped talking.

The big cowboy walked over closer to Mark. "Did you hear us? We think you're an asshole."

Ethan took a step over and said, "Guys we don't want any trouble, let's enjoy the dance."

The smaller guy scoffed, "We weren't talking to you."

Mark had easily moved Allie a little to the side and behind him and he had his hands out by his chest—palms pointed out.

Ethan had left Lindsey behind him and he took another step, poised, in the same position as Mark. "Mark, let's leave the dance."

As soon as he spoke, the big guy took a swing at Mark. Mark deflected the right punch with his left hand and pushed it to his right. As he deflected the punch, his right palm went up and hit the guy in the nose. While blood was spurting out, Mark's left fist hit the guy's ribs. The big cowboy hunched over as Mark's right elbow followed down on his head—within a couple seconds the cowboy was on the ground. The smaller cowboy started to come for Mark. Ethan kicked his right knee from the side and the smaller cowboy fell to his knees and Ethan followed with a wheel kick that smashed his face. More blood, and both cowboys were out of the fight.

Mark and Ethan were in fighting position and the music had stopped. Everyone was frozen in place. They were waiting to see if there were friends that would join the fight. After a few seconds, Ethan turned to Lindsey and Allie and said, "Ladies, I think Mark and I will have to go."

Allie looked at Lindsey.

"We're going with you," Lindsey said.

They walked out through the door and Ethan told the ticket guy at the door, "Sorry about that. We tried to stop them."

They guy looked at them and shook his head. "Those two have been looking for trouble all night."

Clark and Megan and a few friends went out behind them. "Clark, do you have a ride home?" Ethan asked.

A friend of Clark's spoke up that he would give Clark a ride. Clark's friends asked Ethan and Mark if they were okay and then felt relieved when they confirmed they were fine. Allie looked at Megan and took a car key out of her jean pocket and gave it to Megan. With that, Clark, Megan and their group turned around and went back to the dance.

Ethan pulled out his key. "Where should we go?" He asked.

"Let's go to our parents' house," Lindsey said. "We can have privacy and we can also get some ice for Mark if he needs it for his hand." Ethan got in the truck and Lindsey climbed in next to him. Mark got in the back and Allie climbed in.

On the drive over, Allie asked Mark, "Where did you learn that?"

Mark told her about how they had learned Krav Maga together in San Diego, and their father joined them. All three trained in the class together. He looked at Allie. "Sorry, I should have seen them before they reached us. I may have been able to prevent that whole episode."

She asked if his hand was okay and he nodded with a soft "Yes." She scooted over to him and put her head on his shoulder and took his arm and wrapped it around her.

Lindsey navigated Ethan to her farm. Mr. McGregor was on the porch as Ethan pulled up. They piled out of the truck and Lindsey told him that they had met up at the dance and that Ethan and Mark had returned from retrieving their grandparents. McGregor welcomed them and soon Mrs. McGregor was out with their youngest daughter Cali. Lindsey mentioned that they left early because a couple of guys were causing trouble.

Mr. and Mrs. McGregor and Cali left them and went inside the house. They were soon alone on the porch. Allie excused herself to get a bag of ice for Mark. Lindsey asked Ethan and Mark if they wanted a beer and went to look inside the refrigerator.

Ethan looked over at Mark. "You okay bud?"

"Yes, how about you?" Mark asked.

Ethan nodded. "You looked good there, about two-three seconds. You remembered what they told us, you have three seconds before others join in."

Mark smiled. "Good kicks. The first messed up his knee but the wheelhouse was the finale."

Allie came out with the ice pack and two drinks. She gave Mark a beer, put her drink down, and put the ice pack on Mark's right hand before placing herself next to him and the icepack and right arm around her as they settled on the bench.

Lindsey came out on the porch with two drinks and gave Ethan a beer. She suggested that she show him the grounds and they headed for the barn hand in hand. Once in the barn, she took Ethan toward some bales of hay. They sat down and he couldn't help but kiss her. It was a tender and passionate kiss and they kissed for ten minutes then broke apart as he held her. They started to talk, to share their pasts, and their dreams. Ethan told her about their trip to and from Wisconsin with their grandparents.

Out on the porch Allie asked Mark questions about his life growing up. In return, Mark asked about Allie. After an hour, the ice had melted. Mark took the pack and put it on the table and when he turned around he saw Allie and her green eyes focused on him. He looked into her eyes and felt hypnotized. Gently he kissed her lips and his mind went fuzzy. He couldn't think of anything but the taste of her. They kissed for a while and then broke apart and Allie came closer to snuggle. They talked and talked until they saw Ethan and Lindsey come out of the barn.

It was 1:00 a.m. when Ethan told Mark they should head back to the farm. Ethan turned and kissed Lindsey and said something about talking tomorrow. Allie reached up and kissed Mark on the cheek. She pulled out her phone and asked Mark for his cell phone number.

As they drove back to the farm, the guys were quiet and deep in thought. Ethan broke the silence. "Those girls are certainly something." Mark didn't say anything. Ethan looked over. "Mark?"

Mark turned to him. "I really like Allie. I like how I feel with her near me. It's funny how I miss her and almost feel like having you drive me back to her."

Ethan chuckled. "I really like Lindsey. I'm going to go see her again tomorrow."

Chapter 66

Trieste

CHRIS AND MIKE STOPPED at a small establishment and had a cappuccino and pastry, then went down toward the harbor. They stopped and asked questions along the way. They wanted to know where the fishermen kept their boats. It was 9:30 a.m., and the pier was not busy. They saw an older grizzled man with white hair working on his boat.

Chris came up the dock. "Excuse me sir, do you speak English?" The man shook his head no and studied them for a few seconds, then went back to work. Chris didn't see anyone on the other few remaining boats and walked back.

They saw a small store across the street and walked over. Mike opened the door and they walked in. There was a man in his midthirties at the counter. Chris asked again, "Do you speak English?"

The man at the counter was clean shaven with short brown hair. "Yes, of course," he replied.

Mike selected a couple of sodas and put them on the counter. Chris asked, "Is this where fishing boats arrive and depart?"

"Yes," the man said.

Chris continued the conversation as Mike put down a five-euro note. "When do they leave, and when do they return?"

The man took Mike's note and counted out the change. "They leave before sunlight and usually come back midafternoon. If fishing is poor, they return early evening. They have their own schedule."

Chris had one last question. He asked where the guys went for a drink after returning for the day. The cashier confirmed the bar name they had been given the night before.

They took their sodas and thanked the man. Chris and Mike strolled the two blocks and paused outside of the bar.

"Back at the bar by 6:00 p.m.?" Mike looked over at Chris.

Chris nodded. "We have to find someone to take us down the coast a little."

They stopped for lunch on the walk back to the hotel. After arriving back at the hotel they decided to take a nap and then meet in the lobby by 5:30 p.m.

At 6:00 p.m. they were back at the bar. They walked in and proceeded to the counter. Chris wouldn't say it was crowded, but it wasn't empty. There were eight men positioned around the bar; a couple of fisherman sat by themselves in a corner, drowning the sorrows of their bad catch. There was another group of four in the middle, and then another couple of guys at the other end of the bar drinking in solitude.

Mike and Chris decided to work the room independently. They found two open stools side by side, one by the foursome and the other by one of the loners. They approached the counter, sat down and within a minute the bartender approached them for their drink request in English. They asked what beer he recommended and he gave them a couple names of local brews. Mike and Chris looked out the corner of their eyes to see if anyone was looking. Chris was sitting near the single fisherman who looked at him. Chris asked," Which beer are you drinking?"

The fisherman answered back in broken English, and Chris looked at the bartender, "I'll have the same." It was one of the beers that the bartender recommended so he was pleased as he poured the brew. Mike didn't get much of a glance from the other four who were busy telling stories and laughing hard, he ordered the same as Chris.

Chris lifted his glass and clinked with Mike and then did the same to the fisherman at his side. The fisherman held up his glass and Chris said, "Cheers."

Chris struck up a conversation with the man and found out that he had been fishing for twenty-five years and that today was a mediocre day for catching fish. His partner was out sick with the flu. It was difficult fishing on your own. He was going to try another route the next morning, traveling down past Piran, a coastal Slovenian town. The four men next to Mike had fished that area successfully—that's why they were so jovial. They had a great catch between their two boats. He explained to Chris that Slovenia had a small coastal area on the Adriatic, but most of the coast was in Croatia or Italy.

Mike wasn't getting any attention, so he grabbed his half-filled beer and walked around to the other side of the bar and sat between the other solo drinker and the two men. In a couple of minutes he was engaged in conversation with both parties on either side of him.

Over time the bar started to fill up. By 7:00 p.m., there were twenty-five men in the bar; the counter became a happening place.

Chris told his fisherman friend that he and Mike were here for business, that they'd sailed over from the United States. He explained that they were open the next couple days before returning to Italy.

"Do you want to fish for a day? I'll pay you," the fisherman joked.

Chris replied, "I've always wanted to see Piran. You may have a deal if you can get us close enough so we can see the town."

"Yes, I can get close enough, but I don't want to get too close. The Russians seem to be leaving the coast open now with the exception of a couple of guards at each harbor, but I don't want to take a chance. Anyway, I would give you both 30 percent of the profit from my catch if you are interested." The fisherman replied.

"If we want to join you, where do we meet you?" Chris asked.

"I'll be at the fisherman's dock at 5:00 a.m.," the fisherman answered.

Chris nodded. "I think we may be there. It sounds like a different adventure for us. Good night."

Chris rose from his stool and walked to the door, he paused until Mike noticed him, then nodded and continued out the door. Chris exited the establishment with Mike joining him minutes later.

They shared notes and Chris told Mike that they had an opportunity to go fishing around Piran, they'd help the man fish before the return to Trieste. They'd ask to be dropped off near Piran.

Mike had similar info: no hassle by the Russians along the coast, but they'd heard that the border crossing was difficult. The Russians were closing the land borders with the second priority large harbors.

Chris and Mike stopped at a small restaurant and ate a terrific seafood pasta dinner before walking back to the hotel. They scheduled a 4:00 a.m. wake-up call, at the counter and then went to bed.

Before Chris knew it, the phone alarm was ringing. He dressed, packed, checked out at the counter of the hotel, found Mike and they walked down to the pier. Chris spotted the fisherman, who looked pleasantly surprised. Chris introduced Mike to the man.

The fisherman brought them onboard. After stowing their backpacks in his cabin, the man navigated them swiftly through the mist—he knew where they were fishing for the day. They passed another boat and the fisherman explained the boat were two of the men at the bar last night.

After a while, the fisherman slowed his engines. Chris and Mike helped throw out the nets. When they brought in the nets they were teaming with fish. They dispersed the nets back out to sea and brought more fish aboard. The fisherman was excited and they repeated this process many times until the boat had reached its capacity.

They stored the nets and Chris asked the fisherman if they could go by Piran. The fisherman suggested that they skip Piran and go back to sell his fish and celebrate with drinks. Chris reminded him that this was part of their deal.

They hugged the coast on their return to Tireste until the fisherman pointed ahead toward some structures. As they got closer, Chris could identify houses.

"Piran" is all the man said.

As they passed by, Chris and Mike looked for activity in the harbor. Neither of them saw anything that looked dangerous, Mike flinched his shoulders to Chris communicating that it looked fine to him.

"Can you drop us off at the pier?" Chris asked.

"No, could be Russians," said the fisherman.

Chris looked at the fisherman and he briefly thought about pulling out his gun to force him to dock, but he wanted this option only as a last resort. "Look, we'd like you to drop us off along the coast. We will not take our 30 percent, it's all yours. We want you to drop us off and forget about us."

Mike had retrieved their backpacks with their Glocks inside. Mike pulled out his Glock and stuck it in his belt with the jacket over it. The fisherman saw it and he understood the request was serious.

"Not in Piran, private harbor near Ankaran," the man replied.

They continued up the coast and finally he looked over and pointed. "Be ready at this pier, I will only stop long enough for you to jump off—then you are on your own."

Mike and Chris looked at him and Chris spoke, "That's great, it'll be best if you don't remember us."

The boat was alongside the pier and Mike and Chris jumped onto the dock. They wore their backpacks with their hands free. They walked fast off the pier: they were exposed and didn't want to draw attention to themselves. Chris glanced back and the fisherman had pushed the boat away and was heading back to Trieste.

In a couple of minutes, they were off the pier walking to Ankaran, which was a couple of kilometers away. In twenty minutes, they were in the town. Chris saw a bus station and went up to the counter and asked for Ljubljana. He held up two fingers and pointed at Mike. Handing the attendant a one-hundred-euro note, Chris received change as well as connection information that he didn't fully understand. According to the clock and the board above the ticket window, they had an hour to wait for the bus departure. They decided to sit and wait on the bench.

As it got closer to departure time, more people gathered. Finally, a bus drove up and Chris and Mike walked up the bus steps. Chris paused a second to look at the bus driver. "Ljubljana?"

The bus driver nodded and so they continued aboard and selected seats across the aisle from each other. The bus was only half full and Chris and Mike sat a couple rows behind the driver.

They stopped at every town and small city in that part of Slovenia. They remained in their seats as the bus gained and lost passengers at each stop: fluctuating from one quarter full to three-quarters full. At one stop, the bus driver turned around, made eye contact with Chris and motioned for them. The driver told them to get off, and as they exited he held up four fingers and called out, "Ljubljana." Chris and Mike examined the schedule information on the display. Mike saw that bus 4 connected to Ljubljana and was scheduled to arrive in thirty-five minutes.

It was 8:00 p.m. when they arrived at the bus stop in Ljubljana. There were several Russian soldiers positioned at the station as they studied passengers arriving and leaving the buses. Chris climbed out first and moved directly to the right and kept walking. Mike followed right behind him as they quickly left the train station.

Chris recalled when he and Carly had visited Ljubljana on vacation years ago. In some ways, it seemed like yesterday and in other ways it seemed like a lifetime ago.

Mike and Chris were blocks from the river and they cautiously walked to the river until they spotted a restaurant. They chose a table with their backs to the restaurant wall and a waiter came over to take their orders. They pointed at what they wanted on the menu and tried to use the Slovenian names.

As they ate dinner they saw two Russian soldiers stroll along. They continued eating and didn't look directly at the soldiers. The soldiers were half-heartedly looking around at the people strolling along the river and at the people dining at the restaurants. They didn't linger on Mike and Chris as they kept walking down the walkway.

Mike paid for their dinner and they left, continuing along the river. As they walked, the same two Russian soldiers approached from a side passage. It was too late to avoid them without appearing suspicious. As they passed, one Russian said something. Chris and Mike looked at each other and then back at the Russian and shook their heads. Chris assumed they were asking for identification and it sounded like they were speaking Russian, so not knowing what they were saying was not unreasonable. However, people knew they had to have identification.

Suddenly an argument materialized a half of a block down at another restaurant. A man was very upset and shouting. The Russian soldiers immediately turned their heads in the direction of the noise. One of the soldiers held out his hand giving the command for Mike and Chris to stay as the soldiers walked toward the restaurant. As they approached the argument, Chris and Mike pivoted and walked away. When they hit the corner, they turned away from the river. Out of eye sight, they started jogging.

They kept in that direction, then turned left until they were several blocks from the soldiers. They needed a place to stay. In a few blocks Chris saw a sign for a hostel. Chris knew that these were typically low cost and low frills with many people from other countries typically staying in one room. He didn't know if they would have room but he walked through the door with Mike. There was a woman at the counter with brown hair with pink streaks and a small ring in her nose. Chris held up two fingers and pointed at himself and Mike and then put down a fifty-euro bill. She took the bill and gave back change and led them to a room with ten beds; they appeared to be the only ones in the room but one bunk had some items on top of it. She showed them where the bathroom was, handed them a key and left.

They took turns showering and still nobody arrived. They conceived a plan where they would need to return to the bus station in the early morning to buy tickets to Lake Bled. They went to bed and Mike suggested that they have their guns handy at each step of the trip. Mike stashed his gun under his pillow.

At 1:00 a.m. they heard someone come in; it was a guy dressed in dreadlocks that looked stoned or drunk. He made a lot of noise and staggered to his bunk before climbing in. The dreadlock dude was asleep and snoring before they could get back to sleep.

At 3:00 a.m. Chris heard some noise at the counter. He looked over and Mike had his head up. He'd heard the same commotion. They heard footsteps, and then their door opened. The girl with pink highlights unlocked the door and stood back to the side as two Russian soldiers walked in. She returned to her desk but the soldiers marched into the middle of the room and shouted something. Mike and Chris sat up in their lower bunks with their feet on the floor but the dreadlock man was still fast asleep. One of the soldiers was irritated and walked over and started shaking the dreadlock man who was startled and still half stoned. He started flailing his arms, half asleep. The Russian soldier now grew very angry and started punching him.

The other soldier walked over to Mike and demanded papers. Mike stood up and reached for his backpack by his pillow. The guard made eye contact with Mike and they both recognized each other from earlier in the evening. The Russian's eyes widened as Mike reached up in one swift stroke and hit him in the throat. He gurgled and dropped to the ground. The other Russian guard stopped hitting the dreadlock man to turn around. Mike had his pistol out and pointed it at him, shooting him between the eyes.

Both of the Russian soldiers were dead and the dreadlock guy was knocked out for a while. Mike looked over. "Chris, I think we can fit in the Russian uniforms. Try putting on the uniform and put our clothes in the pack."

In two minutes, Chris had on the soldier's pants, boots, shirt, jacket and hat. They had their clothes in the pack. It was too tight and they couldn't fit everything in. Chris saw the dreadlock's backpack and dumped out all the man's possessions on a nearby bunk. Chris stuffed their extra clothes in the third pack. They had the Russian rifles, handguns and ID's as they walked out of the hostel room. Before leaving they dragged the Russian's onto beds, each covered under a blanket.

At the counter sat the girl with pink highlights. As they walked by Chris put a finger to his lips and shook his head no. She nodded, and they walked out.

In four blocks, Chris saw a bakery truck loading fresh bread and pastries. The driver walked around to the side of the truck. Chris walked to him and held his pistol to the driver's forehead.

"Lake Bled," Chris demanded.

Mike already sat in the middle seat bench of the truck, pistol out, and two backpacks on the passenger side. The deliveryman confirmed "Lake Bled" and slid up into the driver seat. Chris closed the driver side door and walked around and placed his backpack with the other two on the floor. The space was cramped but he got in and closed the door and the driver took off.

The sun was rising when the driver deposited Chris and Mike in the town of Lake Bled. Mike waved the pistol to tell him to pull over and the driver pulled into an empty driveway. Chris climbed out first with the three backpacks.

Mike got out last and then Chris stepped forward. He pointed to the driver and then the direction they just came from. "Ljubljana," Chris directed him to return.

The driver nodded and made a U turn toward Ljubljana. Instead of being disappointed in a delay to his day, he was pleased to be alive and away from the crazy Russian soldiers.

Chris and Mike walked along the lake and approached a car at a stop sign by the Lake. Chris walked up to the driver and pointed the handgun and motioned for the guy to roll down the window. The driver rolled down his window. He had a woman in the passenger seat. They were wearing sport gear and had two bicycles on a rack on top of the car. Chris demanded "Lake Bohinj" and the guy looked at his passenger who must have been his wife or girlfriend and then he opened the locks to the rear doors. Mike and Chris got in the back seats with their backpacks on their lap.

When they reached Lake Bohinj, Chris pointed to the lake and the driver pulled off. Chris and Mike climbed out with their backpacks and then Chris motioned to the driver to take off. He eagerly left them behind.

Mike looked at Chris. "Now what?"

"I think we need to change our clothes back to Slovenian civilian clothing and find a ferry operator that has a son named Drago," Chris replied.

"We should keep the Russian rifle and handgun." Mike suggested.

They walked along Lake Bohinj and came to a thicket that was not visible from the road or trail. They quickly took off the Russian clothes and put them in the dreadlock backpack. They dressed in their civilian clothes. As they walked by a trash can, Mike dumped the dreadlock backpack with the Russian clothes inside.

They hiked to the dock and saw a ferry moving halfway across the lake heading toward them. They noticed a few people at the dock waiting for the ferry. Chris walked up to the ticket window and asked to purchase two tickets by holding up two fingers. Mike hung back with both rifles. Since they were carrying the Russian rifles, they decided to wait over to the side and further away from the other customers. Their biggest fear at the moment was running into Russian soldiers.

When the ferry landed, they waited for everyone to disembark. Chris waited so they were the last to climb onboard, he then walked up the platform with Mike behind him. There was a middle-aged guy that looked like the skipper at the top of the platform. He was collecting tickets and exchanging pleasantries with his customers.

Chris knew he was taking a chance, but he whispered when he handed their two tickets, "Do you know Drago?"

The captain looked into Chris's eyes for a few seconds and gave Chris a piercing look, trying to determine his intentions. He replied, "No," then made a notch in the tickets and handed them to Mike as they climbed aboard.

Chris felt exposed and not sure what to do next. He and Mike went over to one side of the boat away from the other passengers. Because of the rifles, they were not blending in. Mike knew that they were now exposed as Americans and Chris wondered if the captain would radio the Russians regarding his suspicious customers. Mike watched all the tourists. They were now crossing the lake and Chris wondered what the next move would be. Was there another ferry owner? When he first saw the middle-aged captain, he'd felt it could be Drago's father.

They were halfway across the lake. The captain walked over to them. "Who are you?"

Chris felt that he didn't have anything to lose. "We're looking for Drago. We think my daughter is with him. She is an American. I'm her father and we've come to bring her back to the US."

The captain was trying to decide whether Chris was telling the truth. "What is her name? What can you tell me about her? How did you get here?"

Chris gave Jessica's name and for five minutes he told their story of traveling across the Atlantic on Dan's boat and how they had made it inside Slovenia and found their way to Lake Bohinj. The captain listened intently as he absorbed the story.

Finally, he said, "Get off the boat here at this dock. There should be no Russians in this immediate area. Hide the rifles or they will think you are Slovenian Nationalists. I would recommend staying near the café. When I finish for the day at 6:00 p.m., I will come by and find you."

Mike and Chris were the last to get off the ferry and they walked to the café and found an empty table by a wall. They placed their rifles on the other side of the wall and set their backpacks on top of it. They pulled out their lightweight jackets and spread them over the rest of the exposed rifles that were now hidden. Mike watched their things and remained at the table; Chris walked over and purchased two drinks with food and brought them back to the table. They had time to kill so they ate slowly and people-watched. Chris went back to the counter for more drinks and food, a couple of hours later to justify keeping the table. Finally, it was getting near 6:00 p.m.

A few minutes after 6:00 p.m., the captain sauntered over to the café table. He sat down and asked more questions about Jessica and why she was in Slovenia, and he asked about her line of work.

After ten minutes of questions and answers he sighed. "Okay, I have a car in the parking lot. I will leave; two minutes later you will come to my car and get into the back seats." He gave Mike and Chris the description and location of his vehicle. They waited two minutes and then reached over the wall and grabbed their jackets, packs, and rifles and followed his directions to the parking lot.

Chris and Mike quickly put their rifles at their feet as they swung into the back of the car. The captain exited the parking lot and drove down the road. He didn't say a word until he pulled up to a house. "Walk quickly inside."

Chris and Mike walked into the house and the captain quickly followed behind them. They entered into a living room and he closed the front door behind them. A woman shouted something from what must have been inside the kitchen and he shouted back. In thirty seconds, she walked into the living room and eyed both Chris and Mike. She studied them from head to toe, didn't say a word, then pivoted around and went back into the kitchen.

The captain suggested Chris and Mike sit down, and they moved over to the sofa. Before the captain sat down, he pulled out his gun and laid it on his right thigh. He demanded, "Tell me more."

The wife came out of the kitchen clutching three beers and set them down in front of the men and left. Chris felt it was odd: their hosts were being very hospitable considering the captain had a gun on his lap. Chris went back to the beginning of their adventure and over the next hour he filled him in on the rest of the story, this time more details. Now the captain would hear the whole saga. When Chris finished, the captain set his gun on the coffee table and walked into the kitchen. He came out with three more beers and handed them to Mike and Chris.

"I have to believe this story because I don't think anyone could make up quite a tale like this. Please—no hard feelings, our lives and the lives of our family and friends depend on your story being accurate. We are at a crossroad in history. We are not friends with the Russians and they know it. I have an idea of where Drago and Jessica are, or at least the area. You will eat and sleep here tonight and I will take you part of the way tomorrow to get you started. I will call my assistant and have her take my ferry shift tomorrow morning until I return later in the day."

With that said, he asked them to follow him. He took them upstairs to a room with two beds. He showed them where the bathroom was and gave them a couple of towels. He said that dinner would be in twenty minutes; to please clean up and come downstairs.

At dinner, the captain shared that they would head up to the mountains the next day. After dinner, he took them down to his basement and they rummaged around until he found a couple of canteens and hiking packs. He gave them some other camping gear. Chris offered to pay him for the equipment but the captain insisted that he would not take any money. After Chris's third attempt to offer compensation he looked Chris straight in the eyes. Chris could feel his burden of a heavy heart.

The captain spoke in a clear but hushed voice. "Look, I want a favor in return. I want you to find Drago, my son, along with Jessica and their friends, and I want you to take them across the border to Italy. My favor is that I don't want Drago to come back to Slovenia. Whether he decides to live in Western Europe or the US, I don't care. I want him to start a new life and not return to Slovenia. Perhaps someday we will be able to visit him. That is my favor and how I hope you will repay me."

Chris reached out with his right hand and held the captain's. "Yes, we will do our best to get them to safety." They gathered the packs and equipment and climbed up the stairs to the kitchen. They packed canned food, and the captain's wife handed them apples and bread. They filled the canteens with water from the faucet and packed their clothes with the food.

The captain left and came back minutes later with a map. He motioned them over and spread it out on the kitchen table. Mike and Chris came over and pulled chairs and sat down. They understood that it was a detailed hiking map of the Julian Alps. The captain brought a pencil eraser to a specific point at the map and turned to look at them. "This is where you will start."

He then showed them trails toward Italy, and then he showed other trails leading to Austria. He highlighted the areas that would still have some snow and then he paused and left them at the table. He went down to the basement and came back five minutes later with crampons for the snow and ice. He showed Mike and Chris how to put them on, then handed them over to be packed.

Chris and Mike's backpacks were no longer needed and they asked the captain if he wanted them. He told them to put them by the door—he would put them in the basement the next day. And then they all went up the wooden stairs to bed for a good night's sleep.

As they lay in bed, Mike had one last thought. "Chris, I know that we had some action at the hostel, but I have a feeling that we may run into more situations in the mountains. I've let you take the lead until now—but I think it's best if I take the lead from now until we get to safety."

Chris raised his head from the pillow. "Yes, I agree. And I am thankful to have you with me. Thank you for doing this, Mike—I don't know what to say and words are not enough."

"I know you appreciate this. Good night!" Mike answered as he fell into a slumber.

Chapter 67

Cheese house in the Julian Alps

JESSICA SAT OUTSIDE AT the picnic table talking with Nancy and Sam when she saw Drago quickly come down the hill toward them. She had been around him enough now to know that something was wrong. She stopped Nancy midsentence and pointed to Drago. They rose from the table, stood, and took some steps in his direction.

The owners of the cheese house had returned for the spring a couple of days ago, and the wife came outside and walked over to them. Her husband was still working in the town and he would join her on the weekends until summer season.

As Drago neared, Jessica asked, "What's wrong?"

Drago pulled up to where they were standing and took a settling breath. "Now is the time. We will have to pack soon and leave. We must now cross the mountains into Italy."

The others knew there was something driving the urgency and they looked at him, waiting for him to share the rest of the information. "There was an incident yesterday where Nationalists killed three Russian soldiers. The word is that the officer in charge at Lake Bled will be sending more Russians to patrol the mountains and find the Nationalists that killed their soldiers. The Russians heard that we have people in the mountains but they ignored it while they were securing the borders. The commanding officer now wants retribution."

Drago added, "We will pack and head up the route we had marked on the map to Italy. If we leave now, we should have a twenty-four-hour head start over the Russian troops who should arrive at the ski lift tomorrow."

"Has the snow receded enough so that we can pass?" Jessica asked.

"We have to pass; we can wait no longer," Drago replied. "We've heard maybe 100 or more Russians will be coming up here."

"What happened exactly and where did it happen?" Sam had to know.

Drago stopped and looked at him. "I heard that a patrol of four Russians decided against taking the tram. They came up the back way along the old dirt road with a four-wheel drive jeep. They drove up part of the mountain and parked the jeep, then went on a hike. They surprised some Nationalists that were hiking along the route. One Nationalist was killed, one was wounded, and three Russians were killed. One Russian made his way down to Ribcev Laz to give a full report to his comrades."

This was the last of the discussion. "Now let's pack up. Think about what you'll be doing. Make sure you take everything and are thorough."

They went up to their rooms and packed. Drago had them always half packed in case they'd need to leave on short notice. In ten minutes, they had their backpacks on the picnic tables. They listened as Drago verbally went through the key items for their survival in an effort to make sure they had everything packed.

Drago finished reading everything on his list. The owner of the cheese house stood in the doorway; Drago turned and walked over and hugged her while saying something in Slovenian. He returned and grabbed his gear, then walked out the door. Jessica and the others followed Drago and waved goodbye.

Drago had a few words for them as they prepared to depart. "We will keep a steady pace. If you need to stop then let me know—but I would prefer if we are mostly quiet. Have the rifle ready. We will always hike single file with a minimum of ten meters apart. I will lead."

Drago took off on the trail and Jessica went second; Nancy and Sam took the back two spots. In thirty minutes, they had their distance and stride while following Drago's pattern. Every ten minutes or so, he would stop and methodically scan the landscape in a 360-degree view. This gave everyone a minute to catch their breath.

Jessica was anxious and she could see the same tense looks on the faces of Sam and Nancy. The time had come to find out if they could leave Slovenia.

Chapter 68

Brownfield

OVER THE PAST DAYS, Mark and Allie were inseparable. Mark was either at Allie's farm or Allie was at the farmhouse, or they were together doing something in town. Ethan was seeing Lindsey when he could, but she was getting ready to resume classes at Tech and graduate with her Communications degree. They spent each evening together.

It was evening before Ethan and Mark would leave for Norman and Dallas. They ate dinner at the farm: Carly fixed a big dinner and the grandparents joined at the table with Clark. Allie sat next to Mark, and Lindsey sat across the table from Ethan. The four of them were at the center of the table.

Ethan planned to drive to Norman and drop Mark off before continuing on to Dallas. Mark would finish the semester and then return to the farm for the summer. Ethan would continue to live and work in Dallas. He and Lindsey were trying to figure out when he could come back and visit for a long weekend. She was graduating from Tech in June and was also interviewing.

Carly could tell that there was some big news yet to be shared. Mark and Allie kept looking at each other. Carly hoped they weren't going to announce a marriage engagement.

Finally, Mark said, "Well, Allie has some big news."

All eyes turned to Allie and her cheeks were a little crimson as the others paused and looked at her. Allie cleared her throat. "I decided to choose OU for college. I will start next fall." Both she and Mark had big smiles.

Everyone at the table gave their congratulations and the discussion drifted to the Big 12 and the rivalries. Lindsey started teasing Ethan about Baylor and Ethan hugged her and told her, "Thank goodness you're a Techie and not an Aggie."

After dinner, the grandparents helped Carly clear the dishes and let Mark and Ethan and the girls escape to the front porch. Clark went into the living room to read.

"I really like the girls," Grandma H shared.

"And the boys really seem fond of them," Ma K added.

"They both make good-looking couples," Grandpa H interjected.

"They seem natural and easy together," Pa K observed.

Carly listened and blurted what was weighing on her mind. "I wish Chris were here to meet them. I really wish that Jessica and Chris were here—and that Ryan and Abby were here more often."

They finished cleaning the dishes and then left the kitchen to join Clark in the living room. They found their books and soon all of them were positioned in a comfortable spot in the living room.

Mark and Allie took a walk down to the barn. Allie asked, "Mark, will you be able to come back for my graduation?"

"The semester is now more compact." Mark shared. "I'll have to look at the new revised spring schedule—I'll send it to you and we can try to plan out the next couple of months. It may be hard for me to get over here from Norman, but I'll be here this summer and we'll both be in Norman next fall."

Allie turned him around and looked in his eyes. He bent his head down and gave her a gentle but passionate kiss and they kept the kiss and connected closer. Mark felt so different now and he was trying to put a finger on it. If someone had asked him, he would have had trouble identifying it.

Ethan and Lindsey were on the front porch sitting on the bench. Ethan looked at Lindsey. "I really wish we weren't so far apart. There aren't many opportunities for good finance jobs in Lubbock. I don't see many openings here for hedge funds or private equity."

She reached down, grabbed his hand and intertwined her fingers with his. "You know, I was looking the other day at companies interviewing at Tech and there are a number of opportunities in the Dallas area that I can interview for—and they look like really interesting positions."

Ethan looked at her warmly. "That would be terrific, Lindsey. I would like that."

He pulled his hand away from hers and put his arm around her and pulled her close. He would miss Mark and his family, but he'd miss Lindsey in a different way. She was very attractive and she brought him excitement, but she was also very calming to him. They hadn't known each other for long, but it felt like they had known each other for years.

At 1:00 a.m., after long hugs and kisses, the girls left the farm. Lindsey drove off with Allie riding in the passenger seat.

Ethan looked at Mark. "Bud, let's go to bed. We have a long day tomorrow."

As they walked to the porch, Mark confessed to Ethan, "Ethan, I don't know how I'm going to make the next two months without seeing Allie."

Ethan looked over and smiled. "I know, I feel the same way about Lindsey. She'll look at jobs in Dallas and I'm really hoping she will find one."

As they walked to the house, Ethan blurted, "Mark, she may be the one."

Mark nodded. "I know that we're young and Allie has a couple of months to finish high school, but I'm feeling the same way."

Chapter 69

Julian Alps

THE CAPTAIN TOLD MIKE and Chris that the tram was too dangerous for travel, so he used his four-wheel drive vehicle to follow a mountain trail up the back side of the mountain. They climbed a steep trail that the captain liberally called a road. They kept moving up and around bends until he finally pulled over and stopped, turning off the engine.

"This is where I will drop you off."

Chris and Mike climbed out and pulled on their packs. Mike unfolded the map and spread it out on the vehicle's hood. The captain pointed to a spot on the map. "This is where we are."

He moved his index finger and they followed a small trail to another point on the map. "This is the cheese house. I know that Drago and Jessica and their friends stayed there. Our friend owns the place and she will be there now that it's opening for spring. Good luck!"

He looked at Chris. "Please find them and take them to safety."

They shook hands. Mike had the map, they turned around and Mike led them along about fifty feet. Chris turned around again: the captain and his four-wheel drive were gone. Mike was focused and moved along the trail at a steady but quick clip. Chris noticed he stopped every quarter of a mile to survey the landscape.

Chris asked after the third stop, "Are you looking for anything specific, or memorizing where we are?"

Mike looked back and smiled. "Both, but I'm also getting a feel for the Julian Alps."

They walked another half hour and came to a bend in the path. There was a building, in fact there were a couple of buildings. Mike stopped and pulled to the side of the trail and hunched down, staring at the structures.

"Well, according to the map, this is the cheese house. Let' stay here five minutes and observe. This is a good time for a drink of water."

They sat for a little over five minutes and didn't see any activity. Mike then led them forward as they quietly headed up to the house. They reached the house and the door was ajar. They stood there listening for any sounds. They heard a woman's voice singing and Mike cautiously walked in. Chris paused a few seconds and then followed. The woman was at her oven singing and pulling out a tray.

Mike broke the silence. "Hello."

She almost dropped the tray as a small shriek escaped her mouth. Mike and Chris had their hands up with palms out trying to show her they meant no harm. She stood and stared at them. Chris decided to break the ice. "Do you speak English?"

The woman stared at him.

"We are looking for someone. Jessica? Drago?"

No response.

Chris pulled out a picture that he brought on the trip. It was a picture of his family at Christmas with Finley. It showed Chris and Jessica and the family in one of their best-ever moments in San Diego.

"Jessica," he said as he pointed to the young blonde woman in the picture. Then he pointed at himself in the picture. "Chris or Father." She was looking at the picture and then looking at him.

Chris had to keep trying, and he pointed at Mike and himself, "Americans, United States! I'm here to find my daughter."

Finally, she smiled. "Yes, I know her and her friends. They leave."

Mike walked over and pulled out the map and spread it out on the table. He asked her to come over to view the map with him. Chris walked over to the window and looked outside. He saw some shapes coming up the trail about one hundred yards away.

"Mike, we have some visitors."

Mike and the woman came over to see who was coming. All she said was "Rusi."

Mike and Chris knew what that meant. They counted four of them walking up the trail. Mike and Chris looked at the woman and she said, "Come" and quickly walked out of the kitchen and out of the house through a side door and led them into the adjacent cheese house. They carried their packs with them and she brought them into a room that had large cheese discs stacked on the shelf. She pointed to a back room that stored all her equipment, then she left the building and closed the door.

Chris and Mike placed their packs in a corner of the room, their rifles leaning near them. They had their handguns out. Mike also had his knife accessible and went to the side of the door leading to the room where the owner made the cheese. He was not standing behind the door but on the other side so he could easily arm sweep with the knife. He motioned for Chris to position himself at the back of the room facing the door.

In minutes, they heard voices. They heard angry men's voices and they heard the owner trying to respond. Then they heard a big smack sound like someone had been hit. They remained still even when it sounded like the soldiers were searching the woman's house. Then they heard boots approaching. The boots walked into the first room that stored the cheese, then they heard the boots approach the door where Mike was positioned. The footsteps stopped. Chris's throat was parched and his body tensed with his gun pointed at the door. Mike was poised but still like a statue. His eyes didn't even blink. The door swung open and a soldier appeared in the door-way with rifle raised. He was swinging it, canvassing one side of the room to the other. Before the Russian solider could zero in on Chris in the back corner of the room, Mike had the knife across his throat. The soldier went down instantaneously, blood spurting and gurgling sounds. Mike jumped out in the doorway with his gun in a ready position to make sure the solider was alone. He was satisfied and turned around and hissed to Chris to bring him the rifle.

Chris moved across the room quickly. He grabbed the rifle and fol-lowed Mike out to the main cheese room. Mike had his knife in his left hand and his gun in his right. He was listening for sounds and then he motioned for Chris to follow him.

Mike walked out of the cheese house, through the narrow corri-dor, and into the main house. He saw a soldier with his back to him. The Russian soldier was facing the woman. She was bent over the counter and Mike saw some blood dripping down from her mouth. Obviously, she had been slapped. That was probably the noise they had heard in the beginning. The soldier was busy chastising the woman and didn't notice Mike as he quietly came up from behind and slashed his throat in one swift movement. The woman stared at Mike with big eyes and he brought a finger to his lips to signal for quiet. Then with his eyes he questioned where the other two Russian soldiers were.

She understood and pointed one finger up the stairs and then pointed again with her finger to outside the front door. Mike put his knife and Glock away and took the rifle from Chris. Mike looked at Chris and pointed upstairs and then pointed for Chris to stay in place and watch the stairs.

Mike quietly walked to the front door. There was a Russian soldier at the picnic bench standing with one foot perched on the bench. He had a cigarette dangling from his mouth and had a map on the table. Chris thought he was the leader of this patrol. The picnic table was about thirty feet away and completely in the clear. Mike brought up the rifle and fired two shots at the soldier. They were clean head shots and the solider died instantly.

As soon as Chris heard the shots he knew that the soldier searching upstairs in the bedrooms would be alarmed. Within seconds he heard boots coming down and Chris had his body balanced and poised with the Glock. As soon as he saw the Russian's chest he pulled the trigger. The Russian did not even see Chris and he started to tumble and crash down the stairs. As soon as he hit the bottom of the stairs, Mike was back in the house and moving toward him. The Russian was bleeding but still alive. Mike looked at the Russian and pulled his pistol out and shot him in the head.

He looked at Chris. "We can't have any witnesses if we want to get out alive."

Chris nodded. The woman had not moved, and Chris walked over. "Are you okay?"

She didn't say anything, but nodded.

Mike spoke to Chris. "We need to collect all the guns, knives, or anything that looks valuable."

He looked at the woman. "Where do you want us to put the bodies?"

She looked at him, stunned, and they thought that maybe she didn't understand the question. After a few seconds, she told them to follow her. She brought them through the back of the house and through the back door. At the end of a clearing there was a ditch. She motioned for them to put the bodies in the ditch.

Mike and Chris went back in the house. They started with the guy at the picnic table and took his rifle, handgun, knife, and pack and placed it on the kitchen table. They dragged the body around the house and into the ditch. They repeated the process with the two soldiers in the house and then the one in the cheese house. In ten minutes, they had the four Russian soldiers in the ditch. They then went through the packs and took some food and eating utensils. They kept two rifles and Chris took a knife. They left the rest of the goods with the woman but she didn't want the packs. They went out back and threw the packs in with the bodies.

Mike then used one of the Russian knives to cut two branches. He gave one branch to Chris and asked him to go over all the footprints in the backyard as he left for the front yard. Mike was back in ten minutes with a shovel. They placed the branches on top of the bodies and Mike began shoveling dirt in the trench to further cover up the bodies.

Mike stopped when he had a couple feet of dirt on the bodies. He looked at Chris. "This will hopefully eliminate the stench."

They cut a few more branches and laid them over the dirt. Now that the bodies were not visible, they walked back into the house. While they were outside, the woman had done a good job of cleaning up the blood inside. Her house was again Spartan but spotless. They also noticed that the other rifles, guns and knives were gone and she assured them that she had them well hidden.

Mike brought out the map again and he put it down. The woman came over to look at it.

"They left yesterday and they are going this way." She pointed to a trail.

Mike and Chris noticed that the trail led to Italy. Chris looked back at the woman and she started ushering them out of the house. Chris thought it was for their own safety but it was also for the woman's safety.

"Go! Find them and bring them home safe. I'm fine, watch for Rusi! Many Rusi in these mountains today!"

Mike and Chris stood by the doorway verifying that it looked clear. Mike knew which of the trails to take to follow Drago and Jessica. It was a steep hike up the mountain.

He looked back around at Chris. "Until we make it across the border, assume that a Russian is around every corner or behind every tree or bush. Jessica and her friends have a day ahead of us, so we'll try to make good time today—we may hike through some of the night if we have some moonlight. Our goal is to catch up with them by the end of tomorrow."

Chris nodded. "Let's go," he agreed, and they started climbing up the trail. As they reached the knoll, Mike looked ahead and to the side. Chris looked back at the house to see the woman standing in the doorway. She was watching them hike the short segment and she waved to Chris and then walked back into her house. Mike finished his scan and started on the next part of the trail with Chris in step ten yards behind him.

Part 3

Chapter 70

Trail to Italy

Stopping for lunch at a trail junction, Drago explained to the others that this would be their last opportunity to change directions on the trail. From then on there would be only one trail leading to Italy.

"God willing, we may reach Italy in two days," Drago shared.

Sam took his left shoe off and tried to knock out a few shale pebbles that had somehow made their way into his boots during the steep climb. Nancy and Jessica retrieved bread and cheese from their backpacks and set sliced bread and cheese on a flat rock for everyone to eat.

Drago spread the map out on an adjacent rock, as he studied the terrain. The junction was a beautiful spot. There were a few large and mature trees that provided shade, and a number of rocks to sit upon with just enough brush to keep them from being too exposed.

There had been little conversation during the hike, but Nancy broke the quiet with her declaration of desiring a hot bath. "You know, all I have been thinking about is a nice, hot bath. I think I want bath salts—no, I want bubbles. Yes, I want a bubble bath, and I want to be there all day and have breakfast, lunch, and dinner brought in. I wouldn't leave the bathtub the whole day."

"I want a big steak and potato and fine wine and ...," Drago wistfully let his vision carry him as his world trailed off.

"I want to spend the day in a sports bar, one that has fifty beers on tap. I'd order a deli plate with sausages, meats and cheeses," Sam interrupted.

They all turned and looked at Jessica, who was deep in thought. "All I want is to have my family together for a celebration. My mom would be cooking my favorite foods and Finley would be pestering me to throw the ball."

They all laughed at Jessica's vision, then started eating their lunch of bread and cheese. Five minutes later, Nancy took four apples out of the pack and shared them with the others. They would eat their apples as they hiked.

Drago planned for them to hike another five hours. He had a location in mind that would be a good spot to camp for the night. They finished their last bites of cheese and bread, grabbed their apples, put on their backpacks, and continued following Drago on the trail.

They hiked for almost five hours. Drago knew the others were exhausted. However, he felt that they were close to their destination for the day. As he turned the next bend, Drago saw something out of the corner of his eye. Dropping to his knee, he silently motioned for the others to do the same. With caution, he brought his rifle to a ready position.

A soldier up the trail was relieving himself. His back to Drago, he hadn't seen them. Drago kept his rifle pointed at the soldier as he retreated slowly before stopping by a bush about ten meters from the others. Turning around to check on the others, Drago made eye contact with Sam, who had his rifle leveled and ready. Drago held his index finger to his lips, the universal motion for quiet, then turned around again and watched the soldier.

The soldier finished relieving himself. Zipping up his pants, the soldier continued to walk uphill and away from Drago's location. Drago waited motionless for ten minutes before backtracking down to join the others.

"I saw a soldier going to the bathroom." Drago spoke in a hushed voice. "He didn't see me. I couldn't tell if he was Russian or Slovenian. I want Sam to move up to where I was beside the bush and observe: they appear to be staying where I had planned for us to camp tonight. I want to get closer and determine who they are fighting for."

Sam positioned himself by the bush, his rifle ready for action. Drago took his pack off and placed it behind a bush, then quietly proceeded around the curve a few meters before disappearing off the trail to the right.

Jessica felt like he was gone forever, but in twenty minutes Drago returned, motioning for Sam to follow him down the trail to strategize with the others.

As soon as they all gathered, Drago shared. "They are Russian soldiers, and there are eight of them. I don't think we can go around them. They have two men positioned at two different vantage points observing both sides of the trail. We don't know if there are any other soldiers ahead of them on the trail to Italy. I think we should head back to the junction and find another path out of Slovenia."

He sensed the disappointment from the others. Jessica agreed that they only had one choice, so she spoke up. "Then let's go!" Grabbing their packs, they started moving quickly down the same trail they had labored hiking up all afternoon. Jessica wondered if Drago planned to make it back to the junction by nightfall; and if they could successfully navigate the trail in the dark.

After traveling for one and a half hours, it was dark. Drago paused as they gathered in darkness. He gave them the disappointing news that they had covered only half the distance to the junction.

They were near a stream that ran parallel with the trail. "This is a good spot to spend the night. It's too dangerous to continue on." Drago led them across the stream and found a secluded area a safe distance from the stream that was shielded by two trees and a few bushes.

"This is where we will sleep. We should keep watch tonight by the stream. If a group is hiking the trail and they appear to be moving through, let them. If they stop at the stream, then we all need to be awakened," Drago advised.

They couldn't risk a fire. The girls took out some leftover cheese and bread from the packs and they ate quickly. Drago determined their shifts for the night watch: Drago took the first watch while the others fell asleep. The other three were so tired from the long day's hike that they didn't have time to fret over the detour and change of direction. They were just happy to rest.

Chapter 71

Hiking Julian Alps

MIKE LED CHRIS UP the trail at a brisk pace. He stopped frequently for short water breaks and to allow time for them to catch their breath. Chris knew the breaks were mostly for him. Mike was focused and quiet; communication was now mostly performed with hand signals. They didn't stop for lunch; instead, they took a snack now and then from the pack and ate while they traveled.

Sometimes when they approached an area where Mike felt exposed; he would hesitate before proceeding, taking longer to stop and observe. At times, they would detour and create their own trail to stay clear of areas that made him uneasy. Chris didn't complain; he knew Mike was avoiding potential risks.

It was approaching 6:00 p.m., and although Chris was weary of moving at a brisk pace, they pushed to take advantage of the daylight. Mike commented that a half-moon that evening would provide enough light to continue hiking.

Mike was still in the lead position by ten meters—as he turned a corner, he froze, and pulled up his rifle. There were two men positioned on the side of the trail. One stood behind a tree on the left, the other sat crouched behind a rock on the right. Looking further up the trail, there were three men on their knees, rifles pointed their way. Mike stayed still, his rifle pointed, trained on a soldier kneeling on the trail. Chris pulled his rifle up and cautiously approached Mike. He saw five soldiers, all with their rifles pointed at them.

One of the three men on the trail barked an order that Chris didn't understand. Chris took some comfort in the fact that they weren't wearing the Russian uniforms he'd seen the past few days. He glanced at Mike who nodded and whispered, "Yes." Mike and Chris gently lowered their rifles.

The soldier who had spoken approached them and took their rifles. He walked a couple steps away and leaned the rifles against a rock. Turning to Mike and Chris, he asked, "Od kod prihajate?"

"Do you speak English?" Chris replied.

"Are you Americans?" the leader asked.

"Are you Slovenians?" Chris countered.

The leader thought this was funny and chuckled. "We have our guns pointed on you, yet you are asking the questions."

"Yes, we are Americans. We're on holiday, and we are lost," Chris explained.

That appeared to be the ice breaker. The leader said something to the others, who lowered their rifles. The leader motioned for Mike and Chris to come and sit down next to him.

"You are a funny man," he said in English. "Come, tell me your story. We are headed in the same direction, but you have been traveling faster. You seem to be in a big hurry."

Mike and Chris didn't say anything but stared at the man.

"Yes, yes, we are Slovenian. We are not Russians. I think we may have a common enemy. Come, tell me your story," the soldier encouraged them to speak.

Chris and Mike sat down on nearby rocks. They shared their story, and why they were traveling through the mountains. During the conversation, it was confirmed that their new friends were Slovenian Nationalists. Chris and Mike discovered that the soldier behind the tree was a young woman.

The leader knew Drago. He had seen him in the mountains with three friends. "Yes," he recognized Jessica's picture when Chris showed him the picture and confirmed that she was one of the friends with Drago.

Mike pulled out his map and showed the trail that they were trying to follow to Italy. "We think that they are on this trail and trying to cross to Italy."

The leader smiled. "The Russians are bringing a lot of troops into these mountains. They have airlifted many soldiers to the borders and they are working their way down the trails. Meanwhile, there are two hundred Russians that will be assembling near the tram that intend to break into patrols and go up the trails. Yes, there are more soldiers than what was first reported. Their plan is to trap all Slovenian Nationalists and kill us."

"And it looks like you arrived in time for this operation," he said while smiling.

"So what is your plan?" Mike asked.

The leader looked into Mike's eyes. "These are our mountains. We are moving up to the junction and we will ambush and kill the Russians one by one. Yes, we are only five; but there are ten groups of us—just in these mountains. The Russians will not win. This is our home. The mountains are our backyard."

Mike and Chris processed this information in silence. The leader continued to observe them.

Finally, the leader said, "Well, let's travel together to the junction. I'm worried that Drago and your daughter will run into Russians on the way to Italy. They may need your assistance."

Mike and Chris fell in in line with the nationalists and continued up the trail. They traveled single-file with ten meter spacing, similar to how Mike preferred, but they took more breaks. Breaks were often used to let one of them climb a knoll and observe from a vantage point. The observer would return after a few minutes to give a report in Slovenian, then they would continue onward. Chris and Mike listened to hear if there was any excitement in their voices, however, the reports appeared to be nothing of importance. Chris thought the nationalists were more earnest in looking for Russians than the Russians were looking for Slovenians.

It was getting dark quickly, and they stopped for a short break. The leader communicated that they would hike for another hour. There were too many clouds in the sky, blocking the moonlight and making night travel dangerous. They wanted to reach a safe place where they could camp. The next day's hike would be three hours from the camp to the junction.

Hiking in the dark meant moving at a slower pace, suddenly they moved off the trail and continued hiking five hundred meters up a mountain. It was difficult climbing: sometimes Chris had to drop to all fours, before they eventually came to a knoll. That was their camp site for the night, and it had a great view of the trails below them. The nationalists quickly gathered and circled stones for a fire, and a sentry shift was established to watch the trail below.

The leader motioned for Mike and Chris to put their packs down on the ground near the fire ring and to sit down and rest. Walking to his vantage point, the sentry focused his attention down the mountain. Two other nationalists gathered firewood while another prepared dinner. The leader pulled out his flask, took a drink, gave his head a sudden shake (followed with an "Ah"), then passed it to Mike and Chris.

"Can we contribute some of our food?" Chris suggested. "We have bread and cheese and several cans in our backpack."

The leader waved his hand. "It's not necessary, but if you want to add some bread and cheese, that would be welcomed."

Chris pulled out some bread and cheese from his backpack. One of the soldiers came back with a stack of firewood and Mike went over to help him start a fire.

Working together, they quickly had a fire going and began to eat dinner. They were conversing and sharing stories along with the food and drink.

"Do you think you can chase the Russians out of Slovenia?" Chris asked.

The other soldiers looked at their leader, who was older. Chris guessed that he was in his early sixties. He had a beard that was mostly gray that he stroked while he answered.

"You know, I remember living under Russian rule—I won't do it again. I have an advantage over the Russian soldiers. I love my country, and I'm okay dying in these beautiful mountains. On the other hand, the Russian soldiers don't want to die on a foreign mountain in a foreign country."

Looking around, Chris saw the other soldiers were captivated by the leader's words. They all nodded as he spoke. The Slovenians were content in these mountains and willing to fight to their death for freedom. Chris thought that this aligned to what he had read of the Americans that had participated in the Revolutionary War. The statement was more than the Slovenian's words—the leaders' message was a heartfelt feeling he expressed. The Nationalists had peace with their fate, regardless of the outcome.

Chris and Mike assisted with clean up, arranged their packs, and went to sleep by the fire. They knew they had a tough day ahead of them. They each offered to take a turn as sentry but were told not to worry. The Slovenian nationalist leader explained that they would travel to the junction before noon. Then they would leave Mike and Chris and let them continue their pursuit of Jessica, Drago, Sam and Nancy toward the Italian border.

Chapter 72

The junction

DRAGO WOKE THEM AT sunrise to start early on the trail and ensure that the Russians didn't catch up with them. Eating a breakfast of fruit and bread, they hiked down the trail. By midmorning, they reached the junction. This was a great time for a break, but to be safe, they continued a quarter of mile and off to the side of the trail thirty meters behind several trees.

Pulling out the map, Drago looked at several alternative routes that would lead them to Austria. He was contemplating two different trails. Looking at the elevation of both, he chose the longer trail at a lower elevation.

Calling them over, Drago showed them the new trail they would follow. Jessica listened, and thought that they had to trust Drago. He knew the mountains; they were depending on him to lead them out of Slovenia. Drago shared that he chose a path that was a little longer, but he feared that they would encounter snow near the mountaintops. He felt traveling with less snow would allow them to escape Slovenia in a shorter time period despite the longer distance.

Soon they left the junction behind as they took a northern route to Austria. After two hours Drago took a break, leaving the others on the trail as he climbed a knoll. Trotting down, he explained that a patrol would pass them in ten minutes. He thought it was a nationalist patrol, but he wasn't sure—he suggested they hide fifty meters above the trail. They hiked above the trail and stashed their packs behind a couple of rocks. Drago instructed them to lay down flat on their stomachs behind the brush. They had only two rifles; Drago and Sam pointed them in the direction of the trail.

In ten minutes, a nationalist patrol walked down single-file. Jessica counted six figures. When they were directly below, Drago shouted, "Dobro juto!" Jessica knew from her weeks in Slovenia that this meant "Good morning." The nationalists froze; each dropped to a knee with their rifles pointed toward Drago's voice.

Drago continued speaking in Slovenian, and then the Nationalists stood up and lowered their rifles. Drago stood up, waved at his countrymen, and motioned for his colleagues to collect their packs and join him.

Jessica, Sam, and Nancy stood nearby listening to a lot of Slovenian. After ten long minutes, Drago came over to them. "The Russians are sending two hundred troops up the tram today. This patrol is meeting up with some other Slovenian patrols to prepare for an ambush. He warned me that the Russians dropped troops along the borders—they will be coming down the trails. The Russians we saw on the Italian trail might have been an airborne group making their way down from the border."

Drago paused. "We need to keep moving. The good news is that they have not seen Russians the past couple of days."

Jessica studied the faces of the Nationalists while they were talking to Drago. She felt a connection with them. Similar to Jessica, Sam, and Nancy, they were in their twenties. The leader was older but still relatively young as he appeared to be in his thirties. The Slovenians had parents, siblings, spouses—maybe even children. Jessica wondered if those they'd left behind were safe at home.

Waving goodbye to the Slovenian patrol, the two parties headed in separate directions. Drago led his friends up the mountain trail while the Nationalists headed down toward the junction to join their countrymen.

The rest of the day was spent climbing, stopping, crossing creeks, climbing knolls and summiting overlooks. If it had been a vacation day—it would have been fantastic. Drago, Jessica, Sam, and Nancy finally stopped hiking around 5:00 p.m. to camp at a secure spot on a knoll. Hiking since 6:00 a.m., they were tired.

Drago allowed a fire, so they cooked some of their canned goods—it was nice to eat something besides bread and cheese. At six it quickly turned dark, so they cleaned up and snuffed out the fire. There were some yawns and Drago suggested sleep. He explained that the trail was too difficult to travel at night. They were sufficiently far enough from the trail now and he thought they were in a safe place for the night. Drago advised that he would watch the trail for another hour, before joining them to sleep.

Jessica had trouble sleeping even though she was exhausted. Her mind raced and she cycled through the events of the day. She heard an owl hooting above them. She must have been laying there for an hour because she saw Drago return to camp. He settled down a couple of feet from her, leaning his rifle against a tree that was within reach.

"Jessica, are you still awake?" He whispered, trying not to wake Sam and Nancy.

"Yes. For some reason I've had trouble sleeping tonight. I was reflecting on everything that's happened the past two days. We moved toward Italy, we ran into Russian soldiers, moved down the mountain—and now we are hiking to Austria and climbing another set of mountains. I looked at the patrol today—I looked at their faces and I wondered if some of them would die the next day when they fight the Russians."

Drago sighed and laid his head down. "Yes, there is a lot of uncertainty. In some ways things are complicated, but in others, it's very simple. At times, I feel I should be on patrol to fight the cause of chasing the Russians out of our country. But it's equally important that I get you, Sam, and Nancy out of Slovenia. So this my challenge—that God gave me."

Jessica had nothing to say and a minute later Drago added, "We have a long day tomorrow. We need to get some rest. Jessica, think about good things. Think about reuniting with your family in Texas."

They were quiet for a couple of minutes. The only sound was crickets in the night.

"Jessica, I will get you out of these mountains. You will see your family."

Jessica took his advice and had visions of all the family with Finley. She hadn't seen the farm in Brownfield, but she created a picture in her mind of the farmhouse. She soon had a smile on her face and fell fast asleep.

Chapter 73

Trail north

WAKING UP EARLY, THEY ate a cold breakfast. The nationalist leader told Mike and Chris that it was quiet and calm that morning, but that it might end up being a big day. As they finished breakfast, they packed and hiked down to the trail. From there, they continued in the direction of the junction.

After three hours of hiking, they reached the junction. Pulling out his map, Mike called Chris over and showed him a trail that led to Italy. They took a drink from their canteens while studying the trail. Their nationalist friends were waiting for two more groups to join them; then they would leave to ambush the Russians arriving on the tram that day.

Mike and Chris gave their thanks and said their goodbyes. They were warned again to be cautious on the trail. After shaking hands, they turned to begin the trail toward Italy. Chris felt excitement that they may reach Jessica that day.

Mike stopped every ten or fifteen minutes on the trail to listen. Chris understood that Mike had been embarrassed when caught off guard the other day by the nationalists: being surprised by the Russians could be fatal.

After an hour on the trail, it was noon. Mike stopped at a small overlook so they could eat lunch. As they ate, they spotted a dot coming up the trail behind them, moving very quickly. Laying down their lunch they positioned themselves, rifles out and ready as they crouched by the side of the trail.

In five minutes, the nationalist woman turned the corner. She stopped when she saw Mike and Chris pop up.

"Drago go to Austria," she said with a big smile.

Chris must have had a puzzled look on his face because she pointed up the hill. "Rusi! Drago and your daughter take different trail. Quick, follow me back."

Chris looked over at Mike, who shrugged as they both went to retrieve their backpacks. Within minutes, they were following the nationalist woman back down the hill.

Chris thought, I hope this isn't a mistake! I don't want to have to climb this part of the mountain again. He thought how the leader had spoken about Russians hiding in many locations with a big offensive prepared on the mountain that day.

In an hour, they were back at the junction with another twenty nationalists. Their nationalist guide brought them to her leader. He smiled. "I'm glad she found you before you ran into Rusi."

He yelled over to another nationalist, a thirty-five-year-old man, who ambled over. He smiled at Chris and Mike and the two nationalists spoke in Slovenian for a minute.

Finally, the leader spoke to Chris. "This man's patrol was coming down this trail." The leader pointed to a spot on his map. "They passed Drago and three travel companions. Drago told him that they were traveling on the Italy trail but they saw Rusi on the trail and thought that it was unsafe, so they backtracked here. Now they are working their way toward Austria."

"Pull out your map?" the Slovenian instructed.

Mike pulled out their map, and the nationalist pointed at a trail and a spot.

"This is where they saw Drago." The nationalist pointed his finger on the trail and then over to a second trail, then a third trail. "This is where they are headed. They have half day or more on you by now. Be cautious: there are many Rusi all over the mountains now." With that, he shook their hands. Before they could react, he shouted in Slovenian and the nationalist soldiers assembled. They were now forgotten and on their own again. Mike and Chris turned up the mountain trail and headed north in the direction of Austria.

Climbing three hundred meters, they stopped for a water break. Chris looked down toward the junction—no sign of the nationalists. They were off to fight the Rusi. He was thankful to these people trying to fight for their homeland and independence. He prayed that they would be successful and that many would survive.

Chapter 74

Rusi

Drago was extra cautious as they climbed; they moved slower now. The altitude was challenging, but Jessica found it manageable as they took a break every ten or fifteen minutes. She was tired, but she was holding up well. Nancy and Sam looked ragged—she wasn't sure they'd survive without the breaks.

Drago explained that they would turn off onto another trail in an hour. At each break, he reviewed the map and took a couple of minutes to glance around at their surroundings and search for landmarks. They continued up the mountain single-file with Drago in the lead, Jessica and Nancy followed, and Sam brought up the rear with the second rifle.

They made good time. As they approached the next trail, Drago paused under some trees about five hundred meters from where Drago thought the next turnoff would be.

"I am concerned. As soon as we reach the next trail, we will have to climb a steep switchback," Drago shared. "The worst part is that it's open and we won't have many trees, rocks, or bushes to shield us. We will be exposed for a couple of miles. We are stopping here because I recommend once we turn off to this other trail that we don't take any breaks until we reach the top. We will hike almost two miles uphill without a break."

Drago looked primarily at Sam and Nancy, who both nodded. "Let's all hydrate and eat a snack before we tackle it," Drago recommended.

After fifteen minutes, they continued along the trail; in five hundred meters Drago turned onto the smaller trail. They hiked one by one, spaced ten meters apart. Drago maintained a brisk but steady pace. After thirty minutes, they were halfway up the trail of endless switchbacks. Jessica turned her head and noticed that Nancy and Sam were now fifty meters behind them, bunched up and spaced only a couple of meters from each other.

"Drago, Nancy and Sam are having trouble keeping the pace."

Drago turned and shook his head. "We can't stop up here, we are exposed."

He looked up and saw a lone tree ahead. "Go up ahead to that tree and hide behind it and get a drink." He handed his rifle to Jessica as he watched her pass him on the trail.

Drago walked back down the trail and caught up with Sam and Nancy. "Drago, I'm sorry—I need to stop and rest," Sam huffed, face red and sweat rolling down his cheeks.

Drago shook his head. "Quick, both of you give me your packs. Do you see the tree that Jessica is almost at? You have to reach the tree. I will carry your packs. Let's go." Drago placed a pack over each shoulder and marched up the trail. Nancy and Sam slowly followed behind him.

Jessica had her pack off as she watched her colleagues and sipped water from her canteen. She saw Drago carrying the packs; then out of the corner of her eye, she saw some figures marching like ants below at the trailhead. She couldn't determine if they were nationalists or Russians, but she instinctively had a bad feeling.

Drago was close, and she warned him, "Drago, there are soldiers below that have spotted us." Drago didn't stop walking. As he reached Jessica, he wordlessly dropped the two packs, took off his own pack, and dropped to his knees. Following her pointed finger, he squinted. "Shit!"

He didn't look at Jessica. "They are Russian soldiers."

As he spoke, Jessica saw one soldier stop. She heard a shot, followed by more shots. Nancy dropped to the ground on the third shot and collapsed, tumbling down a couple of feet on gravel. Sam stopped and looked at Nancy.

Drago took off running down the trail in the direction of Sam and Nancy, shouting. "Sam, run! Run!"

Sam was dazed but moved up the hill as fast as he could. Shots were coming frequently now; the soldiers below were firing at Sam.

Drago passed Sam yelling, "Run!" Drago threw his body down on the ground next to Nancy. He felt her neck for a pulse and couldn't find one. Drago stayed down. Turning her body over, he saw that she was shot in the heart. Blood had already soaked the front of her shirt: Nancy was dead. He took a deep breath and jumped up. Bullets were hitting all around him, creating puffs of dust and bits of rock, where they hit. He sprinted up the trail toward the tree.

Drago caught up with Sam and helped him the last twenty meters to the tree. They finally reached Jessica and dropped immediately to the ground. The tree couldn't conceal all three of them; Drago lay flat on the trail and scrambled to some nearby rocks that concealed him as he looked down the mountain.

Jessica looked at Drago. "Nancy is dead, shot in the heart," Drago told her.

Sam looked distraught. "It's my fault. She slowed down for me. It should be me dead back there, not Nancy!"

Drago was short with Sam. "Sam, it happened; and now we are in trouble. We are exposed here on the mountain and I have counted seven Russian soldiers down there. I need for you to focus."

They stayed still for five minutes. "Drago, can we climb the trail in the dark?" Jessica asked.

Drago nodded and looked at her. "Yes, that is what I'm thinking. We will hold the Russian's off until dark, then we somehow have to get off this side of the mountain. I'm sure they are thinking the same thing."

"Sam, how are you doing? I want you to give Jessica the rifle and drink some water and eat," Drago directed.

Sam handed the rifle to Jessica. Drago continued, "Jessica, you were shooting well back at the cheese house. I want you to stay concealed; stay down low behind the tree but find a spot where you have good visibility."

She took a few minutes to get situated in a spot where she felt comfortable and had a clear line of shot. "If we have thought about waiting until dark to escape, then the Russians have also thought of this," Drago added. "They may rush us before dark unless they have other soldiers positioned above us that hike down. Sam, your job is to focus on the top of the mountain and tell us if you see anyone. Jessica and I will focus on the soldiers behind us."

There was no activity in the next two hours. It was mentally fatiguing to stare down below so intensely. Drago and Jessica took turns switching off, giving their eyes a break.

Jessica thought she saw some movement. There were four bodies moving slowly toward the trailhead. She whispered to Drago, "I think they're making an attempt to go up the trail."

"I see them. If you get a good clear shot then take it, but don't waste the ammo unless you have a decent shot," Drago responded.

Jessica stared at the trailhead. She saw one soldier move and try to run to the trailhead. She fired a shot. She missed, then saw a second soldier try to run. She shot again and the second Russian went down. A third ran immediately after and made it safely to the trailhead. A fourth soldier laid down near the wounded soldier, then jumped up to drag his wounded comrade back to safety. Drago took aim and shot. The fourth soldier went down to his knee, holding his shoulder as he continued to drag the wounded soldier the last few meters to safety.

Drago whispered, "Good shooting. Keep an eye on the two that made it to the first switchback. They are hiding behind the big rock."

"Sam, are you still with us? Do you see anything?" Drago inquired.

"I don't see anything above us," Sam answered back.

"We only have two more hours before the sun sets. Then we can continue," Drago said to both Jessica and Sam.

"What about Nancy?" Sam asked.

"We will have to leave her, Sam. I'm sorry, but we have to make sure we get out of here."

Sam started sobbing. "I don't think I can do that."

"Sam, we have to get out of here alive. She is dead—we can't do anything for her," Drago tried to rationalize with Sam.

It was quiet for ten minutes. Suddenly Sam stood up and ran down the trail toward Nancy's body.

"Sam, come back!" Drago shouted.

Sam made it halfway down the trail to Nancy before shots rang out. Rocks and dirt were kicked up around Sam—and he was shot. Clutching his side, Sam kept moving toward Nancy's body. He was hit again as he fell down, but he still crawled to Nancy. He was shot two more times before Sam finally stopped moving.

Drago had a hopeless look on his face and Jessica had tears streaming down her face. There was nothing to say as they looked below. The two Russian soldiers at the first bend made a break down the trail to reach their comrades.

After an hour, Drago whispered, "I see two guys coming up behind the Russian soldiers. Do you see them?"

Jessica focused her gaze and saw two ants scurrying. "What are those guys doing? Who are those guys?"

Chapter 75

Reunion

CAUTIOUSLY MOVING UP THE trail, Mike studied the map at each break. He was looking for the turnoff onto a smaller trail. Suddenly he heard shots in the distance: several rifle shots fired in quick succession. Chris heard them and nodded to Mike.

Mike tucked the map away and they increased the pace. Fifteen minutes later, Mike stopped, dropped his pack, and motioned for Chris to do the same.

Chris dropped down next to Mike as Mike pointed below. "Russians." Mike pointed up the mountain toward a lone tree. "Someone's up there." Their eyes followed the trail down until they saw two bodies.

"Stay here. I'm going to see how many there are and where they are positioned," Mike whispered.

Chris focused his sight on the Russians below. There appeared to be four soldiers. Two were injured: one was trying to attend to his injured comrades, while the fourth soldier had his rifled focused on the tree. Chris prayed that Jessica wasn't one of the bodies on the trail.

In five minutes, Mike was back. "There are seven Russian soldiers. You can see the four down below. Around the bend, three more are positioned with their rifles focused toward the tree on the mountain. Can you take these four? I would recommend shooting the guy with the rifle first, then the Russian attending the two wounded men, then finishing the last two wounded soldiers. I'll go around the bend. I think I can kill two of them quickly. The third will be a challenge."

Chris nodded and Mike added, "When I say, we'll start a count to two hundred. When you reach two hundred, you fire first and I'll follow. Let's start now. One, two, three …"

They counted together using the same cadence—before they had reached number ten, Mike had disappeared around a boulder.

Chris counted 195, 196—he had the Russian soldier in his sights. He recalled Mike's instructions to breathe out and pull the trigger slowly. At two hundred he shot twice, and the soldier went down. Moving his rifle quickly to the helper, he shot twice and was again successful. A wounded soldier shot in the leg grabbed for his rifle and Chris shot him next—he was still. The last soldier, with the shoulder wound, now stood up to try to run to the other side of the bend toward his comrades. Chris calmly found him in his sights and the Russian went down.

Chris paused for a half a minute, studying each soldier. The helper soldier was showing some movement. Chris shot again—no movement.

Chris was so focused on his mission that he had tuned out the shots from Mike and the Russians around the bend. He now heard more shots. Cautiously he ran down, briefly checking the Russians to confirm that they were dead. Quickly Chris moved in the direction of the shots.

Mike had anticipated correctly. As soon as he'd heard Chris's shot, Mike had killed one soldier and shot the second soldier before he was even able to turn completely around. However, the third soldier threw himself behind a tree and was now safely concealed. Mike decided to wait a few minutes and then move around to see if he could get a better angle. He wondered if the soldier would make a run for it, but the Russian didn't move.

Mike decided to shift to the left. He moved cautiously; within minutes, he could see the soldier's arm and shoulder. Taking aim, Mike shot and hit the shoulder. The Russian rolled down, shifting from behind the tree.

Mike waited a couple of minutes before deciding to shift his position more to the left. In minutes, he had another possible shot. In his peripheral vision, he saw Chris on his right move in quietly. He worried that Chris could be exposed, so he took another shot at the Russian but missed. The Russian bolted from the tree with his Glock, unknowingly running straight toward Chris.

Chris was quietly looking for Mike, thinking that Mike was either hunting a Russian or lying somewhere badly injured. He decided that Mike could be injured—he had to find him. Chris saw the bodies of two dead Russians; he moved around bushes to get a better viewpoint. All of a sudden, Chris saw a wounded Russian running straight at him.

The Russian was twenty-five meters away but sprinting at him. Chris raised his rifle and shot him. Chris remained still, looking for Mike in his peripheral while watching the Russian for movement.

Mike knew this was the last Russian soldier. He didn't want to spook Chris.

"Chris, I'm okay, I'm over here and coming out, don't shoot!" Mike shouted.

Mike appeared in view seconds later, and Chris walked over to him. Mike looked at Chris questioningly. "Got them, as you choreographed," Chris reported.

Mike nodded. "Let's search for ammunition and any food."

They split up and quickly searched the Russian backpacks. They found ammunition, rifles, and a couple of chocolate bars that would work well as quick energy boosters. Walking back to their packs, they repacked with their new items. In five minutes, they were done.

"Let's see who is up the mountain behind the tree," Mike suggested. From a distance, they could identify a man with his arm around what looked like a woman. They were both holding rifles.

Mike and Chris went to the trailhead and started the climb. In thirty minutes, they found Nancy's body. Chris felt sad but guilty that he was also relieved that it wasn't Jessica. They found Sam's body a few meters up; he was also dead. Up ahead, Chris saw Jessica and a young man.

Chris didn't realize that he had started running. Jessica had also started running to him, her expression filled with disbelief. They met and he gave her a hug like he wouldn't ever let go. They stayed like that for minutes, without saying a single word. Finally, he pulled away.

"I'm so happy to see you safe!" Chris exclaimed. "I'm so relieved that wasn't you below."

Jessica couldn't talk but nodded her affirmation. Then she brought him over to meet Drago. Chris shook Drago's hand. "Hello, I'm Chris."

Mike walked over and introduced himself, then brought them back to the situation at hand. "We've heard that there are Russians all over this mountain range. We need to get up this mountain and find cover."

Jessica and Drago looked over at Nancy and Sam's bodies as they bent down to pick up their packs. Mike looked at Sam and Nancy's packs. "Do they have anything in their packs that we should bring with us?"

Drago stopped to think. "They have some food that we can take," Jessica reported.

Jessica and Drago each looked into a backpack and found food that they distributed among the four of them before continuing the trek up the side of the mountain. Drago took the lead, Mike brought up the rear. He constantly looked below to make sure it was clear. Chris and Jessica had so much to share, but it would have to wait until they reached safety.

In half an hour, they reached the top of the ridge. Drago informed them that they had thirty minutes before the sun went down. He suggested a camp spot another ten minutes further and about five hundred meters away from the trail.

Drago led them up the trail, then moved off to a small clearing. The camp spot met Mike's approval and they quickly set up camp. Deciding not to start a fire, they sat down and ate cold canned goods, spooning the food directly from the can.

Now that they could relax, Jessica and Chris began swapping stories. It was getting later in the night, but Jessica wanted to hear details of her father's and Mike's story. Chris gave a condensed version of their experience in Bohinj and the mountain trails. He promised that he would tell the rest of the story later.

They were exhausted and agreed to go to sleep early, knowing they had a full day ahead of them. Since they were off the trail and hidden, they decided to forego the sentry so everyone could get maximum rest.

Chapter 76

On the Run

WHEN CHRIS AWOKE, HE saw that Drago was already up. Drago had found a stump some twenty meters away and had his map spread out, studying it.

Chris rose and walked to the stump. Drago nodded in recognition as Chris peered down at the map. There were more trails detailed on Drago's map than the map Chris and Mike had purchased back in Barcelona. Drago traced his finger over part of the map and stopped at a particular point. He was deep in thought; Chris was quiet so as not to interrupt his concentration.

The sun started to rise and light filtered in through the trees. Mike woke up, reached for his rifle, then waved at Chris and Drago as he took off toward the trail. Chris assumed Mike was off on a bathroom break. Chris noticed Jessica stir in the camp area.

"Planning our route out of these mountains?" Chris finally spoke, breaking the silence.

"There are a number of trails," Drago answered and then looked up from the map. "The question is if we can safely navigate through them. I'm trying to determine which route is best for avoiding Russians. I have my top two choices; both of them use the same trail for two more days, but then we will have to make a choice. Of our choices, one is longer and at a lower altitude and the other is shorter at a higher altitude."

Chris took all this in, then changed the subject. "Do you care for my daughter?"

Drago's eyes moved from the map to Chris. "I care for her very much—I think I'm in love with her. I was going to talk to you about this when we had a quiet moment. Do I have your permission to date her?"

Chris smiled. "Yes," he reached over with his right hand. Drago smiled and shook his hand.

Jessica was up and walking over to the stump. "I'm the last one up," she noticed unhappily. "So what is the plan?"

"Drago reviewed the best trails out of the mountains," Chris summarized.

Mike returned to camp and observed the sunrise. "I plan to walk back to the top of the mountain to look at what we climbed yesterday and to see if there is any activity. Will we be pushing on soon?"

"I think we can take ten minutes to eat breakfast and then head out. Does that sound good?" Drago offered.

The others nodded. Mike pulled out some bread and cheese, leaned his pack against a tree, and with his canteen and rifle walked back to the overlook. It was around a half of a mile away and he didn't intend to take long.

Chris, Jessica, and Drago rummaged through their packs and pulled out something for breakfast. As they ate, Drago shared the advantages and disadvantages between the two trails he was considering.

Chris asked Jessica how long it had been since she was last able to call home and talk to her mother. Drago asked Chris about his mom and dad. He enjoyed hearing the story about Chris and Mike approaching his father at the boat on Lake Bohinj and how his parents had welcomed them into their home.

"I hope that they don't get into trouble with the Russians," Chris expressed his concern.

"My father is very careful—I doubt it. Besides, my dad has an alternative plan. He's always packed to leave at a moment's notice. He has a cabin up in the mountains—if he senses any trouble he will take my mother and they will hide up in the cabin."

Drago paused, reached for his rifle, then stared behind Chris and Jessica. Turning their heads, they strained to see what he was looking at.

There was a shape jogging in their direction—soon they recognized that it was Mike.

Drago, Jessica, and Chris stood up immediately, reaching for their rifles as they walked over toward Mike. Mike pulled up, took a couple of breaths and then shared. "We have company down below. There are fifteen Russian soldiers gathering their dead comrades at the junction below. They left five soldiers to bury their dead—ten soldiers are hiking up the switchbacks right now. I ran back as soon as they began the climb."

"Let's get started," Drago suggested, new urgency in his voice.

They got their backpacks packed and in minutes, they were ready to move on the trail.

"We should not be as exposed today as we were yesterday on the side of the mountain," Drago shared. "There will be sections where we could be seen from a distance. I will lead. We will have to move quickly but cautiously—I am unsure if there are other Russians ahead of us."

"I'll take the rear," Mike cut in. "I may drift back a little from time to time, so don't panic. Drago, let me know if we plan to change trails."

"My best guess is that we won't switch trails until midafternoon. We will be on this trail for a while. Mike, stay closer after lunch. If the trail is good and we make good time, it could be early afternoon."

Drago took off, followed by Jessica and then Chris, all spaced ten meters apart. Mike was following about one hundred meters behind—sometimes Chris couldn't see him for an hour at a time.

They didn't stop for lunch. When they had a quick break, they would drink water and grab a snack to eat as they continued along the trail. The pace was brisk, but everyone kept up.

Mike rejoined them in the early afternoon. He told them that he hadn't seen the Russians.

Thirty minutes later, Drago slowed the pace. Looking primarily to the right side of the trail as he moved forward, he finally stopped at what could be construed as an animal trail. Drago told everyone to wait as he walked off the main trail. Chris didn't see much of a trail: it was mostly covered with grass and plants. Drago was back in five minutes. "This is the trail."

After one hundred meters, they were swallowed by a forest. Chris saw that they followed a slight path; they continued until he could hear the sound of water in the distance, similar to freeway traffic. The forest prevented them from seeing too far ahead, but they focused on their ten-meter spacing and the person directly in front of them.

In another half of a mile they left the forest and approached the river. Drago paused, deep in thought as he slowly nodded to himself while looking at the river. Whitewater cascaded down the mountain at a thirty-five-degree angle, and Chris noticed large boulders in the river. The river hit several rocks, and the current looked dangerous as it swirled around them. Chris, Mike, and Jessica rested while Drago surveyed the situation, climbing up and down the boulders several meters along the river. Drago went downriver about forty meters, then hiked back up. "I think down below is a good place to cross. We can walk back up along the river and catch the trail again. Follow me."

They had their packs on as they intently followed Drago. Drago paused at the water's edge, then began hopping from rock to rock. He would take two jumps, then wait for Jessica. Chris and Mike followed his movements carefully. As soon as Drago and Jessica safely reached the other side, Chris started to cross, followed closely by Mike.

They made it across successfully. Chris felt sweaty from the focus and effort of hopping and balancing. Drago didn't want to rest at the water's edge, and they followed him up forty meters to the trail. From here they could see more of a trail. Drago kept them moving along for about a half of a mile until they entered another dense forest. There, he stopped for a brief rest.

"This trail is on most of the detailed maps" Drago stated. "The Russians will have to decide if they will take this route or follow the main trail. If they decide to follow both trails, they will need to divide their forces."

The group didn't respond but nodded as they sat down and opened their canteens for a drink of water. Mike suggested they eat a small snack to keep up their strength.

They continued on the trail after their break and started to climb switchbacks. The good news was that the forest gave them a lot of cover, the bad news was that they couldn't see if the Russians were following them and if they were, how close were they?

Drago maintained a consistent pace. They hiked briskly, stopping periodically for short breaks of water and a snack. Because of the dense forest, the afternoon light quickly disappeared over the mountain.

"It will be pitch-black in thirty minutes," Drago commented as he looked at the sky. "I have a place in mind for camp, but it's about one and a half hours away. We have two flashlights—we can continue the hike—but we will have to be spaced closer together. Should we try to continue?"

They were tired, but they agreed to keep moving to the campsite. They hoped to distance themselves from the Russians if they were indeed being followed. Drago took a flashlight and reached over to hand one to Chris, who was third in line. Chris would make sure that both he and Mike could see. Drago would ensure that Jessica could see ahead. In twenty-five minutes, Drago and Chris turned on the flashlights.

The hiking was now a lot slower. It took them another one and a half hours on the trail after sunset. Jessica silently wondered if they would ever find the place. Finally, Drago stopped and flashed the light off to the side of the trail. Walking ahead a few steps, then a little further, he found a small trail and turned up the path. Jessica and the others followed close behind him. After fifty meters, Drago found what he was looking for: a little clearing that was by a shallow creek.

Drago stopped and scanned the area. "I think we should stop, eat and sleep here, then continue first thing in the morning."

They took off their packs. With the flashlights and manual can opener they were able to eat cold, canned food and more of their bread and cheese. As soon as they finished, Drago went to the outskirts of where they were camping and dug a hole in the dirt before asking them to bury the cans. Mike collected the empty cans and dropped them in the shallow hole; Drago covered them up with dirt, and then threw his stick in the forest.

"I have some water purification tablets," Drago offered. "We need to drink as much water as we can for tonight—then we should fill up the canteens and put in the tablets. We will need full canteens for tomorrow."

Using the flashlights to guide them, they found a rock in the middle of the creek where they could easily squat and fill up their canteens. The water was cold and refreshing from the snow melt in these upper mountains. Drago gave each of them the tablets, which they popped into their canteens before returning to the campsite.

It was pitch-black without the flashlights—they shared the light as they prepared for bed. Drago praised them, "We made good time today."

"The first person to wake up in the morning and see a shimmer of sunrise should wake the rest of us," Drago continued. "We'll need to eat quickly and move back on the trail. We should take advantage of all the daylight possible."

Chris walked over and kissed Jessica on the forehead. "Good night."

As they lay down to sleep, Jessica asked her dad to tell more of their travel story. Chris and Mike obliged and shared about leaving San Diego for Texas and then Texas to Florida. He had yet to tell the story of the Caribbean voyage to Barcelona.

After an hour, Chris was very sleepy. "Jessica, can we share more of our adventure story tomorrow night?"

He was asleep within two minutes, and so was the rest of the party.

Chapter 77

Trekking the Alps

JESSICA AWOKE AND WONDERED how she could be refreshed and tired at the same time. She had slept well but her legs and body ached. Her legs felt heavy, and she could feel many muscles throughout her body as she stretched. Her back was sore from carrying the backpack. She noticed that her dad and Mike were moving slower than they had been the day before. Most of their trail the day before had been uphill, she expected the same would be true for that day.

They had some bread and fruit for breakfast as they had eaten most of the Russian food as snacks the day before. Drago estimated that they had enough food for two full days or three light days. Taking a vote amongst the four of them, they decided it was prudent to ration for three days.

Drago gathered the others to look at his map. He shared that if they continued at the same pace, they would face a decision the next day regarding which trail to pursue next. His goal was to camp near the trail junction that evening so they could sleep on it.

"I'm planning to cover a lot of ground today. Only short breaks for water and snacks throughout the day."

"Yes, I am prepared for another full day of hiking," Chris responded, trying to sound enthusiastic.

Drago informed them that they would be on the same marked trail all day. However, he was becoming nervous about the possibility of intersecting Russians.

"I would like to create more space between us, in case of an attempted ambush," he explained as he looked at each of them. "I would like us to be thirty meters apart instead of ten meters."

"I plan to drop back time to time like before to ensure we don't have Russians gaining on us," Mike replied.

Drago led them up the hill at a steady pace. They traveled through forest and open meadows; at midday, they came across some snow. Most of the snow was in dark, shady areas but they sometimes hiked through deeper sections exposed in the sun. Drago stopped when they reached a large area of snow, giving the others a small break as he searched to find the trail.

Quietly, they moved along through the country. Jessica and Chris kept the thirty-meter spacing that Drago had requested. Mike dropped back, often out of eyesight. Chris would see him catch up to them once every two hours. The trail had an incline and they were now traveling due north. Throughout the day they saw deer and an abundance of squirrels and birds.

By midafternoon, Mike had caught up to them. He told Chris he would stay with them for the rest of the day. He hadn't seen any sign of Russians following them.

It was now late afternoon, Drago studied the map, at each break. He didn't say much, other than that he thought they were going to make the junction by nightfall. He continued walking at a brisk pace.

SsHHH. Walking along the trail, the sound became louder. Drago had not stopped for a break in a while; they knew they were racing against the setting sun. It was nearing twilight and they had limited time before darkness set in. Finally, Drago brought them to a little knoll on the trail and stopped. The others caught up with him and saw below them a river that cascaded down the mountain.

Drago watched intently for any activity—anything that looked out of the ordinary. Chris noticed that adjacent to the river, one trail continued to the right and northeast, away from the river while the second trail split off to the left and across a small rickety bridge over the river, continuing up the mountain.

Drago told the others to wait as he traveled down the knoll toward the river. He took ten minutes to methodically look around, then ventured up the right trail for a few minutes. He returned down to the junction and crossed over the bridge before hiking up that trail for a few minutes. Returning to the bridge, he crossed back over and paused for another two minutes. Finally, he was satisfied: Drago waved for the others to join him.

As they approached, he pointed to the right side. "This trail is a little longer, but it's not as high in elevation. I think we should have fewer issues with the snow."

Then he pointed to the old bridge and the trail across the river. "Trail is shorter, but it's at a higher elevation. I fear it may be slow moving through the snow. We'll have to make a choice. Across the bridge, we can go off a trail one hundred meters to a small clearing. We will spend the night and discuss which path we want to travel tomorrow."

They followed Drago across the bridge and he made a remark that the bridge was very old. The water came down fast; mist sprayed them as they crossed. It was a cold mist, but it felt terrific and refreshing after a hard day of hiking. Chris hoped that the bridge would hold up for at least one more day as they crossed over.

"Remember the old bridges across the Pacuare River in Costa Rica?" Chris reminisced. Jessica smiled and nodded as she recalled the family vacation.

Drago found an opening between two bushes that created a small path. They followed him for fifty meters toward a large tree, behind which was a small secluded clearing.

Dropping their packs, Drago suggested they risk building a fire. There was only a slim chance that the Russians would travel after dark. He suggested that two of them take the canteens and fill them up with water using the tablets. One of them could gather firewood and one person could start a fire.

Chris and Jessica volunteered to fill up the canteens, which was more of a challenge now than the other day at the small creek. Chris hopped onto a rock on the edge of the riverbank three feet wide; from this position he successfully filled the canteens. Chris jumped back off the rock, Jessica took his place and in a few minutes she had her own canteens full.

When they returned to camp, Drago had the fire started and Mike had collected a nice stack of wood. Chris offered to assist Mike in gathering more wood before dark.

Jessica placed tablets in each canteen, then found cans of food for dinner. Opening the cans, she handed them to Drago.

Soon enough they were eating by the fire. Drago suggested they let the fire naturally die out as they cleaned the dishes and buried the trash and cans. Soon they were again sitting by the waning fire. Jessica asked to hear about the voyage across the Atlantic, and Chris asked to hear about how she and Drago had ended up in Slovenia. They conversation was animated. Drago helped Jessica with her story out of Croatia and Mike helped Chris with portions of their voyage adventure.

After a while, yawns materialized. Drago used a stick to push some of the fire apart until there were only embers burning with an orange glow. The weather was colder at this higher altitude, and they wore their coats to sleep, using their packs as pillows. They were soon fast asleep.

Chapter 78

Choosing the trail

DRAGO OPENED HIS EYES to notice a bright sun and broad daylight. This meant that they had slept in almost two hours past sunrise. Rubbing his eyes, he stood up. Mike sat on a log about twenty meters away, looking through the trees.

"Good morning," Drago greeted as he walked toward Mike. Mike stared ahead. Drago saw that he was looking at a doe grazing on grass in the small clearing.

"I feel something big will happen today," Mike announced. "We'll need to be alert."

Drago didn't know anything about the man other than that he was ex-military and a serious individual. "Yes, I will be cautious. How long have you been up?" Drago inquired.

"Just fifteen minutes. I got up to go to the bathroom and saw the doe. I can't believe we slept through sunrise."

Drago stood by Mike for a couple of minutes in silence as they watched the doe feed. She was beautiful and moved gracefully. The dew on the grass, the sun filtering through the trees, the birds singing—it all made Drago yearn to stay there for hours. It was captivating, but he broke himself away to walk back to the camp.

Drago whispered for Chris and Jessica to wake up. Mike had joined them now as they rifled through their packs for breakfast.

"Let's all vote on the path," Drago started. "My choice is the longer path at the lower elevation. It is longer but I think it will end up being faster." Jessica and Chris confirmed agreement immediately.

"What is the difference in the terrain?" Mike asked.

"The longer route has more forest and is less exposed. We wouldn't be exposed on the mountain, but soldiers could hide behind the trees. The shorter route has some exposure, perhaps a lot of snow, but there are fewer places they could hide for an ambush."

"I'm with you on the longer route," Mike agreed with the team.

They packed up with rifles in hand and followed Drago back to the trail. Walking across the bridge, they stopped midway to feel the cool mist of the river cascade over the rocks. Jessica smiled as she looked at the four of them facing the waterfall.

"This is our morning shower," she teased.

Crossing the bridge, they broke out in single file with Drago in front, followed by Jessica, Chris, and Mike. Mike reminded them to keep their spacing. Drago started up the trail; Jessica waited until he was thirty meters ahead, then followed.

They were only ten minutes on the trail before Drago pulled off to the side of the trail abruptly and dropped to his knee. He motioned back with his hand to hold. Jessica pulled to the side and gave the sign to her father and Mike. They were now all on a knee in the ready position with their rifles.

After a minute of silence, Mike crossed over to the left side of the trail and moved up directly across from Drago. Drago placed his index finger to his lips, then moved his finger to his ear. The others listened carefully; they heard faint voices in the distance. It was quiet, but in the forest, voices and sounds carried.

With their rifles positioned toward the trail, Mike motioned for Jessica and Chris to fan out to Drago's right. Chris continued until he was ten feet outside of Jessica. A couple of minutes later, they saw movement accompanied by louder voices. Men were hiking their way down the trail.

Chris hoped the voices were from more Slovenian nationalists, but he couldn't see clearly. He knew that Drago would be able to confirm soon if they were friendly. Soon, the hikers were more visible. Chris could see for himself what appeared to be two Russian soldiers traveling swiftly down the trail. Fifty meters behind the two soldiers, in the distance, he could make out more movement.

Drago turned to Mike, then Jessica and Chris, shaking his head side to side. They knew immediately with his head shake that they were not Slovenian revolutionaries approaching but a squad of Russian soldiers.

This was the dilemma: the two soldiers would easily see them run back down the trail, but they would also see movement if they tried to move further back into the brush and away from the trail. They would

CLIFF HUCKLEBERRY

also spot Drago and Mike if they remained where they were currently positioned. Independently, the four of them reached the same conclusion.

Drago pulled up his rifle and Mike, Jessica, and Chris followed his lead. The two Russian soldiers were busy sharing a story as they moved quickly down the trail. Drago fired first, hitting the first soldier in the chest. The solider collapsed as Mike fired two bursts; the second soldier fell.

"Move down the hill!" Mike ordered.

Drago assisted Jessica onto the trail and they moved quickly. Chris reached the trail and turned and glanced at Mike.

"Quick, get down!" Mike urged Chris. "I'm right behind you."

Chris heard a couple of shots as he ran down the trail. In minutes, he approached the junction and saw Drago and Jessica. Drago made the decision to lead Jessica across the bridge. Chris ran toward the bridge without slowing his pace. Once across the bridge, the three of them found a tree and two rocks to hide behind. They waited for Mike with rifles ready.

Mike burst into the clearing, and Drago popped out from behind the tree with a wave and shout to Mike. Mike saw him and without breaking stride ran for the bridge. Drago moved back behind the tree, rifle pointed toward the trail.

Chris was positioned behind a rock and Jessica moved from her rock, settling on a tree. Mike was on the old bridge as Russian soldiers spilled out from the trail. The Russians saw Mike, and stopped the pursuit as they raised their rifles.

Drago, Jessica, and Chris fired randomly on the Russian soldiers. The first Russian soldiers went down. The other soldiers were perplexed for seconds, but soon five Russian soldiers scrambled for cover. Recovering quickly, the Russians started to fire on Mike. Drago, Chris, and Jessica continued firing back at the Russians, trying to give Mike cover. One Russian soldier on the ground didn't move, but two others were wounded as they tried to crawl back to foliage.

Mike was almost across the bridge when he stumbled, caught himself, paused for a second, then continued across the bridge. Chris wondered if he had taken a bullet.

Mike made it off the bridge, continuing until he was out of the line of fire. He lowered himself down on a rock that was shielded by a large boulder.

Chris fired again at the Russians: one more fell, and did not move. Chris was keeping a tally in his head: two dead and two wounded. *Were there eight soldiers total?* Four Russians were now behind trees, firing randomly.

"Are you okay, Mike?" Chris called out.

"Yes, but I think one of them shot me in the right thigh," Mike replied.

"Drago, Jessica, please keep the bridge covered!" Chris shouted. "Mike's been hit—I need to move over to him."

Chris ducked down behind the rock, staying low to the ground as he scrambled toward Mike. A large crimson spot was blossoming on Mike's right thigh.

Mike stood up and carefully dropped his pants so they could examine the wound together. They could see that the bullet went through the flesh part of his thigh: it was more than a graze; a significant flesh wound.

Chris pulled out a small medical kit from his backpack while Mike gave him instructions. Chris worked diligently disinfecting the wound. He applied a bandage, then rummaged in his backpack until he found one of his old shirts. Per Mike's direction, Chris used his knife to cut his shirt and then wrap it around Mike's thigh. Chris required sufficient fabric to apply pressure on the wound. They needed to stop the bleeding to ensure the bandage would stay in place.

Mike told Chris it was an "inconvenient wound." Chris seemed to have staunched the bleeding, but the best care for Mike would be to stay off the leg and rest.

"Stay still while I speak with Drago and Jessica."

"We need to keep moving before more soldiers gather," Mike countered.

Chris put his hand out, palm extended, motioning for Mike to stay seated on his rock. Chris grabbed the rifle, and stayed low while he moved over to his original rock overlooking the bridge. He was now only ten meters from Drago and Jessica. The Russians had pulled their two wounded comrades to safety over behind some trees completely hidden and out of sight. Chris couldn't see any movement; it was very quiet.

Chris reported Mike's injury status to Drago and Jessica. He told them that Mike's wound was clean and bandaged, but that ideally Mike shouldn't be moved.

"What will the terrain be like in the next few miles?" Chris asked Drago.

Drago had the trail memorized and he responded from memory. "The next two miles are very steep. It is a climb until we come to a crest. If we can make it to the crest, it will be a good vantage point for us; a safe place to rest."

"Perhaps we should rest here for a while," Chris suggested.

"These Russians have a radio and we know there are probably patrols on each trail." Mike had been listening. "If we stay here too long, then we'll have more Russian soldiers—perhaps they will surround us. We need to keep moving."

"Drago, is there only one trail to the crest?" Chris asked.

"Yes, only one trail and straight up the mountain."

"How long do you think it will take Mike to get up the mountain?" Chris asked as he glanced back at Mike.

Drago made some calculations in his head, then looked over at Mike as he responded. "Two miles uphill—if he's struggling, maybe a little less than two hours."

"You've watched me hike—how long will it take me?" Chris asked.

"Forty minutes, assuming no breaks."

"Drago and Jessica, I think you take Mike up the mountain to the crest," Chris proposed. "I'll guard the bridge. After an hour, I'll follow. We should all meet at the crest in less than two hours."

Mike grunted and nodded. Drago thought it over.

"Dad, I'll stay with you and guard the bridge. Then we can join up with Drago and Mike," Jessica volunteered.

Chris shook his head. "No, Drago has to lead and keep an eye out for Russians that could possibly be coming down the trail. We need you to bring up the rear after Mike."

Chris paused for a couple seconds. "I'll be okay, if we've guessed correctly that they've communicated with their comrades, they may not know when I leave. They may still be waiting for reinforcements. Make sure that they can't see you leave me and they'll think we're all still here."

"After one hour, I'll move quickly up the trail," Chris expanded on his plan. "I have an advantage—I know you three are up ahead, and I don't have to be cautious going up the mountain." Chris looked directly at Jessica. "I can go quickly for two miles."

Drago and Jessica moved slowly from behind their trees. They went through Mike's pack and distributed some of the heavier items to their packs. Mike had insisted that he keep his pack, so they made it as light as possible.

Chris moved from his rock and discovered the best spot to view both the bridge and the clearing was in front of the bridge from behind a large stump. He parked himself there.

Opening the medicine kit, Chris popped three Ibuprofen tablets in his mouth and swallowed them with some water from his canteen. The tablets were to help with his muscle soreness; he tucked six more pills in his pocket. He wanted every advantage while he was climbing the two miles. He had a left knee that had been operated on a few years back with arthroscopic surgery to clean out some loose cartilage in the knee. His left knee had been sore on these hikes, but he was pleased that it had held up well.

Drago and Jessica gave Chris a wave as they assisted Mike to his feet to begin the ascent. Jessica was the last to leave and she gave Chris a long look. He smiled back to her with a nod. After they left, Chris grabbed a snack out of his pack, then sunk further behind the stump. Quietly he watched. The Russians were very silent. He had heard one of the wounded men cry out, but he hadn't seen any movement. Chris's phone battery was long dead; it was by habit that he relied on his phone for the time. He looked up at the sun in the sky and guessed it was approaching noon with the sun directly overhead. He estimated where the sun should be in about an hour's time. There was a lot of daylight left.

Chris guessed about forty-five minutes had transpired, and nothing had happened. He played mind games to stay alert.

Suddenly, Chris saw movement in the foliage. It was across the water and approaching the bridge. He had been on high alert for any activity. His first thought were birds or bunnies were moving in the brush. For a couple of minutes there was no movement, and he almost pulled his focus away from the bushes. He thought it was his imagination, but then, he saw slight movement again, continuing in the direction of the bridge.

He focused on the area intently. He had to be aware of everything else around the bridge. He caught a small glimpse of something illuminated by the sunlight that appeared to be camouflage material. He tried to recall details of the Russian uniform. The movement was now three meters from the bridge. Chris focused on the camouflage, breathed out, and slowly fired his rifle. Instantly, he heard a scream. A human scream, followed by thrashing in the bushes. Chris took aim again, slowly exhaled and shot twice. The screaming and movement ceased.

For five minutes there was nothing but quiet. Chris calculated in his head the three dead, two wounded, and three healthy soldiers left. If one healthy soldier stayed behind with the wounded, then only two soldiers could chase him up the trail. The million-dollar question remained: When would the Russians receive reinforcements? Chris prayed that he could leave before that happened.

Looking again at the sun, Chris noticed it was positioned where he had calculated for one hour. Reaching for his backpack, Chris found the last Russian candy bar. He ate slowly, keeping his eye trained on the bridge and clearing. When he had finished his snack, Chris laid on his side and relieved his bladder.

He planned on move quickly up the trail. He waited another ten minutes and was packed. Scanning ahead, he didn't see any movement from the other side of the stream. Crawling from the stump through the brush while holding his backpack in his hands, Chris crawled a couple of meters, then stopped for a minute to check behind him. He repeated this process four times. When he finally reached the trail, Chris remained low to the ground and moved up the hill.

Chris decided to keep a steady rhythm to his pace as he hiked up the trail. He didn't look back; he just kept climbing and climbing. He didn't stop for water. When Chris thought he was halfway to the crest, he was sweating profusely and stopped for a drink from the canteen. He took the opportunity to glance down.

All was clear below him. He put the cap back on the canteen and continued the same pace up the trail. In another ten minutes, he saw a crest ahead. *Drago is excellent on estimating time and logistics, he marveled.* He didn't see anyone ahead, so kept pace. In another ten minutes, he reached the crest.

Chris saw both Drago and Mike immediately. Drago was hidden behind a tree as he watched Chris climb. Mike was ten meters away, leaning against a tree in the shade.

Chris looked at Drago, and Drago's eyes immediately flashed up the trail. Chris followed Drago's eyes to where he saw Jessica fifty meters above them. She was positioned behind a fallen tree, watching the trail. She gave him a smile and a thumbs-up, then turned back to focus on the trail. As Drago continued to scan the bottom trail, Chris walked over to Mike.

"How are you feeling?" Chris asked as he sat down next to Mike.

"Hoping you weren't so quick, so I could have more of a rest." Mike smiled as he looked Chris in the eyes.

Drago spoke as he kept his eyes on the trail. "We arrived ten minutes ago. His wound started bleeding again and I just put on a new bandage. I've reviewed the map, trying to consider rest spots within one-to-two-mile increments. The next spot is in one and a half miles. I think we wait ten more minutes, then try to make it to the next stop."

Chris nodded and opened up his shirt pocket. As he reached in for a few more Ibuprofen, Mike asked Chris if anything had happened at the bridge. Chris told him about shooting one more Russian. Mike looked pleased. "One less Russian following us," he commented.

Chris smiled and closed his eyes. He must have taken a cat nap, because the next thing he felt was Drago gently shaking him awake.

"Chris, it's time to move to our next spot."

Chapter 79

Through the snow

DRAGO AND MIKE PACKED up and walked over toward Jessica, who was waiting by the trail. Chris told Drago that he planned to wait five more minutes before following them. He wanted to make sure that the Russians were not following close behind.

"The trail will not be as steep," Drago assured them.

Drago reminded them that he wanted thirty-meter spacing, then turned to proceed cautiously up the mountain. He didn't want to stumble upon a Russian patrol as they traveled down the mountain.

Chris caught up with the group in fifteen minutes. Mike was moving slow, but he was performing admirably considering his injury. They moved steadily up the trail, Drago announcing many water breaks to allow Mike time to recover. They now hiked through larger snow patches that were a little slushy in areas but easy to walk through. Chris was concerned about Mike slipping in the slush, but he looked strong with his slow and steady pace.

At the next stop, Drago suggested a longer break, but Mike convinced Drago that he was fine and that they should keep going. They ate a snack and continued marching along the trail. Chris waited five minutes before following: this gave him the opportunity to watch the trail behind them.

Each rest area was marked on Drago's map; these were designated by Drago as locations where he felt less exposed. It was now late in the afternoon. Drago asked if they thought they could make one more segment which was another one and a half miles away. They confirmed that they were fine, and to keep moving.

Drago, Chris, and Jessica didn't say a word, but they understood it was taking them twice as long to hike the trail. Mike kept moving, but it was obvious he was in pain.

When they reached their last stop for the day, the sun was low. They were near a craggy cliff with great sun exposure during the day, melting the snow. The good news was that less snow on the ground meant they would be dry tonight. The bad news was that they would sleep on a hard rock shelf.

Rifling through their packs, they pulled out all their clothing. They were going to wear several layers tonight to keep warm; what they didn't wear would become their bedding, the empty backpack would become their pillow. They were only forty meters from the trail, but they were tucked around the side of the mountain and not easily visible.

There was a little daylight left and they were famished. Jessica found more cans of food and the last of their bread. Supplies were now running low, but nobody verbalized what they were thinking: they had rationed food for three days, but at their current pace, they would need food for five days.

"Let's take out all our food and see what we have," Drago suggested after they had finished dinner.

Rummaging through their packs, they gathered all food items. In front of them sat a small pile of food. Mike saw their solemn expressions as they looked at the small pile of rations.

"Drago, is there a four-star restaurant at the top of this mountain?" Mike asked, trying to lighten the mood.

They laughed, and Drago separated the food into two piles, one for each day. Drago took one pile and Chris took the other, placing it in their backpacks.

Lying on their makeshift beds, Drago was awake and explaining their position on the map. "We may reach the summit by the end of tomorrow. Possibly the day after, depending on how fast we can travel, and the condition of the trail. We are only two to three days from Austria based on these same assumptions."

Jessica and Chris had redressed Mike's wound minutes earlier: he'd lost a little more blood, but was wide awake and spoke up. "If the report from the Nationalists is correct, there could be a Russian patrol dropped along the border. We should be extra cautious until we reach Austria."

"We also need to keep looking behind us," Jessica added. "If reinforcements make it to the bridge, they could decide to follow us and catch us before we reach the border."

They nodded. Chris then looked up at the sky: clear and magnificent. Chris was in awe of the beauty.

"Look at those stars, people. Look at the show we have before us tonight."

Chapter 80

Top of the mountain

THEY SLEPT SURPRISINGLY WELL considering their bed was a rock. The sunrise was on their side of the mountain and served as a natural alarm clock. Chris wondered in his mind which was more spectacular: the stars last night or the sunrise this morning. All he needed was a cup of his favorite Costa Rican coffee, but not today. He rose with his typical morning aches and ambled around the corner to relieve himself by a tree. Walking back, he dropped a couple Ibuprofen tablets in his mouth, swallowing them dry. The walking and stretching made him feel better; his body starting to warm up.

Approaching camp, he saw Jessica stir. Chris walked over and sat on a rock close to her.

"Mom will be so excited when we get you home," Chris whispered.

Jessica beamed. She glanced over to where Drago was still sleeping and her eyes swept back to Chris. Chris knew what she was thinking.

"Yes, I understand that you two are becoming a couple. Drago is welcome to come with us to begin life again in the US. I like him—I know your mother will love him." Jessica smiled and nodded.

Mike started to wake up and Chris rose up from the stone and walked over to him. Kneeling down, Chris asked Mike about his wound. Mike pulled up his blanket to show the bandage on his thigh was still in place. Their discussion awakened Drago; minutes later they had the day's food on a rock, and worked to determine what to eat for breakfast, and what would be their snacks for the day. The remainder would be dinner.

"Drago, if you were a Russian patrol, where would you set up camp and wait for the nationalists?" Mike asked as they ate breakfast.

Pulling out the map, Drago studied it before responding, "I can think of two possible places—but one in particular would be the best. It is a narrow canyon—we will come across it this afternoon."

"Well, today we need to be careful. I suggest extra caution when we approach these two locations, especially the canyon." Mike suggested.

They were packed up in minutes, and moved out on the trail. Mike was fresh and he did well the first couple of hours, but later in the morning he started slowing down. They kept moving steadily, snacking periodically to keep up strength.

At 2:00 p.m., they took a small break. Drago figured they were two miles from the canyon—what he considered the best spot for the Russians to wait for an ambush.

"Drago, why don't you go up ahead, take your time and watch the area from a safe distance?" Chris spoke as he made eye contact with his three companions.

"We'll rest for another ten minutes and give Mike a little more time," Chris added. "Then we'll continue on the trail and meet you below the canyon. Leave your pack on the trail where you want us to stop. It will probably take us one and a half hours. We'll meet on the trail later."

Drago nodded and started to put on his pack. Jessica walked over to Drago.

"Make sure you're cautious and that they don't see you. Be safe!"

She gave him a hug. Drago turned, gave Chris and Mike a slight wave, then started up the hill.

They rested another ten minutes. Mike insisted that he was okay and that Chris and Jessica shouldn't hold back. Chris suggested that Jessica take the lead; he would follow at the rear. They started a steady pace, traversing through snow in many areas. Patches of snow made Drago's footsteps easy to follow.

An hour later, Jessica suddenly stopped and stepped over to the side of the trail beside Drago's pack. Mike walked up near her, found a nearby log, and sat down. Chris held back fifty meters, keeping watch behind them. Ten minutes later, Jessica saw someone walking in their direction: Drago. He motioned them toward the old log on the side of the trail that Mike was sitting on. Chris brushed off the remaining snow from the log and sat down next to Mike and Jessica.

"There are Russians in the canyon," Drago reported. "At first I didn't think anyone was there, but then I saw one soldier move off and relieve himself. In thirty minutes, I counted five more Russians, so six in total. I observed this from a quarter of a mile away, off the trail. This canyon is narrow and doesn't allow us to avoid them. I don't know how we should continue?"

Mike asked for specifics on where he thought the men were positioned along with Drago's estimated dimensions of the canyon. Drago drew a map on the ground with a stick. He estimated the length of the canyon then the position of each soldier. Mike listened to every word and asked detailed questions. When they'd finished, Mike drew up a plan. The reality was that they couldn't go back down the trail. It was certain there were more Russians behind them, following them up the mountain. Nobody brought up the fact that they were so close to Austria.

They rested for two hours waiting for the sun to set. They used this idle time to check their rifles and consolidate their additional ammo. They went through Mike's plan three times. Each person knew their specific role and objective. As the sun disappeared, they continued up the trail. Drago paused before a bend and suggested they find a place to hide their packs.

It was almost completely dark as they moved into position. Drago recalled that the right side had the most cover; and four of the Russians were stationed at the center of the canyon—with one soldier each on the right of the trail and another on the left side.

Mike and Chris moved to the right, traveling as far wide as they could before it was pitch-black. They stopped periodically to observe their target until they eventually saw the lone soldier. They were in position at the correct time. Chris kept an eye on the watch he had borrowed from Jessica.

Jessica and Drago found a location with plenty of cover at the center of the canyon. They were positioned ten meters apart. Drago frequently checked the time on his watch. He would fire the first shot, and try to hit one of the soldiers. Then he and Jessica would take cover and fire randomly to distract the Russians.

At 6:30 p.m. the sun was down, and it was dark. Drago could see a faint glow from the Russian soldier's cigarette. He thought about how foolish the soldier was, giving away his position with his smoking habit. Drago aimed for the cigarette, relaxed, and fired two rounds.

Mike and Chris heard Drago's shots from their position hiding behind a log. Mike moved first; Chris followed behind him. Mike was very low to the ground; he must have had a jolt of adrenaline because he was moving well toward the distracted sentry on the right side of the canyon.

As they approached, the Russian soldier faced the direction Drago and Jessica had fired from. The Russian had his rifle pointed in that direction. Mike zeroed in on him from behind a tree. Mike heard more shots from Drago and Jessica—he'd been waiting for an opportunity to disguise his own shots—then squeezed his trigger twice. The Russian went down.

Cautiously and quickly, Chris and Mike moved to the dead Russian, keeping low to the ground. Mike checked the soldier's pulse to confirm he was dead.

Chris and Mike moved in a half crawl behind the sentry location. The plan was to move deeper behind the other Russians, then attack while they were distracted by Drago and Jessica. They hoped the Russians would not expect anyone circling behind them as they were near the border and Slovenian nationalists should all be below them. Mike and Chris could see three Russians ahead of them, behind cover, firing randomly at Jessica and Drago. Mike looked at the other soldier positioned on the opposite side of the canyon.

Per the plan, Chris would eliminate the Russian on the outside flank. Mike had argued that he could take the soldiers in the center. Drago's first shot had reduced the soldiers in the center to three, making their objective a little easier. Mike would wait until Chris was in position for a good shot on the outside sentry.

Chris planned to strike quickly, finish his sentry, and then assist Mike. He had to surprise the Russian and get a clean shot. Chris moved quickly and quietly, careful not to make any noise with the crunching of snow underfoot. The Russian was focused on Drago and Jessica, as he fired two rounds in their direction. Taking advantage of the distraction, Chris inched closer to the Russian. The soldier paused, looked for movement near the trail, then fired another round.

Chris moved closer; he was now fifteen meters away and behind a tree. Zeroing in on the Russian, he was ready to shoot when he heard shots come from Mike's direction. Something must have happened to require Mike to shoot early. The soldier's head swiveled in the direction of his comrades and Chris locked in, firing two rounds per Mike's instructions. The Russian went down and was still. He appeared to be dead, but Chris walked over to confirm there was no pulse. Retreating backward, Chris circled back to where he had left Mike. He heard more shots—it sounded like Mike needed assistance.

Mike was twenty meters behind the Russians and could see all three soldiers. There was one body down from Drago's shot; Mike determined the sequence to shoot the Russians and had decided to go right to left. The Russian in the middle of the three had fired his last round toward Drago and Jessica before turning around to sit down and reload his rifle.

The soldier loaded the clip quickly and then by chance looked up and saw Mike. Mike had to react quickly: he brought his rifle up and shot the Russian twice. The Russian hunched over to the ground. The other two Russians heard this and immediately turned around, searching for the shooter. Mike was able to kill the second soldier using two rounds.

The third and last Russian took three steps forward, then dove behind a tree. Mike followed him carefully, trying to anticipate his next move. Would the soldier run?

Chris approached on Mike's right side. He saw the two Russian bodies in the snow, and witnessed the third Russian scramble behind the tree. Chris decided to move up toward the right side and look for a good angle, while reminding himself to stay out of Mike's line of fire. He moved a few feet at a time until he saw a swatch of uniform. He continued moving until he could see half of the Russian.

Chris took aim and shot. It looked like he hit the arm. The Russian jerked farther away from him and around the tree.

Mike heard Chris's shot and saw the Russian soldier moved closer to him, but not close enough so that Mike could see much of him. Mike focused on the soldier's hand, then his arm and shoulder; he shot and clipped the Russian on his left shoulder. Watching for a minute, Mike saw no movement. Cautiously he moved closer.

Chris also moved toward the Russian. He heard Mike's shot, but didn't know if Mike had made his target.

Mike and Chris kept moving toward the tree, rifles ready. The Russian was not moving and Mike and Chris could now easily see each other's movement in their peripheral vision. Mike moved to the left and Chris to the right.

Finally Mike spotted the soldier slumped over, his back to the tree. Walking cautiously, he came within ten meters.

"Hands up!" Mike shouted.

The Russian raised his head and looked at Mike. He had two wounds: one on his right upper arm and the other on his left shoulder. He couldn't raise his arms. The shoulder wound looked nasty and was bleeding profusely.

Mike closed the distance until he reached the soldier. Chris now stood next to the soldier and took the Russian's rifle and patted him down, searching for other weapons as he removed a handgun and knife. Mike kept his rifle on the soldier while Chris walked forward, shouting for Jessica and Drago. Climbing on a rock, Chris waved his right arm with rifle in hand to let Drago and Jessica know it was safe to join them.

"What should we do with him?" Chris asked Mike as the Russian followed their voices with his eyes.

"I'm not sure if he'll live through the night," Mike responded. After a few seconds, he continued. "But we should try to treat his wounds."

Soon Jessica and Drago approached the center of the canyon. As they walked up, they noticed the wounded prisoner.

"Why don't the two of you retrieve our backpacks?" Chris suggested. "I'll check the other Russian soldiers and make sure they're dead. We can take a quick inventory of the camp and give Mike a chance to rest and keep an eye on our prisoner."

"After you return, Mike and I will try to treat this Russian's wounds," Chris added. "We'll check Mike's as well. Then we can go through their supplies and weapons and decide which items to take with us."

Chris turned and looked at the tent structure behind them. "It seems like this may be the safest place to spend the evening."

The next thirty minutes were busy. Chris confirmed that the other soldiers were dead and that the tent would be a good place to sleep. Jessica and Drago returned with the packs and placed them in the tent, then Drago watched the Russian while Jessica and Chris took Mike into the tent to examine his wound.

Mike's wound had opened. Although he had lost more blood—he seemed strong. Chris wasn't sure if it was adrenaline that had kept Mike going. Jessica redressed his bandage and Chris found a Russian chocolate bar and offered it to Mike for a snack. They propped him up in a comfortable spot inside the tent on a sleeping bag and discovered something he could use as a pillow.

Jessica and Chris left the tent and walked over to the wounded Russian. Chris pulled off the Russian's heavy coat and then his shirt to examine the two wounds. Chris wadded up the Russian's shirt, holding it against the shoulder and applying pressure. He tried to stop the bleeding while Jessica cleaned and bandaged the arm. Next, they focused on the soldier's shoulder. Chris pulled off the shirt that he was using for compression, and Jessica quickly tried to apply medication. Chris held the gauze as Jessica taped the soldier's shoulder.

The Russian was weak. Chris left to find him a clean shirt in the tent; rummaging through a pack, he found a clean shirt he used to redress the man.

Drago, Jessica, and Chris decided they would need a sentry while they stayed in the Russian camp. The fear was that that Russians reinforcements were in pursuit.

"We need to skip Mike for sentry watch," Chris declared. "We should split the shifts amongst the three of us. Perhaps each of us take three-hour shifts?"

The Russian would remain outside for the night in close proximity to the sentry. They would bundle him up to try to keep him warm. However, they knew they couldn't trust him: they couldn't be sure that he wouldn't try to attack them in their sleep if he regained his energy. Jessica discovered more blankets and wrapped a couple of them around him. He appeared to be in critical condition as they tried to feed him some food for nourishment.

Jessica had the first shift; Chris chose the last shift. Jessica positioned herself with a view of the trail below her. The Russian soldier was ten meters away, under blankets and propped up against a tree. Chris walked inside the tent, noticing that Mike was fast asleep.

Drago went through the supplies again and created a nutritious dinner utilizing a Russian portable stove to heat the food. Chris found coffee along with a coffee pot. He brewed a pot of coffee so that they had something warm to drink.

Drago fed Mike, then brought some food out to Jessica. He also had a plate of food for himself and for Chris.

Chris poured a cup of coffee for Mike, who had just finished his dinner. He poured three more full cups and walked with both hands full. Drago had given Jessica her food and was talking with her. She ate while talking and watching the trail.

Chris brought over a cup of coffee and handed one to both Jessica and Drago. She took a sip and set it by her plate and Chris continued toward the tree. He gently touched the Russian on the head—there was some movement in the blanket, then a head popped up, two eyes looked directly at him. The Russian couldn't move his arms, but he nodded as Chris bent down and brought the cup to his lips.

He stayed outside ten minutes with the Russian. After the Russian finished his drink, Chris pulled out a chocolate bar, opened it, and gave the Russian a block at a time. The Russian didn't say anything, but his eyes showed gratitude. The Russian knew they were making an effort to keep him alive.

Chris returned to the tent and found Mike back asleep. Chris ate his food and enjoyed the warmth of coffee. Within a few minutes, he too was asleep.

It was 4:00 a.m., and Chris was just one hour into his shift. He had made one more pot of coffee before starting his shift. The coffee wasn't that good, but he savored it like it was the best ever.

He saw movement out of the corner of his eye and froze. Setting his coffee cup down, he raised the rifle. *Was it his imagination, or was it something?* He didn't flinch for five minutes: then he saw something walking, and then another, and another. His eyes focused on the movement, his pulse raced, and he was ready to warn the others that the Russians had tracked them. He sighed with relief as he realized it was only a herd of deer.

Chris couldn't relax after this jolt—eventually he picked up his coffee cup which was now cool. Throwing out the cold coffee, he walked to the stove and refilled his cup. He forced himself to breathe deep and slow; making himself relax allowed him to focus for the rest of the night.

Chris decided he would delay wake-up until 6:30 a.m. He studied each tree and log within visibility. With the snow covering the landscape, there wasn't much else to see. Chris thought about his family and wondered what they were doing. He couldn't wait to get back to the farmhouse—the thought of a big family celebration when they returned made him happy. They had to make it back to Texas alive.

Chapter 81

Julian Alps

DRAGO STEPPED OUT FROM the tent, and stopped momentarily to rub the sleep out of his eyes before walking over to Chris. It was a little after six: Chris was admiring the sunrise while watching the trail below. It was quiet; only the sound of birds chirping and singing from the trees broke the silence.

"Good morning," Drago whispered as he approached.

"It's a beautiful sunrise. If you take my watch for five minutes to enjoy the sunrise, I'll start a fresh pot of coffee."

Continuing over to where Chris was standing, Drago glanced at the Russian who had slept under a bundle of blankets. Then he turned his head back toward the trail.

Chris scooped coffee in the pot and fired up the portable stove. Once he had everything in place he walked back, nodding his appreciation to Drago as he resumed his post, recapturing the view of the sunrise.

"I found snow shoes among the Russian supplies that I think may be useful," Drago spoke up. "I think we should try to find a pair that will fit each of us. Some of their other supplies could be useful, but we can carry only so much. Between, food, ammo, clothing—we need to make some choices on what is worth taking."

"Yes, the Russians were well supplied," Chris agreed. "They were prepared to guard the trail for a couple of weeks."

"How many days do you estimate till we reach the Austrian border?" Chris asked.

Drago pulled out the map from his coat pocket. He unfolded half of it and held it out as he took a step closer to Chris, his finger pointed.

"This is where we are right now. This is our trail. We will need to ascend and descend a few times on this mountain range before we drop down into Austria. If Mike were healthy, we could make it tonight, but based on how much ground was covered yesterday, it will take at least two full days."

Drago paused for thirty seconds to let this sink in.

"The snowshoes will come in handy," he continued. "Without them we may have faced an additional two days of travel. I was hoping we would have seen less snow."

Chris nodded, stepped over to the coffee pot, and poured two cups. He handed one to Drago. Chris was about to take a drink when he noticed the Russian stirring. Walking over to the soldier, a head emerged from the sea of blankets, awake and staring at the coffee cup in Chris's hand.

Chris extended his arm to hand him the cup, forgetting for a moment that the Russian couldn't hold it. The soldier's better arm was still very weak from the bullet wound. Now in the daylight, Chris could examine the man's face. The Russian had a little scruff for whiskers, blue eyes, brown hair, and he was young. Chris guessed he was in his midtwenties by his slender frame.

Chris gave him a sip of coffee, waited a few seconds, and then gave him another. After the second sip, he set the cup down a couple of feet away and left the Russian soldier. Chris walked back to the stove and poured another cup for himself and joined Drago.

"What are we going to do with him?" Drago motioned his head toward the soldier.

Chris looked at the Russian, then back to Drago. He was trying to process the options.

"I think we should get him comfortable inside the tent, surround him with water and food, and then leave him behind. We can't take him with us—we're slow enough as it is. He can't follow us. If we are correct with our prediction, the Russians will have more soldiers here in the next day or two."

They finished their coffee in silence. Chris went over and gave the Russian a few more sips of coffee while Drago scanned the trail. Chris walked over and stuck his head into the tent, gently calling out to Jessica and Mike.

"It's time to wake up."

In five minutes they were standing outside the tent. Mike still looked a little weary: he was typically a "rise and shine" type of guy ready to embrace the day, but the wound had weakened him.

They fixed a hearty breakfast using the Russian supplies. It was their best meal of the past week as they feasted on eggs and sausages. When Chris and Drago finished eating, they took turns feeding the Russian.

Chris and Drago shared their thoughts of going through the Russian supplies to stock up on food, ammunition, and any clothing they needed. Chris suggested they pack medical supplies for Mike's wound, and anything that could be used in an emergency. Drago told them about his discovery of the snow shoes and recommended that they each try to find a pair that fit.

They were all in agreement that more Russians could soon arrive; they needed to move quickly to take advantage of the sunlight.

"We need to move. We don't need to guard the Russian because he's weak. I think we should just concentrate on leaving camp," Chris spoke up.

"Are we leaving the Russian behind?" Mike asked.

"My vote is to leave him behind," Chris responded. "He can't track us or follow us, and he could be rescued in the next day or two. Plus, caring for him would either slow them down or cause them to leave one to two soldiers behind with him."

They agreed with the plan and quickly divided the chores. Mike and Jessica gathered the supplies that they should consider taking to Austria and divided it into three piles to pack.

Chris and Drago gently brought the Russian to his feet and assisted him inside the tent. They propped him up in a seated position, wrapping blankets around him to keep him warm. They set a canteen and some food close to him. Hopefully he would be strong enough to take care of himself for another day, or until his comrades reached him.

Chris could see the relief in the Russian's eyes: he looked thankful and appreciative. Until now, the soldier had been unsure if they would kill him.

Their canteens were full and they each had a pair of snow shoes for the next part of the journey. Chris and Mike left the crampons behind at the camp. Their backpacks had been repacked with food, clothes, and medical supplies—Mike had insisted he carry as much as the others. They agreed with him so as to avoid an argument. However, without Mike's knowledge, Chris and Jessica made sure Mike carried lighter items.

It was 7:15 a.m., and they had a full day ahead of them. Drago walked onto the trail and Jessica and Mike followed him at a distance. Chris walked back into the tent one last time to check on the Russian. The soldier was propped up where they'd left him and looked up at Chris. Chris gave him a wave, then walked out toward the trail. Chris then took his position at the rear of the group.

The trail was inconsistent: patches of snow mixed with areas of dirt. As they continued up the mountain they encountered larger sections of snow, and by midmorning it was all snow.

Drago stopped for a break and waited for Chris to catch up to them.

"We should put the snow shoes on," Drago recommended.

Drago motioned to a snow-covered rock and brushed off the snow, sat down, and put his snow shoes on. The others followed his lead, and found a place to sit down. Drago helped Mike with his shoes, then checked with Jessica and Chris to make sure they had them on properly.

They continued on the trail that Drago had mapped out. They traversed up, then down, then back up the mountain. They were now on the side of the mountain which had less sun exposure, so the snow was deeper.

Jessica and Chris often asked Mike during their breaks how he was doing, and he always responded, "Great." Mike was keeping pace, but Chris thought his eyes showed that he was tired. The pace was slow and steady, but Drago kept them moving along. Chris would drop a quarter of a mile back at times, keeping watch below, but he did not see or hear anything alarming.

Drago decided to take a longer break for lunch. As they ate lunch, they were entertained by a bunch of loud ravens harassing squirrels. This was the only noise they had heard all morning, and the raven's *cahs* echoed off the mountain.

When they finished lunch they continued their trek, and began climbing up the mountain again. After two hours, they took a small break. Jessica turned back and pointed behind them: they could see the ravens flying and circling overhead, the faint *cahs* echoed in the distance. The four stared at the spectacle.

"Something has disturbed the ravens," Mike broke the silence.

"It could be a few things," Drago agreed. "My concern is that we are not alone on this trail."

"What are the chances that they are Slovenian nationalists?" Chris asked.

"Slim." Drago shook his head. "They should be at a lower elevation, ambushing the Russian patrols."

The reality of the situation sunk in. Nobody said it, but they knew the obvious conclusion: a Russian patrol was tracking them.

"In thirty minutes, we will come to a mountain outcrop providing a view below us," Drago blurted out. "If we must, we can defend ourselves at that point or elect to continue on the trail. Let's make it to the outcrop and confirm if anyone is following us."

They continued on the steady climb until they saw a mountain cliff with a small rocky trail and an outcrop extending out. Dropping their packs, both Mike and Drago surveyed the area from the outcrop as Chris and Jessica guarded the trail behind them.

"Drago is correct, there are a number of people hiking up the trail," Mike announced after he and Drago returned from the viewpoint. "From a distance, we can't determine if they are Russians, but that should be the assumption. We need to prepare and find the best position to defend ourselves."

They each selected water, food, and ammunition out of their packs and agreed on a plan. If Russians were following them, they would wait to shoot until they were within easy shooting distance. Mike would fire the first shot on the lead Russian before proceeding to the second soldier. Drago would target the last soldier and work his way up the line. Chris would have the third soldier, Jessica the fourth, and then they would continue firing randomly.

It was 3:00 p.m. They only had a couple of hours of daylight left on the mountain—if they couldn't kill all the Russian soldiers, then they would have to wait until dark. At night, they would try to escape up the trail utilizing Drago's mountaineering expertise as an advantage. If they were Slovenians, then it would be a big relief and a possible reunion for Drago.

They saw the first Russian fifteen minutes later. He wore snow shoes and a warm full length military coat as he moved quickly up the trail. Chris counted more Russians coming along the trail: fourteen total. Then per Mike's direction, he focused on the third soldier in the pack.

They had a great vantage point that showed the lead Russian moving briskly up the trail. Halfway up the trail, he froze, sensing a possible ambush site. He held up his hand, and everyone behind him stopped.

The last soldier stopped ten meters from the tree line, barely exposed. However, every one of the soldiers had stopped in their tracks and had their rifles poised. The scout motioned again for them to stay in place, as he alone continued up the trail toward the outcrop.

This was not the ideal situation. Mike focused on the soldier as he approached, at the same time Drago tracked the last soldier, which would be a challenging shot. Chris and Jessica had their soldiers in their sights, waiting for Mike's signal.

The Russian soldier walked ten meters, then stopped again and studied the outcrop. He repeated this process three times, until he was forty meters away. Mike had worked to hide Drago, Chris, Jessica and himself as best as possible. However, Mike knew the soldier would eventually spot one of them with their rifle in position. When the Russian stopped again, Mike pulled his finger; two bursts and the lead Russian fell. Mike quickly moved down to the second soldier in the line.

As soon as the others heard the first shot from Mike, they fired at their respective targets. Chris shot the third soldier who dropped to the snow and scrambled to get his rifle in position. Chris continued on to another soldier. Jessica took her target down with two bursts and he didn't move, two Russians down. Drago hit the last soldier in line and moved up to the next soldier in line. They continued shooting as the Russians scrambled off the trail. The soldiers in the rear tried to move back into the tree line. The others looked for a rock, log, or tree to hide behind.

Mike wounded his second soldier, but by then, all the Russians had dropped out of sight. Mike, Drago, Jessica and Chris shouted to each other, tallying how many Russians had been shot. They agreed on the numbers: five wounded and three dead. This would leave six healthy soldiers below.

"Hold your fire unless you get a good shot," Mike communicated to the others. "Stay with the original plan."

The original plan was to hold out until dark, when Drago would lead them from the outcrop. The fear was that the Russians would make a move toward their position at night when they wouldn't be seen.

They rested, conserved their energy, and kept an eye below. The Russians had little opportunity to surprise them in daylight. The white snow would fully expose them if they tried to approach. It was impossible to rush them with the required snowshoes.

"How far do you think we are from the border?" Chris quizzed Drago.

"I estimate about one and a half days based on today's pace," Drago responded while unfolding his map.

"Keep in mind that the guys below us may not stop at the border," Mike shared his intuition. "They may be bold enough to venture inside the border a couple days within Austria, especially if the terrain is like this."

"After we cross into Austria, we have one day like today." Drago said. "The second day is mostly downhill with some flat terrain. The third day in Austria we should come to a small farming village."

They were quiet as each person thought about what might lie ahead of them. Soon the sun began to set.

"Take some time now to eat and hydrate. We need to be packed and ready to move," Drago instructed.

Chris thought it was nice eating the Russian food for variety. They wouldn't be able to eat through the night.

"Mike, try to get some sleep," Chris suggested. "I'm wide awake. I'll let you know if we see activity."

It was almost dark; the mountain blocked the sunset. The moon had been exposed since late afternoon, but now it was being filtered by clouds that aggressively closed in, before it began to rain.

Chris strained to look below through the blackness and he felt a tap on his shoulder. He jerked his head around and relaxed when he saw it was Drago.

"It's time to go. Jessica and Mike are up the trail waiting for us. Stay low and follow me closely. Step exactly where I step. Ready?" Chris nodded.

They moved slowly along the outcrop, close to the ground. Drago was deliberate in his footing and Chris concentrated and stepped exactly as he stepped. In five minutes, they had left the outcrop and Jessica and Mike were there waiting for them.

Now raining heavily, Drago advised that they should put on their snowshoes for the wet snow. Traveling would be slow; the rain would make the trail slushy. The moon was completely hidden from them and it was pitch-black. Drago insisted not to space out but to bunch in close together. They would travel very slowly in the dark for a quarter of a mile as the trail circled around the mountain. Drago explained that it'd be safe to use the flashlights after they'd reached the quarter mile point.

It took thirty minutes to cover the quarter mile. Drago paused.

"Is everyone okay?"

He received confirmation, before pulling out two flashlights. Keeping one, he handed the other to Jessica. He changed the formation: Drago would lead, followed by Mike, Jessica, and then Chris.

"We will continue a little faster now with light, but it should still be slow and steady," Drago instructed.

"There is a good chance that the Russians will move in on the outcrop tonight and discover that we left." Drago looked at Chris. "They will decide either to chase us in the night or to wait until daylight. If they chase us tonight, they will also need to use the flashlights. So turn around periodically to look for lights approaching us!"

"Yes," Chris acknowledged.

The travel was slower than expected. The rain made the snow very soft and slushy as Drago had predicted. The snow shoes helped, but relying on only two flashlights in the pitch dark made it challenging. Drago took a break almost every hour.

At 5:30 a.m., they came to what Drago thought was the tallest point of the trail. He anticipated a slight descent for the next major portion. There would be some up and down, but they had climbed the worst part. As they stopped for a break, Drago's flashlight went across Mike.

"Wait!" Jessica called out, as she shone her flashlight onto Mike's leg. His thigh had a large red spot on his pants.

Mike dropped his pants so Jessica and Drago could look at his wound. The bandage had fallen off and the wound had opened again. They spent ten minutes working on him, applying disinfectant and patching him up. Chris positioned himself at the bend, watching behind them. When they'd finished the new bandage on Mike, Chris rejoined them. Looking at Mike,

Chris could tell that he was exhausted. The travel in the snow took a lot more out of him.

At the next break they were quiet, as they ate a snack from the viewpoint. Chris spotted lights a distance below them and moving up the mountain. It looked something like fireflies bobbing around. He counted five lights bouncing.

"Drago, Jessica, come over and look at this," Chris called out.

As they approached, he pointed below. "I think we're being followed. Drago, how long do you estimate before they reach this spot?"

Drago looked at the lights for thirty seconds, then pulled out his map. "I think they will be here in an hour."

"Where will we be in an hour?" Chris asked.

"About here." Drago looked at the map, pointing at a spot.

"And how long will it take them to reach where we will be in an hour?" Chris questioned further.

"Maybe thirty minutes," Drago responded. "They are traveling about twice the speed of us."

"I'm ready to go," Mike interjected.

They resumed their positions and continued on without a break. In one hour, they reached the spot that Drago had shown them on the map. Drago gave them a short break.

"You think they will reach us in less than thirty minutes?" Chris asked. Drago nodded.

"How far from the border at our current pace, and how far at their pace?" Mike inquired.

Drago thought for a few seconds and studied the map.

"About one day at their pace, and at least two days at our current pace."

"Here is the plan," Mike interrupted. "I'll find a good spot to engage with them and you three make it to the Austrian border. If I can give you an hour or two head start, you should be able to make it. Without me you should be able to go at the same pace as the Russian soldiers."

Chris shook his head looking at Mike, "No, you and I will ambush these guys while Drago and Jessica make it for the border. When we finish with the Russians, we'll rejoin them in Austria."

"No, we won't leave you behind," Jessica jumped in. "We will all make a stand!"

"No, you two make it to the village and then wait for us," Chris argued. "We'll be behind you. Look for us to show up a day or two later.

This is where Mike has experience; we'll stop these guys. This allows us to take our time to the border—we can rest along the way. The two of you are in great shape, you can quickly reach the village."

Jessica shook her head, disapproving of the plan.

"Here is the information of where Dan and Ali are staying in Barcelona until the wedding," Chris continued, ignoring her disapproval. "I know where it is—you should keep the information. We need to make this wedding. Dan is so excited. After the wedding, we'll take his boat back across the Atlantic Ocean to Florida."

"Jessica, trust me!" Chris paused. "We can do this. Let's continue on the trail. Mike, you tell us to stop when you have found a good place to make our stand."

They continued on the trail until Mike found a setting that he liked. The trail was narrow and near a fallen log. Mike suggested that he be positioned by the trunk of the fallen log. Chris would be further back; behind and alongside the log at a forty-five-degree angle from the trail. This gave them good cover. It was also similar to many fallen trees that they had passed this morning. Mike felt that this setting would not be alarming to the soldiers.

Mike and Chris got in place and Drago and Jessica found branches to erase their tracks off the trail before they continued on the trail toward the border. They hoped that would keep the Russians focused on the trail and vulnerable to an ambush. Mike told Chris that he would fire first, then Chris should pop up and shoot at the rear soldier and work his way to the center. They assumed there were five soldiers. Mike had gone over and showed Chris where he wanted him positioned, and once satisfied, he went over to get himself settled. He advised Chris to have his rifle, Glock, and knife accessible.

Jessica had helped Mike to get situated. He was partially buried in the snow except for his head and upper torso which were hidden behind the trunk and low branches. His rifle looked like one of the branches.

Drago had assisted Chris into position. Chris was half buried behind the log: he wouldn't be spotted until he popped up. He had his knife with the blade face-down in the snow, his rifle in hand, and his Glock leaned against the log. He was in this final position when he looked over and saw Drago cleaning the snowshoe tracks near him.

"Drago, this is important, listen to me. Mike and I will do everything we can to stop the Russians. We intend to meet you in Austria. I want you to take Jessica and I want you to move quickly to the village. Under no circumstances do you come back, do you understand? If you don't see us in five days, proceed to Barcelona. I gave Jessica the address; we have friends there. If we don't show up after the wedding, then go to Florida with Dan and his friends. I promised Jessica's mother that I would bring her back. I want you to promise me that you will do this, despite what Jessica says."

Drago stared at Chris. Chris waited for five seconds.

"Drago, I spoke with your father. He does not want you to return to Slovenia. He asked that you go to the United States or Western Europe and build your own life there. The instructions that I just gave you are my wishes as well as your father's. You have the hopes and wishes of two fathers that you should respect. Do you understand?"

Drago looked directly into Chris's eyes. "Yes, I understand." Not another word was spoken as Drago put more snow on top of Chris. Soon only his head, knife, Glock, and rifle were exposed behind the log.

Jessica rifled through her backpack and took out some of her food and made eye contact with Chris and Mike, setting it behind the log, just out of eyesight. She looked over to where Chris lay.

"Love you, Dad."

"I love you honey. See you in Austria."

Drago kept the branch in one hand, then took Jessica's hand as they proceeded up the trail. Chris watched them until they disappeared from sight.

It was quiet, providing Chris time to reflect on his life. He thought about his family and how they were all safe except for Jessica. But Jessica would be home soon, and Mike and Chris were making their stand. It was now win or lose or, as Carly liked to say during a critical part of a card game, the moment of truth. A different win or lose than in the business world. No higher stakes were imaginable. This was it. But it didn't bother him. Chris had known deep inside that he would face a moment like this on this adventure. Instead he thought about how happy Carly would be to have Jessica home. He thought she would really like Drago.

But now Chris chased those thoughts away. He wanted to join his family back in Texas, and so he had to prepare for this big event and get in the right frame of mind. This would be the biggest test of his life. He was getting mentally focused and began to regulate his breathing: nice, slow, and quiet. He could now hear every sound in the forest. The snow falling from a branch nearby was loud, and he needed to listen closely.

Was that a footstep? More footsteps followed, and he thought he could discern a pattern. Chris concentrated, then heard more steps that he could tell came from snowshoes. They were close.

"*Be ready,*" he thought, then he heard two shots by Mike.

Chris popped up, completely focused on what he needed to do. He was ten feet from the rear soldier, perhaps too close for the rifle. He pointed his rifle at the middle of the soldier's chest. The Russian was looking to where Mike had fired his shots; then he saw Chris. The soldier turned toward him creating a bigger target. Chris released his two shots and the Russian dropped. Chris moved up the line to the next soldier, but this soldier had his rifle trained on him. The Russian and Chris shot at the same moment. Chris felt a pain in his left shoulder that immediately pulled the rifle down. His shot had hit the Russian in the thigh, and the Russian dropped to his knees onto the snow. The soldier brought his rifle up again and Chris dropped down to safety behind the log. His shoulder hurt as he set down the rifle and reached for the Glock. *Would the Russian come for him or wait him out?*

Meanwhile, he heard a few more shots. Were the shots coming from Mike or a Russian? Chris crawled five feet forward in the snow until he was further up the log. He hoped to surprise the Russian with a new location; he braced himself as he got ready. He would have to push off the log with his injured shoulder. He popped up with the Glock in his hand. The Russian had been focused on the spot where Chris had originally gone down; he was surprised to see Chris and reacted by swinging his rifle toward him. Chris had just enough time to fire two rapid shots. One hit the Russian in the chest and the soldier went down.

Chris looked over at the stump. Mike was on his back and a Russian was on top of him with a knife. Chris bolted toward them. Mike had both hands on the Russian's hands, trying to push him back. The Russian had leverage, and the knife started to come down toward Mike's head. Chris stopped, pointed the gun at the Russian's back, and fired two rounds. The first round stunned the Russian and caused him to pause. The second shot allowed Mike to throw the Russian off of him. Chris ran over to them. The Russian was alive and struggling in the snow. Chris fired one more shot to the chest, and there was no more movement.

Surveying the landscape, Chris saw two more bodies. One was six feet from Mike; the other one was ten or more feet from Mike. Chris assumed that these were the first two Russians Mike had been able to kill. Chris looked at Mike and was alarmed to see red spreading across his abdomen. Chris saw a little red on the side of Mike's face.

"Mike, how badly are you hurt?"

"I have more wounds. First let's make sure the Russians are dead."

Chris checked each of the five soldiers. They were all dead, so he holstered his Glock. Walking over, Chris seized his pack with his right hand and pulled it out from under the snow and brought it over to Mike. Dropping the pack, he knelt down beside Mike.

Mike saw that Chris had been shot in the shoulder. "We were both hit. Let's try to see if we can fix each other up." Mike had been knifed in the stomach area a few inches left of his belly button. There was a lot of blood. Chris took out one of his spare shirts from the pack and folded it neatly, pressing it firmly against the wound with his right hand.

"Two new wounds?"

"The stomach wound is bleeding the most. I think I'm lucky—the blade didn't go in that far. The Russian was reaching for me, but he didn't get full extension."

"I got the first Russian easily," Mike continued. "The second soldier was trying to bring his rifle up but I got him as I popped up, still kneeling. The third Russian took a shot and missed my head, but he grazed my ear. My shot hit his right hand. He came toward me, with his knife and lunged for me and cut me in the stomach. I hit him in the head, but I fell backward and then the Russian jumped on top of me. I was holding him off, but I was getting weaker. Fortunately you came by and shot him."

"I knew the third soldier was the wild card," Mike summarized. "I thought this third one would be the most difficult."

"I thought the second Russian would be a challenge," Mike continued with his postanalysis. "I had an advantage because the first Russian went down before they knew what was happening."

Mike took a breath, then asked, "How is your wound?"

"The second soldier shot me in the shoulder. It hurts."

"Push the pack over to me so I can get the medical box," Mike instructed. "Keep the pressure on my stomach and then you'll need to disinfect the wound. Put some tape on me to seal me up."

Chris focused on Mike's stomach wound. He used disinfectant and a large bandage with a lot of tape. He then pulled out another clean shirt and placed it on top of the bandage. He asked Mike to hold it and to apply pressure.

"Well, hopefully we got this wound taken care of."

Chris looked at Mike's ear. He was missing some of the lower ear, and a lot of blood ran down the side of his face and onto his neck. Chris tried to bandage it the best he could.

"Mike, when you go in for cosmetic surgery, you can ask them work on your ear." It was a lame joke, but Mike gave him a smile.

"Let's look at your shoulder," Mike suggested.

They discovered it was Chris's upper arm that had been hit. The bullet had gone in and out of his arm, and he had a lot of blood that had soaked into his shirt. Chris was able to apply disinfectant with his good arm. Pulling out some bandages, he leaned toward Mike. Chris applied pressure on Mike's stomach while Mike used his two hands to bandage Chris.

Chris felt that there was additional damage from the gunshot wound. He would have to find out later if he had muscle or ligament damage. At least it was a clean bullet hole and he was relieved to have limited use of his arm—he felt grateful to be alive.

Chris sat down next to Mike in the snow and grabbed a water bottle and food that he offered to Mike.

"We got them, didn't we?"

Mike smiled.

"Your plan worked well, Mike."

Chris returned the smile and noticed that it started to rain again. He pulled out his poncho, found Mike's, and then pulled it over his head and down around him. Chris collected all the Russian backpacks and brought them over near Mike. He searched the dead bodies for weapons using his healthy arm.

Chris discovered a Russian pup tent. Between Mike's two arms and Chris's two legs and one arm, they were able to unfold the tent and they assembled it near Mike. Chris dragged their two packs inside the tent, then continued rummaging through the soldier's packs for dry clothing to use to make a bed for Mike.

"Mike, this will probably hurt, but I need to get you out of the rain. I'm going to try to pull you into the tent and then surround you with clothes."

Mike nodded. Chris winced, wrapped his arms under Mike's shoulders, then heaved. Keeping his hand on his stomach wound, Mike tried to push off with his good leg. It took five minutes to travel six feet into the tent, but they made it.

Chris took two of the coats from the Russian bodies and brought them into the tent. Using them as blankets, he laid them over Mike. Then he brought the Russian guns, knives, and ammo into the tent. Finally, once he felt Mike was in a good position and they were safe; he brought in one Russian pack at a time into the tent. Chris searched every pocket of the packs, keeping food, water, medical supplies, and any warm clothing. Inside the tent, he collected a small pile of food and medical supplies. Outside, away from the tent, he piled the discarded items including the Russian packs, in the snow. Chris showed Mike the food they had accumulated and asked him what he wanted to eat for dinner.

They ate a little, but the adrenaline had left them and they were tired. Chris asked Mike if he was okay and he rechecked Mike's wounds. Mike's abdomen was still bleeding. It was less than before, but Chris didn't know what else he could do. He hoped and prayed that the bleeding would stop soon. Mike's ear was bleeding slightly, but that wasn't as threatening of an injury; it looked worse than it actually was. His thigh was now a less critical wound than his abdomen.

Chris checked his upper arm. His bandages were bloody, but not saturated with blood like Mike's stomach bandage. Chris laid down near Mike.

"Mike, I'll be glad to get off these mountains. I can't wait to see valleys, farmland, and then Barcelona."

"Yes. That will be pleasurable." They were quiet in thought for the next three minutes.

"Chris, we both know that you'll have to leave me," Mike broke the silence with his thoughts. "I can't walk out of here."

"No Mike, that's not an option. We're both getting off this darn mountain—I'm not leaving you here. Rest up. We'll start down tomorrow."

"Chris, I can't walk. With my stomach wound, I can barely move."

"I know," Chris admitted he came to the same conclusion. "I'm going to find a few good strong branches in the morning, and make my version of the Indian travois. I'm going to drag you off the mountain."

"Besides, Drago explained that it's mostly downhill from here," Chris added.

Mike had a frown on his face, but he didn't respond. Chris was tired and knew he needed every ounce of strength for the next day.

"Let's rest, Mike. We'll need our energy for tomorrow."

Chapter 82

Austria

JESSICA AND DRAGO MADE good time descending the mountain. It was their second day since leaving Mike and Chris. As they left the snow, they took off their snow shoes and Drago reviewed the map.

"We are out of Slovenia now." He added, "But we must continue to push. I'm not certain the Russians will stop at the border." He took out some food from his pack and motioned for Jessica to do the same.

They now hiked in and out of valleys as they continued to descend. It was late afternoon when they came to a bend and hiked down another hill. Jessica abruptly stopped.

"Drago, are those houses? Is that a village?"

Drago paused, staring in the direction that Jessica pointed. "Yes, I think you are right, Jessica."

They didn't converse further but proceeded briskly down the path. A large brown dog stood up ahead in the middle of the trail, staring at them. Jessica tried to determine what type of dog he was, but she couldn't. Perhaps a mix, she thought. As they approached the dog, he wagged his tail and joined them as they made their way down the path.

They came across fields, passed some cows eating tall green grass in a pasture, and soon found themselves approaching a farmhouse. Without hesitation, the dog turned down the dirt road. Drago and Jessica paused, glanced at one another, then decided to follow the dog home.

As they entered the yard of the farmhouse, Drago shouted, "Guten Tag!" Then he stopped fifteen feet from the farmhouse. Jessica stood next to him.

Jessica heard a voice, then saw a man walk out of the barn. One minute later, a woman was out on the front porch. Drago continued speaking in German—within a couple of minutes they were escorted into the family living room.

Drago discovered that the couple spoke some English. Over a glass of water and snacks, Drago and Jessica proceeded to tell them their story. The Austrian couple listened intently and at times they would utter a "Ja," encouraging them to continue. After they shared their adventure, there were more questions in German. Drago attempted to answer them to the best of his ability.

The couple now understood that Jessica and Drago were waiting for Chris and Mike to return from the mountains. Drago told Jessica that they graciously invited them to stay at their home for the next few days. Jessica said thank you many times, and Drago said, "Danke." The woman smiled broadly, then showed Drago and Jessica to their bedrooms and pointed them to the bath area. The woman handed them fresh towels for the bath.

"You can take the first bath," Drago offered to Jessica. Jessica didn't hesitate as she grabbed her towel, stepped into the bathroom, closed the door, and drew up a hot bath.

After both of them had the opportunity to clean up, they walked downstairs to the living room. The farmer urged them to sit down as he brought them two drinks. Jessica didn't know what it was, but it was warm and delicious. They rested until the woman called them for dinner.

They had a hearty dinner with the farm couple and discovered they had two grown children. One daughter was married and living in a nearby village with her baby and husband. The farmer's wife showed them delightful pictures of her grandchild. They also had a son that was away studying at the University in Berlin.

The conversation was mostly small talk as they learned more about each other. Jessica could converse with them in English but when they had a quizzical look on their face, Drago would translate a portion in German.

After dinner, Jessica and Drago cleared the table and helped clean and dry the dishes. Then Jessica and Drago excused themselves to go outside, they wanted to explore the front of the farmhouse. The sky had cleared and it was a perfect opportunity to gaze at the stars.

"Drago, how long do you think it will take them to arrive?" Jessica asked.

Drago thought he saw a shooting star—he wondered if it was a sign.

"I guess they'll take at least a couple more days. We needed two days, so maybe an additional two for them."

He reached over and put an arm around Jessica and drew her close. "Your dad and Mike are resourceful. I wouldn't be surprised to see them both here soon."

He looked at Jessica. She looked up at him and he moved his head gently down and kissed her. It felt warm, it felt right, and he felt strong.

"Jessica, your dad had me promise that we wouldn't go back into Slovenia," Drago told her. "He told me that my father asked him to ensure that I not return to Slovenia. Your father suggested I travel back to the US."

"Traveling back with us in the old United States would be terrific," Jessica responded, smiling. "I bet you could get a transfer in our company."

"There is something else," Drago interrupted. Jessica paused, waiting.

"Your dad told me to wait for a few days in Austria. If he and Mike don't show up, then we are to head to Barcelona without them."

Jessica didn't say anything but Drago felt her body stiffen. They were quiet for a few minutes.

"I don't want to disobey your father, but I can't do that," Drago continued. "I think the next two days we hike for a few miles to the top of that hill and have a picnic and look for them. If on the third day we don't see him, I will backtrack to try to find them. I want you to stay back here if I have to do that."

"No. If you go, I go. We're a team, and it's my father."

Drago didn't say anything but nodded in the darkness. He'd known that would be Jessica's response. He hoped that if Chris became his father-in-law, he would forgive him for going back on his promise. They would find Chris and Mike, then they would all travel to Barcelona.

They remained outside for another fifteen minutes gazing at the stars in silence. Then, without a word, they turned and walked back into the house, where they joined the husband and wife as they watched a television show in German.

Jessica didn't understand any of the dialogue. It didn't matter: she was deep in thought, enjoying the warmth, comfort, and safety that her hosts provided. In less than half an hour, they excused themselves and entered their respective rooms to sleep. It was early, but they had experienced many long days and weeks, and they were looking forward to sleeping in a warm bed.

Chapter 83

The Travois

CHRIS HAD BEEN WORKING since early morning. He'd uncovered two long sturdy branches to use as poles and had found smaller branches to go across. They looked strong enough to support Mike. It took some time because he had to search and dig in the snow.

Next, he found rope from one of the Russian backpacks. Using the rope to tie strong crossing sticks on both sides, he worked to make a harness that he could put around his chest to pull the travois, similar to a yoke for an ox. His left arm was sore and weak, so he did most of his work with his right arm. He dragged sections to Mike, who tied the knots.

Chris brought out the Russian shirts that they'd used for their bed in the tent. He used these to tie sticks to the poles, then he used blankets to complete the bed of the travois.

They would leave most of the supplies behind—they would only carry water, food, ammo, handguns, knives, and one rifle in the travois. Chris used a pair of trousers to create straps to tie Mike into the travois and make sure he wouldn't slip down. Chris had one strap around Mike's calf and one around the upper chest, under his arms. Mike's stomach and thigh wounds were free and without straps.

Finally, around the middle of the day, Chris finished the travois and changed Mike's bandages. Mike's stomach was still bleeding regularly, but his thigh was only bleeding slightly. Chris asked Mike to refresh the bandage on his arm. Chris gave Mike food rations with a little water, then ate some food himself. It took Chris a half hour to get Mike onto the travois. With considerable effort, Mike was strapped in. Chris tightened the harnesses over him and took off.

Chris kept the Glock and knife on him. He left the one rifle and ammo with Mike in the travois, and hoped that he wouldn't need the rifle for an emergency. They had to travel light and he had to focus on getting them down the mountain. He had his snow shoes on and the rope harness around his chest. It was easy dragging the travois in the snow. When he came across rocks or partial snow, Chris had to slow down and be careful not to jostle Mike more than necessary. Travel was slow, but steady.

They took breaks, but kept moving until it began to get dark. They didn't have room for the tent; fortunately, they didn't need it. The weather was nice at the lower elevation. Chris fed Mike and helped him to relieve himself. He thought it would be better for Mike to sleep on the travois—the blankets would make it softer than any bed he could create on the ground.

They had two extra blankets—Chris took them and found a dry patch of ground next to Mike. He was so exhausted he fell asleep within two minutes.

The sunrise woke him. Looking over, Chris saw that Mike was already awake. He helped Mike go to the bathroom, then they ate breakfast. Chris checked Mike's wounds and took the bandage off in order to clean the stomach wound. Mike was a good sport and didn't complain in spite of the pain.

Intuitively Chris knew that Mike was weaker. Chris also knew he needed to cover more ground that day, and he planned to take fewer breaks.

They started to descend. Chris was careful that the weight of Mike and the travois didn't travel too fast and run over him. Travel was still slow and Chris was straining more today. His arm and shoulder ached. When they stopped for lunch, he had Mike help change his arm bandage, which was red with blood. It wasn't healing; it was burdened with the effort of pulling Mike's travois. Chris changed Mike's stomach and thigh bandages; the stomach bleeding had stopped, but there was now a worrisome ooze. Chris pulled out a clean Russian shirt for Mike and threw the old bloody one away on the trail.

That afternoon, Mike was quiet. He did not respond to conversation even during their breaks—when they would usually banter. Chris pushed Mike to eat and drink even small amounts of water. The snow was inter-mittent and the snow patches were not as deep. Chris had more rocks to avoid with the travois.

Chris was spent. Finally, near nightfall, he found a clearing without snow. He took care of Mike's wounds, and they both ate very little. Mike wasn't talking, and Chris was too tired to make an effort. Soon he fell into a deep sleep.

* * * * *

On the third day, the snow started to disappear on the trail. Chris made the decision to take off the snow shoes and pack them on the travois. If he didn't need the snow shoes for the rest of the day, he would leave them on the trail. They had a light rain, which made the travel slow with mud. He kept the extra blankets on top of Mike to try to keep him dry.

During lunch, Chris changed Mike's stomach bandage as usual. There was more ooze, and the skin on the outside of the wound had red streaks. Mike looked at the wound as Chris changed it.

"Chris, I think it's infected." Chris didn't say anything about the infection. He realized he had to get Mike to a hospital.

"Mike, I think we're getting close. When we reach a village, we'll summon the local doctor. Let's eat something to keep our strength and rest. I plan to cover a lot of ground."

Chris attempted to change his own shoulder bandage when Mike looked over at him.

"Chris, your wound isn't healing. Make sure you use some of the medication. You're pulling me down the mountain. I need you to be strong."

Chris used some of the medication, but he realized that his shoulder wouldn't heal until they had reached safety. He was tired, but they needed to keep moving down the trail. He rose and began to pull Mike and the travois further down the mountain.

Chris was becoming weaker; he fell down at times now. He tried blaming it on the rain and mud, but he knew the truth: each hour he lost more strength. He knew they had both lost a lot of blood, and he could feel his wound bleed as he pulled Mike.

If we could just reach a village, we could have a doctor attend to Mike, and I could let my shoulder rest, Chris thought often as he pulled them down.

That night he changed Mike's bandages. The redness and oozing were more pronounced. Mike was exhausted and weak, but he wanted to talk to Chris.

"Chris, thank you for taking me on this adventure to find Jessica."

Chris thought Mike was joking, but he looked up into Mike's eyes and saw that he was serious.

"Mike, I'm the one that could never thank you enough."

Mike cut him off. "No, you don't understand."

Mike proceeded to tell Chris that ever since he had returned from the war, he had not been coping well. He lacked purpose in his life and had searched for direction. He felt guilty that he had come back alive from the war in one piece while some of his buddies didn't. He'd prayed that God had brought him back for a purpose. The trek to Texas, the adventure to find Jessica and bring her back, had confirmed his purpose. He felt complete now.

Chris had to look away while his eyes misted. Mike had become a very good friend.

After they finished cleaning themselves, they ate the dwindling food rations and continued to talk. It was a deep discussion sharing their failures, their fears, and their dreams. It was just the two of them out in the mountains and under the stars. They had been through a lot together—there were no secrets anymore; their souls were laid bare.

Throughout the night, Mike had some coughing bouts. Chris brought him water and tried to calm him. Mike was sweating and Chris knew he had a fever from the infection. He'd been giving Mike Ibuprofen every four hours—they were both taking the Ibuprofen, but he had increased Mike's dosage.

The next morning, Chris woke, and if it was possible, Mike looked worse. The redness and oozing had become significantly worse overnight, and Mike was drenched in sweat. Mike didn't say much, and Chris only asked questions that required *yes* and *no* answers. Mike often responded with a nod or shake of the head, he ate very little, and even then only enough to appease Chris.

Chris knew that he needed to get them off the mountain that day. He took only one break that morning to give Mike a drink. Mike was so weak he could only sip and smile. Chris felt blood drip down his side from his shoulder but he didn't stop moving forward. He kept going, but decided to stop for a brief lunch. He would change Mike's dressings, they would eat a little, then continue. They were descending and dropping elevation—if they were lucky, a village might be near.

Stopping and pulling over to a good spot to rest, Chris set down his end of the travois.

"Okay Mike, we'll stop for a quick lunch and to change our bandages. Then we'll need to keep going. I'd like to find the village before dark."

As he looked for the medical supplies, he glanced over at Mike.

"Mike, are you hungry?"

No response. Mike stared straight ahead.

"Mike?"

Chris moved to Mike's side and looked into his eyes. He reached over to touch Mike's neck as he felt for a pulse.

"Mike, you can't leave me now. We're too close, Mike. Don't leave me now."

Chris couldn't feel a pulse. His heart raced—he wasn't a doctor or nurse, so he must not be doing it correctly. Chris picked up Mike's wrist but still couldn't find a pulse. He gently took hold of Mike's right shoulder and shook him a little with his good arm.

"Mike, wake up. Mike I think we're almost in Austria."

Finally, the realization hit. Mike was dead.

Mike had known he was dying; that was the basis of their talk last night. They had had their last discussion, their last confession, their last moment together.

Chris dropped down to the ground and couldn't stop the tears. He sobbed and couldn't stop. The culmination of everything they had been through the last few weeks poured out.

Chris didn't know how long he sat there, grieving for his friend. A raven broke him out of his trance as it swooped to a tree nearby and made so much noise that Chris had to turn and look at it. Seeing the placement of the sun in the sky, Chris realized he'd been there almost two hours.

Chris determined to give Mike a proper burial, but he didn't have a shovel. The terrain was tough, and he had only one good arm. He saw a number of rocks off the trail and decided that he would bury Mike beneath rocks so animals couldn't get him. Chris was tired and weak, but he untied Mike from the Travois and dragged him off, laying him underneath a tree not too far from a small ledge with rocks.

Wrapping Mike in both the blankets from the travois, he laid him down and then began to set rocks on top of him. He used another blanket to drag the rocks with his good arm. He didn't stop: he worked continuously, putting each rock carefully in its place. It was getting dark when he finally finished. He had only minutes before it was pitch-black. He gave a heartfelt eulogy that only Mike, God, and Chris could hear.

Chris ate some food for sustenance, but couldn't taste it. He drank water only because he knew he had to. He looked over at what they'd brought with them to this point. He decided to sling the rifle over his good arm, then selected the knife, Glock, canteen, and a small amount of food. He bandaged himself the best he could, and used up the rest of the medication as he poured it on his wound. He placed the remaining Ibuprofen tablets in his coat pocket. He chose the flashlight, then left everything else. There were no clouds in the sky this evening, only a modest moonlight. With flashlight in hand, he continued the quest down the mountain trail.

Chris finally came to a stream in the middle of the night. He was so exhausted he decided to take a brief nap. He found a patch of grass not far from the stream and laid down. It felt good, and he slept.

Chapter 84

Mountain trail

CHRIS FELT RAINDROPS ON his face. He vaguely recalled many dreams from his restless sleep; most were of his family, first in San Diego and then in Texas. He sat up, drank some water, and ate some food. He'd brought minimal food, he didn't have much left. Just required enough to provide some energy.

He started walking down the trail, taking inventory of his body. He was weaker today. His arm throbbed even with the triple dose of Ibuprofen. However, Chris was thankful that he hadn't bled too much the past night. His right arm and legs were sore but working. He thought, *Just keep walking at a steady clip. Take it step by step.*

As he walked along the trail he started to lose awareness. He tried to stay focused on the trail, but Chris's mind wandered to many faraway places. He was throwing the ball for Finley in their San Diego backyard. He was thinking of the sock hops with his daughters, ball games with his sons. He flashed through the lives of his children including school, sports, and scouts. He thought of Carly, their wedding and their thirty years of marriage. He thought of their favorite vacations and pictured the family playing on Hanalei beach in Kauai.

As he trudged along, he thought of his childhood, his parents and grandparents, all the significant moments in his life, the moments that had defined him. As he approached a steep part of the trail littered with rocks and gravel, he awoke from his daydreaming and traversed down the trail. He didn't have good use of his left arm which impacted his balance and forced Chris to concentrate. Suddenly a bird overhead started to squawk. Looking up, he lost his concentration and began to fall. Dropping the rifle, he tried to rebalance himself when his feet went out from under him. Chris fell hard on his right side and rolled into a log. He landed on his left arm and shoulder; a sudden sharp pain pulsated through his body.

He decided to lay still until the pain subsided. Chris tried to take inventory of his body and pain: after fifteen minutes he was still in pain, but it was a little better. His head felt groggy. Ha*d he hit his head?* He could feel that his left arm was wet and knew that his shoulder wound had opened.

Chris slept or passed out. When he came to, he was still lying next to the log. He had to get up, but he struggled to convince his body to make the attempt. He flashed back to Texas—his father telling Ethan, Mark and himself to "survive." He hoped the boys were back in Texas, along with Carly's parents. Another flashback: Chris, back in Texas, Carly telling him to find Jessica and "come home." He had found Jessica. She and Drago should now be safe in Austria—hopefully preparing for the journey to Barcelona and then onward to Texas. But the route between Texas and Europe was a difficult trek and the return trip would also be a challenge. He needed to make sure she got safely home.

This thought gave him a surge of energy. He pushed away from the log and onto his knees. He paused, and then said out loud, "Survive," and "Come home." He was standing now, and he slowly turned and saw the rifle. Chris thought about walking up the hill to retrieve it, but he shook his head. He needed to travel lighter: the Glock, the knife, the canteen, and the Ibuprofen in his pocket was all he would take.

Chris continued down the hill. In his mind, he repeated "survive" and "come home" over and over. He focused on the trail. The sun was out and the birds sang, but it was all background noise to him.

Chris took short breaks to drink water. He slipped a couple more times but was able to catch himself from tumbling. Once he fell on his rear, another time onto a knee, and once he landed on his right side. But each fall took a little more out of him. Soon it was midday, and he needed a break. The trail finally led to a stream where he stopped to fill his canteen. He found a log nearby and sat down, using the log as a back rest. He intended just a short rest but promptly fell asleep.

Chris dreamed of camping in the Sequoias with his family. They had a tent, with their previous dog named Cody. He saw the creek by the camp spot and the children jumping on the rocks. Then, a disturbing noise. Chris woke to see two squirrels upset with each other and arguing on a branch directly above him.

He needed to continue. "Survive and come home," he muttered. It was hard getting up, but he made it to the trail.

He was traveling considerably slower: there were more stumbles or near falls that took more and more out of him. The blood from his arm had trickled down to his waist, and now the blood made its way down his left leg. He muttered to himself but kept pushing forward. He found a nice branch that worked as a walking stick, and kept him steady on his feet.

Continuing on the trail as the sun set, Chris found a stump only twenty meters from the stream. He sat down, refreshed himself with a drink of water, popped a few more Ibuprofen, and rested. He was exhausted. Chris laid down and was soon asleep, dreaming again of his family. The dream twisted into a nightmare: his mind suddenly filled with fighting Russians and then burying Mike.

He woke up suddenly. *What was that by the stream?* His hand felt for the Glock. He remained still and stared at the moving shapes, giving his eyes a chance to adjust. There was filtered moonlight, enough for some visibility. He looked at two, no, three moving shapes. *What were they? How did they track him?*

Wait, they had more than two legs. Were they deer? They were now drinking water from the stream. His heartbeat dropped to normal and he sighed. His sigh made the deer freeze, but after five minutes they continued drinking, before they were startled by something else and abruptly left.

Chris pushed and pulled himself up. He thought he saw a faint light indicating the sunrise. He took his pain medication and water. He was now breathing a little heavier even while sitting. *I need a good day today; it may be my last. I need my best effort, my mind focused, the right frame of mind,* he thought.

He filled up his canteen and splashed some water on his face. Chris thought of looking at his wound, but he didn't have any bandages left; besides, it would hurt too much to unbutton and then take off part of his shirt.

As soon as he had enough light, he started walking. If today was in fact his last day, then he had to give his best and use all the daylight. He made slow progress, leaning heavily on his walking stick as he meandered his way down the mountain.

It was near noon, when he began feeling dizzy and started to lose focus. He played mind games, pushing himself to just make it to that next tree, next rock, or the next bend in the trail. Then he would pick the next closest landmark. This helped him through the morning. When he felt lightheaded, he walked over to the stream and splashed water on his face. Chris hoped this would help him, even if only temporarily. He was able to continue like this for another hour. His first landmarks had been fifty meters away; now they had shrunk to ten meters.

He daydreamed once more of the family gathered together for a big celebration dinner. He was not sure what was being celebrated, but everyone was gathered and talking.

It was early afternoon, and he now stumbled often. His knee was scraped up, his pants torn at multiple places. His backside had a tear from a root that had grabbed him during one fall. He now coaxed himself to take one step at a time. He made a game: one step was "survive," the next step was "home." Survive. Home. Survive. Home.

This mantra continued for a couple more hours until the trail flattened out. As he approached a valley, Chris followed both a stream and a path through the heart of the valley. He chanted "survive" and "home" while thinking to himself *make it through the meadow.* Halfway across the meadow, Chris's hiking stick went into a hidden hole, his stick broke, and he tumbled face down into the tall grass.

He tried to get up but it was futile—he fell back down. Rolling onto his right side, he tried to get up by pushing his right hand into the ground. He made it up and shook as he took three steps, then fell down, hard. Propping himself up, he pushed again and stood up. Shaking, he took one step, before falling again onto the grass. He focused with all he had, rose, then staggered ten steps before falling. Chris rested for five minutes and tried again, but he couldn't get up. He rested another ten minutes, got himself up, but fell down in two steps. He then rested fifteen minutes, and got up but fell on his first step.

Chris lay on the grass. *Is there anything else I can do?* He had maybe two hours of sunlight left until it was dark. He couldn't get out of the meadow. He felt his Glock in his holster, pulled it out, and looked at it. Pointing it up to the sky, he fired three rounds.

Chris put his right arm and Glock down, and his arm hung across his chest. He was slipping from consciousness. As he blacked out, he mumbled, "Carly, I'm sorry. I'm so sorry. I tried."

His mind went to other places, dreams, and thoughts. He had a strong dream that Finley was licking his face. The dream was so realistic that he thought he could feel the tongue on his cheek.

Chapter 85

Austria

Jessica and Drago finished breakfast with the farmer and his wife and were working on a second cup of coffee.

"What are you planning to do today?" the farmer's wife asked.

Drago looked at Jessica. "It's been a couple of days—we thought we'd hike up the trail to see if my Dad and Mike are coming down," Jessica responded.

"Take Balko with you. He roams the hills and valleys—if you get lost, he can bring you home," the farmer offered.

Jessica and Drago helped clean the dishes, then went upstairs to pack for the day. They came down with their rifles and filled their canteens in the kitchen. The farmer's wife prepared a lunch for them in a small backpack.

Walking out the door, they found the farmer and Balko waiting for them out in front of the house. Balko ran over to greet them, surprisingly understanding that he was spending the day with Jessica and Drago. Balko followed them down the trail and within minutes had taken the lead. Sometimes he disappeared off the trail for several minutes, but he always returned to check in with Jessica and Drago.

Drago knew that Jessica was tense. He elected to stay quiet most of the time, but when he spoke he made his best effort to be positive.

"It appears the weather will be nice today," Drago broke the silence while watching Balko run back from the stream.

"Yes. We should keep an eye on time and how far we travel, to allow time for our return," Jessica responded. "We should look for a good vantage points where we can see for a distance."

Jessica knew that Drago was considering her comment, so she kept mum as they continued along the trail. It was uncanny how much they understood about each other.

"We need to walk all morning," he commented. "Then we will come across a small hill with a valley and a stream below and a mountain to the side. I think we may have a good vantage point from that mountain."

Jessica and Drago hiked and exchanged small talk along the way as they discovered more about each other. Around 1:00 p.m. they reached the hill overlooking the valley and decided to have a quick lunch. The farmer's wife had made some hearty sandwiches with large dill pickles and home-made cookies. It tasted delicious and they attacked the sandwiches with a hearty appetite. Balko had a couple of bites of sandwich but he was more interested in scouting the valley.

After lunch, they packed the containers. Drago pointed to the mountain on their right side.

"Jessica, this is what I was talking about earlier this morning. I think we can climb to the top of the mountain in an hour. If I recall correctly, this valley leads to a series of hills and then reaches an upper valley before continuing up into the mountains."

"Yes, let's scale the mountain," Jessica readily agreed.

Drago whistled. Soon they saw Balko's head pop up over the grass in the valley below. He came running toward them, eager for more adventure.

They climbed up the mountain and Balko stayed closer as they ascended. In an hour's time, they reached the peak and scanned the trail below, the one leading to Slovenia. They could see the hills and the upper valley in the distance. Drago took out a pair of binoculars and used them to study the terrain. After five minutes, he handed them over to Jessica.

"Jessica, I don't see anything. Why don't you take a look and see if you can spot them."

They alternated back and forth but were unsuccessful in sighting anyone. At 3:30 p.m., Drago looked at his watch and then glanced at Jessica.

"Jessica, it's 3:30 p.m.—we should head down the mountain. Descending should take half the time, so it will be around 4:00 p.m. when we reach the valley floor. Then we will have only two hours until dark. I have a flashlight in the pack, but we shouldn't walk four to five hours in the dark, even with Balko."

She nodded. "Balko!" she yelled, and in seconds the dog appeared at her side.

Hiking down the hill, they reached the valley before long. They stopped and looked across the meadow one more time—Drago knew that Jessica was conflicted between leaving and continuing up the trail toward the farm.

"Jessica, we need to get back to the farmhouse tonight. We can start earlier tomorrow, and go farther up the trail. We can even bring more food and carry supplies so we can spend the night."

Jessica nodded reluctantly and they turned to go back. Balko raced up front to lead them back to the farm. Bang! A gunshot. Two more shots followed; three shots in total. They stopped and looked at each other in puzzlement.

"It sounded like it came from that direction." Jessica pointed across the valley, in the direction of the hills and the upper valley.

Balko was back at their side; he'd heard the shots and his ears were up, his face pointed toward the upper valley.

"Yes, the shots came from that direction," Drago agreed. He had his rifle in his hands, and Jessica swung her rifle off her shoulder.

"Let's go, but we need to be careful," Drago cautioned. "We don't know who fired the shots."

Drago took off toward the upper valley with Balko ten meters in front. They didn't speak; their eyes were focused on the horizon while listening for more sounds. They crossed the small valley quickly and were soon hiking the hills to the upper valley.

At the top of the second hill, Drago pulled out the binoculars and scanned down below. Pulling the glasses down, he shook his head.

"I can't see anything." He handed the binoculars to Jessica. "See if you can spot anything."

Balko had taken off. He ran in the upper valley through the grass and he soon approached the center of the valley.

After two minutes, they heard barking. Drago looked at Jessica and suggested.

"Let's go. Be ready to fire."

They went down quickly but cautiously, following the way over to Balko's barking. Balko barked often, as though encouraging them to hurry. Finally, they saw Balko, standing by a body. The person wasn't moving. Drago didn't see anyone else, but he was concerned that someone else could be near.

"Did someone shoot this man?" Drago said out loud, but to himself. Jessica ran ahead.

"Jessica, be careful!" shouted Drago, rifle ready. Jessica was halfway to Balko.

"It is Dad!" she shouted.

Drago moved forward, head swiveling as he continued looking to see if they were alone. "He's alive," Jessica shared, checking his pulse. As he reached Jessica, Drago could see that Chris was not responding to her.

Drago knelt down beside her to look at Chris. His eyes followed the blood and he examined Chris's left side.

"He's lost a lot of blood."

Drago rose and walked the immediate perimeter. He was looking for Mike while hoping there weren't Russians in the area.

Jessica saw the Glock lying near Chris's right hand.

"Drago, it was Dad who fired the shots with his handgun."

Drago returned quickly, standing near Jessica and Balko.

"Jessica, we need to bring your father back quickly to the farmhouse. He is in bad shape. I want you to carry my pack and rifle. I will carry him on my shoulders."

They pulled Chris up with difficulty; he was dead weight. Drago struggled but finally maneuvered one arm and shoulder through Chris's legs and hoisted him onto his shoulders. Jessica attached the pack to her back with the rifle over one shoulder. She also carried Drago's rifle and took the lead with Balko. Drago moved surprisingly well in spite of the extra weight as they climbed the hill above the lower valley.

They had at least four hours of travel to the farmhouse. Drago and Jessica didn't take a break but walked deliberately. Soon, the sun was setting. Pulling the flashlight from the pack, Jessica turned it on and tried to provide some light on the trail for Drago.

Drago's face dripped with sweat, but he maintained a determined look on his face. Jessica prayed that he had another two hours of strength left in him.

Another hour passed. Thirty minutes. The trail became easier as they approached the farm and village. Balko had left them minutes earlier, running up ahead. Ten minutes from the farm, they saw the farmer approach with Balko and his rifle. Once their eyes met, the farmer ran to them.

Drago and Jessica intersected him on the path to his house and paused. Jessica looked wearily at the farmer.

"This is my father. He's badly injured—Balko found him. Where is the nearest doctor or hospital?"

The farmer nodded, turned around, and ran back to the farmhouse. When Drago and Jessica reached the farm, he had his truck pulled out. The farmer's wife had blankets unfolded in the truck bed. The farmer climbed into the bed of the truck and motioned for Drago and Jessica to bring Chris over and lay him in the truck. The farmer took Chris's upper half and Drago swung him gently into the truck. Balko followed and jumped into the truck, circling twice before lying down next to Chris.

Jessica and Drago climbed next to Chris while the farmer climbed behind the wheel and his wife sat in the passenger seat. The farmer sped off, and in fifteen minutes they entered a small town. The farmer drove straight to a doctor's clinic, stopped the vehicle, and the farmer's wife bolted into the building. Three people rushed out the doors pushing a gurney. They placed Chris on the gurney and wheeled him inside.

Jessica followed as they pushed Chris to a prep room. One nurse took Chris's vitals while another nurse cut off his shirt and unlaced his shoes.

Drago remained in the lobby with the farmer and wife. Drago discovered the farmer's wife had called the clinic as they'd driven, so the clinic was prepared. The clinic was the closest medical facility within an hour of the farmhouse. The farmer's wife tried to reassure Drago that although the place was small, they had the latest technology.

Ushered out of the room by a nurse, Jessica joined the others in the waiting room. Jessica and Drago filled the husband and wife in on the details of their day. A doctor emerged an hour later from behind closed doors.

"Your father has lost a lot of blood. His wound is infected, and he's dehydrated. We're giving him blood and hydrating him intravenously with antibiotics. It is too soon to gauge how his body will respond. Bringing him in when you did will at least give him a fighting chance."

The doctor paused. He seemed to be holding something back.

"He was shot in the arm. Do you know what happened?"

Jessica looked up at him. "We were leaving Slovenia and had Russians pursuing us. He and his friend stayed behind to let us escape. If we are to hear the story of what happened, you'll have to save his life."

"Tonight will be critical for him. He will have nurses observing and caring for him all night. They will call me if I'm needed." With that, the doctor shook their hands and exited through the same double doors.

Drago and Jessica walked back and they thanked the farmer and his wife profusely for bringing them to the clinic, then urged them to return home with Balko. Drago and Jessica decided they would spend the night at the clinic, and Drago promised that they would call the couple if they received a significant update on Chris.

After the couple left, Drago and Jessica found two unoccupied chairs without arm rests. They sat down and leaned next to each other. Jessica had her head against Drago's shoulder as they took naps. They received a few updates throughout the night—no progress, but Chris was stable, and didn't seem to be getting any worse.

Chapter 86

Texas

CARLY HAD JUST FINISHED the morning dishes, and Clark was working on the morning chores. Her mother and mother-in-law were folding laundry, and her father and father-in-law had left for town immediately after breakfast to pick up supplies.

Things had settled down not only for her family but for the Texas Federation. Mark was doing well at OU and Ethan was back at work putting in long hours. Carly's father-in-law was responding well to chemo: he was now on maintenance with only one day of chemo sessions each month. They had all settled into a routine, accepting their new home at the farm.

Abby had called the night before to say that she and Ryan had adjusted well to Austin and their new jobs. They were coming up to Brownfield that weekend to see Carly and the grandparents.

At times Carly had difficulty transitioning to her new life in Texas. Memories of leaving their home in San Diego and never being able to return made her melancholy. She loved the people in Brownfield, but she missed the ocean and beautiful weather of San Diego.

She worried often about Jessica and Chris. The phone rang as she was hanging up the dish towel. Rushing to her phone, she answered on the fifth ring.

"Mom?"

"Jessica?"

"Yes, it's me. I'm calling from Austria."

"Oh! It's good to know that you're safe and out of Slovenia. I'm relieved to hear from you. Is your dad with you?"

There was silence. Jessica searched for the right words.

"Jessica, is everything okay?" Carly asked again. "Is your father okay?"

"Jessica?" Carly asked again, this time with more concern.

"Mom, I'm at a small hospital. Dad is in bad shape and almost died. We brought him in last night. He survived the night, but they're telling us to take it one day at a time."

"Jessica, what happened? What is wrong with him!" Carly demanded.

"He was shot while crossing the mountains. Drago and I left Dad and Mike in the Slovenian mountains to stop the Russian soldiers pursuing us.

Mom, I don't know what happened. Drago and I went back along the trail with a farm dog yesterday afternoon and found him lying in a valley. He was unconscious. He'd been shot, and he lost a lot of blood."

"Jessica, what valley? How did he get there? What happened?"

"I don't know! Only Dad knows that story. Mom, you wouldn't believe the last few weeks. We need to pray for Dad. I'll update you when I have more news. I'm safe, and Drago is with me."

Carly didn't say anything as multiple thoughts ran through her head. She wished she could be at the hospital—she wanted to be at the bedside of her husband.

"Mom, the doctor said that last night was the first big test," Jessica added. "He said that if Dad lived through last night, his odds of surviving doubled. Each day is critical. They've been giving him blood, hydrating him, and pumping him full of antibiotics. He's still alive, Mom."

Carly was nodding to herself as she listened to Jessica. She was trying to push out the fear and negative thoughts.

"Thank you for the call, Jessica. I'm glad you're safe and that you're out of Slovenia. Is Mike with you at the hospital?" Carly asked.

"I don't know what happened to Mike—he wasn't with Dad. Drago looked briefly in the valley for him but couldn't find him. We had limited daylight, and we had to move out quickly to get Dad to the hospital. Drago had to carry him the whole way back to the farmhouse. We're staying with a nice Austrian couple. We'll have to find out about Mike when Dad can talk, but I don't think he made it to Austria. How is everyone else?" Jessica transitioned, trying to change the subject.

Carly gathered herself to go through the family updates. She shared how everyone was doing well. She sensed that this was what Jessica needed to hear; good news and the knowledge that there was some normalcy back home. They chatted for ten minutes, then Jessica interjected.

"Mom, now that you know I'm safe, I'll check in again daily to give you an update. I'll call right away if Dad's status changes."

Carly and Jessica said their goodbyes and Carly staggered to the sofa, sat down, and didn't move for five minutes. Her mother came into the living room to ask if they should wash the curtains but stopped when she saw Carly sitting down, motionless.

"Are you okay?"

"Yes. I just received a call from Jessica—she's in Austria."

"And she's okay?" her mom inquired.

"Yes."

"What about Chris?"

"He's in the hospital. He's not good—they're trying to save him. Jessica said it's good news that he survived the night. She doesn't know what happened the past few days. And Mike is missing."

Carly looked at her mom with tears in her eyes. Ma K walked over, sat down, and hugged her daughter without saying a word. She knew that this was the best she could offer Carly at the moment.

Chapter 87

Austria Hospital

JESSICA AND DRAGO SPENT the first night and the second day in the waiting room. The second day there were few developments. Jessica spoke with the doctor and the nurses and learned that her dad's vitals were improving. They updated the farm couple on the status and the farmer's wife insisted that Drago and Jessica needed to look after their health and that they should come to the house in the evening. The farmer picked them up in the early evening and brought them home for a home-cooked meal and to sleep in a warm bed.

After dinner, the farmer handed the car keys to Jessica and Drago. He told them to use their car to visit the hospital. He suggested that they return each evening for dinner and to spend the night. He warned them that the recovery would likely be slow and reminded them again that they needed to take care of themselves; the hospital would take good care of Jessica's father.

On the third day, Jessica and Drago entered the hospital first thing in the morning. The nurse walked out to greet them with excitement. She'd explained to Jessica that her father had started to stir during the night, and earlier that morning he'd opened his eyes for the first time. Thirty minutes ago, he'd asked where he was. The nurse cautioned her that he was still very weak, but that Jessica and Drago could go into the room and visit him.

Entering the room, they quietly navigated around the equipment and toward the bed. Jessica noticed that her dad's eyes were closed, and she motioned for Drago to sit down. When they reached the two empty chairs, they quietly carried them over near the bed.

Chris was napping, but when he heard Jessica and Drago sit in the chairs, he opened his eyes. A half hour earlier, he'd been told by the nurse that he was in a small hospital in a small town. Hoping he was in Austria, Chris was too weak to inquire further. Seeing Jessica and Drago, Chris smiled.

He felt elation, but also relief. A myriad of thoughts swirled inside his head. Jessica and Drago had made it to Austria and they were safe, which meant he was probably in Austria.

"Hello," Chris whispered.

Jessica reached over and placed her hand on top of his. He had some tubes inserted in his arm, and she knew he was tired and weak. She and Drago spent the time talking to Chris, telling him about their trek to Austria and then finding the farm. They shared how they had searched for him with the farmer's dog, and how they'd heard the gunshots just as they were leaving the area, and how Balko found him in the valley.

"Drago checked afterward, and the valley was just inside the Austrian border." Jessica paused. "Dad, you made it to Austria."

Jessica explained how Drago had carried him on his back to the farm. Balko had guided them the whole way.

"Thank you," Chris whispered to Drago.

Jessica explained that she'd called her mother; everyone was good back home, and she spent time sharing news about each person. Jessica spoke for two hours. When Chris nodded off she would just pause, then continue when he awakened. He kept the smile on his face while trying to absorb all the information.

Jessica and Drago left as the nurses and doctors changed bandages and performed their tests. Drago left the hospital grounds to walk to the village to find lunch for Jessica and himself. Jessica took this moment to call her mother.

"Mom, Dad is alert. He is weak, but he said hello and a few other words. He's trying to understand where he is, and he's listening and under-standing us."

Carly felt as if she had been holding her breath for an eternity. She exhaled a sigh of relief.

"Have you found out more about what happened?" Carly asked.

"Mom, this is a one-way conversation right now," Jessica responded. "Dad is too weak. We'll have to wait until he's stronger to tell us the story."

"Everything here is good," Carly provided a report for Jessica. "Abby and Ryan visited yesterday, and they look happy." More small talk transpired before Jessica said goodbye to her mom and promised to call when she had more news.

Drago returned in twenty minutes with kaiser rolls, cheese, and fruit. Jessica and Drago ventured outside to enjoy the beautiful day. Drago spotted a grassy area where they sat down and had a picnic. Jessica had a confession for Drago.

"Drago, when we found my dad in the valley, and you had to carry him back—I didn't think he'd live. Now I think he'll survive."

She had a tear in her eye as she paused, and took a bite to give herself more time. She swallowed, then gazed back at Drago.

"I'm happy, and I'm very grateful to you for carrying him back."

They finished lunch in silence, then spent the afternoon in Chris's hospital room. They took breaks when the doctors came in to examine Chris or when the nurses performed more tests. Chris's vitals were stable; Jessica continued talking to her dad as Drago filled in parts of the stories.

In the evening Jessica kissed her dad good night and explained that they would be back the next day. Drago drove them back to the farmhouse, where they shared the positive news with their friends.

Chapter 88

Hospital

WITH EACH PASSING DAY, Chris became stronger. The doctors, through a blitz of antibiotics (along with constant cleaning of his wounds), had staved off the infection. His wounds were now healing, and he was hydrated and alert. The tubes were scheduled to come out that day, and he now drank water and other liquids. The blood transfusion had helped him to regain strength. That afternoon, Chris would attempt his first exercise since being admitted to the hospital: a walk down the hall.

Chris had received from the nurse his schedule for the day while Jessica and Drago were visiting. He was excited that he could finally leave the bed and walk around.

Jessica noticed a big difference from days ago when her father had first opened his eyes. He was alert and engaged in conversation. For the first time, she felt he could tolerate a deeper discussion.

"Dad, what happened after Drago and I left you on the mountain in Slovenia?"

She instantly regretted asking the question when Chris's smile faded. His mind drifted back, remembering. He looked at Drago and Jessica, sighed, and began slowly. He gave them details about the ambush, including Mike's and Chris's wounds. He had tears in his eyes, and had to pause a couple of times when he spoke about Mike. He told the story up until he collapsed in the valley and fired the three shots before passing out. Jessica didn't ask any questions. She had a couple, but she knew she had to let them go. Her fears about what had happened to Mike had been confirmed. Changing the conversation, they encouraged Chris to focus on getting stronger so they could all return home to family in Texas.

Jessica and Drago visited for another hour before a nurse entered the room. She was polite but firm in excusing Jessica and Drago, explaining that she needed to check Chris's vitals, draw blood, and then feed Chris. Jessica suggested they return in the afternoon.

Chris ate his first solid meal in days, and his stomach handled it well. An hour after his meal, he was able to walk down the hallway. He didn't need much assistance as the attendant followed behind him.

True to their word, Drago and Jessica visited in the afternoon.

"Jessica, what is today's date?" Chris asked with concern. "How far away is Dan's wedding?"

Jessica looked at Drago, trying to recall the day of the wedding. Chris had told them the date at the top of the mountain.

"I think it's in five days?"

"Can you figure out the best way to get to Barcelona?" Chris asked, looking at the two.

"Dad, you can't leave yet. You're just now regaining your strength— you're on your way to recovery, but that's a long journey."

Chris put up both hands as Jessica finished talking. Jessica knew her father well enough to know he might push his recovery beyond what was reasonable.

"I'm making good progress. It doesn't hurt to find out how we can travel to Barcelona. I'll ask the doctor what I need to do or what he will need to see from me in order for me to be released. I promise I won't go until the doctor gives his consent."

Jessica gave him a wary look. She knew that he'd work hard to convince the doctor to release him.

"Besides, I'll let you and Drago carry anything heavy. I can just sit and enjoy the ride to Barcelona. After we get there, we can rest some more," Chris added. "I told Dan that I'd be back for the wedding. I would like to honor that commitment if I can."

Jessica and Drago left the hospital and drove back to the farmhouse. Jessica vented to Drago, who was smart enough to just listen and drive.

"It's crazy to even think of attending a wedding. It was only days ago that he almost died. If I told Mom what he's contemplating, she would lose it."

Jessica stopped and stared at Drago, expecting a response. Drago stalled for a few minutes to buy time, but he knew he had to respond.

"Look at the progress he's made. He's willing to listen to the doctor—that's a positive thing. Let's make sure we're there to hear what the doctor says tomorrow. If that motivates your dad to work and get stronger, then maybe it's a good thing?"

"As long as the doctor says it's safe," Jessica conceded with a strained voice.

Drago thought for a few seconds about the next steps. In some ways, it was relief that he could have a task, rather than sit in the hospital.

"Tomorrow, I will drive you to the hospital—we can share our concerns with the nurse and doctor. Then, I will explore possible transportation options to Barcelona whether it's by car, train, or bus."

That night at dinner, the farmer was distraught. His old milking cow was sick and about to die. Dinner was a somber event, and Jessica and Drago were left alone with their thoughts about Chris's health and Barcelona. After dinner, they sat with the couple in the living room and had a chance to share life stories in more detail. It was a good diversion from the decisions at hand.

The farmer brought out a bottle of wine and they sat and talked by the fire. The farmer changed the topic to his current challenge: he needed to buy a new cow. Losing his old cow was like losing a good friend. Since money was tight, he might have to buy milk in the village for a while. He and his wife would have a chance to save their money to buy a milking cow in six months.

As Jessica slept that night, she thought about the couple living in the foothills of Austria. Life was simple: all they needed and wanted was a milking cow.

Chapter 89

Austria

JESSICA STAYED IN THE room as the doctor examined her father and studied the latest tests and reports. As he examined the wound, the physician checked Chris's pulse and looked into Chris's eyes. The nurse changed the bandages.

"You've recovered nicely. It appears you're on track for a full recovery," the doctor stated. "My best advice is to rest and give your body a chance to fully recover."

"When are you thinking I'll be well enough to leave?" Chris asked.

The doctor thought for thirty seconds as he packed the instruments away. When he turned and walked over, he stood and looked Chris in the eyes.

"If you keep making progress and don't experience any setbacks, perhaps two days."

"When you say relax with full recovery," Jessica interjected, "Are you talking about staying in bed, or sitting in a chair?"

"No," the doctor replied. "He should continue walking and strengthening his body. Certainly, he's not to lift anything with his left arm for two weeks. And no heavy lifting for a month."

"Is it safe for him to travel to Barcelona?" Jessica blurted, moving straight to what Chris was angling for.

"I'd like to head to Barcelona in two days," Chris jumped in, eager to plead his case. "I'll take it easy. A good friend is getting married, and I promised him I'd be there. I can rest for a couple weeks in Barcelona.

"I would rather have you rest here for two weeks so I can check you regularly," the doctor confessed. "But if you promise to take it easy, I think that it's workable. But you *must* rest for two weeks. We'll wrap your left arm in a sling. I have a colleague from medical school that has his medical practice in Barcelona. I would like for you to check in with him each week you're there."

After the doctor left, Jessica voiced her concern about traveling too soon. Chris knew that she spoke out of love and that she had a valid concern.

"Look, I agree that I need to recover. I promise to take it easy and rest," Chris agreed.

Changing the subject, Chris inquired about the farmer couple. Jessica explained how hospitable they'd been, and how the farmer allowed them the use of their car each day to drive to the hospital and provided dinner and a warm bed for them each night. Jessica hesitated, then also shared how the farmer was in angst that his milking cow needed to be euthanized and how the cow was special to them.

"Then let's buy them a new cow," Chris suggested. Jessica smiled and agreed.

Drago joined them in the hospital room an hour later. He'd researched the best route to Barcelona and found a bus route with a few train connections.

"Drago, this is good information," Chris praised. "Let's book three tickets leaving two days from now. Purchase first class tickets on the train—since both the doctor and Jessica stressed that I need to take it easy. Also, I'd like you to go into town and buy the best milking cow available for our farmer friends."

"Jessica, will you bring my wallet?" Chris pulled out his debit card and gave Drago his pin number.

"Buy a cow that can be delivered to the farm," Chris instructed.

Chris asked Jessica to check on the medical bill and settle it before he was checked out. His last request was to use Jessica's cell phone. He'd lost his phone on the mountain and he wanted to call Carly while they ran their errands. Handing over her phone, Jessica left the hospital room with Drago. They agreed to check back in before heading to the farmhouse for the evening.

Chris dialed Carly's cell phone. He knew it was an odd time to call and that he might wake her up. He heard a muffled response.

"Hello, Jessica? Is everything okay?"

"Hello, honey! It's me," Chris answered. "Sorry to wake you, but I needed to call you and hear your voice."

The other end was quiet. Chris spoke again.

"Carly, are you there?"

He could tell now that she was crying. He waited for her to speak.

"Yes, I'm here. I was so worried when I didn't hear from you and then Jessica told me that you might not make it. Are you okay?"

Chris shared his latest medical status report. He boasted that he was eating by himself, walking down the hospital halls on his own, and that he would be discharged in two days. He could tell that Carly was encouraged by his improvement.

"Jessica, Drago and I will head to Barcelona once I'm discharged," Chris informed her.

"Do you think that's wise? Shouldn't you rest a little longer?"

"The doctor ordered rest for two weeks. He's fine with the travel as long as I promise to take it easy and rest two weeks in Barcelona. My plan is to go to Dan's wedding, then rest. My doctor has a colleague in Barcelona I'll visit each week for follow up."

They had a good ten-minute conversation before they were interrupted by a nurse checking Chris's vitals. Before hanging up, Chris promised to check in with Carly when they reached Barcelona.

At 6:00 p.m., Jessica and Drago entered Chris's room just as he was finishing his dinner. The two reported the purchase of the bus and train tickets. Drago had found a milking cow for the farmer and scheduled delivery for the next day. Jessica held the estimated hospital bill for Chris to review and confirmed that she would settle it the next morning.

"Thank you for letting me use your phone." Chris handed the cell phone back to Jessica. "Mom says hello."

They visited for another thirty minutes before Jessica and Drago were ready to return to the farm. They had a full day ahead of them: in the morning Jessica would pay the hospital bill while Drago would remain at the farm to ensure the cow was delivered. They planned to visit Chris in the afternoon to discuss any other business to take care of before they left town. Chris pointed at the bag of clothes that he'd worn down the mountain.

"Jessica, would you have the time to buy me clothes tomorrow? I only have the clothes that I wore when you found me. They're bloody, dirty, and have rips and holes. If you could buy a few shirts and two pairs of pants, that would be terrific. I also need socks, underwear, and one pair of shoes."

Jessica nodded, and Chris reached over to pick up a pencil and pad of paper on the night stand. He wrote down his US sizes, knowing that she'd have to translate them to Euro sizes. Chris was excited to leave the hospital. He was recovering and grateful to be alive, but he needed to distance himself from the mountains, the memories of Russians, and the thought of Mike buried up on the trail. He felt guilty leaving Mike, but he hoped that his nightmares would subside.

Chapter 90

On the move

EARLIER THAT MORNING, THE doctor shook Chris's hand and wished him luck. Chris had a feeling the doctor wanted to say more, so he lingered a few seconds before exiting the hospital.

"Remember to take it easy for two weeks." Chris nodded as the doctor winked his right eye. "It's not often that you get a second chance in life. Make it count."

The farmer and wife insisted on driving Drago and Jessica to the hospital. They picked Chris up at the hospital loading area and transported the three of them to the bus stop. The farmer was grateful for the cow and thanked them profusely. Chris explained that it was the least they could do in return for their friendship and hospitality. After exchanging phone numbers and email addresses, the farmer's wife presented a huge care package filled with sandwiches and goodies for their trip to Barcelona.

Chris, Drago, and Jessica strolled across the street to the bus stop. Dressed in a new outfit, Chris wore a navy blue sweater, a new pair of charcoal-gray slacks, and black loafers. The clothes were a little loose, but Chris knew he would gain back some of the weight he'd lost over the past weeks. Drago offered to carry Chris's backpack, Chris was about to protest, but Jessica gave him a look, reminding him that he promised to take it easy. He let it go.

As they boarded the bus, Chris turned around and saw the farmer and wife waving goodbye. Drago carried two backpacks onto the bus, and Jessica ascended the steps with her pack slung over her shoulder and cradling the food container. They had decided earlier to leave their rifles with the farmer, but they'd kept their handguns and knives in their packs. Chris wasn't sure how Jessica and Drago felt, but he was nervous without his usual weapons.

The bus route offered a scenic ride through the country. They saw forests, streams, farms, and picturesque villages. In one hour, they approached a larger town and exited at the stop. Drago walked over to a man standing nearby and conversed in German to acquire directions to the train station.

After some discussion that included pointing and hand waving, Drago turned around and nodded for Jessica and Chris to follow him. At the train station, Chris was surprised to find that he was winded just from walking a few blocks. He chose a nearby bench for a quick rest as Drago left to see if the train was on schedule. A few minutes later, he confirmed that they had forty-five minutes until they could board, and their platform was about a five-minute walk away.

When they did board, Jessica quickly located their first class seats. Chris, Jessica and Drago enjoyed the ride. They spent time chatting, often turning their heads to look outside the window and take in the beautiful countryside. Chris got to know Drago better, the more time he spent with him, the more he liked him. After two hours, they changed trains. Chris followed Drago and Jessica to their new seats, where Jessica brought out the lunch container from the farmer's wife; a fabulous lunch. The time flew as they traveled through Switzerland and France. Finally, they found themselves on the last leg to Barcelona.

During the last train transfer, Chris borrowed Jessica's phone to call Dan. Dan was pleasantly surprised to hear from Chris, and expressed excitement that Chris would arrive that night. Dan was adamant that he would meet them at the train station and asked for the arrival information.

"How is Mike doing?" Dan asked near the end of the call.

Chris tried to say something, but he struggled to find the words. It was almost like his mouth and tongue were cemented shut.

"Chris, are you still there?"

"Yes." Dan remained quiet while Chris mustered the strength.

"Dan, Mike's gone," Chris finally managed to say. "It's a long story. I'll give you details when I arrive."

Chris was depressed after talking about Mike. He tried to be upbeat as he spoke with Drago and Jessica, and after a while he felt a little better. Chris knew that Mike had put his life on the line for Drago and Jessica and the future they represented. Chris would never be able to repay what Mike had done for him, and he would probably carry some guilt and sadness forever.

When they arrived in Barcelona that evening, Drago grabbed the two packs stored above their seats, and Jessica took both her pack and the empty lunch container. They stepped down to the platform, Chris following close behind them. Chris had taken some naps on the train—he'd made a conscious decision to rest, but he was still tired. He was glad their trip was finished.

Walking twenty meters along the platform behind Drago and Jessica, Chris looked ahead, and paused.

"What's that crowd up ahead?"

His eyes rested on Dan and Maria amongst twenty other people that he soon recognized to be Maria's family. Chris pointed to Drago and Jessica.

"Over there!"

Dan saw Chris at the same moment. He spun around and his entourage started moving toward them. Dan reached Chris and hugged him gently. Dan noticed the sling and blocked Maria's relatives from bumping into Chris.

"Be careful, don't touch his arm," Dan announced to the greeters.

Chris introduced Jessica and Drago to Maria's relatives, who showered them with endless greetings and hugs. Two relatives took their backpacks, and soon they were all marching out of the train station.

Dan ushered Chris into the front seat of his car, motioning for Drago and Jessica to climb in the back seat. Maria rode with her parents, and other family members hopped into their own vehicles.

In thirty minutes, they arrived at Maria's parents' home. In forty-five minutes, all the relatives from the train station were gathered in the courtyard. Maria's mother brought out food, and her dad opened bottles of wine. It was a prewedding celebration mixed with Chris, Jessica, and Drago's arrival.

Chris had one glass of wine but made sure he didn't have a second as he wasn't sure if it would affect his antibiotics. He found a chair off to the side and enjoyed the festivities from a safe distance.

Maria's family insisted that Chris, Jessica, and Drago stay with family members. Drago and Jessica would have rooms at Maria's uncle's home, who lived a block away. Chris would stay with Maria's parents; they had the same bedroom prepared. Chris was suddenly exhausted. Saying good night to Jessica and Drago, he walked over to Maria and Dan and then Maria's parents, telling them how grateful he was for their welcoming hospitality.

"I'm sorry, but I'm very tired. I think I need to rest."

"I'll walk you to your room," Dan offered. "I have your backpack on the bed."

Chris followed Dan to the bedroom and Dan opened the door. Chris saw his backpack lying on the foot of the bed.

"Dan, Mike died up on the border of the Austrian/Slovenian mountains," Chris blurted. "It's still hard for me to talk about it, and I think about it constantly. Mike was very honorable and brave and he saved not only my life, but Jessica's and Drago's as well. I'm very tired, but if you have time tomorrow morning, I will tell you the whole story. The story from when we left you weeks ago to our arrival today."

"I know you've been through a lot," Dan acknowledged quietly. "Jessica told me that they didn't think that you would live, and I know you pushed your recovery to make my wedding. I appreciate you being here, and I insist that you rest. Please sleep as long as you can. When you wake up, we'll have breakfast, and I'll make a big pot of coffee so we can talk. I'd like to hear your story, but only if you are up to it." Dan walked over and started to close the bedroom door.

He paused midway with the door. "I can't believe how many relatives Maria has in town for this wedding. More are coming tomorrow."

Before he could close the door, Chris suddenly remembered his earlier question, "Where are Ali and Lisa? With all the excitement and people celebrating, I somehow forgot about them."

"Ali and Lisa took a trip to the south of France. They're due back tomorrow around midday. I'll tell you more about them tomorrow. Go to sleep and get rest. We'll have plenty of time to talk."

Part 4

Chapter 91

Barcelona

CHRIS WOKE UP EARLY while it was still dark. He dressed quietly and walked down to the courtyard. He watched the sunrise and enjoyed the quiet as he reflected on the past few weeks. He made a call to Carly, remembering to borrow Jessica's phone the night before. Chris wanted to let Carly know that they'd arrived safely in Barcelona.

His second call was to fill in his boss, Dale. Dale had heard from Dan the day before, so he knew that Chris had arrived in Barcelona. The Southern California territory was obviously no longer in existence, but Chris's boss had mentioned that they might find a place for him in Texas. Dan had a field application engineering position waiting for him on arrival to Florida. Thinking about work was the last thing on Chris's mind, but he was grateful for a possible job opportunity when he reached his new home in Texas. Dale was a good man.

Dan walked down the stairs past the sunrise, and over to the courtyard, where he sat down in a chair next to Chris. Minutes later, Maria's mother walked out from the kitchen with coffee and pastries. She left a pot of coffee on the table before returning to the kitchen. Chris shared the entire story of the Slovenian adventure with Dan. Maria's family gave Chris and Dan space; they understood that the two were having a serious conversation. Discussing Mike turned Chris melancholy. When he finished the story, he abruptly changed the subject.

"Tell me about Ali and Lisa."

"Well, there is a lot to share," Dan said with enthusiasm. "They've become very close. They announced that they're going to get married. They're planning a small wedding a week after our wedding. They'll be excited to see that you arrived in time for both weddings."

Chris was stunned. He was trying to calculate in his head how long ago they had found Lisa in the Caribbean.

"They plan to marry and make a new home in Europe," Dan continued. "One of Maria's aunts has a family business in Sete, France, and they've offered Ali and Lisa good jobs. They left to visit Sete and the company facility to decide if they will accept the offer. We expect them to return this afternoon."

Chris took a sip from his cup and thought about the two of them. They both had recently lost their families. Getting married and living in Europe were big changes in their lives. However, the few weeks Chris had seen them together, he'd noticed how they complemented one another. They were able to help each other grieve and heal from their losses, and they appeared to make each other stronger and happier. Chris felt that they would thrive as a couple.

Dan suggested that they join the others in the kitchen, and they walked inside to eat more breakfast. Chris wasn't too hungry after eating the pastry, but he selected a banana to help his body recover.

Maria and Dan had wedding errands planned for the afternoon. Dan had said they would return by late afternoon, in time for Ali and Lisa's expected return. Dan and Maria departed and thirty minutes later, Jessica and Drago arrived from the uncle's house.

Jessica and Drago made plans for the day. Jessica wanted to go shopping and look for new clothes. Chris had promised the doctor and Carly that he would rest. He gave Jessica her cell phone and his ATM card and asked if she would buy him up a couple more outfits including a formal outfit for the wedding. Chris asked Jessica to purchase a sport coat, a buttoned-down dress shirt, slacks, socks, and a pair of dress shoes.

Chris rested in the courtyard, and after lunch he went up to his room to take a nap. He woke suddenly when Maria's mother opened the door quietly, checking to see if he was okay. She saw him breathing heavily, and quietly pulled a blanket over him and closed the door. Chris was touched, he knew Maria's mom had heard that he'd just been released from the small Austrian hospital. Nobody could be sick or injured on her watch.

In the middle of the afternoon, Chris rose from the bed and walked down the staircase to the courtyard. Maria's mother poured him a hot cup of tea with a little shot of something. Whatever it was, it tasted good and relaxed him. Around 5:00 p.m., a muffled noise came from the direction of the living room. Maria was home and busy filling her mom in on details of their day. Dan walked into the courtyard and gave Chris a one-minute summary on the wedding cake and flowers.

Thirty minutes later, Ali and Lisa arrived. Chris thought they both looked terrific. There was a sparkle in Lisa's eyes and Ali stood tall, looking relaxed and happy. Chris stood up as Ali shook his hand and Lisa gave him a careful hug to avoid the injured shoulder. Dan motioned for them to join them and sit down. Soon Maria and her mother brought out some freshly baked cookies. With cookies in hand, everyone turned and looked at Lisa and Ali.

"We love Sete!" Lisa exclaimed. "It's small, but charming. We found an apartment that we like—it's not far from the bay. We made a deposit."

"The town seems safe," Ali added. "Maria's aunt's business is focused on boat supplies, and it looks interesting. Maria's aunt wants to expand the business, so that would be our objective. If we like the business, and we succeed growing it over two years, she'll discuss a plan for us to become part owners."

Ali put his arm around Lisa, who looked at him and smiled.

"Ali and I plan to get married a week after Dan and Maria's wedding," Lisa brought her gaze to Chris. "I would like for you to give me away."

Chris was speechless but moved. He found his voice.

"Yes, I would be honored."

Ali's eyes swept around the courtyard. Chris knew instantly who he was looking for.

"Where's Mike?" Ali looked directly at Chris. "I need to ask Mike something."

Chris's smile disappeared. He looked at Dan, then back at Ali.

"Ali, can we step aside and talk?"

Ali knew something was wrong. Both he and Dan followed Chris to the living room, but Chris didn't sit down. He turned to look at Ali, extended his good arm, and placed his hand on Ali's shoulder. He had tears in his eyes as he explained to Ali that Mike had died.

"I was planning on asking Mike to be my best man," Ali blurted out. As soon as the words were out, Ali colored with shame for thinking of himself and the wedding first. "I'll miss him so much. I was going to try to talk him into staying in the area and working with us in Sete."

"I won't have a best man," Ali declared after a moment of silence.

"We're all sad about Mike. Nobody can replace him," Dan responded. "I'll be away on my honeymoon, but, I think there are a number of people here that would be honored to stand beside you."

Ali was quiet ten seconds. A string of emotions cycled through him. Finally, he nodded.

"Dan, I appreciate the offer. Sorry for the hesitation—I'm very sad about the news. I need a day to give it some thought."

Ali, Dan, and Chris returned to the courtyard. Lisa glanced over at Ali as he walked into the courtyard. She'd heard from the others about Mike and she could see that Ali was in a dark mood. But soon, Maria's father returned from work and Ali got distracted discussing other matters.

Maria's mother always had the right food and drink for the occasion. Before Chris knew it, everyone had a glass of champagne in their hands. Jessica and Drago had returned from shopping, and Lisa and Ali had returned from their trip: why not have another celebration? Chris gave a toast to both engaged couples. Maria's father followed with a toast in Spanish that Chris didn't understand, but it brought tears to Maria's mother's eyes. It was a special moment and Chris could feel the joy and happiness refreshing his soul.

After drinks, Jessica and Drago took Chris aside to show him the outfits they'd bought. He opened the bags and pulled out a dress shirt and jacket. He asked for their help as he tried them on. It took a while to take off and exchange shirts, but the new shirt and jacket fit perfectly. Drago helped him take the shirt and jacket off, and hung them in the closet. Chris asked Jessica for help changing his bandage while his shirt was off. He walked to the bathroom to get the supplies provided by the Austrian hospital.

Afterward, Chris tried another new shirt with the shoes. Drago helped with the slacks, inserting the belt through the loops. Everything fit well. Chris looked in the mirror and told Jessica and Drago how grateful he was. Jessica said he looked very sharp, and Chris was touched. He knew that he still looked frail and worn.

Jessica had also purchased another pair of casual pants and a shirt. He tried them on to make sure they fit. The outfit was comfortable, and Chris decided to wear it as he walked downstairs to dinner.

"I need to buy a cell phone," Chris announced at the bottom of the stairs. "Perhaps you can ask where I can get one tomorrow?"

"Dad, you can just use my phone when you need it," Jessica offered.

"Thank you, but I need to get my own phone. Then your mom can reach me while we're in Barcelona. Because of the time difference, she might call me in the middle of the night."

They agreed to find the best place to buy a phone the next day as they continued walking into the courtyard.

More guests arrived for dinner. More of Maria's relatives had arrived earlier that day in Barcelona. Chris sat at a table with Jessica, Drago, Lisa, and Ali, and they had great conversation. Chris mostly listened, but he had a lovely time watching Lisa as she animatedly explained her wedding plans.

Maria and Dan were the couple that received most of the attention. Dan spent the majority of the dinner meeting his new relatives. Chris lost count of all the hugs and kisses that Dan received.

"Dan gains one beautiful wife, and one hundred new close relatives," Chris whispered to Jessica.

Drago asked Ali if the trip to Sete had been difficult, and Ali explained the train connections from Barcelona to Sete.

"We were cautious," Lisa added. "There have been terrorist attacks the past couple weeks in major cities in Spain. We've had a number of terrorist bombings at city squares, bus and train terminals, and popular restaurants. Fortunately, they intercepted a possible terrorist plot planned for the soccer game last weekend."

"Be very aware and cautious shopping or going anywhere in public," Lisa advised, looking directly at Jessica and Drago. "I'll be relieved when we can move to Sete. Every day we hear about some terrorist activity here in Barcelona. Sete is small—not a target for terrorists."

The conversation was energetic, but Chris found himself nodding off. He finally had to excuse himself. Walking up to his room, he started the lengthy process of undressing. He was so tired that he left his shirt on for a minute as he sat down to regain his strength. As he laid back further against the bed pillow to rest, he paused and was soon fast sleep.

Chapter 92

Wedding

CHRIS SAT IN THE pew of the church. Jessica and Drago were seated to his right, Lisa and Ali to his left. Dan and Maria stood at the altar, exchanging wedding vows. The church was packed with Maria's family and friends in attendance. Maria looked elegant in her long flowing white dress. Her sisters, brothers, and cousins represented the wedding party.

Chris's eyes swept through the church. Dan had explained to Chris the other day that it was six hundred years old: Maria and her siblings had been baptized there. Chris wondered how many weddings had been performed in the church over the centuries. As Maria and Dan were pronounced man and wife, the audience stood up, and the bride and groom walked down the aisle and through the crowd.

When it was time for their row to exit, Chris followed Lisa down the aisle and outside of the church. They would have the chance to speak with Dan and Maria later at the reception, so they let friends and family mob the wedding couple with their best wishes. Maria's parents had rented a big hall for the wedding reception about a kilometer away from the church. Dan, Maria, and the wedding party climbed into automobiles and were promptly whisked away to the reception. Guests had the option to walk or drive over to the hall.

Jessica and Lisa had asked Chris, Drago, and Ali their preference earlier in the day. The weather had been forecasted to be pleasant—the only concern had been in regard to Chris. He's assured them that if they strolled slow and steady, he would be fine and would even enjoy the walk. They walked at a leisurely pace to the reception. Drago took the lead—he had the location of the reception on his cell phone. Jessica, Lisa, and Ali followed, and Chris trailed close behind. He was thankful that Drago took the initiative.

Lisa and Jessica discussed Maria's wedding as Lisa shared her wedding plans with Jessica. Lisa hadn't had a lot of time to prepare, but Maria's family had provided assistance. Lisa had decided to use Maria's people for the cake and flowers; it would be a smaller wedding during the weekday, which had allowed them to secure the church. The reception would be held in Maria's family courtyard.

Lisa was pleased that Jessica showed so much interest. Lisa and Ali had pooled their own funds to pay for the priest, church, and cake. Chris had a surprise for them: he'd told Ali and Lisa days earlier that he had their honeymoon taken care of; he'd give them more details later. Maria's parents had assisted Chris in finding a romantic resort off the coast of Spain. Chris had made the deposit and would pay the balance in a couple of days. Lisa and Ali didn't know where they were going, but they were told what to pack for the week.

Chris strolled along behind Drago and Ali, listening to the girls. He reflected how uplifting it was to see happy couples: Lisa and Ali, Drago and Jessica, and Maria and Dan. There was so much to look forward to for these three couples. He reflected back on when he and Carly had started out. They had nothing, but they really had everything. He thought of Abby and Ryan, Ethan and Mark; he appreciated his family.

They arrived at the hall and lined up in the queue to walk through the reception line. Maria's parents were so excited; her father vigorously shook hands with each person. Maria's mother, overflowing with enthusiasm, gave Chris a big hug that was a little painful. He disguised his wince and gave her a big smile while offering his congratulations. Dan's smile stretched from ear to ear, and Maria had never looked more beautiful than at that moment. *Radiant* was probably the best word to describe her.

Through the reception line and handshakes, Drago found their table. It was off to the side, but not too far from the wedding table. Chris could see everything in the room without getting up from his chair. It was a little warm, but Chris left his coat on. He secretly had his Glock under his jacket; he couldn't leave it behind, especially after Lisa's warning about terrorists. He'd hoped that in a few weeks he might be able to relax and take a stroll in the neighborhood without wearing it. But right now he still looked for Russian soldiers at every turn and corner.

One of Maria's aunts, along with other family members, filled in the rest of their table. Since they'd met the relatives earlier at Maria's family home, they were able to easily continue previous conversations. The food was excellent and abundant and Chris enjoyed listening to the music and watching the dancing. Chris had fun watching Drago and Jessica and Lisa and Ali "show their moves" out on the dance floor. Dan and Maria danced to every song as a long line of relatives eagerly waited to cut in and dance with the bride or the groom.

After a few hours, the reception began to slow down. Dan and Maria announced their departure from the wedding reception, and a crowd gathered to cheer as they left in a car decorated with streamers.

Chris, Jessica, Drago, and Lisa, walked back to the house of Maria's parents. As planned, Maria and Dan changed their clothes, and waited for the others in the courtyard. The party would continue at Maria's parents' house with just the immediate family. Tomorrow morning, Dan and Maria would leave for their honeymoon to the Basque area. They'd rented a place on the northwest coast of Spain, courtesy of one of Maria's relatives.

Chris and the others entered their rooms and also changed into more comfortable clothes. Jessica and Drago had brought a change of clothes since they were still staying at the uncle's home nearby. Once they reconvened in the courtyard, Maria's father brought out some of his nice bottles of wine. Maria's father asked Drago to help him uncork the wine and let it breathe. When the immediate family was present, everyone was handed a glass, another round of toasts took place, and everyone settled into relaxed conversation.

"Dan, I'm so happy for you," Chris announced when he saw Dan available. "You and Maria make such a great couple."

"Thank you for making the effort to attend the wedding. It means a lot." Dan smiled and clasped Chris's extended hand. "We'll miss Lisa and Ali's wedding, but we should be back when they return from their honeymoon. We'll be gone for two weeks. After one week in the Basque country, we'll travel down into Portugal. Apparently another one of Maria's relatives owns a second home on a southern beach below Lisbon."

Dan continued to tell Chris about their travel plans. Chris took mental notes of places that sounded interesting and that Carly would enjoy. Someday, it might be safe to travel the world again.

Chris walked over to a table that seated Ali, Lisa, Drago, and Jessica. Pulling up a chair, he waited until there was a lull in the conversation.

"Lisa, are we shopping tomorrow?"

"Yes. We need to get you, Drago, and Ali fitted for tuxedos. I also need to confirm the cake and flowers. Ali asked Drago to be his best man, and I just asked Jessica to be my maid of honor. And I'll need to go shopping for a dress," she added.

"Sounds like a terrific day." Chris smiled. "Do I get the opportunity to sample the cake?" He assumed the lack of response meant that he would have to wait for the wedding.

They chatted for a while, and then Chris zigged-zagged his way over to confirm with Dan when they would leave in the morning for their honeymoon. He wanted to be up to say goodbye.

"Chris, when will you be able to travel across the Atlantic?" Dan asked afterward.

"I have a couple more doctor visits, but I hope to be able to go in three weeks. I'm feeling stronger each and every day; the shoulder needs a little longer. With the food that Maria's mother is feeding me, I may have to lose a few pounds before we go."

"This could work out perfectly," Dan laughed regarding Maria's mother's abundant food, patting his stomach. "When I return from the honeymoon, I'll need a week or more to get the boat ready to sail. I will need some assistance."

Dan looked around and saw Maria still engaged in conversation. He realized that this would not change.

"I think now is a good time to say good night! And with that, Dan walked over to Maria, interrupted the conversation, and whisked Maria up to their bedroom.

The others were tired; one by one the couples excused themselves. Finally, it was just Chris and Maria's parents. He walked over and gave them a handshake and hug with a big smile that he hoped conveyed everything he felt.

Chapter 93

Texas

CARLY STOOD IN THE kitchen cooking lasagna, apple pie, and fixing a big salad with her mother and mother-in-law. Abby and Ryan planned to visit from Austin that evening and they'd said they spend the night. Abby had expressed that she and Ryan would be sharing big news.

Carly wasn't sure what the news would be, however, it was always pleasant to spend time together. She wished Ethan and Mark could join them for dinner. Carly knew that Ryan had been working very hard at his new job, and she wondered if the news could be a promotion.

They had an hour before everyone would converge at the kitchen. Clark was outside mending a fence, and Carly's father and father-in-law were at the store buying wine, sparkling cider, and fresh bread to go with the lasagna. They were also purchasing some miscellaneous items for the farm at the hardware store.

Carly thought how well they had adjusted to life on the farm. She appreciated all the assistance: the grandparents eagerly participated with the chores around the house and Clark relished the farm life. Carly would miss Clark when he started school at Tech that fall.

Finley barked and ran out the open front door onto the front porch. He was animated and focused on the driveway, tail swinging wildly from side to side. Carly heard a car pull up to the front of the farm and she walked toward Finley. She smiled when she saw Abby and Ryan. She waited until the car stopped, then opened the screen door to let Finley out. Finley rushed over to greet Abby, wiggling and talking as he made his greeting sounds. He finally calmed down after Abby spoke to him while stroking his back.

Abby and Ryan walked up to the porch where Carly stood and exchanged loving hugs. Just then the grandfathers pulled up in the driveway. Ryan sauntered over to help bring the groceries into the kitchen and they all gathered in the kitchen where the grandfathers stocked the groceries. Abby and Ryan commented on the good smells coming from the pies and lasagna in the oven. Once the groceries were put away, they entered the living room to visit.

Ten minutes later, Carly heard Clark walk in the house from the back door. Carly hollered to him that they were in the living room. Seconds later, Clark greeted Abby and Ryan, then asked Carly if he had time for a quick shower.

"Yes, but come down as soon as you shower and change," Carly suggested. "Ryan and Abby have some news to share. We'll stay here in the living room."

"Should we get the wine and sparkling cider?" Grandpa H suggested to Pa K.

They left the living room to uncork the bottles in the kitchen. In two trips they delivered the wine and sparkling cider to the others, setting the glasses and bottles down on the coffee table.

Clark returned quickly and found an empty chair. They sat attentive, staring at Abby and Ryan. Abby felt embarrassed at the attention; her face turned crimson.

"We have some exciting news. Something we wanted to share with everyone. I wish Dad, Jessica, Ethan, and Mark were here."

"Well, what is the news?" Grandmother H couldn't wait for the suspense.

Abby looked at Ryan and then blurted out, "I'm pregnant!"

Ma K raised her hands to her cheeks; Grandma H was speechless.

"Congratulations!" the grandfathers exclaimed; as they stepped over to pour the drinks.

Carly was misty eyed as she walked across the room to hug Abby and then Ryan. After the year's challenging moments, it was nice to have something positive happen. Carly paused to reflect; at that moment in time, her family was safe with the hope and promise of a new life. She felt blessed and thankful; she just needed Jessica, Drago, and Chris home.

Toasts were made. Each grandparent made their own toast, and Carly gave hers with tears. Clark gave the last toast.

"We need to call Ethan and Mark!" Carly exclaimed.

"You call Ethan, and I'll call Mark," Carly said while looking at Abby. "We'll put them both on speakerphone."

Ethan and Mark were connected in a minute, and Abby shared her news. They were stunned but happy and gave their congratulations. Fortunately, Grandmother H remembered the food in the oven, and Ma K and Carly joined her in pulling out the pies and checking the lasagna.

Dinner was a huge celebration. There was a lot of laughter and sharing of stories. Ryan and Abby shared the latest on their jobs and their new place in Austin. The grandparents told past stories. Clark shared about signing up for classes at Tech. It was a great evening and Carly didn't want it to end, but the grandparents became tired. Soon it was time to end the night.

It was late at night when Carly dialed Chris, who was just waking up. It was the next day in Barcelona. He answered and Carly couldn't contain her excitement.

"Abby is pregnant!"

"What!"

"Ryan and Abby are expecting a baby."

Chris wasn't expecting this news. He gave up trying to button his shirt and sat down on the bed.

"Wow, that is terrific news."

"Will you tell Jessica?" Carly asked. "We called Ethan and Mark last night when she shared the news."

"Abby and Ryan are at the farm?"

"Yes, they drove down this afternoon and had dinner with us. They'll drive back tomorrow after breakfast."

"Is everyone else doing okay?"

"Yes, we're all fine. What about you and Jessica?"

"Dan and Maria had a beautiful wedding. They're leaving in an hour for their honeymoon in the Basque area. Then they plan to drive down the coast of Portugal. Lisa and Ali are getting married in a few days."

Carly was surprised by the news of Ali and Lisa. She could only remember Ali as a young man and recovering from his parent's death.

"When are you planning on coming back?" Carly questioned.

"The doctor says I'm doing well. Dan and Maria will be back in two weeks—Dan thinks he'll need an additional week to prepare his boat. The timing appears to line up well with what the doctors are telling me, so we may leave in about three weeks."

Carly was quiet.

"Lisa and Ali will be on their honeymoon for a week after the wedding," Chris went on. "They're going to work for Maria's relative's business, so they'll move up the coast into France. A number of things are happening the next couple weeks."

"How do you like Drago?" Carly asked.

"I like him a lot. Actually, the more I'm around him, the more I like him. Similar to Abby and Ryan, Drago complements Jessica well. They make a good partnership."

Chris asked about current events and Carly told him that the Texas federation had expanded. It now included every former state with the exception of California, Oregon, and Washington in the West, a few central states such as Ohio and Michigan who were making overtures that they would still join, minus New York, New Jersey, Pennsylvania, and the New England states in the Northeast. The government capital would relocate to Austin, Texas. Business was almost back to normal on a state level, and some domestic flights were reinstating routes within Texas.

"Chris, when you reach Florida, you should check if air travel is a possibility. We may have flights available from Florida to Austin or Dallas in a few weeks. They say that in eight months, international travel may resume in select locations, and domestic travel could be inside six months."

Carly shared more about the grandparents' good health, the farm, and then they ended the call with "love you." Carly went to sleep and Chris walked down to see Dan and Maria. He entered the courtyard where

Maria's mom had left hot drinks and pastries. Dan and Maria had their bags stacked and looked anxious to leave. Chris knew he would see them in two weeks, so he just gave a handshake and hug.

"Have fun." Chris couldn't think of anything else to say.

After Dan and Maria left, Chris sat down with Maria's dad to eat a pastry with a cup of coffee. They couldn't say much because of the language barrier, but they still enjoyed each other's company.

Minutes later, Lisa, Ali, Jessica, and Drago were out on the patio eating their breakfast. Maria's mother joined them in the courtyard. The young adults knew some Spanish and were conversing with Maria's parents.

Maria's father announced that he had to leave for work, causing the others to decide that breakfast time was over. They brought their cups and dishes into the kitchen, where Maria's mother insisted they leave the dishes in the sink and not bother to wash or dry them.

Lisa announced the first errand of the day and Drago plugged the route information into his phone. After thanking Maria's mother for breakfast, they walked out the front door. Drago took off down the street, leading the way to the first stop. Lisa, Ali, Jessica, and Chris strolled behind him, enjoying the sights.

Chris told Jessica about Abby's pregnancy and the other news that Carly had shared with Chris the night prior. Jessica responded with enthusiasm and delight: she'd received a brief call from Abby earlier in the morning and she knew about the pregnancy. Jessica listened attentively to the other news, peppering Chris with a number of questions he couldn't answer.

"I need to get more details from Mom," Jessica decided when it was clear that her father had shared all that he knew. "I wonder when she'll have a baby shower. We need to get home soon."

Chapter 94

Second wedding

CHRIS WALKED LISA DOWN the aisle and brought her to the altar, handing her to Ali, who waited nervously. Chris nodded to Ali, and Lisa winked at Chris before leaving to stand near Ali. Chris pivoted around and walked over to the first row and sat down. It was a smaller wedding than Maria and Dan's, but Maria's mother and father and the Barcelona family were present.

Ali looked both anxious and happy at the same time. Chris reflected on Ali's life, and the night Chris had encountered Ali's parent's killer: they'd buried Ali's family and left San Diego. Ali had made the trek to Texas and then Florida, followed by the voyage to Europe. Now he was in Spain, getting married. Chris's thoughts shifted to Lisa and her family murdered by pirates. Now she was in this medieval church, marrying Ali. All these events had taken place in less than six months. Lisa and Ali were both very young but they were good together, and they certainly deserved a new start in life.

An hour later, they were back at the courtyard for the wedding reception. The small reception was done nicely by Maria's mother: a lovely food buffet outlined the perimeter of the courtyard. Maria's father had his signature wine uncorked, and he generously poured wine for all the guests.

Chris quietly pulled Lisa and Ali aside for a quick discussion between the wedding and reception. He held an envelope out to Ali.

"In this envelope are two train tickets for tomorrow. I've arranged for you to have a beach house for a week on the Spanish coast. The refrigerator is stocked with food and drinks for breakfast and lunch. The beach is just outside your door, each evening there will be a private dinner at a table on the beach. A woman will come midafternoon to prepare the food. All the information is in the envelope—call me if there are any questions or issues."

Lisa had tears in her eyes as she gave Chris a long hug. Ali shook his hand, decided that wasn't sufficient, and hugged Chris. They both thanked Chris profusely, but truth be told, Chris felt elated to do something nice for them.

Lisa and Ali would spend the evening in Barcelona before boarding the midmorning train the next day. At 9:00 p.m. they departed the reception, to pack for their honeymoon.

Jessica had taken Lisa out the day before to buy her a summer outfit: her wedding gift to Lisa. Drago had done the same for Ali.

As Lisa and Ali left for their rooms, Jessica and Drago strolled (glasses of wine in hand) toward Chris. They interrupted his thoughts.

"It was a smaller wedding than Maria and Dan's, but just as special and beautiful," Jessica said with a smile.

"In some ways I like the small and intimate weddings better," Drago confessed.

"The weddings were both beautiful. I think both marriages will be successful," Chris commented with a smile.

There was a pause as they reflected on the weddings. Chris shifted his feet and broke the silence.

"Well, I have another doctor appointment tomorrow. We have some time before Dan and Maria return, but we should start thinking about what we'll need to buy for the voyage back home."

Chapter 95

Preparation

DAN AND MARIA RETURNED from their honeymoon looking refreshed. The very next day, Ali and Lisa returned from their honeymoon. Chris was pleased to hear that they'd had a wonderful vacation: they returned tanned and relaxed.

Ali and Lisa met with Maria's aunt in the afternoon. They made arrangements to leave in two days for their new jobs and new home.

Chris thought about how he would miss both Ali and Lisa. When things became safe, he would bring Carly over for a vacation in Spain, and they would visit Lisa and Ali and Maria's family. It would be a perfect excuse to travel to Barcelona.

Dan shared his checklist of chores to be completed before departure; his list included checking the motor and sails, but also painting the boat.

Food supplies would be purchased the day before leaving Barcelona. There were five making the voyage back to the old "States:" they wouldn't' have Mike, Ali, or Lisa, so they were losing some sailing experience. Dan suggested a couple of day trips in the Mediterranean (including an overnight trip), so Drago, Jessica, and Maria would feel comfortable on the water. Dan scheduled a short voyage to take place after Lisa and Ali left for their new home.

As their departure date approached, Chris sensed that Maria's mom was a little depressed. Her eyes would mist up whenever she looked at her daughter; Chris knew she would miss Maria dearly. Dan had invited Maria's parents to stay with them in Florida whenever they wanted to visit. Chris thought that once travel conditions improved, Dan might have his mother-in-law visiting on a regular basis.

In addition to Maria and the other family guests leaving, Maria's mother was also going to miss Lisa and Ali—even if they would be only a couple of hours away by train. Lisa told Maria's parents that they had a second bedroom/office and they welcomed them to visit often. Maria's parents countered with an open invitation for Lisa and Ali to visit them in Barcelona anytime. Chris marveled at how gracious and warm Maria's parents were; it made him think of his Carly. Carly was happiest with her family at home, and friends were always welcome.

Chris was healing well and walking further each day to increase his endurance. He worked through daily physical therapy exercises for his arm and could tell that he was getting stronger. He thought he would be able to help Dan and the others prepare for their voyage if things kept up.

At the same time, Chris felt exhausted from lack of sleep. He wondered if he was anxious to start the voyage back home.

Days later, Chris was in the courtyard talking with Jessica. They were sitting in a couple of chairs to the side.

"Jessica, are you ready to go back home?"

"Dad, yes! I'm anxious to see Mom, Ethan, Mark, Abby, and Ryan," Jessica couldn't hide her anticipation.

"How does Drago feel about the trip?" Chris queried.

"He's fine. I think he's excited for a new adventure, but I think he's also sad to leave his family behind. Although, he told me that he thinks the Slovenians will chase the Russians out of the country,"

"He is confident he will be able to come back someday and see his parents and siblings," she added.

"Yes, they have some remarkable people in Slovenia," Chris agreed. "I hope he's correct that they will triumph in the end."

Maria's mother suggested they all travel to the bus station the next morning to see Lisa and Ali off. She had everything organized for the send-off. Lisa and Ali had one bus ride and then one train ride to reach their final destination. After the send-off for the young newlyweds, Dan, Maria, Drago, Jessica and Chris would head toward Dan's boat in the late morning and take it out for a sailing adventure.

Maria shared with the others her father's concern that her mother may become depressed over the next few weeks. With no visitors, weddings, or parties to host, it was likely that Maria's mother would become bored.

Chapter 96

Goodbye, Lisa and Ali

LISA AND ALI'S ENTOURAGE walked through the bus station. Maria's mother and father led the way with Ali and Lisa following and pulling their roller bags. Drago and Dan each lugged a duffle bag for Lisa and Ali. Maria's mother had given Lisa dishes, silverware, and towels: essentially a starter kit for their new home. Many boxes had been shipped and would arrive in a few days to their new residence. Maria, Jessica, and Chris followed the others as part of the procession.

As they approached the LED display listing buses and platform numbers, Maria's mother and father discussed something in Spanish, then headed toward the number nine platform. They were early; there was plenty of time to say their last goodbyes. Hugs, kisses, and handshakes were given to Lisa and Ali along with well wishes. Chris's healing had improved considerably; big hugs were no longer painful.

Dan and Drago placed the bags in the storage bin underneath the bus. Lisa and Ali waved one last time, then walked up the steps onto the bus. Lisa had a window seat so she could look and wave to her friends as they waved back enthusiastically. Maria's mother had tears in her eyes even though she had arranged to travel and visit them in three weeks' time.

The bus was loaded; Chris estimated it was about three quarters full. The bus driver closed the door, and the bus started to slowly pull away. Chris noticed a strange dirty white van coming down the ramp quickly into the bus area. Nobody else from the group had noticed it—they were too busy waving at Lisa.

"Isn't this area only for buses?"

The others looked up and followed Chris's eyes to now see two commercial vans driving down the ramp. Chris's heart sank as he realized that they were not confused drivers. For a split second he thought of LAX.

"No!" Chris screamed as the two vans accelerated.

The first van rammed into the side of the bus with Lisa and Ali. Both minivan and bus instantaneously exploded into a ball of fire. The second van targeted an adjacent bus and seconds later, another explosion and fireball.

Chris and the others stood frozen in shock. Helplessly they watched the flames that claimed their friend's lives. Bus authorities scrambled everywhere, ushering people off the platforms and into the station. Chris followed the others inside to watch the chaos through the Plexiglas windows.

Fire trucks arrived and firefighters were quickly able to eliminate the flames, but there was not much left of either bus. Both buses were charred black skeletons, it was difficult to imagine that they had been waving goodbye to Ali and Lisa moments before.

Police were on the scene and made their way inside the station. Two policemen approached the group and asked them questions.

"What did you see, sir?"

Chris felt numb. He didn't know what to say. He finally managed to mumble a response. He looked around the station at the people wandering aimlessly. Others sat in their seats, and several stood frozen in place. Many were sobbing; it was terrible.

Later police confirmed, what everyone already knew. No one had survived the terrorist bombing. The police asked people who knew the passengers to leave their contact information.

Finally, Dan said, "Let's go!"

No one said a word as they moved like robots back to Maria's parents' home. Maria's dad looked at the wine bottles that he had brought out on the patio table for celebration and shook his head to no one but himself. No celebrations today. Instead, he brought out a bottle of alcohol that looked brown and brackish, and he poured everyone shots. They were strong shots, but even so, two shots were not enough for Chris to erase the grief.

No one spoke; they were all thinking about Lisa and Ali. It had finally appeared that their futures were bright.

"Those terrorists just killed a great couple," Chris broke the silence. "And over one hundred more innocent people."

Drago looked straight ahead and didn't move. Dan was shaking his head and muttering something. Jessica had a pained look on her face. Maria and her mother had tears running down their faces. Maria's father just kept pouring more of the brackish liquid into the empty shot glasses.

"I'm not sure what else we can do here," Chris spoke again. "I think we should head back. Dan, Maria, Drago and Jessica, can we start working on our supply list this afternoon? I know that there isn't much left to buy, but I'd like to ensure that Lisa and Ali have a decent burial and service, and then I'm ready to travel."

Dan, Drago, and Jessica stood up while Maria rose and held Dan. Chris was the first to leave the house. The others followed him as they made their way to the harbor.

Jessica turned back before she left the courtyard to see Maria's dad hug Maria's mother, who was sobbing. They were going to have to work this out in their own way—no one would be able to erase the vision of the bus exploding with their friends onboard.

Chapter 97

Funeral

THEY GATHERED IN THE cemetery for Ali and Lisa's funeral, caskets positioned to be lowered into the holes as soon as the priest finished. Ali had told Lisa before they'd been married that he would convert to Catholicism, so the decision was made to bury them both side by side in the cemetery. The weather was dismal that midafternoon with overcast skies and a constant light rain. Chris stood under his umbrella, looking at the others. Dan and Maria shared an umbrella, their eyes focused on the graves. Drago held an umbrella for himself and Jessica, who stood by Chris's side. Jessica glanced over at Chris and forced a smile.

Maria's family had thoughtfully come in full force. They'd only recently met Ali and Lisa, yet they'd quickly embraced them into their lives. Ali and Lisa had many people gathered around them for a last goodbye.

The priest finished and the caskets were lowered. A line formed to place dirt on the caskets. It was more like shoveling mud on the casket. When they had finished the symbolic gesture, they walked to their vehicles.

Nobody spoke as they drove back to the house of Maria's parents. Walking inside, they visited their bedrooms, changed clothes, then gathered in the kitchen. There was a pot of coffee brewing, and Chris sat down at the table near Dan, Drago, and Jessica.

"I think we are in good shape," Dan said out loud as he studied his list.

"What is left for us to do?" Drago asked.

Dan went through the list item by item. Most of the supplies on his list, were last minute food items. That past week they'd successfully taken a half-day trip. However, they hadn't yet tried an overnighter. Dan suggested they carry out one overnight trip the next day. The overnighter would be their last test before departing across the Atlantic Ocean. They brought just enough food for a few meals, they would do their heavy shopping before their final departure.

The thought of everyone leaving had Maria's mother weepy the last few of days. Chris hoped this would not put a strain on Dan and Maria. Maria was excited to build a life in the United States, but she naturally had some reservations of the unknown.

Maria's father distributed warm drinks to Chris, Jessica, Drago, Dan, and Maria and they exited to the courtyard. When they'd finished the drink, they returned to the kitchen to assist Maria's mother in cooking the meal. Everyone made an effort with conversation, but nobody felt like talking. After dinner, they helped with clean up before retreating to their individual rooms. Since they would wake up early the next day, they wanted to get enough sleep. Chris called Carly to share the latest developments, then fell fast asleep.

* * * * *

At 5:00 a.m., the alarm went off. Chris dressed quickly and was downstairs in minutes. Dan was already drinking a cup of coffee, and he'd packed the food for the next two days in an ice chest. Soon Maria, Drago, and Jessica joined them. They each drank a cup of coffee, then departed for the dock.

The guard at the dock recognized them. They'd been down at the dock every day the past week, and the guard signaled an informal salute as they walked toward Dan's boat. Climbing aboard, they set their backpacks and ice chest down on the deck. Maria brought the supplies down below into the cabin and stored them away. Meanwhile, Dan went through his checklist with the other three before pulling out of the harbor.

Dan motored out of the harbor. The sails were staged and ready for his signal. The weather would be nice that day since the recent storm passed; sunrise was already breaking through the darkness. Maria busied herself making a pot of coffee in the galley and brought up cups for Dan and Jessica.

Dan set course to sail along the coast toward the south of France. The plan was to go out to sea, spend the night, then return the next day to Barcelona. Each person was scheduled to take a turn both "navigating" and "on watch" duty, including a shift for both day and night. Chris felt comfortable on Dan's boat, but, the other three hadn't experienced the first European voyage. Everyone knew their lives depended on how each person handled their job.

Sitting on the deck, Dan explained his intended route back to Florida. He planned to return using the same route as when they'd come to Europe. Chris knew this route, but listened as Jessica, Drago, and Maria asked questions. Dan shared new information he'd recently gathered from the Spanish harbor police. The area from the Mediterranean Sea through the Strait of Gibralter was well patrolled and expected to be safe. However, once they left the Strait, they might encounter pirates traveling up from Africa.

The pirates from Africa targeted small boats before they had the chance to venture too far out in the Atlantic. Their goal was to capture the boat on the Spanish or Portuguese coast, then take the vessel and cargo down the African coast. Chris didn't want to scare the others, but he agreed that this was an undeniable reality. If they were forced to face this challenge, they'd need to fight to the death. To surrender would mean selling the women; the men would be killed or used for ransom.

The day was easy sailing: the water was calm, and they passed a number of fishing boats. After Dan walked through the map and the travel plans, Chris brought up the topic of protection. It was confirmed that everyone knew how to use a handgun; a shotgun was brought out, and they discussed the situations on when to use it. After the shotgun discussion, Chris brought up the rifles they had stashed below. Once they started traveling, they would need to keep them readily available and loaded. Most of this information was for Maria. Drago and Jessica had already experienced tense situations in Slovenia.

Finally, Chris brought out the antimissile weapon that Mike had bought in the Caribbean. Chris went over the weapon many times with Drago and Dan, discussing how to use the weapon, explaining that it was the best protection against attacking vessels. Maria's eyes got big, but Dan reassured her that they hadn't needed it for the voyage to Spain.

At dusk, Dan sailed deeper into the Mediterranean Sea. He gathered them around to go through instructions. Dan planned to supervise Drago,

Jessica, and Maria at the helm before going to sleep; he'd let Chris navigate on his own.

* * * * *

Drago shook Chris to wake him up, then returned back up on deck. Pulling on pants, Chris poured a cup of coffee, put on his light jacket, and went up the stairs to the deck. Dan stood at the wheel; he turned around when he heard Chris approach.

"Are you fresh enough to navigate six to seven hours?"

Chris smiled and raised his coffee cup. "Yes, I had a good sleep."

Dan told Chris that at sunrise he should set the course back toward Barcelona. Chris confirmed the steps which put Dan at ease. Satisfied that Chris knew the course, he retreated below for much—needed sleep.

Chris was wide awake. Even though he hadn't slept well, the combination of the fresh, cool, salty breeze and the strong cup of coffee made him alert. It was so quiet up on deck: he'd forgotten how much he enjoyed the feeling of being out on the water. He would probably never love it as much as Dan, but he enjoyed feeling insignificant out on the water, at the mercy of Mother Nature.

Two hours later, it was still pitch-black, when Chris saw a light in the distance. It was a small light, but it was heading their direction. Chris watched as the light came closer. After five minutes, Chris noticed it was still targeted toward them. He turned the wheel thirty degrees off course, in the direction of France. For ten minutes, he told himself that he was being paranoid and overreacting, but then the light changed its course. It was moving toward their boat, and gaining on them.

Chris changed course another thirty degrees. The boat was now on course for the shoreline. In another ten minutes, the boat altered its course, following Chris. This confirmed Chris's fears.

"Hey, guys, wake up! I need you up here—quick!"

In two minutes, everyone was on deck. Dan studied the light approaching them, took the wheel, and quietly tried to calculate their distance from the French coast.

Dan suggested that they take advantage of the breeze and adjust the sails for maximum speed. Then they moved to ensure that they were well-armed. Drago and Jessica had rifles and handguns; Dan told them to be ready with the rifles before the boat got too close. Maria took the shotgun and was told to wait until Dan instructed her to use it. They would only use the shotgun if their pursuer tried to board. Chris had Mike's antimissile launcher in place and he would be the first to fire.

They were slicing through the water fast, but the mystery boat still gained on them. The sun was rising and Chris was thankful he wouldn't have to shoot in the dark. Dan estimated that they were about one hour from the French coast. He looked over to Maria.

"Maria, will you take the wheel?"

Dan pulled out his binoculars and studied the approaching ship. Drago and Jessica had positioned themselves, rifles ready. Chris was also loaded and ready.

"I think it may be the French coast guard!" Dan shouted so they could hear.

He took the wheel back from Maria and changed their direction a few degrees to the west. Maria reclaimed her shotgun.

"I'm ready to fire!" Chris shouted to all. "We'll have to make a quick decision. Jessica and Drago, you need to wait to fire, but decide your first target and second shot. Make your decision strategic. If it is the coast guard, we'll put our weapons down. If not, we'll need to make a stand."

Chris had his sights locked on the ship's hull. Was the ship the coast guard, or an imposter?

Finally, the coast guard boat was almost parallel to them. The sailors saluted as they passed by. Chris lowered his weapon. As soon as they were a boats length ahead, Chris laid down his weapon.

Dan sighed. "Well, that was an adrenaline rush. A good warm up for our trip back home."

"They were playing games by tracking us." Chris was ticked with the French ship. "If they weren't tracking us so closely, I wouldn't have been so spooked."

"You did the right thing," Dan responded. "We can't get complacent. Drago, Jessica, Maria—that could have been a pirate boat, or a pirate boat disguised as the coast guard. We have to be cautious. Our lives depend on it."

Chris suggested that Dan go back to sleep, but Dan said he'd had enough sleep. Chris packed the missile back in the case and Drago, Jessica, and Maria put their weapons away. They decided they were hungry and needed a big breakfast, so Maria, Drago, and Jessica made another pot of coffee along with pancakes and sausages.

Dan set a new course, hugging the coast as he duplicated some of the course from the day prior. Once Dan had established his revised course, he took the helm from Chris. Chris ducked down below, filled his coffee cup, and came back with a second cup for Dan.

"Dan, I hope we have a very boring voyage back home. I think we're overdue for a quiet and safe trip home."

"Chris, I'm not sure what's ahead of us, but I've had enough excitement to last a lifetime! When we get back to Florida, I hope to have the most boring ten years ever. I want to have a couple of babies with Maria, stay home, work, and take the boat out on a weekend. I've had enough adventure."

Chris nodded but didn't answer. He was deep in thought, wondering what life would be like when they returned to the old United States—the new Texas Federation. Would he have a job? Could life resume as it had in San Diego? He knew it wouldn't be the same, but perhaps it could be different, but still good. If their family was safe and thriving, he and Carly could adjust.

Chapter 98

Preparation

IT HAD BEEN TWO days since their overnight sailing trip. The prior day had been a day of rest, and today they would focus on their detailed list of supplies to be purchased. Maria's mother assisted by suggesting where to buy produce, meat, bread and canned goods: Maria knew these establishments well, but she kept mum so as to allow her mom the opportunity to participate. Dan remained on the boat for the day, working on his miscellaneous checklist. Maria, Drago, and Jessica were in charge of food and any food related supplies. Chris was responsible for purchasing the fishing gear and ammunition. As items were purchased, they were brought immediately to the boat for storage.

That night, they would sleep on the boat and disembark before sunrise. At 6:00 p.m., the five of them arrived on the boat and went through the list a second time to make sure nothing was forgotten. Dan smiled in satisfaction as he rattled off the last items on the list; they were ready.

A half hour later, Maria's parents walked down the dock; Maria's father had a picnic basket in hand. Maria's mother requested they stay one more night at the house; she even offered to invite relatives for a final goodbye. Dan declined. They were ready to go, and he wanted to stay close to his boat now that it was stocked with supplies and ready to cross the Atlantic. The incident with Ali and Lisa had illustrated to him that anything could happen. Besides, it would be hard for Maria to see all the family again.

Maria had mixed emotions about leaving. She was excited to start a new life with Dan, but she was also very close to her family. Leaving them behind was difficult for her.

Drago had never visited the US, but he was ready to embark on a new chapter in his life and strengthen his relationship with Jessica in a normal environment. Chris and Jessica were anxious to get back home and see family. Jessica felt the same way as Drago: she wanted a balanced life; the opportunity to grow their relationship with less stress.

Maria's mother had packed a feast. Dan intercepted them on the dock and assisted Maria's father in lifting the picnic basket onto the deck. They unpacked the basket, spread the blanket out and began to enjoy a wonderful picnic dinner. Maria's father, not one to come empty-handed, had brought two bottles of wine. Chris wondered if his supply of wine was unlimited. The sunset was beautiful, and the temperature was idyllic: just a slight breeze.

After dinner, they enjoyed the last of the wine. It was obvious to Chris that Maria's mother was stalling to avoid the imminent goodbyes. Chris had a silly thought: could Maria's mother be a stowaway for their trip back to Florida? At last she rose with encouragement from Maria's father. She hugged the others and approached Maria last. She held her for what seemed like an eternity, not wanting to let go. She finally released Maria, placing both hands on each of Maria's shoulders.

"You need to be very careful. Perhaps you should wait a few months to see if things become safer?"

Maria's father gently tried to pull her away. Dan searched for something to say.

"I'll take care of Maria. We'll arrive safely in Florida. When it's safe to travel, you'll both need to fly over and spend time with us."

That thought seemed to pacify the mother; she let go of Maria. Tears ran down her cheeks. Maria cried quietly as Maria's father shook hands with Chris and Drago, gave a hug to Jessica and Dan, and then embraced

Maria. Afterward, Maria's parents left the boat; they didn't turn around once as they walked off the dock and through the gate.

Each of them were deep in thought as they went through the motions of cleaning up from dinner. Dan opened a bottle of wine and poured each a glass. They sat on deck, waiting to see who would be the first to speak.

"We should start with armed shifts tonight," Dan suggested, breaking the silence. "We can split into one and a half hour shifts 9:00 p.m. to 4:30 a.m., rising at 4:30 a.m., and leaving by 5:00 a.m."

It was one in the morning when Chris was on deck for the third shift. He had thirty minutes left until Drago's shift. It was quiet, with no activity, but, Chris was restless. He hoped his feeling was the result of the "new normal" he had yet to adjust to and not a premonition of something ominous waiting for them. The route was set: the boat would cross through the straits toward Madeira, then rest for a day or two, before making the voyage across the Atlantic. Dan had a couple of alternative routes planned in case of inclement weather; the forecast promised sunny skies and calm seas.

Drago relieved Chris, who decided to use the opportunity to call Carly. Chris assumed he'd lose cell coverage the next day.

"We leave Barcelona in a few hours," Chris told Carly.

"Make sure you stay very alert," Carly instructed Chris. "We're all excited to have you, Jessica, and Drago home."

"We're prepared, and we'll be cautious. What's happening back in the States?"

Carly paused for a few seconds to gather her thoughts. Chris had walked onto the dock and down a few meters so as not to awaken the others.

"Well, the Texas Federation told California, Oregon, and Washington that they have ninety days to join—or else they're out. The consensus is that Washington and Oregon may join. That would leave us with the Northeast US and possibly California that may not join. The odds are fifty-fifty on California and the Northeast. There's a rumor that the Northeast will form a coalition and break apart to form a new country."

"What are the fundamental changes from the old United States?" Chris asked.

Carly tried to recall the key changes from memory. She knew that Chris was anxious to understand what he was returning to.

"The concept of government has changed. The government is now considered a service—they say it was the intent of our forefathers in the late 1700s. The Texas Federation will have military, international diplomacy, and border control. There will be limited social programs, some speed rail development between the twenty-five largest cities. Social security and Medicare will still be in place with some modifications for the younger generation. State governments will focus on schools, police, and fire departments, as well as infrastructure for roads and utilities like water, sewer, and electricity. Most other services will be cut from the budget. There will be a flat federal tax, and states will be encouraged to offer a flat tax. There will not be any sales taxes in any states. More details are in negotiation."

"What about school, welfare, and immigration issues? Those were two of the hot topics before the collapse of the US."

"Education programs will be similar to other parts of the world. Teenagers will take an exam and qualify for either college or trade school. We'll have two-year trade schools, including an apprenticeship, to ensure students are qualified to enter the workforce. They'll pulse the top twenty trades for the next two decades—that's where the training will be focused. The welfare system will have another name, but welfare will be limited to a specific amount of time. To collect welfare, you'll need to attend a trade school for adults and have acceptable attendance. The intent is to train people for jobs, get them employed and independent."

Carly paused. Chris was quiet, he listened and thought about what Carly had shared. She continued talking to Chris.

"The immigration question is far more complex. There's some movement to grant some people amnesty under certain conditions. I think there will be more debate before they reach a consensus."

"This sounds promising. The kids are okay?"

Carly confirmed that they were either hard at work or studying at school. They chatted a little longer before Chris told her that he had to get some sleep. He told her not to worry; he might not be able to call her again until he reached the States.

Chris ended the call, then he went down below deck and found his bunk. He took off his shoes, slid into the bunk, and was sound asleep within minutes.

Chapter 99

The Strait of Gibralter

JESSICA HAD THE WHEEL and Drago stood next to her, chatting and holding a warm drink. It was 8:00 a.m. and already a bright and sunny day. Traffic on the water had picked up as they'd approached the strait. The whole experience was fascinating for Jessica, Drago, and Maria: the boat activity while traveling through the waters was fantastic.

Dan would navigate them through the strait and take over for Jessica in about thirty minutes. The strait was heavily patrolled; not so much for fear of pirates, but because of heavy congestion on the waterway. After leaving the strait, they would need to be cautious of pirates and other threats until they safely reached Florida.

Dan was now at the wheel as Maria stood next to him, taking in the sights. Drago and Jessica moved to the port side while Chris stood on starboard. They were to report to Dan anything that looked suspicious. A few Moroccan and African boats might travel too close without respecting the spacing. The last thing they wanted was for one of those boats to ram into them and damage Dan's boat.

Dan was exhausted. It wasn't necessarily the length of time at the wheel, but the intensity of the congested waterway that was mentally fatiguing. He'd had six cups of coffee in the last three hours alone to keep alert. They were almost through the passage. The moment they made it through the strait, Dan would set the course for Madeira Island and allow Chris to take the wheel.

Dan set the course for southwest, toward the Madeira Island. They shut off the engine with the sails up, taking advantage of the northern wind. They could see both Europe and Morocco fading behind them.

Chris grabbed a bottled water, then climbed back on deck to relieve Dan. Drago and Jessica remained onboard to keep watch; Dan and Maria went below to rest. After a nap they promised to make sandwiches for lunch and bring them up on deck.

Chris, Drago, and Jessica turned the discussion to the Texas Federation. Chris summarized the information he'd received from Carly.

"It appears that business in the new Texas is starting to return to normal. Domestic air travel has picked up—we may see some international travel routes by the end of the year."

Jessica and Drago confirmed that they'd both been in touch with their company back home. Drago had notified them that he was en route to the United States.

"Our company is trying to expand into Dallas," Jessica explained. "This is great timing for us. They want us to contact them when we arrive. We have a standing appointment to meet the site manager at the Dallas facility."

"Have you been in contact with your company?" Drago asked Chris.

"Yes, I contacted them while we were in Barcelona. My boss, Dale, understands that Dan and I are trying to make it back to the US. They may have an opening for me in Texas, but I need to discuss it further when we return. Dan should have a position in Florida."

As they spoke, Chris kept an eye on the surrounding water. There was minimal activity around them other than one boat directly behind them. They could see traces of both Europe and Morocco on the horizon.

"I'm excited about going to the United States. My dream is to be successful," Drago shared.

"My father is close to retiring in a couple of years. At least that was the plan before the Russians invaded our country," Drago continued. "If Slovenia can push the Russians out of the country, I would like my parents to move to the United States. My mother may resist moving to North America with her relatives in Slovenia, but I think my father would favor the move. Hopefully he can convince her of the benefits."

Chris smiled, and they watched Dan and Maria come up to the deck with sandwiches and fruit. Everything looked fresh and delicious.

"It appears we're almost all alone, with the exception of that boat trying to pass us on the right. It amazes me that we have all this space, and some of these boats still insist on traveling right next to us," Dan commented as he scanned the open sea.

Jessica noted how delicious the fruit tasted, and Maria shared that the produce vendor back in her Barcelona neighborhood was a friend of the family. They always received the best fruit and vegetables.

"Honey, you told me the same thing about the baker and the butcher!" Dan laughed.

"It's true! My parents and ancestors have lived there for a long time." Maria smiled but her response was firm; this was a serious topic. "We have many friends in the community."

"Yes, I know." Dan took a step toward Maria. "Life will be different in Florida, but I think you'll like it." He gave her a kiss on the cheek.

"I am sure I will. I can't wait to get there."

Chris, Drago, and Jessica observed Dan and Maria with amusement, then Drago glanced behind.

"That boat is getting closer to us," he said urgently.

Dan released Maria and quickly pivoted around.

"Chris, why don't you change direction? Portside."

Chris made the adjustment and veered off to the left. The boat behind them gained on the starboard side, and made the same adjustments. Dan looked through the binoculars.

"They aren't European. It appears the crew is Middle Eastern and African. They're either playing with us or they're intentionally following us. We need to arm ourselves."

Within a minute, Drago and Jessica had their rifles ready and Maria went below to retrieve the shotgun and shells. Dan took the wheel and Chris went below to get the missile. Chris hoped that it was a false alarm; a replay of the French coast guard incident in the Mediterranean.

Chris was quickly back on deck and prepared, but the boat still gained on them. Dan altered the course again, running south and parallel to the Moroccan coast. Chris moved to his best vantage point; Drago and Jessica were in position. Dan turned to Maria and asked her to take the wheel as he started the engine.

Dan waited a few more minutes before they moved closer to the coast. He asked Drago and Maria to bring down the sails. It was then that Drago glanced over to the shore.

"Are those two motorboats coming toward us?"

Everyone followed Drago's eyes. "Oh crap!" Dan exclaimed.

"I was warned some of the pirates could have motorboats." Dan shouted. "Often, they have one large boat with two motorboats that are agile. The motorboats allow them to board easily."

"Chris?"

"Yes?"

"How many missiles do you have?"

"Two."

"Get ready to use one. If you can target and hit the big boat coming up on our starboard side, then I can turn us away from the coast and go further out into the Atlantic."

"Loading now!" Chris responded. "Mike gave me detailed instructions on how to load and shoot this thing. He bought these on the black market—hopefully, it works."

Dan nodded to himself more than anyone else. They needed to execute crisply.

"Jessica and Drago?" They looked over at Dan.

"I need you to track the two motorboats. From what I've heard, they'll try to come alongside the boat: one boat portside, one starboard. Then, they'll try to board us. After Chris hits the larger boat with the missile, I'll turn ninety degrees away from shore. They'll probably try to overtake us before we get out too far. Make shots that count. I'd suggest aiming for the man at the wheel—for the first shot."

Drago and Jessica went below deck to grab more ammunition. They were positioned at the back of the boat, one on each side. Chris was almost ready. He was on the starboard side, his sights on the pirate boat.

"Bring all the shotgun shells and load the gun," Dan directed Maria. "If they try to board, your job is to shoot both barrels and then reload and shoot again!"

Dan had them at full speed, but the pirate boat and the two motorboats were still gaining. They could now see the motorboats, each loaded with six pirates per boat.

"How soon before you fire?" Dan shouted to Chris. "I want to make sure I hold us steady."

"Give me two minutes," Chris responded. "I'll shout *ready*!" I want to make sure I'm locked."

The boats were gaining; Chris could clearly see the individuals on the larger boat. He estimated they had twenty people on deck.

Mike's instructions ran through his head. *Be ready, take a deep breath, stay calm, lock and fire.*

All of a sudden he heard a sound from the large pirate vessel. The pirates fired and landed a blow middeck. Dan and Maria dropped to their knees when they heard the blast: they landed splayed out, lying on the deck. No one was injured. Chris was thrown to his knees when the shot hit; he was scraped up but untouched.

"Dan, Maria, Jessica, Drago, are you okay!" Chris shouted. He kept his eyes focused on the pirate ship.

Dan recovered, he was on one knee with his hands back on the wheel. Rising up, he pulled Maria up with one arm.

"Yes, we're fine."

Chris heard from Jessica that she and Drago were unharmed. He was in position and almost ready.

"Ready!"

The boat was now traveling a little slower. Chris stabilized himself on deck and locked in. Mike's voice was still in his head, instructing him. *Breathe. Exhale. Fire.* The missile exploded on impact. One second the boat was gaining, pirates on deck and excited in anticipation, the next second, the boat was a ball of flames.

Seconds after the explosion, Dan turned the boat away from the pursuing motorboats. The two motorboats did not hesitate; they mirrored Dan's turn, into the Atlantic. The motorboats were now directly behind them.

Jessica and Drago locked on their first targets.

"Jessica, I'm about to fire. Remember, nice and easy," Drago reminded Jessica.

Chris reloaded the second missile. The boats gained as Jessica and Drago shot at their respective targets. The pirates responded with their own fire.

The motorboat on portside was still gaining. Jessica was focusing on her next target—she shot the pirate at the wheel. The motorboat began to turn. As the pirate's body splashed in the ocean, another pirate secured the wheel and steadied the boat.

Drago was emboldened by Jessica's hit and now decided to join Jessica portside. Drago shouted for Jessica to stay focused on the pirate manning the wheel as he shot at the pirate standing at the rear of the motorboat. Drago hit one pirate after a few shots, and Jessica hit the next pirate at the wheel in the shoulder. Holding on with only his good arm, the injured man stepped back to give the wheel to his colleague. Then Drago wounded another pirate in the back of the motorboat. Finally, the motorboat slowed down—the remaining pirates elected to call off the pursuit.

The motorboat on starboard was closer. Chris positioned himself with his last missile ready to fire.

"Ready!" Chris yelled, and Dan let up on the speed. Chris was poised and ready, when the pirate motorboat on the starboard side slowed and pulled out.

It was possible that the pirates gave up the chase because they were concerned about being too far from shore, or they saw Chris positioned with the missile and knew they may face a similar fate as their larger ship. Yet another argument could be made for the effectiveness of Jessica and Drago's precise shooting. In the end, it didn't matter: all the crew aboard Dan's boat were now safe.

Dan kept them running at a good clip for five minutes. When the motorboats in the distance became the size of ants, he reduced speed and shut down the engine. Chris unloaded the missile and stored it below deck. Drago and Jessica followed Dan's instructions and had the sails up in minutes. Maria brought out a bottle of her dad's wine that he had given her for a special occasion. She uncorked the bottle while Drago kept watch from the rear; not a word was spoken. You could only hear the water slapping the side of the boat, and the clinking of wine glasses.

Dan gave Maria the wheel and walked around the deck and the cabin below as he surveyed for damage. He inspected his boat in silence for twenty minutes.

When Dan was ready to share his damage report, Drago, Chris, Jessica, and Maria gathered around him. The sun was setting over the water, a remarkable orange and red sunset.

"Well, the good news is that the boat has not been compromised. We're seaworthy and the mast and sails are fine. However, we have some bad luck. They hit our antenna, as well as the electronic box, and our VHF radio. Communication is down. There's a good-sized hole in the cabin; above water level. We need to cover the hole with a tarp to keep rain or large swells from filling the cabin."

Dan rifled through their options: they could fix the electronics, but that would require a return to Spain or Portugal. It seemed dangerous to return and travel the same stretch of water outside the strait where they had just left the pirate motorboats. It would also be dangerous to head toward the Moroccan coast, and Dan had his doubts that they could fix or replace the electronic equipment.

Dan added that they'd used a lot of fuel during the pirate pursuit. There were two other options: one was to set sail directly across the Atlantic (without communication and with the tarp covering the cabin), the other was to find a nearby island and repair the cabin only, but not the electronic equipment. Dan believed it was doubtful that anyone on the islands would have the expertise to fix their electronics. Either way, they would sail without the safety of the electronic navigation and communication equipment.

"Can you navigate without the electronic equipment?" Chris asked Dan when he had finished.

"I've read a number of books: I feel confident I can navigate by the stars," Dan responded. "I can teach you to find the major constellations—we can observe the stars each night and adjust our course if needed."

"I have a concern about the Madeira islands as a destination," Dan continued. "It's a popular stop for boats. I'm unsure if there could be more pirate activity."

"What about the Canary Islands? It's just south of here," Maria spoke up. "It's been influenced by Spain over the centuries. It's a popular European vacation destination, but over the past year it has been deserted. There is limited boat travel and no planes can fly in."

Dan pulled his map open and moved his finger until he found the Canary Islands. He looked over at Maria.

"That's a possibility—it may work well. We're probably as close to the Canaries as we are to Madeira. The winds are taking us in the direction of the Canaries anyway. Maria, how confident are you about your travel information?"

"I read an article about it last week in our newspaper."

Dan received affirmations from the others, and they set sail for the Canaries. Minutes later, the sun was down and the stars were becoming visible.

"After dinner, we'll have our first navigation lesson," Dan suggested. "It should be a clear night."

Dan turned the wheel over to Chris and Dan excused himself and descended down into the cabin to look for a tarp. He solicited Drago and Jessica's assistance to help him cover the opening to the cabin. Maria kept out of their way and started dinner.

Once the tarp was fastened and appeared capable of withstanding heavy wind and rain, Dan climbed down into the cabin and created a list of repairs to be made when they reached the islands. Jessica and Drago helped Maria prepare dinner; minutes later, Jessica came up on deck and brought Chris a beer. She had a mug of tea for herself.

Chris took the beer and had a long swallow. Looking up to the sky, he took a minute to appreciate the beauty of the constellations.

"It seems that there's never a dull moment," Chris commented wryly.

"Everything seems calm and quiet at the moment," Jessica countered. "We'll get to visit the Canary Islands. We can buy mom a postcard."

Chris smiled and saw Drago walking over with two plates of food. Handing one plate to Chris and the other to Jessica, Drago took the wheel.

"Take a few minutes to eat. Maria and Dan are below eating alone. I'll get my dinner once you finish. Maria is nervous about traveling across the Atlantic and Dan is trying to calm her. I think today really scared her."

"I think everyone was nervous today." Chris confirmed. "I was trying to recall everything Mike told me, so I could hit the boat. I was also concerned that the missile could have been a dud. Mike may have saved our lives again."

Chris and Jessica ate in silence. Chris handed his plate back to Drago and took the wheel. Drago ate next to Jessica in silence; when they finished their dinners they went below to assist with clean up.

Chris was alone for an hour before the other four joined him on deck. Dan began his first astronomy lesson and they located the North Star, the Southern Cross, and other constellations. He had four eager students who understood that their survival now depended on being able to navigate by the stars.

Finally, Dan concluded the first lesson. He planned to teach for thirty minutes each evening: they could practice relocating constellations during their night shifts. Dan created a shift schedule for that night and the next morning. He planned to personally take two shifts until they reached the Canary Islands.

Maria, Drago, and Jessica were down below in the cabin, preparing for bed. Dan was up on deck, visiting with Chris.

"Chris, Maria remembers the Canary Islands from her vacation days. If there is one thing we've learned, it's that the world is different now. With tourism down, who knows what we'll find. We'll have to be very careful. I think we should stay just long enough for repairs, then gather any fresh produce we can find."

"Well, fortunately we have one missile left," Chris searched for optimism. "It would be good to keep it in our back pocket. If we need to, we'll use it. I agree we need to be careful—we should be ready to leave at any time."

Dan stared up at the stars. "Look! A shooting star! Make a wish—this is a good sign!"

Chris thought that it was more than a good sign—he believed it was a sign, perhaps assurance, that God was watching over them.

Dan went below to get some rest and Chris spent some time in silent prayer at the helm. As the boat moved southwest toward the Canary Islands, he sent up the same prayer that he'd been communicating for several weeks.

"God, bring us home safely."

Chapter 100

Canary Islands, La Gomera

THE GROUP ENJOYED THE sunshine and beautiful skies up on deck as they sailed further out into the Atlantic. Only water was visible in every direction.

Maria shared more information about the Canary Islands: it was a popular travel destination for residents of the UK, especially for winter holiday. The islands were one hundred kilometers (or sixty-five miles) from Morocco, a common vacation destination for Maria's family when she was a girl.

They agreed to avoid the more populated islands. Dan was concerned that high unemployment might make the locals more aggressive, their group might become a target for crime.

They sailed to a small island called La Gomera, located behind the popular Tenerife Island. Maria explained that years ago, people had elected to stay on Tenerife, taking a ferry across for day trips to visit the nice beaches on La Gomera. Over the years, several hotels had been built on La Gomera, making it a final destination.

La Gomera was the second smallest of the Canary Islands. History documented La Gomera as the island that Columbus embarked from in 1492 to leave for the Americas. Columbus had brought sugarcane cuttings to America from La Gomera.

Drago pulled out the fishing gear and asked Dan if he wanted to join him. They had been successful the past two days in catching Dorada. Dan had explained to them that while many classified the fish as a Sea Bass, it was actually a Gilthead Sea Bream. All Chris cared about that was that it was a good sized fish that tasted great.

Jessica was at the wheel, and Chris had a cup of coffee as he watched Drago and Dan fish. He thought about Ali, and how much he had enjoyed fishing. Ali had become quite adept at catching fresh fish for dinner. Maria traveled up to the deck with two warm drinks: she handed one to Dan and kept the other for herself as she sat down next to the two fishermen.

"When should we reach La Gomera?" Maria asked Dan.

Jessica was the first to see land on the horizon.

"I think I see land!" she shouted, answering Maria's question.

Dan and Drago reeled in their fishing lines. Drago stored their equipment below deck and Dan swiftly cleaned the fish and packed them into the ice box for a future dinner.

Dan reviewed the map with his colleagues, then relieved Jessica at the helm. The island of Tenerife was ahead; Drago, Jessica, and Chris were armed and on watch. They weren't sure what to expect: they didn't see activity on the water with the exception of a few fishing boats, but they couldn't be sure. Maria stood near Dan, shotgun in hand. Dan maintained a cushion of two kilometers from Tenerife, bypassing the island. They reached the south end of the island and left Tenerife waters.

"Well, we seem to have made it past Tenerife," Dan commented, breaking the silence. "That should be La Gomera." He pointed to another island in the distance.

"Yes, that is the island," Maria confirmed. "San Sebastian, the capital city, should be on the east coast."

Dan navigated the boat to the east side of the island. Soon they saw buildings and a coastline with large mountains in the background. The buildings grew larger as they got closer to land, and Maria pointed out to Dan a dock in the harbor that was empty with the exception of one other boat. They took down the sails and Dan started the engine, guiding his boat toward the dock.

They had been spotted from a distance; two people in uniform greeted them on dock. A woman and a man, both of average height, wore uniforms of charcoal pants and black shoes. Chris searched in his mind for the name of their shirt uniform color. Carly joked that he only used blue, yellow, and red to describe colors—he stayed with the primary colors. The uniform shirt color was a faded gray-blue; he thought to himself, Carly would be proud. Chris grew serious when he saw the holstered handguns and rifles.

The woman shouted something in Spanish as they neared the dock. Drago set his rifle down, leapt onto the dock, and caught the rope that Chris threw to him. Maria conversed with the woman. In minutes, the boat was secure and Maria translated for them.

"They are the Civil Police. They're concerned that we're carrying weapons. They asked us to set our rifles and shotgun down. The police-woman asked who we were and why we're here. I explained that our destination is the United States, that we encountered pirates after leaving the Strait of Gibralter, and that we're concerned for our safety—which is why we're armed. I've also told her we have damage to our boat from the pirates, and that our intent is to repair our cabin quickly, then continue across the Atlantic."

Chris and the others listened intently. Chris sized up the two police officers: he wondered how much English they could understand. He concluded it was minimal, because they listened intently to Maria as she translated.

"They asked us to put our weapons down, again" Maria translated. "They want to board and inspect the boat immediately. Once we clear their inspection, they want us to bring our paperwork with us and sign the register inside the dock office. They can provide us information on who may help us with repairs. As we thought, all flights and cruise ships have stopped service to La Gomera. The ferry travels once a day from Tenerife. We will be the big news of the day. She said crime on the island is almost zero. Most of the restaurants and the hotel owners have closed up until regular travel service returns to the island."

Dan stepped off the boat and onto the dock. Everyone set their weapon down and joined him. It felt good to stand on land, and they waited while the armed policeman and policewoman searched the boat. They didn't have anything to hide: their weapons would be the only item of concern.

The policewoman emerged from the cabin and spoke in Spanish. Maria climbed aboard the boat and they disappeared into the cabin. Minutes later, they both stepped off the boat. The woman conversed in Spanish with her fellow officer as they walked back to the office. The others turned to Maria.

"They want us to bring our documentation. She insisted we not carry weapons off the boat when we enter their town."

"Perhaps you and Maria should go with the officers? We can stay here?" Chris suggested.

Dan nodded and climbed aboard to retrieve his boat documents. He was down inside the cabin for a minute before coming back on deck and stepping off his boat onto the dock.

"Why did the policewoman ask you to go down in the cabin?" Drago asked Maria.

"She saw the antitank missile launcher," Maria smiled. "I explained that it saved our lives and how Chris was able to hit the large pirate boat. I think she understands why we're so well armed, but it makes her nervous. She asked multiple times that we not carry arms off the pier. I think they will watch us closely while we're here."

Dan and Maria walked down the dock and disappeared into the office. Drago and Jessica discussed the first things they wanted to do on shore. Chris strolled up and down the dock, stretching his legs. He eyed the other docked boat and wondered how long they'd been there.

Ten minutes later, Dan and Maria walked back down the pier toward the boat. Chris thought Maria seemed more relaxed off the boat: she definitely preferred land. Dan loved the water, so she would hopefully become more comfortable with sailing over time.

"The officers said we're okay to travel into town," Dan announced. "We were reminded again to leave our weapons behind. There are some restaurants open if we want to eat. We have a map of the town; it's marked where we can buy groceries and supplies at the hardware store. The policewoman gave us three names of carpenters that should be able to fix the cabin. Maria will help me call them to set up appointments and then get estimates this afternoon."

"And we found out about our neighbors," Maria added. She pointed over to the boat even though there was only one other boat.

"The blue-and-white boat next to us is owned by a retired couple who have been stranded in the Canaries since the terrorist activity began. They have supposedly been traveling to all the islands. Once it becomes safe, they will sail back to the UK."

They told Maria that the dock was secure, but I think we should have someone on watch," Dan interjected. "If we're walking unarmed on land, I recommend we should travel in twos."

"Why don't I take the first watch," Chris volunteered. "Dan, you can check to see if they have a good option for lunch. Jessica and Drago can buy food at the market and explore the town. If you and Maria make appointments for the boat repair, I'll walk over and eat when you return."

Everyone seemed to agree with the plan and took off. Chris walked below deck, grabbed a beer from the galley, and went back over onto the dock. He turned over a box to use for a chair. He sat down and thought about how fortunate they'd been so far. Crossing the Atlantic again would certainly be a continuation of their big adventure.

Chris finished his beer, and felt relaxed and sleepy. He stood up, walked over to the boat, and climbed aboard, looking toward the shore. He spotted two people walking down the dock wearing beachwear. When they were twenty feet away, the white-haired man gave Chris a wave.

"Good day!" he called. He and his wife stopped by Chris. She had dyed brown hair, wore sandals, and had on a beach cover up over her swimsuit. She was clearly younger than her husband, who wore a shirt buttoned halfway, a large Panamanian hat, sandals, and multi-colored swimming trunks.

Chris smiled and stepped off the boat.

"Hello. We just came in less than an hour ago."

"I'm Mick. My wife is Natasha," the man introduced themselves. "We went for a swim and came back to rest for the afternoon."

"Care for a beer?" Chris motioned to the galley.

Mick looked at his wife, who nodded. They accepted the offer and boarded the boat behind Chris. Chris continued below and popped back up with three beers. They found a place to sit on deck and soon Maria and Dan were walking toward them. Chris made the introductions and the group continued chatting.

Natasha disclosed that they'd retired three years ago and purchased their boat. They planned to leave England in the winter after Christmas, sail across the channel, and then make their way down the French coastline, continuing past Spain and Portugal and across the Strait toward the Moroccan coast. The end of their trip would be marked by arrival in the Canary Islands. In March, they planned to return to England, stopping by Madeira on the way.

In July, they planned to take a two-month trip to Denmark and continue on through Scandinavia. The final destination was St Petersburg, Natasha's birthplace. She'd married Mick years ago and had become a UK citizen. They would return home via Estonia, Latvia, and Lithuania.

The first two years of travel had been perfect. However, this year, when it was time to return to England, travel had become unsafe. They'd decided to stay in the Canary Islands until things settled down. They were still waiting. They had a small home near their daughter and son-in-law in a quaint village on the east coast of England. While they were away, the daughter cared for their home.

"We're retired, and we don't really need to be anywhere at any time," Natasha added. "But we're getting a little bored with the Canary Islands. The smaller islands are safe, but the lack of tourism has created some crime on the larger islands."

Mike and Natasha looked at Dan, Maria, and Chris—waiting for them to reciprocate with their story. Dan became their spokesman.

"How about having dinner with us tonight? We have a long story to share. Maria and I need to contact some people about repair work before the end of the day, and I think Chris is ready to go on shore."

Mick and Natasha quickly accepted their dinner invitation. As they left, Dan asked. "Do you like fish?"

They confirmed that fish would be terrific and left, Dan looked over at Chris.

"Why don't you take some time for lunch? Are you okay by yourself?"

"I'm more than okay. I'll leave my Glock behind, but I'm taking my knife. Is there anything specific that I should buy for dinner tonight?"

"How about fresh bread and wine? Drago and Jessica are buying fresh vegetables and fruit."

Chris nodded and gave a two-finger salute. As he left, he heard Maria speaking in Spanish on the phone to a carpenter. Soon Chris was in town, wondering if his Spanish would be sufficient.

Chris found a modest lunch spot. He ordered by pointing to what the locals seated next to him were eating—wrinkled potatoes with a spicy sauce. He was told that it was a "mojo picon" sauce. Since Chris liked spice, he said "Mojo picon" a couple of times, trying to preserve it in his memory bank. He enjoyed his lunch and thought he would try that menu item again.

Chris left and found a bakery. Through pantomime he was able to acquire many loaves of bread.

Before leaving, he asked the woman at the bakery, "Vino?"

She walked out of the store with Chris and pointed down the street to the right. She motioned for him to walk down, turn right, and then to the left. Chris strolled down the street, looking at the store fronts. Finally, he approached a shop with wine bottles in the front window and walked inside.

The store was empty, other than the man behind the counter. He came up to Chris with inquisitive eyes.

"Rojo?" Chris asked.

The man understood and motioned for Chris to follow him to the back of the store. Chris was afraid he would show him the most expensive wine, but the man pulled out a bottle from the shelf and pointed at himself, communicating that it was his favorite. Chris glanced at the price: only ten euros. He put up three fingers, encouraging the man to select two more bottles. He maneuvered around the wine displays before returning to the counter.

Twenty minutes later, Chris approached the boat with a bag of wine bottles and a large bag of bread. He saw two men on the boat with Maria and Dan, inspecting the cabin and speaking in Spanish. Chris went straight down in the galley and unloaded the bread and wine. Fifteen minutes later, the two men left.

Dan looked over at Maria, who was writing down numbers. They both looked over at Chris.

"First estimate?" Chris asked.

"Yes. We have two more today," Maria responded. "They are hungry for business and insisted on coming out today. The appointments are scheduled forty-five minutes apart."

"It looks like you were successful finding bread and wine," Dan acknowledged.

"If you two are okay, I'd like to go back out and see more of the town." The two gestured him off the boat.

Chris walked off the pier, but this time headed toward the beach. The warm sun and gentle breeze made it perfect for a stroll. He was in his shorts and he took off his shoes and walked down to the water, continuing along the beach.

In the distance, he saw two people playing in the water. Drago and Jessica. He stopped, then strolled back up and away from the shore. They must have bought swimsuits in town. He figured they needed some quality time together: the past two months had been so intense; they needed an afternoon of fun.

Chris instead walked along the shops and found a clothing store. Fifteen minutes later, he walked out with swimming trunks in a shopping bag. He found a gelato stand that carried pistachio, one of his favorite flavors. He sat under a tree in the shade overlooking the bay. He ate the gelato and pulled out his phone to see if he could get a signal. The phone showed a couple of bars. It was early morning back in the States. Too early? He might as well try.

Carly answered on the fourth ring. Chris could tell that he'd wakened her.

"Carly, I'm sorry I woke you. We're safe in the Canary Islands."

Chris and Carly exchanged the latest updates. In the moment, Chris almost felt normal again.

When they finished the call, he headed back to the boat. He wondered if he'd ever be able to fall back into a normal routine when he returned home. He didn't share with the others that he had nightmares every night. Most nights he dreamt of Russians, then Mike, and then burying Mike. To watch Drago and Jessica enjoy the beach, and having the chance to talk to Carly that afternoon was therapy. His step was lighter and the sun was brighter as he approached the dock.

Chapter 101

San Sebastian

THE GROUP FEASTED ON fresh fish caught earlier in the day, and a big salad that Jessica made, fresh bread from the bakery, and wine that the shop-keeper had recommended. The stars were out and the warm breeze felt invigorating. Mick and Natasha dressed up a bit for the evening: they came wearing nice shorts, tropical shirts, and sandals. They made a striking couple. Without the towels wrapped around them, you could see they were trim and sported a nice tan.

Chris noticed that Jessica and Drago had new outfits, Maria wore a new sundress, and Dan displayed a new shirt. Chris felt underdressed for dinner in his best shorts and shirt.

Mick explained how he'd met and fallen in love with Natasha thirty years ago during a business trip to St. Petersburg. They'd moved through-out Europe and finally settled near Mick's hometown in England. Natasha discussed their current situation stranded on the Canary Islands and waited for the opportunity to safely return to England.

They shared information about their past two years of travel through-out Scandinavia, the French coast, and the Canaries. Chris listened, enjoy-ing his Spanish wine. As Mick and Natasha told their story, he got a weird feeling. He couldn't explain the uneasiness that he felt.

Midway through dinner, Natasha asked about their story. Chris let Dan tell the story from San Diego to Texas and then on to Florida. When Dan paused, Chris interjected, and took up the rest of the story. He didn't want to share as many details as Dan had shared. He omitted sections, skipping the Slovenia portion altogether, as he jumped to Barcelona and the meeting with Drago and Jessica in Austria. He didn't reference any part of the Russian and Slovenian story. It wasn't just because of the emotional experience; there was something he couldn't quite articulate.

Natasha listened intently, asking questions about Austria and where they had stayed. Chris answered crisply before moving quickly back to Barcelona. He spent a lot of time describing Dan and Maria's wedding in Barcelona.

As Chris finished the story, Jessica, Drago, Dan, and Maria watched him intently. They could tell that he had purposely edited specific events from the past weeks. For the remainder of the evening, they followed his cue. Everyone was pleasant but guarded with their responses.

"So how long will you be here in La Gomera?" Natasha asked.

"We'll have some work done on the boat as we rest up," Dan replied. "Then we'll be off. We don't know yet if that is a couple of days, or a week."

"How long will you be in San Sebastian?" Jessica asked Natasha.

Natasha looked at Mick. Chris wondered if they were stalling to think of a response, but Mick responded.

"We'll stay until we get bored; then we'll drop down to the island of El Hierro for a couple of weeks."

After another hour, Chris yawned. Mick caught the cue and nudged Natasha. "We should let our new guests of San Sebastian get a good night's sleep." After thanking them for the wonderful meal and conversation, Natasha and Mick left quickly.

Chris gathered the empty wine and water bottles with Dan while the other three cleaned the dishes. Chris and Dan left the boat and walked down the dock toward the trash can near the gate.

"Chris, don't you trust them?"

Chris looked over at Dan and dropped his trash. He closed the top of the trash container and paused.

"I can't give you anything specific, but I get weird vibes. They were asking a lot of questions earlier. But I recall that the epidemic and terrorist activities were escalating over six months ago—why would they venture down to the Canary Islands near Africa and the Middle East? Something doesn't add up. Why would someone travel, with all that turmoil?"

Dan opened the adjacent trash lid and carefully placed the empty wine bottles in the dispenser. Chris closed the trash lid, turned, and walked back to the boat.

"Let's help the others clean up. We need to digest the estimates from the contractors," Dan suggested. "I want to get the work finished on the cabin so we can head home ASAP."

Chris nodded as they approached the boat. "Yes, I'd like to continue our voyage as soon as possible."

"So would I," Dan chuckled. "Although I think Maria would be okay if I sank the boat and we stayed here for the next decade."

They climbed aboard Dan's boat and descended the steps into the cabin. Chris found a dishtowel and assisted Drago in drying dishes. As the last dish was put away, Dan cleared his throat.

"Can we go up on deck? Maria and I want to share the three bids along with our impressions of each contractor."

Up on deck, Dan went through the bids. At the end, he highlighted the price along with the estimated repair time.

"But who do you like the best? Who do you trust to do a quality job?" Chris asked Dan.

"The one I like the best has the longest lead time. His price is in the middle of the three." Dan glanced over at Maria to see if she agreed. "He's six days—the others are quoting three and four days. But I think he's being honest."

Dan kept his gaze fixed on Maria. He stopped to let her comment.

"Yes, I get the feeling he is the most honest."

"I think you should go with your gut feeling," Chris recommended.

"So what's your gut feeling about Mick and Natasha?" Jessica asked Chris.

"I'm not sure, but I'm uneasy. I may be wrong, but I think we should be nice but guarded on what we say."

There was a half minute of silence while they replayed the dinner conversations in their head. Chris wondered if he can be cautious without being paranoid.

Dan broke the silence and concluded that he and Maria would call the contractor in the morning. The meeting ended.

"Should we create a schedule so one of us is always on the boat while work is performed?" The thought just popped into Chris's head. "That way, others can enjoy time on the beach or island?"

They agreed to break the day into three segments so each group would have a shift. Chris volunteered to be alone for his segment. Dan and Maria were still extending their honeymoon, and Drago and Jessica were enjoying their time together.

They debated whether they should keep watch during the night. The town seemed harmless, and they did have the dock security gate with only one other boat at the dock. Chris felt uneasy, so he volunteered to sleep on deck and the others agreed that this would suffice.

Chris didn't feel like it was a sacrifice: the weather was pleasant, and sleeping under the stars sounded delightful. He would have to sleep in the cabin on the voyage back—this was an opportunity for fresh air. Chris got ready for bed and brought up his pillow, mattress, and blanket to the deck. He also brought his pistol and wrapped it in his T-shirt. He was comfortable stripped down to his boxer shorts under the blanket.

Looking up at the stars, Chris tried to find the constellations. Dan's astronomy lessons helped him to find the Big Dipper, then, at the handle of the Dipper he found the orange star of Arcturus. *Now where is the Southern Cross that Dan showed us the other night? Is that it?* The next thing Chris knew, he was fast asleep.

Chapter 102

Exploring San Sebastian

Maria called the contractor, who confirmed that he would gather materials in the morning and start midday. Dan and Maria decided to take off in the morning, then return before noon to meet the contractor. They planned to remain on the boat all afternoon to answer any questions he might have. Chris volunteered for the morning shift so as to allow Drago and Jessica to have the whole day off. Jessica and Drago wanted to head into town to explore the mountains.

Jessica and Drago walked over to the police station. In broken Spanish, they asked where they could hire a mountain guide. The policeman pointed them toward a corner restaurant with instructions to ask for Lucia. They found Lucia at the counter, and after talking to the two, she immediately made a call on her cell phone. In five minutes a young man named Jaimie arrived at the restaurant. He quoted an acceptable price to lead them up to the mountains for the day.

Drago paid Lucia a few euros for bagged lunches and bottled waters. Jessica and Drago put the lunches in a backpack and followed Jaimie out of the establishment.

Jaimie hiked like a mountain goat; Drago and Jessica stayed right with him. The hiking was similar to what they had experienced in Slovenia just a few weeks earlier, but without the snow. The country was wild and beautiful.

They had hiked for over an hour when they suddenly heard a whistle. Jaimie froze to look around and spotted a person across a ravine. Jaimie whistled to the other man and Drago and Jessica watched as each exchanged a few whistles. Then the man disappeared from sight.

"Were you communicating?" Drago asked Jaimie.

"Yes, Silbo Gomero," Jaimie responded.

"That's called Silbo Gomero?" Jessica tried to clarify.

Jaimie, in decent English, explained that it was an ancient communication system used by the islanders. He'd learned it from his grandfather, and it was still commonly used. Jaimie took a few minutes to show them how to whistle. Drago had almost mastered it after a few tries, but Jessica had little success. After ten minutes, they continued on their hike.

Jaimie showed Jessica and Drago the volcanic plugs in the center of La Gomera. Later, they stopped for lunch under a shady tree. Jessica and Drago were able to ask Jaimie more about the island and learn about the way of island life. Jessica relished hiking in the mountains. It was fun to hike without concern of an ambush around each bend.

Drago and Jessica enjoyed their day on the mountain. By midafternoon, Jaimie had them back in San Sebastian. They paid Jaimie the negotiated fee and Jessica offered a nice tip. On the way back to the boat, they found a gelato stand with some interesting flavors. It was a perfect way to end the day: eating gelato on the stroll back.

When they returned Dan and Maria were talking to two local men on the boat. Dan greeted Jessica and Drago and told them Chris had recently left for the beach before resuming his discussion with the workers.

Drago and Jessica went down below deck. Drago dropped his day pack on his bunk and Jessica walked to the cooler for two bottles of water; tossing one to Drago.

"Are you interested in a dip in the ocean?" she asked Drago.

Drago gulped and drained half the bottle. The hike had made him thirstier than he thought.

"Sounds terrific," he answered.

Jessica went into the bathroom and put on her swimsuit. Drago pulled on his swim trunks, and grabbed two towels before they headed for the beach. They found a spot for their towels, then they sprinted into the water.

Meanwhile, Chris explored the coast. He walked to the remote end of the black sand beach and took off his T-shirt as he walked out into the water. His wound had healed, but the warm water was still very soothing. He enjoyed floating and swimming in the ocean, but he didn't go beyond where he could touch the bottom of the ocean floor. He'd dropped a lot of weight on the trip. He'd lost weight on the voyage across the Atlantic Ocean, but hiking in Slovenia was what made him lean. He estimated he was about the same weight as when he'd first met Carly over thirty years ago. He might need to invest in some new pants and suits when he returned to the States.

Chris floated and wondered if he could stay in shape. It all came down to the many snacks he ate back at home. Mountain hiking with packs was not easily duplicated in the gym. *Perhaps he could modify the weights and stationary bike to emulate mountain exercise?* After he had been out in the water a long time, he climbed out to dry off.

As Chris emerged, he saw two people sitting near his towel. As he continued up the beach, Chris recognized that it was Mick and Natasha sitting in the sand by his towel.

"Hey! Enjoying the day?" Chris called out.

He walked to his towel and started drying his upper body. He noted the time as he sat down and looked over at his neighbors.

"How was the swim?" Natasha asked.

"It was relaxing. The water temperature's perfect. I was out for over an hour."

"We were swimming and decided to take a walk. Natasha spotted you out there," Mick added. "You wandered far from town."

"Well, I did the opposite of you," Chris responded. "I took a walk, then decided to go in the water."

Natasha was eyeing his wound and Chris gently pulled the long-sleeved T-shirt over his shoulder.

"You have a nasty wound there. Bullet wound?"

"A stupid injury that never should have happened. I'm fine." Chris's shirt was pulled down. "Not much to discuss. So what are you two going to do for the rest of the day?"

"We were thinking about walking to town and grabbing a drink. Would you care to join us?" Mick offered.

"I've been gone longer than intended," Chris smiled, trying to make his excuse seem sincere. "I told Dan that I'd be back to review the work on the boat. Can I take a rain check?"

With that, Chris sat up and grabbed his towel.

"See you later," Chris offered as he walked to the dock. He gave himself a pep talk as he left. *Don't be so paranoid. They're only trying to be nice.*

Chris reached the boat and found Dan surveying the work for the day, two workers with him. Maria stood with him, assisting with the translation. After five minutes, the workers gathered their tools and left for town.

"They're doing a good job," Dan looked over at Chris. "They're telling me three more days of work."

Dan disappeared down below into the cabin and Chris spotted the gentleman from the civil police office walking down the dock toward them.

The policeman saw both Chris and Maria and hesitated, before speaking to Maria in Spanish. They went back and forth, before Maria translated for Chris.

"He wanted to tell us that there will be a fiesta tonight. It should be safe, but they'll leave their station early and have the gate locked."

Chris nodded to the policeman. "Mucho gracias."

The policeman smiled and turned away. After two steps, he turned and spoke to Maria, then gestured in the direction of Mick and Natasha's boat. She looked at Chris.

"He asked if we would relay the information to Mick and Natasha."

"I'm sure it's the same old stuff for them since they've been back and forth for months," Chris responded. "Besides, this is their third year."

Maria spoke to the policeman again: he paused and frowned before responding. After a two-minute conversation, they echoed their pleasantries as he continued off the dock. Maria looked at him and then turned to Chris.

"I asked how this celebration would be different from past celebrations since Mick and Natasha have been here for a while. That's when he gave me a funny look—he told me that they arrived five days ago. He's never seen them before."

"Well, maybe he's new."

Maria cut him off. "He has worked here for twelve years."

Drago and Jessica approached, ending the conversation. Jessica wore a large straw hat, and Drago had his long-sleeved T-shirt draped around his neck. They talked about their wonderful day exploring the island.

Dan popped up on deck with a few cold beers and water bottles. They all sat down and heard about Jessica and Drago's adventure hiking in the mountains. Drago and Jessica had already heard from Jaimie about the town celebration taking place that night.

"Who would like to use the shower first?" Jessica asked. "Let's clean up and prepare dinner," she suggested.

They took turns taking showers at the facilities. Chris was the first in the shower and the first one dressed. He made the salad in the galley while Drago grilled the last of his fish.

Chris looked out a porthole and saw Mick and Natasha return for the day. When Chris finished the salad, Drago exclaimed that the fish were ready, and Jessica brought out fresh bread. Dan and Maria uncorked two bottles of wine and they enjoyed a nice dinner.

Chris was tired; he encouraged the others to enjoy the town's festivities. He planned to relax and watch the celebration from the boat. Dan and Maria promised they wouldn't be out too late—they planned to come back early so he could experience the town party. Dan explained that the two workers were returning for repairs early the next morning—he didn't want to be out late. Chris nodded, but truthfully, he felt like taking a nap under the stars.

Dan, Maria, Jessica, and Drago headed out to town and the beach. Chris stood on deck, enjoying the beautiful night. He planned to test himself on the constellations again.

A half hour later, Mick and Natasha walked by. Chris waved, then looked back to the sky in search of Orion.

"Aren't you going to enjoy the festivities?" Natasha inquired.

"I'm tired from the swim—I told the others to enjoy. I may go out a little later."

Mick and Natasha smiled, but didn't move on. Chris felt mild irritation, he wanted to be left alone to find Orion.

"I wanted to ask you," Mick blurted. "You mentioned that you were in Austria. We've contemplated a trip to Austria, perhaps over to Slovenia. Have you been to Slovenia?"

"Oh, yes," Chris replied quickly. "My wife and I vacationed in Slovenia and Croatia a few years ago. I'd highly recommend it."

"Were you able to hike the Julian Alps? I hear they are lovely," Natasha asked.

"Yes, we spent a little time in the Julian Alps." Chris smiled, then changed the subject.

"You've been to a number of the local festivities, correct?"

"Yes, we've been to a number of them," Mick confirmed. "I hope we see you later."

They turned and walked out the gate toward the crowd. Chris studied them until the gate closed and they were out of sight. Finally, he turned his gaze upward, searching again for Orion.

Chapter 103

Festival

CHRIS TOOK A SHORT nap, and woke to the sound of the gate closing. It took a few seconds for him to focus before Chris saw Dan and Maria walking under the lights toward the boat.

Maria must have had a couple glasses of wine—as she came aboard she was animated, and talking quickly. She talked about riding horses on the beach and the crowds of people gathered along the shore.

"Chris, you should go out and see it. You can catch up to Drago and Jessica," Maria suggested.

A frown formed on Chris's face. He wasn't sure if it was accurate, but he was under the impression that Dan and Maria wanted the boat alone.

Dan offered directions on where Chris could find Jessica, Drago, Jaimie, and friends. It was a bar located on the outskirts of town, owned by Jaimie's uncle. Dan gave the "you can't miss it" phrase, which Chris worried might become a jinx.

Chris decided to venture out and make an appearance to give the newlyweds time alone. Chris left the gate and followed the sounds of the festival. The noises blended into a small roar. He paused for one full minute to digest it with his ears, and to focus his eyes.

As Chris made his way through town, Jessica and Drago spotted Chris before he found them. Chris walked over to a table where Jessica and

Drago sat with four other people. A number of empty glasses were stacked in the center of the table.

Jessica jumped up to meet Chris and give him a hug. She introduced Jaimie, a man with dark hair and eyes; a medium build. Chris then met Jaimie's cute girlfriend, and Jaimie's best friend and best friend's girlfriend. Three good-looking young couples sat at the table, plus Chris.

"What would you like to drink? We have a special drink in mind," Jaimie said to Chris.

"A local beer would be great," Chris answered. He wanted to keep it simple.

"Cerveza!" Jaimie shouted toward the bar.

Chris discovered that Jaimie was a local living his entire life on the island. In a short time, it became clear that he was either related to or good friends with many of the patrons in the bar.

As they made small talk, a crowd formed on the beach below. Suddenly Jaimie and his friends bounced up from their chairs, suggesting to Jessica, Drago, and Chris that they move quickly to the shore. Chris had just arrived minutes before—he had half a beer remaining in the glass.

"You, guys, go ahead. I'll join you in a few minutes."

Jessica paused like she was considering staying back with Chris. Chris gave her a nod and a wave of his hand, encouraging her to join the others.

"I'll be there as soon as I finish my beer."

Jessica relented and left him to join most of the town as they made their way to the shore. Only Chris, the uncle bartender, and two waitresses remained in the small bar. The waitresses took advantage of the lull to clean the tables.

Looking down at the mob gathering at the beach, Chris was startled by a "hello."

Mick and Natasha. They stepped over to his table and sat down on either side of Chris.

"You decided not to join the rest of the crowd?" Chris asked with a smile, waving his hand in the direction of the party on the beach.

"No, this seemed like the perfect time to come up for a drink while the others gather on the beach," Mick responded.

Chris drained the last of his beer. Mick saw him set down the empty glass.

"I invited you earlier for a drink, what can I get you?"

"I'm okay," Chris told him.

"No, I insist that I buy you that drink."

"All right, thank you. I'll take another beer."

Mick walked up to the bar and Natasha scooted her chair closer to Chris and touched his shoulder. The wound had healed well, but Chris slightly flinched. "So tell me, Chris. How did you get that nasty, but sexy wound?"

Chris wondered what she was up to—he gave the standard, cliché joke.

"If I tell you, I'll have to kill you."

"Are you telling me you are a spy, Chris?" Natasha laughed.

"I think that is one profession that I would be terrible at." Chris chuckled. "No, I am in the tech industry. Well, I was until the world events that unfolded these past months. But I hope to return to my job soon."

"So how does that explain the gunshot wound?" Natasha rubbed Chris's shoulder. "It must have been a bad transaction."

Mick showed up with three drinks, none too soon. He handed Chris a beer in a full glass.

"The bartender said this is a local draft we should try." Mick set the beer down, and handed Natasha a glass of white wine.

"Cheers!" Mick held up his glass.

After his toast, Mick drained a quarter of his glass and Natasha took a sip of her wine. Chris sampled his beer as the bartender walked over and plopped a bowl of nuts at the center of the table. In a swoop, the bartender grabbed the empty glasses, then paused to look at his patrons.

"To San Sebastian!" Mick proposed the second toast.

Glasses raised, they clinked and then took another drink. Before the bartender left their table, Chris needed to use the restroom.

"Bano?" he asked the bartender.

The bartender motioned for Chris to follow him. When Chris stood up, he felt a little woozy. He thought perhaps he'd been out in the sun too long. The bartender pointed to a restroom fifty meters away, toward the beach.

Excusing himself, Chris stepped toward the restroom. He was dizzy. Chris focused on making it to the restroom by taking one step at a time. He saw an outline of a man next to an arrow indicating the men's room, so Chris continued to the right side of the building. He had to urinate, but Chris felt poorly. He wasn't sure if he was going to be violently ill. Walking through the door, he gripped the sink and turned on the water full force. Splashing cold water on his face allowed Chris to momentarily regain focus.

Chris fumbled with his zipper as he walked over to the urinal, then leaned his head forward on the wall as he peed. He finished, zipped up, and stayed another minute, leaned up against the wall. Staggering over to the sink, Chris felt even worse. He could barely hold on to the sink as he splashed more water on his face. He heard the door open and close, and there was Mick standing three feet away.

"Chris, are you feeling all right?"

"No, I'm feeling sick. I think I need to head back to the boat."

"I would like to ask you some questions first. Were you in Slovenia a couple weeks ago? What were you doing there?"

Chris shook his head sideways while attempting a step. Mick blocked him at the doorway and gave Chris a little shove when he tried to go around him. Spinning forty-five degrees, Chris fell to one knee but balanced himself, trying not to go completely down.

"Chris, I don't think you're telling us the truth. We think you're a spy, a special services agent with the former United States. We think that you were recently in Slovenia."

Chris looked up to see that Mick had a knife in his hand. Mick took a step toward Chris and leaned closer. Chris was still on a knee, trying to focus.

"You need to talk to me, Chris. Then we can go on our merry way. I just need information, Chris."

Chris wished he had his gun and knife that were stashed back on the boat. How could he fight this guy when feeling sick? Was he sick? No, not sick. They'd drugged him. Mick had dropped something in his *beer.* Chris tried to think clearly. He shook his head from side to side. I have to get out now but how?

Mick bent over and clutched Chris's shoulder. He tried to pull Chris up off his knee.

"Let's get you up, Chris—so you can tell us the real story."

Chris flashed back to Krav Maga—listening to the instructor in class. *Your elbow can be a weapon in many ways. First, we will show forward elbow, then upward thrust. Stay balanced.*

Mick pulled him up by his left shoulder. Chris used this motion to his advantage to push off, thrusting his free right elbow into Mick's chin. There was a crack, and Mick dropped the knife and fell to his knees. Chris dropped down also to his knees—now their heads were six inches apart. Chris whipped his head forward with a head butt to Mick's nose. Blood spurted over both of them and covered the floor. Mick screamed.

Chris had to stand up. "Get up," he muttered. "Get out, now!"

Using Mick's shoulder, he pushed up, got up, and staggered to the door. Mick swore while holding his nose. Chris recalled the other instructor at Krav with her favorite phrase. *If there is one asshole, then there is most likely a second.*

Natasha! (Where was Natasha? She might be outside). Chris could barely stand, but he knew he must be ready to face her as well. He saw the knife on the floor and held on to the wall, bent down, and picked it up.

Chris pushed the door open and staggered outside with his back to the wall. Chris held the knife in front of him and saw Natasha four feet away, watching. He had some of Mick's blood on his shirt from the broken nose. He made a swing with the knife: not to hit her, but to warn her. In retrospect, he must have looked wild: a drugged man, blood spattered on his shirt, swinging a knife.

"Get out of the way," he grunted to Natasha. She backed away five feet.

Where should he go? The crowd below? He decided to make his way in the direction of the crowd. Safety in numbers is what his mind told him. *Move your feet,* he told himself as he staggered forward onto the beach with the knife.

In his peripheral vision, he saw Natasha move into the bathroom to check on Mick. Chris needed to move quickly toward the crowd gathered on the beach.

It must have appeared as if it was the first time he had ever walked. He staggered and swayed as he leaned forward. He threw the knife in the sand and moved near the crowd. He kept saying out loud, "Right, left, right, left!" He was very close now, but the people had their backs to him. They were watching something in the water. He was losing control.

He fell to his knee. He looked up—the closest person was ten meters away.

"Help," Chris whispered. It took him ten seconds, but he rallied himself; he would shout through his diaphragm.

"Ayuda!" It was louder, and all he could muster.

Chris fell to his hands and knees with his head down. *Did anyone hear him?* He was now lying down on his stomach, his knees down in the sand.

"Help! Ayuda!" he cried, but it came out softly. He didn't think anyone could hear him. His head spun.

Hands were suddenly on him. He was being turned over. *Focus. Is it Mick or Natasha? Is it someone else? The person looked young. Was it the young man who was with Jessica and Drago? Jaimie? Was this Jaimie?* The man shook Chris a little. Chris tried to stay connected, but he couldn't. He slipped into darkness.

Jaimie recognized Chris when he turned him over. He looked at his girlfriend.

"Bring Jessica and Drago over! It's Jessica's father."

Jaimie looked up from the area that Chris had staggered from and he saw the outlines of two people: a man and a woman that he couldn't recognize. Then, they disappeared. He turned his focus back to Chris. Jessica and Drago were now approaching and Jessica ran to her father.

"Dad?" She bent down and then looked over at Jaimie.

"I think he was drugged. I need Drago's help. We should take him to the doctor right away."

Jaimie dialed a number, spoke for a quick minute in Spanish, then (with the help of Drago) picked Chris up. They paused, trying to decide how to carry Chris. Drago made the decision.

"Get him on my shoulders, and I will carry him."

Are you sure you can do it?" Jaimie asked.

"I have done it before. We won't have to go too far this time."

Drago carried Chris on his shoulders as he followed Jaimie and his girlfriend into town. Jessica followed behind Drago and looked around for anyone who appeared suspicious.

In less than ten minutes, they reached a building and met a small man in his midfifties. A blanket of white hair covered his head, and he had a kind face. He looked as though he had been waiting for them. He spoke rapidly in Spanish; Jessica and Drago couldn't understand him because he spoke so quickly. But Jessica felt at ease: the man worked like he knew what he was doing. He instructed them to rest Chris on a bed and then ushered them out (with the exception of Jessica, who insisted on staying). Jessica conceded only when the doctor promised that he would come out and provide a progress report as soon as possible.

Jessica and Drago reluctantly sat in the waiting room. Jaimie left for his uncle's bar and returned soon after with coffees. The doctor walked out a long thirty minutes later, reporting to all assembled that Chris was going to be fine. Jaimie translated to make sure they understood clearly.

"What caused this?" Jessica wanted to know.

Jaimie repeated the question in Spanish and received a quick reply from the doctor. Jaimie thought about it for a moment before translating.

"His best guess is that he was drugged. It's something the doctor typically doesn't see here."

Jessica stared over at Drago, who returned her gaze evenly. Jaimie translated another statement by the physician.

"The doctor insists that Chris spends the night."

Jessica decided to spend the evening curled on the chair in Chris's room. The others dispersed. Drago indicated that he wanted to stay, but Jessica encouraged him to return to the boat and report back to Dan and Maria. They needed to be extra careful: whoever drugged Chris might try to approach one of them next.

Chapter 104

San Sebastian

OPENING HIS EYES IN a strange room, Chris first saw Jessica curled up in a corner chair. He mustered a "Hey," and her eyes opened, and she smiled.

"Where am I?"

"You're at the doctor's. You were drugged last night. You're okay now, but the doctor said that you need to rest today."

"Mick and Natasha drugged me," Chris answered.

"We heard from Jaimie's uncle that they were drinking with you after we left the bar. When we returned, they'd already left. Drago said that their boat is gone," Jessica explained.

"Where are the others?"

"Dan and Maria are with the contractors. The boat cabin should be completely repaired by midday tomorrow. It's the afternoon now. Drago is buying provisions with Jaimie, and Dan says we're going to leave as soon as the boat is repaired and you feel strong enough to travel."

"I need to thank Jaimie—he's the one who saw me."

"You'll see him later. He's the one who called the doctor and directed us here. But you need to rest. The others will come to visit later today."

* * * * *

It was late afternoon when Drago and Jaimie came by to see Chris. Chris thanked Jaimie profusely, but Jaimie waved off his gratitude, insisting that it was what anyone else on the island would do in the same circumstance. Drago announced that he'd bought a lot of supplies: he only needed to buy more fruit and vegetables, which he planned to do the next day. The young men left after a half hour.

Soon after, the doctor came in and recommended that Chris stay the night and leave the next morning. Chris agreed, then asked Jessica to approach Jaimie's uncle to see what he could give Jaimie as a thank you gesture.

Jessica agreed. She would ask, then buy the gift the next morning. They chatted a little longer, and then Jessica and Drago left Chris for the evening.

Forty-five minutes later, Dan and Maria visited. They knew the whole story; Maria had confirmed with the civil police woman that she had first met Mick and Natasha a week ago. Jaimie's uncle had never seen them before that evening. Dan and Maria wanted to know more details of what had happened and Chris shared the bar, bathroom, and beach story.

"They thought I was a US spy. They somehow correctly surmised that I was in Slovenia. I'm guessing they work for the Russians!" Chris exclaimed.

Chris switched the topic to the boat. Dan was excited the cabin would be finished the next afternoon. Dan studied Chris as he spoke; providing a detailed report.

Chris found the timing ideal: he would be discharged first thing in the morning, and they could then leave midafternoon. The thought of leaving the island was a boost to his morale.

"Are you sure you will be okay to travel?" Maria asked.

"Yes, the doctor said I'm fine. The drugs should be out of my system. He's being extra cautious by having me spend the night."

Chapter 105

Leaving the Canary Islands

DAN WENT THROUGH THE checklist for his boat, and everything was found to be acceptable. It was time to leave San Sebastian. The woman from the Civil Police station stood on the dock alongside their boat, waving good-bye. When they left the harbor, the dock would be completely empty. Dan started the engine and within minutes they were pulling out of the harbor, past the few fishing boats.

Once out of the harbor, Dan set their course for Florida. The electronic equipment would be out of commission for the rest of their trip, but they could continue to navigate by the constellations. Chris studied the stars and felt he could add value on their course. The civil police at San Sebastian had confirmed that the weather report looked good for the next couple of nights.

The sails were unveiled, and in no time Dan had the boat moving through the water at a good clip. Drago pulled out the fishing gear to try to catch dinner as Jessica kept him company. Chris stood over by Dan as he went through the watchman shifts for both the day and evening.

Chris still felt a little groggy; some of the after-effects of the drug still lingered in his system. He made an attempt to flush the toxins out of his system by drinking a lot of water.

"How are you doing, Mr. Spy?" Dan smirked as he glanced over at Chris.

"Boy, were they really off base. How could they think that I was in the special services? All we've been doing is trying to stay alive."

"Where do you think Mick and Natasha are headed?"

Chris had a blank look on his face. He'd given this a lot of thought while he'd been lying in the clinic.

"I have no idea, but it appears that Russia's planning for another Cold War. Perhaps they want to secure their old empire. It certainly seems like they are utilizing spies to report back secrets from many locations. It's like a rollback from decades ago."

"Well, if you retire from the tech industry, you have a new second career," Dan quipped.

"Dan, in all honesty, I would like to have a boring life. These last few months have been too much."

"Yes, let's just hope from now on, we have a simple and boring voyage across the Atlantic," Dan agreed.

Chris went below to the galley and quietly made some coffee. He brought Dan a cup and they chatted for a bit. Eventually Chris offered to man the wheel for a few hours, and Dan walked over to check if Drago had had any luck with fishing. Dan was impressed to find that Drago had already caught two decent-sized fish. Confident that things were under control, Dan continued below deck to take a nap with Maria.

The afternoon was uneventful, and the weather was terrific. The trade winds blew them along at a good clip. They ate Drago's freshly caught fish for dinner along with a salad and fresh bread. After dinner, they gathered above deck with Dan to analyze the stars. Dan confirmed that they were headed in the right direction, then dispensed instruction on stars and constellations. After thirty minutes, they disbanded. Dan was pleased to find that they retained most of their knowledge.

"Can you show me the Southern Cross, Chris?" Dan asked.

Chris searched up in the sky. He'd been practicing on his own.

"Well, that is the south celestial pole," he moved his arm. "And there is the Southern Cross, and the Pointers."

"Excellent. For the rest of the trip, if we can follow the Southern Cross, then we'll head in the correct direction." Dan emphasized this point with his arm and hand extended.

"Since you enjoy history, you might be interested to know that the ancient Greeks used the Crux—even Amerigo Vespucci used it in the early 1500s."

Chris filed the trivia away in his head. He gazed up and admired the cross, a friend to sailors for centuries.

Everyone was now comfortable behind the wheel, the course was set, and the weather was nice: Dan scheduled each person with a two-hour shift between 9:00 p.m. and 7:00 a.m. Maria created a schedule, and wrote it down and placed it in a visible location in the cabin. For the next five days, they would rotate and work different shifts. Maria was pleased to have created an equitable system, and Chris was pleased that nobody had tried to drug him or kill him in the last forty-eight hours.

Chapter 106

Sailing the Atlantic Ocean

THE WEATHER WAS FANTASTIC for the first two days after leaving San Sebastian. The days held clear skies, and nights were filled with ethereal stars that directed them onward to their course home. The affable breezes increased to a gentle wind, and Dan pointed out that the swells were getting larger every few hours. By the end of the third day, the winds were no longer gentle. The swells were larger and ominous clouds hung overhead.

Maria, Drago, and Jessica were by now familiar with being tossed in the ocean, and the violent waves made Maria very sick. She stayed below in the cabin with a bucket. Drago was unable to fish. They could no longer make meals in the galley—they just snacked when they got hungry.

Dan asked everyone to wear life jackets. It was evening; clouds blanketed the stars. Dan decided to modify the shift schedule to exclude those feeling ill. Jessica started to feel seasick, so she joined Maria down below for the evening and tried to rest. Dan, Chris, and Drago agreed to each take two hour shifts. Dan was still confident that they were on course for Florida.

Dan wore a whistle around his neck that he insisted the navigator on deck wear. If there were an emergency, the whistle was to be blown. The howling wind made it difficult to hear voices: the whistle was a safety precaution.

As Chris went up on deck to start his shift, Dan confirmed the course. The swells had grown larger; the wind was blowing hard. An hour after Dan went below, the skies opened up and rain began to pour down. Chris donned rain gear and pulled the hood up to cover his head. He couldn't see beyond the stern, and the boat was tossed with each swell. Chris held on tightly to the wheel to maintain Dan's course. Even with the hood covering most of his head, rain beat down on his face and seeped under the hood.

The last hour seemed the equivalent of four hours. When Drago emerged on deck with rain gear and a life preserver, Chris handed him the whistle. Chris was now fond of Drago; he trusted him. Chris decided to pass along some advice he'd received on the voyage to Europe.

"Drago, stay at the wheel, and keep a steady grip. Don't let go or walk to the edge of the boat without assistance. Any question, blow the whistle, and we'll come up. Don't risk falling overboard: we will never find you, if you go over."

Drago nodded and grabbed the wheel firmly. Chris waited a couple of minutes, then went below to take a nap. He was exhausted, but once he climbed up into his bunk, he swayed so much that he didn't think he would be able to fall asleep. However, the rocking finally put Chris to sleep. He slept for four hours, until it was time to relieve Dan.

Drago was asleep in his bunk. Chris put on his life vest and climbed above deck without a word. There was still heavy rain and strong wind. Large swells formed at regular intervals. Dan's head pointed toward him as he held out the whistle.

"Nothing new to report," Dan shouted to him even though they were standing near each other. "The storm is still strong. Hopefully we can run it out."

"I'm good. Go rest. This weather is similar to my last shift," Chris shouted back to Dan.

Dan went below when he saw Chris take a firm hold of the wheel. He was thankful that Dan had been meticulous about the boat's upkeep.

They cycled through another shift. On Chris's next turn, the swells were smaller, and the rain was light. The wind was not as strong: it was still dark and overcast, even though it was midmorning.

The weather was consistent for the rest of the day and through the night. The following day, the wind continued and the swells were still a good size. The rain alternated between light and heavy downpour. Because of the cloud cover, they were unable to see the stars and constellations. Dan hoped they were still heading in the direction of Florida.

Maria and Jessica were not as sick as they had been a couple of days before, but they continued to eat light. Dan, Chris, and Drago continued alternating shifts; the system seemed to be working well. It remained dark outside, regardless of day or night.

Finally, after two and a half days, Chris came up for his 2:00 a.m. shift to relieve Dan. He was pleased to find that there wasn't any rain. The clouds were still overhead, but the wind and swells had subsided.

The next day at noon, the clouds started to break up. Blue sky and sun peeked through the clouds. Maria and Jessica climbed up on deck for the first time in days to feel the sun.

By afternoon the swells were normal and Drago managed to catch a few fish for dinner. That evening, they stood above deck trying to help Dan identify the stars. The skies were still partly cloudy, which created a challenge for Dan. Chris held the wheel as Dan held his chart, hoping to identify specific stars. Dan gathered the others after thirty minutes.

"It's hard to judge exactly where we are because of the clouds. I think we've been heading too far south—we're on course for South America. I think we should be heading west to northwest." Dan held his right arm stiffly, pointing to the right of the stern.

Dan made the course correction, then decided to keep the wheel for a couple of hours as he continued to view the visible stars. When Chris took the wheel, Dan waited for a few minutes.

"What are you thinking?" Chris asked, knowing that Dan was problem-solving in his head.

Dan took off his hat with his left hand and scratched his scalp. He sat down and looked up at Chris.

"I'm trying to figure out our current location, in addition to our corrected direction. We had the wind with us for a number of days during the storm. I think we may have covered a lot of nautical miles."

"Well, maybe we'll arrive in the Caribbean and have to work our way back up to Florida?" Chris joked.

"Or we land in Venezuela or Brazil," Dan responded, less jovial. "We may be more than a little off course."

Dan left Chris and went below to sleep. Chris wondered how they could have gotten that far off course. He hadn't paid attention to the news of either of those countries. Were Venezuela and Brazil safe? Chris couldn't identify many of the stars he saw overhead. He guessed on the constellations, but tried the best he could to test himself as they continued their voyage across the Atlantic.

Chapter 107

Atlantic Ocean

CHRIS BROUGHT A CUP of coffee to Dan, who was stationed at the wheel. With a nod of appreciation, Dan took a sip. Chris briefly wondered how they would cope without their stash of coffee. It was his responsibility to restock at each port.

"The others are fixing dinner and it should be ready in fifteen minutes. Why don't I take over for you?" Chris offered.

Dan nodded and stepped aside, pausing to study the sky. The past twenty-four hours had been good weather, but new clouds were approaching.

"I was hoping for a clear night so we could confirm we're sailing in the right direction," Dan shared with disappointment.

"Are you concerned? You seem tense."

"I'm not positive that we're headed in the correct direction. I wanted to verify our course tonight. I don't think we're on course for Brazil, but we may be headed toward the southern part of the Caribbean, a large area. Originally, we were hoping to avoid the Caribbean to arrive in Florida."

Dan sighed again and looked out to the ocean. There was something else on his mind.

"What else, Dan?"

"If my hunch is incorrect, we may be heading for the Bermuda Triangle, into another storm that will reach us in a few hours."

"We may have another adventure ahead of us," Dan stated after a minute of silence. "We need to get back home,"

"I feel the same way, but hopefully, we're close. Dan, the boat is behaving beautifully," Chris tried to cheer Dan up.

"Chris, I'm worried. I'm not sure how much Maria can take living on the boat. She's been sick for most of the voyage. There's no chance she would have survived your Slovenian adventure. I hope I didn't make a mistake trying to bring her to Florida."

Dan stood a step away from Chris. Chris stretched out his arm as far as he could reach and put his right arm around Dan while his left hand remained secure on the wheel. He pulled him in so they were side by side. Chris was much taller, so he looked down at Dan.

"Dan, you need to continue to be strong. I think if we are strong and confident, then Maria will be okay. If we lose our composure, she might become distressed. You've done a terrific job navigating—we *will* get back."

They stood in silence for a couple of minutes as the wind picked up and more clouds headed their way. The swells increased in size, and Chris was concerned that they had another significant storm on the horizon. He kept the sentiment to himself.

"I'd better go down below and help so we can eat dinner before the brunt of the storm. We'll bring you a plate," Dan offered.

Dan was ready to step down the cabin to the galley when Chris spoke.

"Dan, I'm different now."

Dan turned and studied Chris but didn't say a word.

"We will get back home," Chris continued. "I'm more determined than ever. I am now a 'shoot first and ask questions later' person. I think that has to be our attitude. The world is crazy right now. There are a lot of bad things happening. However, from talking to Carly, the new Texas Federation sounds promising. I think it will take us to a safe and prosperous country. A great place for my children and for Maria and your future children."

Dan focused his eyes on Chris, then nodded. He didn't say a word as he went below. Chris took a sip from his cup and felt the warmth permeate through him. He didn't know it, but he said out loud, "Yes, I'm tired too." Chris looked above, hoping to recognize a star or group of stars. He couldn't decipher anything in the partly cloudy sky, which was becoming more ominous by the minute.

Chris thought of the Bermuda Triangle. As a boy, he'd been fascinated by the Triangle: stories of the airplanes and boats that entered the triangle and were never heard from again. Some people thought the black hole was real, that you could travel into another dimension.

As Chris took the last sip from his cup, Jessica came up the stairs with a plate of food. She set it down next to him, and reached for his empty cup.

"Would you like a refill?"

"That would be great, but I can wait until you finish eating. Thank you for the plate."

"Are we heading into another storm?" Jessica asked with a worried voice.

"It appears so. But we're also getting closer to home. I'm sure you won't be as sick this time."

"Dan told us about the storm, and Maria's face went white. I know Dan loves the water, but he may have a hard time talking her into a long trip again."

"Well, with the pirates, storms, and Russian agents, she may never be interested in another long voyage." Chris laughed.

"Dad, do you think the world will settle down again?" Jessica asked. "Will it be safe to travel? Or more importantly, to just live our lives without fear?"

"Your mom gave us an in-depth report when we were leaving Spain. The new Texas Federation seems solid, Jessica. The majority of the states have joined, and I think our country will be better than before. It may take a few years for the Texas Federation and other countries to stabilize, maybe even longer for the second and third tier countries, but I think we'll eventually live in safety again."

"I think Drago is concerned about the immigration process," Jessica shared. "Our company assured him that they'd have it in place by the time we arrived, but he's still feeling anxious."

"If your company can grease the skids, I think he'll be fine. He has a large employer backing him. From what I've heard, we're tougher about monitoring people entering our country. I think it will be different from the country we left months ago. From what your mom told me, the age of political correctness is over. Our new country will be fair, but follow the laws explicitly. Special interest groups are taking a back seat to the majority."

Jessica stepped over, kissed her dad on the cheek, then took his empty cup and disappeared below deck. Chris looked at his plate and started eating the fish. Drago had been successful fishing in the calmer ocean. If they had several more days of storm, that might be the last of the fresh fish for a while.

Two hours later the sky was covered with clouds. The wind had picked up, and the swells were higher. Chris was enjoying his third cup of coffee. A bundled shape that Chris recognized as Drago walked toward him to take the next shift.

Chris stepped aside to let Drago take the wheel. The storm was becoming progressively worse, and both men expected rain to fall any moment. Chris took the string with the whistle from around his neck and handed it to Drago. They were now taking three hour shifts: Dan had volunteered to take Maria's shift since she was starting to feel ill again. Jessica felt fine now, but both Drago and Chris had volunteered to take her shift, or split it. Chris offered to Dan to split Maria's shift, or go back to the three-man shift.

Concentrating on his footing, Chris walked down into the cabin and found Dan and Jessica asleep in their bunks. Maria was lying still in her bunk. Chris walked by and noticed her eyes were open.

"Maria, is there anything I can get for you?" Chris whispered.

"No, thank you," she mouthed back to him.

Chris stepped to the galley and set his cup down. He was very tired. With robotic movements, Chris walked over to his bunk, and took off his rain gear, jacket, shoes, and then pants. Climbing under his blanket, he rocked with the swells, and he was asleep in ten minutes.

Chapter 108

The Americas

FOR SEVEN DAYS, THEY experienced poor weather. There was not one clear sky, day or night. They would make it through a bad storm that was followed by a mild storm, but then they would confront another severe storm. Maria had been sick for seven straight days now: either very sick or mildly sick. At the worst moment, she had threatened to jump overboard before Jessica and Dan were able to successfully calm her down.

Every minute brought rain. Even with the rain gear, their clothes were wet and the cabin remained damp. Jessica was not as sick as the first storm, which freed them to work a four-person rotation with three hours per shift. This worked well: three hours on, nine hours off.

All the fresh food from the Canary Islands was long gone. They now ate from a bag of rice, a bag of beans, and the remainder of the canned food. Even during the mildest parts of the storm, the water was still too rough to fish.

Fortunately they had a strong wind that allowed them to cover numerous nautical miles. Dan was still concerned whether they were on the path to the Caribbean or Brazil. The successive storms made it nearly impossible to keep a precise course.

Chris finished his shift at 10:00 p.m. Dan took over, still half-asleep as he clutched a cup of coffee. Coffee was their staple and Chris felt comfort knowing they still had a one week supply. They had just made it through yet another bad storm, and now had a light wind with rain. Chris scampered below, took off his wet jacket, and poured a quarter cup of coffee. He needed something to warm him and get rid of the chill before retiring to bed. The warm drink did the trick: Chris climbed into his bunk and pulled a blanket over himself.

Shriek! A sound interrupted his dream and Chris lifted his head up and felt groggy. He saw Jessica and Drago with their heads up, and Maria was struggling to wake up. They heard another shrill sound coming from the deck.

"It's Dan and the whistle!" Drago shouted.

Quickly slipping on their pants and shoes, they grabbed their jackets as they reached the stairs. Drago made it up onto deck first; with Jessica close behind. Chris was two steps away, and Maria stumbled behind him on the bottom step. Then they heard a scraping sound, seconds before the crash. The impact was like an earthquake and they shook.

Chris held tight to the railing, trying not to fall down the steps. After the significant jolt, he maintained his balance and continued up the last two stairs to the deck. Behind him, he could hear water rushing into the cabin. Chris glanced behind to find Maria by his side.

Drago and Jessica scrambled to their feet. Dan lay prone on the deck, struggling to climb up to his hands and knees.

"We hit some rocks!" Dan shouted. "I didn't see them until the last minute. I couldn't avoid them."

Drago and Jessica rushed to the stern, Chris and Dan right behind. They'd hit a rock; the boat no longer swayed.

"Looks like we hit a reef," Dan confirmed.

"There's water rushing into the cabin," Maria shouted.

Dan snapped into emergency mode. He'd rehearsed a few different scenarios with the others.

"Drago and Jessica, get the raft ready. The boat may stay on the reef for weeks or months, but it could only be minutes. We need to move quickly."

"I'll go into the cabin to check on the damage," Dan added. "Chris, get the spotlight. I want you to look for land."

"Maria, come down to the cabin. If the damage is significant, we need to bring our essential items from below deck and start loading the raft."

Chris followed Dan and Maria down into the cabin. Dan found the spotlight, and Chris quickly found his way back on deck. He glanced over at Jessica and Drago working efficiently; they would have the raft ready in minutes.

Chris stood perched at the stern. The rain was still steady, it was past midnight, and with the night sky and cloud cover, it was pitch-black. Chris did a 180-degree turn, sweeping the light in arcs in front of him. He thought he saw something. *A rock? A tree?* He moved the light up a few degrees and saw some fronds. *Yes! A palm tree?*

"Yes," he confirmed to himself in a whisper. *Now how far was it to the trees? A mile?* Chris was challenged with judging distances over water. Guessing it was in the ballpark of a quarter mile, Chris turned off the light. He walked briskly across the deck and he stuck his head down into the cabin.

"I see land ahead! One rock and what appears to be palm trees," Chris shouted.

"We have a mess down here," Dan responded. "We're starting to take in a lot of water. We're about a foot deep—we need to bring essentials up to the deck. "How are Jessica and Drago doing with the raft?" Dan questioned.

Chris lifted his head and looked over at Jessica and Drago.

"How much more time do you need?"

"Just two minutes, and we can load," Jessica shouted back.

Maria brought food up to the deck. Chris brought up all the guns, ammunition, and missile launcher. Dan took out a tarp, and a sports bag stuffed with various tools, binoculars, and maps.

Drago tied a rope to the deck and attached it to the raft. He and Jessica lowered the raft into the water. Drago hopped down into the raft and motioned to Jessica that he was ready to receive the supplies.

Jessica assisted Chris and Maria in bringing the chosen supplies to the side of the boat and lowering them down to Drago. Chris and Dan brought the fresh water containers. The ocean water was now two feet deep inside the cabin.

They took turns going down into the cabin and bringing up their individual backpacks with clothes. Jessica suggested packing another pair of shoes, a minimum of two outfits, and a hat. She went below and packed some items for Drago.

Drago, Jessica, and Maria were in the lifeboat with Dan and Chris handing down the last of the supplies. Dan left Chris for a few minutes to make sure they didn't leave anything critical behind. They had limited room in the raft, requiring difficult decisions on what to bring and what to leave behind.

Chris finished loading the last bag, then climbed into the raft. Drago held the rope, keeping the raft close to the boat. Dan's head appeared with a book in his hands—his book on stars and constellations. Untying the rope on the boat, Dan dropped into the raft and landed awkwardly. He was about to fall backward into the ocean, but Drago and Jessica grabbed each arm to help him steady his feet. Chris used an oar to push the raft away from Dan's boat.

Spotlight on, Chris focused it in the direction of the palm trees. Dan and Drago had the oars working in rhythm, moving the raft forward. As they got closer, they saw a small beach area with the large rock off to the left that Chris had first spotted. Chris shifted the light to his left hand and pulled out his gun. The beach area was clear, dotted with palm trees thirty meters from the shore.

The rain was steady but light as they landed uneventfully on shore. Chris did a 180 scan: the rock was fifty meters to the left, and there was only beach to the right. He cast the light on the trees ahead of them. Beyond the trees was low-level vegetation. Chris couldn't see anything beyond that. Climbing out of the raft first, Chris directed the light for the others. Jessica was next off the raft, then Maria. Chris handed Maria the light and asked her to walk up the beach ten meters, with the light in hand.

After Chris handed the light to Maria, he turned to Jessica, who was on shore and ready.

"We don't know where we are. There may be enemies here or wild animals. Be cautious—have your rifle ready."

Jessica walked next to Maria with her rifle positioned. Together they walked ten meters toward the palms, looking for any signs of life.

Drago was now off the raft. Dan exited last and heaved and pulled the raft further up shore with the help of the others. They were armed now; Dan with the shotgun and Drago with the rifle.

"Dan, is there another light?" Chris asked. "You stay with the raft and Maria can hold the light for you. Drago, Jessica, and I will look around to make sure we're safe before we think about unloading the raft."

Dan didn't say a word as he turned back to the raft and pulled his tool bag out. He brought it up to the front of the raft, unzipped it, and rummaged around until he found the LED flashlight.

Chris and Drago walked ahead ten meters until they reached Jessica and Maria.

"Have you seen anything?" Chris asked.

"No, not yet," Jessica responded.

"Maria, we need your light so we can scout around," Chris told her as he reached out with his hand. "You and Dan are going to stay with the raft. He's waiting for you."

Maria handed Chris the light and walked back to Dan. Chris looked over at Drago and Jessica meaningfully. Placing his rifle over his shoulder, Chris pulled out his handgun.

"I can hold the light. You both be ready with your rifles. Any thoughts of where we should go first?"

"We should search back one hundred meters beyond the palm trees and make sure the beach area is secure. Then we can go further along the shore in each direction," Drago suggested.

"Sounds good," Jessica agreed.

Chris nodded and started walking to the palm trees. He continually moved the light from side to side. Jessica was on his left side and Drago on his right; they cautiously moved away from the shore. When they reached the first palm tree, Chris paused and slowly panned the light. There appeared to be little vegetation, then more sand and water ahead of them on the other side. They didn't see any movement, so they exited the palm trees and continued walking straight ahead. In fifty meters, they were standing on another beach on the other side of the island.

"Well, exploring this island may not take too much time," Jessica shared what they were all thinking.

They walked one hundred meters along on the left of the shore, keeping the palm trees as a landmark of where Dan and Maria were waiting by the raft. They could see the end of the island now as they headed back to the other shore. They walked through knee high vegetation, then found themselves back on the shoreline. Leading back toward Dan and Maria, Chris passed the large rock that he had first spotted from the boat. In a few minutes, they were back at the raft.

"It appears that this is a narrow island," Chris reported to Dan and Maria. "Fifty meters beyond the palm trees is the other shore. We walked one hundred meters to the left and crossed over to the other side of the rock. It's all clear on the left and also straight ahead. We'll go to the right side and then return."

Drago, Jessica, and Chris walked to the palm tree, turned right, and slowly stepped through the vegetation. Sweeping the light from side to side, they could see both shores. They walked about two hundred yards, where both shores narrowed until they soon reached a point at the end of the island.

"Well, we're on a small uninhabited island," exclaimed Drago.

They reported back to Dan and Maria. Chris, Dan, and Drago pulled the raft further up on the shore. Dan took out the tarp, and they chose to create a shelter utilizing the palm trees. Jessica and Drago started to fasten the tarp to one tree using the rope. It was soon apparent that they would need more rope to tie all sides of the tarp to the palm trees.

"Why don't we unload the raft's contents by the palm tree," suggested Dan. "I can go back to the boat and bring more rope. Anything else that we may need?"

"Should we wait for the morning light?" Jessica wondered.

"I'm worried that my boat will break up and we'll lose supplies," Dan confessed. "It may not happen, but I don't want to take the chance. I can move around that boat in the dark. I know every inch of it."

The others nodded.

Maria thought that they would need cooking utensils, silverware, matches, cups, and plates. Jessica suggested they bring clothes to help shelter them from the sun, and anything waterproof. They made a mental list, deciding that Drago and Jessica would return with Dan to help him bring the additional items.

Chris tied two of the four ends of the tarp before he ran out of rope. Holding the other end up with his arms extended skyward, he kept the area dry as Maria brought the backpacks and food items out of the rain.

Dan navigated the raft to his boat quickly, and soon the three of them returned to shore with the provisions. They unloaded the raft and carried the supplies to a dry area under the tarp. Dan and Drago then dragged the empty raft completely out of the water.

Jessica handed the additional rope to Chris. Together they tied down the remaining two corners to a third palm tree. They couldn't create a rectangle with the tarp, but they had a nice triangle large enough for them to keep themselves and their key supplies dry.

Maria opened some canned goods and they ate an early breakfast under the tarp. Dan's watch said 4:00 a.m. It was drizzling, and as soon as he finished his breakfast, he rummaged through his backpack. Dan found a detailed map of the Caribbean that he studied under the flashlight while the others finished eating.

"Any idea where we are?" Chris asked Dan after five minutes of silence.

"Unfortunately, no," Dan responded with a sigh. "We need to keep an eye on the raft. That's our most important possession now. I'm hoping that this small island is part of a larger island chain or close to a mainland. Once we get more clues, I can venture a guess. A reef and a small island with a few palm trees and sand is not enough information for me to make an educated guess."

Chris, Dan, and Drago brought the raft further up shore until it was close to the tarp. Chris volunteered to take first watch so the others could sleep. Drago suggested that Chris wake him at 6:00 a.m. to take a watch and Jessica volunteered for the 8:00 a.m. shift. They agreed that rest was vital and hoped that the storm would break and they could explore the island in the daylight. With the binoculars they could look for land nearby.

The ideal situation would be to paddle the raft from island to island until they found mainland (without having to venture in the open water).

Dan asked Maria for all the containers, which he positioned outside the tarp to collect rain water.

"Our raft is the first priority, but drinking water is second. Let's be careful with it. We should only use our water for drinking."

With that, Dan scooted over beside Maria, laid down, and fell asleep. Chris looked over at Drago and Jessica, who had also snuggled to sleep.

The sound of water lapping upon the shore mixed with the slight wind soon relaxed Chris. In the two-hour watch, nothing happened. They were alone on the island, their only neighbors—some industrious crabs. He woke Drago at 6:00 a.m. and fell asleep the moment he put his head to the ground.

Chapter 109

Islas La Roques

DRAGO AND JESSICA EXPRESSED their pleasure that it wasn't raining for the first time in a week. The sky was cloudy, but visibility was good: they could see their shipwrecked boat in the distance. They chose to walk around the perimeter of the island in daylight. When they returned, everyone else was up. They gave a quick report that confirmed that the island was void of life. They could see another island in the distance from the other shore.

Drago retrieved a fishing pole with fishing gear from the evening's excursion back to the boat. He walked over to the large rock to cast out, Jessica beside him. Chris was encouraged by their report of visible land on the other shore. Picking up the binoculars, he marched over to the other side. He zeroed in on the island that Drago had spoken about. It appeared to be only a few miles away, and all he could see was sand and another small island similar in size to the island they were already on. Chris gazed to the left, then to the right of the sandy island, it looked as though there were more small islands behind the sandy one. Looking further in that direction, Chris thought he saw a larger island beyond the smaller ones.

Chris walked briskly back to camp. Maria was busy taking inventory of the food, and Dan had gathered kindling for a fire. He'd collected palm fronds, coconut husks, and some dead leaves before digging a small area away from the tarp and gathering small rocks to form a fire ring.

"Drago caught a fish!" Jessica yelled over from the large rock.

Chris's spirits soared: fresh fish for breakfast. He walked over to Dan, who was preparing the fire ring.

"I saw the island that Jessica and Drago reported—it looks like there are smaller islands behind it. I can't tell, but there could be another larger island further behind. Do you want to take a look?"

Chris handed Dan the binoculars, pointing in the direction of the islands. Dan waved a hand toward his pile of kindling.

"Will you prep for a fire? Maria, are you ready with the beans?"

"Yes, they are in the pot," Maria answered.

"Let's start the fire and cook the beans. When they're finished, Drago might have more fish to cook." Dan held the binoculars as he walked to the opposite shore.

Ten minutes later, Dan returned. The fire was established and Chris had the pot of beans cooking. Dan said that he couldn't tell if the last island was a large island or a string of smaller islands. Chris suggested that he should look for land at other viewpoints. Chris took the binoculars from Dan and walked over to Jessica and Drago.

"How's it going?" Chris inquired.

"Drago has caught three fish," Jessica reported.

"Terrific!" Chris replied. "Maria and Dan are cooking the beans now. We'll be ready to cook the fish in about ten minutes."

Drago looked back to smile at Jessica and Chris before returning his focus to the task at hand.

"Drago, we are so fortunate that you've turned into such a good fisherman," Chris commented.

"I'm going to the end of the island to take another look. I looked at the island you found this morning: it appears to be small, but there are more. I hope to find a larger island or more small islands beyond it. After breakfast, we might explore them."

Chris spent five minutes looking from the left end of the island. All he saw was an expanse of blue ocean. He walked back on the opposite shore of Drago and Jessica to observe the same islands he had looked at earlier that morning. Chris continued until he reached the right side.

He saw a small island in the distance. To the left of the island toward the other smaller islands, he saw an additional island. Chris wondered if one of the islands might have people.

Soon the beans were cooked and cooling off to the side. Dan had salvaged a grill from the boat and three cleaned fish sizzled on the grill.

"Drago is cleaning two more. We have five fish: one for each of us," Dan announced with a pleased look on his face.

Drago joined them shortly, adding the last two fish to the grill. The fire was more smoke than flames, but created enough heat to do the job. Chris shared that he had spotted more islands on the right side: they had islands directly ahead of them on the opposite shore and islands to the immediate right.

"After breakfast we should clean up, pack up, and head out to explore the islands," Dan announced. "I'm hoping that one of these islands will have habitants. We need to stay alert and be prepared as we travel. I'm not sure where we are, but there could be pirates or drug runners. It's possible we may run into a good situation, but we might also stumble upon a bad situation."

"Or we may be on an island chain without any habitants," Dan added after a pause.

They were packed in the raft, paddling for the first island straight ahead. The weather cooperated, filtered sunlight shone through the scattered clouds. Chris sat in the front of the raft, scanning ahead with the binoculars. He knew that the island in front of them was uninhabited, but what was beyond? As they reached the first sandy island, they navigated around and discovered two more islands behind it. An added benefit was the better view of one of the distant islands to the right.

Between the two islands and directly ahead of them was a more visible island with palm trees. Chris couldn't tell anything further from his vantage point, but it held promise. They decided to raft between the two islands to get a better look. If the islands ahead weren't promising, they could always move to the island positioned on the right.

They were now through the strait between the two islands. A larger island loomed ahead. Chris had his binoculars focused ahead to where he could see a long beach. He passed the binoculars to Jessica and Drago who saw the same view as Chris. The decision was made to paddle around the large island, observe it, and then go ashore.

Chris couldn't see any visible structures, but the island was larger than any of the others they had seen. They circled the island counterclockwise until they were positioned behind the island.

"I think I see something!" Chris exclaimed.

"What do you see?" Maria asked fearfully.

"It looks like a dock extending out into the ocean."

A couple of minutes later, Chris saw what looked to be man-made structures. Upon closer inspection, they appeared to be huts.

"I think this is a resort of some kind," Chris mused as he surveyed the area intently.

They rowed closer to shore for a better look. Chris was nervous: he didn't see people; it looked deserted. He reminded himself that if this was a resort, it *would* be vacant since people weren't traveling on vacation at the moment. Through the binoculars, Chris could see a large group of buildings beyond the dock that he assumed might be the reception and restaurant areas. On either side of the beach were several bungalows.

The group guided the raft alongside the beach and paused forty meters from the dock. Jessica and Drago jumped out to wade in the water ten meters from the shore. They scanned right to left but didn't see a soul. Maria was now out of the raft; she joined the couple as Dan and Chris dragged the raft onto the beach. They enlisted Drago's assistance since it was heavy with supplies.

The five were armed and cautious as they walked along the shore toward the dock. There was still no sign of life, so they climbed up onto the dock. In front of them stood a large building with a covered patio area. It was enclosed with glass windows and appeared to be one of the main buildings.

"Restaurant?" Dan stated what everyone else was thinking.

"Dan, do you and Maria want to stay here on the dock while Drago, Jessica, and I explore?" Chris asked.

"Sure, we'll stay here," Dan agreed. "Don't venture too far, and keep checking in with us."

Chris looked at Jessica and Drago, then slowly scanned 180 degrees. He was concerned that he was missing something. There was a vanishing edge pool overlooking the beach, and a patio to the right. To the left were bungalows. Chris's eyes snapped back to the pool. The water looked clear and clean. Was someone maintaining the pool?

"Should we go into that large building?" Chris asked Jessica and Drago as he pointed ahead.

"I think that's a good plan. I'll lead," Drago offered.

Drago went forward and Jessica and Chris spaced themselves as they followed. Drago came to double glass doors and opened them slowly before stepping inside. It was quiet. Jessica entered next, seconds later, Chris joined them inside.

It was indeed a dining room. An empty dining room that looked like it hadn't been used in a while. Tables and chairs were in place but the tables were empty. There were doors leading from the side of the room and a door at the back, that Chris assumed led to the kitchen. Drago pointed and then started walking to the back of the room, the others following behind.

They met another pair of double doors, these were metal with only glass windows at the top. Drago peeked through the window, then slowly opened the door. Jessica and Chris followed. The kitchen was deserted, but there was food on the kitchen counter: fresh fruit and vegetables. Jessica saw it first and pointed, Drago and Chris nodded.

"There are people on the resort," Chris whispered.

Walking back into the dining room, they exited the side door onto a deck overlooking the beach. Chris turned in the direction of Dan and Maria, who could see them in the distance. He gave them a wave.

Drago moved toward the other large building they'd assumed to be the reception area. Drago and Jessica entered side by side, Chris following behind. The lights were on and there was a middle-aged man and woman behind the reception desk, guns pointed at them. An older man stood by the elevator, also with a gun. And still yet, there was an older woman behind the lobby sofa holding a gun. Chris, Drago, and Jessica stood with their guns pointed back at them.

The man behind the reception desk shouted something in Spanish. Chris turned to Drago and Jessica with an inquisitive look. The man yelled again and Drago gave a curt reply in Spanish. There was a strained exchange back and forth and finally Drago put his gun down and looked at Chris and Jessica.

"They asked who we are, and I asked who they are. My Spanish is not very good, but this is what I learned," Drago shared. "This is a resort, and it's been temporarily shut down. This is the crew who was left behind to keep the resort in good condition. They're as nervous of us as we are of them."

Drago held up his bare hand and pointed outside. Chris and Jessica put down their guns and followed Drago outside. The four resort employees dropped their guns and followed. Once outside the lobby, Chris saw that there was a younger man and woman armed and positioned outside the doorway. In total, six resort workers that had been left behind.

Drago said something to the resort workers and pointed in the direction of the dock. Everyone followed his arm.

"We found caretakers. We're all walking toward you," Chris shouted to Dan and Maria.

"Maria, we need your Spanish," Drago called. "I understand enough, but they want more details of where we came from and where we are going."

Maria walked forward and had a five-minute conversation with the middle-aged man and woman.

"These people are three married couples that are caretakers. They were left behind to watch things and keep the resort clean and maintained. The younger couple maintains the outside garden and pool. The older couple works inside; she cooks and he does inside maintenance. The middle-aged man is the manager, and his wife is in charge of maintaining the rooms."

"They had a small group of pirates stop here weeks ago," Maria continued. "They had to scare them off and even shot a few, which is why they are nervous now. They didn't think we were pirates, but they couldn't understand why we were out here in a raft. I told them we were shipwrecked. We are invited to come inside: they offered to help us pull our raft up. We should bring all our key valuables with us."

"Wait! Please ask where we are." Dan couldn't hold the suspense.

Maria had a two minute back and forth conversation with the manager before turning to the others.

"We are on Isla La Roques, one of a string of islands. It's a natural preserve that attracts divers. Right now, there aren't tourists. There are very few people on this whole island chain."

Dan searched in his brain, trying to register the name of the islands. He would have to pull out his map when he retrieved his backpack.

"Maria, where are we in relation to mainland? What is the closest well-known city or landmark?"

Maria spoke with the manager again. As he spoke, he pointed behind himself. Then he spoke again, and pointed off to the side.

"He says we are on islands off Venezuela, about one hundred miles away. To the side is Bonaire about one hundred miles, and off Bonaire is Curacao, then Aruba."

Dan and Chris looked at each other, and then Chris looked at Jessica and Drago. What was there to say? They were south of Florida, but fortunately also north of South America.

"Why don't Jessica and Maria go up with them to the lobby. We'll start unloading the raft," Chris broke in.

Drago, Chris, and Dan went down to the raft, and the younger caretaker volunteered to help them. They each carried two bags and walked back up from the dock. Chris could tell that Dan was beating himself up on their location.

"How could we be so far south?" Dan spoke rhetorically.

"Dan, you did a great job," Chris was quick to the point. "We're alive, and we made it across the Atlantic. Let's unload our supplies and then we can talk with these people about options to get back home. We'll need to understand all the possible sea routes."

Dan felt discouraged and shuffled off, hands full of supplies. Chris followed behind him.

"Dan, we have to keep moving forward. I'm just sorry about your boat."

They brought most of the possessions inside in two trips. Drago and the young caretaker went down to the beach and pulled the raft way up and off the shore before bringing in the remaining items. All the supplies soon stood stacked in the center of the reception room.

As he entered the lobby, Chris found that the caretakers had prepared rooms for them. Maria and Dan had a room—much to Maria's delight she gathered her personal items and quickly showed Dan to their room. Jessica and Drago had separate rooms nearby. Drago returned with the caretaker, quickly gathered his personal items, and left with Jessica. This left Chris standing alone in the lobby.

The middle-aged woman reached out and handed him a key. As he took it, she turned around and led him to his room. He grabbed his backpack, shouldered his rifle, and then took the bag with the missile launcher in his other hand and followed her.

Fifteen minutes later, they were all back in the lobby. Their hosts suggested they leave their food, water, and generic supplies in the store room off the reception area. The consensus was that everyone wanted a shower. They would meet back in the lobby in approximately an hour: Dan and Maria requested a discussion on transportation and geography at that time.

Chris went back to his room and charged his phone only to discover that there wasn't cell coverage. He had hoped to call Carly for a few minutes, but that was not going to happen. He shed his clothes and walked into the shower like a statue, basking under the hot water. It felt good. After twenty minutes he climbed out and looked for the cleanest clothes he could find. The middle-aged woman had told them to bring their dirty laundry to wash. Chris had all his other clothes in the bag ready to bring to the lobby. After their voyage, *everything* he had was dirty laundry. The hosts had given him fresh towels, with a shaving kit, and it felt good to shave.

Finally, he laid down on the bed to rest, it felt heavenly. He was so grateful that they had found the resort and the nice hosts. It felt like an angel was looking over them. Chris fell asleep dreaming of an angel, until he was abruptly roused by a knocking on the door.

Jessica and Drago stood at his door. Chris was still half asleep as he opened the door wide to greet them. With a grunt he left the door open. Chris stumbled over to a chair, found his pistol holster, and reached for his rifle.

"Really, Dad? You need your rifle?" Jessica questioned.

Chris looked at her, shrugged, and then went over and laid it down on the bed.

"I'm starting to feel more comfortable with it."

They were last to arrive in the lobby; everyone was waiting for them. The hosts wanted to hear their guests' stories. Dan and Chris provided a quick summary, then suggested they could elaborate with more detail over dinner. Chris, Dan, Jessica, Maria, and Drago wanted to understand more about the surrounding areas and learn the best options for a safe passage to the States. The manager told Chris and Dan that they could discuss later all these details in the reception room.

In the reception room were bottles of wine and appetizers. Chris was surprised at the effort that the hosts had made. Chris waited until each of his colleagues had selected a glass, then proposed a toast to the hosts as he expressed his gratitude for their hospitality. Maria gave a quick translation and smiles formed all around.

Drago attacked the appetizers and finally decided to pick up the entire tray while sitting down by Jessica. Jessica got one or two bites in before Drago cleared the tray.

Dan soon had the map on the table. Leaning over, Dan motioned for the caretaker gentlemen to position themselves around it. Chris took his glass of red wine and sat in a chair to the side of the table. He understood where Venezuela was and where Aruba was located. In his mind, Chris tried to recall all the countries they would need to cross following a land route through Central America and all the islands to pass for a Caribbean route to either Texas or Florida. Was one route safer than the other?

Dan confirmed where they were on the map, then looked at Maria. "Will you ask if there is regular transportation off the island by boat or by air? Or if something could be chartered?"

Maria held a conversation in Spanish. There were gestures and all three of the resort men participated. Then the middle-aged woman brought out a tray of more appetizers and joined the dialogue. Each of them watched the exchange except Drago, who eyed the new appetizer tray. The Spanish conversation ended and it was quiet. Everyone looked to Maria to summarize in English.

"There is an airstrip on the island. When the resort is open, there is a daily flight to Caracas. This has stopped until they reopen for tourism. However, the owner of the resort has a small charter plane that flies in every other week to bring in supplies and to make sure that everything is fine. The next flight arrives in four days. The flight comes in from Caracas and returns the same day."

"When they are open for tourists there are a few boats at the resort, but they have all sailed back to Caracas," Maria continued, trying to spill all the information before she forgot anything. "One boat was for deep sea fishing and the other for scuba diving. There is a man on the other side of the island that has a charter boat. He sometimes takes long fishing trips for three days to a week. He is still on the island. He has a house on the coast and lives with his family. He's waiting for tourism to bounce back. There was a ferry to Bonaire and then to Aruba, but it has also stopped service at this time."

"So we have two choices," Dan stated. "One, fly back to Caracas in four days. Two, try to talk to the guy with the boat."

Maria nodded slowly. It was quiet.

"Venezuela isn't overly fond of Americans, right?" Dan asked. "Weren't they kidnapping and ransoming family members of major league baseball players who came from Venezuela? And this was *before* all the craziness in the world."

"What do you, guys, think?" Dan turned and looked at Chris, Jessica, and Drago.

Drago stopped eating off the new appetizer tray. He had been listening closely, but now needed to respond.

"Where would the guy with the boat be able to take us?" Jessica spoke up.

Maria asked Jessica's question and received multiple answers from the hosts. When they stopped talking, she looked at Jessica to share the response.

"His typical trip is up to a week, but he's been known to take customers a little longer and farther. But he never strays from the Antilles or Venezuelan basin. They say we should talk to him. There's been no business for a while—he may be interested in a longer trip if it pays well."

"Will you ask how safe it is in Caracas for Americans?" Chris asked. "My concern is that a land route would go through Venezuela, Colombia, Central America, and then Mexico. Honduras is very dangerous, as is Guatemala, El Salvador, and other specific areas. We know Mexico has a major drug war that's existed for decades. The safest travel areas that I'm aware of are Belize, Costa Rica, and Panama.

"I'm assuming we can't fly anywhere safe from Caracas?" Chris added.

Maria confirmed with the hosts that traveling in Venezuela would be risky and that there were not many flights from Caracas other than to Colombia and other South America countries. Chris listened and studied the map with his colleagues.

They spent another half hour asking more questions. The consensus was that the younger caretaker would take them to the other side of the island the next morning after breakfast to talk with the boat owner. They expressed gratitude to their hosts for the valuable information before parting ways.

By then, it was late afternoon. The island hosts had prepared a nice dinner in their honor. The weather was clear: partly cloudy with some sun. The hosts expected the evening to be beautiful; their plan was to dine out on the patio overlooking the ocean. It was an evening experience that many tourists would pay a couple hundred dollars a night to experience. Chris smiled as he heard Maria and Dan tell their hosts how much they loved the resort.

The young caretaker woman pulled Maria aside and said something to her. Maria looked at everyone.

"She asked if you would like a tour of the grounds before dinner. She can give us a tour of the resort and then we'll have time to pick up our laundry, and maybe swim in the pool, before changing for dinner."

This was well received by all. They gathered around the young woman, who led them out of the lobby.

The tour was given in Spanish. Maria translated the key information. The young woman was in her midtwenties: she was no bigger than five-foot tall, slim, and with jet-black hair, white teeth, and an infectious smile.

The resort was large. It was not hard to imagine people scattered on the beach, at the pool, and in the Jacuzzi. They had beach volleyball, paddle boarding, and kayaks that were in storage. They even had a motorboat that pulled an inner tube around the bay. This was an all-inclusive resort for water activities including snorkeling tours and scheduled diving excursions.

They thanked her for the tour. Chris especially appreciated new understanding of the significance and beauty of the resort. After picking up their laundry, they thanked the middle-aged woman. She was about fifty years old with long black hair that had just a touch of gray. She was not slim, but was still petite. Chris thought that perhaps she was the mother of the younger woman that had showed them the grounds.

They were offered loaner swim outfits that they happily changed into in the bathrooms by the pool. Soon they jumped into the pool to swim. Jessica and Drago swam to the waterfall and the water poured over their heads, in five minutes they climbed out and entered the Jacuzzi. Maria and Dan kept to the shallow end, immersed in private conversation. Chris took the time to swim a couple of laps before floating on his back. He slowly swam two more laps before getting out. It felt good to stretch and test his shoulder. Before dispersing to their rooms to change for dinner, Chris held up his hand.

"There's no ATM on this island. When you go back to your room, calculate how much cash you each have. Include the old US currency and euros. When we have our discussion with the captain of the charter boat, we'll need to figure out our best and safest way back. It may include a combination of events and a number of payouts. I think we should collect all ideas and understand what cash we have on hand as we explore our options."

Dinner was wonderful. It was served at a large table on the patio with a breathtaking view overlooking the grounds and the ocean below. The hosts lit tiki torches along the perimeter. The weather was perfect, the moon was visible, and the stars sparkled. They spent two hours sharing their story. They each told sections, but Chris condensed the Slovenian part. It was too long, and it held too many haunting memories. Their hosts gasped at parts and were amazed by the adventures. One of them told Maria it was like a movie, or perhaps even more adventuresome than a typical movie.

At 10:00 p.m., everyone looked tired. The oldest hosts noticed that their guests were weary and suggested that it was time to end the evening. Before retiring to their rooms, the hosts confirmed breakfast at 8:00 a.m. in the dining room. The guests would be escorted from there to the other side of the island to meet the captain of the charter boat.

Chris and Jessica offered to help clear and clean the dishes, but were told not to worry about it. Secretly, Chris was glad. He was so exhausted he didn't know if he could stay awake much longer without caffeine. They walked back to their rooms in a daze. Once inside, Chris closed the door and sat on the bed. He took off his shoes, lay down, and quickly feel asleep. It was the first time in weeks he felt safe enough to fall into a deep sleep.

Chapter 110

Other side of the island

AFTER FINISHING BREAKFAST THE next morning, Dan, Maria, Chris, Drago, and Jessica walked to the front lobby and out the doors to climb into the jeep. Each of them wanted to go on the field trip to see the charter boat, even Maria. She expressed her apprehension regarding another voyage, but Dan sat in the back seat with Maria on his lap and next to Drago. Jessica sat in the front seat, and Chris squeezed in next to her. When they were all settled, the young man drove off on the dirt road.

In five minutes, they reached an overlook. The driver said something in Spanish, then pointed to a dock sheltered in a small cove. There were two boats moored at the dock; nearby sat a modest but rustic house with peeling white paint and a large satellite dish.

As they drove up to a small parking area by the dock, the driver stopped, stepped out, and shouted "Miguel?" A response came from one of the boats. A man in his early forties waved from the larger boat, then turned back toward his project. As they approached the boat, they could see the man working on the engine, his son beside him holding a couple of wrenches. There were two dogs onboard the boat: one a midsize mongrel that was tan and black, the other a small gray puppy (also a mongrel) that looked like he had some schnauzer in him. The dogs were happy to see someone new and jumped off the boat and ran onto the dock to greet the visitors.

Some Spanish was exchanged before the driver motioned for them to follow. They all walked back to the rear of the house and he stood near the picnic table. The dogs joined them, lying down under the shade of the picnic table. Maria and the driver spoke and Maria translated.

"Miguel asked for five to ten minutes to finish his work. He'll clean up when he's done and meet us here."

Chris seized the opportunity to glance at the grounds. He saw a chicken coop and a laundry line with some sheets blowing in the wind.

"Simple life," he commented. "But there's something appealing about it."

Ten minutes later, Miguel walked down the dock with his son. He had a towel in his hand and wiped grease from his hands as he walked over. Miguel's son continued walking to the back door of the house and went inside. Miguel shook everyone's hand, then looked at the driver and started the conversation in Spanish. Midway through, Maria jumped in. Drago and Jessica tried to follow the best they could, but they could only catch key phrases.

At a break, Maria translated the conversation into English. Dan and Chris listened intently.

"It's true that business is slow because of lack of tourism. He's open to take us somewhere, but he doesn't travel far, and he doesn't trust his boat to go further than Aruba to the west and either Grenada or Trinidad to the east."

Dan pulled out his map and spread it out on the table. Miguel and Dan quickly found their current location on the map, then looked at destinations to the west and north.

"Does he understand we eventually want to arrive in Florida or Texas, or somewhere in the new Texas Federation?" Chris asked Maria. "Does he have any ideas of how we can get there, or at least get closer?"

Maria spoke with Miguel and he moved his finger along the map while he spoke in Spanish. When he traced east he shook his head while looking at Maria and the others, then his finger traveled over to Aruba and he shrugged his shoulders.

"He said that if he takes us to Grenada or Trinidad we would have to find another boat to head north," Maria translated. "But he warns that there are many pirates through the Caribbean on the way to the Bahamas. If we travel to the island of Aruba, then we can reach Colombia and continue inland. He says that Venezuela, Colombia, Honduras, and Guatemala are all very dangerous, especially for Americans. Mexico is also very dangerous: drug lords have defeated the government army in some locations. And the border between Mexico and the new Texas Federation is very tough to get across. In short, he doesn't have any ideas of what we should do. He suggests that we stay at the resort until things get better."

"What about Cuba?" Jessica asked studying the map. "That would get us close to Florida."

Maria spoke with Miguel, who responded with a shake of his head.

"Miguel said that once terrorism accelerated, Cuba shut down. There is no travel in or out of Cuba. If we enter, we won't get out."

"Ask him, if he were us, and wanted to get back badly, what would he do?" Chris didn't want to give up yet.

Maria asked again and Miguel threw up his arms. Maria looked at the others and shook her head. Miguel saw the disappointment on their faces, and spoke again. Maria listened and then shared.

"If it were him, he would take his boat to Aruba. He has a friend who has a small plane in Aruba. From Aruba, he would fly to Jamaica or another place in Central America like Belize. It wouldn't take us to the States, but it would take us halfway to the States."

Dan, Chris, Jessica, Drago, and Maria looked at each other. Jessica spoke first.

"Should we have him contact his friend to see if he is willing to fly us?"

"Find out the cost for five passengers," Dan added. "How much money for Miguel to take us to Aruba?"

"And then how much to fly to Jamaica or Belize?" Jessica added.

They looked at Maria as she spoke with Miguel. Miguel nodded and turned away toward the garage.

"He has a CB radio in his workshop. He asked for a few minutes to try to get the information we requested."

In ten minutes, Miguel walked back. He sat down, looked at Maria, and spewed information.

"Miguel's friend will be flying to Jamaica in a few days," Maria shared. "Then he plans to continue to Belize before returning to Aruba."

She quoted the price to fly to Jamaica plus the price to continue on to Belize. Then she shared Miguel's price to travel by boat to Aruba.

Chris looked at Miguel and Maria, then suggested that they take time to discuss the proposal. He thought they should also discuss the option of flying to Caracas, Venezuela. Maria spoke with Miguel briefly. He nodded, walked to the back door of his house, opened it up, and yelled inside. A woman who must have been his wife came to the door holding a baby on her right hip. A young girl stood by her other side, peeking around her mom at the guests. The teenage boy reappeared, and Miguel and his son walked down to the dock to continue work on the boat.

"The prices seem a little high," Dan shared as soon as Miguel was out of earshot.

"Maybe we should ask our driver how much we can negotiate?" Drago suggested.

They agreed for Maria to speak with the driver. He hemmed and hawed but finally gave her a response.

"He says that we should be able to get the price a little below half of what Miguel quoted," Maria told them. "He suggests we offer a third—he thinks it will end up somewhere between a third and half the price."

"Let's review all our options," Jessica suggested. "First, we can fly back to Caracas and it sounds to me like that would be asking for trouble. A country that doesn't like Americans and that is currently in turmoil. Plus, it's a large city. Secondly, we can go to Aruba, then onto Columbia. It's a country that has its own set of problems, not to mention we would travel through dangerous territory in Central America and Mexico. Additionally, we would need to find transportation."

"I agree that there's a high likelihood that we'd run into problems along the way," Chris interjected.

"Or we can have Miguel take us to Aruba," Jessica continued. "Then have his friend fly us and drop us off in Belize."

"Maybe we can catch a boat over to Texas," Dan cut in. "Or worst case, find transportation through Mexico?"

"I would prefer a safe route that didn't include more travel by boat," Maria chimed in.

"Remember that travel in Mexico is difficult and dangerous because of drug lord wars and the government," Drago reminded the others.

"But Belize should be a safe destination," Chris added. "It gets us closer to home. Jamaica is right below Cuba, which would be a problem for us right now. I think Belize gives us options."

"Should we vote?" Jessica asked. "Who likes the idea of going to Belize?"

Everyone waved a hand; there was no need to vote on the other options. They asked Maria to try to haggle with Miguel. Maria warned them that they may have to leave in the middle of the negotiations and to follow her lead. She spoke with their driver and gave him instructions. He nodded his understanding.

They walked down to the dock. Miguel saw them approach and stopped his work and exited his boat. Maria, as planned, offered a third of the price for Miguel's boat trip, and also a third of the price for his friend to transport them to Belize. Miguel shook his head while Maria spoke. After he'd responded, Maria left him and motioned for her friends to come over and join her at the picnic table.

"He's calling his friend. He warned me the price I gave was far too low, but he said he would call and ask his friend if he can reduce the price and if he has room for five people on the flight."

Five minutes later, Miguel approached the picnic table. He spoke with Maria in animated conversation; raised voices on both ends. Finally, Maria spoke to Miguel and motioned for them to leave. The others got up and headed toward the jeep. Chris expected Miguel to come after them—he recalled past negotiations in second and third world countries. But Miguel didn't chase them, and Maria did not flinch.

Maria explained on the ride back to the resort that he had offered half price for both the boat and the plane. She wanted to compromise at forty percent of the original price. Miguel said that the price was too low, and Maria said that they had other options and would consider those.

When they arrived back at the resort, Chris wondered what they would do. Certainly the shuttle flight back to Caracas was too dangerous. He didn't want to stay on the island for months or years. As soon as they entered the lobby, the middle-aged woman approached them and spoke with Maria. Maria smiled as she addressed the others.

"Miguel called the resort asking me to call him back."

Their hosts ushered Maria to their CB radio in a back room. Maria contacted Miguel and listened. She made a couple of comments, and Chris heard "si" a couple times. Maria finished the conversation and turned to the others who were waiting with anticipation.

"Well, both the voyage to Aruba and the plane ride to Belize is at 40 percent of the original price."

There were smiles and congratulatory words for Maria for her handling of the negotiation. But she wasn't done.

"However, we leave this afternoon," Maria went on. "His friend must take off in a few days. Miguel has finished the work on his boat engine, so he and his son will take us to Aruba. Departure is in two hours."

The middle-aged woman was still standing at the counter. Maria had an exchange with her.

"They'll feed us lunch in an hour. We need to pack and bring our things here. Miguel warned me that we have to travel light. Apparently, his friend has a small plane, and with the weight of the five of us, it's almost at his weight limit, including the cargo. We need to pare down our possessions for the flight."

Chris was soon back in his room. He decided to take a hot shower—he wasn't sure when he would have his next hot shower. He enjoyed it, then packed his clothes and belongings. Drago and Jessica were waiting in the lobby when he arrived; five minutes later Dan and Maria arrived. They left their belongings in the lobby and walked to the dining room. Their hosts were already gathered at the table, ready to present a farewell lunch.

The lunch was magnificent. Once they had finished, they walked back to the lobby with the driver. Just fitting everything in the jeep turned out to be a challenge. All six hosts stood out front for hugs and handshakes. They'd only met their hosts the other day, but they were treated as old friends. Chris, Jessica, Dan, Maria, and Drago wedged bags in between and on top of each other as they climbed in the jeep.

Chris turned his head as they left the resort. In different circumstances, it would make for a fun vacation destination. Perhaps he and Carly might return someday. He looked out at the blue ocean and the sun's sparkly reflection. It was a beautiful sight.

Chapter 111

Chartered fishing boat in the Caribbean

CHRIS, JESSICA, DAN, DRAGO, and Maria sat at the table in the galley, looking at the map. They had been on Miguel's boat for almost two days now traveling to Aruba. Miguel had been pushing hard: he hoped to arrive in Aruba that evening.

Miguel shouted below, announcing that they would land in one hour. Miguel's friend Jay-Jay was supposedly already waiting for them at the harbor. He would pick them up and transport them to his plane. Miguel reminded them that Jay-Jay was in a rush to deliver his merchandise.

They had packed the guns, ammunition, and a few changes of clothes. Chris had the antimissile case with one round left. He had determined that this was a necessity as they'd made difficult decisions of what to bring. His reasoning was that it had saved them once before off the Moroccan coast. The missile would have to be part of the deal.

Miguel explained that Jay-Jay had told him that his flight plan would leave Aruba for Jamaica, then hopefully to Belize, and then the Yucatan.

His flight plan could often change depending on business and weather. However, Yucatan was as far north as he would travel. They would learn the final flight plan when they landed in Jamaica. This concerned Chris. He didn't say anything but looked at Dan as Miguel shared.

Miguel confirmed with Jay-Jay that it was not advisable to travel in Mexico by land. Chris and Dan were unsure if traveling by boat to the new Texas Federation was a viable option. Rumors said that the Texas Federation borders were closed to Mexico.

They paid Miguel half of his fee up front when they boarded with the balance due when they landed in Aruba. They had pooled all their cash together and divided up the payments. Maria had the money set aside in her jacket pocket for Miguel. For the airplane travel, they would pay half up front; Drago kept the money in his left pocket. They would pay the balance when they landed in the Cancun area or Belize—Dan had this final payment in his pocket. Chris and Jessica carried the leftover cash with hope that it would cover the balance of their travel costs.

If they had cell coverage in Aruba, Chris planned to call Carly before their departure. Drago and Jessica planned to take the opportunity to call the headquarter office to ensure that the company had contacted the correct departments for Drago so that his visa would be waiting for him. Dan planned to call his boss, Dale, to update him that he and Chris were still en route to the States. Miguel made it sound that they would be pressed for time, so they planned to call while riding to the plane.

Miguel and his son were nice, hardworking, and great hosts under the circumstances. Miguel told them that he and his son would stay the night in Aruba, then return home to Islas Los Roques the next morning. He was very appreciative of the business and thanked them.

Soon they were on deck with their packs, watching the harbor. As they landed, Maria paid Miguel the final installment and thanked him again. He shouted something in Spanish to his son, and Miguel left the dock to escort them. A smile spread on his face when he saw a parked black SUV. He walked to the vehicle. A black man with dreadlocks, big brown eyes, and a few golden teeth jumped out of the car. Miguel greeted Jay-Jay with a half hug and hand slapping, then pointed toward the others. He introduced each one, saying their names out loud.

They all shook hands with Jay-Jay, who proceeded to open the back door of the SUV to place their packs inside. When Chris handed him the case for the missile, Jay-Jay shook his head.

"We have to take this," Chris insisted.

Jay-Jay frowned at first, then smiled, and told them to get inside.

Jay-Jay got them inside the SUV quickly with Drago claiming the front passenger seat. The windows were down, keeping it cool. The five travelers waved goodbye to Miguel as Jay-Jay explained that they had to leave quickly for Jamaica. They would be at the airport in fifteen minutes. Jay-Jay confirmed the price for the flight and Drago pulled out half of the fee and placed it on the console between his seat and the driver's seat.

"This is half of the agreed price," Chris explained. "The balance will be paid when we land in Belize or the Yucatan."

"Which will it be? Belize or Yucatan?" Jessica asked.

Jay-Jay smiled his gold teeth. "Yo, man, won't know till we reach Jamaica."

Chris found cell bars on his phone and dialed Carly. He saw Drago and Dan also search the contact information on their phones. Chris sat in the middle row with Jessica, and Dan and Maria were back in the third row. Chris was thankful that they had some space. After six rings, Carly picked up.

"Hello?"

"Hi, honey, this is Chris. I have Jessica, Drago, Dan, and Maria with me. We have about ten minutes to talk. I'll fill you in, and then let you talk to Jessica."

"Where are you?" Carly asked.

"Aruba. I need you to let me talk for a couple of minutes. We had a series of storms in the Atlantic and we drifted further south, almost to South America. We hit a reef and had to abandon the boat. We navigated by raft to an island with a resort, then chartered a fishing boat. The fishing boat took us to Aruba, and now we're paying to ride on a small private plane to Jamaica, then hopefully continue to either Belize or Yucatan, Mexico. We aren't sure how we'll get home from there, but we'll be close."

"Is everyone okay? When will you know where you'll land?"

"Everyone is fine," Chris assured her. "We won't know until we reach Jamaica. If we have cell coverage in Jamaica, we'll try to call and let you know. If not, we'll try when we land at our final destination."

Chris paused and then asked, "How are you and everyone else?"

"Mark is coming home after his finals this weekend. Ethan should be coming down for the weekend. Abby is doing well but has morning sickness. She and Ryan may try to come down this weekend if she feels well enough. Your father is responding well to chemo, and your mom and my parents are fine. Clark is really responding to farm life. We'll miss him once he starts at Tech."

"But how are *you*?" Chris insisted.

"Physically okay, but I really want you and Jessica home."

"We're getting close, Carly. We're all doing fine. I'm going to hand you to Jessica."

Chris handed the phone over and Jessica started talking to Carly. There was the happy buzz of conversation in the car. Drago spoke with his company while Dan left a detailed voicemail for their boss. Chris looked out the window and saw that it was getting dark. The black SUV moved down the road at a fast clip.

Chris thought they were going to the international airport, but Jay-Jay took some narrow roads without signs. Finally, he turned down a road where a plane sat on a small dirt runway.

"Yo, man, this is the stop."

Jay-Jay drove up to the plane. There were two more men here: one was armed and the other loaded boxes. Jay-Jay pulled up and opened the back door of the SUV. As he climbed out of the SUV, they seized their belongings in the back and carried them to the plane. Jay-Jay did not introduce the other two characters. The one loading boxes set the last box in place and walked over to Jay-Jay, who flipped him the keys. The man climbed into the SUV and drove off.

Jay-Jay looked at them. "Let's get going."

They climbed aboard the plane with guns and backpacks in hand. Drago and Jessica had rifles, Dan had his shotgun, and Chris was the last to board with his rifle, backpack, and the case. The armed guard looked at the case, then back at Jay-Jay.

"Do you really need that, Man?" Jay-Jay asked.

"Yes, we need it," Chris smiled.

Chris climbed in. He noticed that the others buckled in with rifles down and packs near them. Chris found a place to store the case, then took a seat.

Jay-Jay surprised them: he was the pilot. Chris hoped Jay-Jay had flown many successful legs within the Caribbean. Jay-Jay's companion, the armed guard, rode up front next to Jay-Jay in the copilot seat. Chris noticed he had no intention of setting his gun down. Chris glanced back to the rear of the plane and saw stacks of boxes. He wondered what the cargo was, and why such a rush to fly to Jamaica? He was afraid that he knew the answer, but hoped he was wrong.

Jay-Jay told them all to relax: the flight would take a few hours. Once they arrived in Jamaica, he would make a phone call to confirm his next stop. Chris prayed that the plane was maintained well, and was solid enough to get them to their destination. The weather looked clear and perfect for an evening flight.

After a half hour in air, Chris looked over to discover that Jessica and Drago were fast asleep. Dan was awake, but Maria was asleep with her head on his shoulder. Chris knew that Maria was relieved to be off the boat. He nodded at Dan, then rested his head back and closed his eyes. He might not be able to sleep, but he would at least try to rest. He needed to keep an eye on Jay-Jay. Jay-Jay was very friendly, but something was not quite right. Chris guessed that they were transporting illegal contraband to Jamaica.

Chapter 112

Air travel

CHRIS'S EYES WERE CLOSED, but he was wide awake as he sat in the row directly behind Jay-Jay and the guard. Jay-Jay was talking to his guard in a hushed voice, which was difficult for him since he was an animated person. Chris couldn't decipher what was said, but it raised the hair on the back of his neck. He kept his eyes closed, but Chris made sure he didn't fall asleep. Two hours into the flight, he heard some rustling; Drago and Jessica were awake. Opening his eyes wide, Chris looked at them.

"Drago, is your visa all set for entry into the States?"

"Yes, they say it is ready. They asked if I could identify our entry port. I told them I didn't know, but my best guess was Houston, assuming we land in the Yucatan or Belize."

Jessica told Chris about her conversation with Carly; there really wasn't anything new to add. Soon Dan and Maria were awake and joined the conversation. They hadn't had an opportunity to eat dinner that day and they hadn't brought any food for the flight, so Chris felt hungry. Dan unbuckled his seatbelt and walked up to Jay-Jay.

"How much longer until we reach Jamaica?"

"We should be there in two hours."

"Is there anything available to eat or drink on the plane? If not, will we have time to get something at the airport?"

Jay-Jay let loose a huge laugh. "No, not at the airport we're stopping at. We do have a few bottled waters in the back. Help yourself."

Chris looked at Drago and Jessica, then he motioned for them to join him. Chris spoke in a loud voice for Dan and Jay-Jay to hear.

"We'll look for the water bottles."

Chris climbed out of his seat and walked to the back of the plane. He spotted a case of water bottles. When Drago and Jessica had reached him, he selected a few of the water bottles from the case. Chris grabbed each by the arm, head close as he whispered to them.

"Something isn't right. You need to be ready to fight at a moment's notice. I don't know if they'll try to rob us, or what they'll try, but I feel uneasy."

Drago and Jessica took extra water bottles for Maria and Dan. Chris had two water bottles for Jay-Jay and his guard. He walked up to the front of the plane and offered them each a water bottle.

"How long will we stay in Jamaica?" Chris asked Jay-Jay.

"Only to unload, load, and refuel. I'll make a two-minute phone call to confirm our next stop."

Chris walked back to his seat and wondered if they would have cell service. It was doubtful if they weren't landing at a major airport. There was only one type of merchandise he was aware of that needed to be unloaded and loaded at 1:00 a.m. at an obscure landing strip. These guys were clearly distributing drugs.

Chris sat down. He looked over at Drago and Jessica and nodded to them. Dan and Maria weren't aware of what he suspected, but he couldn't talk to them without alerting Jay-Jay.

* * * * *

In the distance were a few lights outlining the coast; Jamaica was on the horizon. The empty resorts were well-lit, even in the evening. Jay-Jay turned the plane away from the resorts and coast, as they started the descent. In ten minutes, he approached a landing strip with just a few lights outlining the runway.

Jay-Jay landed with only two soft bounces, guiding the plane in the direction of a building with fuel pumps. This appeared to be a private strip in the midst of a farmer's crop field. Chris could not determine the crop in the darkness.

Once Jay-Jay stopped the plane and shut the engine, he confirmed they would unload, load, refuel, and then immediately take off again. He pointed at a secondary building for use if they needed a restroom.

Five guys waited patiently on the tarmac. Once the door opened, two men jumped onboard and slid the cargo boxes toward the open door. The other men picked the boxes up and carried them to a small warehouse.

Chris preferred to stay on the plane. Jessica had to use the restroom, along with Maria and Dan. Chris knew Jessica would share their suspicions with Dan and Maria once they walked away from the plane. Chris told them he would wait onboard during their break. Both Drago and Jessica nodded. Chris kept a close eye on the backpacks and their missile.

The guys finished unloading the boxes from the plane, and disappeared into the building with Jay-Jay and the guard following them.

Ten minutes later, Jessica, Drago, Dan, and Maria were aboard the plane. Jay-Jay returned to check instruments on his control panel—the plane was still refueling. Chris was ready to walk over to the restroom, when he suddenly recalled that Dan had vacationed in Cancun.

"Dan, was Cancun the place you vacationed a few years ago?"

"No, it was Cozumel, an island off the Yucatan. It's a decent-size island, but it's slow-paced. Some boats stop by, but it's not crowded like Cancun."

"Is there an airstrip?"

"Yes. Some people can fly in, but they had a boat shuttle from Cancun. That's what we used for arrival and departure."

"Interesting." Chris ended the conversation and thought about what Dan shared.

Chris stepped off the plane and walked toward the restroom. He took the long route in order to walk past the warehouse window. He peered in and noticed an open box. Inside the box were bags filled with a white substance. One of the men pulled a bag out of the box, examined it, and walked to a table. Chris had seen enough without being noticed; he continued and entered the restroom. In minutes, his bladder was empty and he climbed back onto the plane.

Dan was engaged in a conversation with Jay-Jay. The other men were now loading other boxes onto the plane.

"So do you know where we'll land?"

"Yeah, man, we have one small detour, then we'll go north toward Cancun and drop you off."

"Where is the detour?"

"San Pedro. We won't be long. Then we'll head near Cancun in Merida."

Chris knew that San Pedro was a city in Honduras—they'd been warned not to travel there. Merida was more inland than the coastal Cancun.

"Any chance you can go to Yucatan first, then San Pedro?" Chris asked.

"No. I have an anxious customer waiting for us. It won't be a long stop—we'll be back in the air en route to Mexico in no time. If you prefer, I can drop you off in Cancun and then continue to Merida."

Chris didn't say anything. He was concerned that Jay-Jay offered to go to Cancun now instead of Merida as a compromise. For some reason he wanted them to make the trip to San Pedro. Drago and Jessica looked at Chris. He nodded and reclined back in his seat.

The guard climbed into his front seat next to Jay-Jay. The last box was loaded, and the doors to the plane were closed. Jay-Jay finished his instrument check and received a "double thumbs up" from the worker replenishing the fuel. Jay-Jay started the engine, then slowly turned the plane around. He didn't waste time; as soon as the plane was positioned on the runway, Jay-Jay immediately started to accelerate.

Soon they were airborne, heading west in the direction of Honduras. Chris looked at Drago and Jessica. He caught their eyes and then looked down to his right hand which he formed as a handgun. They nodded.

They waited about twenty minutes, until the Jamaican lights were way behind them. Chris took off his jacket and used it to conceal his Glock. He rose slowly from his seat and stepped gingerly toward Jay-Jay and the guard.

Drago and Jessica nodded at Dan and Maria who released their seatbelts with guns up as they followed behind Chris. They knew that they didn't want a Wild West shoot-out while airborne, risking damage to both the plane and pilot.

Chris asked a question as he approached the two sitting in the front. Jay-Jay had his eyes focused straight ahead at the sky, periodically glancing at his instruments. The guard looked over at Chris.

"Jay-Jay, what's the time difference from travel to Yucatan vs. travel to Honduras?"

Jay-Jay looked at him in surprise, wondering why he specifically mentioned Honduras. The guard's eyes met Jay-Jay's, and the guard began to turn his rifle toward Chris. Chris dropped his jacket and revealed the pistol pointed at the guard.

"Jay-Jay, I insist that you take us north to Mexico first. Then you can travel down to Honduras. We don't want to go to Honduras. Miguel told us the route would be Jamaica, then Yucatan or Belize."

"Yo, man, I just have to make the delivery."

The guard made an attempt to surprise Chris—Chris didn't hesitate. He shot twice, and the guard dropped the rifle as he slumped down in his seat. His shirt turned crimson. Chris pointed the Glock on Jay-Jay, who shook his head.

"Yo, man, you don't have to do this."

"I'm sorry, but he shouldn't have made a stupid move. I want you to change course to Cozumel right now. No Cancun, no Merida. You take us to Cozumel. If you take us there now, we'll let you go. If not, we will no longer need you," Chris explained. "We have a pilot that can fly the plane."

Jay-Jay didn't say anything, but he nodded. Chris turned his head toward his companions.

"Drago and Jessica, we need your assistance. Pull the guard out of the chair. If he's dead, lay him down in the cargo area and make sure he doesn't have any weapons. If he has a pulse, try to stop the bleeding. We'll have to keep an eye on him."

They dragged the guard out of the seat. Chris used a towel to wipe the seat clean of blood before he sat in the copilot seat. He kept his gun trained on Jay-Jay.

"Dan?" Chris yelled to the back of the plane. "Can you come up?"

Dan was there in a minute, looking at Chris.

"Dan, you took flying lessons?"

"Yes, but that was awhile ago."

"I want you to carefully frisk Mr. Jay-Jay. Make sure he doesn't have a weapon in his pockets. I want his phone and wallet. Take everything out."

Dan patted him down, starting at the shoulders and working down toward the pant legs. He pulled out a pen and phone from Jay-Jay's shirt pocket.

"Jay-Jay, be still. If you twitch, I may shoot," Chris warned. "Then we'll have Dan flying us to Cozumel."

Dan finished the search. He found a knife and a handgun on Jay-Jay. He handed these to Chris, who kept the cell phone and asked Dan to take the rest of the items. Dan placed the weapons in his backpack, then returned to the front of the plane.

"Dan, we want to head to Cozumel. Will you double check and confirm that we're headed in that direction?"

Dan checked the instruments and confirmed their course. Chris asked Dan to take the seat behind Jay-Jay and watch Jay-Jay pilot the plane and advise them if he saw anything concerning.

"Now tell me"—Chris's eyes were focused on Jay-Jay—"what was waiting in Honduras?"

"A powerful man in San Pedro, a pissed man. I'll be in trouble for this."

"What was going to happen in Honduras?"

"I needed to make my shipment."

"What was going to happen to us?" Chris asked again, irritation in his voice.

"I was asked to bring you. They were going to decide if you stayed or left."

Chris looked at Jay-Jay to continue. When Jay-Jay didn't elaborate, he probed further.

"And ransom us? Kill us? At a minimum, rob us?"

"Yes," was all Jay-Jay said. "This is messed up," he added.

Jessica walked over to report that the guard was alive but had a weak pulse. They applied pressure to try to stop the bleeding, but weren't sure he would make it. Chris shook his head. Even if it was inconvenient, they had to try to keep the man alive.

"Still keep an eye on him," Chris instructed. "If anything changes let us know. We're heading to Cozumel."

They flew in silence for the next hour. Chris had his Glock in hand, resting on his right leg. Dan kept an eye on the instruments, satisfied they were heading in the correct direction. Chris asked him for an update every fifteen minutes, just to be sure.

Drago made his way to the cockpit and sat down next to Dan.

"The guard died. We found a blanket and wrapped him."

Jay-Jay shook his head and then let loose with an outburst.

"You, guys, don't understand. Cozumel airport will have police there who will inspect the plane. We can't land there with a dead body and cargo. They'll throw us in prison."

Jessica and Maria stood between Drago and Dan in the aisle, listening to Jay-Jay's confession.

"Well, we have to get rid of the body and the cargo," Chris responded.

"We can't get rid of the merchandise, or I'll be killed!" Jay-Jay exclaimed. "We'll all be killed."

"I would rather take that chance instead of being arrested by the police in Cozumel," Dan offered his opinion.

Chris looked at Drago, Jessica, and Maria, who all nodded. Chris then glanced over at Jay-Jay, who was mumbling under his breath and shaking his head.

"We need to throw the body and the cargo in the ocean before we land," Chris summarized. "Dan, if Jay-Jay can get the plane low enough over the water, can you hold it steady?"

"Yes. But I'd like to fly it beforehand so I can get a feel for the plane. Perhaps I can get ten or fifteen minutes of flying?"

Chris looked over at Jay-Jay. "Jay-Jay?"

No response.

"Jay-Jay?" Jay-Jay looked over at him.

"This is what we are going to do. Get up and let Dan fly for a while." Chris assumed that Jay-Jay had missed the previous conversation with Dan.

"Then you will take us to a lower altitude over the water," Chris added. "Dan will take over and you and I will throw the body out with the cargo. Jessica and Drago will follow us and keep their guns on you. If you create any problem, they'll shoot you, and we'll throw you out the door with your friend's dead body. Do you understand?"

Chris looked at Maria, Drago, and Jessica sitting behind them. He asked them to secure a life jacket and to buckle in. Dan exchanged seats with Jay-Jay and took control of the plane. Jay-Jay moved to the copilot seat and glowered at Chris.

"Okay, I'm good now," Dan declared after fifteen minutes. "Jay-Jay can take control."

Jay-Jay took control of the plane again. Jessica walked up with two life jackets which she handed to Chris and Dan.

Chris fastened his life jacket as Jay-Jay eased the plane lower toward the ocean. They continued descending until the plane skimmed the ocean. As Jay-Jay leveled off, he relinquished control to Dan.

"I have control; you can drop the merchandise."

Chris motioned for Jay-Jay to rise. Jay-Jay walked to the back of the plane and Chris followed. Chris asked Drago to get out of his seat as he handed him his Glock.

"Keep it pointed on Jay-Jay. If he does anything questionable, shoot him. No questions."

"Go ahead and open the door," Chris instructed Jay-Jay.

Jay-Jay opened the door and looked over at Chris as they walked toward the dead guard wrapped in the blanket. Chris grabbed the legs, and Jay-Jay took the shoulders. Together they approached the door.

"I will count to three. On three, we throw him out," Chris instructed. "One, two, three."

The wrapped body dropped to the ocean, falling below the ocean's surface.

"Now we throw out the boxes."

Drago had the gun trained on Jay-Jay while Chris and Jay-Jay threw out each and every box into the ocean. Chris noticed that Jay-Jay struggled with each box thrown into the water. When they had thrown the final box, Chris paused and looked at Jay-Jay.

"Is there anything else that the police will be concerned with onboard the airplane?"

Jay-Jay shook his head, but Chris asked Jay-Jay again.

"If we have a problem, I'll shoot you in front of the police. You need to be certain that we don't have anything illegal onboard."

Jay-Jay looked at Chris, then pointed to the front of the plane. Jay-Jay confessed he had something under the pilot's seat. Chris reached under the seat and pulled out a small box. Inside were a couple of bags of the white powder and an additional bag of marijuana—Jay-Jay was skimming off of the shipments. Chris walked to the back of the plane and threw both bags out the door and into the ocean.

Chris had another thought. He walked over to his missile case stored in the back, after two minutes he picked up the case with the antimissile launcher. He walked over to the open door and threw the case into the ocean.

Chris motioned for Jay-Jay to close the door. Once secured, they returned to the front of the plane, Jay-Jay reclaimed his pilot seat and brought the plane to a higher altitude. Dan rode copilot and the others went back to their seats. Chris sat behind Dan, with a good view of Jay-Jay and hoping they would arrive in Cozumel.

Chapter 113

Cozumel

JAY-JAY AND DAN APPROACHED the runway. Jay-Jay contacted the radio tower to make them aware of their arrival. Drago and Jessica had found a long bag that Chris repurposed to store the rifles and shotgun. He placed it alongside their luggage and backpacks.

Chris instructed Jay-Jay to fuel up and leave Cozumel immediately. They didn't care where he went, but they did not want him to stay in Cozumel. Jay-Jay asked for additional money to help cover the cost of flying to a new home. He argued that he could never return to Honduras, Cancun, or Aruba ever again. Chris agreed to pay the original price but not a cent more: Jay-Jay would do well to consider that a more than fair offer considering the circumstances.

At 5:00 a.m., the lit runway was in sight. Jay-Jay brought the plane down toward the runway. The wheels touched down gently and Jay-Jay brought the plane forward to a complete stop. A vehicle approached carrying three policemen and a dog; they quickly piled out and pointed their rifles at the airplane door. Chris suggested that they put all their handguns in the bag with the rifles. He opened the bag and they handed him the weapons.

Jay-Jay shut the controls down and opened the door. The guards shouted instructions in Spanish; Maria translated that everyone must get off the plane. They exited single file and the policeman led the dog onto the plane to smell for drugs. Meanwhile, the other two policemen engaged Maria in a lengthy conversation. Finally, Maria turned to her companions.

"They want to understand why we landed here. I told them that we were shipwrecked in the Caribbean near Venezuela, and explained our story about navigating the raft to a populated island, then taking a fishing boat to Aruba and chartering Jay-Jay to take us here. They asked our intentions—I told them our ultimate destination is our home in the States or the new Texas Federation. They laughed; the only flight out of here is the daily flight to Cancun. Only commercial ships from Mexico can land in the Texas Federation, this might not change for two years."

The policeman with the dog leaned out of the airplane and reported to one of the other policemen, who nodded as the dog and policeman walked away. The policeman in charge spoke with Maria, gestured at Jay-Jay, and then Maria gestured at Drago.

She translated for the group as Jay-Jay listened.

"Jay-Jay, you can stay here, pay for fuel, and then leave without checking your passport."

"Jay-Jay, that is the best option," Chris interjected with authority.

"I told them that I have a Spanish passport, and that Drago has a Slovenian passport. The rest of you are from the States," Maria continued. "We'll have to go through their customs check station inside the building. We can grab our bags and head over there now. He warned us that we may be in Mexico for a while."

Drago climbed back on the plane and brought the luggage near the door. He began handing the backpacks and bag off the plane. Once everything was unloaded, Drago made the last payment to Jay-Jay. Jay-Jay didn't thank Drago, and Chris gave him a lingering look as a reminder of what they had discussed.

One guard stayed with Jay-Jay as they waited for the fuel truck. The policeman with the dog walked to a small office about one hundred meters away and disappeared from sight. The policeman in charge said something in Spanish, then turned toward the largest building. He paused at the entrance, then motioned for them to follow him inside.

Drago walked into the building first and the others followed. The officer that escorted them inside, turned, and exited toward a small building across the tarmac. They saw a sign that said Customs; standing beside it were two Mexican uniformed policemen with side arms holstered on their side. Nobody else was in the building except the two middle aged potbellied officials. One sported a mustache, the other wore wire rimmed glasses. Both were of average height.

The man with the mustache spoke in Spanish.

"They will check our passports, and then we separate." Maria translated. "Men go to the right, women go to the left. They will search our bags and if necessary, question us further."

Dan, Chris, and Drago gave her an odd look.

"Why do we need to be separated?" Dan asked.

"I asked—he said that is the procedure."

As the officers checked passports, they spent more time with Drago's and Maria's: Maria translated all questions and responses as they passed the first stage of the customs process. The customs agent with the mustache motioned for the women to follow him into the next room, as the agent with the glasses motioned for the men to follow him. Drago carried the long bag with the ammunition and weapons. Chris tried to envision a scenario where they'd be able to pass through with their weapons.

They opened the backpacks carrying their clothes. The long bag was last to pass inspection. Drago unzipped it to reveal the rifles, shotgun and handguns. The agent didn't spend much time searching this bag, but he spoke to Drago. Drago understood enough to respond. The guard looked at each of them carefully, then motioned for Drago to zip the backpacks up and proceed without the large bag.

Chris was wondering how to rescue their weapons bag when they heard a loud thud, and then a bang against the wall. The agent was startled; he immediately left for the room that contained Jessica and Maria. Drago, Dan, and Chris followed behind. The guard opened the door and froze. Maria held a gun that was pointed straight at him. Dan, Drago, and Chris entered slowly, questioning Maria with their eyes. Jessica stood over the mustachioed agent lying on the floor unconscious.

The bespectacled agent reached for his gun, and Chris immediately clutched his arm. They locked eyes, and the agent froze.

"What happened?" Chris asked.

"We walked in here," Maria began. "The agent looked at our packs and then told us that he would need to pat us down. He was feeling us out and then told us to take our tops off. We refused, and he walked over to force Jessica. She kicked him in the groin. He went down, writhing in pain, and then reached for his gun. Jessica kicked him in the face and knocked him out. His gun fell to the floor, and I picked it up."

The agent standing by Chris spoke to Maria in Spanish. She responded with a lengthy explanation as they went back and forth. Meanwhile, Jessica repacked her backpack.

"The agent is asking me to put the gun down," Maria told them. "He'll need to explain to higher authorities why Jessica struck the agent. He keeps saying that it's individual discretion of the agent to insist on a more invasive search. I don't think Jessica will be treated fairly."

"What should we do?" Dan asked the others.

"I think our stay in Cozumel will be short." Chris had already reached the conclusion.

"My vote is to handcuff the guards, make sure they can't shout for assistance, and then hide them. Then we hustle to get off the island." Chris paused to see if anyone had a better idea.

"I didn't see the Cancun boat shuttle." Chris continued. "Drago, can you check to see if Jay-Jay has taken off? Don't let the police see you. Jessica, find handcuffs to handcuff the agent on the ground with his hands behind his back? Maria, search him and take any weapons; on second thought, take everything out of his pockets, then find something to stuff in his mouth."

Chris looked at the agent standing next to him. He still had his hand on the agent's right arm. With one motion, Chris seized the agent's gun.

"Dan, find the handcuffs. Handcuff his hands behind his back, then pull all personal belongings out of his pockets. Place them with the items that Maria's pulling from the other agent."

In minutes the guards were handcuffed; all their possessions (including car keys, cigarettes, lighter, money clips, gum, and other miscellaneous items) were in a pile. Maria found a clothes bin, and Jessica held the gun on the agents while Maria stuffed socks in their mouths.

"Jay-Jay has taken off," Drago announced as he walked back in. "There aren't any airplanes on the tarmac. The police are in their offices. It's deserted."

Chris located a door on the other side of the room.

"Dan, can you see what that door leads to?"

Dan disappeared for a minute, then returned.

"It's a small office."

"Let's take the bodies into the office and lock the door," Chris suggested as he and Dan moved to escort the standing agent to the office.

"Drago and Jessica, take the two sets of car keys and see if you can locate the agents' cars? I'm guessing there's a nearby parking area. Hopefully one vehicle will be able to transport the five of us."

Drago and Jessica left the room and Dan and Chris walked the agent to the adjacent office. Chris kept the gun on the agent as Dan dragged the unconscious agent into the room. Chris looked over at Maria.

"Maria, will you look for something to clean the blood off the floor?"

Chris discovered a closet door, he motioned for the agent to walk in the closet. Chris followed the agent, confirming the closet was empty with the exception of two boxes. Chris pulled the boxes out of the closet, pushing them in a corner of the office. Dan lugged the body of the other agent into the closet, once inside, they closed the door.

"Chris, let's drag the desk over to block the door," Dan suggested.

Dan and Chris pushed the desk against the door, then walked out of the office and locked the door. Maria found a bottle of cleaning liquid and paper towels in the bathroom; she quickly cleaned the blood off the floor.

"We found a van," Jessica reported when she walked back in. "Drago successfully started it and drove it around to the back door. We need to grab our bags, then leave."

Chris motioned for her to leave with Maria and Dan, who walked to the customs area and located the long bag. Jessica had her backpack plus Drago's. Maria held her backpack and Dan's. Chris took the towels from Maria and told them he would be right behind them.

Chris worked on cleaning the last few spots on the floor. Unless someone examined the floor closely, they wouldn't be able to see blood. Chris picked up the old towels and cleaner bottle and threw them in the trash. Then he picked up his pack and walked out the back door.

Six feet from the door, Chris saw a rusted fifteen-year-old van idling. Drago sat in the driver's seat, Jessica rode shotgun, and Maria and Dan sat in the far back.

The side door was open. Chris hopped in, put his pack on the empty seat next to him, and closed the van door in one motion. He nodded at Drago, and Drago pulled away from the building to access the only road out of the parking lot. The clock on the van said 5:45 a.m. This was supposedly a sleepy island. Chris hoped they had some time before people started their day, and left for work. He hoped it would be hours before the custom agents' absence was noted.

"Where do we go?" Drago asked once they had left the parking lot.

"We need to find a dock and then a boat," Dan suggested.

Jessica and Chris nodded. Drago approached a fork in the road. One road appeared to head in the direction of the ocean and Drago chose it. Within minutes, they reached the coast. Drago drove along the coastal road until Jessica spotted a small harbor with a dock. Drago navigated the van toward the dock and pulled off the road into a dirt parking area.

"I saw two people down there on a fishing boat," Jessica reported.

"We need to see if we can pay one of them to take us to the mainland," Dan spoke loudly from the rear. "If we can pay more than what they expect to make from an average day of fishing, perhaps they'll be interested."

"Great idea," Chris agreed. "Why don't you and Maria go down to the dock. We need to get off the island immediately."

Maria and Dan clambered out of the back seat. They walked cautiously to the dock, backpacks slung over their shoulders. They conversed with the two men on the dock for about five minutes. Chris was concerned that the fishermen were refusing the offer, but Maria remained on the dock as Dan returned.

"We agreed on the price. It was a little more than we wanted to pay, but he and his brother are willing to leave now. We push off in less than ten minutes."

Dan pulled the long bag out of the van and started down the path. Chris was climbing out when inspiration struck.

"Drago, why don't you drive the van a half mile from here, somewhere near a residence. You can jog back. It may confuse the police into thinking a local stole the car—if you leave the keys in the car. I'll take your backpack to the boat and we'll wait for you. Hurry!"

Drago agreed and drove off as Jessica and Chris walked to the fishing boat. This boat was smaller than Miguel's or Dan's boat that had sailed them across the Atlantic and Caribbean successfully. They nodded hello to the two brothers as they climbed aboard. Dan showed them where to store the backpacks; Maria was already in the cabin area storing the bags. Chris left the packs next to the long bag as Jessica went back on deck to wait for Drago. Chris pulled out his money and handed it to Maria. She divided it in half, kept half and handed Chris the balance. Maria and Dan left to pay the fishermen the first installment.

Chris put the remaining money in his pocket and pulled out his phone. He had cell reception! It would be early, but he called Carly.

She answered on the fourth ring, "Chris?"

"Yes. I only have a couple of minutes. We landed in Cozumel, but we had problems. We're taking a fishing boat to the mainland."

It was quiet for ten seconds. "Isn't Mexico unsafe? We keep hearing about drug lords and military battles on the news."

"Yes, it's not our first option, but we're closer to the States. It's urgent for us to get off the island. I can fill you in later."

"Where are you going to go? Is Jessica okay?"

"We haven't figured that part out yet. I'll call back when I can. We're all fine. Is Mark home?"

"Yes, and Ethan will arrive today. Also Abby and Ryan."

Chris saw Drago jog down the dock toward Jessica. The fishermen brothers were ready and waiting for them to climb aboard.

"Honey, we're pushing off. I love you. Tell all the others I love them too."

There was silence. Chris added, "We're getting closer to home."

They said their goodbyes. Drago and Jessica came below deck and Chris pulled out the rifle bag and brought out the handguns, handing one to Drago and Jessica. He left the rifles in the bag, then walked out of the cabin to join Dan and Maria on deck. Jessica handed Dan his gun and holster. One of the fishermen looked at them and Maria provided an explanation.

The boat owner nodded and went back to work. Dan asked Maria what she said.

"I told him that we've had a lot of unfortunate experiences and that you all feel naked without your guns. And that they don't need to worry: we don't want their boat, just a safe passage."

Chris looked back as the harbor became smaller. It was still early in the morning for Cozumel. With any luck the agents wouldn't be found for another three hours; by then they would have disappeared on the mainland, out of sight. They needed to consider their next destination now. They could not stay in Cancun. The Mexican police would rank this as the most likely destination. Chris suggested they go down into the cabin for a group discussion.

Once below, they sat down. Dan pulled out his Caribbean map.

"Where do we go next?" Maria asked.

They discussed going north through Mexico but were warned this was a bad idea as it was not safe. They ended up with two possibilities: one was to head south to Belize. Belize City was a problem area, but the country spoke English. They could blend in better because the country was diverse with a mix of blacks, Mayan Indians, Hispanics, and some white. Outside of Belize City they should be safe.

The other option was to go further into the Yucatan. Other than Cancun, they could hide in a village in the Yucatan, where they might be safe. But they would be stuck there for a while, and Maria was the only one of the group that spoke fluent Spanish. After discussion, they agreed to head to Belize.

They climbed back on deck and enjoyed the fresh air. It was a rare opportunity to relax until they reached the mainland; then they would have to be sharp. They agreed that three of them should take advantage of the situation and nap. Chris took watch with Dan. They had Dan's map out and looked over logistics of how they would move after landing on shore. They kept an eye out for Mexican police, boat or air. Chris wanted to keep watch on the brothers to ensure that the fishermen would not be tempted to radio the Mexican authorities.

Chapter 114

Mainland

MARIA SPOKE WITH THE fishermen, and they agreed to drop them off at Akumal, south of the famous Playa del Carmen, which was also south of Cancun. The distance was less than twenty-five miles.

In an hour, they approached their drop-off. One of the fishermen announced, "Akumal." Chris and Dan walked down to the small cabin and awakened Drago, Jessica, and Maria. Gathering their packs and the long bag, they went up onto the deck. Chris and Dan had decided to double the fishermen's money—they instructed Maria to request that the fishermen keep the voyage quiet. The fishermen agreed to fish and take their time returning to Cozumel.

They stood on the dock and waved to the two fishermen departing into the sea. As they stepped off the dock, Dan and Chris proposed their plan to Drago, Jessica, and Maria.

"We should look for a bus to Chetumal," Dan began. "Chetumal is located on the Mexico and Belize border. From there, Chris remembers a ferry there that runs to Ambergris Caye, an island in Belize. We need to get out of Mexico quickly. The agents at the small airport will be upset and vindictive once they are found."

"From Ambergris Caye, we can ferry to Belize City," Dan continued. "But Belize City is not a great area—we don't want to spend much time there. When we're in Ambergris Caye, we can plan our last route back to the States."

After everyone agreed with the plan, they started walking down the street. Maria asked locals for directions to the bus station. The information was consistent and the group followed Maria. An idea popped into Chris's head as they approached the bus ticket window.

"We should buy our bus tickets individually or in groups of two; we should also board separately and split up to sit in different locations on the bus. Drago and Jessica could be paired as a couple, same with Maria and Dan. I should appear to be alone. The police bulletin will profile us as a group of five—this may help us go undetected."

"I can take the rifle bag," Chris volunteered. "I think we should pack our handguns in our backpacks. The bus will require me to check and store the rifle bag underneath because of its size, but we need to be armed and mobile in case something happens."

"It might be less suspicious if Drago and I carry the rifle bag and load it on the bus," Jessica suggested. "A couple traveling together seems less suspicious with luggage."

Chris and the others agreed, so Drago reached over and picked up the rifle bag.

They walked around a corner to where they weren't visible, then quickly opened and transferred the guns into their backpacks. They left for the ticket counter a minute spaced apart, so it didn't appear as though they were traveling together.

Maria and Dan went first to buy their bus tickets. Dan left the kiosk to briefly stand by Jessica; he handed her his bus ticket to disclose the route information. She memorized the information, then went to buy her own tickets. Dan walked over to a bench and sat next to Chris to share the ticket information once more.

They waited for the bus on separate benches. Chris took the opportunity to call Carly and tell her about the plan to reach Ambergris Caye. They had vacationed in Belize a few years earlier with Mark and Jessica, so Carly felt a bit relieved with the updated plan.

After an hour, the bus arrived. Maria and Dan climbed the steps so as to be the first to board the bus. A few people boarded after Maria and Dan, then Drago placed the rifle bag in the underneath luggage area and boarded the bus with Jessica. The two sat a few rows behind and across from Maria and Dan. Chris waited until several passengers had boarded, then climbed the stairs and walked to the back of the bus and chose a window seat.

The bus filled up quickly. A local woman carrying a baby took the seat next to Chris. In some ways, this camouflaged Chris—if you looked in his direction, you would see the woman and baby, then Chris wearing a cap that covered most of his face. It would be easy to assume they were traveling together.

The bus ride was scheduled to take four hours. Chris leaned against the window to doze, his backpack lying at his feet. Chris woke from time to time and saw Dan asleep by the window, Maria's head on his shoulder. Jessica napped with her head resting on the window while Drago stayed awake, vigilant as he looked out the window. Drago was cognizant of who was getting on and off the bus at each stop as they traveled further south toward Belize.

Upon reaching Chetumal, they departed the bus. Drago retrieved the long bag, and the driver closed the baggage doors and took off for his next stop.

Maria and Dan were the first off. She quickly asked a local person the direction for the ferry to Belize. Once the others were off the bus, they proceeded to the ferry. Jessica and Drago followed twenty meters behind. As soon as Chris made it safely off the bus, they continued the journey to the ferry at a faster clip. When they were two blocks from the bus stop, Dan and Maria waited for the others to join them so they could travel together.

Chris stopped them about ten minutes into their walk. He recalled that Belize had strict gun laws, so they discreetly transferred their handguns into the rifle bag. Chris offered to carry the heavier bag.

When they reached the ferry, Maria was first at the ticket window with Dan as the others hung back. Dan motioned for the others to hurry to the window. Once they were near, Dan advised that there was one ferry leaving that day for Belize, and it was leaving in ten minutes. Their timing was perfect, but they needed to board now. Dan pointed toward a white ferry boat and told them to wait in the adjoining area. In a couple of minutes, Maria and Dan distributed ferry tickets to each of them.

They climbed aboard and handed their tickets to a man dressed in a white uniform. Chris handed the rifle bag to a crew member to store it in the luggage compartment. Keeping possession of their backpacks, they walked along the deck and found seats. Maria explained that this was a three-hour ferry ride: they would land at Ambergris Caye around 5:00 p.m.

On the ferry ride they developed a plan upon landing in Ambergris Caye. First, they would find a place to stay that was safe and low profile, then they would find dinner. During dinner they would develop a plan for their return to the States.

Chris sought out the crew member that had packed the rifle bag. He walked over to the young Hispanic man dressed in white, who was now standing alone. He recalled that the man had spoken some English when he had handed him the bag.

"How long do you dock in Ambergris Caye?"

"Just one hour. We're told to get something quick to eat, then we start boarding passengers back to Chetamul."

"You know the bag I handed you to pack?" Chris gambled with his words. "I would rather not have the custom agents in Belize looking through that bag. Is there a way to get the bag ashore without going through inspection?"

The crewmate was quiet and Chris guessed what he was thinking.

"I know it will be a hassle. I'm willing to pay for the trouble. I assure you, we are not carrying drugs."

The crewmate was still quiet. Chris thought it could go either way, so he decided to keep trying.

"What would be a fair price?"

"Two hundred dollars sounds fair," the man responded.

Chris nodded, swallowing his panic at the large fee. Their cash was depleting fast, but he shook the young man's hand.

"Good. What's your plan?"

"Leave the boat without the bag. When I finish here, I'll take the bag like it's my own. When you get off this boat, you'll walk two blocks straight ahead, then turn left. There's a restaurant with a bar area. Sit down at an outside table, and I'll come by and drop the bag where you are sitting."

Chris nodded and fished out a hundred-dollar bill. He shook the man's hand again, leaving the Ben Franklin in his palm.

"The second hundred dollars will be paid when the bag is safely delivered."

* * * * *

The weather was calm and the afternoon ferry made for a pleasant ride. The island of Ambergris Caye loomed ahead as the crew prepared for landing. The captain announced that they would disembark in ten minutes.

As the boat docked, Chris identified custom agents waiting for them at the edge of the pier. He took only his backpack as he followed the line of passengers. The agent looked at his passport, surprised that he had arrived from Mexico. He asked what he was doing in Belize.

"Vacation." Chris wanted to say as little as possible.

The agent looked through his backpack thoroughly, noticing only two outfits and nothing else. He studied Chris suspiciously, then reluctantly let him go.

Chris walked ahead thirty meters and then pulled off to the side, pretending to fiddle with the straps of his pack. Instead he opened the pack and rearranged his clothes.

Chris saw that Jessica was next in line. She walked up with Drago to the other agent. He checked their backpacks, then studied her passport and then Drago's passport. He commented to the other agent, who glanced over and responded with a shrug of his shoulders. The agent conversed with Jessica before releasing them. They passed Chris and stopped on the opposite side of the dirt road in front of a food stand; pretending to look at the menu from a distance.

Maria and Dan came to the same agent that had reviewed Chris's passport. He searched their bags, then let them through. As soon as Dan and Maria passed the checkpoint, Chris walked forward and passed Jessica and Drago. He made a left turn down the street, following the crewmate's instructions. The others followed him at a distance.

Chris found a table on the edge of the establishment with six empty wooden chairs around a weathered table. Chris chose a chair underneath some shade. Drago and Jessica sat across from him, and a minute later Dan and Maria joined them. A waitress came by as soon as Maria sat down. They ordered drinks and perused the menu.

The waitress brought their drinks and they ordered sandwiches. After the waitress left, Jessica told Chris that the agent had asked the other agent the name of the American that had gone through. Then he'd asked if they were related since the unusual names were the same. She'd confirmed that Chris was her father. He'd asked why they were visiting, and she replied, "*Vacation,*" as planned. She told him that the agent was suspicious that they didn't have a hotel reservation when he asked where they were staying. The agent had demanded they return to the station later that day to confirm where they were staying. He'd written down both of their passport numbers.

Ten minutes later, Chris saw the crewmate turn the corner and head toward them, rifle bag in hand. Chris pulled out five twenty-dollar bills from his wallet, setting the dollars on the edge of the table. The young man walked by their table without acknowledging them, picked up the one hundred dollars, stopped five feet at an adjacent table beyond Chris, and dropped the bag. He pulled out a pack of cigarettes, lit one, then proceeded down the road with the bag left behind.

Chris stood up, stretched, and walked over to push the bag close to his chair. He set his backpack on top of the long bag. Chris needed to use the restroom and excused himself. As he passed by the bar to the restroom, he saw the waitress bring the sandwiches to the table. Two minutes later he walked back past the bar. Two men were at the bar; it was obvious they'd had a few too many drinks. One of them pushed away from the bar.

"Okay, I'm done. I need to use the restroom, then I'm ready to head back to Caye Caulker."

Chris passed them and then hesitated. Caye Caulker was a sleepy island not too far away. It was not as busy as Ambergris Caye. Jessica and Drago had to check back with the customs agent—a risk. Turning around, he approached the man who'd just spoke.

"Excuse me. I just heard that you were heading to Caye Caulker. My friends and I were talking about how we would love to see that island. It's supposed to be very relaxed there. Do you recommend it?"

The man broke out in a huge smile. His friend was now by his side.

"Yes, it's great for living. I come over here for business sometimes, then head back to Caye Caulker. Most of my business is out of Belize City, but I come over to Ambergris about twice a month."

"Hey, if we paid you a small token, would you consider taking us over to Caye Caulker?"

The guy looked at his friend and then over to the table where Jessica, Drago, Dan, and Maria sat eating lunch.

"Sure, why not? Are you ready to go?"

"Yes, as soon as we can settle our bill. What can we pay you?"

The man looked at his friend and tried to think—this was difficult considering his condition. Finally, he pointed at a bottle of whiskey.

"Buy us a bottle of that fine whiskey, and we'll be square."

Chris motioned the bartender over and asked to buy the bottle of whiskey. Chris pointed toward his table and asked the bartender to put it on his tab. The two new friends said that they needed to visit the restroom. Chris handed them the bottle, then walked back to his table.

"Eat fast. We're moving out in two minutes, or whenever those two leave the restroom."

Chris sat down, grabbed his sandwich and took a huge bite as he stuffed in a couple fries.

"What's happening?" Jessica asked for the group that was chewing.

Chris took another bite and spoke with his mouth full.

"We're taking a boat ride to Caye Caulker. I'm nervous that the custom agents will do a background check on us and look at recent reports from Mexico. These guys at the bar are shuttling back to Caye Caulker—where they live. Seriously, eat up. We need to leave soon."

"What was the price?" Dan asked, concerned about their dwindling cash situation.

"They wanted a bottle of whiskey." Chris took another bite, chewed, and swallowed.

"Look, we need to go somewhere safe to reset and figure out how to get to the States," Chris added between bits. "Nothing happens in Caye Caulker, and we can easily hop to Belize City. If we need to, we can go to a more remote place within Belize."

Chris managed another bite before he continued. "Reminder that they don't like guns here. It's a crime to carry one—we will have to be discreet."

Chris had now eaten half of his sandwich between discussion. "I think we need to hold onto the guns until we safely reach the States."

The others were quiet as they ate. Chris saw the men walk out of the restroom. He put on his backpack and reached for the rifle bag, and the remainder of his sandwich. The others rose from the table as the men walked over to introduce themselves.

The local men left for their boat with Drago, Maria, and Jessica close behind. Dan pulled out some cash from his pocket and put it on the table to pay for lunch and the bottle of whiskey. Chris followed, sandwich in hand. They hadn't eaten much for two days: he was determined to finish his sandwich!

The men walked to a different dock about a half mile away and boarded their boat with their five guests behind them. Chris placed the rifle bag with the backpacks below in the cabin. The man with the bottle of whiskey went immediately below to safely pack it while his friend prepared to push off.

When the man came back up on deck, he mentioned their backpacks. "You guys don't pack a lot, do you?"

"We're only planning a night or two on Caye Caulker," Chris replied. "We'll return to Ambergris Caye, where we have the rest of our belongings." Chris wanted to change the subject. "After you push off, can you give us your favorite restaurants and things to do on Caye Caulker?"

Chris got the men talking about Caye Caulker and then their life story, deflecting the conversation away from themselves. Before they knew it, they were approaching Caye Caulker. As Chris remembered, there weren't police or custom agents at the dock. He recalled the only officials they had seen on their vacation were the officials sitting in boats at the reef, checking permits. They were diligent about protecting their tourist industry that revolved around scuba diving and snorkeling, ensuring that each visitor had purchased a permit.

The new friends invited them out for drinks that evening, but the sun was setting and they'd had little sleep the past two days. They asked for a rain check, and the men looked disappointed. The skipper recovered and gave Chris his business card, stating that he would head to Belize City and southern Belize in the morning, but would be back to Caulker in three days. Chris told him that if they decided to stay longer, they would try to catch up for drinks. They thanked them and walked off. Jessica recalled the layout of the small island and took the lead, guiding them to some local hotels and B&Bs. They decided that they would like one bedroom for Dan and Maria, and either a three bedroom for Chris, Jessica and Drago or a two bedroom with a sofa bed. They strolled down the dirt road a couple of blocks to get their bearings.

As they stood on the dirt road, they chose their top three locations based on exterior appearance. Maria and Jessica inquired on price and looked at the rooms; the guys agreed to follow their recommendation. While they waited outside, Drago found a tiny market and went inside to buy three cold beers. The clerk popped off the tops and Drago walked out seconds later with cold drinks. They sat at an empty picnic table under a tree overlooking the blue water.

They waited thirty minutes. A couple of times they would see the ladies walk out and step over into the next establishment. Finally, the women returned. Their first choice had two rooms side by side, both with two bedrooms. They could pay cash without sharing their passports. They gathered the cash for a two-night stay. They informed the manager that they might stay longer.

They checked into the rooms. Drago planned to stay in the extra room with Dan and Maria. The rooms were very nice and the complex included a small pool area. They had a view from the roof to the ocean water on both sides of the small and narrow island.

After checking in, they decided to explore the island. Although they'd eaten only two hours prior, they voted a snack as a high priority during their stroll. They stashed their handguns under their pillows and pushed the rifle bag under Drago's bed before they left their rooms.

They walked down the dirt road, enjoying the pedestrian-only traffic. Chris recalled from their past vacation that only a couple of service trucks were allowed on the island.

The lack of world tourism had also affected the island. Chris commented to Jessica that there were less people on the street than when they had vacationed a couple of years ago. Chris saw locals beginning to gather at some of the restaurants and bars.

"Do we want to spend time in a restaurant tonight?" Maria asked the group.

After some discussion, the final vote was to stop at a local market to buy some fruit and bottled water, then walk back to their complex. They shopped quickly, returned to their rooms, washed the fruit, then climbed up on the roof to enjoy the view.

The stars were shining, and they could feel the trade winds blow. The smell of fresh salt air was intoxicating. Looking down, they could see light reflecting on the water. They were together, but sat alone in silence.

"What is the plan for tomorrow?" Dan spoke, breaking the silence.

"I think we should split up and explore all possible options to travel by boat or plane from Belize to the States," Chris shared. "We can consider a ferry to Belize City as an option. I still think we should try to avoid Mexico."

Chris finished his bite of banana. "We need to consider that we may be flagged by a Belize custom agent when we try to leave Belize."

That was the end of the conversation. The five tired travelers left and quickly fell asleep in their rooms.

Chapter 115

Searching routes

DRAGO WOKE UP EARLY. He took advantage of the time and walked two blocks to the store and purchased a bag of coffee and some pastries. He walked over to Chris and Jessica's room and knocked on the door. Jessica answered and Drago entered the kitchen area to prepare a pot of coffee. Within minutes, Dan and Maria walked down the hall to join the others as they ate fruit and pastries, enjoying the ocean view.

This day was to be slow and relaxing. They would approach any service company with access to a boat or plane for potential passage to the States. They planned to also inquire if Belize City airport might have flights to the States soon. In the past, Houston to Belize City was a frequent air route. Dan and Maria would work as a team and take one side of the island; Chris, Drago, and Jessica would make up the second team and work the other half of the island. Chris and Jessica knew they had to be extra cautious since the custom agents had their last name. Chris and Jessica bought wide-brimmed hats at a local store: the hats covered a good portion of their face and hopefully made them less recognizable. Chris was also pleased with the sun protection.

They dressed in T-shirts, shorts, and sandals: an attempt to blend in with the locals. Business didn't open until midmorning, so they enjoyed the view a little longer and took a second cup of coffee. The plan was to reconvene for a later lunch at 2:00 p.m. at a rustic spot only a block from where they were staying.

Chris, Drago, and Jessica took turns approaching the businesses—scuba diving and snorkeling excursions, fishing excursions, and private charter boats. The businesses didn't venture outside their territory, and certainly kept within Belize. The story was the same: business was slow. But not slow enough to consider a voyage to the Texas federation. They had some tourism within the surrounding countries in Central America—just enough to stay afloat. Until the world became safer and the economy returned close to normal, businesses would struggle.

Chris engaged a middle-aged woman in discussion at a charter boat service. She looked bored and had time to talk. She confirmed that flights from Belize City to Houston were suspended. She heard it would be at least three months—maybe longer—before regular flights resumed. She laughed at the thought of taking her boat north toward Mexico or the Texas Federation. It was not even worth considering the risk.

Chris, Jessica, and Drago finished canvassing their section of the island. Jessica noticed when it was about 1:45 p.m., so they walked over to their designated lunch spot and sat down at the establishment's table. Thirty minutes later, Dan and Maria appeared.

"Any luck?" Dan asked. The response was three heads shaking slowly back and forth.

"We didn't uncover a solution, either." Dan sighed. "We're late because we decided to speak with each person on the dock. We received confirmation that there are large ships in Belize City—used mostly for commerce. The routes are between their Caribbean neighbors. We were warned again to be careful traveling in Belize City."

Chris reported that the airport wouldn't run flights to the States for at least the next few months. Dan and Maria confirmed they'd heard similar news.

"I guess we'll just have to stay here for a few months," Maria blurted out. She was trying to be uplifting, but it didn't hit the mark.

They ordered lunch and did their best to enjoy the food and small talk.

After lunch, they strolled back to their rental units. Jessica and Drago elected to check out the beach and Maria decided to lay by the pool. Chris went grocery shopping again—before everyone dispersed, he solicited their input, and made a short grocery list.

Chris found most of the items on the list and returned to the rental. He stored the perishables in the small refrigerator and left the packaged and canned items on the kitchen counter. Walking down the stairs to the pool, Chris saw Maria swimming laps as Dan lay under the shade of an umbrella. He dragged a chair over from a nearby table and sat down next to Dan.

"We're starting to run low on cash. We may need to visit a bank or ATM in Belize City. While we're there, we should inquire about chartering a boat or plane out of Belize. We might have more success at the harbor."

"That may be a good plan." Dan propped himself up on an elbow. "We can leave the others to relax for the day. We can take the early shuttle over tomorrow morning and take the shuttle back in the evening."

Chris moved over to an extended lounge ten feet away and took a long nap by the pool. When he heard voices, Chris started to return to consciousness. He opened his eyes to see Drago and Jessica sitting nearby, sharing their beach experience with Dan and Maria.

Dan disclosed the plan for the next day. Jessica, Drago, and Maria wanted to travel with them to Belize City, but Dan explained that five of them might be too noticeable. Chris suggested that they canvas the island again to see if new boats arrived in Caye Caulker. They reluctantly agreed. Jessica and Drago offered to show Maria the "split," the narrow waterway that split the island in two—formed during a hurricane years prior.

Chris left the pool area and walked down the road a few blocks to the dock to confirm shuttle times to Belize City. The shuttle would arrive at 9:30 a.m. and leave at 10:00 a.m. for Belize City. He walked back to inform Dan.

They decided to cook dinner in the apartment and then bring their dinner to the rooftop to eat and enjoy the sunset view. It was beautiful and relaxing to feel the trade winds gently blowing.

After dinner, Chris called home with Jessica sitting next to him. Ethan, Mark, Abby, and Ryan were visiting the farm and they were eating supper. Jessica and Chris sat alone on the roof while Dan, Drago, and

Maria took the dirty dishes back down to the apartment. Chris's phone was on speaker as they spoke with their family.

"If you can't figure out how to get back home, we'll have to come get you." Mark joked.

"One of my friend's parents have a boat docked in Houston. I'm sure we could head over," Ethan added.

Chris and Jessica laughed. Chris shared their plans for the next day: they would continue to seek transportation options out of Belize City. The report from Texas was good, and the grandparents shared some stories.

As they hung up, Chris looked over and saw a smile on Jessica's face. It was therapeutic for them to talk to the family. Chris thought how they needed to get home. It had been a while; he was tired of the nomadic life, and he missed Carly very much. He always joked with Carly about packing their roller bags to embark on a long vacation around the world, but he wondered if he would ever want to travel again. At the very least, he would need some time before they traveled.

Chapter 116

Belize City

CHRIS HAD A GOOD night's sleep and felt well rested. He and Dan strolled down toward the dock wearing their backpacks. Chris wore his hat and snacked on a banana as they walked along the main dirt road. Chris contemplated about bringing a gun on the trip, finally deciding to carry one in his pack. They'd been warned often about how perilous it was in Belize City, and he thought about visiting the bank or ATM and walking around with money. The water shuttle between the two Belizean ports was a short trip that wouldn't require any police inspection.

They were a block away when Chris looked ahead to see how many people were gathered at the ticket office. It was a small queue of about eight people and there were about twenty-five minutes until departure. The shuttle had just arrived from Belize City and people were exiting the shuttle and walking off the dock.

Chris froze and grabbed Dan's arm. Two armed custom agents walked from the water shuttle and approached the ticket kiosk. They politely cut in line at the window and showed papers to the person inside the kiosk.

Chris motioned to Dan to cross over to the opposite side of the street. As they walked past the ticket kiosk, they slipped into a shop and pretended to look at clothing merchandise. They kept their eyes glued to the ticket window. The two agents left a few papers at the kiosk, then headed down the street away from Chris and Dan. The agents split up, each working a different side of the street. They approached each establishment and showed the piece of paper.

Chris and Dan walked across the street to the kiosk that now had a line four deep. Chris received a dirty look as he walked up to the front of the line to look at the paper lying on the counter. It had his face and Jessica's face with their last name printed underneath their photos with the words "Possible Fugitives." He stepped hurriedly over to Dan without drawing attention.

"They have my picture and Jessica's on those papers. They're canvassing the island to see if anyone has seen us. We need to head back to the others. This island is small—the chance that someone will recognize us is high. We need to leave the island now."

They couldn't go back down the beach street in the direction where the agents were traveling. The agents had five blocks to travel before making it to their rental. Dan and Chris walked a block over to the main street, then ran four blocks and slowed back to a brisk walk before cutting back over to the beach street. They ran up the stairs. Chris and Dan knocked on their respective doors and Maria and Jessica answered within seconds.

"Pack up!" Chris barked. "We need to be out in five minutes. I'll explain later—the Belize police are coming down the street looking for us."

Fortunately, they didn't have many items to pack; they were ready to go in four minutes. Chris led them down the stairs and out of the complex. They walked over to the main street and then cut over, stopping a half block from the shuttle boat kiosk. Chris noticed the police had covered two blocks and were halfway to their complex.

"Maria and I will buy five tickets to Belize City," Dan offered. "You three stay here."

Chris looked at his watch. They had seven minutes before the shuttle departed. He smiled at Jessica and Drago.

"I was ready to leave this island anyway," Jessica replied.

"Jessica, we need to keep our hats on low," Chris told her. "We should try to avoid eye contact if possible."

Dan and Maria left the kiosk with the tickets and walked to the side of the building, out of eyesight of the person manning the kiosk. Dan nodded and Chris, Jessica and Drago walked over to Dan and Maria. Dan handed Drago a ticket and told him to go board. When Drago climbed onboard, he handed the rifle bag to the crew member for storage. Dan handed Jessica a ticket, and Maria and Jessica boarded as a pair. Dan and Chris would board last.

Chris handed his ticket to the captain and kept his head down. With his wide brimmed hat down low, his face wasn't noticeable. He stored his backpack in the baggage area, noticing where Drago had placed the rifle bag. He placed the backpack alongside it. He found a seat in close proximity to the others, but pretended he wasn't part of a group. Drago did the same, giving the impression he was traveling solo.

The shuttle left the dock on schedule and they were on their way to Belize City. They passed some very small islands; some were inhabited and others consisted of mostly mangroves.

Soon they were approaching the Belize City dock. They left the boat in the same groups that they had boarded. Jessica and Maria walked down the long dock, then pulled over to the side of a building. Drago was next and he walked off, then paused to stand next to passengers sorting through stacked luggage at the base of the dock.

Chris and Dan walked slowly off the boat with their heads down. Chris pretended to search for something in his unzipped backpack as he walked slowly past the women. Dan and Chris stopped about forty meters beyond Jessica and Maria. There weren't any custom agents on the dock, nor did they see any police.

Drago bounded over in five minutes with his pack over his shoulder, the long rifle bag in hand. He kept walking and the others followed at a distance until they were two blocks away, then they huddled together.

The first priority was to find a bank or ATM where they could each withdraw money. They agreed that an ATM was safer than a bank. Then, they would check to see if any boats were heading to the States, or if they could charter a boat. If that didn't work, they would try to cab over to the airport to see if there were small private planes available to charter. They agreed that they wouldn't spend the night in Belize City.

Jessica entered a nearby store with Drago and asked a worker for the closest ATM. In four blocks, they found the ATM. Each pulled out the maximum dollar amount allowed before walking to the harbor.

Here they divided up again. Dan and Maria planned to check the schedules of commercial boats. The commercial dock was a good distance away, so they would cab over. Chris, Drago, and Jessica would solicit private boats.

They determined a time limit of three hours and arranged to meet back at a designated coffee shop at the closest harbor. It was now 11:00 a.m. Dan hailed a cab and left with Maria.

Chris switched off with Drago carrying the rifle bag. Walking along the shore, they didn't find too many people. A few worked on their boats, others looked as though they had just come in from the ocean, and a few seemed to be prepared to head out. They didn't approach a boat unless it was over thirty feet long per Dan's guidance—this limited the number of prospects.

Because of the global situation, boat owners were not interested in heading through Mexican waters toward the former United States. They had heard horror stories of boats being held for weeks in the States, waiting for clearance. The new Texas Federation had issued a warning to international boats and planes: there would be a long delay. They were working on improving the process—in a few months, it would be substantially better. Carly had told Chris that the new government had a new system scheduled for installation, but it wouldn't be in place until fall. A few boats were leaving for Honduras.

Leaving Belize to travel south toward Honduras was not even in discussion. It simply wasn't safe. Chris could see the dejection on Drago and Jessica's faces after each rejection. He reminded them that they only needed one viable path to the States. When they finished canvassing two docks, it was 2:00 p.m. They were late to meet Dan and Maria, so they walked briskly to the designated coffee shop.

Dan and Maria sat at one of three tables outside the coffee shop. They each had a cup in hand, packs stacked on one empty chair to the side. Chris asked Drago and Jessica what they wanted to drink before walking up to the counter. He brought back three drinks and set them on the table before joining the conversation.

Dan explained that there were limited ships going to the States. There were a few ports open at that time—this number would expand in the coming months. The issue was that the crew could not enter the States.

The current procedure required dropping off the cargo and then immediately heading back to sea. They found one boat bringing cargo to Cuba and Jamaica, and then ending up in the Bahamas, but this journey would take a month, not to mention that the captain didn't seem too receptive to taking passengers. Dan explained that the captain feared that harboring stowaways on his voyage could land him in trouble and possibly end with his boat getting confiscated. Drago and Jessica had already shared with Dan and Maria that they were unsuccessful in finding options.

"Should we go to the airport to investigate options there?" Dan looked at Chris as he asked everyone around the table.

"We can find a taxi once we agree on the next step," Chris agreed. "There was a taxi line, two blocks from the water shuttle landing."

In ten minutes, they walked the three blocks to the taxi line. Chris saw a large taxi sedan—it would be a tight fit for the five of them. He asked the driver if he would take them to the airport. Drago put the long bag in the trunk and they piled in, three in the back and two up front. Chris sat in the front middle seat. The driver turned toward the heart of town. Chris recalled from their vacation years ago that they didn't have to travel through the center of town to reach the airport.

"Hey, we want to go to the airport."

"Yes, we are going to the airport."

"No, this isn't the way. Please go to the airport."

The driver shook his head and mumbled under his breath.

"Stop the car," Chris instructed, reaching over to grab the steering wheel.

The driver stopped in the middle of the street and cursed at Chris. Dan, Drago, and Jessica opened the doors to get out while Chris stood frozen with his hand on the steering wheel.

"Open the trunk," Chris ordered.

"Pay me first."

"Open the trunk now!" Chris stared at the taxi driver until he lifted the trigger to the trunk. When Chris saw in his peripheral vision that Drago had the bag out of the trunk, he climbed out and threw a bill on the passenger seat.

Once they left, they walked back to the taxi line. Chris noticed that there weren't any taxis idle.

"Why did you pay the driver?" Dan inquired.

"We don't want him so upset that he complains to the authorities. If we were in a different situation, I wouldn't have given him the money."

Drago saw an empty taxi driving by and waved the driver over. Chris walked over to the driver's window.

"We want to go to the airport and not through the city."

"Of course, we won't go through the city," the driver assured him.

Climbing in, they left Belize City and headed in the direction of the airport. They were dropped off at the curb, where Chris paid the taxi driver. Dan offered to go inside to ask about chartering a plane, while the others sat on a bench outside the terminal.

After twenty minutes, Dan walked out of the terminal and joined them. He exhaled with a big sigh.

"Well, we face the same issue with planes as we do with ships landing in the States. They may be held for a couple of weeks if they land uninvited in the Texas Federation. It's actually worse than that, because the crew can't stay on the plane. The pilot will be fined and restricted to a holding area until cleared. Even if we offer to pay the fine, pilots don't want their airplane impounded for weeks, nor are they willing to sit in jail."

"Did they have any suggestions?" Jessica asked.

Dan laughed. "Only to vacation and enjoy ourselves for a few months until things open up."

"I'm going to walk down to the bus area and see what the options are," Chris announced as he stood up. "We need to leave Belize City and find a place where they won't look for us so we can rethink our plan."

Chris walked over to the bus station and approached the counter.

"Can you show me bus routes?" Chris asked the lady and she responded by pulling out a laminated map of Belize.

Chris recalled from his previous trip that there weren't many highways in Belize. He followed the routes while studying the road north in the direction of Mexico, close to the border. They could go north, inland toward Guatemala, or south. If they went south, they would remain along the coast; they wouldn't want to travel as far as Honduras. Chris saw a Hopkins route and recalled that Chris, Carly, Jessica, and Mark had vacationed there. They'd rented a house on the beach and chartered a boat to snorkel. One day they'd kayaked along a river with mangroves. He recalled that the locals were Garifuna, descendants of West Africa or Central Africa. It was a small town, but off the grid. A few Europeans lived there; some owned restaurants and shops. A Chinese family owned the sole grocery store. It was a mixture of people and cultures that called the place their home. It was a place where you could blend in.

"When does the bus go south along the coast?" Chris followed a line on the map with his finger.

The woman looked at a list of bus departures and told him the bus would depart in twenty-five minutes. She provided the bus line number and Chris thanked her before taking off. He walked over to the bench and briefly described Hopkins to the group. Jessica helped provide a description of the town since she'd also been on the trip. Chris ended by suggesting that they hide there for a couple of days.

"We need to catch our breath and reset."

"I agree that we need a break." Dan chimed in, and the others agreed. The group followed Chris over to the bus counter without further discussion.

Chris bought five tickets: the ticket lady pointed to where the bus would depart. After the purchase, they walked over to the departure area and found two empty benches. The others sat down while Chris walked twenty meters and called Carly. She picked up her phone after two rings.

"Hi, honey. We're at a bus station in Belize City. I only have fifteen minutes before we board and leave. We can't find a path home by boat or plane to Texas. Mexico is too dangerous to travel through via the mainland, and everyone is telling us to hang tight for three to four months, until the new Texas Federation is open for travel. To make things worse, our incident in Cozumel followed us to Belize. Jessica and I are on a watch list—the authorities have our names and pictures. We're taking a bus to Hopkins. Remember Hopkins, the town on the beach? We're going to head there and lie low for a few days, see if we can come up with another plan."

"Hang on a minute, I want to put you on speaker," Carly interrupted. "Mark, Ethan, and Abby—Dad's on the phone and doesn't have much time. The group can't find a way home, but they're heading to Hopkins on the central coast of Belize. They plan to stay there for a few days."

"Dad, I checked with my friend—we can borrow their family boat," Ethan chimed in. "It's fifty feet long, and it's moored in Galveston. His father's retired and was excited about the opportunity to sail to Belize. I checked at the office and I can get time off from work, and Mark is home on summer break. We can sail down and bring you back to Houston. Is everyone traveling with a passport?"

"Yes, we all have a passport." Chris answered. He walked over to the benches and stood next to the others so they could hear him talking.

"Drago should have a visa from his company," Chris added, and Drago nodded. "Maria and Dan have their wedding certificate and her Spanish passport. I think we all have documentation."

"Dad, my friend's father has the route planned—he said it's about a two-week trip. They're ready to go at a moment's notice. Why don't you stay in Hopkins? We can find you. Mark's been there with you on vacation—he'll help us find you."

"Ethan, you're going to have to watch for pirates," Chris warned, thinking of the risks his son might face. "And storms can come raging through the gulf without notice."

"Yes, my friend says that his father is an experienced sailor and the boat is well equipped. I'll contact him and let him know the trip is on."

"I don't know, boys. This sounds like it could be dangerous."

"Dad, we're coming," Mark interjected, cutting Chris off.

"Okay, we'll head to Hopkins. We'll start looking for you in town. We'll try to rent a house on the beach."

Chris spoke with Carly for a few more minutes, then saw the bus approach. They said their goodbyes and Chris walked over with his traveling companions to join the other passengers waiting to board. Drago placed the long bag in the luggage compartment underneath the bus. The bus was only half full, so Chris chose to sit by himself in the far back. He hoped to take a nap. Dan and Maria took a seat near the middle of the bus, and Drago and Jessica sat across the aisle and back a couple of seats.

As they left the airport, Chris lost cell coverage. With no other obligations, he was finally able to take a series of small naps. The bus stopped often, and they lost passengers and gained passengers. The bus stayed about half full. As they passed Mayan villages, the road sometimes left the coast and ventured inland but they always returned to the coast.

After a couple of hours, they approached their stop. The five stepped off the bus with two older black women. One carried a roller bag and the other a shopping bag. Chris guessed they had been visiting friends or relatives in Belize City.

The bus continued on its route and the five followed the women to the main street of town. Chris and Jessica glanced around, trying to remember landmarks. Not much had changed over the past few years.

They approached a 'Realty' sign on the exterior of a small but well-kept office and they decided that Dan and Maria would walk in and look for a nice rental on the beach for up to two weeks. Dan and Maria walked out minutes later with smiles on their faces, Dan gave them a thumbs-up sign.

A minute later a man exited the office, locked the front door to the building, and turned over a sign that said, "Back in fifteen minutes." He motioned toward his SUV and quickly realized the size of their group. His SUV only seated five people. Drago loaded the long bag in the back of the SUV as Chris asked the property manager for directions to the house. He offered to walk and meet the others at the house.

Drago insisted that he would walk with Chris. Chris discreetly pulled Drago to the side and out of hearing range.

"Drago, travel with the others in the car. We need you to keep an eye on the bag. Besides, I want to walk the town first and see if everything appears okay."

Chris walked back to the driver side of the SUV. The realtor pointed south and told Chris the house was about a mile down on the beach. Chris nodded and began walking at a leisurely pace as the SUV departed, navigating potholes in the dirt road.

Chris enjoyed the walk. He saw locals living their daily lives: the Chinese market had vehicles parked in front with patrons walking in and out with bags of groceries, he saw a homeowner burning trash in his yard. A pack of dogs ran past Chris and he stopped to visit with an older couple as he passed the produce stand. The dogs reminded him of Finley; Chris wondered if anyone was throwing the ball for Finley while he was gone.

Chris passed a small, freshly painted church, then walked further, through a small grove of trees. He turned down a dirt road toward the ocean until he spotted a parked brown SUV. Nearby were a couple of houses built in close proximity to each other. Chris found one exec-style house among the local houses that was elevated on stilts. It had wooden stairs with a gate leading to a deck with a locked metal gate. Jessica stood on the deck and waved at him. He continued walking toward the house and climbed the stairs. The realtor walked down the steps and gave Chris a friendly greeting as he left.

Chris closed the metal gate and walked along the deck. Jessica greeted him and led him to the front of the house. There were two wooden doors with embedded glass inserts outlining the main entrance to the house. He looked inside and saw Dan, Maria, and Drago sitting in the living room. The house had two bedrooms. Maria and Dan planned to take one, and Jessica would take the second. Chris saw a hammock on the deck and suggested that Drago take the sleeper sofa in the living room; he enjoyed being outside and wouldn't mind sleeping in the hammock with a couple of blankets.

Chris set his pack down along the wall in the living room. It was getting late: Dan and Maria suggested that they visit the market. Chris volunteered to stay behind while the four went food shopping. He walked out to the deck and sat down on a teak chair, content to stare at the waves lapping the shore. He was excited that Ethan and Mark were coming to get them, but he was also nervous for them. He prayed they wouldn't encounter some of the difficulties that they'd faced in the Caribbean and Atlantic Oceans. He felt relieved that Mexico was well policed in the Yucatan. Ethan and Mark would have to watch the weather and keep an eye on the reef and small islands. There were a lot of things to worry about, but it would be good to see them.

The others returned from the market lugging a couple of large bottles of drinking water along with three bags of groceries. Chris helped them unpack, then they cooked dinner together in the kitchen; once finished, they brought the food outside to the deck. There was a table with two chairs. Chris brought over the large teak chair from the other side of the deck, Drago brought two chairs from the inside dining area, and the five of them sat down and enjoyed their meal. The breeze from the trade winds paired with the twinkling stars in the sky above them and the rhythmic sound of the waves made for ideal ambience.

After dinner, Dan opened a bottle of wine. They remained seated outside, enjoying the pleasant breeze. The wine was mediocre, but the company was great. Drago and Jessica expressed their desire to explore the shore the next day, and Maria said she wanted to swim in the warm water. They looked over at Chris and he lifted his hands palms up.

"I just want peace and quiet tomorrow. A stroll along the beach sounds great."

They were quiet on the deck. Each person sunk deep in thought, reflecting on the past, present, and future. They'd been through a lot: it was good to have peace. Every once in a while they would hear a noise from a nearby house that would temporarily startle them, but they were off the grid. For once, they did not need to be concerned.

One by one they left the deck to go to sleep, until only Chris remained. He climbed into the hammock under two blankets. He had his gun in his shoe—the shoe was on the deck beneath him. Chris anticipated a quiet night, but he'd had thought that before and been surprised. He was done with surprises. The hammock was comfortable, and the glass of wine helped take the edge off the day. Chris listened to the soothing pattern of the sounds of the ocean waves as they came to shore and soon fell fast asleep.

Chapter 117

Texas

ETHAN AND MARK STOOD in the living room by the front door, luggage stacked to the side of the entry. Grandpa H carried a backpack toward them; he was trailed by Pa K. The grandmothers and Carly entered the room from the kitchen to survey the situation. Ethan and Mark looked at their grandfathers who were packed and ready for the trip.

"We decided we're going with you to Belize," Grandpa H spoke first.

"I was stationed down in Panama. I've been in that area," Pa K added. "And your Grandfather H was in the navy. We think we can be useful. We can shoot and fight if necessary. We want to help bring your dad and Jessica home."

Ethan and Mark looked at each other for a few seconds. Ethan walked over to his grandparents.

"I know that you would be helpful. We only have four of us sailing to Belize, but it will be nine of us returning. My friend's boat can't hold more than ten people; the nine of us on the return will be stretching it. Mark has been to Belize—he'll know where to look for them."

"We really appreciate you wanting to join us, but our time on Hopkins in Belize should be short," Mark added. "The town is small. We're hoping to locate the group and leave within hours."

Carly walked over to where her sons, father, and father-in-law stood. The truth was, they all wanted to be part of the rescue team.

"I understand. I also originally thought about going," Carly shared. "I agree that you would add value to the mission, and I understand how it's hard to hear bits and pieces and wait so long for them to come home. Ethan and Mark had the same conversation with me—we agreed it should just be the two of them."

Grandma H and Ma K walked over to their husbands and told them that they agreed—they should wait at the farm. Reluctantly the men lowered their packs. Finley barked, and Carly took two steps to the window to see a truck travel down the driveway. Grandma H joined Carly at the window to see two blond girls pop out and approach the porch.

"It's Lindsay and Allie McGregor!" Grandma H exclaimed in recognition.

Ethan and Mark opened the front door to meet the girls in the driveway. Ma K walked over to peek through the window by the front door.

"I think we'll get to know the McGregor's very well in the future," Ma K observed slyly.

Carly and the grandparents walked outside and stood on the porch. Ethan held Lindsay in his arms and on the other side of the truck, Mark had Allie in his arms. They talked and hugged for a couple of minutes before walking to the porch.

It was time to go: Ethan and Mark hugged their grandparents and kissed their mother. The McGregor girls followed them to the truck as the young men packed their luggage in the truck bed. After a kiss and hug, Ethan climbed behind the wheel. Mark sat in the passenger seat. They waved goodbye; Mark yelled "adios," out the window as Ethan drove the truck down the driveway.

"Ladies, would you like to join us for some coffee?" Carly offered.

Lindsay and Allie looked at each other, and Lindsay accepted. "We'd love to have a cup."

They walked back to the kitchen and they sat down as Carly started a fresh pot of coffee. Grandma H brought pastries, to the table and Ma K retrieved the milk and sugar. The grandparents set coffee mugs and plates down and settled in for a good chat. They were worried about Ethan and Mark but relished the opportunity to know the McGregor girls better.

* * * * *

Meanwhile, Ethan and Mark drove to Houston and then on to Galveston, where Jake's father's boat was harbored on the Gulf of Mexico. Ethan had confirmed with Jake their ETA and Jake had given Mark detailed directions to the dock along with a description of the boat. Other than a coffee and bathroom break, the brothers drove straight through to Galveston. They temporarily forgot about home, sourcing their energy toward mental preparation for their next adventure.

Hours later, Ethan and Mark recognized Ethan's friend Jake on the dock. Ethan and Mark had their backpacks slung over their shoulders and each carried a duffel bag. Carly had packed some food and water for the trip that was stashed in their bags. Ethan yelled a greeting to Jake, who responded by walking up the dock to greet them.

Mark had met Jake a couple of times previously, in Dallas. Jake had attended Baylor with Ethan. After graduation, they'd both entered the work force. Jake had decided to return for his MBA that fall semester, and he'd treated himself by taking vacation for the whole summer.

Jake introduced his father, who insisted he be called Roy. Roy had retired from work a year prior. Jake divulged that his dad was excited for an adventure. Jake's mother, Sue, was in the cabin helping with the preparation, but she would not travel with them to Belize. She had boxes of food in the back of her SUV and asked the young men to transport the boxes to the cabin.

An hour later the supplies were packed, and they were ready to set sail. Roy and his wife lived nearby in Houston and had spent the past two days getting the boat ready. Sue made them promise to be careful and to check in when possible, then left.

Before they left the dock, Mark called his mom and put her on speakerphone. Carly told Mark and Ethan to be careful and to bring Jessica and Chris home safely. Carly had been watching the weather: the forecast predicted ideal weather and sailing conditions in the Gulf.

They traveled out of the harbor, in the early afternoon. Jake instructed Ethan and Mark and Roy to set the course for Belize. When the sails were up, Jake motioned for Ethan to follow him below deck. They returned with four beers: Ethan handed one to Roy and Mark as Roy reviewed the plan. After reviewing his estimate for travel time and confirming the course, Roy shared his concerns. Afterward, he allowed Jake to take the wheel. Jake would have the first shift while Roy gave Ethan and Mark a detailed tour of his boat. Roy planned for them all to have two or three hour shifts at the wheel under his supervision until Mark and Ethan felt comfortable sailing.

Roy showed Ethan and Mark the fishing gear and suggested they try their luck. Roy had all the latest equipment and until that point had used his boat primarily for fishing. He explained that Sue didn't care for the boat much—she'd nixed his original dream of traveling the Caribbean together.

"I've been anxious to get out of the Houston area this past year. This is an excellent opportunity to take my boat on an extended trip," Roy smiled.

Ethan and Mark each caught fish and were pleased to contribute to the main course for dinner. Ethan took the following shift at the helm while Jake and Mark fished for a couple more hours, adding two fish to the total catch for the day.

After Ethan's shift at the helm it was Mark's turn. Ethan and Jake cleaned the fish; afterward Ethan grilled the fish while Jake cooked rice and prepared a green salad. They had enough produce stocked for about a week; they'd need to buy more fresh vegetables and fruit in Belize for the return trip to Galveston.

After dinner they cleaned the dishes and Roy again expressed how pleased he was with Ethan and Mark navigating the boat. They planned to take three hour shifts throughout the evening. The weather was perfect and the stars were bright and shining. They enjoyed the evening as they searched for the constellations. Jake took the first shift at 8:00 p.m. The others left him on deck and retreated to their bunks for sleep.

Chapter 118

Hopkins

CHRIS THOROUGHLY ENJOYED THE sunrise each morning. The hammock faced the ocean to the east, allowing him to wake at the first light. The first thing Chris did each morning, was to quietly open the sliding glass door to the kitchen and start a pot of coffee. He prepared the coffee and water the night before and set clean mugs out on the counter. He pushed two buttons on the coffee maker, then walked back to the deck to enjoy the sunrise. He didn't want to disturb the others so early in the morning.

Chris tied his tennis shoes, pulled on a T-shirt, and poured himself a full cup of coffee before walking along the shoreline. He saw fishermen and a number of stray dogs. After strolling about one and a half miles up the beach, he'd return. He alternated the direction each day. One day he'd walk north along the beach toward town, the next day he' travel south, away from town.

Chris watched boats take off, trailing them until they became dots on the horizon. He was curious about their life and wondered about their typical day in Hopkins.

Chris held discussions with Dan, Maria, Jessica, and Drago soon after they arrived at Hopkins. They agreed to keep to themselves and try to avoid conversation with the locals. They'd be polite but would refrain from engaging in conversation. This was a challenge: they were a novelty to the small town currently devoid of tourists. It was an art to be friendly and have a brief conversation without really saying anything.

When Chris returned from his morning walk, the others were usually waking up. Chris ate breakfast on the deck while Jessica and Drago ran along the beach.

Drago and Jessica enjoyed the water each day. The first day they found snorkel equipment at the house and decided to snorkel each day (if the water was calm). They described the fish to Chris during breakfast, then looked the fish up on a website so Chris could see the pictures.

Maria was more of an evening person; she didn't usually wake up until 9:00 a.m. Dan would wait to have breakfast with her. Afterward, they would relax, then take a walk along the shore. Often Maria chose to wade in the water.

Chris typically took a midday walk into town to buy groceries then returned home. He enjoyed the water a couple of times a day, but would venture out only in front of the house. The others knew he was on edge, always on lookout for the Belize police.

They found one other place to shop for food. There was a produce stand two blocks from the house. Jessica and Drago's daily task was to buy fresh produce each day, and so far, the selection of fruit was outstanding. Chris enjoyed the variety and was always interested to see what they would bring back each day.

In the evenings they ate dinner together. Maria had found board games in a cupboard, and after dinner they often played a game and sat on the deck and talked. They discussed past experiences, but their conversation usually focused on the future and what each was most looking forward to back in the States.

At noon on the sixth day, Chris walked along the dirt road. Deciding to pass the market, Chris headed to the main intersection and continued a couple blocks before circling back. It had been five days since Ethan and Mark had left Galveston; Chris wondered if the boys were close. Wearing his wide brim hat low, he saw vendors sitting under an umbrella by their kiosks. A couple of restaurants ahead of Chris served the locals lunch at outside tables. Across the street, a few people sat out on a picnic bench eating packed lunches. His typical response to the people glancing at him was to wave and smile while he continued walking.

Chris reached the market and pulled out his list of items to purchase. Some of the goods were scarce; a number of items were repeated from their previous grocery list. He typically bought one large water container and carried it back with one arm, his other arm devoted to a bag of groceries. He worked hard to balance on his walk back to the house.

The market proprietors of the grocery store were Chinese. They never attempted to carry a conversation, so it was safe to shop in the store as long as you kept some distance from the locals. Chris deliberately chose to shop at midday because there were fewer customers in the store.

Chris was at the register counting money to give to the impatient cashier. After handing the money to the cashier, Chris lifted the water container with his right hand and held the bag of groceries in his left. He navigated through the exit doors and stepped outside, then froze for a few seconds as he caught sight of a car twenty meters ahead. Two police officers climbed out of a car and walked across the street in his direction. Keeping composure, Chris continued walking down the steps, pretending to focus on his bag and water container as he put his sunglasses on. With his head down, his full brim hat would hopefully conceal his face. He took the last steps and was on the street. In a snap decision, Chris turned to the right to walk in the opposite direction of the house.

The two officers focused on him as they approached from the side of the road. Out of his peripheral vision, Chris saw that the officers were of different heights.

"Hello," said the shorter of the two officers.

Chris ignored the policeman, pretending that he didn't know he was speaking to him. He was trying to put distance between himself and the police, but they didn't lose ground.

"Hey, we're talking to you!" the taller one spoke up, indignant.

Chris turned his head and smiled. He had a sudden memory that a number of Europeans lived in this coastal town. The police were not locals; they were passing through. Quickly he tried to recall some of his high school German.

Chris turned completely around to face the officers. He kept his hat low and left his sunglasses in place.

"Guten tag!"

The police officials stared at him. The shorter one broke into a sheepish smile and waved his hand as a gesture.

"Have a good day!"

They turned and walked back across the street to the little restaurant, where they selected a table with visibility of all the activity on the street, 150 meters in either direction.

Chris exhaled, then turned back around and walked steadily for two blocks. He made a sharp right toward the ocean. When he reached the beach, he turned right again to head back to the rental house. He hoped the buildings shielded him from the main street. He was soon parallel to the market, and kept walking along the shore until he reached the beach house. He didn't break pace as he continued up the stairs, unlocked the metal gate, and walked into the house. He set the groceries down on the kitchen countertop and stored the water container in the designated corner area of the floor in the kitchen. Dan and Maria were eating lunch. Ten minutes later, Jessica and Drago climbed up to the deck. They'd been swimming and were still a little wet, so they sat down to dry off on the deck chairs. Chris finished unloading the last of the groceries, then asked Maria and Dan to walk out onto the deck with him.

Jessica and Drago sat down in chairs with feet propped up on the wooden rails. Chris sat down in an adjacent chair and looked at them, then at Dan and Maria who walked out the sliding glass door.

"There were police at that small restaurant across from the grocery store. They said hello to me and were irritated when I didn't respond," Chris told them.

"What did you do?" Dan asked.

"Since there are several Europeans here, I responded in German. They shrugged it off, and I walked away from the direction of our house, then down to the beach. I circled back to the house. I don't think they're looking for us ... I just think they were passing through on some other business and stopped for lunch."

"But I would stay out of town today if possible," Chris added. "I think we're okay, but you never know,"

Chris walked inside the house and pulled the rifle bag out from under Jessica's bed and brought it outside. Dan and Maria made sandwiches for Chris, Drago, and Jessica. Chris took a few bites but remained focused on cleaning and inspecting the rifles and shotgun. Mike had instructed him several times on how to clean them, drilling him why it was important to clean them regularly as he explained how it could save their lives. Chris had learned this first-hand these past months, and he was thorough in his cleaning. Finally he was satisfied. He felt calm after spending two hours on the weaponry.

The group kept in close proximity of the house for the rest of the day. No more walks or swimming. They cleaned their handguns in the afternoon, played two games that Maria had been wanting to play, and then cooked dinner together.

"Well, it's been five days since Ethan and Mark left," Jessica announced. "Ethan and Mark may show up within the next two days. We need to be ready to leave quickly."

"We will also have to decide soon if we need to add a week's rent," Maria reminded them.

"Can we pay for a couple more days, or does it have to be in weekly increments?" Drago inquired.

Maria shrugged and put her right hand up as a gesture. "I'm not sure, but Dan and I can stop by the realtor's office tomorrow and chat with him."

"We just don't want to draw any attention to ourselves." Chris cautioned. "If adding one more week's rent is the best path to lessen any suspicion, I'm fine with that."

Chapter 119

Off the coast of Belize

THEY'D BEEN AT SEA for a number of days without any issues. Roy had successfully navigated them between Cuba and the Yucatan without any trouble. He'd told them ahead of time that he didn't want to drift too close to either region. They'd implemented two-man shifts as a precaution as soon as they'd approached Mexico and Cuba. Roy had them on six hour shifts: one person would take the helm for three hours, then switch with the other person who was on guard and armed with a pair of binoculars.

It was early afternoon when the four of them were on deck listening to Roy explain that they were getting close to Hopkins. They were miles off shore from the Belize mainland and the islands south of Belize City. Roy was slowly angling them closer toward the shore.

Mark had been at Hopkins on vacation with his family years ago; he recalled that there wasn't much to the town. The plan was to dock south of the town near the mouth of the river. Roy and Jake would remain onboard while Mark and Ethan searched for their family and friends. Roy reminded Ethan and Mark that they weren't allowed to have guns on shore.

"If the conditions stay the same, I anticipate we'll land in Hopkins around midmorning tomorrow." Roy confirmed. "Jake and I will wait at the dock for you, but please return by the evening to provide us with a status report. If you're unsuccessful in finding your family, you can start out early the next day and search again."

Mark went to the edge of the deck and stared out at the water. Ethan came by and sat down next to him.

"What are you thinking, bud?" Ethan asked.

"I'm trying to remember the town. I think the dock is two to three miles south of town. People are friendly—we may be able to bum a ride. Dad said they would try to rent a house on the beach. Cell coverage in Hopkins is terrible. I'm wondering if we should split up and cover twice the area, or stay together. There's not too much to Hopkins besides the main road and beach."

"How safe is the town?" Ethan asked. "Should we risk bringing handguns in the backpacks?"

"I think we can take our handguns if they're concealed. We're only going to be there during the day." Mark advised. "The town had some sketchy areas and I'm not sure if it's the same now or if it's better or worse. We should stay on the beach or down the main road but not drift from there. Dad and Jessica should be looking for us."

They were quiet for the rest of the afternoon as they mentally prepared to land in Hopkins. They kept their normal shifts through the night. Roy and Mark shouted out the next morning at seven that they were moving toward the mouth of the river. Ethan and Jake immediately climbed up on deck to see the coastline with trees, sandy beaches and homes. As Jake went down below to prepare breakfast, Ethan and Mark took turns watching on deck. While one stood watch, the other worked to pack his backpack with food, water, and clothing articles wrapped around the gun.

They finished eating all their fruit for breakfast. The last of the bread and cheese was packed in their lunch, and Jake and Roy reminded them to buy fresh produce if they had the opportunity.

The mouth of the river was soon visible. The young men took down the sails and Roy started the engine. Roy navigated them through the mouth of the river, which looked familiar to Mark. Roy knew that the dock was up the river several hundred meters, and he continued up the river slowly. They spotted the dock and Roy pulled them closer. There was one boat on the dock preparing to take off. They waved at the captain of the boat as he passed. Roy pulled them within feet of the dock, and Jake and Mark jumped off to secure the boat.

Once secure, Jake climbed back onboard while Roy stepped off to find the manager and negotiate a stay for the day and evening. Ethan handed Mark his pack before following Roy into the office. Ethan checked for cell coverage—as expected, he couldn't get a bar on his phone.

Roy approached a man stationed at the counter and asked for the rate to stay one night. He agreed on the price, and Roy pulled out his money clip and paid him. Once the transaction was complete, Mark spoke up.

"How far is it to Hopkins town?" Mark asked.

"Just a couple of miles up the coast," the man responded as he cleaned his counter area.

"Would anyone be heading in that direction?" Mark pursued.

"I'm sending one of my guys into town in about half an hour for an errand. "The man volunteered.

Mark kept eye contact but said nothing. The room was quiet with the exception of the hum of a boat's motor in the background.

"I guess he can head up there now," the man offered.

Mark smiled and nodded. He and Ethan were anxious to start the search.

"We would really appreciate getting a ride now," Ethan spoke up. "It'll just be the two of us."

Ethan and Mark waited outside the building while Roy walked to the riverbank toward his boat. Once alone, Ethan looked at Mark.

"Mark, you take the lead on the search. Tell the driver where you want to be dropped off."

In five minutes one of the workers walked into the office. He came back out thirty seconds later with keys in hand.

"You, guys, heading to Hopkins?"

"Yes, sir, and we appreciate the ride," Mark responded. The worker motioned with his hand for them to follow him.

Mark and Ethan followed him to a rusted truck parked behind the office. They opened the passenger door and climbed in. The truck needed reupholstering: some springs were showing. However, the ride was only a short distance. The driver turned on the ignition and proceeded to drive the truck down the dirt road, maneuvering around large pot holes.

In five minutes, they reached the outskirts of town. Mark directed their driver toward the main intersection and asked him to pull over, about fifty meters from the intersection. Ethan pulled a twenty-dollar bill from his pocket and handed it to the driver.

"Can you pick us up here at 6:00 p.m. to take us back?" Ethan asked. "I'll have another twenty dollars for the return trip."

The driver looked pleased as he pocketed the twenty in his front shirt pocket.

"I'll be here." He made a U-turn and took off to run errands for the boss.

Mark pointed at a restaurant with tables outside by the road. It had a good view of both ends of the street. Ethan and Mark walked over and sat down, placing their packs on an empty chair. Mark checked for cell coverage—still no service. They ordered cold drinks, took a few sips, and glanced up and down the street.

"I think one of us should stay here and the other should do a long loop," Mark suggested. "Walk a mile up the street, walk over to the beach, and then walk two miles back along the beach; coming back to the road and walking the mile back here. We can take turns walking. We should use this as our base today: order drinks, then eat lunch."

Ethan nodded to Mark's plan. "I think Dad will be looking for us."

Mark offered to take the first walk. He grabbed his backpack and started walking north on the road. He didn't recall the area, but there were house rentals available. As he ambled along, a few people saw him and waved. One dog ran over to greet him. Mark patted the dog on the head, and the dog decided to travel with him. After what he judged to be about a mile, Mark walked down a dirt road to the beach and sand. Once on the beach, he made his way back parallel to the restaurant, passing the intersection and market.

Mark kept walking until he stopped at a familiar spot; one he recognized from when they had vacationed years ago. His new canine companion briefly left, sauntering up to a house outlined by palm trees. The dog smelled the base of one of the trees, marked it, and then returned to Mark.

Mark looked out to the ocean. He identified a few boats in the distance that he thought were fishing boats out for their morning catch. He continued walking with his canine friend.

A few minutes later, Mark contemplated whether to turn back toward the center road when he heard his name called. He looked around for the source and heard it again. It was a woman's voice—for some reason, he was expecting his father's—a man's voice. Looking toward a two-story house, he saw someone waving at him. Soon there was more than one person. She moved across the deck in a hurry and then raced down the stairs. He now recognized the woman running to him as his sister, Jessica. The man remained at the railing, peering down at Mark from the deck.

Jessica didn't slow down as she ran into his open arms. Mark hugged her and lifted her up in the air.

"Mark, I've been watching for you and Ethan these past two days. Dad said he thought you would arrive today."

Jessica excitedly waved to the man standing on the deck, beckoning for him to come down. Minutes later, she introduced Drago to Mark. Mark looked back up to the deck and glanced up the beach.

"Where's Dad? Where's Dan and his wife?"

"Dan and Maria went up the beach for a swim," Jessica pointed up the shore. "I think those two small dots are them in the water. Dad left ten minutes ago for his daily walk up the road to the market. He should be back in thirty minutes—we can go find him."

"Let's go find him. Ethan is sitting at a café near the intersection."

"I'll get Maria and Dan to come back and we'll meet you back at the house," Drago volunteered.

Jessica went up to the deck to retrieve her shoes, then she and Mark turned away from the beach and walked toward the center street. They passed between an older house and an unfinished cement house, both owned by locals. They reached the main street and turned in the direction of the market.

In the distance, Mark noticed that Ethan had a visitor standing at the table. As Mark and Jessica approached, Mark recognized his father talking with Ethan. At that moment Ethan turned his head and saw Mark and Jessica approach. Ethan jogged over to give Jessica a hug while Chris rushed over to hug Mark.

Chris motioned for them to sit at the table so they wouldn't draw too much attention. Ethan and Mark explained that Roy's boat was at the dock—they needed to keep an eye on the time. They had a prearranged ride at 6:00 p.m. that would take them back to the boat. Mark pointed to the exact spot where they would meet their ride.

"We should head back to the house soon," Jessica suggested. "Drago went down the beach to get Dan and Maria from their swim."

They pushed away from the table. Ethan went inside to settle the bill and was back out in two minutes. They walked down to the beach and headed for the beach house.

After twenty minutes of walking and chatting, they reached the stairs and saw that Dan, Maria, and Drago were waiting on the deck for them. Ethan was introduced to Drago and both Ethan and Mark were introduced to Maria. Once the introductions were complete, they sat down. Ethan and Mark relayed the plan again for the benefit of Drago, Dan, and Maria. Ethan and Mark thought the crew could all fit in the truck: five could sit in the bed of the truck. Ethan and Mark added that they needed to buy groceries and fresh produce for the return voyage.

A plan was established: first, they would pack; the top priority was to be ready for the 6:00 p.m. ride. Chris advised that he was already packed—he packed each morning. While the others packed, Chris and Mark would travel to the market to buy food Items. Jessica and Drago thought that they could pack up in five minutes, then join Ethan to buy produce at a roadside stand. They needed enough produce for nine people on a weeklong voyage. Dan and Maria would visit the realtor and inform him that they would be leaving the property by 6:00 p.m.

They finished their errands early and still had a couple of hours left before meeting the truck. The seven of them sat on the deck as Ethan and Mark peppered Chris and Jessica with questions. Mark and Ethan explained the situation with Roy and Jake, then described Roy's boat. Dan asked specific questions about the boat, more than Ethan and Mark could answer.

At 5:30 p.m. Ethan and Mark walked to the location where the driver said to meet them. The others were going to wait by the side of the road near the rental house. They thought it would be too noticeable for all seven to wait near the main intersection. They had their packs and groceries and huddled together.

When the driver returned, Ethan explained to him that they would pick up some additional passengers about a mile down the road. The driver didn't care. In a couple of minutes, Ethan and Mark saw their family and friends on the side of the road. Ethan and Mark hopped out of the truck and pointed for Jessica and Maria to take the seats in the cab. Ethan and Mark helped the other men load the groceries and bags into the bed of the truck and the men climbed into the back with their provisions.

The men sat in the truck bed using their backpacks for support. They could feel each and every pothole, as they bounced up and down and to the side. Chris thought it was like an amusement park ride without the seatbelt and he wondered if his rear would develop a bruise.

The driver pulled up to the dock and his passengers quickly climbed out and unloaded their supplies. As promised, Ethan had a crisp twenty held out for the driver, who briskly pocketed the bill. As soon as their cargo was unloaded, he started his truck and headed home. Ethan and Mark grabbed their packs off the ground, then snatched a grocery bag in each arm.

Ethan saw Jake and Roy on deck right away. "Hello!" he hollered. The dock was void of any other vessels. Roy and Jake came forward with enthusiastic introductions, each grabbing a grocery bag from Jessica and Maria before climbing back onboard. Roy and Jake showed them where to store the groceries and where to place their packs and bags. Roy explained it would be tight quarters: they would have to switch off sleeping on the bunks.

Roy noticed the long bag that Drago carried. "Son, what do you have in there?"

"It's our survival equipment. We've used it against hostile boats," Chris answered for Drago. "I'll show you what we have in the bag."

Chris requested that everyone gather as he opened the bag. He pulled out the rifles and the shotgun. He had towels wrapped around an object that he lifted as he unraveled the towels. From the unwrapped towel, Chris pulled out a couple of pieces that Dan, Jessica and Drago recognized. It was the antitank missile launcher. Chris pulled it out and assembled it.

"I thought I saw you throw the case out the door of Jay-Jay's plane!" Drago spoke with surprise.

"I didn't want to throw it out. I wondered if we would need it one more time on our return journey," Chris answered with a sneaky smile.

"Roy and Jake, we had a colleague named Mike who acquired this at the start of our journey," Chris continued. "It saved our lives once fighting off pirates near Morocco. If we get into a sticky situation, it may save our lives again."

"The Mexican custom agents didn't say anything?" Dan asked, still sorting through the past events.

"They saw the rifles and shotgun—I assume they just thought it was another rifle." Chris nodded.

They finished unpacking and stood out on deck. The sun set in the background.

"Well, we can head out now while there is still a bit of light and pass the reef and set sail," Roy asserted. "Or we can spend the night and head out in the morning."

"I vote on leaving now," Chris interjected without hesitation. "And Roy, I can't thank you and your son enough for coming down here to bring us home."

Dan, Maria, Jessica and Drago agreed that they would prefer to leave immediately.

In ten minutes, Roy had them motoring along the river. Fifteen minutes later, they had the sails up and the route established for the States.

Roy offered to take first watch while the others prepared to eat dinner. While the others ate in the galley, Chris grabbed two plates and went up on deck to eat with Roy.

"So I've heard you've had quite the adventure, but I haven't heard many details," Roy said.

Yes, it has been a challenge," Chris answered carefully, his mouth full.

"Would you like to share it?"

"Sure, but it's a long story. And you may have trouble believing some of it."

Roy looked at Chris and smiled. "Hell, we have all night."

Chapter 120

Caribbean Sea to Gulf of Mexico

BEFORE LONG THEY ENTERED the Yucatan channel that divided Mexico and Cuba. From there, they would leave the Caribbean Sea to enter the Gulf of Mexico. The channel separated these two countries by 120 miles of water.

Before they left, Roy learned that territorial waters extended twelve nautical miles from shore. He planned to navigate the boat in the center of the channel. Traveling too close to Mexico could be problematic: not only did they face the issue of pirates, but the Mexican navy might try to board, using the excuse that they were looking for drugs or other contraband. If you traveled too close to Cuba, they might bring you to their closest port and possibly confiscate your boat. Once in Cuba, it would be a *long* process to return to the States. Neither option sounded attractive to the nine sailors.

Everyone stood on deck either as a scout looking for other boats or to enjoy the nice weather. The sun shone off the water, a few clouds outlined the big blue sky.

Roy calculated that he'd brought them a little closer to Cuba than Mexico; by his estimation they were still twenty-five miles away from the Cuban shore. Jake, Dan, and Ethan had success in fishing, catching enough for a hearty dinner that evening. They all attempted to catch one more fish before calling it a day.

Mark gave Roy a break at the helm, and Roy went down to brew another pot of coffee. Chris stood near Mark and asked about summer plans and his class schedule for the next semester. After a while, Chris decided to switch topics.

"Mark, your mother told me that you're interested in a girl named Allie."

"I really like her, Dad."

"We've talked about a future together." Mark added after a few seconds.

Chris nodded. He walked closer to Mark, looked him in the eye, and gave him a one-armed hug. Mark was a young man of few words, but he'd just told Chris a lot.

Maria was engaged in conversation with Jessica and Drago at the stern. Mark shouted a request to the three of them.

"Please keep watch, as you enjoy the fresh air."

Some ships passed in the opposite direction; leaving the Gulf for Central or South America. These were commercial ships either loaded with cargo or empty from unloading their cargo in the Texas Federation. According to Ethan and Mark, the sea trade with the Texas Federation was now fully operational.

Dan caught another fish and the men announced that they were done. They reeled in their lines, and Dan quickly volunteered to clean the fish while Jake and Ethan put away the gear. Ethan gathered the fishing poles. When he glanced up, he saw something in the distance approaching them at a forty-five-degree angle from the Cuba side. He kept this information to himself—the boat was way off in the distance. But a couple of minutes later he looked again: the boat was closer, and on a course to intersect them.

"Hey, everyone, it's probably nothing ... but the ship behind us is on course to intersect us. I noticed it two minutes ago, but now it's gaining on us."

Chris left Mark's side and yelled down to Roy. "Roy, where are your binoculars?"

Roy came up moments later with the binoculars. He looked at Ethan in question, who pointed toward the ship. Roy made his way back to Ethan and focused on the dot that loomed larger by the second.

"I see the Cuban flags. It has a red triangle with a white star and white and blue stripes," Ray responded. I wonder what a Cuban Navy ship is doing this far out in the channel. We have to be a minimum of ten to fifteen miles out of their territorial waters."

Roy walked over to Mark with a suggestion.

"See if you can move us toward the center of the channel."

After a couple of minutes had passed, the Cuban ship was still on course to intersect Roy's boat.

"I think we need to be well armed," Chris suggested to the others. In silent assent, a few of them went below to retrieve their rifles.

Chris brought up the antitank missile, others brought their rifles, and Dan held the shotgun to use in close quarters. Roy reported that although Mark had tried to gain distance, the navy ship was moving quickly toward them. Roy heard a message on his radio in Spanish.

"Maria, will you come here and translate this?" Roy asked.

Maria walked over briskly, but the person speaking had stopped talking by the time she arrived. Roy held his hand out, motioning for her to stay. A minute later, they received another message. Maria listened intently until it was quiet again.

"It's the Cuban Navy," Maria confirmed. "They're ordering us to stop to let them board. They think we may be smuggling people or illegal contraband."

"Tell them that we're returning from Belize," Roy directed. "And that we're far from their territorial waters and that we won't stop. Tell them we're en route to the States."

Maria responded in Spanish. Soon after she finished, she received a reply.

"The captain is insistent that they search our boat," she translated.

Roy turned to Mark and suggested that he navigate the boat closer to the channel center. Roy shouted for Jake and Ethan to pull the sails taut to secure maximum speed. A few minutes later, the Cuban ship had closed the gap between the two vessels. They could see individuals on the boat. Roy looked at Chris as he began to load the missile.

"Chris, what are you thinking?"

"I have one more missile left, and I'm planning on using it. We've come too far to fail now. I don't think any of us want to spend the next few months—or possibly years—in Cuba."

Chris focused as he prepared the launcher. When he was ready, he looked over at Maria and Roy.

"When I give you the word, have Maria tell the captain that he has one last chance to turn away. You can even tell him that I'm locked onto him with a missile. Give him ten seconds to pull away. If he doesn't; I'm going to sink them. I'm going to the helm to focus on my target.

"It'll help if you can loosen the sails to slow us down," Chris now directed his conversation to Jake, Ethan, Mark and Roy. "I'd like to have our boat sailing as smooth as possible when I fire."

Chris moved to the helm but was struck with another thought.

"In case I miss my target, have the rifles ready to start picking them off. Jessica and Drago, get in position. Ethan and Jake … not sure how accurate you are with rifles. If you're skilled, now is a good time to get in place. Remember, someone needs to lock in on the captain. He's the first to go. Roy and Mark, if I don't get a direct hit, bring the sails taut and try to keep as much distance as possible. Hopefully their boat will be impaired— if not, we'll need as much time as we can for our rifles."

They slowed down as the Cuban ship gained speed. The Cuban ship was still engaged in conversation over the radio, but Maria didn't respond. She waited for Chris's direction.

Finally, they were close enough where Chris felt he had a ninety percent chance of hitting the ship. He yelled to Maria that he was "locked in." The Cuban vessel sent another message, and Maria responded. While Maria translated, Jessica called out that she had a lock on the captain. Drago, Ethan, then Jake also responded that they had their targets in their sights. They were set and ready.

Chris's gaze fixated on the captain of the Cuban Navy ship. The captain had binoculars trained on them. When Maria finished speaking, he swung his glasses over and froze on Chris. Chris was in the proper launching position that Mike had taught, locked on the ship. The captain shouted an order. Chris began his count the moment Maria concluded her conversation. He was at number seven, praying that he had a good missile, when the Cuban ship started to slow and then began to turn back toward Cuba.

Chris stayed locked in position until the Cuban ship was completely turned around. Only then did Chris relax and stand. He walked back to Mark, Roy and Maria.

"They had one second left," Chris muttered out loud to himself.

"Would you have shot at exactly ten seconds?" Roy asked.

"No, I was going to fire at eight." Chris confessed. "I saw him give orders, but I didn't know what those orders were. If they didn't turn immediately after receiving those orders, I was going to shoot. He had until the count of eight."

Drago and Jessica decided that it was prudent to continue watching for Cuban vessels. They positioned themselves so that they faced the Cuban coast for the next hour. After the adrenaline rush had subsided, Chris broke the weapon down. They stored the rifles (with the exception of the two that Jessica and Drago carried).

Dan finished cleaning the fish and solicited Maria's help to cook dinner. It was late afternoon and they had skipped lunch, so everyone was hungry. Jessica and Drago handed their rifles to Mark and Ethan before going below to prepare a salad using the fresh produce from the Hopkins stand.

They took two shifts to eat dinner. After everyone had finished, Mark, Ethan, Jake, and Chris did the honors of cleanup while Dan kept them on course for Galveston. In the evening, the stars were out and shining brightly. They were far from Cuba and Mexico and now well into the Gulf of Mexico. With a cold drink in hand, they could relax. Roy took the opportunity to prepare the crew for the evening shift. They would continue watch with two person crews. As before, one person would be armed and on lookout while the other navigated.

The weather report predicted great sailing conditions for the next couple of days, and the course was set for the new Texas Federation. Drago was apprehensive of what to expect in the new Federation, and he spent time quizzing Mark and Ethan. Chris spoke with Jessica—they both felt uneasy and unsure of what to expect; they'd been away so long.

Maria was excited to step off the boat and see her new home. Dan promised to attempt to find a flight from Houston to Miami, then rent a car so they could drive home. He hoped his insurance would cover his lost boat and that he'd recoup enough money to buy a new one. Maria was not enthusiastic about buying another boat—she shared her feelings openly. Dan told Chris that the insurance payment would take awhile; he'd give it some time. He hoped Maria would be more receptive to sailing in the future.

The next couple of days were routine, filled with fishing and sailing. They shared more dreams and plans as they neared Galveston.

Chapter 121

Texas arrival

THE GROUP LANDED UNEVENTFULLY at Galveston. It was the first time Chris, Jessica, and Dan had ever been to Galveston and the first time Drago and Maria ventured into the old United States.

They arranged their passports in proper order; Dan held his marriage certificate. He and Maria talked to one customs agent and Jessica and Drago to another. Their company had filed the paperwork correctly, so Drago just needed to methodically go through the process, which would take a few hours. Ethan and Mark helped Roy and Jake clean the boat while Chris was checked through customs. Their original US passports were still valid for one year, but eventually they would need to be replaced with new Texas Federation passports. Chris went back to assist the others in cleaning the boat after he successfully cleared customs.

Chris approached Roy and asked if there was something he could contribute to his boat as a token of appreciation. Roy refused the idea of any gift or payment, so Chris asked Ethan to speak with Jake and inquire if his father had a wish list for his boat. Of course, the gesture would be symbolic. Roy had given them the priceless gift of time … not to mention that he'd rescued them from Belize.

Chris called Carly to let her know that they had safely arrived in Galveston. She asked when they would be home. He informed her that Drago and Maria first had to clear customs, then they would be on their way. He estimated they would arrive in Brownfield late that night.

It was midafternoon when Maria finally cleared customs. Roy and Jake were chatting with Ethan, Mark, and Chris when she and Dan arrived back at the boat. Roy offered to drop Dan and Maria at the Houston airport on his way home. Dan checked online using his smartphone and found a direct flight to Miami and booked two seats. They would need to move quickly to make the early evening flight.

A quick departure was a positive situation: it limited the goodbyes to a couple of minutes. They only had time for hugs and handshakes. Dan and Chris agreed to talk later in the week on job possibilities. Roy and Chris got along well in their short time together, so they discussed the possibility of a get-together with their wives. Chris offered to host them at the farm, or suggested they find a midpoint location to meet, such as Austin.

In minutes, Roy, Jake, Dan, and Maria left. Chris, Ethan, and Mark picked up their packs and bags and walked over to wait for Drago and Jessica. The rifles cleared customs—Chris had dumped the antitank missile and launcher into the ocean when they were within fifty miles of Galveston.

When Drago had finally passed through, it was time for dinner. Ethan and Mark directed them to their truck parked in the long-term parking lot. It was exactly as they'd left it, which seemed like ages ago. They loaded their limited possessions and crammed their bodies into the two rows of seats. They took a quick vote and decided to stop and eat something on their drive back to Brownfield. They now expected to arrive early in the morning of the next day. There was a strong desire from each of them to reach home as soon as possible.

Mark called Carly, then passed the phone around to Chris, Jessica and Ethan.

"Don't try to wait up," Chris told his wife. "We'll wake you when we arrive."

They were cruising the highway when Ethan reported that they had less than a half tank of fuel. They'd need to stop for gas in a couple of hours and could use the opportunity to grab something to eat. Mark confirmed that they still had nine hours until they reached the farm, which was a little less than five hundred miles away.

"How is everyone doing?" Ethan asked. "Can everyone last a little longer?"

Ethan received confirmation that he should travel further, so after a stretch, they decided to drive for another hour. When they approached an hour's time, they kept their eye out for truck stops that offered both gas and fast food.

As they turned off the highway, Ethan and Mark spotted a truck stop. Mark planned to clean the windshields, while Ethan pumped gas in the truck—then they could join the others inside.

Chris, Jessica, and Drago entered the building and discovered a separate indoor eating area outfitted with tables, a small store, restrooms, and a sandwich shop. Drago headed for the men's room.

Chris and Jessica had a list of everyone's sandwich preference, so they walked up to the counter. A middle-aged woman was busy making sandwiches for a couple at the counter. The couple paid, took their bag, and exited out the door to the parking lot. Finished with her prior customers, the woman met Chris and Jessica at the other side of the long counter to take the order. Drago joined them at the counter and Jessica departed to use the restroom.

Chris waited at the counter for the sandwiches to be completed, and Drago left to find seating for their group of five in the designated eating area. He told Chris he'd stay there and save a good table.

Chris selected five bags of potato chips, then confirmed that they also wanted five water bottles.

"Leave me alone."

Chris pivoted his head and saw Jessica turn the corner, followed by two large men. One tried to grab her while the other said something that Chris couldn't understand. Jessica pushed the man that had grabbed her and moved quickly to the counter.

"What's going on?" Chris pushed forward toward Jessica.

Jessica shoved the guy one more time to distance herself from the largest of the two men. One man was about two hundred pounds; the other appeared to be three hundred pounds. Chris wondered if they were truck drivers or just degenerates looking to cause problems. The bigger guy had a beard, dark hair in need of a shampoo and cut, a faded flannel shirt, soiled jeans, and old boots. The smaller of the two men wore a long-sleeved cowboy shirt with pearl snaps, jeans, and boots. He sported a small goatee with thin strands of oily hair gathered together to form a ponytail at the nape of his neck. Both were probably in their thirties.

"Guys, we just want to grab our food and move on," Chris warned them.

"Old man, stay out of our business," the larger man spat back.

"We found something we like, and we aren't going to leave just yet," the smaller of the two added as the larger man grabbed Jessica's arm and pulled her back.

Chris wished that he had his Glock—he'd stored it in his backpack, which was under the truck seat. He'd been too optimistic in thinking trouble was over now that they'd reached the States. He had a sudden flashback from their old Krav instructor: *Don't appear threatening. Maintain your balance. First combination, head up and revolving; move quickly.*

The big guy pulled Jessica back, she clawed at a shelf to try to avoid being dragged back. The big guy outweighed Jessica three to one; fortunately, Jessica slowed them enough so Chris had time to approach. Chris was four feet away when the big guy let Jessica go and turned to face Chris. The woman behind the counter shouted something that Chris didn't comprehend as the pony tailed man disappeared from sight. Chris wondered if he might come down another aisle to surprise him—he knew he needed to move quickly. He had his hands up, palms out: he didn't want trouble. But at this point, he knew trouble couldn't be avoided.

The three-hundred-pound man had some strength, but he wasn't quick: he telegraphed his moves. Chris wasn't surprised when he swung with his right hand. Chris deflected the blow with his left hand, pivoting on his foot to immediately strike with his right palm, a square hit to the nose. Blood spurted out of the man's nose as Chris immediately followed with a left punch to the man's ribs. The large man doubled over in pain. Chris took advantage of the man's prone position and thrust his palm into his throat, causing the big man to collapse.

"Dad, look out!"

Chris swiveled to see the two-hundred-pound man behind him. The man lunged, and Chris barely had time to move to his left. He used his right foot to trip the man and his right hand to deflect the punch. He wasn't quick enough—the punch grazed Chris's head. He felt a little jolt from the impact of the punch, but was able to keep his balance.

Chris's right foot caused the man to fall down and land on all fours. Chris rebalanced and kicked with his right foot, catching the man on the inside of the head. The man dropped low to the ground and reached into his pants pocket to pull out a knife. Chris kicked the knife hand with his left foot, then followed with another right kick to the ribs. The knife fell to the floor, but Chris kept kicking the man in the head and ribs until he didn't move. Chris turned around to find the three-hundred-pound guy recovering on his knees. Blood poured down the large man's face, and he muttered something as he looked at Chris and then glanced at the knife that lay on the floor.

Chris was closest to the knife. He shuffled two quick steps and squatted to pick it up with his right hand. The three-hundred-pound man was now on his feet and moving toward Chris.

"I will kill you," the man muttered.

The man was focused on the knife in Chris's right hand. This distraction allowed Chris to move forward with his left foot to kick the man in the groin. The man dropped to his knees, allowing Chris to move in with his right knee, slamming it up and into the man's chin. The man was now on all fours and in agony as Chris connected his left foot to the man's face. More blood poured from the giant man's face; his arms shook. Chris gave him a couple more kicks for good measure. His mind was no longer in Texas: he was now in the Julian Alps, and these men were the Russians who had killed Mike. Chris walked over with the knife in hand and lifted the man's head by the hair.

Chris felt a tug on his right arm.

"Dad, stop! Let's get out of here."

He shifted back to the present, to reality: he was at the Texas truck stop.

Chris looked at Jessica, his brain cycling and processing.

"Dad, we can go. They won't bother us now."

Chris turned to see the woman at the counter frozen in horror. She looked down at the two men lying on the ground, then back up at Chris. Drago entered the room with mouth open, trying to figure out what had happened. He walked up to Jessica and Chris.

"Are you okay?" Drago asked.

Jessica nodded. Chris was silent, then suddenly walked toward the counter, and the completed sandwiches.

"Take them. They're on the house," the woman offered. "But go. I'll call the police so they can pick these two guys up. I may have to make an insurance claim on the damage to the shelves. I'll say that I didn't see anything. They'll think it was a fight with one of the other truck drivers—it'll probably end there."

Chris didn't say a word to the woman.

"Drago and Jessica, will you grab the food?"

Chris turned and asked the woman behind the counter for her hand towel. She handed it over the counter and Chris wrapped the knife in it. He took the towel with him and walked to the restroom. He washed, then walked out of the restroom, where he found Drago and Jessica waiting for him. He reached into his wallet and threw two twenties on the counter.

"Thank you. Sorry for the mess."

The woman nodded. Chris kept the towel with the knife as he followed Jessica and Drago outside. Mark and Ethan had parked the truck about eight spaces away and were getting out of the vehicle.

"Stay there. We're leaving!" Jessica yelled to them.

"I thought we were eating here?" Ethan asked, puzzled.

"Change of plans," Drago responded curtly.

"I need to use the restroom," Mark complained.

Jessica held up her palm to Mark.

"We'll fill you in," Jessica announced with authority. "But trust me, just get in the truck and drive until the next rest stop."

Chris, Jessica, and Drago climbed in the truck and sat behind Mark and Ethan. Mark took off down the highway. Chris was deep in thought, so Jessica retold the events.

Mark still needed to use the restroom, so they took effort to find a rest stop. While Mark and Ethan used the restrooms, Chris walked over to the trash can outside the bathroom and delicately dropped the towel and knife into the garbage container.

Everyone was back in the truck quickly, and Mark had them back on the road toward Brownfield, Texas in no time. Jessica and Drago handed out sandwiches and chips that they ate as they traveled through the Texas countryside.

Jessica took the wheel at nightfall. Chris rode shotgun, staring out the window into the black void. Drago couldn't legally drive, so he was stuck in the middle back seat with Mark and Ethan seated at either window. The brothers used shirts for pillows as they napped, heads against the window.

"Dad, are you okay?" Jessica broke the quiet.

"Yes." After a minute, he added, "I'm just tired. I want to be home with family. I need to decompress."

"I'm a semiconductor salesman," Chris reflected. "I've never had the formal training that Mike shared with us. The past few months isn't something I'm used to. We've been in survival mode for so long that it's become a part of me that I don't particularly like. I'm glad you tugged on my arm."

"Did you know what you were doing at the truck stop?" Jessica asked.

"I'm not sure. I'm actually afraid to answer that question. I was in a zone: the same survival zone that we experienced in the Julian Alps, where we fought to survive. I thought I was back in the Alps, trying to escape from the Russian soldiers." Chris paused for a minute and then added. "We need to get back. *I* need to get back. We all need to go back to work. Mark needs to finish school. We need to just do those things that are ordinary. We need normalcy, Jessica."

Jessica didn't say anything, and Chris looked over at her.

"How are *you* doing?"

"I'm okay, but I know what you mean. While you were hitting the big guy, I kicked the pony tailed guy. Something came over me and I wanted you to kill him and I wanted to kill the other guy. But then I tugged on you and thought, this isn't who we are. We have to return and become the people that we are."

"I'm really looking forward to seeing everyone," Jessica added minutes later. "I'm excited to see what life will be like with Drago and our new assignment. I think these things will help me recover."

Chris smiled. He also started thinking about what the future may hold.

"Yes, we have some exciting things ahead. I'm going to check and see if they have a new territory for me. I think I want to work at least a couple more years." Chris shared. "Maybe then I'll retire or do something else. Moving from San Diego will require adjustments by everyone. We're the last in the family to begin the adjustment."

They drove in silence until they had to stop again for gas and coffee. Chris took the steering wheel for the final leg home. He was wide awake and anxious to be home. The long drive allowed him to process and start to decompress, if only just a bit.

When they were within thirty minutes of home, Chris woke the others. They helped him to navigate and find the road to the farmhouse.

* * * * *

Finley woke Carly by climbing on the bed and giving her a kiss, then he jumped down by the door. Groaning, Carly put on her robe and glanced at the clock: it was 2:00 a.m. Finley beelined straight to the front door. Carly looked out the window and saw truck headlights approaching the house. She rushed to the door and held Finley by his collar as she walked out on the porch. The truck stopped and she let Finley go. He raced to the truck. In seconds, everyone was out.

Carly saw Ethan, Mark and someone she didn't recognize. Jessica came around from the front passenger seat and Finley intercepted her. She hugged him and then ran to her mom. They all met in a big embrace. Finley moved next to Chris, who bent down to receive Finley's kisses. He tried to calm Finley as he his whined and moaned in joy.

Chris stood up with Finley at his heels and walked to Carly. She finished her embrace with Jessica and took a step toward Chris. Chris gathered

Carly in his arms, and though no words were uttered, volumes were spoken. Carly cried as they embraced.

"Welcome home, Chris!" Carly finally managed to choke out.

Jessica interrupted to introduce Drago to Carly. After a couple of minutes, they retreated to the truck to grab their backpacks and bags. They dropped them inside on the living room floor, and though they tried to be quiet, they awakened the grandparents.

Now everyone was in the kitchen. Chris sat on the floor with Finley as they enjoyed coffee, cookies, and good conversation. Carly and the grandparents wanted to hear the story, but the travelers were exhausted. They agreed that they needed sleep first—they would reconvene at breakfast. Clark, who was asleep in the other farmhouse, would be able to join them then. It would be a long discussion told over a big breakfast.

Ethan and Mark located their packs and suggested to Drago that he follow them to the older farmhouse. Jessica would sleep in the extra bedroom inside the new farmhouse.

Chris entered the bedroom and dropped his pack. He stripped down, took a long hot shower, and found a clean pair of boxers inside the dresser. He headed straight to the bed. It was now 5:00 a.m., and he was tired and going down fast. Carly was already in bed with Finley snuggled next to her. Chris climbed in.

"Do you want to share some of your story now, Chris?"

"If it's okay, honey, I really need sleep. I can give you details tomorrow and answer any questions after we share with the others at breakfast."

Carly looked a little hurt and Chris spoke. "You need to know that a lot has happened that you don't know about. I'm a different man than the one who left. I'm a little damaged right now. But I believe and have faith that I can recover. I'll just take some time."

She was quiet. Chris wasn't sure if Carly was hurt or letting him sleep.

"I love you. At times the thought of coming back to you and the family was all that kept me going. It was what I focused on. It drove me and encouraged me when I needed it most. I just need a little time," Chris repeated.

With that, he lay back in bed. Carly came over and rested her head on his chest, and Finley found an empty space by their feet. Chris was asleep and snoring within a minute. For the first time since leaving San Diego, he felt safe enough to fully let go and rest. He was home.

Chapter 122

Home

Everyone gathered in the kitchen the next morning, the room abuzz with conversation. Fresh coffee, orange juice, stacks of pancakes, and sausages were on the table. Chris told the story about driving to Florida, sailing Dan's boat across the Atlantic, and the trek from Spain to Slovenia. Jessica and Drago told their story, beginning at the company meeting, then the vacation in Slovenia and Croatia, up until the moment they met Chris and Mike on the trail. Drago told the part about Nancy and Sam's death on the mountain.

From that point on, Jessica told the rest of the story. Chris shared some events about Mike, but he experienced some difficulty so he skipped many details. There was a heavy sadness that fell over the room upon hearing of the deaths of Mike, Ali, and Lisa, but everyone listened intently to Jessica until she reached the part of meeting Ethan and Mark in Belize. From that point, Ethan and Mark told the remainder of the story.

It was now 10:30 a.m. Clark had to leave the kitchen for the necessary chores, and the grandfathers left for town with the grocery list to buy supplies. Ethan and Mark traveled to the McGregors to see their girlfriends. Jessica and Drago called to confirm when they should report to work, and Chris called his boss, Dale. He was given good news: they had a territory ready for him. He could use the farmhouse as a base and set up a home office. He would need to travel infrequently to nearby states, but could do most of the work from home.

The McGregors invited the family over the next day for a midday meal. The grandmothers baked apple pies and cheesecakes in preparation, and Carly had fresh produce from the local market to make salads. The McGregors were to prepare fried chicken, mashed potatoes, and gravy. Carly offered to show Jessica and Drago around the farm later, and Jessica asked to drive into town with the grandparents to help with the shopping and to see the town with Drago. The next day was Saturday, so Abby and Ryan planned to travel down to join them for the celebration lunch.

Midafternoon, Chris took a long walk of the property with Carly and Finley. Carly had more questions, and Chris gave her more details … but some parts would require more time. Memories of Mike, Ali, and Lisa were difficult topics that he hoped might be easier to reveal in the future. At the moment, it was therapeutic to walk and spend time with his wife and dog in a peaceful setting.

Friday night was quiet. Lindsey and Allie McGregor joined the family for dinner, and Ethan announced that he would have to drive to Dallas on Sunday. Jessica and Drago would also leave on Sunday; they'd been instructed to report to the office on Monday. Mark had an internship in Houston and planned to leave in one week. Chris also had one week before starting work. They had a relaxing dinner together, and afterward a few of them retreated to the family room while others walked out to sit on the front porch.

Chris expressed to Carly and his parents and in-laws how thankful he was that everyone was safe. Grandpa H and Grandma H informed him that his brother, Jeff, and family in San Francisco were also fine. His brother Scott, who had left his Orange County home to stay with relatives in Nevada, had ended up moving to a suburb outside Denver. He and his wife now had jobs and a new life in Colorado.

Carly's brother in Portland was fine: there hadn't been any changes—he still lived in and enjoyed Oregon. Carly shared that Ryan's mother and sister were flying to Texas in a couple of weeks for a visit. Pa K and Ma K had heard an update from their relatives: the motorcycle gangs in Wisconsin were under control; they'd been driven out of northern Wisconsin. Their relatives were safely back at their home in Fish Creek.

The next morning they prepared for the McGregors. Carly and Jessica made three large salads and set the bowls on the kitchen counter. The grandmothers had the pies and cheesecakes ready on the counter. The grandfathers bought wine at the market.

Abby and Ryan arrived at the farm. Chris and Jessica were happy to see them. They visited with them exclusively for a good thirty minutes on the porch. Chris and Jessica wanted to hear about their new home in Austin, about their jobs, and about Abby's pregnancy. Abby and Ryan wanted to hear about the adventure and Chris and Jessica gave them the short story while suggesting they find time to talk again later.

Everyone helped pack the food in the vehicles before they caravanned in three vehicles over to the McGregors. Ethan and Mark wanted to travel on their own because they planned to stay longer. Drago and Jessica were able to meet the McGregors for the first time. The McGregors wanted to know the detailed story of the entire journey, but Chris provided a high-level summary. In some ways, telling the story was cleansing; but in reality, he needed space from the events of the past couple months. He had a feeling he would see the McGregors on a consistent basis over the years, there would be many more opportunities to talk.

The food was excellent and the company was terrific. Everyone had a great time. Chris was surprised to see how comfortable and witty Clark had become; he'd changed a lot over the months that Chris had been away. Clark looked older, was more confident, and Chris was amazed at how Clark took ownership over key parts of the farm. Chris looked around the table and saw all the paired couples.

"Fast forward this picture a few years and we could be seeing a new son-in-law and two new daughters-in-law," Chris whispered to Carly.

Carly smiled. "Yes, and I like them all."

At 5:30 p.m., Ethan and Mark remained as the rest of the group left the McGregors to travel back to the farm. Chris helped Clark and the grandfathers check the grounds, ensuring that the animals were fed and okay. Finley got his two scoops of food, and Clark took off to see a girl. Carly shared that Clark had met a girl at a town dance, and they were becoming an item.

"Another possible couple in the future," Carly added.

Chris and Carly sat on the porch talking with Drago and Jessica. They shared information about the upcoming week. The corporation had company apartments for temporary living, and generously paid the first month's rent. Drago and Jessica would find permanent housing starting in the second month. The two had discussed the housing situation in Dallas with Ethan, who had helped provide information on where they should look for apartments. Ethan offered the contact information of a realtor that he had successfully used in the past. When it grew late, Chris and Carly decided to go to bed.

Chapter 123

Goodbyes

It was going to be a difficult day; everyone was packed and ready to leave.

Ethan was leaving for his job and apartment in Dallas. Jessica and Drago were packed and ready to settle into company housing in Dallas.

They'd elected to follow Ethan for most of the drive to Dallas. Abby and Ryan were packed and ready to head back to their home in Austin. Over a period of one hour, they all left the farm except for Mark, who had one more week before he headed to Houston.

Chris knew that Carly was feeling down. He left her alone, and she eventually verbalized that she would miss the kids.

"We're closer to Ethan and Mark than we ever were in San Diego," Chris pointed out. "We can see them more often. And Abby and Jessica are both close by."

"I'm not sure I want to be on this farm for the rest of my life," Carly commented.

"Carly, let's at least start our new life here. I think we need to find stability for a couple of years. Our parents are helping a lot, and Clark will help until he's off to school. I plan to work a couple more years ... then perhaps I'll retire."

"Clark really likes it here. He's thinking of becoming an agriculture major," Carly shared.

"Maybe that's his calling—he'll be a farmer or rancher. Carly, let's give it a couple years and then you can pick where you want to live. We can move somewhere else in Texas, or now that we're almost one country again, somewhere else in the new Federation."

In one week, Mark went off to Houston for a two-month internship before returning to OU for the fall semester. Chris started work and although it wasn't the same, it gave him a chance to settle in. He had his same boss, Dale, that he liked, and he was able to work with Dan and Bill again. Working from the home office was terrific: he still had to travel, but he was typically home on the weekends so he could help with the farm chores.

Clark headed for Tech late in the summer. He promised that he would come back some weekends. Clark knew he would miss the farm; he was his happiest working on the farm ... not to mention he now had his girlfriend in Brownfield.

Finley was introduced to a female golden over the summer and became the father of some fuzzy puppies. Chris and Carly picked a male puppy from the litter and loved having two dogs running around the farm.

Abby and Ryan had a beautiful baby girl in the fall. Carly went to Austin for a week to help with the newborn. Mom and granddaughter were healthy and doing well, and Ryan's success at his work made for a happy home.

The grandparents were healthy and helpful with the chores around the farm. They met several neighbors in the community and established a network of new friendships. Dividing the chores made farm life easier during Clark's absence. It was a good year for the family. The Texas Federation became established—it was a stronger and better country than the former United States. People were generally happier with the smaller government.

In the fall, international flights resumed to most locations in the world. Other than isolated incidents, the terrorist groups were mostly defeated.

Chapter 124

Next twenty years

Life continued at an accelerated pace. The next two decades brought joy, peace, and fulfillment to Chris and Carly. However, they did have their share of grief. The grandparents passed away one by one from natural causes. They'd asked to be buried under a large tree about fifty meters from the old farmhouse. Chris built a small picket fence, sectioning an area for his parents and in-laws. Their legacy lived on inside Chris, Carly, and their children. There were family gatherings each year that became larger events as their children's families grew. Chris and Carly thoroughly enjoyed and looked forward to each event.

Ethan and Lindsey married and built their lives in Dallas. They bought a small ten-acre ranch outside Dallas where they raised a family. They were very happy and Ethan fulfilled his dream of building a six-car garage for his Land Rover and a couple other vintage cars that he collected. Ethan started his own hedge fund with one of his best friends from Baylor. Lindsey managed the household and the activities of the three children.

Jessica and Drago married and also settled in Dallas. Before they married, Drago joined another company, eliminating a possible conflict of interest in the work place. They bought a home in Highland Park that was an easy commute for both to their offices. The close proximity allowed them to work a full day and still be home in time for family activities. Both rose to the VP level of their respective companies, and parented two children who became close to their nearby cousins.

Abby and Ryan bought a nice home outside Austin that sat on a couple of acres; enough space for their four children. Ryan started his own technology company with a friend and loved his work. Abby taught, then shared a split contract to devote more time to the family. Their oldest daughter enrolled at UT in Austin, which added another Big 12 school to the rivalry.

Mark and Allie married and lived in Houston. Mark moved up quickly within an energy company and the couple bought a nice two-acre place on the outskirts of Houston. They had three children, and Allie focused on managing the household and worked part-time in communications. Mark traveled internationally for work. On occasion Carly and Chris would stay a couple of weeks watching the children and allowing for Allie to travel with Mark and add vacation time to the end of his business trip.

Clark married a girl from Brownfield. He decided to become a farmer after finishing his agriculture degree at Tech. Chris and Carly offered to sell the farm to him over an extended period of time. Instead of financing with a bank, Clark paid Chris and Carly a monthly payment—in essence, they created an annuity. Clark and his wife had three children. He became a pillar in the farming community. His children assisted with the chores around the farm.

Chris and Carly stayed and worked on the farm for seven years. Chris retired from technology sales after four years. He needed the next years to decompress: going back to familiar work and the weekends on the farm with family helped him to accomplish this. Chris and Carly became involved with some charity organizations and explored a number of hobbies.

After they struck the deal with Clark, they stayed two more years to help Clark get established. Instead of leasing the farmland, Clark started farming. He bought a tractor and other necessary equipment.

After six years, Chris mentioned to Carly that he was ready for a change. He asked her if she was ready for a move. The children were all settled and Clark and his family needed some breathing room. He pulled out the map of Texas and they discussed where they should go. It was a tough decision since they wanted to see the family often. They made a decision to live near Waco so that they were centered between Dallas, Austin, and Houston. They found a home that was large enough to host all the children and grandchildren. Travel time to Dallas and Austin was only one and a half hours; travel time to Houston was less than three hours. It seemed to be a central area and they planned to rotate on weekends to attend their grandchildren's activities. Chris had all the schedules of their activities written on Carly's large calendar so they could support each grandchild at least once a month.

They were often invited to stay at their children's homes. They loved staying with their children and grandchildren and frequently watched the grandchildren while the parents went away on a much-needed *couple* vacation. Finley's puppy was named Finley II and later, Finley II continued the legacy with another male golden retriever puppy. Chris's best friend was now Finley III. Finley III traveled everywhere with Chris, rarely leaving his side. He could be seen at the market or in the car, riding shotgun on the way to a destination. Carly tried to convince Chris into giving Finley III another name, but Chris stood firm on preserving Finley as the name of their retrievers.

Chris and Carly traveled on a few international trips. Chris lost all desire to travel years earlier, but Carly had interesting destinations in mind. The children and grandchildren all wanted Finley III to stay with them when they traveled, so Finley III always had a place to stay while they were gone. Life was terrific for Chris and Carly as they grew older; they were able to stay active. But then Chris recently began to have more trouble. He went to the doctor at Carly's urging but received a report that he was fine, that he was just getting older.

Thanksgiving approached, and Chris pushed hard to have the family in Brownfield. He thought it would be a great idea to visit with Clark and the McGregors, and to visit his and Carly's parents' graves. Carly sold the children on making the trip out to Brownfield.

Mark and Allie flew into Dallas on that Wednesday evening to spend the night with Ethan and Lindsay. Mark rented a SUV and the group planned to caravan to Brownfield. They discussed that Ethan and Mark could drive one car while Allie and Lindsay drove the other. The children could choose to ride in either car. This would give them the opportunity to visit during the five-hour drive to Brownfield.

Abby and Ryan and their children arrived at Chris and Carly's Waco home a day earlier to spend the night and then caravan together to Brownfield in the morning. They would all arrive at the ranch midday to spend Thanksgiving at the ranch.

Jessica was on business travel, so she would arrive late Wednesday evening. Drago, Jessica and her family would then drive to Brownfield as part of the caravan with her two brothers.

Clark arranged a block of rooms in Brownfield for Thursday night. They would visit half of Friday, then caravan back to their homes.

Chris had been feeling a little under the weather. He told Carly he didn't think it was contagious, but it made him less energetic. He suggested that she drive or perhaps a grandchild could help drive part of the way. Chris typically liked to drive, so Carly knew that he wasn't feeling strong. She hoped he would feel well enough to enjoy Thanksgiving with the family.

Clark still had the big country table at the center of his kitchen. He brought the table from the old farmhouse and placed it in the living room with a couple of other tables for the Thanksgiving feast.

The families started to arrive around 12:30 p.m. Old McGregor and his wife were excited to see their daughters, sons-in-law and grandchildren. The first couple of hours were festive and filled with laughter, good conversation, and appetizers.

Finley III got along with the other dogs, but Finley III found two tennis balls and preferred to chase the balls instead of playing with the other dogs. Chris spent some time with him throwing the balls out in the front yard. The other dogs would show some interest in the ball, but Finley III was like his father and grandfather before him: he was obsessed with the ball, and was always first to the ball. Chris indulged Finley III in playing fetch for twenty minutes straight, then told Finley III that they would have to resume playing ball after dinner. Chris wanted to visit more with his family.

Clark took the family on a brief tour of the farm. He'd had a great crop last year and was anxiously waiting for spring and a new harvest. Chris and Carly noted how excited he was speaking about the crops and what he planned to plant for the spring. Chris couldn't walk too far, he didn't feel as strong as usual.

They had a midafternoon Thanksgiving meal. Chris asked if he could speak before Clark gave the blessing. Chris held a glass of wine that Drago had poured minutes earlier. Chris asked Carly to come up next to him as they stood in the living room.

"I want to tell each of you how proud I am of you. I think you know that we love you all, but we want to let you know that each of you is a terrific individual. I couldn't have asked for more in life. I am blessed beyond measure with my children and grandchildren."

Carly was misty eyed and choked up, so they all drank to the toast. Clark and his wife mixed up seating arrangements by pulling names out of a jar. It was a fun spin to Thanksgiving and created interesting and lively conversation. The McGregors appeared to enjoy themselves thoroughly.

After dinner several adults elected to clean up the dishes in the kitchen while others turned on the television to watch the Cowboys football game. The grandchildren weren't too interested in either.

"Why doesn't Grandpa Chris tell you a story?" Carly suggested.

Chris leaned over and kissed Carly. "I love you," he whispered as he walked out onto the porch.

Soon Chris had all the grandchildren gathered on the front porch, listening attentively. He found his favorite chair as his grandkids found seats on the old swing, chairs, and porch steps. He had all his grandchildren and Clark's children surrounding him. He looked at each of them: the youngest was eight and the oldest was nineteen. He needed a special story that would hold all their attention. So he decided to tell them an old story, a story that Chris hadn't shared for decades. It was a new story for his grandchildren, but a story that Chris remembered well.

The story took about an hour to tell. The porch was silent for the full hour. Not one of the grandchildren left or stirred as he spoke. Chris was able to tell it without the emotion it had evoked years earlier. He finished and looked at each of them. They were all very quiet.

"Who wants to check on the pies?" Chris asked.

"Grandpa, was that story make-believe?"

"It was true. It was quite an adventure," Chris acknowledged with a smile.

Finley III emerged on the porch with the ball and Chris rose up from his chair.

"I'm going to go visit your great-grandparents' graves. I'll be back for pie when I finish. Will you tell your grandmother?" He bent down and threw the tennis ball in the direction of the graves and followed Finley III.

The grandchildren went into the kitchen as the grandparents finished clean up. They told Carly that Grandpa was visiting the graves.

"Where is Slovenia?" one of the younger grandchildren asked.

Jessica had a dishtowel and walked over to hang it up on the oven door handle. "Between Italy and Croatia, and below Austria. Why?" she asked suspiciously.

"Have you been there, Mom?"

Jessica's youngest child looked at her inquisitively. Jessica finished hanging the towel, then turned around.

"Yes, I have been there. With your father and grandfather."

There was a pause.

"Were there pirates in the Caribbean?" another grandchild asked.

A couple of the kids tried to pull up maps on their cell phones. One grandchild had a map of Europe and another pulled up the Canary Islands; still another had the Caribbean. They all looked at the images and asked more questions.

Carly looked at them all and said, "You need to ask your parents about the maps."

Immediately they all scattered. Ethan and Mark's children went into the living room; Jessica's children grabbed Drago and brought him into the kitchen. Abby and Ryan looked at their children and told them that they might want to hear more from their aunt and uncles; they had a different story about coming to Texas.

Chris sat down under the tree and looked at the graves. He'd deeply loved each of the individuals buried there. Finley III tirelessly retrieved the ball and Chris continued to throw it. Finley would immediately return to repeat the process. Finally, when Finley had had enough, he decided to lay down beside Chris in the shade. Chris was happy and satisfied. He'd lived a good life, and he closed his eyes to rest.

* * * * *

There was a scratching at the door. Abby opened it to find Finley III. He ran in and went straight to Carly, nudging her and then heading back for the door. Carly walked toward him and looked out the front door, searching for Chris.

"Where is he, Finley?"

Finley went out in the direction of the old farmhouse and continued on toward the grave markers by the big tree. Abby joined Carly and they trotted after Finley. Finley ran ahead and then returned, beckoning them to hurry. Around the farmhouse they could see Chris slumped under the tree.

Abby reached the tree first and touched her dad. Carly was close behind. When Chris didn't respond to Abby, Carly felt for a pulse. She couldn't find one.

* * * * *

Two weeks later the family gathered at the gravesite. Finley III stood by Carly's side. The family circled around a casket that was ready to be lowered into a hole in the ground. Carly learned that Chris had been diagnosed with cancer two months earlier. He'd been told that it had spread into his vital organs and that he only had a couple of months to live. He told his doctor that he wanted to keep the information quiet; he wanted one more opportunity to enjoy his family. She now understood why he was insistent on having the family together at Thanksgiving.

As they lowered the casket, Carly was consumed by overwhelming grief and peace. Simultaneously, her children looked at her as she searched for her voice.

"He loved you more than you will ever know. He had a good life!"

About The Author

CLIFF LIVES IN SOUTHERN California with his wife, Cathie, and their beloved golden retriever, Finley. As in the book, they have four grown children. Upon retiring from the technology industry, he wrote and published *Indomitable*, his first book.

CPSIA information can be obtained
at www.ICGtesting.com
Printed in the USA
BVHW081026061218
534938BV00001B/13/P

9 781642 982947